the hand holding the knife

More by Brooke Shaffer

The Timekeeper Chronicles

The Chivalrous Welshman
Time to Kill
Tick Tock
Windup
Stopwatch
Free Time
Leap Second
Imminence
Synchronization
Turning Point (Summer 2024)

The Hands of Time
In the Hands of the Enemy
The Hands Pulling the Strings
The Hand Holding the Knife

The Lone Wolf
Wolf Pack
Alpha Wolf
Lone Wolf

The Akari-Bearer
Bearer of Bad News (Winter 2024)

Singles
Of Saints and Sinners
Chasing the White Bear

the hand holding the knife

Book Three of The Hands of Time
The Timekeeper Chronicles

Brooke Shaffer

Black Bear Publishing

Published in Michigan by Black Bear Publishing.

This novel is a work of fiction. Names, characters, places, and incidents are either products of the author's imagination or used fictitiously. All characters are fictional and any similarity to persons living or dead is purely coincidental.

ISBN:
Hardcover: 978-1-953113-34-4
Softcover: 978-1-953113-35-1
eBook: 978-1-953113-36-8

For Shane and Gabby

Maine, 2013

kokumbo

It was a beautiful house in a quiet neighborhood, if it could be called such. The closest neighbor was a quarter mile away. On the one hand, it didn't seem to match the personality of the homeowner who enjoyed flaunting himself at every opportunity in every way imaginable, and some ways previously unimaginable. On the other hand, seclusion afforded him certain abilities, like being able to host self-aggrandizing parties that lasted far longer than they might have if there were any next door neighbors to disturb.

He'd had one of those parties a couple nights ago. Almost no one had showed up to the flagrant display of self-worship, and those who did had primarily come for the finger foods and the company of each other over the homeowner. The man was not well-liked by anyone but himself, but he supposedly had a great tactical mind that kept him relevant.

Cassius was going to test that tactical mind tonight.

The only real reason he was hesitating was because of the security system. Technology had jumped tremendously in the last forty-five years, though cameras and alarms were hardly anything new. There were plenty of more advanced races in the universe with more advanced systems. But Cassius was having a hard time believing that this system was so cut and dry. The man was an Akarin officer. He had no real need for such a system; few could ever hope to sneak up on him if he was home, and there was little that anyone could want if he wasn't. Even if something was stolen, it wasn't as though he lacked the means to replace it. There had to be more to it.

"If I wanted to trust the protection of my stuff to technology, how would I do it?" Cassius murmured.

Well, considering he had the ability to mold the fabric of the universe, it might be beneficial to give himself access to as many aspects of the universe as possible. A flash of light, maybe, to use Light, a noisemaker to invoke Sound, maybe some metal pieces for Magnetism. All of this would be in addition to common forces like

Gravity, Time, and so on. Except most of those things were already well available. Even invoking the Energy of electricity wasn't much of an inconvenience in such a house.

A well-manicured hedge provided excellent cover for Cassius to sneak all the way to the west wall. There he put his hand to the brick, invoking Energy to trace the electricity. Cut the power to the security system and —

There was no power to the security system. The cameras, the alarms, all dark. All for show.

He removed his hand from the brick. Well, that just made this too easy. And the unlocked windows made it criminally easy. The man was begging for someone to break in. Of course, he was also so self-absorbed that he could barely get friends to come over, so his best chance for home entertainment was showing off his strength or Akari abilities. And winning the fight wouldn't hurt his ego either. Turn a common criminal over to the police and be heralded a public hero, another dose of ego. Considering the man was only five-foot-six, Cassius couldn't help but wonder where he put it all.

The carpet inside the house was plush and there was no need to use Sound to muffle his footsteps, though he did mask the closing of the window. Cassius tried not to stare at the self-aggrandizing imagery in the room. Most objects in the house were homages to the homeowner or his various accomplishments. Photos, paintings, statues, trophies, a selection of diplomas or certificates, and a wide assortment of papers detailing massive contributions to various causes.

This was not to say the house was overly cluttered. It was bigger than the one he'd lived in some years ago, the first one Cassius had broken into, providing ample room for more egotistical displays, and Cassius looked for any and every bare spot on the wall to focus on as he quietly left the room and made his way down the hall. He now used Sound to augment the breathing of the only other person in the house. He also used Thermodynamics to ensure there wasn't anything else lurking around. He found no dogs or cats, just a few lines of ants and a dozen or so spiders.

A long time ago, Cassius had lived in a palace as a personal hired mercenary to the Crown Prince of Rid, or one of them anyway. This house wasn't a palace, but he could get used to living in a three-story mansion. His only lament was that he wouldn't be able to get rid of all the self-centered decor, not if he wanted to pull off this little switch. The ego he could mimic; he just had to pretend to be Rifun. The tactical mind he was less confident in. He wasn't stupid; he just preferred to do things more directly. He didn't play chess. He couldn't think five or ten moves ahead. Two, maybe three on a really good day with an easy plan.

Pushing open the door to Doug's third-floor bedroom—and throwing up in his mouth a little at some of the more erotic self-imagery—Cassius was actually still surprised that Rifun had not only allowed but orchestrated this plan. Normally he balked at such killing. Oh, he'd run out onto the battlefield a time or two, but when it came to individual men and women, suddenly there were morals to contend with.

The only light in the room, aside from faint moonlight filtering through thin curtains, was the green glow of a small clock on the nightstand, the numbers announcing 3:59 am. This illuminated the lumpy figure under the light blanket, the person evidently facing the wall.

For all the power available to Time Agents and Akari-bearers, whatever their great physical prowess or however silver their tongue, sleep was the final vulnerability, the ultimate risk. It was also, unfortunately, a biological necessity. Oh, Cassius could have tried to take Doug on in open combat, but the chance of being found out was too great. This was one kill that had to be completely silent, completely anonymous.

He'd no sooner considered this than a sudden, jarring noise almost put him through the roof, and he had just enough time to realize it was the alarm clock going off at precisely 4:00 am. Not half a second later, the blanket was thrown back and Cassius was treated to a horrifying visage of a naked Doug Templeton with a straining erection. It wasn't that the man was overweight or otherwise bad looking, it just wasn't something Cassius had been prepared to see.

The man had thrown off his blanket dramatically, but his mind was evidently on other things. Despite the pressing and secretive nature of his mission, Cassius found himself pausing to watch in fascination. Even after the man had finished, Cassius did not make a move against him. Doug heaved a sigh and stared up at the ceiling, still oblivious to the murderer just a foot away. The alarm clock was still buzzing obnoxiously but he ignored it.

"All right," he huffed. "Another day." He groaned as he sat up. "Greg's waiting for me—"

He paused as he swung his legs over the side of the bed and finally made contact with Cassius. He looked up.

"Your first words should be 'thank you,' " Cassius told him.

The man leaped out of bed, putting a good five feet between them. Neither reached for an Akari ability. Doug put out a hand, blindly pawing for a pair of shorts on the back of a chair.

"I should thank a burglar?" Doug wondered. He grasped the clothing and slid the shorts up to his waist, his eyes never leaving Cassius who was starting to grow hard himself. "This should be an interesting argument." He noted Cassius' bulge. "I know I'm handsome, but I don't think you broke in here to rape me."

Somehow, the statement made Cassius even more disgusted with the man, and he didn't think that was possible.

"No," Cassius replied. "I'm here to replace you."

The man was probably still wondering why he should thank a burglar, and it was that split-second of curiosity and indecision that gave Cassius the advantage, closing the gap in a single stride. Doug reached for a Band. Cassius easily matched it and used Time Tendrils to lock them together. Sound might have been unnecessary, but Cassius wasn't going to take a chance.

Doug moved back, heading for the door, trying to keep at least three feet between them. Cassius only needed to touch Doug, just once, just for a moment. His old Harvesting abilities would do the rest, quietly, and basically instantaneous.

"I know who you are," Doug stated warily. "Cassius. Kokumbo."

"A good portion of the universe knows my name," Cassius chuckled. "What of it?"

Outside the room on the opposite wall was one of the many paintings of Doug, resting in a heavy metal frame. Before Doug could reach the door, Cassius raised his hands, exposing the metal bangles on his wrists. Using Magnetism, he ripped the painting off the wall and struck Doug squarely in the back of the head. The glass shattered, causing Doug to stumble forward a step or two, the canvas buckled, and the four sides of the frame broke apart at the seams. The frame continued to fly through the air, still attracted to Cassius' bangles. Releasing the Magnetism, he grabbed a long piece and a short piece. The other two, he oxidized in midair so that they fell to the floor as nothing but a small pile of rust flakes.

Cassius continued to advance on Doug, raising one of his improvised weapons.

Suddenly, everything went dark. Doug cut all Light in the room. Cassius reached for Sound, but it was his Reflexive Band that saved him, slowing Time and alerting him to some object that was attempting to penetrate the back of his head. He jumped forward, just enough to the side to get out of the way of the object, and whirled around, swinging the longer metal piece. To his surprise, Doug was already there, within his range. Cassius brought up the shorter piece and managed to strike the man under the jaw.

Doug made an over exaggerated fall and roll, but it put distance between them.

"You're not as dumb as you look, I'll give you that," Doug huffed. "You really messed up the Akarin with your little memory stunt. Forty years later, I—"

Already sick of hearing the man talk, Cassius invoked Gravity, using himself as the anchor and attaching the track to Doug. The man was jerked off his feet and came flying through the air toward him. Just a touch was all he needed.

Thinking fast, when he got within reach, Doug grabbed the end of the long metal piece in Cassius' hand. He then took the energy from the Gravity and channeled it into Force, turning straight motion into circular motion, effectively causing Cassius to throw Doug out of the room and down the hall, now putting the distance between them at a good fifteen feet.

"Calis Cutthroat," Doug said. "Instigator of the Dispersal, slayer of the Gentleman Killers—"

"Unlike you," Cassius interrupted, drawing near in long strides, "I don't rub off to my own titles."

This time he threw the metal pieces, using Force to augment their speed and Gravity to guide their trajectory. The combination would have made them lethal to any common man, but in the moment, as Doug dodged, it only made them dangerous to the drywall, blasting through like a couple of crossbow bolts before sticking into the outer brick.

But if Doug thought Cassius was just going to leave them there, he was sorely mistaken. Oh, Cassius rushed him, certainly, wanting nothing more than to bash all his teeth in and make him choke on them. As he moved, however, he did the same thing in reverse. The Force needed to overcome the pieces being stuck in the brick was tremendous but beautiful, and another Gravity track got them going in the correct direction. Cassius ended the Gravity track about three inches from Doug's head, just so he wouldn't notice it. Then, as Cassius got within striking distance, he raised his fist and made a swing as if to punch the man. Doug brought his arms up for a solid counter, but Cassius took his moving energy and amplified it with Force.

It didn't do quite what he wanted it to do, that is, snap his head back with Force, meeting the Force of the metal pieces, and the collision of the two Forces would cause his head to explode completely. Regardless, the result was the same, with Doug dead on the floor. The metal pieces, which had once been part of a frame of a painting of himself, were now lodged in his head, one sticking out through his shredded right eye, the other protruding from his mouth. Multiple teeth were scattered on the floor and the blood was demonstrating a new color of stain for the hardwood floor in the hallway.

Now this Cassius would rub off to. And he did.

There was no need to worry about hiding a body, though he wouldn't say he wasn't disappointed that he couldn't show it off either. He had a suspicion that not a few of the Akarin would thank him. This time, however, he was obligated to keep it a secret. So he simply knelt and, with a combination of Time and Matter, simply decayed Doug's body. The bloat, the rot, the withering of flesh as it fell off the bone. Eventually even the bones became brittle, cracking, breaking, dissolving. And the whole of Doug Templeton's body, all five-foot-six, one hundred seventy pounds, was but an unfortunate pile of dirt and dust on his hallway floor.

Cassius satisfied himself a second time, then went to find some cleaning supplies.

Doug's bedroom was in the corner on the third floor, giving him a panoramic view of the surrounding landscape, including the roofs of his neighbors' houses, equally rich and large down on the flat ground, though his house had been built up into a hill. Rifun would appreciate the view, but Cassius wasn't the reflective type. At the same time, it was perhaps the best view in the room considering the only other option was just more self-worship.

He was just heading down the stairs when he heard the front door open. Bad enough the man had an alarm set for four in the morning, but who was this that was coming in at the same time? A personal chef to make him breakfast? Actually that didn't sound like a bad idea. Cassius descended two more steps before recalling that he was supposed to be Doug now. Whoever this was, they would be expecting five-foot-six, one hundred seventy pounds, white with brown hair, not five-foot-nine, one hundred ninety pounds, black with a shaved head.

Reluctantly, he donned a Disguise. He had no shortage of reference material as he fitted the skin suit, though he elected to utilize more clothing than just a pair of shorts. On the other hand, it wouldn't surprise if Doug had just strode about his house completely naked so he could stare at himself in one of the many mirrors that also graced the walls.

In the first floor kitchen, he found the intruder. A woman, maybe forty years old, white, black hair tied back in a ponytail. Every part of her was what a normal man might call unfortunate. Scrawny, rather than skinny or thin. A forehead that was too high, nose too big, cheeks too angular, eyes too baggy. Her chest was almost nonexistent and terribly disproportional to her hips that were just too wide.

How did he interact with this woman? Were they friends? He didn't even know why she was here.

"The usual?" she asked, not really looking at him as she set a backpack on the floor and a tote purse on the counter.

Usual? Seemed safe. "Sure, let's do that!" he said boisterously.

"All right, I'll just be a minute."

Rather than going for the milk in the fridge, however, she grabbed the backpack and disappeared into an adjacent room, shutting the door behind her.

Curious, Cassius elected to wait and see what happened. A few minutes later, the woman emerged, dressed in a rather scandalous outfit.

Maybe Doug was attracted to such things—indeed, Cassius was more surprised that he would be attracted to anything that wasn't him—but Cassius found it almost as appalling as the man himself. Was that the point? Had he intentionally hired an ugly woman and put her in an even uglier costume so that he could feel better about himself? If Cassius would have had the power to kill the man again, he certainly would have. He might have tried to murder his Disguise in some way, but he wasn't sure how to do that, or if it was even possible.

The woman leaned against the doorframe. "Hey there, big daddy. You wanna go shoot some guns?"

He was supposed to have sex with this thing? What was actually going on right now?

"Maybe we can change it up just a little," he said, trying to buy time. "How about a blindfold? On you."

"Ooh, spicy." She said it with all the enthusiasm of a woman who didn't really care how it got done, only that it did so she could go about her day.

Still, the woman dutifully put on a blindfold—at least that wasn't too unusual, seeing how she had one in her bag. Relieved, Cassius Banded and dropped his

Disguise.

First he made sure there weren't any other interlopers hanging around who might stumble into the house. Then he went to the woman's giant purse and started snooping. A lot of trash, a handful of small bills, melted chocolates and crushed mints, hair supplies, makeup, an ID that proclaimed her to be Annabelle Marie Richards, and a small planner detailing her monthly schedule. "4a, Doug T." with a certain symbol he could not identify was listed for every other Thursday, but that was about it. He was the only one listed for today, but most days saw her visiting between three and five people. It was not lost on him that all the names appeared to be male.

He set the purse down and went to the backpack. The clothes she had walked in with were stuffed in a large front pouch, along with a small assortment of accessories he assumed were from other costumes. In the small front pouch he discovered various drug paraphernalia, including some questionable substances. In the main portion of the bag, he found a collection of items that piqued his interest. He dropped the Band.

"Don't speak," he said, bringing out a few things. "And just do as you're told."

She wasn't Isthim, that was for sure. He was pretty sure he'd had more fun with a literal limp dishrag. Only the bonds made it in any way enjoyable, though he could barely finish. Reluctantly, he donned his Doug Disguise, then went to work releasing her, against his better judgment.

"You felt bigger than usual," she said, removing the blindfold. "You been taking pills or something?"

"Or something," Cassius-as-Doug replied. "Is it going to cost extra or do I get a discount?"

As far as he was concerned, she should be paying him.

"Two-fifty for the day, same as always."

"You get yourself cleaned up and I'll be back."

He ducked out of the room just as fast as he could. He made his way back up to Doug's bedroom, figuring there might be some cash stashed in there somewhere. Or maybe it would be in an office? Well, it would give him an opportunity to go snooping anyway.

Cassius really didn't want to go looking through the man's stuff, if only because he didn't want to come across anything weird, or weirder than what was already on display. Maybe he could get rid of the stashed stuff. Not that Cassius expected to actually spend a whole lot of time here, but when he did, he would need a reprieve.

On the other hand, opening up the door to the rather expansive closet, maybe he could utilize some of the stashed stuff. There was quite a collection, far more than what whatsherface had in her backpack. Maybe he could take it back to the ruins on Sadurnon and use it on Isthim. Now there was an idea. If he was expected to fuck that drug-addled slut downstairs every two weeks, he would need something like that in his head in order to push aside whatever the hell was waiting for him downstairs.

Maybe that was the reason for the obnoxious personality, Cassius mused, finding a stash of cash in a drawer. He was trying to detract from his darker sins.

By the time he returned to the kitchen, the woman had started some bacon and sausage and was busily arranging an assortment of household cleaners, picking out this and that.

Cassius tossed the two hundred fifty dollars on the counter just as she turned around. "How about you finish breakfast there and then take the day off?"

She stopped, startled as though slapped, and looked at him. "What?"

"You heard me."

"But—"

"You have three seconds to agree before I change my mind."

She stared at him for at least two of those seconds before snatching up the cash and shoving it in her purse, sputtering feeble thank yous. Cassius wandered off for a few minutes, returning just as the food was being scraped onto a plate. He ate. She washed the dishes and wiped down the kitchen. Neither of them spoke. She packed up her things and her hand was halfway to the front door handle when she turned.

"Are you sure?"

He made a huge gesture. "Of course, of course. You've earned it today. Off with you now!"

And she was gone. Cassius leaned back with a sigh of relief. At least she only came around every other Thursday. After a couple minutes of just sitting and making sure she wasn't going to come back for some reason, he dropped the Disguise and returned to his breakfast. Now what? He was pretty sure Doug had mentioned something about someone waiting for him. Who was it? Where were they waiting? What was he supposed to do? Well, obviously, he was going to miss the appointment. He hoped it wasn't anything important.

After breakfast, Cassius again returned to the bedroom to begin a less than methodical search of the house. He spent a fair amount of time in the closet, going through some wicked paraphernalia. Granted, there were no true torture devices, but he knew how to fix that. He was going to have to bring Isthim here, and it wasn't going to be a suggestion.

When he finally peeled himself away from the treasure trove, there was little else of interest to be found. A little more cash, some credit cards, a driver's license, a ring of keys, and a dozen other cards he did not understand but did not appear to be especially important.

The next room he explored was indeed an office. The ring of keys came in handy there as all of the drawers were locked. Inside he found mountains of paperwork, much of it legal in nature. Cassius' eyes and brain glassed over as he opened up file after file of legal forms and tax work and investment portfolios and other irrelevance. If he found anything useful, it was a small piece of paper taped to the underside of one of the drawers containing what he believed to be some kind of "log in" information for the computer sitting on the desk.

Cassius had never been especially computer savvy, only enough to get by for what he needed. Logging into Doug's computer now, the only good thing he had to say was that at least the picture of him in the background had clothes on. He was shaking someone's hand and appeared to be holding some kind of award. Otherwise, the screen was a mess of icons. He perused through a few of them, got bored, got frustrated, and finally left the room entirely.

More bedrooms, a few bathrooms, another office, a living room, some rooms he didn't really understand the purpose of, a mini kitchen, the full kitchen, a laundry room, and finally a small mud room leading to an enormous garage full of expensive rides and other toys.

He walked back inside, pausing when he got to the kitchen.

"Did you know about the stuff in Doug's closet?" Cassius asked. "Is that why you suggested I take up this insane endeavor?"

"I didn't know until a few minutes ago," Rifun replied, leaning against the counter, "but I do think it might be an incentive for you. Am I wrong?"

"Depends. How long am I supposed to keep this up? I guess he was going to meet someone this morning, but I think he's going to skip today. He can't skip every day."

"You are correct on both accounts." Rifun tossed something to him which proved to be a phone. A "smartphone" they were called. "The code is 261181. If you forget, it's his supposed birthday. Anyway, he was supposed to meet a man named Greg at a local park so they could go for an early morning jog. You could probably still make it."

Cassius scoffed. "I don't want to go for an early morning jog."

"No, but Greg and Doug do."

"Why don't you go for the jog? It's all a Disguise anyway."

"I'm not the one having to keep up the charade. You need to figure out their relationship and what he knows. If I do it..." Rifun chuckled. "Well, then we'll have to have a meeting about what I learned."

Cassius just rolled his eyes.

Rifun shifted his stance. "The elections are coming up in a few months—"

"Six months," Cassius cut in.

"Not that long is the point I'm making."

"Takes half a second to do Test."

"Only if the Akarin think they need to. Don't give them a reason. Go jogging with Greg."

He didn't want to. If he had any consolation, it was that he got to drive a nice car to the park. There he met up with a man named Greg. He appeared to be a simple acquaintance, something about some business dealings and moving money around. Cassius managed to deflect most of the conversation, and he figured he was appropriately flagrant and self-centered in what opinions he did give, but Greg had evidently expected far more from him. Well, they were there to jog in the park, not commit to major business dealings or financial fraud or whatever they were supposed to do.

Thankfully he was not expected to go to breakfast with the guy, and just as soon as he could, he returned to the mansion. The narcissism looked even worse as the sun came up. Dammit he wanted to rip down every photo and painting on the walls, smash every statue and figurine, burn every certificate of false humility. Anyone was a saint compared to this man.

Cassius headed up to the third floor where the bits of dust and dirt that were Doug's remains still sat on the floor, scattered a bit from the central air flow. He stared at it for a few seconds before finally going in search of a broom to sweep up the dirt. As for the blood, even though it had dried, it was still fresh enough that he was able to use Matter to lift it out of the wood.

By the time he was done, it was like it never happened. As far as anyone was concerned, Doug Templeton had woken up, fucked his whore, eaten breakfast, dispensed a bit of mercy to the lower class, gone jogging like he was supposed to, and come home. No one was breaking down his door demanding proof of his identity. Of the two people he had interacted with so far, neither one was so suspicious that they made a big deal about it. Maybe he was having an off day, but it was still in the realm of believability.

Now what was he supposed to do? He still hadn't figured out what the man did as a day job. Sure he'd just been talking business, but what was his title, his position? Cassius wasn't even sure who he worked for. Maybe he worked for himself and it was his own company they'd been discussing. He probably should figure this out at some point.

It would have to wait at least a few minutes as he meandered back to the closet. He had a feeling he was going to be spending a lot of time in here. Maybe there were a few perks to this job that would make the rest of it a little more bearable.

Cassius checked Doug's phone, though that felt like a misnomer. It was phone, mail, music, games, business, accounting, all stuffed into an electronic gadget. It was certainly very convenient, and Cassius had seen similar devices on other worlds, but it also felt like a terrible burden. People could always get a hold of you. Any hour, any moment, someone would be able to reach you, from the catastrophic to the silly or mundane. It sounded annoying and exhausting.

According to the phone, or the digital calendar anyway, he had an appointment for a haircut at 2 pm. Didn't say where, only that he had one. Other than that, today was remarkably free of obligations. Tomorrow and next week appeared rather full, but he seemed to have picked a good day to begin impersonating someone.

Cassius put the phone away. He could skip the haircut. He wasn't here for Doug, because he craved his lifestyle—although the money and the closet were pretty appealing—he was here to infiltrate and undermine the Akarin. The faster he started doing that, going into the elections in the Wheel, the faster he could clear out the vault as it were and get out of here.

With a resigned sigh, he once more donned his Disguise, then opened a portal to the Akarin fortress.

The Hand Holding the Knife

The last time he had been here, the Akarin were still reeling from Isthim's operation to wipe their memories. He thought all memory of the Akarin at all should have been destroyed, but Rifun and Julianna interceded with their conveniently intermittent morality and vetoed the idea.

These days, everything appeared business as usual, not that he would know what that was after forty-five years. Fortunately, the place never actually changed, so all he had to do was run up to the Archives on the fifth floor and bring himself up to speed. The whole time he walked up the infernal staircase, he couldn't help but wonder if anything was going on and if his demeanor was appropriate to the situation. The overall feel of the place was very casual, but that didn't mean that Doug didn't know something was amiss.

Everything the man did was to make himself look good. How would that work in a crisis situation? He would always have a plan, probably, and he would always know just what to say. He would be the one to look to for answers. And yet, what if there was no crisis? What if everyone really was just going about their business, the universe in a rare state of equilibrium?

Cassius mentally shook his head. No. The universe was never in equilibrium, and if the elections in the Wheel were going to be as contentious as Isthim predicted, the Akarin would feel it. True, not all Akarin were Time Agents, but the Time industry was the core political superpower of the universe; everything they did affected everyone everywhere. They would be watching, or the higher-ups would, which included Doug.

He did notice that he garnered a few stares when he walked into the Archives. And why not? Could a man who couldn't shut up about himself really be expected to stay quiet in a library?

He pretended to be on a mission and knew exactly where he needed to go. This was entirely false and he spent a fair amount of time just looking for what he needed. He wasn't even sure what section that would be in. History? Politics? Current events? He didn't even go to regular libraries, how could he be expected to know where anything was in this one?

In the time that he spent there, perhaps an hour or so, he did find some useful information. He learned who comprised the current Akarin council and some of the current concerns. The elections were one of those concerns, but it appeared to be a business as usual. Another election cycle has come around, what do they expect to happen, and has anything come up that might be of interest to the

Akarin? He found no mention of the Cult or any of its leaders. But Doug had clearly known about them and what happened, so—

Cassius spotted the Authored Books, tucked away neatly in their standard case. There were more of them now, he saw. Curious, he approached and removed one he didn't want to consider.

The Hands Pulling the Strings, Book Two of The Hands of Time.

He flipped open to the list of "current" Books and compared it to what was in the case. There was no mention of *The Akari Bearer* series, nor *Chasing the White Bear*. At the same time, *Lone Wolf* was also not in the case and *The Chivalrous Welshman* remained stubbornly future-bound.

The good news was that the Akarin's copy of their first Book was still safely in Cult hands. The bad news was that everything they had tried to prevent by stealing the first Book might have been negated with the appearance of this second Book. Skimming through a few passages, it did seem to pick up right where the first left off, and it ended with their appearance in the modern day. Everything in between—Titik, the Turitians, the Time Trial, all of it—was now almost-public knowledge.

And yet, there had been nothing about it in the Akarin council notes. He and Rifun had only been in the twenty-first century for about a week to ten days. Assuming this Book appeared literally right after their emergence, it couldn't have made the rounds. But still, for there to be nothing about the Cult? Even reading about their own deception with the Disguises and the Borelians and wiping their memories, they didn't even give the Cult the benefit of a footnote?

He placed the Book in the case and left the Archives. He was just heading down the stairs when someone, who he knew as a council member only from his very recent research, came up beside him.

"Another day, another meeting," the alien sighed. It was a quadruped, almost like a large dog, though more insect-like in appearance with a hard, crustaceous outer shell.

"I'm sure it'll be fine," Cassius-as-Doug declared. "I think I know a little more about what's going on."

Pretending as if this was exactly why he'd come, he followed the alien to a third floor meeting room where a respectable gathering of council members stood around a large table. It did not appear to be all of them, but enough to make a quorum.

"All right, I'm here, sorry I'm late," Cassius-as-Doug said upon entry. "What were we talking about?"

Not a few of those gathered sighed or made unpleasant facial expressions at his appearance. Someone he could not presently identify said, "We had not begun, so you are not late and we have begun no discussions from which you were absent."

"Wonderful! Then no one has to repeat himself and I can hear every word."

A few more members showed up and the meeting was called to order.

"Before we get started on whatever agenda we have," Cassius-as-Doug blurted, cutting off another alien who had gotten only half a syllable into some long speech he was sure, "I want to bring up an issue. Now, maybe we've discussed this before, but I'd like to know if any opinions have changed." He went on before anyone could grant or deny his request. "I want to talk about the Cult of the Akari. What's being done about them?"

The reaction to the topic was about as friendly as the reaction to his presence.

"They've been neutered," someone said. "Two of their leaders went missing, and their Borelian alliance has likely seen most or all of them straight into slavery. Unfortunate, yes, but that is the price one pays for dealing with evil."

"And the newest Authored Book?"

"Their obituary no doubt."

"Have you even read it? How can it be their obituary when there is a promised third Book? Are we really just going to ignore the Author's words?"

"We have more pressing matters to attend to at the moment," another member sighed. "The elections in the Wheel are rapidly approaching. The Harvester Lily Guile continues to be a thorn in the sides of the Merchants and the Grandfathers. However, her crop of bought seats this time around is wholly different from what she has done in the past."

"Different how?" someone inquired.

"They trend towards those who have, in the past, favored Merchants over Grandfathers—"

"Hardly surprising, coming from a Harvester."

"Yes, but it seems that these new candidates have a particular animosity toward the Grandfathers. Not necessarily the Borelians, as all are rightfully wary of them, but the Grandfathers as an institution."

Another member spoke up. "It seems to me that it might be a good thing. The

Grandfathers have always kept a keen eye on us. Taking away some of their power and favoring Merchants might do all of us some good."

"Isn't Lily Guile affiliated with the Cult?" Cassius-as-Doug jumped in. "Her Harvester mentor was Julianna Brown herself."

"Then I would suspect that this would be seen as a betrayal," the third member informed him. "The Borelians have had the monopoly on the Grandfathers since the Dispersal. If she is trying to weaken or dismantle the Grandfathers or provoke something from the Borelians, this would be the way to do it. And if the Borelians have not already enslaved the Cult, well, I can't imagine they would be pleased with such turn of events."

"But the Book—"

"Honestly, Doug, you and your group of naysayers exhaust us. Whatever the Cult was planning to do, whatever they managed to achieve with the Dispersal, it's all gone now, and things are back to the way they've always been. Now then, we are here in the present moment, and we are discussing present matters, not issues that were resolved forty years ago through natural consequence."

And that was that. Doug may have had a big personality, but even he could not overcome the will of a couple dozen irritable aliens who shut him down every time he opened his mouth to speak of the Book.

Their disregard for even the appearance of a new Book was surprising, but it made it that much easier to smuggle the Book out of the Akarin fortress afterwards. He thought about taking it directly to the ruins and give it to Rifun or Julianna. Then he thought about it a little and decided to keep it tucked away in the closet for a while instead. It could prove to be a point of leverage later or maybe it would end up being a fancy paperweight. He'd figure it out later.

The important thing was that he had survived a meeting with the Akarin council themselves and none of them appeared to suspect that he was an impostor. He had a hard time believing that if someone had hit him with Test and discovered he was a fake—whether or not they cared about his identity—that there wouldn't have been some kind of reaction.

For all that he had done so far in the day, from breaking into the house to jogging to stealing a Book, it was still only noon on Earth at Doug's house. As far as Cassius was concerned, it was probably something like two in the morning. The question was, did he sleep at Doug's house, potentially exposing himself to harm if someone came snooping, or return to the ruins to his own chambers and hope to simply pass it off as Doug was out somewhere doing something?

This question was not difficult to answer as Cassius considered the bedroom's decor, and he returned to his chambers in the old Elif temple. He fell asleep quickly and soon found himself in darkness, surrounded by heavy smoke. Something beyond him moved, and a moment later, glowing red eyes appeared in the shadows.

"The enemy is weak," the spirit murmured. "They have squandered their time, and the opening you created for us has allowed us to establish a presence among them."

"I took the Book. I'm taking over Doug's life, getting close to them," Cassius said. "They are the ones we face, but there is still the enemy behind me. What do I do about the others?" He went on before the spirit could speak. "We wasted forty fucking years looking for some shit book that wasn't even where we thought it was. Did you know it wasn't there? Couldn't you have warned me at least?"

The eyes lowered and got closer so that Cassius could make out the faintest outline of the dragon's head and especially its teeth. "You are too small to know the greater war, too foolish to understand its maneuvers."

"I understand that I'm just a grunt, here to be your sacrifice on the front lines. Just going wherever my commander tells me, isn't that right?"

"It is. And you should be grateful for such mercy."

"Grateful? Mercy? I'm your fucking puppet. The only reason I give two shits about any of this bullshit anymore is because of this fucking bullet in my face!" He pointed to the spot just below his eye where he knew the lead ball still rested. "I thought I was getting something out of this, something more than just being a lackey."

"You do not even know what you want. You require guidance, a heavy hand of control." The shadows shifted so it was almost like a snake threatening to coil around and suffocate him. "If you are not going to cooperate, I have no shortage of loyal faithful who will."

Cassius immediately thought of Isthim and the Borelians. Liars. Double agents. Slavers.

The dragon must have sensed his defenses dropping as the serpent disappeared. He looked up at the red eyes and grudgingly asked, "What do I need to do?"

"Certain sacrifices must be made—"

"Who? Name them. Doug is already dead, who's next?"

Now the spirit rumbled a laugh. "You will know them."

"Tell me Rifun and Julianna and I'll do it right now."

The dragon turned serious and Cassius went to his knees as his face throbbed in pain, the bullet making itself well known. "You will do nothing I do not command. You are not my only pawn."

Cassius groaned as the pain in his face was alleviated and he was able to stand once more. "Was there anything else...Master?"

The dragon made a gruff humming sound. "Your insolence is noted and will not be tolerated much longer."

"The feeling is mutual, believe me."

Another laugh. "Your tiny arrogance amuses me."

Before Cassius had a chance to respond, the darkness closed in, and the next thing he knew, he was waking up. He might have thought that something external had woken him, but looking around his chambers, he saw nothing out of the ordinary. Everything was exactly where and how it was supposed to be.

He didn't want to impersonate Doug. If they had just wiped the memories of the Akarin entirely and taken all of the Books, they could have crippled or even destroyed the Akarin, and he wouldn't be in this predicament. But no. They had to do this the hard way. Because making things harder on themselves was more moral or something. They were trying to take over the universe for fuck's sake. Morals had nothing to do with it.

Well, unless he wanted to get some lecture or be dragged to yet another meeting, he might as well get back to the mansion and pretend like he cared about anything in Doug's life.

It was seven o'clock, the barely setting sun pouring into the room in picturesque perfection through the great bay windows. Using Light so he could dim the room and find his way, Cassius shut the curtains. Yeah, that view was probably worth a lot of money to someone, but he wasn't trying to sell the house.

Or maybe he should. Maybe he should make Doug go dark, back him away from daily life and have more freedom to do what needed to be done with the Akarin. Now there was an idea. Then he wouldn't have to care about what the man's job was or who his friends were. And Cassius wouldn't mind having a couple million in play money. Not that money really mattered, but he'd always wanted to be rich.

He checked the phone. Some missed calls, a few with voice messages, some new text messages. Opening up an "app," as they were called, he discovered over one hundred fifty email messages. Many of them appeared to be pretty useless, messages from businesses telling him about particular deals or sales. Cassius didn't think anyone would argue with him deleting those. A few emails sounded more personal, many dealing with topics he didn't care about anyway. Then there were the business emails, asking about this deal, what he thought about that move, something about the stock market. All of it sounded very important in some way, and Cassius knew he should probably respond.

Or he could fake his death, he supposed. Burn the house down, plant a charred body to be found, and go dark as he had just considered. Maybe that really was the best way to go about this. And if Rifun complained, well, he could do this impersonation. He had the ego and he cared more about people and their home lives. For fuck's sake, the man had disappeared for years just so he could go live on a cattle ranch or something. Why he hadn't just stayed there Cassius did not understand.

He decided to ignore everything and do a more complete search of the house, see if there were any more little secrets he missed the first time around, any more hidden closets. With a closet like he had, Doug had to have a few skeletons somewhere. Unfortunately, such a search came up empty.

Cassius stood there on the second floor landing overlooking the first floor. So. Here he was. Living another man's life, supposedly. What was he supposed to do? Sit around and drink wine? Rub off to any of the many images of "himself" hanging on the walls? Read a book? Did he really want to take the time to try and figure out just what this man did for a living?

He made a valiant attempt, but his attention was only good for about fifteen minutes when it came to finances and business dealings. From what he could gather, Doug's line of work had something to do with the finances and legalities of certain fighting organizations. That was about as far as he got before his mind glazed over and he decided to call it a night.

He'd figure it out tomorrow or something. For the moment, he just had to figure out how he was supposed to get to sleep with dozens of pairs of eyes of a dead man staring at him.

Rifun sometimes wondered what Turit would look like if its sun hadn't gone nova and destroyed everything except what lay under the protective domes. Looking at the otherwise dead landscape from the edge of the dome, he could almost picture the hills being covered in lush greenery. But what if that wasn't the case? What if this was supposed to be a desert? Or a grassland? From what information he could find, this area had been almost like a transitional landscape, with grassland on one side and scrub desert on the other.

It didn't matter now, he supposed. Now there was only rock, tinted gold from the protective dome. Actually, since his last visit, the city had grown up quite a lot and now spanned multiple domes, connected by small self-driving vehicles that ran along inlaid tracks.

The main part of the city which housed the palace, however, was the same as ever. Maybe a little different landscaping, maybe a fresh coat of paint, but largely the same. Even the formal fashion attire hadn't changed much. The people still wore the belly bands because of some taboo about seeing the midriff—there was no genitalia involved, though it carried the same stigma—with various colors and patterns denoting their precise location in the social hierarchy. Those with military standing also had shoulder sashes and streamers to represent the various battles, wars, and achievements they had been involved in.

Most outsiders agreed that the social constructs of the Turitians were too complex for non-Turitians to fully grasp. Some also said that it was made this way intentionally so that the Turitians could feel smug or self-righteous when dealing with outsiders. While Rifun might agree with the first statement, he was not fully convinced of the second. There were plenty of social norms he did not understand just among the various peoples of Earth. There were many social norms to be observed among the various peoples of the Cult inhabiting the ruins of Sadurnon. He knew he would never learn them all and had unintentionally offended a great many people. But there was a certain understanding among so many people, that it was all right. As long as no harm came to anyone, everything was probably all right and no more than a slight miscommunication.

Or that's what Rifun told himself as he approached the palace and prepared to speak to the royal family Jalar and High Commander General Dira. From what he understood of the situation, the Turitians had pinched their noses about the Cult's dealings with the Psiaco pirate Titik, up until said pirate decided to attack one of their royal cruisers and take their prince hostage in exchange for the third of Richard's journals which the Cult sought. Two Cult-affiliated groups with the same goal to find the journal and turn it over, but very different methods of going about it and ideas of who should be the one to present the gift to those in charge. And each one wanted the other out of the Cult.

If he had to pick which group to keep, Rifun had already decided he wanted the Turitians. Yes, Titik was brilliant and unconventional, but he was one man, one pirate. If something happened to him, the rest of his crew held no loyalty. Titik himself was dubious at best, always claiming that money was the only pleasure in the world. At least with the Turitians he was dealing with royalty and military, two stable institutions that, with any luck, would value honor and negotiations beyond the death of one or two people. The fact that they were still willing to dealing with them after forty years was a good thing, or so he hoped.

The palace boasted two large statues outside its main doors, depicting two great heroes of old. Rifun couldn't help but feel a sense of awe as he passed between them. When he'd first laid eyes on the Turitian palace, he'd had a passing thought that this was how the palaces of the old Malagasy kings and queens must have looked. Whether this was true he did not know, but he had an inkling from the spirits that it was.

According to social custom, as a foreign diplomat, the only people he was considered "inferior" to was the royal family and the top-ranking military commander who, in this case, happened to be High Commander General Dira. This not only esteemed visitors, for even non-diplomat outsiders were treated with high respect, but it made it easy to know which basic turns one should use in any given setting. Walking up to the receptionist inside the palace to announce his arrival, he did not have to wonder about propriety, for he knew that he was considered the "superior" in the interaction, and he would be the superior all the way to the meeting itself. Then he would be the "inferior" party.

Whatever meeting the royal family had been in, it was running long, and

Rifun was made to wait in a rather comfortable sitting room, complete with a balcony. There was a lovely view of the east side of the city, toward the markets. Turning to the south, he could just make out the limits of the southern gardens, purple and white flowers bloomed out brilliantly, while some red ones were just shyly opening up. To the north, the landscape was dead and dull except to look at the other, smaller domes that housed more city districts.

He tried to picture grasslands beyond the golden tint, tall grasses and flowers waving in the breeze, animals grazing contentedly or perhaps running from some predator ambush. He tried to picture scrub desert, with squat plants, tall cacti, snakes sunning themselves on the rocks while an entirely different compilation of fauna awaited the arrival of night. Staring at the dead rock, he could picture the desert more easily than the grasslands.

He went back inside the room, still waiting. It was an odd thing to consider that the last time he had been in the room was forty or more years ago in the grand scheme of things, yet it hadn't been nearly so long in his own life. He was going to approach this very differently than the royal family. While amusing in its own way, he knew he would have to be cognizant of such discrepancies. A lot had happened in forty years, both in Time and for the Turitians in general; he couldn't just walk in the room and pretend like they could pick up where they'd left off.

Perhaps what annoyed him the most about the whole thing was that Cassius had admitted to knowing about this incident between the Turitians and Captain Titik before they went in the cave. It had been an accidental admission, true, but the man had not looked fazed or guilty about it at all. When Rifun pointed out that it had happened well before they entered the cave—at least a couple weeks if he could interpret Cassius' non-answers correctly—he could have resolved this right after it happened and not have had to let this stew and fester for four decades.

Well, Cassius was another matter for another time. Right now he had to deal with the Turitians and try to make them happy again.

He looked up from his seat as the door opened and a servant announced that the royal family was waiting for him. It had only been about an hour. Rifun did not feel an affront to his personal pride so much as annoyance that this had to happen at all.

He followed the servant upstairs to a rather poorly-lit room where the royal family received their guests. He did not understand why it was done all the way on the top floor, nor why the lighting was so bad, but he decided not to complain.

In addition to complex turns and gestures, the Turitians also had a rather strange arrangement when it came to family. From what he understood, family was less about blood ties and more about those who shared common family-oriented goals, could achieve those goals, and could somehow advance them in society at large. There were rules about who could and could not be part of certain families, so while almost none of the current royal family were actually related by blood, they were all of a certain stock of people, a certain caste as it were, a particular pool to pick from.

Queen Aronet had only just ascended to the throne when Rifun last saw her. While use of Time and, perhaps, the Akari had made her aging nonexistent since then, there was a kind of hardened maturity about her countenance now. He had never believed her foolish or incapable of ruling, but some things only came with real experience, and the woman looking at him now was greatly wizened to the ways and politics of the universe. That included hard decisions and even betrayal, he was sure.

Appropriate turns and gestures were made, Rifun now making the "inferior" signs as he deferred to their authority in their own palace.

"Thank you for meeting with us so soon," Queen Aronet said formally, though there was a bit of annoyance in there, Rifun thought. He didn't blame her, but it did make him a little uneasy. "Although it does seem to be a few years longer than what was anticipated."

She made a gesture which indicated he had the right to speak.

"I cannot change the past," he began slowly, knowing that it was true for more than one issue. "Time only moves forward, as must we."

"And yet, every time you move forward and make gains toward your goal, you seem intent on squandering such achievements," Dira cut in, her tone, expression, and gestures all very accusatory. "If you cannot overcome minor setbacks, then there is no reason anyone should fight with you. If your response to major obstacles is to run away from them for forty years—"

"I do not control how Time Traps work. I do not control where and how they are placed. I do not control how they are weaponized. I can only work with what I have."

"For proclaiming such great power through the Author and the Akari, your skills appear to have very convenient gaps or lapses," one of the other royals observed. "Or perhaps one or more of your associates is working against you?"

"Petty squabbles are not uncommon, but it is bad form for there to be such division among the leadership," another royal agreed.

Rifun tried to read their expressions and gestures, but he was not well versed enough to catch more than one or two implications on the fly. He turned his attention back to Queen Aronet. "You have obviously had plenty of time to discuss this matter amongst yourselves. What is it that you are actually asking of me?"

The queen studied him for a long moment. Then, "Whether it is the Zero Hour, the Gentleman Killers, or Captain Titik, your associate Cassius has a way of destroying everything he touches, and the effects of his destruction, be it intentional, malicious, ignorant, or otherwise, are felt throughout the universe for many years to come." While she did not rise from her seat, Rifun could almost imagine that she wanted to be standing or even on a stage as she continued. "We Turitians are known for being a patient people, and we do not take such praise lightly. But even our patience is not infinite." Her expression remained severe, but there was a shadow of understanding as well. "You have favored us with good manners and thoughtful words, and we can appreciate that diplomacy is often the better option. But words have failed and only action remains. If our relationship with the Cult is to continue, Cassius must die."

For a long moment, no one spoke. Rifun did not need to be an expert in alien body language to know that all of the royals were in agreement.

"Given that you are not the first to put a bounty on Cassius' head, am I correct to assume that you are asking me personally?" he inquired.

"We have given you our terms. Our only term. How this is carried out is not our concern, though it may be that you are the only one able to get close enough to him to carry out this task."

Rifun let out a breath and nodded. "I understand. I cannot say that I have not thought something similar, though it is typically poor sportsmanship to murder those who are supposed to be on your side."

"Indeed."

"And once this is done? I assume you will want some proof of death."

"We will, yes. Once it is done, we may proceed with our previously negotiated terms, control over the Scouts, outposts, and so on."

He shifted in his seat. "As I have just said, I have had similar reservations about Cassius for some time, though I find it curious that you have said nothing about Isthim or our alliance with the Borelians."

Queen Aronet made a gesture whose significance Rifun did not understand. "The Borelians rarely ally themselves with anyone unless they cannot conquer them. For all your blunders and missteps, the Borelians have not been able to conquer the Cult. See that it stays that way."

He could tell that there were any number of other things she wanted to say, but that was perhaps the only thing she could say in her position in such a meeting. Or maybe this meeting was what their last meeting, the one that had run so long, had been about, what they wanted to say, what terms they wanted to bring, all of it.

"I understand," Rifun said finally. "Was there anything more you wished to speak about or ask of me?"

The queen and the commander exchanged a look. Aronet made a gesture and Dira responded with one of her own. She looked at Rifun. "As a personal request, if you should get a chance to do the same to the Psiaco pirate Morain leRou Titik, please do so. I will personally reward you for it."

"Revenge" was not a word that frequented the standard Turitian lexicon, and the fact that the concept was coming up now meant that Dira took Titik's successful attack as a very personal blow. Considering that the event was forty years old, well, forty years of patience had allowed that wound to fester well.

"Considering that Cassius did prefer Titik's company over yours, I may be able to use one to find the other," Rifun said, hoping to inject a bit of venomous hope into the situation. It appeared to work as Dira settled down with a certain satisfaction that one of her personal enemies was going to get his due.

It appeared as though even the Good Samaritans had few qualms about killing others in certain situations. Everyone felt the same way at one time or another.

"Was there anything else?" he inquired politely, getting the conversation back on track. He glanced at the other royals gathered, but his focus remained on the queen.

She said nothing for a long time, instead studying him through eyes that looked almost too small for her head, though this seemed to be a common Turitian attribute.

"Nothing that cannot wait until the primary task is complete," she decided at last. "Otherwise anything else we discuss or succeed at is only at risk of yet more destruction by Cassius' wrathful hand."

Rifun dipped his head. "Agreed."

There followed a bit of fluff talk as Rifun expressed his gratitude for the Turitians' continued willingness to work with the Cult, reaffirming their first agreement that the Cult would work with only the royal family Jalar, and reiterating that Titik was not just going to fall by the wayside or sneak out a back door. Then there were more turns and gestures, formal farewells, and at long last, he was on his way. He did not receive an escort as he departed, but he had little doubt that he was being watched. Even so, he left the palace with no words and no trouble and soon found himself in the street under the long shadows and fading light of a tiny sun.

He returned to his chambers in the old Elif temple and made for his shrine in the northeast corner. There he bowed to pray and calm his nerves.

There was a dark spirit within Cassius, an evil using him as a mere flesh puppet in order to kill and destroy, wreak havoc and cause chaos. Rifun had always known there was something very off about the man, but every time Rifun dived into the spiritual world, he discovered new lows for the depths of depravity that walked around in the skin suit of a former, and now permanent, slave.

Himself, a dual-spirited man, his spirit strong enough to see and understand these things with a physical hand capable of slaying both man and demon. But how? Rifun would have gotten rid of Cassius long ago except killing the body would do nothing to stop the demon inside. It would simply leave and look for a new host.

At the same time, they really needed this alliance with the Turitians. Maybe he could kill Cassius, fulfill his end of the bargain, and worry about the evil spirit later. It would manifest eventually, but at least they might be in a more stable position within the Cult. If the reincarnated evil came as a foe, then they would be ready to slaughter it on a grand scale, perhaps put it to rest for good, without the need for secrecy, negotiations, and espionage. A house divided and all that.

But what if it reincarnated as a friend? What if it decided to go after Isthim, considering her connections to the Ul Ik Zol? The Cult and the Borelians were only just maintaining an alliance; such a move would undoubtedly push things in favor of the Borelians. Or what if it went after Julianna, with her weak mind and frail constitution? Choose the most unsuspecting person to be the most destructive, most evil.

Or, ancestors forbid, what if it came after him, because of his dual-spirited nature and connection to the spirits? Could it do that? Maybe it wouldn't possess him, but it could very well kill or cripple him. Then where would he be? Dead, and with an evil spirit still on the loose but with no one to fight against it.

No, he had to figure out a way to destroy the evil spirit first, then worry about Cassius later, assuming there would even be a body to kill afterwards. A small voice in the back of his head said there wouldn't be, that once the spirit had departed, then the flesh would simply collapse and rot away as it should have done centuries ago.

How to go about it, though? Often there were rituals and enchantments to perform, blessings and curses to invoke, even certain talismans that needed to be acquired. The problem was, the shaman he had looked to had not only outlived his usefulness—at the end, Rifun was the one telling him what to do—but he had died because of it. Rifun was at the top of the spiritual food chain as it were, at least among mortals.

Maybe it had something to do with Building. Maybe it even had to do with the Core of the Wheel, the heart of Creation itself. Maybe this evil was so great, so vast —and, judging by Cassius' behavior, it was—that the only way to be rid of it was by undoing it at the existential level. Maybe he had to reach into time and space itself to effectively unmake the demon.

Would that undo all the chaos Cassius had caused? Would it un-murder everyone he had ever killed? Would it undo the Dispersal, the Gentleman Killers, the Tacagans, all of it? Would it cause Richard to un-write the journals?

Rifun sat up from his bowed position and stared at the shrine for a long moment. He was not made different so he could plod along like the rest of them. He was not made different so that he could idle away as a cattle rancher. But if he unmade this demon, would it somehow unmake him? Exactly how far-reaching were these effects? Or could it be completely innocuous, that it would be like killing any other savage beast? The victims of its savagery would not come back, but neither would there be any new victims. Somehow he doubted it would be that simple, but stretching it so far out did seem a tad far-fetched, even to him. There could just as easily be another answer, and here he was, thinking about killing a spider using dynamite. He needed the right tool for the job; he just didn't know what that was right now.

The good news, if there was any, was that Captain Titik was as mortal as anyone else in the universe. If nothing else, he could get Dira's personal request out of the way and maybe win a little favor, a show of good faith as it were.

He left his chambers and went to find Isthim. She was still in the officers building, talking to General Misik in the main hall. It sounded like mundane business, reports from the Grandfathers, all very routine. If either of them noticed Rifun, they gave no indication of it, and he elected to wait patiently.

They wrapped up their conversation, General Misik departed, and Rifun approached Isthim.

"Help you?" she wondered, her tone impossible to judge.

"Don't suppose you know the whereabouts of Captain Titik?" he inquired.

"Last anyone knew, he was hanging around Psia, or that system, anyway."

"Voluntarily?"

"I don't know the details. The only reason I know of it at all is because of some passing gossip between a couple of Psiaco recruits."

Rifun nodded. "Fair enough. I'll check it out."

He left before she could speak, though she had looked more annoyed by his presence.

Why would Titik be hanging around Psia? Had he been cowed in some way? Captured? Was he foolishly provoking his own people to attack? Was it possible that he might just get himself killed so Rifun didn't have to bother with this little side mission from Dira? And, if the Psiaco themselves did it, Cassius would have nothing to complain about, and Rifun wouldn't have to listen to him whine. Well, he would, but the majority of the frustration would not be leveled at him.

At the same time, Rifun was kind of curious to know what Dira's reward would be, and it would be a show of good faith to the Turitians. And if Cassius got angry about it, it might provide an excuse to kill him too, even if he wasn't entirely sure how he was going to be able to kill the evil spirit.

Opening a blind portal to a planet was difficult enough. Trying to pinpoint a single spaceship in the vastness of space was tragic, even though Rifun had been there a couple of times. He called to mind his thoughts and opinions of Titik's vessel. Living space was given little consideration in favor of firepower and cargo holds. Corridors were comfortable for humans to get by, but the larger species of the ship were probably a bit cramped if they had to pass. It was remarkably efficient when it came to design, getting from one important place to another.

This appeared to be true for at least several of the vessels that he found as he searched for a landing spot for his portal. Titik, then. What did Rifun think of him personally?

Huge, compared to the average Psiaco, achieving a bulk that just didn't seem likely given standard Psiaco biology. Moody, gruff, and unbelievably shallow when it came to his larger life goals. Money was fine and all, and a skirmish or two might be interesting, but to make his whole life revolve around just those two things? Had he considered nothing else in the last forty years? Fine, so he didn't want to become a holy monk and swear a vow of poverty, but did he have no other ambition? What was the point of having extended lives if not to use them to their fullest?

His apparent distaste for Titik helped him pinpoint the correct ship and open a portal directly into one of the cargo holds.

The hold was quite full, a maze of containers and bulky items under harsh lighting. He didn't see anyone around and he did not appear to have tripped any alarms, or none that he heard. He paused for a moment, long enough to get his bearings and assess the situation. He did not hear anyone else in the room, which he supposed was to be expected.

With no imminent threat to his person, Rifun made his way through the maze, popping out near a staircase which led to a small landing and a door going somewhere. It was in this doorway that he met his first crew member, a normal-sized Psiaco.

"What—? Who are you?" it demanded. "How did you get onboard this ship with the shields up?"

"That will be a matter to discuss with your captain," Rifun said pleasantly. "Where can I find him?"

"What, so you can slit his throat and collect the bounty from the policing vessels? I don't think so." The Psiaco drew a weapon Rifun could not specifically identify but he figured it to be some sort of firearm.

"If I wanted to kill Captain Titik, I wouldn't have needed to open a portal into the bloody cargo bay," Rifun informed the man. "I could have just opened up to wherever he is, killed him, and escaped with none the wiser. I'm trying to be polite."

Sometimes, the easiest way to do something was to convince someone that you couldn't possibly do it or desire to do it. Of course Rifun was here to kill Titik, but he couldn't very well admit that out loud.

The crewman hesitated, but even for an alien, he looked distracted. Shields up, crew on high alert, mention of a bounty and the policing vessels, there was a situation here. But if the crewman was distracted, Titik couldn't be much better. He'd be too worried about getting out of this predicament to worry much about Rifun.

Finally the crewman made a motion and bid Rifun walk. He did so, acutely aware of the gun aimed at his lower back.

"Even in fear, loyalty runs strong," he observed. "I respect you for that. But why not simply open a portal and escape? The ship, I mean."

"You'll have to ask the captain," the crewman answered.

His words said one thing, but his tone said another. He knew what the situation was, how they'd gotten here, why they hadn't seen fit to leave. Walking through the ship, Rifun thought it felt a little emptier than last time. True, everyone was probably reporting to battle stations, but somehow, that just didn't quite fit the mood of the place. Could it be that Titik was making his last stand with the last of a loyal crew? Why? What had happened that he was suddenly willing to challenge death?

Rifun said none of this out loud as they made their way to a part of the ship he remembered. Up the stairs, down the corridor, and there at the junction was the captain's quarters, or maybe his office.

The crewman pushed a button, a doorbell maybe.

"What?!" came a sharp demand through a small intercom.

"A visitor, sir," the crewman reported.

"By the gods, what do you mean a visitor?!"

Nevertheless, the door opened. Rifun walked in without being prompted and went to stand about in the middle of the room, facing Captain Titik who was standing over his desk like a giant bear over some prey.

"What the—?" Titik sputtered. "What the blazes are you doing here? How did you get on my ship?!" He closed the door remotely, the crewmen disappearing behind solid metal.

"You think the Akari can't penetrate some weak shielding?" Rifun wondered innocently.

"They're Time shields in addition to regular fusion shields, but you're probably right that it doesn't matter to your stupid religion or your stupid cultist followers."

"You seem to be in quite a situation, captain, I don't know that I would be calling anyone names right now."

Titik made a sound like a primal growl. "I don't want your help."

Rifun couldn't help but make a face. "How many Psiaco police vessels are out there? One you might handle. Two if you're lucky. Three just because you took on a Turitian royal cruiser. But how did you get here in the first place? What's all this about?"

Now the captain chuckled, and it didn't sound entirely sane. "You don't care about that. You don't care about me. You just want your stupid book."

"Well, yes, that would be helpful, too."

Titik grabbed something from a shelf behind his desk, whirled, and smashed it on the ground between him and Rifun. "Your fucking book!" He slammed a fist on the desk. "Your *fucking* book!" He took a breath. "Was a fucking *lie!*"

Rifun blinked. "I'm sorry, I don't—"

Now the captain stormed around his desk, seeming to grow at least one foot per step as he neared. "You tried to have me killed! First by the Turitians, then the Borelians! All for a fucking fake!" He made as if to strangle Rifun but held up at the last moment, instead turning and walking away several strides, staring at a blank spot on the wall. "And Pilory...she paid the price for it." He looked back, lips drawn back in an animalistic snarl. "For your deception."

"I did not deceive you," Rifun insisted. "Quite frankly, I'm not entirely sure what you're talking about. If you could enlighten me, that would be most helpful both for my knowledge and so I may be more appropriately intimidated by your display."

For a long moment, Rifun feared the crazed man would ignore the question and instead go straight for the attack. Then he returned to staring at the wall and said, "The book the Turitians possessed was a fake. It did not possess the locked words of the others, the Imprint I believe you called it. I was upset, but there was little to be done for the Turitians were hot against us and our survival took priority."

"Understandable," Rifun said calmly.

"Some years later, from a captured vessel, I acquired an Ururian entertainer, made him part of my crew. As it turned out, he was the one you were looking for, years ago, the one who gave the Borelians the slip." He glanced over his shoulder. "Quite a coincidence, wouldn't you say?"

"I've learned that few things in the universe are truly coincidental."

"Indeed." Composed and civilized once more, Titik faced Rifun. "I interrogated this Ururian extensively. He knew of the journal. He had it."

"What did he do with it?" Rifun asked.

"Took it to Kath, had the Kolkath make a copy of it and keep the real one in a vault somewhere. He'd been sent on a mission from some Akarin Builders, but..." Titik chuckled darkly. "Ururians are not the most noble of characters normally, and this one was especially slippery. He pulled one over on them."

"And the journal? What happened to it?"

Before Titik could answer, the ship suddenly lurched sideways and both men stumbled.

A voice boomed over the intercom, "Captain! They're attacking!"

"No shit," Titik grumbled. Forgetting Rifun entirely, he went to his desk just long enough to push a button and tell whomever that he was on his way.

As the large Psiaco pirate walked by, Rifun grabbed one of his arms. On a normal day, the captain might have been able to shrug him off, but a little Gravity and a little Force went a long way.

"Where is the journal?" he repeated.

Titik tugged, trying to free himself. "I don't give a shit about your stupid book. I have five Keepers coming after me, and we're under attack."

The intercom buzzed again. "Captain! They're boarding!" In the background were shouts and sounds of gunfire.

Titik looked at Rifun. "I'm done."

Rifun let him go and turned. He drew his revolver. As Titik turned to walk out the door, Rifun aimed and fired. A perfect shot to the side of the head, the large Psiaco went down in a heap.

No one said anything. There were no alarms. The ship lurched again, throwing Rifun into a bulkhead. Somewhere down the corridor, shouts echoed, wild cries of defiance cut off by sharp orders and commands.

Rather than flee, Rifun simply waited. A moment later, a dozen or more Psiaco soldiers—if indeed that was what they were—swarmed into the room. They looked ready for a fight and became confused when none met them. Some were distracted by Rifun's presence, others distracted by Titik's body.

"What the—?" one of them finally asked. "Who are you?"

Rifun holstered his revolver. "I think the phrase you are actually looking for is 'Thank you,' but to your question, my name is Rifun Ndolo."

"You did this?" another soldier—judging by the more elaborate insignia on his breast, Rifun concluded he was in charge of this particular party—inquired, gesturing to Titik.

"I did."

"We have orders to take him in alive."

"And I was under contract to kill him."

"By whom?"

"No one you'd know."

"Commander," one of the grunts interrupted. "Um, he's still alive."

"What?" Rifun and the commander demanded at the same time.

The commander gave Rifun a smarmy look. "Psiaco have thick skulls and are notoriously difficult to kill in such a way."

Rifun grunted. "The first part I knew. The second has very quickly become apparent. Although it puts me in a difficult position."

"We will be taking custody of him," the commander informed him, his tone suggesting no room for negotiation. "If you attempt to interfere, you will be arrested as well. As it is, the only reason we're letting you free of this incident is because of Titik."

Rifun considered his options. The Psiaco were indelibly loyal to Time, so it wasn't as though he had to worry about the implication of future alliances going south, or the possibility of them just not liking him or the Cult. But was it really worth it to kill them? Over Titik?

"At the very least, may I look through his computer?" Rifun inquired. "He has information I need as well."

"Titik's body, person, and effects all belong to the Keepers of Psia now. No, you can't kill him, you can't talk to him, you can't look through his things. If he has stolen from you, you can make a claim with the appropriate office; if your items are found, they will be returned in good time."

Even Gravity was not so constant as bureaucracy throughout the universe.

He could still kill Titik, he supposed; it wasn't as though the Psiaco were knowledgeable about the Akari and Akari Bands. Thick skulls or not, it was probably just a matter of a few centimeters in any direction to kill him, something Rifun was far too familiar with.

He decided against it at the last moment. If, by some miracle, Titik lived and was coherent, Rifun might be able to come back and ask him more questions about the journal's whereabouts.

So he quietly assented to the Psiaco commander, opened a portal back to the officers building, and departed.

Rifun had a sneaking suspicion that Commander Dira wasn't one of those who would be satisfied with a "good enough" response, especially if this was a personal vendetta. If proof of death was required for Cassius, proof of death would be required for Titik. He would put it off for now and wait to see if the space pirate even lived through the night. Maybe he would wake up blind. Ha!

Titik said the journal was a fake. The Ururian that Isthim's hunters had tracked down—and recovered yet another fake—had taken the real one to Kath in order to make a copy and hide the real one. Hadn't this all happened before? Just who was this Ururian and what was he up to? What kind of game was he playing with this?

Annoyed, Rifun headed to the Wheel. It hadn't changed any in forty years, and he made his way to the Archives unimpeded. There he looked up information about the Ururians.

They had no home world anymore, after being completely overrun and enslaved centuries ago. Any free Ururians lived in small, scattered colonies or on cohabited worlds, but they weren't the most civilized people out there. They weren't stupid, for they could learn and perform many of the tasks that any sentient, cognitive race could, from learning multiple languages to building houses and large structures to operating spaceships. The difference between them and their neighbors usually boiled down to short-sightedness. Short-term pleasure, short-term gain. They did not consider building monuments to the past, for that was long ago. They did not consider the integrity of the future, for that was far ahead. The only contradiction to this line of thought was their insistence of being called by the names of their fathers, up to seven generations. The reason for this was up for speculation, considering the rest of the culture was based on the premise that now was all that mattered.

From that, Ururians tended to operate on the premise that basically everything was a game. There was always a punchline, always a payoff, always a victim, always a clever orchestrator. This tendency could be tamed, as many who owned Ururian slaves could attest to. In fact, in some circles, "taming" an Ururian was considered a mark of an accomplished slave owner.

So it was unlikely that this particular Ururian was acting out of deeply rooted spite or revenge for real or perceived wrongs. More likely, this was just a prolonged and very frustrating game of keep away. But was it? Would an Ururian really have the foresight to have a copy made and redistributed? If he didn't know what the journal was, that wouldn't make sense. He'd just grab it, play with it, and either hide it or give it back. Why bother with making not one but two copies?

He left the Archives and elected to simply stand there and look around. The elections were coming up fast. Cassius was working on impersonating Doug to get into the Akarin. Isthim was preparing for combat. Julianna was still stuck in the in-between dimension. He had his lead with Tommen Forbes which he had yet to follow up on. But they couldn't just ignore the Book of Commands, could they?

He started walking, having no destination in mind as he decided to focus more of his energy in formulating a timeline of events.

Julianna had given the journal to Andrew O'Dell and Nathan Wilde, both of them long since vanished. At some point, the Ururian Abbal Duma something-or-other had gotten it from them. He takes it to Kath to have a copy made—no. He himself makes a copy first, the bad one which the Borelian hunters had recovered. Then the Kolkath give another copy to the Turitians, making a big scene to draw the Cult's attention that way. Titik attacks the Turitians, retrieves the journal, finds out it's a fake, throws it in Rifun's face.

What then? And now what? Did he go to Kath and hope that the real journal was still there after forty years? Considering the Borelian hunters had failed to capture Abbal Duma, would it be unreasonable to think that he might have returned to Kath to pick it up and take off with it once more? But where would he go? The universe was too big.

Checking the time, he judged it to be only a few hours since the incident on Titik's vessel. Maybe he'd been a bit hasty in his decision to shoot the captain. On the other hand, maybe it had bought him the breathing room he needed to better interrogate the man.

Another hour or so of research pointed Rifun to the most likely place he would have been taken for treatment and subsequent detainment. After their earlier chat, he doubted the Psiaco police would be any more willing to let Rifun interrogate Titik through normal means, assuming Titik had indeed survived. But that was nothing a little Disguise couldn't handle. As long as no one tried to touch one of his fake Psiaco arms, he would probably be fine.

Psiaco medical capabilities were remarkably advanced compared to Earth, at least when it came to the common folk. Similar to Earth, prisoners saw very little of this technology except, perhaps, as an experimental lab rat whose safety and comfort was secondary, if he was that lucky. So whatever the outside world proclaimed, the inside of the Psiaco prison hospital was less than advanced or welcoming.

He pretended to be some high-ranking official, having stolen the uniform's image from his Archive research. He'd also pilfered some official-looking badge, though he hoped no one would look too much deeper than that.

"Sorry, sir, we're just cleaning up from the incident," a lackey said as he led Rifun to a particular room.

"Incident?" Rifun inquired, determined to keep his interactions brief.

"When he woke up, he went entirely savage. Many were wounded, even him."

They stopped at a window looking in on a sad brick room with a single bed and no amenities. Titik, even without the blankets and bandages, appeared far too large for the bed, and also unconscious.

"He is sedated?"

"Yes, sir."

"Wake him."

"That's not a good idea, sir."

Rifun snapped his attention to the lackey. "I said wake him."

Whoever Rifun was pretending to be, he evidently had the authority to order such a thing without too much objection beyond the standard warnings. Doctors and a team of armed security arrived. Drugs were administered, and Titik began to stir.

Aside from a gaping hole in his head, Rifun had left Titik with all of his arms in tact. Now, one was completely missing, another chopped off just below the elbow, and a third missing a hand. All of it appeared fresh, perhaps when he'd gone "savage." Coming around from the drugs, he was not leaping off the bed immediately, although Rifun could see the strength still rippling through his limbs, an animal that does not yet realize it has been caged but knows something is very wrong and wants to be free.

Rifun Banded and shed his Disguise so he could work more comfortably. He Touched Titik, Felt him. He would not pretend to be Isthim or a red or purple Borelian, capable of altering emotions or one's sense of danger, but he did know how to cut off the nerve impulses from the brain to the body. Titik could panic as much as he wanted, but he would have no physical ability to hurt anyone.

"Well, well," Rifun said as Titik's eyes finally found him. "You survived, you hard-headed bastard."

Titik made a hissing or choffing sound.

"Do you even remember who I am?"

"Liars..." Titik hissed. "Traitors...betray your allies..."

"We're not allies anymore, remember? You said you were done." Rifun shifted his stance. "But I'm not. I need to know if you know anything more about the Book of Commands."

"Words...weedy words..."

"What do you know?"

"Know?" Titik choffed a laugh. "Many things...I know..."

"What do you know about the Book of Commands?"

"Lies..." the captain hissed. "Lies...dead now..."

Rifun pinched the bridge of his nose. This was going nowhere. Why had he expected to get anything out of this? Not everyone was so favored by the Author as to regain their faculties after such a devastating blow.

"Lies...dead now..." Titik repeated. "Truth...survives..."

"Yes, it always does," Rifun sighed, looking around helplessly.

"The heart of a black hole...weedy words..."

Now Rifun looked up. "What?"

"Words...words...words..."

"What did you say about a black hole?"

"Black hole's heart...weedy words..."

"The only thing inside a black hole is the Wheel of Time," Rifun stated. He blinked. "Words...you're talking about the Archives. Is the journal in the Archives?"

Titik hissed at him like an animal.

"How do you know this? Who told you?"

Another choffing laugh. "Puppets...and puppet masters...betrayal..." He tapered off into hoarse giggles. "Animals...in a trap...a trap they made..."

"Who told you?" Rifun repeated forcefully.

Now Titik got angry. Had he been able to move, Rifun could easily envision him going berserk, or savage. "Attack! Take the jewel! Punish the allies!" He settled some. "Foolish alliance...stupid Titik. Money is the only pleasure in the world!"

"What jewel?"

"Joy of the sky..." Titik lamented loudly.

"Your ship? We didn't take your ship. I'm sure the Psiaco police—"

"Joy of the sky, free of the wind. Too far, too far..."

Something in Rifun's mind clicked. "You're talking about Pilory, aren't you?" A hiss confirmed this. "Who took Pilory?"

All he got was another hiss.

From what Rifun had read, Ururians weren't that smart, or that vicious. Abbal Duma wouldn't have taken Pilory. The Turitians, perhaps? Rifun inquired about this. He didn't fully understand the response, but it was safe to guess it was a no.

"Cassius and I were gone for forty years," Rifun stated. "Julianna is trapped in another dimension. Isthim—"

Titik made an awful hissing snarling sound. "Foolish alliances...stupid Titik..." He raised his voice again. "Attack! Take the jewel! Punish the allies!"

"Isthim took Pilory," Rifun said. "But what does that have to do with the Ururian or the Book of Commands?"

"Animals...in a trap..." Titik hissed lowly. "Weedy words..."

It almost sounded like he really was trying to say something that made sense, but couldn't.

Rifun donned his Disguise, then dropped the Band and his hold on Titik at the same time. The captain again went savage, lurching against fragile restraints and swinging for the doctors and guards more than Rifun. In the chaos, Rifun opened a portal and escaped.

He spent a short period recovering from repeated portal use in such a short amount of time, then headed off to find Isthim. She was not in the officers building at all, and it was some time before he found her out and about in the city. Her demeanor said she was on some errand or another, and Rifun fell into step beside her.

"I just had the most interesting conversation," he began.

"This one should be equally as interesting if you wish for me to partake," Isthim rebutted.

"Then I'll just get to the point. Where is the Book of Commands?"

She stopped short. He, just in front of her, turned to face her.

"We are all in this together still, right?" Rifun inquired innocently. "As a team? Equal leaders of this organization?" He did not give her a chance to answer.

"Where is it, how did you come to have it, and why didn't you see fit to mention it to the rest of us at some point in the last week since we've been back?"

Isthim glowered at him for a long moment. Then, "The Ururian was captured. He had the Book of Commands. I verified it. Julianna verified it. It is the real journal this time."

"Then we should get it—"

"The Ururian escaped."

"So what?"

"As per the original plan, the journal was kept in a temple in Ancrath. The temple vaults are very old with only one key to one lock and one lock to one key."

Rifun let out a breath and couldn't help but slump slightly. "The Ururian took it, didn't he?"

"He did, yes."

"So where is the key? Or did he give your hunters the slip again?"

"He was captured, yes, but he did not have the key. When he was interrogated, he revealed that it was to be hidden in the Core of the Wheel by the Akarin Builders."

Rifun looked away. "Damn it." He huffed a sigh. "Well, it's a start. At least we know where it is. Again, why not bring this up sooner?"

"Because it is a known thing," Isthim told him irritably. "With Cassius working on impersonating Doug, we have a lead on the Akarin angle, and you have the ability to retrieve the key from the Core. But the elections are coming up and we have Lily Guile to deal with. Priorities were arranged."

He nodded slowly. "Fair enough."

She started walking again, but before she could get more than four steps, he asked, "So where does Captain Titik come into this?"

Isthim paused, then answered, "The Ururian was once briefly affiliated with Titik. Apparently he made a friend—"

"Pilory."

"If she was a Tibidi. She helped the Ururian to escape the hunters for a time."

"So you captured her, too."

"It was more than fair. We should have taken Titik and his whole crew and his ship."

"A little late for that now. He's been captured by the Psiaco Keepers and mortally wounded. His crew is arrested or dead, his ship taken."

Her expression hardly changed. "Our loss, then. Maybe next time we won't hesitate."

Rifun considered Cassius' warning from the cave, about Isthim's plans to get the Cult to effectively enslave themselves. "This is a joint endeavor for social, political, and religious change, not an open air slave market for you."

Isthim shrugged. "Many Borelians would say that enslavement is one of the fastest ways to enact social, political, and religious change in a person."

She departed before he could say anything more.

Considering that she hadn't even so much as mentioned the Book of Commands until now, Rifun could only conclude that her confidence in her plan was growing, which meant all the loose ends and all the ways it could go wrong were slowly being mended, the Cult slowly getting boxed in. Likely she already had plans for the elections coming up.

Cassius' first answer would be to kill her, then kill the rest of the Borelians in their ranks. Even Rifun knew that wasn't going to go over well. They were going to need more men, more well-trained men. The Akarin might help if Cassius-as-Doug convinced them, though that was a serious gamble.

Tommen Forbes. Their paths had not crossed coincidentally. Micaiah Durvin being involved was also not a coincidence. This was providence. This was the Author giving him a way out. Maybe Tommen was another dual-spirited person. With Cassius on one side and Isthim on the other, it might take two to take them both down. He didn't know where Micaiah fit into this, but that would reveal itself in time, he was sure.

And somehow, he was going to have to retrieve the Book of Commands from a Borelian temple of death. With the way Isthim's plan was going, and with the excuse that it had disappeared too many times already, he doubted that she was going to hand it over willingly.

The elections were less than a year away. Time to get moving.

kokumbo

oug's day job was a nightmare of boredom. Business dealings, finance stuff, legal jargon, all of it cluttering up desks and emails and computers until Cassius felt mentally catatonic by noon. The worst part was that he couldn't pawn it off on anyone else in the company because he was not only supposed to be super savvy about such things, but he was supposed to want to show off just how good he was. In fact, others sent him their projects or papers so he could figure them out. Some of these other people did it out of necessity, others because he'd apparently told them to.

Only the advent of computers helped Cassius in any regard, the ability to let the spreadsheet do the work for him. That, and the ability to look up virtually anything on the Internet. Working from home most of the time was also helpful, so he didn't have to suffer through a skin suit, too. He could type out a flagrant, narcissistic email at any time; he didn't know how well he could spontaneously conjure such a physical attitude in an office setting all day every day.

The few times he did go in and do work, it was a miracle everyone survived. How did people live like that? Petty, shallow, narcissistic in their own way, it was a wonder anything got done. And people had the audacity to call Doug insufferable? Did they even know what a mirror was?

Everyone had to go. Before he left Doug's life and this shitshow behind him, he was going to murder everyone. If it wouldn't attract so much attention now, he might have already done it. But if such a thing happened, even if Doug were supposed to be working at home, someone would call him and he would be expected to act. Not by the general public, of course, but the Akarin might be suspicious why he didn't step in and do something. As one of the more powerful Akari-bearers, there were few who could pose a challenge to him, so there should be no reason for him to hesitate.

As Cassius shut down his computer for the day, around three o'clock, he found himself seriously hoping that the elections put a solid end to this charade.

Doug was dead, and his death would be revealed. The Akarin were going to collapse and then they were going to be utterly annihilated. No more of this tiptoeing around, pretending to bid for peace. No more olive branches. No more half-baked schemes to wipe their memories or whatever bullshit. They were going to die, and Cassius was going to ensure that every single one of them was buried. To a man.

Then they could turn their attention to the Wheel and ruling over the universe. Cassius didn't understand how elections were going to solve anything, but Isthim had explained more than once that the general public was incredibly gullible and stupid. As long as things were done lawfully, as they were expected to, then even if the outcome was decidedly poor, they could accept it. Even if they didn't, it wasn't as though they, the Cult, were beholden to them. Ignore the barking dogs and carry on with their plans. Like the Akarin, people were excellent at posturing, but few had the nerve to act.

In the meantime, the best he could do for stress relief on Earth was Doug's little closet of horrors. Rather, Cassius had turned it into a closet of horrors. Doug might have pretended to enjoy certain things, but only Cassius could appreciate what those things really entailed.

He did convince Isthim to come and experiment with a few things, but she was surprisingly less enthusiastic than he expected her to be. It wasn't exactly medieval, but it was, by all accounts, a torture chamber. Padding had been removed, dull edges sharpened to a lethal point, rubber replaced by metal. He'd even added a few new things—he wouldn't call them toys necessarily, for although he enjoyed them, he would never diminish their importance with such a flippant term.

He touched the metal bed frame. The one Doug had used was small, light, aluminum, and it squeaked atrociously, likely intentionally. Cassius had since moved in a heavy cast iron bed frame. Only a great feat of strength, or Gravity, could move it, so anyone tied to it would have no hope of escape.

Isthim had been mildly intrigued when she saw this place, but laughed when he'd described its purpose. A silly game, she'd called it. A silly game for weak men who had to pretend what they could not do.

Her words had cut Cassius in a way he could not readily describe. In the moment, he had tried to force the issue, tried to bind her and show her what it was really about. This was no game.

Except it was, she said. Because she was not in fear. This was a place of pretend fear for pretend pleasure. Even victims whom he did intend to kill would likely know no fear until the very end, when they realized it was not a game. But how much time would be wasted getting to that point?

Cassius grumbled a little and left the room. He didn't want to admit that she was right, but she did have a point. This room was less exciting than the black cells in the Judgment Wing, because this room held expectations, good expectations. The black cells expected only despair and death, and Time could be warped in order to prolong the agony.

Suddenly furious, he lashed out, striking one of the many photos on the wall. The glass shattered, the frame came apart, and the image inside crumpled around his fist before falling to the floor.

This was bullshit. This was not what he was made for and even the joy of the perks had been denied him. At the least, Rifun should be doing this. At the most, they needed to stop pussyfooting around. Jumped forty years into the future, elections coming up fast, Book of Commands still missing thanks to Titik's blunders, and here he was, wasting away dealing with finances and lawyers.

He glanced back into the torture room. Pretend fear for pretend pleasure. He would give Isthim some "pretend fear." He would show her that this wasn't just a silly game to him.

And he might even make a little meaningful progress in their conundrum.

The problem with Harvesters was that they slowly acquired the traits of their victims, so tracking down Lily Guile was going to be more difficult than normal. He could put her name in a search engine, but when fifteen different women popped up, he had no good way to narrow down the search. He had no idea what her profession was either.

On the other hand, he could always go to the Wheel and search for her that way.

So he did. Even better, the Wheel computer still recognized him as the Zero Hour. Whether this was an oversight or because someone had done something he did not know, nor did he especially care. The point was, he had privileges.

For the time being, he just did a simple Time Agent search.

Registered Name: Lily Guile; Current Alias: Lily Guile; Rank: Master Harvester; Coordinates: 1-11-5-4-38-4-4

Region Four, District Four? Cassius quickly cross-referenced the area. Well,

well, Walter and Tommen Forbes. And Micah and Micaiah Durvin. Cassius had first-hand experience with the spirits, and though his opinion of them was rather low, even he could not deny that this was far more than a coincidence. How and why else would there be so many important people in a single area except that it had been ordained?

The Time industry was less concerned about the details of the Agents' day-to-day lives, although he did find a brief biography of Lily in the Archives, detailing an unusually meteoric rise to power and prominence in the Time industry despite being only a Master Harvester.

Curious, he looked for himself, using every name he had ever branded himself with. There was little about Cassius or Kokumbo, save for a few snippets of what amounted to "Wanted" posters or bounties. There was, however, plenty about Calis Cutthroat. While it amused him, he had a thought that he might want to do something about that with the elections coming up. Erase himself, spark the fear anew when they did...whatever the hell they were supposed to do. He rolled his eyes. They were doomed to fail. Divine providence was literally the only thing keeping them afloat right now, and he couldn't figure out why. If he were a god—and he basically was, honestly—he would have left them to die a long time ago.

He strangled a groan of pain as the bullet in his face began to throb, causing his eye to twitch uncontrollably. *Then consider the patience I have had with you,* the dragon spirit hissed. *And know that it is almost out.*

Yes, yes. Cassius tried to shrug it off and walk away, pretend nothing had happened even as he couldn't stop his gaze from darting to every shadow, wondering if the dragon was watching him from every dark corner.

I do not need darkness and shadows to watch you, it hissed, more faintly now. *I am you.*

The bullet stopped throbbing.

He returned to Earth to continue his search for Lily Guile. District Four was large, but at least it was a starting point. All he had to do was type in her name and then start going through a list of states and provinces.

As it turned out, there were four Lily Guiles in District Four, one in Quebec, one in Maine, one in Georgia, and one in West Virginia. Appearances mattered little, and age would necessarily be fabricated. But then, if he were to follow the string of coincidences, why not go with the woman in West Virginia?

This Lily Guile was the head of the Neonatal Intensive Care Unit in, coincidentally, Charleston, WV, living right alongside Walter, Tommen, Micah, and Micaiah. Cassius decided this was the woman. Working with sickly and premature infants, she would have access to entire lifetimes to sell in the Wheel, making her fabulously wealthy and, therefore, highly influential.

He shut down the computer and stood. Honestly, he probably could have just asked Isthim, seeing how she was the one overseeing the handling of Lily Guile. But he didn't want to. For one, she had laughed at his torture room, and for two, he needed to do something exciting because Doug's life was a bag of bricks.

Having been to Charleston multiple times, it was not difficult to open a portal there now. He did not try to home in on Lily's position, deciding instead to look around and observe her from afar.

This was surprisingly difficult, as security at the children's hospital was quite strict. Every door that wasn't a public door required special access. Even when he did go in the public doors, he was heavily scrutinized and denied access to some areas because he lacked the proper wristband or other documentation. It was impressive, Cassius wouldn't lie. It also wasn't a serious problem for someone who could manipulate physics to bypass these obstacles. A Disguise kept him from being recognized as a repeat offender and potential threat in the event he was caught. Electricity or Magnetism could take care of the secured doors, and Time could get him past the security guards. Gravity could forcibly move the elevators, or he could just take the stairs and side-step the hassle.

The whole hospital was a massive facade. Brightly-colored murals graced halls of sickness and death. Stuffed animals and puppets covered up instruments of interrogation. It was beautiful and repulsive at the same time, and Cassius wasn't sure what to make of it.

For all the color and sparkles, the seriousness of NICU bled through it all, permeating the air with anxiety and the literal death of innocence. Currently Disguised as an average white man, Cassius made slow rounds through the floor. He didn't enter any of the rooms, but he studied the tiny boxes filled with tinier babies. Many of them had at least one parent present, though there were a few that were unattended at the moment.

To a Harvester, every living thing had an aura. The color of the aura told the Harvester how many years a person had left. Those with a black aura were on death's door. Those with gold auras, like these little babies, had decades. More experienced Harvesters could see both the Actual and Possible Time of a person, assuming those Times were not reasonably similar. These babies, for instance. All of them had the golden glow of a lifetime ahead of them. Many of them had a silver lining that said their lives were likely to run just that long, barring disaster. But then there were a few whose glow was lined with dark gray and black. For all the medical intervention being done, it just wouldn't be enough in the end.

Cassius had no need for the years. He had whole lifetimes to spare. But what would it be like to watch any of these parents and their sudden realization that their little bundle of joy suddenly went silent, the rhythms on the machine suddenly gone?

Lily Guile was a sneaky bitch, that was for sure, but Cassius found that he couldn't muster up the same hatred as before. He would admit, there was a bit of admiration in there, too. She had found the perfect profession for the silent killer who wanted to be hailed a hero. And to think that she was the one in charge here. How was that for irony?

He stopped one of the nurses.

"Excuse me, I'm looking for Dr. Guile," he said, hoping he sounded appropriately distressed.

"I'm afraid she's not in today," the nurse informed him. "She'll be back tomorrow."

"I can't be here tomorrow, only today."

"I'm sorry. She's not in."

And that was that. The nurse went on her way before Cassius could inquire as to her whereabouts.

He could come back tomorrow, he supposed. There was no real reason he couldn't except that he'd had an idea and wanted to carry it out right away. He'd set out with the intent of talking to Lily Guile; he didn't want to wait until tomorrow. Except now he was stuck between two unappealing choices: wait until tomorrow, or waste a fantastic amount of time looking for her.

A third option crossed his mind as he walked down the stairs. Maybe the hospital kept records of their employees' residences. Of course they did. Doug's company did, so why wouldn't a hospital, especially one with this much security?

The problem he encountered with this path of investigation was that everything was digital and required passwords and other verification. As Cassius had discovered, because computers were so interconnected anymore, it became extremely difficult, if not impossible, to Band them. And nothing of importance was stored in the individual computers, but on servers, which didn't help him at all.

They'd recently made the acquaintance of a Japanese Timekeeper who, having learned the Akari while Cassius and Rifun were away, claimed that it was possible, with careful study, to combine Touch and Electricity on a computer and read the data inside, very much like Feeling a wound in a human being. How true this was, Cassius did not know, and he wasn't in a mood to experiment.

Did no one use the postal service anyone? Was there no actual paper trail to follow?

He couldn't find any.

Frustrated, he returned home. Actually, he kind of liked having a home to return to, in the sense that he wasn't expected to report back to the officers building every night. He could masquerade as Doug even if he wasn't actually masquerading as Doug.

Fine, so he wouldn't be talking to Lily today. By this point, he wasn't even sure why he'd gone looking for her in the first place. What did he expect to do? Tell her to stop Harvesting babies? No, because he was pondering the same thing. Tell her to stop buying votes and seats in the Wheel? Hardly. Tell her to be nice to the Cult and the scary Borelians? He didn't even want to do that. So what was this about exactly?

Well, it would give him something to do, anyway, other than look at emails and spreadsheets and text messages and an empty torture room.

Another night. Another day.

It was Friday, when most of the people in the office took off early. Cassius ducked out at noon even though he was still "working from home." Monday he was expected to go in, but maybe he could accomplish enough this weekend to make it worth his consideration.

And it wasn't like the Akarin were much more exciting. They were almost as boring as Rifun. Constant meetings, whining, complaining. They didn't really care about anything unless it affected them, and even then, they were more likely to just brush it off and wait for things to pass them by. The one time, after the first meeting, he had even brought up a hint of the Cult or a potential threat, the Akarin council told him to shut up about it. The Cult wasn't a threat, and even if they were, the Author would keep them safe. That was the reason for the fortress. That was the reason they had been safe for so long.

What happened to all the energy and excitement? What happened to vigilance? Yes, Cassius wanted to be rid of them, but he really preferred his enemies to at least try and fight back. He liked seeing their expressions when they realized they'd lost. He didn't want to fight a ragdoll.

By one o'clock he was back in Charleston, about half a mile from the children's hospital. He'd thought about just Banding and walking into her office and waiting for her, then decided the subtle approach might be more effective.

He got inside, made it up to NICU. As he asked the same nurse about Lily Guile, he made sure to throw in some frustrated story about having to take a day off of work to do this. The nurse showed very little sympathy but directed him to Lily's office.

Her hair wasn't quite bleach blond but close enough, artificial curls tumbling to her waist. Not especially tall but with the body of a porn star, Lily sat at her desk, four folders open before her. She looked up as he entered, her expression annoyed until she perceived that he was a member of the public and not one of her nurses.

"Can I help you?" she inquired politely, closing the folders and sitting up in her seat.

"I was here yesterday to speak to you, but you weren't in," Cassius said, trying to sound meek as he crossed the room, finally standing across from her.

"Well, I'm here today. How can I help?"

Now he sighed. "I don't like it when I have to wait on people. It annoys me."

He dropped his Disguise.

Lily stood, but that was all she did. Her posture was rigid for a long moment, then she relaxed.

"Isthim can't be bothered to stoop so low, so she sends you to kill me."

"Isthim didn't send me, and I haven't decided if that's what I'm going to do."

Lily scoffed and waved a hand. "Please. That's all you do." She went on before he could speak. "You don't have to lie to me, Cassius or Calis or whatever the fuck you're calling yourself these days. I know why you're here."

"You say that, and yet you're not trying to run away."

She grinned and shook her head. "Forty fucking years. You know, the way I figured it, either you weren't coming back, in which case, fuck Isthim and the rest of you, or else the first thing you were going to do on your return was kill me, so I may as well live it up while I have the chance. And here we are." She made a mild gesture. "So do it. Kill me."

"Not even going to try to beg, plead for some semblance of mercy?" Cassius wondered.

Now she gave him a look. "What, you can't do it unless I do? I admit, I've known a few men like that, but you didn't strike me as one of them."

"I don't need a reason, but it does seem a bit too easy."

"You think it's a trap? That I somehow spent my time coming up with how I would respond if and when you showed up here on a random Friday to threaten me?" She shrugged. "Well, I might have spent some time doing that. But it doesn't explain why I'm still alive. Since when does Calis Cutthroat hesitate?"

He Banded, walked around her desk, grabbed her by the hair, spun her around, bent her back over the desk, and put a knife to her throat. He did not release the Band, but brought her into it.

"Who's hesitating?" he hissed.

She blinked several times, trying to figure out just what was going on, fighting the fear that cropped up when that realization came into focus. She managed a small grin and relaxed as much as her position would allow. "You are. You're one of the most powerful Harvesters in the universe, capable of Harvesting at a touch. Still you rely on knife tricks and fear." With her head held back so her neck was exposed, she couldn't get in more than a short, hoarse chuckle. "You really can't do it unless I do. You can't kill me unless I show you fear. You get off on the fear, the helplessness, the pleas for mercy." She made an indeterminate sound. "Well, you're not going to get it. Not from me. Not today, not tomorrow, not ever."

Cassius snarled, pushed the blade closer, but did not kill her. He released her hair and lowered the blade.

She laughed at him. She laughed at him like Isthim had laughed at him.

"The greatest flame always begets cold ash, Calis," Lily said, still smiling. "Your flame burned brighter and hotter than most, but even you are fading." She chuckled darkly. "I've made sure of that. The Cult has been neutered. And after these next elections, there will be nothing left. You might get a footnote if you're lucky."

"You're working for the Akarin, then?" Cassius questioned.

She waved a hand. "I don't give two shits about the Akarin. I'm returning the Time industry to its roots: money and business. You give me money, I give you eternal life. As it always should have been, before you bastards started bringing religion into it, to say nothing of the politics already in play."

"Going to make yourself a queen?"

"I already am. They just don't know it yet."

Still she showed no fear. Cassius had a notion that he was not the first person to threaten her, nor was he likely the scariest, as much as it pained him to consider it. Perhaps Isthim herself had threatened Lily at some point.

Whatever the case, he was losing his touch. Something must have shown on his face, for she shrugged and said, "Sorry I can't meet your fear quota. You know, most Time Agents only last about double their species' average lifespan. For humans, that's about two hundred years. There are plenty of species that are even shorter-lived." She sighed dramatically. "Point is, you're part of the old generation of chaos and fear, from the days of the Missing Zero Hour and Dispersal. There's a whole new generation of mercenaries out there, and they've actually been around doing things."

"I already took care of the Gentleman Killers," Cassius said weakly.

"Who?" Lily inquired innocently, her tone suggesting she knew exactly who he was talking about.

"Who are these new mercenaries?" he demanded.

She laughed again. Her every smirk, smile, chuckle, giggle, laugh, and spoken word was infuriating, yet it shook him at his very core, rooted him to the ground so he could not move to kill her.

He was old. Yes, yes, he had many more years than most, but suddenly it occurred to him that he was...old. Outdated. Washed up. He was yesterday's news, the terror of a bygone era. The Cult was an ambitious idea sunk in an ocean of weak leadership and bad ideas. He was an ancient mass murderer who apparently couldn't even inspire fear in a helpless woman.

"Sorry, is this getting a little too close to home?" she taunted, twisting that knife just a little more. "Well, I hate to be the one to break it to you, but...you're done. All of you. As far as I'm concerned, this little club of yours is a failed experiment. As far as anyone else is concerned—anyone who matters, anyway— you are nothing more than a footnote." She turned her attention nonchalantly back to the folders on her desk. "Now if you'll excuse me, I have work to do."

Reluctantly, he released the Band and moved back around the desk, not even bothering with his Disguise. Lily returned to her work, speaking no more to him, not even looking at him.

Suddenly devoid of will, Cassius did not even bother navigating his way out of the hospital, simply opened a portal right there, from her office to his. There he made his way behind his desk—Doug's office and Doug's desk, really—and sat down in a heap.

He did not know how long he sat there. Maybe half an hour or so. He genuinely did not know how to respond to this. He wasn't even sure what this was. If he had to pick a word, he might have said...irrelevance. He was irrelevant now. No one knew about him. No one cared. He was feared in the same way any evil man in history was feared: he wasn't, because he was, at least in his case, metaphorically dead. At least before he'd still had the notoriety of the Missing Zero Hour, but even that had since faded.

Lily was right. The Cult was a failed experiment. There was nothing he could really point to as an example of their power being efficiently and effectively managed. They were just another small faction with a big mouth.

He looked at the computer on the desk, quiet at the moment.

He was sitting here. Doing spreadsheets. Fucking—spreadsheets. Impersonating a man no one liked, leading a group that didn't do a whole hell of a lot anyway. And that group didn't even listen to the man he was impersonating. The Akarin were as weak as the Cult. And if Lily got her way in the elections, neither one of them would be relevant come the dawn of the day after.

Angrily, he stood, cleared the desk with a mighty sweep of his arm, then opened a portal to the officers building on Sadurnon. Judging by the lack of activity, it was about the middle of the night. This did not stop Cassius from using Force to fling the doors wide open and Light to suddenly blind everyone in each room as he came to it, stunning them to wakefulness.

The only person who had never actually been a soldier was Cassius—and Julianna, but she wasn't here right now. The rest of them, Rifun and the Borelians, were quite punctual in their response to the sudden wake up call. Cassius did not give a lot of details, just yelled repeatedly that he wanted to call a meeting right away and everyone better be there.

It didn't take five minutes for everyone to assemble in the meeting room, and the most satisfaction Cassius felt about it came from the subtle bewilderment of the Borelians. What had happened? What was this meeting about? How did this affect their plans?

"All right, here's the situation," Cassius began, closing the door. "Actually, here's what we're going to do." He went to the table and put his hands out, leaning on the table menacingly. "We're going to assassinate the Hands of Time. And the Grandfathers." He quickly clarified, "The non-Borelian Grandfathers. And every Time Agent who doesn't want to be part of our group and swear fealty."

Confused glances were exchanged.

"And what prompted this?" General Misik wondered.

"I had a meeting with Lily Guile earlier. Impromptu, as this is impromptu. I find that impromptu meetings get the most honest results."

"Did you kill her?" Rifun asked.

Cassius gave him a look. "No. Believe me, I wanted to. As it turns out, not killing her allowed me to get more information out of her." He looked at Isthim. "You said she had become difficult to handle. I imagine this might have something to do with her plan to mobilize the Hands and the Grandfathers against both the Cult and the Akarin after this next election. She seems to think that this crop of Hands that she's buying in are going to do this. I don't know how, but that is the way things stand."

He went on before anyone could object. "And let's face it, the Hands would have a chance. They would have a very good chance. They have the numbers, they have the motivation. And what do we have? The Akari? Laughable. If the Akari meant anything, we would already be in power and not scrambling to find dusty tomes, worrying about the rescue of useless individuals."

"You helped dictate and write those dusty tomes for that useless individual," Rifun reminded him. "You are effectively responsible for everyone being here today."

"And you are responsible for us being where we are now!" Cassius snapped. "Standing around in a crumbling temple with nothing to show for ourselves, possessing the greatest power in the universe and being threatened by those who have but a shadow of it!" He slapped his palm repeatedly on the table. "I am not—listening to you anymore! My way is the only way that has proven effective at getting things done. Therefore, we will be doing things my way from now on!"

One of the Borelians put up a hand. "So you expect to just walk into the Wheel, kill all fifty-one Hands, slaughter the Grandfathers, then line up every single Time Agent in the universe—all the billions and billions of them—and offer them an ultimatum?"

Cassius gave him a look. "Quite frankly, yes."

"Are you even interested in the logistics of such a thing, or are you more interested in just running off to meet the consequences of your actions?" Rifun asked, sighing.

"Oh, do enlighten me. Tell me about how it will be difficult or tedious or not very smart." He slapped the table again. "Stop—fucking—whining. I've told you this before and I will say it again: we are gods. We have the power and the physics of the universe at our fingertips and you are worried about what people might think. We take our place as gods, we dictate what is right and wrong. If what we say we do is good, then it will be so. We will shape morality to us. As I did when I dictated the journals."

"The journals said that each man should govern his own affairs."

"And he will. As long as those affairs don't threaten us." Cassius continued before anyone could object. "This is no longer up for debate. I'm tired of you bastards sitting on your hands, worrying about timelines and logistics and morality. We have become nothing but a small group of dusty old philosophers." He straightened. "But I am going to change that."

He was getting real tired of Rifun's sighs, and he only just tolerated the one the man gave now as he said, "Well, for as much as you may not like logistics, may I make at least a few suggestions?"

Cassius folded his arms. "You can talk. It's what you're good at. I am under no obligation to heed your empty words."

"Don't try anything right now. Wait until the elections." Rifun put up a hand and there was a minute of them trying to talk over each other before Cassius finally relented. Rifun went on, "The elections, and especially Inauguration Day, are when there are the most number of Time Agents in the Wheel. Officers are required to attend. Get the Hands and the officers all in the Coliseum at the same time. Then kill them."

"It will give us time to coordinate the Grandfathers," General Misik threw in.

Cassius took an even breath, considered their words, considered his options. Finally he nodded. "Fine. But know that when Inauguration Day comes, I'm murdering those bastards and seizing control, with or without you."

"And Lily Guile?" Isthim wondered. "She is not an officer, but she is the most influential person in this election by far. Kill her before the election and—"

"I don't care if things spiral out of control or make things a teensy bit more difficult for those of you who sit in an office all day. I'm the one doing the work.

And now, I'm the one calling the shots. As for Lily specifically, I have my own plans for her."

He could see how uncomfortable he was making them, especially Rifun, and he was enjoying every second of it.

"Furthermore, I'm taking Doug dark. I can't get anything done if I have to sit around worrying about fucking spreadsheets. I don't know what the fuck I'm doing and it's only going to blow my cover." He fixed Rifun in a stare and managed to talk over him, "If you still want me to impersonate him, this is the best idea I have."

"It takes weeks, even months to go dark," Rifun told him.

"Yes, and?"

"And what are you going to tell everyone?" Isthim wondered, her expression suggesting she was not in any real distress over it, more mildly curious.

"The people on Earth can fuck off for all I care. As for anyone who needs to know, I can start spreading rumors about the Cult and some massive thing that I think we're planning. The Akarin council has summarily dismissed me, so it will make it more ironic, I think. Either that, or I'm just a Chicken Little."

He could tell the Borelians were perplexed by the analogy, but Rifun's expression said he understood perfectly.

"This is what we're doing," Cassius stated firmly. "This is what is happening. It's going to be a long time until the next elections, but we don't have that long. So if anyone even hints at delaying this plan, he's either going to have a good fucking reason or a knife in his throat." He straightened. "No questions!"

He whirled around and stalked out of the room.

One last chance, he thought. He was giving them one last chance to prove their worth. As it was, he was going to have to find something to bolster his own reputation, make people fear the name Calis Cutthroat again. What was the point of living longer if you were still only going to be replaced? He could not, would not be replaced.

But you will, the dragon spirit whispered in his ear.

No. I've only stepped out of time on a few occasions, but I — me, I'm still as fearsome as I ever was.

Everyone outlives their usefulness eventually.

You dictated the journals to me, and it seems that the Cult has never been very useful.

Useful enough, and it is not the only project I have.

The Hand Holding the Knife

Don't put all your eggs in one basket, huh?

The spirit did not reply to that, but its tone seemed to be more of a warning. Time was running out for both the Cult and Cassius himself. He had been raised up for a grand purpose but somehow fallen far enough that the dragon was prepared to do a clean sweep of the board and start over somewhere else.

No. Cassius was not going to let that happen. He was going to take charge now and do things the way they should have been done in the first place.

After cooling off for a few minutes, he donned his Doug Disguise and headed to the Akarin fortress.

Going dark was basically outsourcing all the legal paperwork to take yourself out of your current life in society and then put you back in. This was necessary for Time Agents and Akari-bearers from Unengaged worlds who might grow suspicious that their neighbor of fifty years still looked like a recent college graduate. Depending on how soon you wanted to re-enter society, and where and how and everything else, it was entirely possible to just wait it out for a while. Trying to re-enter society was the hard part. Birthdays had to be fudged, documents forged, histories rewritten, witnesses sworn, all of it.

In Cassius' case — or Doug's case — he just had to quit his job and get rid of the house. It was going to be fast and less than graceful, but he didn't care about normal people. Let the lawyers fight it out; Doug Templeton was leaving town quick. Cassius had no plans to re-enter society as Doug Templeton. He was going to be too busy getting people hyped up about something happening in the Wheel with the elections and the Cult.

All he really needed, then, was a bunk. Cassius would have been happy anywhere, but he figured Doug would demand accommodations with a few more amenities.

No one looked happy to see him when he walked in the office and asked for an open bed.

"I'm going dark for a while," he announced so the entire floor could hear him, "so I need a bed. I don't know how long I'm going to be, a few months probably. At least through the elections in the Wheel. Something happens there, I need to be close to hand so you can rely on my knowledge and expertise to get us through."

Cassius was not an expert on alien expressions, but he figured this one was bored and annoyed, both by his presence and his insistence that something was going to happen at these elections. Did no one believe him? Were they that disenchanted or was the Cult that weak? Stupid question, the answer was both.

"I think your bed from last time is currently taken," the office worker sighed. "But there are some other options available. Marchizek just left; you could take the bed he was using."

He didn't know who Marchizek was, but he went along with it. "Sounds good to me! Let's do it!"

There wasn't much ceremony to claiming a bed. There weren't any bills or fees or nightly rates that he was aware of; mostly it just had to do with keeping track of how many beds were taken and who was where and when. The fortress was not actually big enough to accommodate everyone at the same time; rotation was key.

He didn't receive any papers or keys or anything, and he left the office with his head held high, hoping he looked like he knew what he was doing, where he was going, who this Marchizek person was.

The officer barracks were on the fourth floor. There were large bays of military-style bunks for those who weren't staying long or were unconcerned about their accommodations. Then there were proper rooms for those who did care.

Cassius lucked out finding his room, as the label on the door still read "Marchizek." Well, unless there was more than one Marchizek running around, this was his room. Even if there was another Marchizek running around, this was his room. It wasn't much, ten by ten, a large bed, a small dresser, and a desk that was perhaps more of a nightstand.

Disguises couldn't be held while unconscious, which could prove to be a problem if he ever chose to sleep here. Really he was doing this for show, to be close to hand when it hit the fan. He would still be sleeping in the officers building in the Ruins of Meroian. That bed would be an escape from the drudgery of the Akarin, and this bed would be an escape from the ineptitude of the Cult.

Something really needed to happen in these elections. He would make something happen.

What if he slept here as Cassius and someone found him? That would cause a ruckus, wouldn't it? Even a little panic? Maybe mildly startle the one who found him?

Damn it, he needed to get his name back out there. His name was the fearsome one, not Rifun or the Cult at large. Put himself out there, get things stirred up, then maybe these people would take him a little more seriously.

He couldn't threaten the Akarin; they wouldn't take him seriously and it would just turn into a distraction. Threatening the Wheel or the Hands, well, honestly, it wasn't anything they didn't already deal with. He had to make it credible, like when he went after the Gentlemen Killers.

Lily Guile. He had to go after her, but even she didn't take him seriously. He had to get close to her, get that needle under her skin. As Isthim had said on several occasions, give a man just a reason to fear and he will torture himself for you. She did not fear him because she had no reason to. She thought she was ready for death. Thing was, very few people who claimed such a thing were actually ready. He needed to give her a reason to fear. At this point, he was obligated to kill her; he just needed to figure out the best way to go about it.

He returned to Earth, to Charleston, West Virginia. There he donned another Disguise, this time as what he believed to be any average male on the street. Five-eleven, maybe six-foot, white, brown hair, brown eyes, average build, about as plain as plain could be.

He did not enter the children's hospital, did not get any closer than about half a block away. He found a park bench, sat, and pretended to read a newspaper he'd stolen from some corner store. He acquired a phone and ear buds which he used to pretend to listen to music, though his focus always remained on the hospital. He used Sound to decrease the ambient noise of the interstate and city traffic, allowing him to better hear the goings-on around the hospital.

About once every hour, he stood, walked around the block, ducked into an alley to change out his Disguise, then returned to a similar position. Sometimes he had a newspaper, sometimes a regular book, once he had a candy bar that was, in a word, disgusting. He traded that out for a sandwich the next time around.

Finally, around eight o'clock, Lily emerged from the hospital through one of the secure doors marked "Employees Only - Identification Required." He saw her stop, give the vicinity a brief glance, then head out to what looked to be a very expensive car. Halfway across the parking lot, she started undoing her hair and removing any unnecessary clothing. By the time she ducked into the driver's seat, she looked ready for a street corner.

When she turned out of the lot, Cassius Banded so he could get a better view of where she was going. He released the Band, watched her zoom away to a particular intersection where she turned, not even bothering with a signal. This did not bother him as he Banded again, caught up to her position, then released the

Band so he could watch her drive a few blocks more, and turn again. From there, she kept straight on the road for several miles. Cassius continued to follow her to a bar where she met up with a few other people of similar apparent chastity.

Cassius entered the bar about ten minutes later, sitting six tables away from Lily and her cohorts at the bar. He forwent the alcohol and opted for a light appetizer. After the food, he pretended to be interested in whatever sportsball game was on the TV that at least half the bar seemed uncomfortably enraptured by. Eventually, however, he got bored. Lily and her friends were multiple drinks into their evening with no sign of stopping.

He left the bar but, as with the hospital, stuck around to observe. It was past midnight when Lily and four of her friends stumbled out. They all got into another expensive car, the driver clearly sober.

From there it was another hour of following this car on its route to drop off all of the drunk patrons. Lily was the last, of course, swaggering into the condominium complex, laughing hysterically about nothing. Cassius waited for the car to depart before going inside. He was just in time to see the elevator doors click shut, Lily leaning heavily against one side of the car.

He Banded so he could take the stairs and make it look like he reached her condo before she did, even if he didn't actually know which one was hers. He eventually got the right floor and waited patiently for her to unlock the door—which was a far more painfully coordinated endeavor than it should have been—where he slipped inside. With her addled brain, she probably would not have noticed him, but he Banded anyway just to be safe.

He stood in the middle of her living room, not saying a word but itching with delight as he released the Band. Lily stumbled inside, muttered a few curses as she bumped something or other. Her hand slapped the wall a few times before finding the light switch.

"Hello, Lily," Cassius greeting, unable to suppress a grin.

She looked at him. She did not startle, and her expression said she did not recognize him. He waited a moment, waited for that realization, waited for the inevitable fear. It never came.

"Who are you?" she asked. "How...did you get in here?"

"I followed you," he told her, trying to sound as menacing as possible.

"Oh, you did?" She almost sounded happy about it as she approached him and drunkenly patted his chest. "Well you're so sweet, wanting to make sure I get home safe." She giggled. "But I'm safe now."

He wanted to kill her. But she didn't even recognize him. What fun was there in that? The ultimate terror of the universe, whose name once sparked fear in the hearts of millions as he slunk from planet to planet, was making this woman laugh because she thought he was being sweet.

"You're welcome," he said hastily, roughly pushing past her and leaving the condo. He opened a portal to his room in the officers building just as soon as he could.

He paced the room several times, silently panicking. The dragon spirit was going to kill him. If he couldn't even spark the tiniest bit of fear in a woman, what use was he? He couldn't even be angry about it, really; he hated himself at that moment. He would probably kill himself if he wasn't suddenly struck with fear at the thought. And he hated himself all the more for it.

He needed to kill Lily Guile. Even if the dragon spirit killed him afterwards, he had to kill her first as his last act in this universe. But he couldn't kill her if she didn't fear him. He had to see the fear, the absolute terror in her eyes. Clearly just following her around town and speaking to her when she was so drunk she didn't know enough to be afraid wasn't going to do it. He had to do something more.

He would need an easier target first, one who would know to be afraid. He needed to send a message, and he had to make it big.

Cassius went down to Rifun's chambers, mildly surprised to find the man home, not surprised in the least to find him praying. Cassius almost started out with, "I need your help." Then he considered the situation and instead said, "You're going to help me."

Rifun paused in his murmured prayers, sighed, and sat up from where he bowed at some shrine. "Oh? And what task hast thou laid for me, my master?"

Cassius gave him a look but said, "I'm going to kill Lily Guile, but I need to terrorize her a little first. She needs to know that we're here, we're coming for her empire, and we're not the pushovers she thinks we are."

Rifun slowly got to his feet. "Well, as it so happens, I have a few tasks of my own to complete in this ambitious massacre you have planned. Give me a couple of days to gather some information and we might be able to pull something together."

The man could be stalling, but it was more cooperation than he'd honestly expected. After a moment of consideration, Cassius nodded. "You have two days."

4 | Fifandonana

The Caves of Meroian, 2013

Altercation

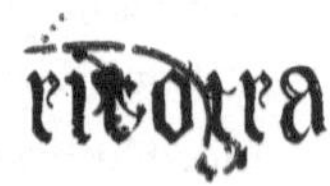

Cassius left Rifun's chambers in a mild fury. It was just as well that their encounter hadn't lasted long because Rifun had a lunch date to keep. He waited a moment more just to be sure the man was gone, then opened a portal to Fianarantsoa, a small alley where he wouldn't be detected. From there, it was half a block to the cafe where Lalao was just arriving, her hand in her son Tomas' arm.

Rifun hoped he did not betray anything amiss as he approached. The way her face lit up at the sight of him eased the worst of his fears. Tomas helped his mother into a chair on the cafe patio, then departed, promising to be back in a couple hours. Lalao waved a hand and told him there was no need to rush.

"Honestly, it's like he doesn't trust you," she huffed, looking at the menu.

"He wouldn't leave us alone together the first time we had lunch," Rifun reminded her.

"You'd think he was a father checking up on his daughter's suitors."

"Is that why he's not married yet?"

Lalao giggled. "Hardly."

He gave her a look. "Oh, come now. You're not feeble and infirm, needing care at every moment."

She met his look. "No, I'm not anymore, am I? Not since the cancer magically cleared up."

Rifun just leaned back, glancing over his own menu. "And they say miracles don't happen anymore."

The waitress came and took their drink orders, promising to be back swiftly.

"Speaking of miracles," Lalao said, turning her menu over to peruse the back side, "any progress on slaying this evil spirit you've told me about?"

"No good progress I'm afraid," he admitted. "He's gone mad recently, wants to kill someone, but first he seems to want to terrorize her by killing others she knows. Then I think he may try to kill me."

"Are you going to stop him?"

Rifun hesitated for half a second. "I don't condone what he wants to do. I don't support it, I don't like it. But I find myself at the crossroads of, if I kill him, yes, I may save the woman or women, but I still don't know how to defeat the evil spirit itself. Everything I know, everyone I've talked to, all the spirits I have prayed to, and no answer has surfaced."

Lalao frowned. "Perhaps it requires a touch of faith, then. Go into the battle not knowing the outcome, have faith that the spirits will guide your hand to strike when and where the time is right. It may be something that can only happen in the moment."

"But if it's not, the spirit gets away, and however it returns, whoever it possesses, it will come after me with a particular vengeance."

She made a kind of disapproving humming sound. "I suppose so, but it doesn't sound like you are going to have a whole lot of time left to spend in study and research. Eventually, you have to get into the fight itself."

He sighed. "I know."

The waitress returned with their drinks, and they gave her their food orders.

"Come now, Rivotra," Lalao said teasingly. "You must be thinking of something. You Disguised yourself as your own son and attended your own funeral. There must be some clever ideas left in that head of yours."

"Plenty of ideas, I don't know how many of them are all that clever."

She shifted in her seat. "Tell me more about what's going on. Maybe I can spark something or help you think it through."

He hesitated. Lalao could appreciate some of what he was experiencing. She understood his longer life, she understood some of his abilities, though she did not fully understand the Akari or the Time industry or any of the larger truths. He tried to shield her from some of the more outrageous concepts, confining everything to the mortal and the immortal, as they had all grown up with.

"Why does he want to kill this woman?" she pressed. "What makes her special?"

Rifun shrugged. "She's rich, she's corrupt. But most importantly, I think, is that she's not afraid of him."

Lalao hummed a bit. "Yes, evil spirits do enjoy fear, don't they? Though there is a certain wisdom in fear as well, understanding that we are only mortal. But there are a lot of people who are rich and corrupt and do not fear evil. Why her?"

"She's buying politicians and rigging courts."

Now her expression turned confused. "Would...would not the spirit then seek to...help her? Protect her?"

"I don't know. There's definitely something off about it. If I didn't know better, I would say he's afraid."

She mulled this over for a moment, frowning. "You think perhaps he displeased the spirit and now is doing this so the spirit does not harm him?"

He shook his head. "No. He has been far too loyal. I can't think of any way he could have displeased such a spirit."

Her expression said she wasn't convinced. "Spirits can be fickle, Rivotra. You know that. And for as loyal as he may have been, however good he is at killing, a dog that no longer listens to its master must be put down."

"Agreed. But that doesn't solve my problem of how to go about it."

Now she got a smirking grin. "A dog that no longer listens is more dangerous to its master than anyone else."

Rifun blinked and shifted in his seat. "Use the weapon against the master. But if he is just a corpse reanimated, there is only the master."

Lalao shrugged but her smirk remained. "It's only a suggestion. I am not a dual-spirited person with an extended life and the power of the razana at my fingertips."

"Maybe not, but you're no damsel in distress."

She waved her hand flippantly. "Bah! A dreadful Western notion! We either stand strong in the face of danger or we crumble. All of us, together. Man and woman, young and old."

Rifun just laughed.

The waitress brought their food. She had gotten a light rice dish while he opted for a marinated steak with rice and vegetables. He didn't need it, honestly; he wasn't especially hungry. But it was delicious. Their first lunch together, he'd tried to order something small. Lalao would have none of it, worrying that he was poor and not eating enough. He needed strength to slay demons. So now he got the bigger meals, reminding himself that he would just have to do some extra hard labor over the next week to work it off. Slaying evil spirits did seem like it might fall into that category.

Tasty food turned their conversation toward happier things, both past and present. Pretty soon, Tomas had returned. His tone was light and words friendly, but his demeanor toward Rifun was still confused. Rifun did not know what Lalao had told her youngest son about him, and he was afraid to ask.

"Same time next week?" he wondered.

"Oh, of course," she said, smiling. "I always look forward to it."

He dipped his head. "I'll be here."

They parted ways.

Not a few times, Rifun had thought about returning to Madagascar in Disguise, then drop it right before he reached the cafe, in the event that Cassius or the others followed him. The last thing he wanted was to put Lalao in danger. He decided against it in a small fit of self-loathing. Yes, he wanted to kill the evil spirit inside Cassius, but that evil spirit likely already knew that Lalao was special to him, and if he was forced to kill Cassius bodily and deal with the spirit later, then he would.

He could not, however, conjure up a similar attitude toward Lily Guile. He didn't know what kind of life she was leading on Earth right now, but if it was anything like her dealings in the Wheel, she was quite the bitch. Rich, powerful, corrupt, and flaunting it at every turn. If she was able to get Cassius this upset, well, maybe she deserved it.

He remembered the first time he saw Lily. Petite, blonde, demure, still following Julianna around, trying to figure out what this Harvesting and Time thing was really all about. Julianna had said that she didn't tell Lily a whole lot about the Cult, mostly because of Cassius, but Rifun wondered how true that was.

How had she turned into this? Had she always been this way and he just didn't know her well enough to have seen it before? Was that really the power and allure of money and fame? He couldn't even say why he was so concerned about it except to wonder whether Cassius was wrong to want to kill her. Cult politics aside, she was everything everyone hated about the Time industry.

He also couldn't shake Lalao's observation, that her work was exactly what dark spirits liked. Why would one dark spirit kill another?

There was something more at work here, something he wasn't seeing. Could it indeed be that Cassius had fallen out of favor with the spirit and was trying to avoid some terrible fate, even his own death?

Unfortunately, the man's erratic behavior was not allowing for as much time to sit quietly and ponder philosophy and religion, and Banding wasn't going to make Rifun feel any better about it. He had chores of his own to take care of before seeing where Cassius intended to take this insane venture.

He returned to the same alley where he opened a portal to Charleston, West Virginia. South Charleston to be specific, and there was a difference he'd learned. Even if it was technically northwest of Charleston proper.

And they say my people are primitive and stupid, Rifun mused, helping himself to a park bench while he reoriented himself and waited for the lingering nausea to pass.

He'd only gleaned information about Tommen Forbes, what he could learn from the Wheel and what might have been written about him in the local or school newspapers.

He'd first appeared in society back in 2005, an eight year old boy hit by a car. The only item on his person was a small journal, believed to be a miner's journal from the old salt cave near town, which was later donated to a museum. There followed a couple years of court records as he was put into the foster system, eventually being adopted by his biological uncle, now-Captain Walter Forbes of Charleston Police and also Timekeeper Captain of District Four. There was one minor newspaper article mentioning him and using him as a poster child for people and children who got left behind in society because they did not speak English well. Rifun couldn't help but chuckle at that. Judging by that evening at the bakery, the kid had learned plenty of English since then.

After that, there were only passing mentions of him, most often photo captions when he was photographed at various school or other local functions. There was never a mention of any awards, particular talents, or anything unusual, though this was hardly suspect.

The next logical step, then, would be observation from a distance. Did he have any Akari talents at all? Was Micaiah teaching him anything? How did he use it, if at all? If Micaiah wasn't teaching him, why not?

In spite of his many world and universe travels, the time differences always jarred him. Not for jet lag, but for the expected activities. He'd just gotten done having lunch in the middle of the afternoon in Fianarantsoa. He might have expected school in Charleston to be just getting out. Instead, it was just getting started. A few late cars scurried into the parking lot, the students running inside, but the bus lane was quiet and what activity he could see through the windows looked minimal.

Curiosity getting the better of him, Rifun Banded and went inside, sliding past a couple of the late students trying to juggle books and bags through the front doors. He looked in a number of classrooms before finally spotting the sophomore he believed to be Tommen Forbes.

Just as in the newspaper photographs, he was pasty white—enough to make Rifun look pretty dark—dark brown hair that looked like it was finally back to normal after a uniform trim, brown eyes, not yet six feet tall, paper thin although in most photos he was shown to be eating something, and somehow looking even less lively than the rest of his tired classmates. Peeking at the papers on his desk, his homework was only half done, his notes nonexistent. On the other hand, he had another notebook with him full of what might have been stories or journal entries. Unfortunately for Rifun, they were all in what he assumed to be Welsh, and he could not read them.

There was nothing sinister to be found, although Rifun hadn't expected to find anything. Maybe he had been hoping to find Tommen Banding in some way—judging by his enthusiasm for his class, he would have wanted to Slow Band his way through, maybe Fast Band to get his homework done before having to turn it in. No such luck.

He found nothing else of interest in the school and so retreated back outside. After a moment of consideration, he paid a visit to the bakery, again Banding so he would not be noticed, or it would be less likely.

The morning rush had ebbed, leaving the twins with a huge mess. This place was far more lively as far as unusual activity, but it wasn't what he'd expected. If Micaiah was still with the Akarin, why were they using regular Time Bands in the kitchen? Why fret over the oven when he had Energy abilities? Why worry about product being overdone or underdone when he could use Matter? Micah, fine, maybe he'd never been brought in. But was Micaiah simply not part of the Akarin anymore? Had he left them after the Time Trial? Rifun may have thought it would be a reason to stick with them, although, from Cassius' reports, the Akarin weren't such a lively bunch these days. Maybe they had abandoned him.

Still more puzzle pieces, but Cassius had decided to flip the table and murder everyone else who was seated.

Whatever he was going to do to Lily, if Rifun could keep him on track overall for the elections and Inauguration Day, it might buy him time to figure out how to make Cassius disappear in the chaos he wanted to cause.

He left the bakery and headed to a park to think and watch people, still in his average man Disguise.

After about half an hour of simple observation, he stood and made his way to the Charleston Police Department. He didn't know where Captain Forbes was at the moment, but it wouldn't hurt to take a quick look around. Or a long look around, for that was the power of Banding.

He found Captain Forbes' cubicle, announced by a paper sign with a crude drawing as from a child. Like every desk in the building, it was littered with papers and folders, a few protocol books and binders breaking up an otherwise flat, unassuming landscape and acting as tables for various case files. The computer was currently resting on the login screen, suggesting he hadn't been gone long. The only decoration to be found in the whole wash of gray was a single photo of his son.

Homicide Detective, Rifun mused, studying the paper sign. How were cases assigned to the detectives exactly? If he could figure that out, if Walter Forbes really was the Owain Fforidd that Cassius remembered, maybe they could have some fun with this.

His next stop was the chief's office, where the man was talking on the phone, typing something on the computer, and reading from a stack of paperwork all at the same time. Trying not to disturb the man too much from his ergonomically-poor posture, Rifun took the computer mouse and started navigating. Or he tried, anyway.

Bringing the computer into the Band let him look at anything currently on that single computer, local files of which there were precious few; most everything was kept "in the cloud" as the kids were saying these days.

He left the office and started wandering around the open layout, shared spaces for the grunts and cubicles for the grunt masters. He checked a few other computers that were currently logged in, but, as one might expect, the grunts knew less than the chief about larger operations. That is, until he decided to check the secretary's computer.

Apparently, there was one person who knew more than the chief, and that was the front desk, an unassuming nameplate reading "Cynthia Amberfield." Even better, she happened to have available a list of the homicide teams and the work they were currently on. Had someone been murdered recently, making this information relevant in the moment? If so, he sent up a silent prayer of thanks for their sacrifice as he grabbed a pen and paper to copy down the information.

If he could decipher the notes correctly, Waterford and Johnson were about to be assigned something. The next team in the list, Spencer and Lane, were noted as being tied up with something from a previous case and were unavailable for new assignments. Then there were two more teams before finally getting to Forbes and Standish.

That might calm Cassius down a little, giving him a warmup. Rifun wasn't going to go running to him with the news; he might have to space it out to ensure that Captain Forbes got the case.

He returned to Forbes' cubicle for a last look. Something caught his eye, if only because the word did not initially make sense to him.

Snowcoming? What was Snowcoming? And why—?

Ah, it was a list of events and scheduled off days for South Charleston High School. As each one passed, it was crossed off with a pen. The Snowcoming which had caught Rifun's attention was listed as being in February, but coming up much sooner was Homecoming in October. He didn't quite know what it was, had never experienced anything like it in his life, but from what he had seen in passing news articles, it had something to do with football and a student dance. That might be something to take advantage of, seeing how Cassius wanted to be seen and feared.

He left the station and dropped the Band. Maybe there was a way to ensure everyone got what they wanted out of this arrangement. Cassius could kill Lily, Rifun could get Tommen. And as for Walter...well, there didn't seem to be much use for him at this point. He had only Time to back him up and no Books that anyone knew about. Maybe he could be persuaded to join his son in learning the Akari, but if not, well, there was something to be said for the fatherly instinct to protect. He would have to be dealt with as the situation demanded.

As for the twins, they were the Lieutenants for this District, which meant they weren't considered Runners. True, not all Akari-bearers were considered Runners, only those that bragged about being an Akari-bearer or held some standing with an Akari-bearer group. Micaiah had held some standing, enough to be in the company of Builders, but even Cassius had said that he hadn't been seen in the fortress awhile. He had to have left them. But why? Something must have happened, probably something Doug himself would be aware of, but Cassius was not.

Of course, just because they weren't part of the Akarin didn't mean Micaiah didn't still have his Akari abilities or that he hadn't taught Micah. Maybe that was the reason. The Akarin had refused to accept Micah for some reason, so Micaiah left. It would be the brotherly thing to do. Considering, however, that they were reported to be able to combine their abilities and make them more powerful, even if they were alone without the backing of the Akarin, they were still a terrible force to be reckoned with.

And the woman, Aklaq White Bear? Rifun did not find anything on her in the Wheel other than she was a Runner who had effectively ghosted. The Akarin didn't have much on her, much like Micaiah. He didn't find anything about her on Earth either, not unless she'd been living in Sacramento for several decades, far, far past what anyone would believe given the non-aging. That didn't mean that she might not be around somewhere or that she wasn't still a threat, but her involvement would be only minor even if she did show up.

So, they had Lily to kill, Tommen to interview and get on their side, Walter and Aklaq to deal with situationally. Micaiah and Micah were wild cards, but their loyalties would be revealed soon enough, once Cassius began his killing.

Rifun returned to the officers building, but Cassius was nowhere to be found. Next place to check, Doug's house.

He couldn't be sure he was in the right house when he finally got to his feet. The walls were bare, with no sign of his legendary narcissism. No pictures, no portraits, no statues, only the barest difference in the color of the walls where the sun had faded around the spots where they used to be. Overall, the place appeared to be very tidy. A happenstance look out into the front yard showed a "For Sale" sign at the curb.

He found Cassius in Doug's office, the only room that displayed any disarray.

"What's going on?" Rifun wondered. "You're selling the house?"

"I'm moving into the fortress so I can be close by when shit hits the fan," Cassius told him, not looking up from the screen. "Right now, my biggest trouble is convincing them that shit will hit the fan, seeing how no one takes our threats seriously, assuming they believe we even exist anymore."

"I see. Well, I may have a few suggestions for that."

"Are they good ones?"

"I don't know how much they will help with the Akarin fearing us, but it may help with your problems with Lily Guile." He added, "And it may also work to investigate Tommen Forbes and see where he stands with the Akari."

Cassius sighed and leaned back in his seat, finally looking at him. "I don't care about Tommen Forbes—"

"You don't have to. I'm just trying to make this as efficient as possible. Do you want to kill people or don't you?"

"Surprised you're going to make such suggestions. Is it right? Is it moral? Those are words you love to toss around."

"Do you want to kill people or not? Do you want to get the Cult back in power or not?"

Cassius stood, angry, but in a tired and grumpy sort of way. "I don't give two shits about the Cult—"

"Except that your dark spirit says you must," Rifun cut in.

Cassius stopped, his expression almost like he'd been slapped.

"Something has happened, and you're trying to get back in its good graces," Rifun went on. "If it requires more blood, I can give you bodies, or point them out to you to kill them yourself."

"And you with your morality and religion, why would you help me do this?" Cassius folded his arms.

"Because I suspect that the Borelians have some evil spirit of their own, and who else is going to be strong enough to take them down? Your pure loathing for slavery is just the catalyst needed to go after them and not be swayed by pretty words and empty promises. And your lack of fear of death means you won't be groveling for your life, begging for slavery just to be kept alive."

It was an absolute lie, but the man bought it. Really, Rifun had had an idea spark, that maybe when the door was open between the spilling of blood and the infusion of that sacrifice into the dark spirit within Cassius, that would be the time to strike.

"All right, who are these bodies?" Cassius asked. His stance and expression still showed suspicion, but also intrigue.

"The first two may be random, but they must be normal people, not involved in Time or the Akari in any way. One this week, one next week. After that, I might have a better idea how to go about the next two."

He could see Cassius wanted to question it, but Rifun identifying his problems with the dark spirit had clearly shaken him. If his problems were that obvious, was he worse off than he originally thought? He needed a fix. He needed a plan. He wasn't so good at planning. Fortunately, Rifun was very good at planning, and he hoped he was indeed uncovering the plan to rid the universe of the evil spirit within Cassius.

Mundane details were briefly discussed, and Rifun returned to Charleston. He stumbled out of the alley and made his way to a bench where he sat down in a heap. His eyes throbbed, his head ached, and nausea threatened to make a fool of him in public.

By the time he was able to get his legs under him and get his body to function, he saw that it was two o'clock. His first stop was South Charleston High School, just a few miles from his current location. By the time he got there, saving his head by not Banding unless necessary to cross the freeway, school was just about out.

Rifun donned a Disguise of an older man—to old to be seen as a credible threat, or so he hoped—then sat on a bench across the street to watch. The buses dutifully pulled into position, obscuring most of the view. Through the windows of the school, he could see the students wiggling excitedly in their seats, some already packing up. Another bus pulled up to a different door and a large group of students all in sports uniforms burst out of the school to run onto the bus, bags bouncing along behind them. It took probably twice as long as necessary for everything and everyone to get ready, but the sports bus still left before the others, pulling out of the parking lot three seconds before the rest of the doors opened and the mass of the student body poured outside.

He did not see Tommen, but he couldn't say he was really surprised by it, with all the buses and other students in the way. The buses waited a good ten minutes from the arrival of the students before pulling away. Doors closed, brakes released, diesel roared to life, and the giant yellow convoy pulled out into the road one at a time.

Rifun waited a minute more, then stood and started walking away, down the sidewalk on the opposite side of the road past the school.

Movement in his peripheral caused him to look up just in time to see the door open and a pale, gangly teenager run outside. His goal was to, perhaps, catch the last bus before it reached the traffic light, but he only just reached the road himself before realizing this was a futile effort. Rifun heard a curse as the teenager, now close enough to be identified as Tommen Forbes, stomped back to the sidewalk in front of the school, digging a phone out of his pocket. Curious, Rifun used Sound to listen to the conversation.

"Bakery na hÉireann, Micaiah speaking."

"I missed the bus," Tommen stated grouchily.

"Is that my fault?"

"No, I...I'm just letting you know."

"Your dad going to bring you in?"

"I haven't called him yet. Otherwise I'm walking."

"I'm sure if you Banded, you could be early rather than late." The older twin's tone dripped sarcasm.

"I'm just letting you know," Tommen insisted. "I'll be there as soon as I can."

He hung up before his boss could reply.

Then, in a turn of events that was arguably only going to make a bad day worse, another student exited the building. Or rather, Rifun thought he was a student. The man was big enough that he might have been one of the sports coaches, or a professional lifter. Considering he had a few others with him, he was probably a student. He noticed Tommen and the whole group changed its course to intercept.

Tommen saw the man coming and briefly made several nonsensical changes in direction, as if trying to decide whether to meet the person or make a break for it. Rifun stayed where he was across the street, still using Sound to listen in.

"Odd to see you here after hours," the man said in a sneering voice.

"I missed the bus," Tommen mumbled. "I'm going to be late for work."

He made his decision to try to turn and walk away, but the man—the bully, stepped in front of him. The rest of the group made a loose triangle around the two.

"You're late?" the bully said in a mock voice. "Is that what your girlfriend said? Is that why she broke up with you?"

"I have to go to work, Tyler," Tommen insisted.

He attempted to leave, but one of the bully's friends grabbed him and pushed him back in the not-quite-a-circle. Rifun saw a flash of a Time Band, as if he used it to cover up a loss of balance.

"Come on, you really work that much that you can't talk to your friends?" Tyler wondered. Every word from him was insulting.

"We're not friends."

Rifun watched the whole scene play out, just waiting for something to happen. Surely Tommen had to know something about the Akari. He couldn't work for Micaiah and not know something. A simple Band, a little piece of Disguise, maybe a flash of Light? Anything to buy him even a small advantage in a fight or a chance to run away. The fact that he hadn't already tried to use a Band to run away said that he probably did want to fight, to prove his honor and manhood, but he knew he was outnumbered and outgunned, so there was an element of diplomacy at play as well.

Again Tommen tried to leave, again he was pushed back.

"He has to go to work," one of the bully's friends said. Rifun would be willing to bet he wouldn't be so tough after one good punch in the mouth, or if he didn't have Tyler to hide behind, but did Tommen know that?

"He got a work ethic," another friend said. Even his demeanor said he was a weakling feeding on Tyler's more domineering presence.

"You think that makes you better than us?" Tyler wondered, stepping forward and giving Tommen a small shove.

"It means I have places to be, now let me go," Tommen told them. "I'm in enough trouble as it is."

"Yeah, it is a long way to walk, isn't it? Maybe you should call your daddy, get him to take you in his cop car."

Tommen's tone turned cheeky. "Maybe I should. At least I know my daddy."

That, apparently, was the trigger for the bullies. The friends shrunk their circle considerably as Tyler came in swinging. Tommen managed to block so it didn't crush his face, but the blow itself was still formidable and knocked him back a step or two. The bully followed up with another powerful swing. This time, Tommen managed to dodge and he got in a solid strike to Tyler's ribcage, but he may as well have hit a brick wall for all the bully appeared to notice. In fact, all Tyler did was twist around to that side and attempt to grapple Tommen from behind.

The maneuver worked. Tyler got one hand on Tommen's shoulder, another on his hip, and he delivered a solid knee to the gut. Tommen went rigid for a moment as he coughed once, but a second knee caused him to go limp. When Tyler let go of him, he went to the ground on all fours. From there, all four bullies took turns kicking him, or kicking at him. Rifun saw multiple Bands go up as Tommen tried to dodge, but dodging one kick was putting himself right in the path of another.

A sudden shout caused the bullies to stop as two men—who they were, Rifun could not say except that they were from the school in some fashion—started running toward the beating. The bullies immediately pivoted and ran away, still laughing and high-fiving for the first ten yards before jogging out of sight.

The two men reached Tommen. One stopped to kneel beside him while the other jogged after the perpetrators for about a hundred feet before giving up and returning to the scene of the crime.

"You all right?" the first male inquired as he helped Tommen to his feet.

"I just got the shit beaten out of me, what do you fucking think?!" Tommen demanded, his anger tempered only by an occasional cough. The adult had a hand uncertainly on his shoulder.

"Should we call an ambulance just to be sure?" the second male wondered, looking at the first.

"Yeah, my dad will hear that and know exactly what happened. Last fucking thing I need." Tommen shrugged off the first man's hand. "I'm going to be late for work."

"Do you need a ride?" the second man asked. "I know where you work; I drive right by there."

Tommen hesitated for a long moment, then finally agreed. He followed the man to a particular car and they left the school.

Rifun watched them go, not saying or doing anything, only thinking. Other than a few quick Time Bands to try and spare himself a few blows, the kid hadn't done a thing. He had not touched any Akari abilities in any way, meaningful or not. He had not appeared to even attempt such a thing. He had not tried to disperse the kinetic energy of a fist or foot in motion. He had not attempted to redirect energy back to the bully, thereby breaking bones. He had not attempted to dissolve the structural integrity of the bully's bones, making them more prone to breaking. He had barely used Time, and even then, it had been Time as taught in the Time industry, not even the Akari.

Wasn't Micaiah teaching him anything? Had he turned his back on the Akari itself, on the Author? Was Tommen completely uninterested? Was he even aware of the existence of the Akari? What was going on here that one chosen by the Author was not even aware of any of this?

Rifun Banded and made his way to the bakery, making sure to change his Disguise just a little bit, on the off chance Tommen had seen the old man watching from afar. Once he was fixed up a bit, he headed to the bench that doubled as a bus stop. He watched the car pull up to the curb. Tommen got out, looking no happier for having gotten a ride rather than being forced to walk. Probably worse in his mind, he'd likely been a captive audience for a lecture on fighting and bullying. Rifun would like to give him a similar lecture, but pertaining more to Time and the Akari, and question why he didn't use his abilities to at least defend himself and get away.

Tommen headed into the bakery. Rifun gave him a thirty second head start, then followed. Whatever anyone told him, no teenage boy was going to be able to just set aside such an incident and carry on with a cheerful smile for every customer. If Rifun was right, if anyone made any comment about it, Tommen was going to be ready with some indignant justification or self-righteous lament about life being unfair in one way or another.

Rifun was not the first one in line when he entered. He watched Tommen serve the two customers before him with a quiet loathing and a thousand silent fantasies about what he'd like to do to his bullies.

Rifun stepped up to the counter, still Disguised as an old man.

"And for you?" Tommen asked tightly, his eyes suggesting his mind was far away. He wanted to beat his tormentors into oblivion, but he didn't for some reason. Why?

"I'll just take a glazed donut," Rifun answered politely, momentarily forgetting that he was in fact expected to order something. He hadn't given it much, or any, thought, but when he Banded and checked the wallet of the man before him who was just leaving, he only had enough cash for a simple donut.

As Tommen grabbed a deli paper and moved to grab the baked good, Rifun continued, "You all right? I see you got a bit of a shiner there. You get trampled by a cow running downhill?"

"I'm fine," Tommen said stiffly.

"You know, if you're going to pick a fight, you might want to at least have some muscle to back it up. Or maybe you're the swift and agile type, light on your feet?"

Now his words got a little testy. "I'm the kind who gets cornered by half a dozen bullies at school, and I'm not exactly acting on a script where I come out on top." He set the donut on the counter between them and rang up the total on the register.

Rifun handed over the cash. "Well, the important thing is, you got back up. Even John Wayne got knocked down a time or two."

Tommen was not impressed, but the sudden appearance of one of the twins prevented him from saying anything more about it. He simply told Rifun to have a good day and mentally moved on to the next person in line.

Rifun did not start on his donut right away, instead sliding into an alley where he wouldn't be seen and opening a portal back to his chambers in the officers building. Only after he recovered from his vertigo did he start on the donut. For someone who liked donuts, it was probably as delicious as their cookies. For Rifun, well, it was edible. Or he thought it was. He couldn't always be sure with

American food.

Maybe he was still distracted by everything that had just occurred. Tommen had not shown any inclination of Akari abilities. None. Not a hint, not a poor attempt, nothing. Even his Time Bands were paltry. True, he'd only been listed as a probationary Timekeeper, but if he was getting beaten up with any kind of frequency, one might expect him to hone his abilities, at least enough to try and escape. Was it possible that he was straight up retarded?

What was Rifun supposed to do with this? Was he going to have to start from square one? Was there really going to be that little resistance from Micaiah or the Akarin? Was Lily Guile really the only thing holding the entire paper fortress of the universe together? If that was the case, then not only would it be easy to take down, but Rifun felt obligated to do it.

He'd already given Cassius the next step in the plan. One death this week, one next week, trying to bring everything together so that Walter Forbes would be on a particular murder. Of course, there was every chance that it wouldn't happen quite as expected; maybe some other murderer out there would decide to kill someone and so throw off the sequence of events. Rifun would have to keep an eye on that schedule and start planning the murder or murders that mattered, namely Lily Guile's.

Where to begin? Lily Guile deserved to die, and Cassius seemed to think he needed to kill her in order to win back favor with his spirit. But she didn't fear him. He wanted or needed her to fear him in order to kill her. Well, it wasn't about killing her but deriving his sick sexual pleasure from it. The way Rifun figured it, if it got done as perfectly as Cassius needed it to be, it would afford him the greatest opportunity to kill the spirit and the man.

There were innumerable ways to incite fear in people. Lily seemed to have become impervious to spontaneous fear, had probably endured plenty of death threats over the years as she manipulated the Time industry. The backing of the Cult had likely contributed to this callousness as such threats were identified and eliminated. Except now she had no such backing. Whether she knew this or not Rifun did not know, but now it was time to start acting on it.

Rifun waited until after Cassius had made his first "padded" kill before approaching him with a plan.

"We need long-term fear to act on Lily," he said, meeting Cassius in the madman's chambers. "She's expecting the jump attack, the sudden fight. She has likely been bombarded with threats for years, but they are always quietly removed."

"So we stop quietly removing them," Cassius stated.

"No. We become them. The Cult has had her back for decades. Now it's time to stab her in the back, as she's tried to stab us."

Cassius folded his arms. "I'm not good at long-term or subtle."

"We don't need subtle, or not entirely. We just need to get under her skin. Women value safety. We need to start cutting the cords of her safety net."

"So are you going to tell me this plan or just monologue about it?"

Rifun shifted his stance, trying to gauge how volatile the man was at the moment. "I'm going to contact Julianna. With her ability to access people and places through the in-between dimension, she can be our eyes and ears while we're doing other things. We're going to hit Lily in her workplace, in some sort of social setting, in her apartment building, anywhere she goes regularly. We're not going to kill her, yet, but she needs to know that we can get just that close." He went on before Cassius could speak. "It's not going to be all at once. We have to strike and then disappear for a time. Strike and then disappear. We have to leave some clues intentionally, enough to make her think that there is some hope of catching and stopping us, and then rob her of that hope."

He could see Cassius' mind working through the plan, wondering if it would be enough to even salvage his favor with the spirit. Was he conversing with the spirit even now? Was Cassius truly dead and this was only the spirit looking back at him, perhaps judging his motives? Did the spirit know what he was trying to do, what the real plan was on Rifun's part?

"When do you expect to put this plan into motion?" Cassius asked at last.

"I'm trying to keep an eye on the police department and its functions. I'm curious as to its responses and operations. I also want to try and make it so Walter Forbes is the one who responds."

"Why do you want him involved?"

"Because I want his son. Tommen Forbes is the Chivalrous Welshman. I am as sure of that as anything. But I don't understand why he doesn't appear to know anything about the Akari, why Micaiah isn't training him if you said he is still listed as active personnel."

Another tense moment of silence from Cassius. Another conversation with the spirit, perhaps wondering if he might not be able to kill this prisoner who escaped his clutches so long ago?

"All right," Cassius agreed. "I still have one more body to make. You contact Julianna and do whatever the fuck it is you need to do. Otherwise, just point me at the person, and they're dead."

Rifun agreed and, in the spirit of quitting while he was ahead, left Cassius' chambers.

His next stop was New York City where a Japanese immigrant named Tadashi Hajiku lived in a rundown basement apartment, spending his days hacking into whatever he could. And when he wasn't doing that, he was slowly amassing a small stockpile of weapons which he kept in an undisclosed location.

It was Tadashi who had figured out a reliable means of communication between the in-between dimension and the primary dimension. It had taken years of trial and error and a few explosions which had been ruled either accidental or terrorist, depending on what blew up, but they now had a line to speak to Julianna without having to stare at computer screens and talk to thin air.

Rifun let himself into the apartment. Tadashi whirled around in his chair, two handguns raised, half a breath from pulling the triggers when he recognized Rifun. He cursed in the light of eight computer monitors.

"Don't you know how to knock?" he demanded.

Rifun raised a brow. "Don't you know to keep your operation away from the front door? And anyway, who else is going to pick that many locks that fast?"

Tadashi just scowled, opened a drawer, rummaged inside for a second, and tossed him a cell phone. The phone had some kind of modified battery pack so that it was twice as big and heavy as it would normally be, but something about it made it so it could connect to a similar phone in Julianna's possession. Rifun didn't understand how it all worked. Tadashi had said something about tapping into the energy of the dimension itself and how it was like a vacuum or something. He flipped open the phone and dialed.

"Hello?" Julianna answered.

"It's me. We need your help."

"Lovely. What do you need me to do?"

Rifun made a motion for Tadashi to listen as well. The kid reluctantly removed his headphones and slumped in his seat as if expecting a scolding.

He explained the plan, as vague as it sounded at the moment.

"If you can follow Lily around and get a feel for who might be good candidates, that would save me a lot of trouble," he finished.

"Do you really think this is necessary?" Julianna wondered.

"Let's just say that Cassius has a vested interest in him being the one to kill Lily, and so do I."

"Honestly, Rifun, I know you are the more rational and elegant one, but I know you have killed. If you want Cassius gone, you know how to do it. Why sacrifice innocents?"

"You know it's not just about the body."

She sighed. "Yes, yes, the dark spirit inside him." A second sigh. "I will follow her around and see what I can come up with."

"Your objection is noted."

"And will be ignored in the order it is received, I know."

She hung up before he did. He tossed the phone to Tadashi. "You're going to have to come down to be with us at some point, too. We'll need you to be the link between us and her while we're on the move."

Tadashi still did not look overly enthused, but Rifun would say mildly intrigued. "You want to leave clues, you're going to need a ride. Cops love chasing down vehicle descriptions, especially vague ones. You want to make a spectacle, you're going to need firepower."

"And here I thought you were an antique collector."

"Fuck you. You are the antique. All of you. I'm the youngest one here."

Rifun put a hand to his chest in mock injury. "The disrespect of today's youth wounds me so."

"Fuck you," Tadashi repeated, turning back to his screens. "And get out of my fucking apartment." He replaced his headphones. When Rifun reached the door, he added—a little too loud, perhaps to compensate for his music which was also too loud, "And fucking knock next time!"

Admonition

ṛokumḅo

Making plans was annoying enough. Changing them was even worse.

They'd had everything all worked out, ready to go yesterday. Julianna had done her part, everything and everyone had been coordinated perfectly. There was supposed to be some kind of distraction in the NICU at the children's hospital on a night when Lily would be working, giving him and Rifun time to kidnap one of the nurses to be killed. Somehow it was all supposed to fall together that Lily would be a witness to it.

Then the bitch had to go and trade shifts. She wasn't even going to be at the hospital that night.

The only thing that made it bearable was that Rifun didn't flip out about it. In fact, he decided it was a most fortuitous turn of events.

"Who did she switch with?" Rifun asked Julianna on the phone.

The two of them sat in the dining room of a house on top of one of the many hills overlooking Charleston. The owners were on vacation, and Tadashi had remotely hacked the cameras so nothing unusual would show up if the owners checked the feed. It was the morning of the day they intended to kidnap the nurse; now they had to rework their plans a little.

"The girl's name is Sam Pietrowicz," Julianna reported, her accent garbled on the touchy line. "Not much taller than me, white, blond hair just past her shoulders, pretty thing, really."

"Very much like Lily when we first met?"

"I suppose, though I think Lily is a bit taller. And Sam seems rather shy, certainly not as...outgoing as Lily."

"You're not going to save her," Cassius cut in.

"Did I say—?"

"You don't have to. I'm just saving you the effort of trying."

Julianna sighed. "My objection has been noted and will be ignored in the order it was received."

"Exactly," Cassius said, cutting off Rifun. "Now then, does she have any kind of schedule or routine? Seeing how it doesn't seem to matter anymore if Lily sees it, this doesn't have to be anything elaborate."

"At Rifun's suggestion—" She seemed to enjoy emphasizing whose suggestion it was. "—I have been observing the NICU for a couple weeks now, learning their routines, their protocols, getting to know how the doctors and nurses operate."

"And no doubt influencing them in their work to save tiny lives," Cassius interrupted sarcastically, "thereby thwarting Lily in her work to Harvest such precious, innocent lives full of vast potential."

"Would you shut up?" Rifun told him, annoyed. "We all know your thoughts. We're trying to make a plan."

"What needs to be planned? We go in, we get the girl, we get out. Nothing fancy, nothing elaborate. You're right; it's good Lily isn't here. It makes this incredibly easy, but you insist on making it more difficult than it really needs to be."

"When she works evenings, starting at three, Sam normally takes her first break at six-fifteen," Julianna said. "Depending on the schedule, her lunch might be anywhere from eighty-thirty to eleven-thirty. Then she'll take a second break at one-fifteen. Her out time is three in the morning. Of course, this might shift a little if an emergency comes up, but those are my observations."

Cassius stood. "That's all I need."

Rifun looked up at him. "Where are you going? It's barely ten in the morning. We have five hours until she even starts her shift." He went on, "This is about Lily, not Sam. We're trying to make the point that her workplace isn't safe, that we can find and get to her even there. In order to send that message, Sam has to be at the hospital, working, doing exactly what Lily should have been there doing."

"I know that. But I have some things to get ready."

"You said nothing elaborate."

"For the kidnapping part, sure. But what I'm going to do to her afterwards—"

"We're not going to hold her hostage for days so you can torture her."

"I don't need days. You said you wanted to dump the body so Tommen Forbes would find it and Walter Forbes would be assigned to the case. You said you wanted to do that during homecoming to make a big scene about it. There will be a little time between kidnapping her and dumping her body. And there will be as much time as I need thanks to Banding."

"Don't rape her," Julianna said, her tone begging. "As Rifun said, this is about Lily, not Sam."

"And as I said, we're doing this my way from now on."

"Is it really necessary?" Rifun wondered.

Cassius barked a disbelieving laugh. "You didn't have a problem with it when I made those two extra bodies, all so you could make sure the right police officer got assigned to the job. Killing those two wasn't a problem, killing this one is just a means to an end, but you somehow draw the line at rape?" Rifun opened his mouth, but Cassius beat him to it. "Your line of morality is very convenient sometimes, you know that?"

"I do what is necessary, nothing more," Rifun informed him.

"You do what makes you feel good, whatever helps you justify what you do. If you did what was necessary, we wouldn't be in this mess in the first place. Your 'morality' got us where we are. No. I'm doing things my way. How I want to do them."

"If you rape her, the police will have your DNA," Julianna piped up, tone desperate.

"The Wheel of Time has already logged my DNA, and I'm still here. Besides, it's not as though evidence couldn't be destroyed later."

With that, he left the room. He didn't go far, though, before he turned back. He did not return to the dining room. Rather, he muffled his steps using Sound, walking into an adjacent room where he used Sound again to listen in on the rest of the phone conversation.

"If he does rape her," Julianna was saying, "do you know enough about Matter...?"

"I will heal her, yes" Rifun promised. "Even if he kills her beforehand, there is still enough life left in the body for a short time to repair the tissue. It will be like it never even happened."

"Thank you." She paused. "Is it really part of his killing ritual?"

"He's trying to get back in favor with his spirit. If the spirit chose him for his ruthlessness and lack of conscience, well, he has to demonstrate that he is still that way, that he hasn't been corrupted by such terrible things like morality."

"Yes, we wouldn't want that, would we?" Julianna sighed. "Well, I've done what I can."

"I might suggest finding anywhere else to be, at least for a little while."

"Thank you, I will."

Cassius rolled his eyes and Banded to leave the house undetected. Did those two honestly expect universe domination to just fall into their laps? Wasn't there some idiom about cracking eggs to make omelets? No one was going to give them control of the Time industry; they were going to have to take it. They were going to have to kill their rivals. In war, people died. So-called innocent people died. This was no different.

As for the rape thing, well, quick frankly, fuck them. Literally, fuck them. Julianna had obviously been alone for far too long; maybe she needed a good reminder of what that felt like down there. If they did manage to break her out of the in-between dimension, Cassius would be right there with a nice welcome back gift. As for Rifun, he was no virgin. And he'd fucked his girlfriend—his bloody cousin—right before making the leap into the future, so it hadn't been that long. But somehow, it all came back to that morality thing. He wasn't married, they weren't too far apart genetically, but it was still just fine. Cassius wanted to do his own thing and suddenly he's the devil.

He opened a portal back to Doug's house. It was for sale, and a few people were reportedly interested, but it all had to do with banks and lawyers and all this other bullshit. He didn't care. He wasn't really living there, just stopped in once every other week to screw the druggie whore who kept the place clean. But he was kind of glad it was still his so he still had access to his little private torture room. This was where he would be bringing the girl once he'd kidnapped her. This was where he'd have his way with her, with or without Rifun's approval.

Somehow, it all came back to morality. Fucking morality. Useless morality. Some described morals as being like fences, to keep people safe. Cassius saw them more like cages, to keep people contained. If the true might of humanity—or any species, seeing how most of them out there had some version of morality—were to be unleashed, nothing could stop them, not even the gods, assuming there were any out there. A fleeting thought of the bullet in his face passed through his mind.

The necessary thing. Cassius could not tell if the thought was his own as the words were accompanied by an image of Rifun. *The necessary thing is coming soon.*

Yes, he thought, nodding to himself, now envisioning Rifun on his torture table. *The necessary thing. I will gladly do that necessary thing. It has been a long time coming for that coward. I should have done it long ago, when he was a mewling fool quivering at the thought of even being touched. Better late than never, though. Just tell me when.*

The spirit did not respond.

He spent the day preparing the room, preparing his tools and instruments. Even though he could Band, he really didn't have a lot of time to do what he wanted. Several ideas had gone through his mind, but by the time he left for the hospital, he was fairly certain about what he was going to do. It would only take a couple hours.

The hospital was surprisingly busy for a Friday night. Seriously, who wanted to go visit a sick kid on a normal day, never mind a night when most people would be going out to do other things? Bunch of bleeding hearts anyway.

Simple plan. Go in, grab her, get out. No muss, no fuss, no collaboration or coordination. As few moving pieces as possible. He checked the time, just turned over to six o'clock. Julianna said the girl took her break at six-fifteen. He'd give her a few more minutes to finish up some mundane task, grab a snack, and settle into a period where she obviously expected to relax for a few minutes, her guard down. He didn't expect any trouble, but it was the psychological impact he was going for.

He half-expected Rifun to appear out of nowhere with more pleas to spare this poor innocent girl's chastity, maybe some short lecture about logic and necessity or some other bullshit. No such thing happened. Surely Rifun knew what time it was, knew he would be hanging around, waiting to strike. His absence sparked a bit of paranoia in Cassius and he almost missed his window of opportunity. It was past six-twenty before he actually Banded and started moving.

He did not waste time lurking around corners or ogling at the bright paintings or wondering what all of these people were up to. More than just busy, there did seem to be some sort of function going on, and his eyes may have passed over the word "fundraiser" on a banner. But he bypassed all of this, heading for the stairs. He did not bother with formality, but utilized a Gravity track to fly him up to the appropriate floor.

NICU did not change, and there was no sign of extra activity or any of the fundraising going on in the lobby. Everything was quiet and sterile, covered in plastic and doused in chemical cleaners.

He began a methodical search of the unit, going room by room, hallway by hallway. He noted that Lily's office was dark and wondered if there might be anything of interest in there. After a moment of thought, he decided not. If he were in the business of information, maybe, or if he cared about any of the neonates in the ward. But he did not care, and he couldn't come up with anything Lily might keep in her office that would be pertinent to the mission at hand. The ultimate goal was her death, nothing more, nothing less, and nothing was going to change it.

One by one, he eliminated rooms and hallways. By the time he finished up with the normal public areas and the nurse's stations, he was starting to wonder. Where was she? He checked the general break rooms, found a different nurse getting something from the vending machine. He checked a few of the break rooms on the outer wings, nothing. Waiting areas, nothing. He headed outside to the smoking areas, found several employees, just not the one he was looking for. He checked the offices, peered down the many aisles of patient records. Still there was no sign of Sam.

Had she called in sick or something? Was she on another floor for some reason? Was he going to have to search this whole damn hospital? Where would a NICU nurse have to go? The morgue maybe?

He didn't find the girl in the morgue, but he did find plenty of inspiration for torture and other things. As he'd told Julianna, he wasn't worried about anyone having his DNA. The Wheel of Time had it and he was still here. What were the local police going to do to him? Besides, these bodies had already been examined; it was just a matter of shipping them out for burial now. No one would know. And even if they did, what were they going to do?

He returned to NICU. Well, there was really only one place left to look. And, really, it would provide perfect cover for the kidnapping when the police went to check security cameras.

The first bathroom he checked was empty, as was the second. Then he got an idea to look in the employee bathrooms. Well, they weren't employee only, but they were hidden back far enough in a mess of employee only rooms that it was not likely frequented by the public.

And there she was, standing at the sink, just reaching for a paper towel from the dispenser.

There was nothing especially remarkable about her. Around Julianna's height, though with a better body in Cassius' opinion. Blond hair was forcibly tied back in a tight ponytail using an elastic band that looked ready to snap. Her scrubs were plain, hospital issue. He didn't give faces much thought, but for some reason he got a minor vision of her and Rifun kissing right before Cassius put a knife in her back. She coughed up blood all over him and he held her in his arms as she died, Cassius looming over both of them.

He didn't know where the vision came from, but he savored it for a long moment.

Tonight was going to be a good night. This was going to help him kill Lily, he just knew it.

She was ridiculously light, and he scooped her up and attempted to fling her over his shoulder. He did not bring her into his Band, so he had to manually position her limbs, but this was no issue. All she would know was that one second she had been reaching for a paper towel, and the next, she would be tied to a bedframe.

He opened a portal right there in the bathroom and stepped through to the secret closet in Doug's house. He laid his catch on the bed, turned, and nearly had a heart attack when he saw Rifun standing there, leaning against the wall, arms folded.

"What the—?"

"I had a hunch."

"And what are you here to do?" Cassius challenged. "Stop me? Beg for me to not rape her or her body afterwards? Are you going to make sure that my torture of her is humane?"

He could see his words unnerved and annoyed Rifun. He could see just a flicker of uncertainty in his eyes. Just as Cassius would never allow himself to be a slave again, Rifun would never allow himself to be cut or tortured again. But what if Cassius tried something? What if he was risking himself by being here?

Cassius kept one eye on Rifun and Rifun kept both eyes on him as he approached the table where his instruments lay, neatly arranged the way he liked them.

"You were never on this side of things, were you?" Cassius asked casually, picking up a scalpel. He examined it, then set it down and went to the bed. "No, you weren't." He adjusted the girl's position and reached for the bindings. "You were always on the receiving end of things."

"Is it really necessary?" Rifun cut in, sounding anxious. "Is this..." He made a vague motion. "Is it necessary?"

Cassius gave him a look. "It's the whole point."

"The point is to frighten Lily, to get under her skin, inside her head."

"Simply executing her isn't enough. We have to show her what we're capable of, what's in store for her later." He added quickly, "You don't have to be here at all. Give me an hour and I will let you know when it's safe for your delicate sensibilities."

"I'm not going to let you chop her up into little pieces just so you can ejaculate over the remains."

"Do you want Lily dead or not?"

"I'll do it myself if I have to."

Cassius shifted his stance. "Oh? Since when? Is your attack dog outliving his usefulness? Is he becoming rabid, or invalid? You've always pawned this off on me because you want to keep your pretty hands clean. What's changed? Just waiting for the opportune moment to strike the demon out of me?"

He crossed the room where he kept the Authored Book. He snatched it up and tossed it across the room. It landed with a thud about three feet from where Rifun stood.

"I read it while waiting for you," Rifun said, making no move to pick it up.

"You know, I'm starting to think you don't trust me," Cassius sighed. "And yet, here I am, still laboring for this pathetic cause." He shook his head and returned to his instrument table. "I never should have come back. Never should have dictated those fucking journals. Maybe I should have just fucking died when that Timekeeper killed me. At least in Hell, I'd be in like company who could appreciate the work I've done."

"And what work is that?" Rifun wondered. "If you had died centuries ago, you wouldn't have done anything more than kill some slavers and Harvest some battlefields. You might have been something of a good guy. A bit questionable, but almost good."

Cassius shifted his stance. "You are here to kill me, then? Or at least try?"

"Quite frankly, I don't give two shits about you. I'm here to kill your evil spirit. I just don't know how."

Cassius barked a laugh. "Well, it's not going to tell you. Assuming I had any inkling of how to do it, it would kill me to stop me from telling you."

"I know."

"So what do you expect to do?"

"Observe. Learn. And yes, stop you from raping her whether she is alive or dead."

Cassius studied Rifun for a long moment, trying to discern his motives. He didn't deny anything. Of course, who could argue with an Authored Book? But he also wasn't trying to embellish or distort or weasel his logic one way or another. There was no story, no plan. Just a simple statement. He was here to kill the evil spirit, but he didn't know how.

It was a stunning admission, coming from this man who always seemed to have an answer to and for everything, and Cassius wasn't sure what to do with it. Some part of him said it was a trap, but why? Why try to trap a man who already knew that you wanted to kill him? Was he trying for a false sense of security, maybe pretending that he was only interested in slaying the spirit while saying that Cassius himself could be saved? Except he'd also said that he really didn't care about Cassius either.

There had to be more.

He would think about it later. Right now, he had a woman to torture.

He picked up a scalpel.

"If you are open to the idea, I have a suggestion," Rifun said, immediately annoying Cassius.

"You? Why would you have a suggestion for torture? Or are you trying to make it more humane?"

"The idea is to make it utterly inexplicable to the police."

Ignoring him, Cassius took the scalpel to the woman's face. Beautiful, delicate, precise cuts. Horizontally, vertically, exactly as he had done to Julianna. He hoped she was here to watch this from her dimensional prison. Of course, that was highly unlikely. More likely, she was somewhere else, worrying, fretting, as all women do. Later she would contact Rifun, maybe cry a little, and he would have to reassure her that everything was fine. Yes, the girl was dead, but it had been a humane death, whatever that was.

When he was done with the woman's face, he turned his attention to her hands. He unbound them from the bed frame and put them together, one on top of the other. Then he took a small knife and pierced her hands, straight through the palms. He removed the knife and began shoving larger objects through the hole. A pen, a slender stick, and finally a metal rod. With the rod through the hands, he wiggled it and moved it around, feeling the shifting of tissue and the popping and crunching of bone.

He glanced at Rifun. Though his expression remained stony, his pallor had turned a noticeable shade of green, which was no more flattering than his normal skin tone.

"So, tell me about this idea of yours," Cassius said. "How are we going to make this inexplicable?"

The sudden change in attention appeared to alleviate the worst of Rifun's revulsion and nausea, though he still appeared quite skittish in his approach, and he never got closer than three feet to the girl. She remained outside of Cassius' Band, oblivious to what was happening to her. He'd figured that she might see it as, one moment she was in the bathroom and the next moment she was tied to a bed. Now, though, it appeared as though she would be in the bathroom one moment, then suddenly dead. He wondered if she had made peace with her God. She had a small tattoo on the back of her shoulder of a symbol resembling a cross. Well, as the saying went, no one knows the day or hour, and death had come for her.

"I will Band her," Rifun said, his gaze transfixed on the girl's face and the perfect cuts that had not begun to bleed, his skin again turning green. "I will do it as I have done to you, cutting off brain and body. And I will plant smaller Bands in her arteries and surrounding tissues. If you cut her throat, I will use Matter to heal over the ends, effectively clotting it shut. The backup of blood into the heart will kill her quickly."

Cassius nodded. "That would be unusual. Cut her throat, but no blood." He shifted his stance. "I'm still surprised to hear such an idea coming from you."

"Not my idea. The Uprising occurred after the second World War. The Allies had suffered greatly, and they wanted to see about new ways to reduce casualties, especially from blood loss. For as much as they demonized the Nazis, the Allies were no different, not really. The Uprising gave the French soldiers plenty of opportunities to experiment on Malagasy prisoners, see how much they could make us bleed, try out new methods, new drugs, new inventions to make the bleeding stop."

"And one of them figured out how to stop a jugular bleed?"

"Not exactly, but he did go on to contribute to the invention of synthetic platelets."

"And you're upset that he didn't give you any credit as his test subject?"

Rifun gave him a look. "I was part of the burning experiments, not the bleeding ones."

Cassius matched his look. "You could have run away at any time. Don't blame me for your stupid pride. You didn't have a demon holding a bullet in your face to make you cooperate."

"For being a master of death and lover of torture, you seem oddly averse to death yourself."

Cassius studied his scalpel, trying to sound ambivalent. "Death is fine. I just don't like being beholden to others."

"You never liked being part of the Cult, then."

Did he? Had he ever? He thought back over everything he knew, everything he remembered, and everything that was in those damned Books.

"I don't know. I don't think so. Julianna tried to play politics in the beginning, make me the Zero Hour, but it never amounted to anything. She didn't understand how revolution really works. I never would have been free of my master if I hadn't killed him and burned down his house. Talking would have done nothing, persuasion meant little. The Dispersal was as close as we ever got to achieving a revolution, bringing real change, and we fucked it up. You guys fucked it up."

Rifun shifted his stance and folded his arms. "The Dispersal came after all of this Missing Zero Hour business, which tells me that you never liked being with the Cult."

"You sound less upset about that than I might have thought."

"It does give one cause to wonder." He clarified his statement without being asked. "You were used to dictate the journals. The Cult has clearly made some astounding blunders, and more than once we would have sunk if not for some intervention on your part which you claim was involuntarily driven by this dragon spirit manipulating or holding the bullet in your face. If you don't do as it says, you're dead. But what would a spirit need with a cult? Why does it need this Cult specifically?"

"I don't know," Cassius interrupted pointedly, "and I honestly don't care. You might be able to stand there and wonder and hypothesize, but I'm the one with a spirit holding a bullet in my face. Believe me, if I do get a chance to face it head-on instead of this mystical dream-walking bullshit it's doing to me, I'm killing it. But it's not going to tell me how to beat it otherwise, so I'm kind of stuck." He used the scalpel to gesture to the woman, still on the bed, hands pierced, face cut. "Can we get back to the real reason I came here today?"

Rifun's aversion to the sight had ebbed once he got on his philosophical pedestal, but he now appeared to shrink back and take on another shade of green, his expression saying that while he recognized that he had made an offer to assist with such a gruesome task and would carry it out in order to save some imaginary honor, he was still no happier for it.

"Fine," he sighed. "Where or what do you intend to cut?"

"I'm going to cut her jugular and remove her throat." Cassius indicated where he planned on cutting.

"Is that really necessary?"

"I'm not called Calis Cutthroat for no reason."

"Maybe not, but..." Rifun shook his head. "Never mind."

Rifun got into what Cassius assumed to be a more comfortable position, perhaps so if he did pass out from squeamishness, then he wouldn't hurt himself on the way down. There was no real way to tell from an outsider's perspective whether the Bands were having any real effect right now, and the only indication that there were dozens, hundreds, maybe thousands of tiny Bands being embedded into the woman's skin was the concentration on Rifun's face and the sweat at his hair line. After a minute or two, he glanced at Cassius and nodded once.

With the same careful precision he'd used when cutting the woman's face, Cassius drew the sharp blade over her throat. As promised, not a drop of blood was spilled, and Cassius couldn't stop a spark of envy as he watched the arteries clot and heal over just as fast as the blade passed through them. The same went for all the tiny veins, the blood of the skin itself. The perfection of the cuts and the surreal beauty of, not a fountain of blood, but no blood at all. It was a new trigger but a familiar sensation as he turned his attention to the throat itself, the trachea.

More precise cuts, and still not a drop of spilled blood. He returned the scalpel to the tray. With one hand, he lifted the trachea from the woman's throat. With the other hand, he unzipped his pants. Rifun's disapproving look and notable clearing of the throat only amused Cassius more.

When he was finished, he dropped the Band.

Immediately, the woman began thrashing, an atrocious wheezing and whistling sound hissing through the gaping hole in her throat. She grabbed at her chest, eyes wide in a panicked frenzy. She rolled to one side, then the other, her movements becoming sluggish and uncoordinated. One hand still rested on her chest, another pawed at her throat. Rifun took her hand in his. She clutched at it, looked at him, but her gaze was already starting to fade. Finally, her whole body went still, her eyes relaxed, and her hand went slack.

"You are absolutely insufferable," Cassius hissed as Rifun closed her eyes.

"Obviously not," Rifun said smartly, not looking at him. Cassius had a mind to put the scalpel in the back of his neck, or maybe shove it into that spot in the back of his head. Then he straightened and turned, his demeanor once again all business. "All right, Tadashi is waiting."

"Waiting?"

At the front door with a beige van, apparently.

"What's all this about?" Cassius asked as they hoisted the body in the back and climbed in. "Open a portal, push her through to wherever you want to dump her."

Rifun slammed the rear door shut and sat down even as Tadashi was already pulling away. "We have to give the police a little bait, a little something to chase, don't we? A body is good and all, but, all things considering, it's not much to go on."

Cassius shrugged. "Who cares? This is about Lily. Fuck the police."

"The next detective in line is Walter Forbes, also known as Owain Fforidd, now the Timekeeper Captain of District Four. Tell me you wouldn't like to have some fun with him, assuming he is your escaped prisoner from so long ago."

Considering all his other problems at the moment, Cassius didn't really care about Fforidd at all. But, he supposed, it might prove to be a fun side venture, assuming the dragon spirit let him pursue it. He heard and felt nothing.

"And," Rifun went on, "his son, his adopted son and biological nephew, is Tommen Forbes, who has been called The Chivalrous Welshman so often in the time that I have been following him that I cannot believe that he is not the Chivalrous Welshman as foretold by Authored Books."

"And have you figured out what makes this one kid that special?" Cassius asked bluntly.

"Not yet, but I'm hoping that this endeavor sheds some light on things."

"How so?"

The van rumbled and shook violently as Tadashi drove it through a portal. Cassius looked out the front windshield to see they were somewhere on the outskirts of a city in the mountains, probably Charleston. They Banded through traffic for the most part, dropping the Band at certain places before picking it back up again. When Cassius inquired for details, Rifun informed him that they were ensuring that security cameras might be able to pick them up, the van anyway.

"Where are we even going?" Cassius whined.

No one answered him, but a few minutes later, they pulled into a dirt lot. It wasn't very big, enough for one or two cars to pull off. A large row of trees separated the lot from what looked like an enormous sports field. This particular field was dark, only a few lights on to deter mischief makers.

Rifun Fast Banded the three of them and the van.

"This is where we're dumping her?" Cassius asked as they climbed out. He looked around, the larger view not much more promising. "How is this going to get noticed or be relevant in any way?"

Rifun pointed to the far end of the field. "Because Tommen and his friends are making laps. The next time they come around, they are going to find a body under the bleachers."

"And you want to see if the kid does something special with the Akari? Are his friends Time Agents, too?"

"Yes to the first, no to the second. But I am expecting him to call for the police, at which time his father will show up."

The more moving pieces a plan had, the more likely it was to fall apart. Cassius rolled his eyes. "What ever happened to the journal? Remember the Book of Abilities that we lost forty years for? Shouldn't we be focusing on the tasks we already had lined up before adding new ones? Lily, Book of Abilities, Book of Commands. Who gives a shit about this fucking kid?"

Cassius went to his knees as he felt the bullet twist in his face. He felt the shift in his sinuses, the movement of soft tissue, and a very stern but silent warning in his mind and soul. Somewhere in the distance, he knew Rifun knelt beside him.

"Obviously your dragon spirit gives a shit."

"Why?" Cassius sputtered. "Is he supposed to replace me?"

He felt a stir in the shadows of his mind, a pulse that he supernaturally understood to be laughter.

"If he is, he's a pretty poor replacement," Rifun said. Cassius hated the man with an intense rage, yet the pain in his face demanded more of his attention. "Or he could be exactly what we need. Only one way to find out."

The pain receded as Rifun stood. As Cassius remained there on his knees in the dirt lot, slowly recovering his faculties, he couldn't help but wonder if there was more between Rifun and the dragon spirit. True, Cassius had become acquainted with the spirit long before Rifun was even born, but there were plenty of spirit workers in the world. What if they were somehow commanding the spirit? What if Rifun was commanding the spirit now, telling it when to punish Cassius and when to let him live?

The pain stopped receding and Cassius heard a whispering rumble in his mind. *No one commands me, small one. Not the Author, not her minions, not any spirit worker, and especially not you.*

And what of Rifun's vow to slay you?

Laughable. He sees the speck upon your soul but fails to acknowledge the plank upon his own. He is nothing.

Cassius knew a moment of terrible frustration, but also a bit of hopeless disappointment. The dragon knew exactly what was going on, was maybe even orchestrating it for its own nefarious ends. What those ends were, Cassius did not know. He was only a means, and he was fast outliving his usefulness unless he could kill Lily Guile and bring the Cult to some prominence again. Why the dragon seemed to need this particular Cult, he did not know, but that was the current mission.

Suddenly, everything was normal again. There was no pain, no fatigue, no cloudiness in head or soul. He was just kneeling there in the dirt while Rifun and Tadashi opened the doors of the van and brought out the woman's body.

Cassius stood. He used Gravity to relieve them of their burden, pushing Tadashi out of the way and almost running over Rifun as he snaked a track through the trees to the nearest set of bleachers. He heard Rifun say something, heard Tadashi grunt a reply, but did not stop or even slow down to make sure they were following.

He dropped the body most unceremoniously under the bleachers, then wandered off to get a look at the kid Rifun seemed fixed on lately.

Not especially tall, messy brown hair, white enough to make any average white person look black, currently burning through a roll of marijuana, there was absolutely nothing about him that showed promise in anything. Not in life, not in academia, not in the military, not in Time, and certainly not in the Akari. What in the hell was so special about him that even the dragon spirit was forcing Cassius to go along with this ridiculous scheme? Did someone know something he didn't? Of course they did. They always seemed to.

He returned to the bleachers where Rifun was kneeling before the woman, putting her in a more noble position. She now sat quietly against the supports, eyes still closed, hands folded neatly on her lap.

"Fucking hell, you're sentimental," Cassius growled. "You think you're winning points with your gods because you do shit like this? You think you're going to be in a lesser circle of Hell than me? It's all the same Hell."

"The ancestors and the razana do not discriminate," Rifun sighed, pointedly ignoring him. "I simply want to ensure that she does not become a forgotten soul." He stood. "As for Hell, there is no worse Hell than the one we make for ourselves."

Cassius shifted his stance. "You do remember that this was your idea, right? You suggested this. And you do know that there will be a few more of these, right?"

"I am very aware of this, thank you."

Cassius trudged back toward the dirt lot. There was a reason he always did his work alone. Less stupidity, less sentimentality. No one to answer to, no one to blame but himself if things went wrong. Plus things tended to get done a lot faster because he didn't have to deal with everyone else's input and suggestions. Dead was dead. It didn't matter if she was sprawled out naked under the moonlight or posed perfectly with roses to line her body.

He reached the dirt lot, surprised to find that the van was now outside the Band, Tadashi was just looking out for traffic on the road, just as if all he had done was pull in and turn around.

Cassius turned as the bushes rustled and Rifun stepped into the lot.

"I'm surprised you don't want to stick around and watch things play out," he observed mildly.

"How do you propose we do that?" Cassius asked irritably.

With a good vantage point and some clever use of Light, bending the light and shadows around them so that they appeared nearly invisible. Once they were set and ready, Rifun dropped the Band.

The three boys continued their lap of the field, talking and joking, hardly anything exciting. Then they came back around to the bleachers where the woman was sitting. Surprise was hardly an adequate word, though Cassius didn't know any more sophisticated ones to describe the boys' reaction to the body. One stumbled back, the second took off running, and Tommen took off after him, tackling him to the ground.

Cassius glanced at Rifun, but the man was watching the scene intently. He was obviously waiting for something, but Cassius couldn't figure out what. Did he expect Tommen to suddenly break out some kind of resurrection magic, make the woman grow a new trachea, heal her artery, and restart her heart? Cassius was more entertained by the show currently going on. Panic, chaos, this only multiplied further when the police did finally show up.

As expected, Walter Forbes was one of the officers on scene. Using Sound to eavesdrop on the conversation, Cassius learned that he was likely to be the one assigned to the case. For as much as he hated to give Rifun credit for anything, especially having a good idea, he found that the thought of Walter being put in charge of the case was rather exhilarating, hilarious even. This man who had murdered his ex-father-in-law and several associates, then later escaped his own death sentence, was going to investigate a murder with the intent of bringing the perpetrator to justice. There was trying to buy your way into heaven, and then there was this. He might have used Sound to muffle his laugh.

He and Rifun stayed put for a little while longer. Finally Rifun crafted a couple of Disguises for them and, shedding the pseudo-invisibility cloak, they joined the growing crowd of curious onlookers. Two police officers were doing their best to keep people back, but the field was a large area to cover and some people could get creative when they really wanted to get close. Behind the officers, the coroner was just finishing up his report, standing and directing some underlings to prepare the black bag.

The two of them dispersed with the rest of the crowd, walking down the sidewalk and finally disappearing through a portal, landing in the officers building.

"Well, that was exciting," Rifun huffed, recovering from the portal.

"It was, I agree," Cassius said. "Wait a day or two, drop another. We got her workplace, so what do you think next? One of her neighbors?"

"I don't think we should move quite that fast, for one. The police don't move that quickly. Captain Forbes is going to take everything he got tonight, dump it into a bin to deal with tomorrow. When he gets to work tomorrow, he's going to spend a fair amount of time drinking coffee and staring at the wall, making a mental list of things he needs to do with this case. Eventually he'll get around to it. He and his partner will conduct their investigation, all according to policy and procedure, chase a few dead ends, then put it on the shelf to go cold."

"We can't just let this go. The elections are coming up. Lily has to be dealt with."

"I'm not disagreeing."

Cassius grunted. He was the one in charge here. He was the one giving orders now. That was what he'd declared. This was his show, and he was going to run things his way.

Before he could speak, Rifun beat him to it. "Perhaps it would be in our best interest to start some rumors among the Akarin about an attempt on Lily Guile's life. Maybe start compiling a list of Akarin who are also still active Time Agents and consider what you might do to spook them a little. Plant those seeds and see what grows."

Hadn't he just said that this was his show and he was calling the shots? Where did Rifun get off barging in and giving orders? Why did he think he could do that? After all this time, knowing that his ideas were the ones that got them in this mess because they were slow and plodding and nonsensical, he still thought he could give orders?

At the same time, compiling that list would give him a chance to kill more later, maybe get the Akarin to pay a little more attention. Maybe that wasn't such a bad idea. But how long did he expect it to last? Fine, wait a few more days for another kill, but was it really going to take that long to compile a list and tell the Akarin that someone was after Lily Guile? And who in the Akarin was going to care about that? The whole reason they were having to do this dog and pony show was because Lily Guile had weathered so many threats that she was basically immune to them now. Idle threats meant nothing. Words were nothing. It was all about the action.

Well, the first action had been carried out. Given the choice between the two ideas now, Cassius decided that the list sounded more productive. And if he could spook those people, those who were both Akarin and active Time Agents, it might give him better standing before the Akarin, that there was a greater threat to be had than against one single person who was routinely opposed.

His first stop, however, was the torture closet in Doug's house. It could have been the reason the house wasn't garnering many, or any, offers, but Cassius wasn't overly concerned.

While normally excited to see the blood and other residue of torture, he was now more enticed by how clean everything was in spite of everything he had done. Cutting the woman's throat should have produced a fountain of blood to soak herself, the bed, the floor, him. And yet, there had been nothing. Not even a tiny drop as from a pinprick. Utterly pristine.

Maybe he would have to take that as a goal, to be able to do what Rifun had done. Not only would it come in handy for this bit of torture, but maybe he could use it on the man himself one day, as Rifun had used it on him on several occasions.

Cassius folded his arms and huffed an angry sigh. What was Rifun's play here? What was he trying to accomplish? What reason did he have for keeping Cassius alive, really? It was not unreasonable to think that simply killing a body would do nothing to kill a spirit, but why let him live anyway? Did the dragon spirit truly dwell within Cassius? He didn't think so. Whether Cassius was alive or dead made no difference to the dragon; he was simply a tool to be used as long as he was both convenient and obedient, both qualities that were fast wearing out.

He did not know whether his lack of epiphany was from his own inability to put things together or because the dragon was purposely obscuring such things. Somehow he had a sneaking suspicion that the dragon would reveal everything right before he died, as a way of pouring salt into his death wounds.

It was coming, his death. He knew it as surely as he knew the smell of it. Time was ticking, and if he didn't figure something out soon, the dragon spirit was going to release its hold on the bullet in his face and kill him.

Cassius left the torture closet and departed Doug's house. First he was going to compile that list of Akarin who were still active Time Agents, starting with those in District Four, closest to Lily Guile. Then he was going to spook them. Maybe he wouldn't kill people around them, but he would give them a good scare, let them know that someone was watching them. Once they were good and riled up, he would take it before the Akarin council and use every ounce of Doug's boisterous personality to try and convince them that something was amiss. If they didn't listen, well, it was their own fault for everything that happened next.

Once that was all taken care of, then it was on to the next event. He was thinking one of Lily's neighbors, let her know that nowhere was safe and she could not, in fact, rest assured about anything. Barring that, maybe one of her friends who went out drinking and whoring around with her. That sounded better, actually. Drive her away from work, drive her away from her social life. Get her all safe and cozy in her bed, sure that she was safe in her own castle. Then kill her.

6 | Fampitandremana
Charleston, 2013

Caution

Apparently unsatisfied with how things might progress too slowly, Cassius had decided to put himself out there. He hadn't gone and waved to any surveillance cameras near the dump site, but he had taken the van and made himself known at a couple of places: a gas station, a supermarket. Of course, he and the van had disappeared, which profoundly frustrated the police, for the short time they paid any attention to the case.

Rifun kept an eye on the case as much as he could, snooping around the police station, following Walter and his partner around, eavesdropping on various interviews, and generally getting a feel for when it was going to be shelved. Actually this came a lot sooner than expected — only a couple of weeks — and Rifun was left with either letting Cassius loose right away or else coming up with some other avenue of psychological torture that would both draw all players deeper into the game and buy a little more time so Cassius didn't blow their scheme too soon.

When he wasn't following Walter, he was following Tommen, and it was not an exciting or heartening thing to behold. From everything Rifun could tell, Tommen not only had no Akari abilities, but he was not even aware of its existence. Micaiah never mentioned a word about it, not even a subtle hint. Rifun might understand how it might not come up when the public could hear or observe, but even alone, he never demonstrated an ounce of skill.

Sitting in the park in Disguise, mulling over his options, Rifun found himself rather annoyed. A chosen one of the Author was not even aware of his talent. He wasn't even aware of how special he was, how honored he should be that he had been chosen. True, Micaiah's first Book showed him in the dark of the truth, but he still had inherent talents that he exploited. Those Books promised the rise of the Chivalrous Welshman. Was he blind to this miraculous coincidence, or had something happened? What was going on?

Rifun stood. Well, maybe it was time to take matters into his own hands and force the issue a little. He might not be able to use Tommen at this time, but he could draw Walter in more.

His first stop was an antique store, although he couldn't decide how he felt about many of the items being classified as antiques. He had seen almost half of these items when they were brand new, had used almost all of them in some way. Now they were tossed out of old homes like trash and given one last chance at life, maybe picked up by some collector or put on display as an ornament.

In the front display case he found a pocket watch. On closer examination, it appeared to be real silver, though whoever cleaned it up hadn't done the best job. Enough to make it look nice and shiny, but hardly the care of someone who understood its true value.

There was no specific reason he chose the pocket watch. It was simple enough, easy to carry around but not easy to miss at a crime scene. It also allowed for the delivery of secondary messages, like the photo Rifun had found of Owain Fforidd in a Welsh museum. It wasn't his mugshot per se, oh no. No, this was the photo of him when he was an upstanding man of London, son-in-law of a wealthy London banker. But even for the overall poor quality of the photo and all the years that had passed, Owain Fforidd was still very recognizable. Same brown hair and bushy blond mustache, same face.

His next stop was a laser engraver. He walked in the shop with no Disguise. If there were cameras, they would catch his face, and the man at the counter would give his description to the police, but that was sort of what he was counting on. Let the police put their faces out there, let Lily know what was going on, who was stalking her. Make a grand show of things, invite a large audience to witness.

The whole thing was shaping up like a stage play, Rifun thought. Different characters entering the stage at different times. Some lay the mystery, others attempt to solve it. And, like actors on a stage, some of the characters had to pretend they didn't know what was going on. Tommen had only the most paltry abilities himself, just enough to get himself into or out of trouble. Walter Forbes could not tell his fellow policemen about Time or the Akari, the machinations of a universe they knew nothing about. How long would they be able to keep up the facade, pretend that they were perfectly normal and as confused and helpless as everyone else?

No. Walter might not be involved with the Akarin or the Akari at all, but a chosen one of the Author didn't get to hide. They were not made differently so they could live like everyone else. No one who had the potential to manipulate the fabric of the universe was going to roll over for a pathetic street thug bully. He would find out more about Micaiah and his situation later. Right now, he had to work on coaxing Tommen into the light, and it started by getting his uncle involved.

"Here you are," the man said, setting the freshly engraved pocket watch on the counter. "Will this be cash or card?"

"This will be cash," Rifun told him, bringing out a money clip. He'd swiped bills here and there from people and now laid them out on the counter, telling the man to keep the four cents change. Then he grabbed the watch and left the shop.

He returned to the officers building, mildly surprised to find Cassius there. The man had been elusive lately, though with surprisingly few bodies to show for it. Rifun decided not to question it. No doubt the evil spirit had caught on to what he was trying to do, and perhaps he was onto something with his theory about there being a moment of weakness when Cassius made a kill, an opportunity to strike at the demon. Now it was laying low, trying to figure out a new strategy to consume such heinous sacrifices. No doubt it was also considering how to turn Rifun into one of those sacrifices.

"Ready for a second swipe at Lily?" Cassius asked pointedly before Rifun could utter a word.

"I had something made," Rifun told him, showing him the watch. "I think it might up the ante a little, bring more players into the game."

Cassius snatched the watch and inspected it, the engraving, the small cutout of Owain. "Thought you were going after the kid?"

"I am. And you are going after Owain Fforidd on the side as I recall. Bring one, get the other, everyone goes home happy."

Cassius tossed the watch haphazardly into the air. Rifun made a grab, caught it. "Fine. Whenever you're ready—" His tone was mocking. "—then we go and take another swipe at Lily."

"You have someone in mind?"

The man shrugged. "Wouldn't be my first choice, but it makes the same point. Julianna told me about some dinner she's planning for Thanksgiving."

"A party guest," Rifun stated.

"No, she's going out to eat. Figure we nab the girl at the next table. Julianna said her boyfriend is going to propose to her."

Rifun raised a brow. "Sounds a bit dark for Julianna, after the fuss she made about the last woman."

Cassius gave him a look. "You made a fuss about the last woman, too."

"Yes, but what purpose does this serve? A coworker, fine. I could understand a neighbor, too. A friend would be very close to her. What is this about kidnapping some woman in a restaurant?"

"I don't know exactly, but Julianna insisted that it would mean something."

"Suddenly you care about her opinion?"

Now Cassius got upset, his posture shifting aggressively as he pointed to his face. "I do what I'm fucking told."

Rifun blinked. Cassius and the dark spirit was one thing, but now Julianna was involved? Was this simply a matter of two interests coinciding, or was there more? Not a lot was known about the in-between dimension, but now he was curious to know what was going on. Was Julianna consorting with spirits? She'd never shown any particular interest before, just a mild respect for beliefs she herself did not hold.

Or could the spirit be impersonating Julianna? No, that wouldn't make sense. If you were going to impersonate one person to sway someone else, you had to impersonate someone that person trusted or respected. It was why Cassius was impersonating Doug, although Doug apparently garnered less respect than they had originally thought.

Just another piece of the puzzle, one Rifun was quite unprepared for. The spirit was making a move, and he had to figure out how to counter it, or how to make it work for him. He nodded once. "Thanksgiving isn't far off. What did you have in mind?"

It wasn't a difficult plan, but then, Cassius wasn't an especially complex person. The idea was to simply watch the woman in the restaurant, wait for her to leave, then jump her as she walked by a certain alley on the way back to her apartment. In the event that her new fiance drove her home, they'd just wait inside for her.

Out of curiosity, Rifun had checked up on both parties of this allegedly impending marital arrangement.

The woman, Cassidy Wilhall, was a tidy housekeeper, thoroughly organized, and looked like she had a good plan for her life. She would probably change her mind on some of the details, but it looked like she wanted to have some kind of good job without it being an all-consuming career, a family with three or four kids, and, eventually, a house of her own rather than an apartment. Maybe a little naive, but nothing overly grandiose or unattainable.

The man, Michael Bailey, did not resemble this lifestyle in any fashion. Rifun would not fault the man for renting what he could afford, as far as apartments went, but that was no excuse for how filthy it was. Holes in the walls and ceiling were poorly patched or covered in faded and ripped posters. The carpet was ripped or burned in several spots, littered with beer cans and drug paraphernalia, and stained thoroughly with dog urine.

Maybe they should kill the man instead and spare the woman this horrendous future. He actually felt less bad about what they were about to do; it almost felt like a rescue mission now. At the very least, Rifun wasn't going to stop Cassius from coming back for the man, too. They'd be doing a lot of people a favor.

Would it be as meaningful if they did kill both of them? Rifun had not asked Julianna for her reasons why she picked this particular woman; truthfully, he wasn't sure he wanted to know the answer. His only guess was that it would somehow resonate with Lily who had lost her husband in World War II. Maybe he had proposed to her in a similar manner. But even if that were the case, why go after her and not him? At least this guy seemed to deserve it, not that Rifun could speak to Lily's husband's personality.

It seemed a sad thing that he was the only one who cared about such details. Going with Cassius to wait for the girl, he knew the dark-skinned man wouldn't care about any of it. He had a target, and he believed that killing this target would somehow satiate the dark spirit enough to let him live a little bit longer and so fulfill the goal of killing Lily Guile. But why did the dark spirit care about Lily Guile? Or was this just about toying with Cassius and seeing what it could get him to do? Then, once the spirit tired of the game, it would just kill Cassius.

The spirit thought Rifun was getting close to figuring out how to slay it. Maybe it thought Rifun had found some kind of ally in Cassius. It wanted to wrap up whatever this particular mission was, accomplish some minor goal, then kill its current fleshy host and flee.

Rifun could hardly imagine living in such a way. Even prison did not seem so cruel. Yes, conditions were poor and the jailers would beat and torture prisoners for fun, but this seemed to be a prison of the mind, the will, the very soul. Cassius had been so intent on never being a slave again that he had willfully enslaved himself to a far worse master.

"What the fuck are you staring at?"

Rifun blinked, his own mind returning to the present where he was, indeed, staring at Cassius. They waited in the shadow of an alley across from the Italian restaurant where the girl was waiting for her boyfriend. While the bending of Light and shadow would generally conceal them from distant eyes, they were still pretty well visible to each other.

"Stop fucking staring at me," Cassius growled.

"Apologies," Rifun said evenly. "I was thinking."

Cassius rolled his eyes, and they turned their attention back to the restaurant.

Rifun had been to the man's apartment. He knew what he drove. The vehicle he rolled up in was not his vehicle. Only because of mandatory inspections did his vehicle look and run as nice as it did, but this one was worth at least a few more dollars per hour, or maybe a lot more dollars. Either he borrowed it, or he got the sticky finger discount.

Watching the girl, she did not look surprised in the least to see him driving such a vehicle, so she probably knew its origins, or else he could lie a good one. She took his hand and they went inside.

"Would you like to go to dinner?" Rifun inquired of Cassius.

"Why?"

"Eavesdrop?"

Cassius gave him a look. "What the fuck do I care? We're here to kill her, not dig up gossip."

Rifun shrugged. "Just a thought."

"Go if you want, I don't give a fuck. I'm here to fucking kill her."

"I have to say, Cassius, I'm a bit put off by your sudden, excessive use of profanity. Not the profanity itself, of course, as Americans seem to be far more sensitive to it than when I lived in London, but just your sudden interest in it. I understand you're not the most eloquent, but it was —"

"I'm doing my part to blend in," Cassius interrupted irritably. "Younger generation likes this shit."

"You're a serial killer, Cassius, and a necrophiliac. You are never going to blend in."

"I blend in more than you do, mutt."

Rifun blinked. He hit the man with Test just to be sure this was Cassius beside him. It was. "I'm sorry, I thought we were on the same side here."

"The only side I'm on is my own."

"Then maybe I'll just leave you to this little endeavor and we can forget any further mention of getting rid of this dark spirit."

"If it means I don't have to listen to you whine about giving her a humane death, then by all means." He spoke again before Rifun could open his mouth. "It is going to kill me. I know that for a fact. And I don't want to spend whatever time I have left listening to you whine and cry and fret over what I'm doing."

Rifun studied Cassius for a long moment, glancing at the restaurant only occasionally where the happy couple was sitting at a nearby window perusing the menu. A waiter came by to deliver drinks; so far it appeared to be standard soda, no sign of wine or champagne yet.

"I will meet you back at Doug's house," he decided finally. "I imagine this kidnapping will be as swift as the previous one, with no need for anything overly dramatic."

"I thought you were leaving me to this little endeavor," Cassius said smartly, not looking at him. "That would imply leaving me alone."

"I would, but I'm still going to watch out for her somewhat."

"Ah, yes, the humane death you are weirdly obsessed with."

"I'm sure you will get plenty of pleasure from Lily. These women are not Lily."

Cassius' expression was mockingly thoughtful as he turned toward Rifun. "And there is that strange line of morality. I will say, thanks to you, I now understand the full implications of drawing a line in the sand. You can reposition it whenever it becomes convenient. Murder is subjective, but somehow less than rape, even if the victim is already dead."

"I'll be waiting at Doug's house."

"Suit yourself."

Cassius looked back at the restaurant. The first course had come, soups for both of them. Still no sign of the engagement. Rifun wondered if he shouldn't Disguise himself and go in anyway, see what was going on. He kind of wanted to witness the proposal, even if he was highly questionable and she about to die. He wanted to see her last happy moment before Cassius took it all away.

Rifun left the alley, heading deeper as if to open a portal. Instead, he rounded the corner, took out the special cell phone, and called Julianna.

"Is it done?" Her tone was forcibly even.

"Not yet; they're only on the first course," Rifun reported. "Actually, I was wondering why you picked her. She holds no connection to Lily that I've been able to find. Yes, Lily is there in the restaurant, probably going to witness this short-lived engagement, but what is all this about, really?"

"Social tragedy. Her workplace is not safe and neither is going out in public." The line sounded terribly rehearsed.

"From everything Cassius and I have seen, Lily rarely goes out alone. Why this woman specifically and not one of Lily's friends?"

"Lily and her friends enjoy going out drinking. If nothing else, she should be sober for such an event." Again, the line was rehearsed but hardly believed.

"That may be true, but it's still not the truth, not the answer I'm looking for. And you know it."

Julianna hummed a moment, and he could imagine her nodding. "All right, fine. I suppose it takes an actor to know one."

"You're not much of an actress, sorry to say."

"Yes, I don't have the face for it anymore, I'm afraid. As to your inquiry, well, Lily's husband proposed to her in a similar manner, right before he left for war."

Rifun grunted. "I wondered if it was something like that. But what would you have suggested if this wasn't all happening? What if he doesn't propose here for some reason? Or what if he wasn't going to?"

"Oh, I had several other plans in mind, don't worry. But you have to understand the history of things. Yes, going after her at her workplace or her social life is very unnerving, but attacking her history is absolutely penetrating. Make no mistake, she will try to brush it off, put on a strong face, make some sarcastic remark or other, but I guarantee that she has not forgotten her husband and she will remember him through this. It won't take much to connect the two murders, and I do believe that you will start to get to her."

He nodded though he wasn't sure if she could see. "I can understand that, though it still feels like a gamble."

"You're taking a bit of a gamble yourself, aren't you? With the watch and drawing in the Forbeses?"

"You can't tell me you don't think Tommen is the Chivalrous Welshman."

"Who cares? That's only a coicidental label. Even so, you were sixty years old before you became involved with the Akari. He's only a moody, hormonal, violence-prone teenager. Do you really want that around so much power?"

"You think he could be worse than Cassius? I don't. Besides, we shouldn't judge him on his faults. He just needs guidance, as all boys his age do. I never got it, and look what happened to me." He went on, speaking over her first few syllables. "Anyway, with regards to the present moment and closer future plans, I think I may wish to make a slight detour."

"Detour?"

"The Book of Abilities, the one left in the cave."

"Yes, what about it?"

"Tommen found it. He went into Forbes Cave to explore and got caught in the Time Trap. But he found the Book of Abilities there and brought it out. It got donated to the museum here."

"Why not just go in and get it?"

Rifun shifted his stance. "I'm thinking I might try to bring everything together, tie up all these disconnected threads and turn them into a singular work of art. Lily and the Time industry, Cassius as Doug and the Akarin, the Cult, all of it needs to be streamlined so we're not running about here and there on disconnected, competing errands."

"Hm," Julianna mused. "Well, I've little enjoyment for what Cassius is about to do, so perhaps I shall instead learn more about the journal and its whereabouts, and perhaps I shall follow Tommen around for a bit, see what kind of routine he keeps."

"That would make my job a lot easier. I admit, I'm a bit worried about Cassius. I think something is going very wrong between him and his demon."

"Why should anyone expect anything less? The Devil always comes for his due."

"I can't let it get away, not when it's this close."

She sighed dramatically. "For God's sake, Rifun, you're a Builder, aren't you? Why are you having such a difficult time with this?" She added hastily, "No. I don't want to hear it. You have exhausted my patience on the matter. You are an Akari Builder and a shaman among your own people. Either this evil spirit is too great even for you or else you're just being lazy about it. Considering that you have proclaimed it far above the skill of the average layman, there is nothing I'm going to do to help, so get to it."

Rifun managed to turn his sigh into something like an even breath. "Well, first we have to get through this evening, and I have to keep Cassius from raping a dead body. Let me know if you come up with anything interesting on Tommen or the journal."

He did not give her a chance to reply as he ended the call.

She was right. He was running out of excuses why he couldn't try something to be rid of the evil spirit, and he was running out of time to do it. How much more power did he think he needed? How much more power was available to him, really? If manipulating the physics of reality wasn't enough, what was?

He opened a portal to Doug's house and stepped through. Looking around at all the torture devices Cassius had brought in, he couldn't help but feel a twinge of doubt. Was evil a tangible thing to be manipulated? Where did evil fit into physics? What if it wasn't part of physical reality and he couldn't manipulate it?

Gingerly, he approached the small instrument table and picked up a scalpel. How many times had he had skin removed and then stitched back on? He Felt his twisted flesh, the lines, the lumps, the odd keloid he was having trouble getting rid of permanently. He Felt the scalpel, knew its metallic composition and condition, knew every dust particle that rested on its shiny surface, every microbe that had amassed since its last cleaning. He again looked around the room, examining the Energy. The Light, the Gravity, the Electricity, the Magnetism, all of the forces at work. All of it, the Matter and the Energy, predictable and precise, all of it governed by mathematical formulae and other basic laws. Action, reaction. Cause, effect. Action, consequence.

What were the mathematics of evil? What did he add or subtract to make Cassius more or less evil? What graph would help him predict his next move? And even if such a graph existed, would it answer the why? And would it answer why different people in similar circumstances chose radically different paths in life? Why did some choose to forgive and others choose revenge? What was it that drove Cassius to such extremes? What force of reality was a spirit?

A change in the lighting indicated Cassius' arrival, to say nothing of the Band that enveloped him. Rifun quickly set down the scalpel and turned to watch him haul the woman through, the exact same way as before. He deliberately ignored Rifun as he laid the woman on the bed, blissfully ignorant of what was about to happen as she remained outside the Band.

There was something he was missing, Rifun thought. Not that he had anything more to learn, in the sense of acquiring new pieces, but that he needed to figure out a new way of putting the pieces together. He personally enjoyed jigsaw puzzles, and for all the pieces in the box, the puzzle only went together one way. He knew the Book of Philosophy well enough. Maybe there was something in the Book of Abilities that would spark an idea.

"Just like last time, then?" Cassius wondered, breaking into Rifun's thoughts. "Or did you have any more strange and brilliant ideas?"

"Same as last time," Rifun told him. "We need to make sure everyone understands that the two murders are related, and the media loves a sensational serial killer story."

He didn't like the look on Cassius' face as he simply shrugged and approached the table of instruments. "Your idea, your call."

Rifun stiffly moved out of the way and went to stand beside the bed. Pretty girl, neat, organized, with plans for her life. He still didn't understand how she got tangled up with the man who was only a short-lived fiance, but he was fairly certain that whatever plans she had would quickly get tossed out the window. Still, she deserved better. If anyone deserved to die, it was the man. But then it wouldn't mean as much to Lily. It wouldn't make her afraid enough to excite Cassius.

Maybe he should just kill Lily himself, ignore Cassius' plight entirely, snub it even, and spare any more women such a gruesome death. Maybe such a thing would aggravate the spirit and give him an opportunity to kill it. He had to do something, and he had to do it soon.

"All right, you ready?" Cassius asked, walking over with the scalpel.

Rifun tempered his sigh and readied the Bands. Microscopic ones, thousands of them, ready to capture every single red blood cell and stop it so that he could use Matter to knit flesh back together. Sever an artery and never spill a drop of blood.

First the face, making neat squares, the same as he had done to Julianna. Next the hands, tearing up tissue and pulverizing bones as he expanded the hole and then secured her hands together.

Finally, the throat. One incision to sever the artery, Rifun holding the Bands like fast-filling balloons, working quickly to use Matter to knit the flesh back together, clotting and healing each end of the wound. The hard part done, all he had to do now was the minor healing as Cassius removed the trachea.

Rifun couldn't say he wasn't fascinated, in a purely scientific sense. He had butchered a number of animals in his time, but there was a morbid fascination with the human body, knowing that they were pretty well similar. Blood was blood, throats were throats. And they were all just sacks of flesh whose souls could be ripped from them at any given moment by a psychopathic necrophiliac.

"That should do it," Cassius declared with far more enthusiasm than Rifun felt comfortable with. The madman stepped back away from the woman, scalpel in one hand, trachea in the other.

Rifun released his Bands and Cassius did the same. The woman immediately lurched into death throes, the same ghastly sucking sound wheezing at her open throat. Perhaps what made it worse was the total lack of blood. There should have been spurts and gushes, splattering everything in a ten foot radius with red droplets. But there was nothing. Everything, including the woman herself, remained absolutely clean. Her eyes rolled back in her head, she pawed at her neck, but her convulsions were growing weaker until they transformed into the final twitches of a body expending the last of its electrical energy.

Cassius was polite enough not to rape the body, but that didn't stop him from satisfying himself anyway. Rifun just rolled his eyes and turned away.

"Another successful mission," Cassius sighed when he was done.

"A successful murder," Rifun corrected. "The body is still here. We still have to dump it somewhere."

"And where would you suggest? Is there some other convenient event in which Tommen will coincidentally happen upon this body?"

Rifun shook his head. "That was just to draw them in, get that ball rolling and test reactions. We don't need to completely ruin his psyche."

"Why not? Boys go to war all the time, or they used to."

"Yes, after some training, receiving some instruction on how to react and proceed. He hasn't received any of that yet."

Cassius just shrugged. "All right, so what do you want to do with her? Or are you going to let me decide?"

"She needs to be found," Rifun stated seriously, "preferably in one piece."

"Or two pieces, as the case may be." Cassius indicated the trachea.

"Keep the throat if you must, but don't do anything else to her."

Rifun could see that Cassius was past warnings and threats; his mind was already going to where and how he would dispose of the body.

"Tadashi isn't waiting for us this time?" Cassius inquired.

Rifun shook his head. "No, he's a little annoyed, I think. With us, the Cult. He either wants to sit in his basement or else shoot stuff up, and we keep dragging him out to go driving here and there every once in a while."

"So it's not just me," Cassius quipped. He went on before Rifun could speak. "Maybe I'll just dump her in the river, shove her into some bushes on the riverbank in one of the parks. Then it will be a surprise whose psyche I permanently damage."

He did not wait for Rifun's opinion. Apparently quite pleased with himself, Cassius scooped up the woman, opened a portal, and disappeared.

Rifun let him go. There was every chance that the man was going to violate the body, but he had to stop focusing on trees and start looking at the forest. He could not allow another woman to die just so Cassius could rub off and feel better about himself and his task to kill Lily. He had to shift things back to the Akari, the Authored Books, and everything that mattered more than one sadist's abominable fetishes.

Cassius returned just as Rifun was about to leave. Still the man was sickeningly upbeat.

"Our next move is going to be the Book of Abilities," Rifun announced.

Cassius shrugged. "All right, so go get it."

"Not yet. I have Julianna keeping an eye on Tommen. I want to see if we can bring him into this in some way."

"You just said —"

"I said I didn't want to damage his psyche with another murder. He is still a chosen one of the Author and an Akari-bearer, even if he doesn't realize it yet. Maybe a little more challenge will encourage him to use his abilities, if he doesn't think he has to hide them."

The dark-skinned man did not appear overly concerned on that part, but added, "And going after the Book of Abilities might get the attention of the Akarin a little more."

Rifun folded his arms and shifted his stance. "I thought you said you had made progress?"

"I said they were letting me talk about it. Given Doug's personality, I can at least get in a few words, maybe a warning, but they're still very quick to shut me down." He added quickly, "And if you don't want anyone to die from me trying to force my opinion on others — and I have been forceful several times without killing anyone — then I have to back down somewhat."

"What about stalking the other Akarin in the area?"

Cassius' expression was unimpressed. "You're the bureaucratic one. You know how slow things move. You have the patience for it. That's why I wanted you to impersonate Doug."

Rifun grunted. "Well, I admit that even my patience has limits." He nodded. "Once the body is discovered and the connection is made, take it before the Akarin council. Do some more stalking of the others in the area and take that, too. Once Julianna comes back with something to work with and we go after the Book of Abilities, make a big deal about that as well. Either they'll do something or else this is going to be the biggest 'I told you so' anyone ever uttered."

"And if they do end up doing something? There's been some whispers that Micaiah is up to something, doing some investigating."

"A man may acquire all the knowledge he wishes and still not be a threat to anyone. I won't be worried until he decides to act on that knowledge, assuming what he finds is true and accurate."

Cassius remained unimpressed. "Shouldn't we stop him from investigating in the first place? Won't that entice the Akarin a little more, maybe make them think we're something of a threat? If we can't stop one man, we're not going to stop all of them."

Rifun nodded. "True. Let's see what he does after the second body. In the meantime, I'll ask Isthim to set the Grandfathers on him and possibly Captain Forbes as well, a little negative reinforcement from the Time industry side of things."

"Box them in, see how they react."

"Exactly."

All that really left, then, was just waiting for the body to be found.

Rifun went to the park where Cassius had stuffed the body in some bushes on the riverbank. The park itself was more of a minor rest area, and several vehicles came and went throughout the evening. But no one went to the river. The water was cold and choppy, the wind fairly chilly. What reason was there to go down? Rifun himself, Disguised as someone else, went down once, only to slide down the poorly-maintained steps that were nearly indistinguishable from the bank. If not for Gravity, Banding, and general quick-thinking, he might have lost his Disguise. As it was, he straightened and got everything smoothed out, a bit flustered as he returned to the picnic table he had been sitting at for at least three hours now.

It was dark. It was windy. No one was going to find the body tonight.

Maybe he should drag it up here to the picnic area, position it respectfully; it would be more in line with the last murder. On the other hand, between rigor mortis and the freezing river, he probably wouldn't be able to manipulate the limbs very well, and he wasn't about to try and warm it up.

He hadn't asked where Cassius had actually kidnapped the woman, if it had been the alley or if he'd had to go to her apartment. He wasn't about to go back and find out. So he just opened a portal near the restaurant and started walking down the sidewalk. At any and all likely locations, he stopped, Banded, and looked around for any signs of the kidnapping. Of course, given that the whole point was to make them virtually untraceable, he was finding himself in a trap of his own design.

The best he got was the discovery of a necklace in one of the alleys they had staked out. It looked like something the woman might wear, though how or why Cassius had had a chance to rip it off her, he did not know. Time to gamble, he supposed.

Rifun left the engraved pocket watch with the necklace in the alley, trying to position them in such a way that it did not look staged, but it might also appear as a logical spot for the items to fall in a small struggle. He did not know quite how successful he was and figured the police would let him know.

He returned to the officers building where he bowed to pray at his shrine. He had watched and even participated in two senseless murders because he was allowing himself to be overwhelmed and frightened by this dark spirit within Cassius. He was getting distracted and worn down when he should be formulating a plan. The spirit was about to kill its own host and flee. Rifun was admittedly less concerned about Cassius, but he didn't want to let this spirit get away.

Regrettably, he had no visions while he was praying, but he did get a strong inclination about the Book of Abilities. So maybe he was on the right track. He had the pieces, he just had to put them together the right way.

Rifun sat up, stretched, stood, stretched again. He wasn't especially tired, but he went to bed anyway, if only so he could run through things in his mind without interruption. Even when he did fall asleep, he still had no visions or other spiritual encounters. He would not say that he was not disappointed, but there came a point when a child had to step out on his own and do the work he had been shown and taught to do.

The Hand Holding the Knife

Eventually he returned to the roadside park. This day was completely different from the evening before. Now it was mostly sunny with just a hint of a breeze. More people came and went, and more of them stayed an extra minute or two, mostly to stand around and talk.

After an hour or so, Rifun went down to the water just to make sure the body was still there to be found. It was, and he returned to the picnic table he had claimed as his own. Cars came and went. Children ran around to stretch their legs and work off some pent-up energy, people took dogs for potty breaks or short runs, and working men double-checked the straps on their load.

Still no one went down to the river. Rifun resolved that if she wasn't found by the end of the day, he would move her up to the picnic table and position her. He could pinch his nose long enough to do such a thing, if only to move this along.

It was just about noontime when his hope flared. A family had pulled in and decided to actually stop for a while. Mom brought out a cooler packed with sandwiches and snacks, and Dad produced a frisbee. The kids couldn't catch worth a damn. Then came the fateful toss, the disc soaring over everyone's heads and sweeping toward the bushes, right toward the area of the body as if guided by a spiritual hand.

Rifun pretended not to be overly interested in the family, staring at a newspaper laid out before him, watching them in his peripheral as best he could. He waited for the scream, though it never came. Reflecting later, this was probably for the best as the parents tried to keep the kids calm and shuffle them back to the car. Glancing up, he saw both parents had gone absolutely pale, stark white like a freshly-bleached pair of socks. Dad was already on the phone, one hand up, futilely trying to tell his wife to stop talking in his other ear.

At some point, the weather had changed, but Rifun hardly noticed. He just stood, folded up his newspaper, and went on his way, ignoring the family where the wife was becoming increasingly hysterical even as she tried to keep the kids calm and occupied.

Unlike the bleachers and the sports field, Rifun did not stick around to see what the police did, if they made the connection, if they called Walter, any of it. They would be too politically correct out in public, bound by protocol to release as little to the public as possible.

What he was really interested in would be spoken of the next day, when the policemen were safely back in the office or the cruiser, going over evidence and discussing theories. He doubted he would be able to sit in on any conversations Walter would have with Micaiah, but the police he might be able to pull off.

It wasn't glamorous, but it was effective. He used a Band to get into the precinct the following morning, then made his way to a dark closet not ten steps from Walter's cubicle. There was no real way he could get comfortable, but he was able to finagle something like a sitting position. Then it was simply a matter of using Sound to generally listen in on the goings-on of the office. Once he heard Walter clock in and offer a few greetings, Rifun homed in on his activities.

No one's morning routine was spectacular. No one's. Not when they got up, not when they went to work, and not when they got to work. Even Rifun couldn't claim that his morning routine was anything worth eavesdropping on, and Walter's certainly wasn't either. Cup of coffee, another run to the restroom, getting on his computer to run through his to-do list, knock out some emails, and figure out the plan of attack for this new case.

Rifun's calves started to cramp up.

The first break came when the woman's sister called to report her missing. With the body now identified, the case exploded into a flurry of activity which Rifun was happy to keep an eye on as best he could. Sneak in the shadows, curious passerby, nameless intern, whatever he had to do to stay in the general loop.

If there was anything he could appreciate about the investigation, or this part of it, it was that the police were just as confused about the choice of victim as he had been. If they were trying to scare Lily, go after coworkers, go after friends and family, send threatening letters. Why bother picking off one random woman who happened to be dining at the same restaurant one coincidental evening?

Well, it wasn't going to happen again if he could help it. He wasn't going to indulge the whims of this dark spirit, he was going to confront it, fight it, kill it. He was going to get the Book of Abilities and see what he was missing, figure out how these pieces all fit together.

He left the investigation circus, headed to a site outside of town and called Julianna.

"Hello?" came the accented voice.

"I don't suppose you've been able to follow Walter and his partner in their police car?" Rifun wondered. "I haven't quite figured out how to pull that one off without alerting them to my presence."

"No, I've been keeping an eye on Tommen, as you asked. This dimension is many things and I can do many things, but two places at once I cannot be."

"All right. Well, the journal is more important at this point, so keep following Tommen. I was only curious."

"But it's not the reason you called."

"Well, I was hoping you might have figured something out about Tommen. Teenagers are not so clever as they think they are; they are still very much creatures of habit, especially when they can't legally drive."

Her grin was in her voice as she said, "Well, he may not be able to drive, but he does seem to enjoy walking home sometimes."

"From school?"

"Or the bakery if he's working."

Rifun shifted his stance. "Julianna, I'm looking at one...two, three...at least three or more interstates or highways here. And you say he walks home from the bakery?"

"Banding is a wonderful thing, isn't it?"

He let out a breath. "It's the only way I can see that he makes it through alive."

"I think the more interesting thing is that his route home from the bakery takes him past the governmental complex, which includes the museum where the journal is currently housed."

He nodded. "That is interesting."

She chuckled. "I may not be there, but I know you're thinking about something." Her tone turned serious, if mildly exasperated. "You're not going to hurt Tommen, are you? If he is the Chivalrous Welshman as you seem to believe, you can't hurt a chosen one of the Author."

"There is a very real likelihood of having to kill Cassius who appears to be a chosen one as well, but I do understand what you're saying. I have no plans of truly harming Tommen. Scaring him a little, maybe. I still think he knows something about the Akari, he's just too...self-conscious to use it."

"Image is everything, and he isn't the most popular kid in school," Julianna agreed. "It would make sense that he would want to minimize anything he thinks is weird or would make him look weird."

"Given that he resorts to Time Bands, I expect his Faith is brittle."

"Nonexistent, really. He proclaims to be an atheist, though he still holds to some old morals."

Rifun frowned. "We'll have to work on that. For now, I think our next move should be to get the journal and confront Tommen. If we can do both at the same time, so much the better."

"I'll see what I can arrange," Julianna promised. "Of course you'll have to be on Earth when I call."

"Naturally. I'll keep an eye on the police investigation into the murders and check in on Tommen when I can."

"And this means no more innocent women will be murdered?"

"Not for Cassius' sick lust, no. No, that was a mistake from the beginning. We need to get the journal and get back on track. Get the journal, get Tommen, kill Lily, take over the elections and the Time industry. At some point, I will have to deal with the dark spirit within Cassius."

"Oh, well, I'm glad that made it into your plans, even as an afterthought," Julianna said sarcastically.

"The journal has what I need. I know it. Find me a rendezvous with Tommen Forbes if you can."

"I can only try."

He did not respond to that, just hung up and observed the cityscape from his vantage point. He did not consider Charleston to be a beautiful city. Its only redeeming quality aside from the landscape was, perhaps, the capital building, golden dome gleaming in the evening light. Other than that, it was a mess of twisting freeways, billboards popping up like giant steel weeds, a few tall buildings like enormous steel tree trunks, and a scattering of ordinary American fare: big box stores, supermarkets, a downtown district, and various neighborhoods of all income levels.

He only needed to be on Earth to receive Julianna's calls. He didn't necessarily have to be here. Yes, yes, he should follow the police around some more, maybe check in on Tommen, but he had things he wanted to do, too, that didn't have anything to do with any of this.

Well, it was still pretty early in the morning back home; everyone would be asleep. Maybe he would check in on Walter, then Tommen, then head back to the officers building to pray and get some sleep before dropping in on Lalao. That sounded like a good plan. Made more sense than any of the other plans he had to come up with in the near future.

kokumbo

For as many words as people used to describe Doug Templeton, impulsive was evidently not one of them.

Among the peons of Earth, all the harping coworkers and lawyers and bankers and assorted businessmen with whom he somehow had to do business, Cassius really wasn't concerned. He didn't care about the legal proceedings or business dealings that he would leave hanging. He didn't care about how their stock portfolios were suffering because of how many important people were reading into some kind of panic on his part. None of that interested or concerned him.

If anything kept them in line, it was the fact that his house wasn't selling. There were plenty of interested parties, but they were so picky and demanding. They didn't like the color of the granite countertops. The refrigerator wasn't smart enough. They wanted him to repaint such and such walls where the color had faded in between where pictures and paintings used to hang.

For fuck's sake, people, he was selling the house as is where is, all furniture and knick-knacks included. Literally turn-key ready, don't even have to bother packing up the old stuff and moving it in.

But it let him have access to the torture room and other various amenities for the time being.

Maybe, when he didn't have to pretend anymore, he would just burn the house down. If people couldn't be grateful for such luxuries, they didn't get such luxuries. Simple as that. Assuming Rifun didn't intercede and try to give the house to some homeless person as some act of charity. Maybe Cassius would open it up to all of the nearby homeless, then burn the place down with the homeless inside. Not only would it teach the rich snobs a lesson, but it would rid the community of a nuisance and the city of a drain of resources. He would be acting in the best interests of the community at large. Besides, it wasn't like the homeless were really going to accomplish anything, however much the naive idealists of the world seemed to think so.

Well, it wasn't long until the elections in the Wheel, so if he was going to do such a thing, he might have to start planning it out. Maybe he should invite the homeless to come check out the house. Maybe he should start his diabolical community service early, invite the homeless in one at a time and introduce them to his torture room. Then he could do all sorts of things to them without having to listen to lectures from Rifun.

And maybe he ought to do something about the housekeeper. In spite of the generous salary he paid her, plus whatever else she got from her other clients, she was almost homeless herself. Five kids from five different fathers, plus half a dozen more kids the state had already taken from her. Addicted to multiple drugs, it was a wonder she could drive or walk or remember what day it was to know where she had to be. Doug didn't do his own housecleaning, and Cassius didn't either, but his own laziness couldn't justify her existence. A little bit of dust on his cabinets was not worth the thousands of dollars the government and courts poured into keeping her alive and basically functioning.

Maybe he could get her to paint the walls and whatever other minor tasks people were whining about, then kill her. Leave her body in the torture room and let it burn with the rest of the homeless he would invite in.

If he was figuring that his cover would be blown with the elections, he needed to start making preparations. He wasn't sure what kind of preparations, but preparations all the same. Maybe he should make himself—Doug—known among the homeless, win some points with them so it would be easier to get them into his house. Maybe he would offer them a little money in exchange for doing simple tasks, then kill them when they were done. That sounded reasonable, too. If they did a good enough job, he might even make it a humane death. Ha!

He figured he was just about ready to kill Lily Guile. Killing these last two women had helped to restore his self-confidence. According to Rifun, Lily was starting to break, at least in private. Oh, she remained snooty and self-righteous when she talked to the police and as she went about her day in the hospital, but whenever she was alone, the paranoia started to make itself known. Checking every room of her condo, keeping all the lights on, timing her comings and goings with her neighbors and others, including when she decided to use the restroom. She knew what was coming, even if she didn't want to admit it out loud. She knew Cassius desired fear, knew what awaited her, and her stony facade would soon come tumbling down.

The Hand Holding the Knife

Cassius sat in the home office, chair turned toward the window. The computer was off; he hadn't checked any emails for a week or so now, hadn't replied to anything in just as long. He had been to the work office once, answered all of three calls. Apparently "I quit" wasn't good enough in the modern era, and even two weeks didn't seem to be enough to shake these clowns that were dragging at his ankles. He didn't know. He didn't care. He was done and moving on to more important things.

He glanced at the clock. There was supposed to be a meeting in the officers building soon, to determine their next course of action. Cassius leaned back in his chair. He knew the next course of action. One more woman to kill, then go after Lily Guile herself. One more woman would not only bring him back to rights, but it would be the final needle they needed to get under her skin. Apparently killing the woman who got engaged was more effective than he or Rifun had expected. Next he figured they would go after one of her whore friends. That would cover her workplace, her social life, and her past. Nothing was sacred and nowhere was safe. Time to die.

He stood and stretched lazily. The meeting was more for Rifun's sake, he supposed. He valued order. He liked plans and lists. Cassius was surprised the man had been able to go this long without a meeting. Either he was in withdrawal and needed to call a meeting in order to feel relevant and useful, or else he was going to fuck shit up. Cassius had a plan. He had announced the plan. They had carried out the plan to great success so far. Did Rifun really think he was going to do any better? They had made tremendous progress, or Cassius thought so, anyway.

He sighed and stretched again, more intentionally this time. Rifun was up to something, he just knew it. He was going to give some kind of lecture at this meeting, something about morals, something about doing things the right way or the humane way, and then he was going to come up with some stupid plan of roundabout reasoning and passive action, if any action at all, that would sound nice but get them absolutely nowhere.

No. Cassius shook his head though he was the only one in the room. No, he couldn't let that happen. He had a plan, he was the one in charge. He was the one making progress. He might have let Rifun influence him a little just to make the man feel better and feel like he was part of a team or something, but this was all on him, Cassius. Rifun was just getting a little uppity about it and needed to be reminded about his place.

Even as he thought it, he felt the tiniest bit of pressure in his sinuses. It was not an outright rebuke or punishment, just a small reminder. Scowling, Cassius stormed out of the room. He headed to the torture room to collect himself so he didn't kill everyone upon walking into the meeting. He still might one of these days, but for now, he might humor the others enough to pretend to care about their words and opinions.

After a minute or two, the pressure in his sinuses released, his muscles relaxed, and he opened a portal to Sadurnon. He did not go directly to the officers building, but rather the usual entry point in one of the tunnels branching off from the main chamber where the ruins lay. In the time he and Rifun were gone, Isthim and some others had perfected the cloak he had once experimented with, making it so the ruins appeared to be just that, quiet and lonely ruins, from the outside. Upon entering the old city, the glamour was revealed and the ruins came to life with the military camp they had turned it into, with the ancient temple carved into the north stone wall as the officers building.

Cassius took his time getting to the officers building, instead pretending to be interested in the goings-on of the camp. Few followers actually lived in the camp. Home world politics aside, few were keen on being potentially investigated for their work and affiliation with the Cult. Instead, many visited the ruins via portal, trained for several hours, then left. How Isthim had it all worked out, Cassius did not know. Honestly, he wasn't too concerned because there had never really been a need for a standing army. It was all for show, as far as an army went. For the individual, well, they weren't exactly soldiers, not to his eyes.

He reached the officers building and made his way to the meeting room, pleased that he was the last to arrive and so had kept everyone waiting. Raised voices abruptly ceased, and General Misik looked as though he had been in the middle of some diatribe toward Rifun.

"Please, don't let me interrupt," Cassius said, ambling up to the stone table which had once been a sacrificial altar. He glanced at Isthim who already looked annoyed. "You look good, is that a new battery for your speech assist? I see you got a newer, slimmer version. Much easier to hide with or without a Disguise, I should think."

"Shut up," Misik snapped.

"Why, what did I do now? I just walked in the room."

"Lily Guile is still alive despite all promises to the contrary. The Book of

Abilities is not in our possession although I have been told that it is so easy to retrieve an ambitious child could do it. I've a mind to go to Earth, take the Book of Abilities, kill Lily Guile, and enslave the rest of humanity!"

"A decidedly poor idea," Rifun said calmly, "at least at this time. At least wait until after the elections, when we have taken control of the Wheel."

"Ah, yes, that," the general scoffed flippantly. "How is that coming along again?"

"Everyone has a role to play, *général*, and it is imprudent for everyone to be in everyone's business at all times."

"You talk so much I cannot believe you have a plan. You are only stalling." Misik took a menacing step toward Rifun.

"We do have a plan," Isthim told him. "The elections will take place as everyone expects. At the inauguration, the Grandfathers and the army here will take over the Wheel. Seeing how all officers vote and all posted officers must be present at the inauguration, it will allow us to decimate the chain of command among the Time Agents. Having all of the Hands both incoming and outgoing in one place will make that a clean sweep as well. Kill and imprison everyone, seal off the Wheel as much as we can, and we will have control."

"And then what?" Misik demanded venomously.

"Then we retrieve the temple key from the Core of the Wheel and get the Book of Commands from the temple in Ancrath," Rifun explained. "With all three journals and the most well-defended stronghold in the universe, we can subdue the Akarin and remake things as we want without interference."

Misik was not overly impressed with Rifun's idea of things, and neither was Cassius, really. It sounded too naive. But then, what, exactly, were they hoping to achieve? Why did they want to kill Lily and take over the Wheel?

Because the dragon says so, that's why, Cassius thought bitterly. *Because we're all just pawns in its game, slaves to be ordered around here and there, doing things under threat of death.*

He didn't like that he thought he could hear it laugh in his head.

"That's all well and good," he interrupted, "but how about our next move? Which of Lily's whore friends should we go after? I think the redhead; I like redheads. Or maybe we should just go straight for her, seeing how Misik is a bit antsy about the whole thing."

"Our next move is the Book of Abilities and Tommen Forbes," Rifun told him. "I'm just waiting for a call from Julianna."

"You get signal here?"

"Very funny."

"Who cares about some inept slave?" Misik demanded harshly. "If these journals are so great, what do you care about these Books?"

"That's enough from you!" Isthim barked.

Misik backed down immediately, and it took Cassius a second to remember that Isthim was one of the few publicly known members of the Ul Ik Zol, the Borelians' Holy Men of War, though only recently publicly known. Still, the general did not look enthusiastic about the state of things.

"There is still time before the elections," Isthim went on. Her new speech assist device sounded much less robotic and her tones more discernible, though it was far from perfect and she usually sounded like she was talking through fan blades. "The more chaos we can cause the better. We have a plan in place for the takeover, with or without Lily Guile, with or without Tommen Forbes. Whatever plan these two come up with to kill Lily or bring Tommen into the fold, they have time to carry it out." She gave Misik a pointed look. "We are not involved in these affairs yet."

The general held her gaze for a long moment but did not reply in any manner. Only when he averted his gaze did the conversation continue.

"Fine, so we get the Book of Abilities, and then we kill Lily Guile?" Cassius inquired of Rifun.

"As far as overarching goals, yes, that is correct," Rifun answered.

"I don't like how you said that."

The white-skinned man sighed. "Yes, the Book of Abilities is very easy to get to and it would be nothing to walk in and grab it. However, in the interest of being efficient and keeping everything moving along in the right direction at the right speed, I would like to bring Tommen Forbes in on this as well. Thus, I await Julianna's call. If I hear nothing in a timely manner, then things may change and we may have to just walk in and grab it."

Cassius blinked. "So when do we kill Lily?"

Rifun sighed. "Honestly, Cassius, is that the only thing you care about? Lily is nothing, she is no one. She was...she is convenient, a tool. Her death was supposed to rouse the Akarin, shake the Time industry, but it does not appear to mean much. The Akarin are slow to care about anything, and the Time industry will carry on as it always has. Even if it doesn't, we are going to take it with or without her. We can kill her now, at the inauguration, after the inauguration, it doesn't really matter.

She doesn't matter."

Rifun looked back at Isthim and opened his mouth to speak, but Cassius slapped his palm on the table, stopping both of them. "No! This was supposed to be my plan! We were making progress!"

"Progress toward what?" Rifun challenged. "You being able to get an erection again? That's not my problem. We're here to take over the Time industry and set the universe back to rights."

"Oh, is that what we're doing? I don't recall that being part of the initial business plan."

"How would you know? You never went to any of the meetings," Isthim commented dryly.

"The original purpose was to unite the broken Akarin, to do away with old and corrupt leadership," Rifun went on. "To exercise this goal fully and follow it to its logical conclusion, the Akari-bearers of the Author must reclaim the Wheel of Time as it was originally intended for them. The Akarin of old—whatever they called themselves—were kicked out for arrogance and pride. Trying to set them straight using the Authored Books only fractured them further. We are their only hope, the only logical conclusion. I am not convinced that Lily Guile is significant enough to warrant any more expenditure of resources. As I have said, the only reason I care about bringing Tommen Forbes in is because of his connection to the Authored Books."

"Does Julianna feel the same way?" Isthim wondered, cutting off Cassius. "If I recall correctly, she thought the Authored Books were heretical and wanted to replace them. That was why she commissioned the journals."

Rifun waved a hand. "She's just upset that the Books don't glorify her impervious and infallible British Empire and she might have to share the spotlight a little, share the love of the Author like siblings must share the love of a parent. The Books are good history—and even she cannot deny the things written in our own Books—but the journals are law. They are absolute."

"So absolute that nothing is being done about them," Misik grumbled.

"In good time," Rifun promised.

"I'm going after Lily Guile," Cassius interrupted hotly. "You're not going to stop me from killing her."

"The thought never crossed my mind. I am simply trying to juggle priorities. If I may persuade you to refrain from killing her for a short period, let her stew in uncertainty for a time, I would like to do so."

Was Rifun giving him free reign, or writing him off? Was he hoping Cassius would turn his back so he could stick a knife in it? What was the end goal here? Had he given up on trying to slay the dark spirit, or was this part of a plan to do exactly that? Was there a way to ask without asking and alerting the spirit? Fucking hell, life was simpler when politics stayed out of everything.

"I have a few meetings with the Akarin," Cassius stated flatly. "I'll see where they stand, if we've been able to convince the sloths to leave their trees."

"Interesting analogy, but not untrue," Rifun remarked. "I will return to Earth and give Julianna a little time to call with any useful observations or ideas."

"You're going to be waiting a long time. Maybe not for the call, but for the usefulness of her existence."

"The public does love a pretty face and soft voice, which none of us can really provide. Her naivete is useful enough."

Cassius wondered if Rifun was aware of his own naivete and how close he was to death at any given moment. But then, looking at Isthim and especially Misik, none of the non-Borelian Cult members or leaders were held in any special regard. They might be given ranks and privileges to make them feel slightly less than miserable, give them some feeling of power over their slave brethren, but a slave in the house was still as much a slave as the slave in the field.

"And if the Akarin do not react to this hostile takeover?" Misik inquired, his tone suggesting he was not particularly interested in the answer.

"All the easier to sweep them away," Rifun told him. "Concerns and priorities. Isthim seems to have the plans for election day and inauguration day worked out, and we all have our list of tasks and wishes."

"So what am I supposed to do?" Cassius demanded.

"I would prefer it if you could hold off on Lily Guile for a short time, but I am not going to tell you what to do. I expect your next major task will involve the razing we're going to do on Inauguration Day, but you will have to ask Isthim. Other than that, you still have your Akarin members you could be stalking, I suppose, or you could pick up some other minor contracts. At the moment, we are simply waiting out the clock as the saying goes."

Cassius studied him, still undecided about his motives. What was he waiting for? Was he testing Cassius? Was he testing the spirit? What did the spirit think about all of this? Why did Cassius feel like the object of contention between two hostile parties? Or was he considered more like collateral damage? Was he one of the game pieces to be moved around, or the board to be walked on?

He brushed it aside and tried to look disinterested. "I guess I'll go see if I can't rouse the Akarin to some action."

"At this point, I don't think the dog is sleeping so much as dying slowly," Rifun mused. "Perhaps your time would be better spent figuring out how best to dispatch it instead."

Cassius sneered. "Humanely, right?"

"If possible."

Cassius scoffed and rolled his eyes before leaving, and he found himself muttering aloud as he traversed the halls of the ancient temple.

"Are mortals the idiots that they think they are significant to the spirits, or the spirits that they play with mortals like immature children with dolls? These dolls are weak, but for some reason the spirits seem to want to keep them alive like limp puppets rather than let them fade into nothing. It's like the life support for the infants Lily works with. She knows what's up. She knows there's no reason to try and save the weakest of the pack. Feed the emotional needs of the parents for a time, but then do what has to be done. Kill it. Take its years for yourself, because you're strong."

As he donned his Doug Disguise and headed to the Akarin fortress, he couldn't help but wonder if that was what the spirit was doing to him. Feed some emotional need for a time, make a sickly child happy, then kill it. Kill him. He had become weak.

But he was trying to get strong again. Rifun was cutting him off, or baiting him into some kind of trap. He had to be careful.

Or could it be the spirit that was testing him? Would he run in blindly for the kill? Would he hesitate? Damn it, he hated this. He missed being his own man, his own mercenary. But for some reason, he still had to slog around with these imbeciles. Why? Was this some kind of cosmic cattle pen and the spirit intended to wipe them out all at once? Were the Akarin in another kind of cosmic cattle pen? Or perhaps they were dog pens, and the spirits would have them fight in some grand spectacle to amuse themselves before shooting any unlucky survivors. Was the Time industry just another dog for the spirits to whip and antagonize to fight at a whim?

He could feel the dragon spirit's amusement as he climbed the stairs to the meeting room. He wasn't even sure if there was a meeting going on right now, but he could look around a little anyway. To use Rifun's analogy, see if the dog was just sleeping or ready to be put down. Either way, they were going to destroy the

Akarin; it was just about seeing how much of a fight they could expect.

There was indeed a meeting going on, though two seconds of listening in determined that it was all the same mundane business it had always been. To liken it to the droll collection of human flesh and voices that constituted meetings in Doug's workplace, it was scheduling, a little bit of finance, some legal talk, ass covering, the blame game where the aggressiveness of the offense and defense was largely dependent on the number of snacks at hand, dithering about sports, daydreaming about the weekend, and, if there was time for it, the topic for which the meeting had actually been called.

"Well, I'm glad to see that everything concerning the well-being of Lily Guile and all related concerns about her assassination and the stalking of other nearby Akarin members has been cleaned up," Cassius-as-Doug said, sauntering in. He leaned casually on the table. "How did that all turn out? What did you guys agree on or do?"

"Has Lily Guile truly been assassinated?" one council member inquired, his tone suggesting that he was about as interested as asking about some particular bit of news in a neighboring area which, if no further convenient information was provided, he would not waste his time seeking out anything further.

"Not to my knowledge, but the fact that you are asking shows that it has become a real possibility. The stability of the Time industry is at stake here."

"Yes, and we should be ready to receive those who will be lost and confused, those who have long relied on greed to sustain them," another councilman stated, his demeanor entirely unconcerned.

"And what do we have to offer?" Cassius-as-Doug challenged. "Dull meetings, petty bickering, everything they probably already have at home?"

A third councilman spoke up. "Many are intrigued by the Akari, if afraid to say so because of the stigma it carries."

The first councilman's expression, though alien, said that not all were in agreement, despite whatever agreement they had allegedly come to. "You have made many arguments in favor of protecting Lily Guile and the Time industry, and you have pointed out several concerns regarding the Cult of the Akari. No one here can deny your spirit or determination, nor your fortitude and stubbornness, although some have questioned why this means so much to you."

"If the Cult is half as powerful as they claim—"

"But they're not. If they were, they would have been a threat long ago. One army as a whole on the march across the universe — or whatever their goals were — not a scattering of lesser-trained misfits and one or two skilled mercenaries who can't decide which way they want to go when given two options." The councilman put up a hand, or what passed as a hand for his race, cutting off Cassius. "Whatever this imagined feud between the Cult and the Time industry, whatever may happen, it does not affect us. We gave it our attention long enough to assess the threat. Upon concluding that there is no threat, we have turned our attention back to normal matters."

Cassius-as-Doug seethed for a long moment. Then, "And if Lily Guile dies because of our negligence?"

"Are we her personal bodyguards?" another council member asked. "She has surrounded herself with the finest protection she can afford and keeps the personal company of the Timekeeper Captain of her home region, or so she claims. Her protection is her business. As for the Time industry itself, a shelter made of paper. Should we cry when it disintegrates in the rain, or rejoice that we have a new opportunity to rebuild correctly?"

"And if we were going to do that, we would have done it by now."

That shut them up for a minute anyway.

"The matter is closed," the first councilman said finally, though he still appeared a bit uncomfortable. "Unless something drastic happens, it would be appreciated if you did not bother the council with every time a new Cult recruit deposits bodily excrement."

There were any number of things Cassius wanted to say, and he couldn't decide whether it was the dragon spirit or his own disbelief that tied his tongue to prevent him from speaking, at least until they were well into the next matter.

So, their official decision was to do nothing. Good to know. Well, if they didn't care about Lily, and Rifun didn't care about Lily, and the Borelians obviously didn't care about Lily, maybe it was time to get rid of this thing that apparently no one cared about yet was causing so much trouble.

He excused himself from the meeting early and returned to Doug's house. Still up for sale, still no takers. The agent had called a few times, suggested lowering the listing price. Cassius ignored the calls or just said that he wasn't in the biggest hurry to sell. Maybe after the new year, he would consider such a thing.

He headed to the torture room, considered it for a long moment, and walked back out. Maybe he couldn't get the council too interested, but what if he set his sights a little lower, kept things a little closer to home?

Being a small business owner, Micaiah Durvin was typically only one of two places: home or the bakery, most often the latter, especially since the orders were starting to pile up for Christmas. Pies, cakes, cookies, brownies, breads, rolls, anything that required baking that people didn't want to do themselves for the holidays.

In true Doug Templeton fashion, Cassius walked in during a huge rush, bypassing the line inasmuch as he sauntered up to the front display case and, upon seeing Micaiah in the kitchen, broke into a huge grin. Micah, who was on the front counter, did not look so enthused.

"Micaiah! I thought I'd find you here!" Cassius-as-Doug boomed. He helped himself around the counter, ignoring Micah who could only get out a brief, breathless, "Doug, wait out there."

From what Cassius understood, Micah did not know Doug as part of the Akarin, but one of Micaiah's annoying acquaintances whom he'd met at some point in the past and had never been able to shake. The ability to jump from here to there via portal did not help matters.

"Micaiah!" Cassius-as-Doug said, spreading his arms wide as he took up a post in the most inconvenient location in the kitchen he could find. True to Doug, however, it was a tactically advantageous position; comfort and convenience were secondary. "My my my, what are we up to today?"

Micaiah paused long enough to glare at him. "Fuck does it look like, Doug? I'm working. Unlike you these days."

Cassius Banded, bringing everything around them to a halt. Micaiah, who had at least a dozen Bands of his own encompassing numerous baked goods in various stages of preparation, struggled to gather them and reconcile them against Cassius' Band.

"What are you doing here, Doug?" Micaiah demanded, his tone and posture toeing the line between angry and furious. "If it's important, I'm sure—"

"You've been looking into Lily Guile's attempted murder, right?" Cassius-as-Doug interrupted, unfazed.

Micaiah sighed, a mixture of annoyance and disbelief. "Somewhat, yes. The Hands didn't like us poking around in their stuff and we got...a warning from the Grandfathers."

"So that's it? You're going to let the Grandfathers, the Borelians push you around? You're a Timekeeper; you're supposed to uphold the Laws of Time. Assassinating a member of—"

"Lily Guile has broken enough Laws of Time to warrant a life sentence encompassing all of the years she has stolen for herself. I have little doubt that she is buying protection from the Grandfathers to that end."

"Then why would she stop you? Why wouldn't she want you to find this would-be killer?"

Micaiah shrugged. "No such thing as bad publicity, maybe. The thought of another collapse in the Wheel, prices are sky high, people desperate to buy as much Time as they can before the fabled end."

Cassius-as-Doug blinked. "You think she's staging the deaths herself? What about the evil Calis Cutthroat? What about the Cult of the Akari?"

Now Micaiah paused. "I don't know."

"Come on, you must have an opinion."

Still the older twin hesitated. After a moment, he said, "I haven't forgotten the Time Trial. The fact that I can't remember much else about them is what gives me cause to think they are a threat. The fact that you have been pushing hard for the council to act on them only exacerbates this."

Cassius-as-Doug folded his arms. "Surprised you've been keeping up. You've been so inactive and made so little progress lately I was considering listing you as a Whisper."

"Aklaq and I have been keeping a low profile; you know that. Maybe a little too low at times. But I'm not eager to tangle with the Cult again."

"And ignoring their threats against Lily Guile?"

Micaiah gave him a look. "I'm not particularly concerned about Lily. Maybe a little scare will do her good to remind her that she is mortal like the rest of us."

"And if she does die? It would be a rather nasty fallout for the Time industry."

The older twin sighed but nodded. "I know."

Cassius-as-Doug shifted his stance. "I don't remember you being so cautious before, Micaiah."

Micaiah frowned and punched a large ball of dough. "I endured a Time Trial. I put my wife at risk in that Time Trial." He stared at the dough as he spoke. "Time Trials don't happen for no reason. At one time, the Cult had control of the Time industry. I know that much. But the rest...it's a mired fog of memories I don't have anymore. I can use Feel, dive into my brain, and I can see that I have been fucked with. To my knowledge, only a Borelian can do such a thing. It's not that I have secret knowledge locked away, it's that I don't have that knowledge anymore, period." He looked up. "It happened to you, Doug, I know it did."

"And I'd like to stop it from happening again, wouldn't you?"

"But where do we begin? The Borelians were rumored to still be in league with the Cult. And they are the premier species used by the Grandfathers in the Time industry. The Grandfathers are preventing any investigation into Lily's would-be assassin. Does that mean that the Borelians are no longer with the Cult? With that kind of access, they could kill her at any time if they wanted to. Or does the Cult already have control of the Wheel in the background and they're just trying to remove someone who isn't playing nice anymore?"

Cassius-as-Doug shrugged. "I'm here for strategy, not politics."

"Oh, fuck off." Micaiah turned his attention back to the dough. "You and your false fucking humility."

"I do get accused of that sometimes, I admit. However, my ego and big mouth have served me very well in life. They would serve the Akarin very well now if they would just heed my words and take this threat even a little bit seriously. I was hoping I might find some sympathy from you given your history and proximity and all, but it seems that either no one thinks the Cult is a threat or else they don't care if they are."

"The universe is a big place. Humans have never been much of a player. We could be cut off completely and few would bat an eye."

"And yet the Cult does appear to be going after Miss Guile." Cassius-as-Doug waved a hand. "Forget the Cult, forget the Akarin, forget the Time industry. Does this thought alone not trigger some innate chivalry within you?"

Micaiah gave him a look. "We both know Lily is no helpless and pathetic maiden."

"Calis Cutthroat and Rifun Ndolo are trying to kill Lily Guile and you don't care?"

"To be honest, Doug, I'm more concerned about why they would be interested in Walter and Tommen. I'm most concerned about Tommen because he has virtually no abilities to speak of."

Cassius-as-Doug shrugged, trying not to giggle. "In all of the Authored Books so far, there is mention of a Chivalrous Welshman. Word on the street is, that's Tommen's nickname. Cult or Akarin, the Author seems to be bringing you all together in the same box and tying you up with a big, pretty bow. I can't speak for Walter other than he's the posted Timekeeper Captain, but Tommen looks like some tender bait."

"That fact hasn't escaped me either," Micaiah admitted, frowning. "And I do have some vague recollection of Rifun reading the Authored Books, or the ones that were available at the time. I also know that he was there at the Time Trial. I'd be willing to bet that he was somehow behind our memory loss." He shook his head. "Walter showed me an article about one Rifun Ndolo being found dead in Madagascar, but I have a hard time believing it."

"So why aren't you doing something? If Rifun took such an interest in you that he put you through a Time Trial and erased your memory, what do you think he's going to do to Tommen, who is far more impressionable? Even if he is dead, what do you think his followers will do?"

Micaiah paused in his work, but he still didn't look at him. "Nothing good, that's for sure." He went back to kneading. "But he appears to be going after the Time industry first. Again. Whatever you want to call it." He used his shoulder to itch his forehead. "Fucking memory loss. I feel like I'm starting from scratch, and yet I'll bet he has detailed notes about what happened. Every move, every word, every strength and weakness."

"And Calis Cutthroat?"

"I wouldn't want to meet him in a dark alley, that's for sure. And I do know, I remember clear as day, watching him resurrect the Bat from death. That memory, I don't think even a Borelian could erase."

"And you think it's a good idea to just let them roam around the universe, give them control of the central hub of the universal economy, give them access to everyone's information, give them access to the Core of the Wheel?"

Finally Cassius saw the light in Micaiah's eyes. Finally he had reached something, some instinct or bit of logic that might actually propel someone to some sort of action. Maybe it was a memory, or the not-quite-shadow of a memory, something important that he knew he should know but couldn't quite reach and never would.

"There are some Akarin members in this district who believe they are being stalked in some fashion," Cassius-as-Doug went on, more serious now. "Tommen may have Authored Books—or he may not—but he isn't some chosen one who will do anything single-handedly. Last anyone knew, the Cult had an army and were still allied with the Borelians. The Borelians, as you said, are the preferred species of the Grandfathers."

"Whatever the Cult does, it's going to be an inside job," Micaiah stated.

"And the elections are coming up fast. Want me to start—?"

"No. Whatever you're about to say, no."

"Why? I'm a brilliant strategist. I've been trying to get the Akarin council to see reason for a while now, so obviously I have plenty of plans to go around."

Micaiah barked a laugh. "Well, your first mistake was thinking the Akarin council would care or get motivated enough to do anything."

"Maybe so, but the council has the political authority and social reach to mobilize a lot of resources at once."

"There is that, yes." Micaiah shifted his stance. "Why don't you keep working on the council? Go around them if you have to, mobilize a small force of your own. I'll keep an eye on Walt and Tommen, and I'll have Aklaq see about the other Akarin in the district, see if there is anything to these stalking claims."

Doug raised a brow. "You ask me to mobilize a force, but what am I telling them to do?"

Micaiah shrugged. "I don't know. What were you going to have them do before you talked to me, pretending that the council had heeded your earlier warnings?"

"Fair enough. Just curious to see if you had anything in mind."

"No doubt so you could tell me what a stupid idea it was and how your plan is so much better."

"I only offer constructive criticism. It's one thing I am good at."

"Fuck you, Doug. Now get out of my fucking store."

For a brief moment, Cassius thought about imitating one of Rifun's irritating bows. He decided against it as he dropped the Band and instead sauntered out of the store with the same arrogance with which he'd entered. He got an annoyed look from Micah and a few curious looks from patrons, but otherwise nothing happened.

His first thoughts centered on Micaiah. So he had married his whore girlfriend at some point after the Time Trial, yet they weren't together. They were trying to lay low. Then along came the beauty of impersonation. Learn a few secrets, give a swift kick in the pants, and now he had control of— At a twitch in his face, he grudgingly adjusted his line of thought. They had control of any Akarin counterattacks. Micaiah would be staying in Charleston, his primary focus being Walter and Tommen and maybe Lily, too. He would send Aklaq to keep an eye on those whom Cassius was presently stalking. And Doug was expected to get some kind of force together to do something or other. What that was, he didn't know yet, but the Cult would be calling the shots, and that was a taste of irony Cassius could savor.

He dropped his Disguise as soon as he could and checked in on those he was stalking, just to reinforce the point and give Aklaq White Bear a little more urgency in her mission. He also started stalking a few more in neighboring districts. It took time for people to realize they were being stalked, that it wasn't just them being forgetful or careless but that some stranger was actually following them, skirting the periphery of their lives even as they were the obsessive life focus of some demented freak. He should see how many people he could frighten before the elections, see how much he could make Aklaq run.

After a while he returned to Doug's house for a quick rest, then donned an unassuming Disguise before heading to the Wheel of Time, the Disguise preventing the Zero Hour cloak from activating as he went through the portal. The Akarin were slow to act, its members too loyal and too attached to the decisions, or lack thereof, of the council. But with the persistent discontent among the Time Agents of the Wheel, maybe he could find a few idiots to get riled up and ready for battle. That was the magic of herd mentality.

It all started with a little manufactured anxiety of his own as he entered the Food Court and started looking around. All the best gossip was found at the tavern, right? What better place to start a few rumors and find a few like-minded revolutionaries? And maybe he could plant a few other suggestive seeds while he was at it.

He found a group of six aliens in some less-than-pleasant conference at one of the many tables. He could not recall all of their species, but he knew they were all at least Engaged Privilege and Scientifically Advancing. On approach, their conversation appeared to be geared toward the elections, as much of the chatter in the Food Court tended to be at this time. But rather than the usual "armchair referee" — a phrase he'd recently become acquainted with thanks to the gross ubiquity of sports in the United States — style of complaining, their conversation sounded more thoughtful, even conspiratorial.

"The Hands expect us to keep things running smoothly and protect the Time Agents, but they don't seem too concerned about us," one grumbled.

"We don't need to jump at every shadow," another said. "There have always been threats."

"This one is real," Cassius mentioned casually, jumping in. "And we're going to do something about it."

"Who are you?" a third alien asked, looking and sounding offended at his intrusion. "And who is 'we'?"

"Who I am is unimportant. I'm here on behalf of Micaiah Durvin, Lieutenant Timekeeper and one of the Akarin." Cassius continued speaking, though for a moment his word was lost in a jumble of protests from the rest of the group. "Whatever you believe about the Akari, the threat from the Cult against Lily Guile and the Time industry is real. The Akarin are too slow to act, too caught up in politics and public relations and whatever internal issues are going on. They are no threat, but they're not exactly a reliable ally either, not officially."

"So what do you or Micaiah Durvin expect to do?" another alien inquired, unimpressed.

"That depends. What do you want to do? Are you interested?"

Even coming from aliens of varying physical appearances, Cassius could tell he hadn't won them over entirely as he might have hoped. Well, get a little closer to the elections and there might be enough fear to drive them further. The six of them exchanged glances.

"You can tell Micaiah Durvin you have our interest, but not our commitment," the first told him. "We may require more persuasion. There are too many ears here."

"Fair enough," Cassius said amiably. "I will let him know."

He got their information—it would probably come back as invalid when he checked it later, but for now he didn't care—and left their group. He made a few more laps around the Food Court, approached a few more groups with mixed results, then departed.

Even with all this danger and uncertainty hanging over their heads, it was surprisingly difficult to actually get anyone to act. Oh, they all talked about it, but no one wanted to be the first guy. No one wanted to be the one to actually pull the trigger. No one wanted to fail. That was the problem with the Time industry. Everyone had a home planet they could run back to and be safe; the Wheel was nothing. Yes, some places were more affected than others by goings on in Time, but there was still that separation.

After they took over the Wheel, they would have to start going after individual planets.

He left the Wheel, dropped his Disguise, and headed to the Ruins of Meroian. It was apparently nighttime here, for activity was minimal in the city and ghostly in the officers building.

The Hand Holding the Knife

How easy it would be to just murder everyone in their sleep. He hadn't figured out Rifun's paralysis trick, but a fast enough Band would suffice, or he could just use his death touch from being a plain old Harvester.

He found Rifun asleep in his chambers. The man never slept well, or so his sheets proclaimed, drenched in sweat and twisted every which way. Rifun himself looked coiled and ready to spring out of bed with hardly a whispered warning. Cassius knew Rifun kept his revolver under his pillow, but why he relied on mechanical intimidation over his own professed abilities, Cassius did not understand.

The polite thing to do would be to let everyone sleep and talk to them in the morning. One thing Cassius and Doug had in common was that they were not known for being polite. Nor was Cassius known for his spiritual reverence. He spied a carved staff among the various paraphernalia that decorated Rifun's shrine. He grabbed the staff, went to the bed, and poked Rifun from a distance.

Rifun was moving before he was fully awake, registering the staff, grabbing the end, and yanking. Cassius let him have the staff, then immediately questioned the wisdom of such a decision as Rifun quickly had it turned around and ready as a weapon.

"If anyone wanted you dead, they wouldn't need to poke you with a stick," Cassius said as Rifun hesitated, consciousness finally catching up with him.

Rifun blinked. His gaze shifted to the staff in his hands. Then he did something Cassius really didn't expect: he hit him in the side with the staff.

"Why did you touch this and remove it from the shrine?" Rifun snapped, straightening and going to replace the artifact, his movements suddenly tender as he briefly knelt to bow, quick prayer inaudible.

"Because I figured that was safer than trying to lay hands on you," Cassius told him flatly.

Rifun finished his prayer, sighed, and sat up. "And if you have time to consider such things, the reason you woke me clearly isn't an urgent one." He stood and faced him. "So what is it?"

"Oh, nothing much, just taking control of our enemy's defenses and wondering if you have any ideas of what to do with them before the elections."

"What are you talking about?" His tone wasn't convinced.

Cassius relayed his conversation with Micaiah as best he could remember, as well as his endeavors in the Wheel.

"Interesting to know about Micaiah and Aklaq," Rifun mused. He wasn't exactly jumping for joy as Cassius might have hoped, but he wasn't brushing it off or giving a lecture, so that was a good thing. "At least one of the cows has been prodded to move."

"We can probably get a few more to move, but we need to act now if we want the stampede."

Rifun gave him a look. "Considering how you were just whining about this being your operation, I find it suspicious that you are suddenly coming to me for ideas."

"But if I didn't, you would whine that I'm not a team player," Cassius countered. "So which is it?"

Rifun regarded him for a long moment. Cassius considered cutting up the man's face just so it matched the rest of his body.

"Fine," the light-skinned African said, not looking at him.

"We'll be going after Lily Guile, then," Cassius stated.

"Not right this second, no."

"Why not?"

"Our next move should be to retrieve the Book of Abilities. Right now, all attention is on Lily, so no one will care about a minor break-in and petty theft. It will be easier to do now than after we take control of the Wheel." Cassius was not impressed, and Rifun altered his expression to match. "Minor logistics, Cassius. Do you want the journal or not?"

Cassius shifted his stance and folded his arms. "I don't know, you're the one claiming to be the closest thing to a god but can't seem to do jack shit about the situation we're in. But that might be attributed more to your morals than your power, which is why I don't have any."

"Morals or power?" Rifun questioned smartly. He stretched briefly. "Was there anything else or can I go back to bed for a while?"

"Beauty sleep will do less for your complexion than the Akari."

"How would you know? Hasn't done a thing for you in three centuries."

Cassius gave Rifun a look.

"Get out," Rifun said, waving a hand dismissively. "I have a few things to do in the morning, then we'll go get the Book of Abilities."

With that, he intentionally pushed past Cassius to get back into bed. Cassius glanced at the staff at the shrine once more before turning and leaving the room.

8 | Fiantsoana

Fianarantsoa, 2013

Invitation

Spirits are all around us, Rivotra, you know that. Good ones, bad ones, blessings, curses. And yet, such symbiosis as you have described doesn't happen every day. Your ascension took many years, many thoughtful prayers and sacrifices, true devotion of the heart and soul. I have a hard time believing that the same would not be true of someone on the...opposite side of things."

Lalao leaned back in her seat and sipped at her tea. She noted Rifun's expression. "You don't think so?"

"Oh, I fully believe it," Rifun told her, staring at his own cup of tea still sitting on the table at the cafe where they met for a late dinner. "And yet I don't." He shifted in his seat. "Evil tends to take hold of weak men. The men they become are strong because of the evil that resides in them—" He stopped when she shook her head. "No?"

"Evil takes hold of strong men, Rivotra. Strong, stubborn, prideful men. Evil itself is weak. It cannot stand up to good, not as it is, so it requires mortals to do the fighting for it. But good spirits choose weak, humble men and makes them strong in order to oppose this evil."

Rifun thought about this for a long minute, taking a drink of tea to buy him a few more seconds. Then, "And when did you become so well-versed in the ways of the spirits?"

Her eyes glittered with amusement. "You've given me a lot to think about over the years, since the night you left. I admit, I may never become so powerful as you, not while I walk among the living, but that doesn't mean I haven't done my own searching and asking and praying."

"You don't think Cassius the man can be saved, then?"

Now she frowned. "Honestly, no. Just going by what you've told me, I don't believe the man himself even exists anymore. If he can be moved from here to there, to do a thing or not do a thing, just by some wound in his face, he is not a man, he is a vehicle, an empty shell to be moved as a game piece."

"He seems to think his time is running out, that the spirit is going to kill him at any moment."

"And it may. You are closing in on it, a hunter stalking his prey. Like I said, evil itself is weak. The ancestors and the spirits, gifting you with the power of the razana, have made you strong. It cannot hope to stand up to you, even with Cassius. Physical prowess has come to mean less and less, and now you are approaching a time when only spiritual strength matters, and you would win without a fight. It would not surprise that the spirit would kill its host and flee rather than face you."

Rifun nodded thoughtfully. "That would explain some things, I suppose." He shifted again. "But where would the spirit go? Such powerful and direct control over someone is considerably rare."

Lalao made a sound of affirmation as she sipped at her tea, finishing it off. She waved off the waiter who came to refill the cup, her gaze never leaving Rifun. "This is true. Depending on the spirit, it might seek to run far away from you and try to cause havoc elsewhere, or it might try to stay close and take revenge on you."

He frowned. "If it did that, I imagine it would strike quickly, before I could identify it again."

"That is also something to consider, yes."

"Hm...maybe the best thing to do, then, at the moment, is back off a little. If I stop trying to dig into its burrow, it might stick its head out to see if I've gone."

"A swift strike and it's done," Lalao concluded.

"Exactly."

It sounded good in theory, except Rifun knew exactly how that would play out. He would back off from Cassius, then Lily, and probably a whole bunch of innocent bystanders, would meet terrible fates in that infernal torture chamber in Doug's house. Lily was the target, yes, but Rifun couldn't stomach the thought of any more innocent women dying.

He would have to think of something.

"You don't look convinced," Lalao commented, interrupting his thoughts.

He again shifted in his chair. The waiter was probably wondering if one of the legs was broken, or perhaps a tack had been set on the seat. "I think I prefer open combat to this game of stealth and trickery and magic. The rules are much simpler."

"Maybe, but the stakes are less meaningful."

"Good. That means we can all go home." At his sarcasm, she gave him a look. He pointedly ignored it.

"Talk to me, love," Lalao said gently. "I don't want to see you upset when you leave."

Rifun sighed, studied his hands for a moment, then looked at her. "How are your boys doing?"

She gave him a look but happily launched into the news of her family, all the things her sons were up to in the last few days. When it came right down to it, there wasn't much to report. Her two older boys had families of their own and were pretty well settled into the mundane routine of life while her youngest son continued to look after her. Although, with her sudden, miraculous healing and new lease on life, as well as the sudden appearance of this mystery man who kept taking her out to lunch, he was finding time to pursue his own hobbies and look for a wife.

Still, the way she talked about her boys only helped to reinforce Rifun's confidence that he hadn't completely abandoned her that night years ago. She had lived a good, full life.

The closure of the cafe prompted the end of their meeting more than anything, though they continued to talk as Rifun walked her home, handing her off to her son at the front door like a boy escorting a girl home from a date and having to face her father. He wished them both a good night, then turned and headed off down the sidewalk.

He wasn't ten steps down the street when the cell phone rang. He gave the caller ID only the briefest glance before answering. Julianna's phone always came up as Unknown, but then, so did every telemarketer.

"Hello?" he inquired.

"Sorry, I didn't want to interrupt your date," Julianna began.

Rifun paused and looked around.

"I'm sorry you went cave diving with Cassius and didn't get to spend your life with her instead."

"It wasn't supposed to take forty years," Rifun murmured, continuing his walk.

"I know. But she had a good life, and you still get to spend time with her now."

Irritation flared in Rifun's chest, if only to cover up the fear and mild paranoia. "Are you calling just to patronize me?"

She immediately got defensive. "No! No, of course not. I was simply acknowledging that you are perhaps the most human out of all of us, and it's rather refreshing to know that there exist more important things than just conquering the universe."

"I aim to keep her safe," he said through gritted teeth. "At any cost."

He could imagine her putting a hand over her chest. "I promise, I will never breathe a word of her to Cassius."

"He read the next Book. He already knows about her."

"Oh. I'm sorry." Her tone was more confused or mechanical than sorrowful.

"So why did you call? Obviously it can't be too important if you waited until after dinner."

"Well, it was nothing urgent, say it that way, given the time difference."

"Something to do with Region Four, District Four?"

"With Tommen Forbes specifically. Having stalked him for a short time now, I am more confident in his movements and routines."

Rifun nodded. "All right, anything of interest?"

"When he walks home from school—a treacherous and dangerous thing I should think on these infernal mountain roads—there are plenty of opportunities to catch him alone or in less populated areas."

"That's not difficult to do," Rifun stated. "With his father's work schedule, I imagine he is home alone quite frequently and could be visited at any time. If this were the goal, I would have pursued such an avenue already." When she was silent for a long moment, he prompted, "Was there anything else of note?"

Julianna cleared her throat awkwardly and said, "When he walks home from work, his route takes him past the governmental complex."

"Which includes the museum, as you said."

"Yes. And I know where the journal is kept as well."

"Well, I haven't taken the tour, but I can't imagine it would be that hard to find."

She sighed. "Why do I feel like you already have a plan and you've just been politely keeping me busy?"

"Not at all," he told her. "I just think a little faster than you. With this new information, I have an idea of how I want to go about this."

"And is the help privy to this information? Perhaps you are going to frame him for robbery, attempting to steal the journal?"

"And tarnish his reputation and ruin his life with a criminal record? Of course not."

"It's not like he isn't known for fighting already. His reputation is already tarnished."

Rifun sighed dramatically. "I don't know about you, but I don't exactly have a pristine past myself. Who am I to judge a hormonal teenager? His true character should be assessed first."

"How do you expect to do that?"

"We are going to give him a chance to demonstrate his integrity and courage, his sense of right and wrong. If he sees someone breaking into the museum, how is he going to react? And how will he react if he sees that the perpetrator might be a Time Agent like him?"

"What about the Akari?"

He shook his head. "He's demonstrated little or no inclination toward such things. At least with the colors of a Time Band, it should catch his attention."

"Rifun, I don't know if you know this, but Tommen is red-green color-blind. He can't see the colors of a Band properly, gets them mixed up all the time."

"Fast is red, slow is blue, what is so difficult about that? He should be able to see at least the blue, right?"

"It's difficult to articulate what you have to take on faith exists, even color. So, yes, he does struggle to remember that red is fast and blue is slow."

He let out a breath. "I do hope he is the Chivalrous Welshman, because I am less and less impressed with him otherwise."

Julianna chuckled. "You weren't so impressive yourself at sixteen, I think."

"I joined a nationalist group and fought for my people," he informed her, mildly amused himself. "I'm just going to help him through the awkward phases. Anyway, I'll grab Cassius and—"

"You're going to bring Cassius on this? He'll kill Tommen."

He shrugged. "As I said, a test of character."

"Testing his resolve when he witnesses a break-in is one thing. Setting him against Cassius is cruel and unusual."

"We'll just have to see what happens, I suppose. Maybe he isn't the Chivalrous Welshman at all. Or maybe he'll just ignore such a crime like everyone else; the police are very close by after all."

He could imagine her disapproving gaze. "I don't like this, Rifun. Do this yourself, leave Cassius out of it."

"If I don't, he is going to go after Lily or another innocent woman. It's a distraction."

Julianna did not respond right away, but he could feel her uncertainty. Finally, "I hope you know what you're doing, Rifun. Men may want to protect their women, but women want to protect their sons."

"And fathers want their sons to be men. But enough talk. There are preparations to make. Is Tommen walking home tonight? It's getting rather late in the year. Charleston doesn't get much snow, but I think there is snow on the ground right now."

"As it happens, his father is working late tonight, so either he'll have to get a ride or walk home from the bakery. Bets on walking."

"Let me know when he leaves the store."

He hung up before she could reply, then opened a portal to Charleston. He donned a Disguise before emerging from the alley and looking around.

It was early afternoon here, though his internal clock said it was mid-morning despite just having finished a late dinner date under the stars. And there was, indeed, snow on the ground. It wasn't much, just enough to make footprints and almost reveal the sidewalk, but dark gray clouds promised more to come later on.

He picked up a newspaper, mildly disappointed to find that the double murder story had slipped to page eight, just a short reminder that there was a killer somewhere in the area and to call the police if any new information surfaced. Written descriptions were given of the suspects as well as their getaway vehicle, but nothing more. In a few days, the story would probably disappear entirely, if not for their little escapade this evening.

Still in his Disguise, Rifun navigated the city streets until he reached the appropriate shopping plaza. He walked by the bakery and glanced in through the windows, but did not actually go inside. Tommen was just ringing up a customer and there appeared to be some other activity in the kitchen, but otherwise the shop was empty.

Tommen was not a big kid. A bit shorter than Rifun, much skinnier, and he didn't look to have a whole lot of muscle on him either. Hell, when Rifun was sixteen, he was taking on men twice his size, or that was how it felt when he lost.

The nationalists had trained him to fight effectively, and prison was no walk in the park either. This kid was soft.

Julianna was right; Cassius would kill Tommen in a fight. Even in a fight that was skewed in Tommen's favor in every way, Cassius would still kill him. It wasn't fair. But it would provoke some very quick decision making, test his character and resolve.

Not all fights are going to be fair, Rifun thought, shivering against the cold and looking for an alley for a quick exit.

He returned to the officers building. Cassius was nowhere to be seen, but he was directed into the city where the man was out and about on some angry stomp.

"Bad dreams last night?" Rifun inquired, falling into step beside him.

Cassius just gave him a look.

"If you're not doing anything, in a couple hours we're going to rob a museum."

No reply.

"It's not going to be a subtle affair, either. Oh, we're not going to trash the place or anything; our focus is still only the journal. But we are going to rig it in such a way that we are going to attract the attention of Tommen Forbes."

Still nothing.

"Assuming we can get him to follow us, you might even be able to rough him up a little, see what he's really made of when he doesn't have to hide his talents. Considering everyone knows you to be a murderer, this will be a true fight for his life."

Cassius gave him a look but did not stop in his angry walk as he finally asked, "And what is the goal here, really?"

"If Tommen doesn't follow, at least we get the journal. If he does, you get to rough him up."

Now Cassius stopped, though his expression was no less displeased. "Is this a test for me? Are you really going to let me hurt him, or is there just going to be some lecture about it later? If all you want to do is push him around a little, why not do it yourself?"

"Because you are the face of murder in Charleston right now. He needs to be confronted with real danger and real fear. High school bullies, however annoying, just don't provide the same...desperation."

For a long moment, Rifun thought Cassius would refuse. On the other hand, he wasn't sure he was ready for the man to accept the challenge either. Would he show any restraint, or would he actually try to kill Tommen? Would the Author let that happen, assuming Tommen was the foretold Chivalrous Welshman?

"A few hours, you said? Not next week, not next month, nothing where you have to do ungodly amounts of planning and calling meetings and all this other bullshit?"

Rifun nodded once. "A few hours, no real preparation needed. No meetings."

Cassius studied him. Then, "Fine. I'm going to be in the officers building in exactly three hours. If you're not there—"

"I will be. Don't worry."

Rifun departed, trying to stay calm and not looking to see if Cassius resumed whatever tirade he'd been on.

His best means of whiling away at least some of the time was traveling to Charleston yet again, donning a Disguise, and going through the museum as a regular patron. Yes, yes, he could easily just Band at the time of the heist and figure out what he needed to know, but some things were best done in the moment, and he had at least a few of those to spare. So he got on the escalator with half a dozen other people and descended into the first area of the museum.

An hour or so later, he had all the information he needed, and he returned to the officers building to both pray and sleep off the migraine that had bloomed in his brain. His eyes throbbed and there was stabbing pain in his old head wound.

He had no dreams, and he could not say that he slept especially well, but his migraine had ebbed so he might be able to function when he woke and found Cassius standing there in his room. Well, at least he hadn't touched anything at the shrine this time.

"Three hours," Cassius said, sounding in a slightly better mood. "Let's go."

Rifun rubbed his eyes and sighed as he stood, minding his throbbing head. "All right, fine. Lead the way."

Cassius did not make any pretense of formality, but opened a portal right there in Rifun's chambers directly into an alley in Charleston, about half a block from the museum. Rifun was momentarily overcome by nausea and he knelt near a wall to get his bearings.

"So what's the real plan?" Cassius asked while Rifun recovered.

Once he was confident that words and not vomit would come out of his mouth, he answered, "Julianna should be calling at any minute to say that

Tommen has left the bakery and is walking home. He'll go right by the museum. When he does, we intentionally trip the alarms, intentionally use Time Bands to get his attention, hide a short distance away, and see what he does. If he decides to pursue, we'll lure him to a place where we may speak freely and assess him. If he doesn't pursue, we head back to Sadurnon. Either way, we get the journal."

"And by assess, you mean I get to beat the shit out of him and make him fear for his life."

"If the second did not depend on the first..." Rifun sighed and stood, one hand on the nearest wall. "Yes. In the event that things don't go quite as planned, we'll meet back up in the officers building in a few hours."

Cassius gave him a look that was almost a sneer. "Well, if I find you sleeping again, maybe I'll just leave you alone."

"That would be appreciated. And don't touch anything, either."

Cassius took over the Banding as they left the alley and approached the museum. The cold air eased Rifun's discomfort, and by the time they reached the door, he was almost back to normal. It would all be fully erased with the portal to return to Sadurnon, but at least then he would be able to sleep it off.

At Rifun's direction, Cassius dropped the Band. Almost immediately, the cell phone rang. It was Julianna.

"You're on speaker," he told her.

"He's just left the bakery, but he's in a Band," she reported, sounding a tad frantic.

"Great, less waiting around," Cassius said sarcastically.

"Alert Tadashi and have him ready to disrupt or erase the cameras," Rifun instructed.

He hung up without ceremony. At the same time, Cassius erected another Band, and the two entered the museum. The escalators no longer ran, but that was hardly a hindrance. The locked door proved more of a challenge, but a simple use of Matter to manipulate the locking mechanism was no trouble at all. Because a key would not trip the alarm, they would have to do it intentionally when they left.

"I thought museums were supposed to be big open buildings with everything locked away?" Cassius commented as they followed the exhibit path.

"Visit many museums, do you?" Rifun retorted. "I'm surprised."

The foreign oddities led into the prehistoric geology display which transitioned into the Native American exhibit, and on and on through a tumultuous history before finally reaching the exhibit crossroads. On the one side, the general store and happy home life of the past. On the other side, the coal mines and other inhumane work practices of the past.

The journal itself was nothing terribly special, as far as the museum was concerned. It was kept in a small display case near the exit of the mine exhibit, a brief description stating that it was a journal of a miner gone mad from the darkness and the dangerous gases and chemicals used in old mining. Rifun knelt to politely pick the lock.

"If they knew what it really was, they'd have it on a pedestal," Cassius grumbled.

"Weren't you the one who said you regret even dictating it? What do you care what they do with it?"

The lock clicked and the lid released. Rifun lifted the glass lid and removed the journal. It was, as expected, just a normal book, old, yellowed pages bound in leather. Opening it up, the markings were still pristine, though Imprinting the text so that different pieces of each letter were out of sync with each other made it look like gibberish, haphazard dots and small scribbles, like a bad form of Braille or archaic Arabic. When he released the Imprint, words came into immediate focus. Time, Matter, Energy, detailing the properties of each and how to manipulate them. Much of this Rifun had already learned, but this would help him refine his abilities even more according to proven theories, or even just different ways of thinking about a concept.

"We got it, let's move," Cassius interrupted.

Rifun closed the book and turned. "Quite right. Tommen is heading this way as we speak, I imagine."

They left the museum, heading back upstairs to the lobby. The building had been designed in such a way that the plaza was the main focal point, and the main doors faced inwards to this end, facing some piece of art, indistinguishable in the dim light. As such, they had to use a side door that faced the street in order to wait for Tommen Forbes.

Julianna had already said that he was in a Band. If Rifun had to hazard a guess, because it would make no difference with the snow and cold, Tommen was trying to give Micah and Micaiah the slip. In order to do that effectively, he would have to use as tight a Band as his probationary abilities would allow, which could still be enough to make it appear as though everything around him had stopped. The Band that Cassius was using now was far more powerful than that; it would make it appear as though Tommen moved at regular speed, maybe even slower.

"Ease up on the Band," Rifun said, "just a little."

Cassius, who was busy looking through the gift shop for unknown reasons, did so without a word. Rifun remained where he was at the door.

Finally, there was movement in the sea of stillness. The same angsty teenager from the bakery was trudging through the snow, his expression clearly questioning why he had done such a stupid thing but knowing that he was fully committed to it.

"He's here," Rifun announced. "Let's go."

Cassius strengthened the Band enough to allow for their escape to a nearby street, then relaxed it enough that it would be visible to Tommen and weak enough that he might be able to push into it and follow them.

It took the kid a minute to realize what was going on, and for a few moments, Rifun was afraid he wouldn't follow them, despite clearly noticing the Band wake left behind. Then he started walking into the wake, his steps hesitant at first, then more confident as he pushed into the Band. Rifun nudged Cassius, and they retreated.

"All right, deserted alley," Cassius said as they found one.

Before he could drop the Band, Rifun stopped him and said, "No. A little farther, just down to the river here."

"But—"

"He's sixteen, he's not the smartest kid in the universe. He'll follow. It's just down the street and down to the river."

Cassius looked annoyed but followed him anyway.

They emerged into a small wharf where fishing charters bobbed quietly in the water and several docks were marked as being reserved for fire or police boats. There they leaned against the wall of a nearby building and waited for Tommen. Cassius dropped the Band.

The teenager jogged into the wharf, stopped, and looked around.

"Good God, you're right," Cassius said, loud enough that Tommen could hear him. "He is stupid."

That was not what Rifun had said, but he did not bother to correct him as they stepped away from the building and approached Tommen. The most he could do right now was, "Now, Cassius, we mustn't be rude. After all, he is only a probationary Timekeeper, and he has done well to follow us here."

They stopped a polite conversational distance away.

"Because you wanted me to follow you," Tommen stated. He straightened, maybe tried to make himself look mildly imposing. "My dad is a Captain and he'll be here."

Rifun put a hand to his chest. "Oh, how cute. Daddy to the rescue." He sighed. "Well, I suppose we should thank you after all."

"Thank me?"

He held up the journal. Tommen's expression turned disbelieving as he pointed at it. "That? You killed two women...for that?"

"A simple case of mistaken identity," Rifun said before Cassius could speak. "One mistake we will not be making again, I can assure you."

"And who are you?"

"Ah, so the good captain has not released my name because many would find such things impossible. But for you, I will introduce myself. My name is Rifun Ndolo." He did a sweeping bow, making sure to shift his body so Tommen saw the revolver at his hip. Now, he was not only outmatched in numbers, but there was a symbol of physical danger which he was very familiar with, to say nothing of what he might have perceived of their Time abilities.

"So what's in the journal?" Tommen wondered. "And why haven't you killed me?"

Everyone was so fixed on death, so afraid of it, that they never considered alternate and far worse means of punishment.

"Ah, dear child," Rifun sighed. "What did you expect from me? That I would lure you here, divulge my evil plans by way of a Shakespearean monologue, then leave you to my henchman to be killed, only for you to weasel your way out of danger and report my activities to the police where this all comes to a dramatic climactic Western-style shootout, and everyone goes home safe and sound, and I am led off stage in chains?"

Tommen blinked. "Well, that would be helpful."

Rifun laughed, but he really couldn't say why. It wasn't even that funny. Maybe it was just disbelief. "Ah, dear child. How naive you are. The only plan I shall divulge to you tonight will be the one where I do not tell you my master scheme, and instead leave you here to be killed and Harvested by my henchman, while I make an escape to you know not where."

With that, he turned and headed down to the dock, to the smallest, most inconspicuous boat he could see, throwing over his shoulder, "You know where to meet me, Cassius."

So many options, he thought as he got into the little wooden boat and started unraveling the mooring line. What would Tommen do now? Fight? Flee? Try to talk his way out? The boat started bobbing away from the dock.

The favored course of action seemed to be ignoring Cassius entirely and going after Rifun, which the man would admit he was a little surprised by. But Tommen's Bands were paltry, and Rifun was able to match it with his own Akari Band. As Tommen jumped into the boat, his Band wake trailing behind him, Rifun used the Energy from both the use of Time and the physical movement to construct a Gravity track. With a little Force to augment it, he effectively wrenched control of Tommen's movement away from the teenager and slammed the kid into the bottom of the boat.

As soon as Rifun let go of the Bands and his Akari maneuvers, Tommen came up, fists flying. Uncoordinated school bullying had nothing on years of military discipline, however, and Rifun soon had Tommen face-down in the boat once more, arm twisted behind him, Rifun's boot on his back. They were now well into the river, floating downstream.

"You've got spirit, kid," Rifun observed. "A real fighter. I like that. I could use you. See, that's another good thing about me not telling you my master plans. No skin off my back if I decided to let you go right now. You run to daddy, train really hard to be the best Timekeeper you can be. But you'll always remember this night, and you'll always want your revenge for how I defeated you. Maybe then we'll talk, hm?" He knelt down into a more comfortable position, the rocking of the boat doing nothing for his head. "What's your name, kid?"

"T-tommen."

"Tommen. Nice name. Well, Tommen, can you swim?"

"Huh?"

With barely a grunt of effort, Rifun grabbed Tommen and rolled him over the side of the boat, his splash nearly invisible in the dark water.

Still no Akari abilities to speak of, Rifun thought, sitting down and trying to steady himself, brain sloshing. But his spirit and quick thinking were undeniable. Maybe once he'd had a chance to more permanently sleep off this migraine, then he would formally introduce himself to Tommen.

The splashing of water near the boat alerted him to some mischief. With only minimal abilities, Tommen was not able to stealthily pull himself back into the boat, but his apparent anger fueled his determination. Rifun simply stood to meet him. Tommen Banded just as soon as he could. Rifun needed little more than Reflex Bands to see the punch the kid was trying to throw, and he used Force to augment his own block. Tommen stumbled back, going from angry to startled, tripped over something, and went down.

"You're persistent," Rifun said, head throbbing. At this point it had gone from annoyance to a real problem, and this was not helping his disposition. "But we're done here."

He drew his revolver, aimed it in Tommen's general direction, and fired. Truthfully, he was just going for a shot into the water, but his vision was starting to get spotty with frustrating moments of blindness. He didn't know if he'd actually hit Tommen, but the sudden water at his feet let him know that he'd hit more than just river water.

Cursing, Rifun jumped into the river.

Between his migraine, his growing blindness, and the frigid water, the mission was starting to fade into the background, replaced only by survival. He kicked his way to the surface and managed to stay there in the gentle current, but he had to wait several moments before there was a minor break in the pulsing in his head and his vision returned. As soon as he saw land of any form, he started that way, falling into a rhythm that he might keep moving even when his vision went dark.

Pulling himself onto shore, he threw up twice. Oddly enough, this calmed his migraine some and his vision returned, for the most part.

Although he probably could have slept right where he was, he knew he couldn't stay there. For one, he'd freeze to death. For two, someone would spot him and probably call the cops on a vagabond.

His stomach unhappy with the idea but now empty, he managed to conjure one last portal, directly into his chambers where he passed out before he fell into his bed. He wasn't even concerned whether or not he made it; he'd sleep on the stone floor if he had to.

In spite of the pain in his head, true rest proved elusive as he woke up several times. At one point, he realized that he had indeed fallen to the stone floor, and he crawled his way into bed. Even then he did not get the rest his head desired.

He woke to a jab in the ribs. His mind registered what was happening before he did, and at the next attempted poke, he grabbed the end of a stick. The staff from his shrine. Again. When he yanked on the staff, Cassius did not let go as he had before.

"Where's the journal?" the black man demanded.

"What?" Rifun wondered dumbly.

"Where is the fucking journal?!"

"Give me the staff, I give you the journal." Rifun again tugged on the staff.

Cassius glared at him for a long moment, then released the staff.

Rifun sat up. His head felt like lead, but there was no real pain and the nausea had gone. He stood, turned as if to reach for something, then gripped the staff and swung at Cassius, feinting one attack and striking true with the follow-up. Cassius stumbled. Rifun took the opportunity to cut the Energy in his spinal cord and paralyze him from the neck down, leaving him with only the ability to breathe.

"When I say don't touch my stuff, especially the shrine, I mean, don't touch my stuff, especially the shrine," Rifun warned, putting the staff under Cassius' chin. "Do you understand?"

"Where's the fucking journal?" Cassius spat.

Rifun turned and replaced the staff, bowing to pray briefly. Only when he rose did he release the paralysis on Cassius. The man twitched violently for a moment before getting to his feet.

"It's on my person," Rifun told him. "There was a bit of a mishap and some fisherman will be missing his boat by now, I imagine. I did it to keep it safe."

"I already checked 'your person'," Cassius said. "You don't have it. Where the fuck is it?"

"It's right—"

It should have been in one of his pockets, and he'd slept in his clothes. He checked the bed, but there was nothing. The whole room, no journal. He sighed. "Must have fallen in the river when we went in."

"Looks like we know what's on your agenda for the day," Cassius said in an angrily sarcastic manner.

Rifun had had full intentions of not using portals at all for at least a few days. He wasn't overly thrilled by the prospect of a cold water swim, either, but he knew he wasn't going to get out of this.

Reluctantly, he returned to Charleston, to the same spot where he'd crawled onto shore. It was early morning now, the sun just climbing over the mountain peaks. Even this far across the river, he could see that the wharf had been taped off and was being canvassed by police. A police boat bobbed in the water, an officer in the boat talking to a diver in the water. Hm, so the cold water swim might be out of the question for the moment. On the other hand, maybe he should just check the evidence room first.

He jumped at Cassius' voice behind him.

"I have a better idea," the man said.

"Better than just Banding, walking into the evidence room of the police station, and stealing it back?" Rifun questioned.

"That might be easier, but my plan is better."

"For all the complaining you do about how I routinely choose the most difficult way to do things—"

"And for all the complaining you do about how I'm too simplistic and don't think far enough ahead..." Cassius countered. "You like to do things the hard way, so let's do them the hard way."

The demon was getting ready to kill him, maybe kill them both. Whatever was coming, it wasn't going to be good. Rifun briefly wondered if Lalao hadn't been correct in her assessment that Cassius himself was long gone and this was only the spirit speaking now.

"How about we don't?" Rifun suggested.

"How about you shut the fuck up?" Cassius snapped. "Make sure the cops have the journal, but don't steal it."

"Why?"

"Because I fucking said so. You don't like it when I ask questions, and you usually lie when you do answer."

Rifun blinked. "I have been rightly called many things, but a liar, I am not."

Cassius continued as though he hadn't spoken. "Go find the journal, make sure the cops have it, don't steal it, then go do whatever it was you were going to do if you hadn't fucked things up."

The rage and obvious angry spittle, if not the increasing profanity, was a good indication that verbal argument would go nowhere. On the other hand, this might be Rifun's best opportunity to see what the Book of Abilities had to say about vanquishing evil spirits. He couldn't let this slip by if he wanted to stop whatever Cassius was planning.

He meekly took the out, Banding and using Gravity to get himself over the river without getting wet. He checked the boats and other vehicles first, just to make sure the journal wasn't hiding in any of them presently. When he found nothing, he started walking to the police station.

He really wasn't a fan of cold weather, however much he had endured while living in Europe. He used Thermodynamics to take the edge off the chill, but he really was grateful that the station wasn't far away. Even better, they had the heat turned up.

The evidence room was nothing remarkable, the attendant looking rather bored. His log book was still open and one of the latest entries was, in fact, the "unknown leather-bound journal, case #103-4176." He'd even been thorough enough to log where the journal could be found, the aisle, bay, and specific box.

Rifun followed the directions perfectly and was rewarded with the Book of Abilities. It did not appear damaged in any way. He wasn't sure how this had been accomplished, what Cassius or any of them had done to it to make it so perfectly waterproof, but he wasn't arguing.

Time, Matter, Energy, where did he start? Where was the section on killing demons? How did spirits, both good and bad, fit into an otherwise logical narrative of observable, mathematical science?

Within the science itself, he reasoned. In the characters and the spaces in between. The majority of life was simply empty space, after all, except it wasn't empty. It was in that space that the razana flowed, a river filled with good and bad spirits. And Cassius had become a festering pool of death and decay, dominated by an evil spirit. It wasn't enough to kill the body; the filth would only flow somewhere else, into something or someone else. He had to destroy it from the inside out.

Rifun helped himself to a chair and read through the journal several times. He retrieved a pad of paper and a pen so he could take notes and write down some theories. He'd always been a studious note-taker in school; maybe it would help him come up with something now. He knew how to wield the razana, the Akari, but how did he get into it and change it? Was this a matter of sacrifice, not an animal, but perhaps himself? Was that why such dual-spirited people were rare, not only because of the evils they alone could face but because defeating such evil required that ultimate sacrifice?

He leaned back in the chair, book still open in his lap. He had not been made different so he could plod along with the rest of them. He had never been permitted to forge true, lasting bonds in family, friends, or assorted causes. He had to remain separate, so that when the time came for him to put his life on the line, he was not held back by anything or anyone waiting for him.

A random thought floated through his head about Julianna. It wasn't anything specific, but this thought gave way to a thought about the Land In Between. The in-between dimension. The spaces in between. Julianna had tried on a handful of occasions to describe the dimension and some of the unique abilities she could wield, such as being able to travel at near-teleportation speeds, witnessing any past event although she could not change or influence them. But there had been one occasion where she mentioned something about white animals and black animals. She dismissed it as a shadowy anomaly, but now Rifun wondered.

Julianna held no love for the Authored Books, but there was mention in at least a couple of them about Whites and Shadows. Good and evil spirits, as one might expect. The space in-between, where the spirits resided.

This minor revelation made Rifun a bit jealous, actually, that she was physically closer to the spirits than he was. But then, there was something mentioned in the Book of Abilities, in the Energy section, about how dimensions might theoretically work, and how one might theoretically access them. It was one of the most advanced things in the journal, but maybe it would provide a clue going forward, show him the path to take at least.

He couldn't kill Cassius in this primary dimension, to use a term from the journal. This was the physical, mortal dimension. Only physical, mortal things could be harmed. But if he could access the spirit world, the spirit dimension, or even just get into the Land In Between, he might be able to kill the evil spirit itself.

Of course, it wasn't called the Land In Between From Which No One Has Ever Returned for nothing. It was likely a one-way journey. Well, at least he and Julianna could keep each other company, although he wasn't sure that was anything to look forward to.

He ended up copying the entire section on dimensions and dimensional energy. If he was lucky, it would take a few days for Cassius to figure out what he wanted to do, giving Rifun enough time to study and try out a few things. Maybe he could rescue Julianna from the in-between dimension, figure out that secret so he wouldn't end up trapped there.

When he was done copying, Rifun replaced the journal, gathered his notes, and left the police station. He donned a Disguise before he dropped the Band, and he walked around the block a couple times for some fresh air. His migraine had vanished, though a headache still lingered, and it was only augmented when he opened a portal back to the officers building. It wasn't three seconds before Cassius confronted him.

"And?" he demanded.

"They do have the journal," Rifun confirmed. "It is in tact and unharmed in police custody."

"Good."

Cassius pushed past him, but before he could stalk off into the shadows, Rifun asked, "What now?"

"Now you go back to whatever the fuck it was you were doing and don't fuck up my plans."

And he was gone.

Rifun stared at the spot where he'd disappeared for a few seconds more before turning and making his way to his chambers. On the one hand, he had some peace and quiet for a short while. On the other hand, he had no idea what was going on with Cassius, so he didn't know how much time he had to study and make plans of his own.

He wasted no time sorting through his notes and the copied passages, rewriting everything several times before he was confident he could begin working with the information, though how much progress would be made with a throbbing head...

Working with Time, Matter, and Energy was daunting for any beginner when first presented with the Akari. Rifun felt similarly as he began to dive into dimensional theories. If he was understanding things correctly, it worked like an offshoot of Schrodinger's cat. Most people tended to assume that dimensions were simply two different places, that they occupied two separate areas of any given space, one building and another beside it, flour and sugar measured out separately. In fact, according to Cassius' dictation, they occupied the same space, but at an offset, although this offset was too small for anyone to perceive. It was one building inside another, flour and sugar mixed together.

The reason the dimensions could coexist so tightly together and yet feel worlds apart, the reason Julianna could not be seen or heard though she might be standing right next to someone, was because the offset changed the vibration of atoms, changed how they moved and interacted. It wasn't enough to rip someone apart, but alter them just enough to be invisible, sure. It was no different than sound frequencies that were too high or too low for the human ear to hear; that didn't mean they didn't exist.

Thinking about it, it was very much like Imprint and how they locked the journal, keeping pieces of letters out of sync with the rest of Base Time. Rifun leaned back where he sat on his bed. There was more to it, he knew. He wielded the razana like magic, but there was logic embedded in there, too. Unfortunately, he'd studied architecture, not science.

What, then, did that mean for the spirits? Were they bound by atoms and molecules? Maybe to a certain extent. Even if there was an all-powerful evil spirit residing within Cassius' body, it was still bound by the limitations of that body. There was only so much a body could handle, so much he could lift, so far he could bend.

Evil is weak, Lalao had said. Rifun nodded to himself. *That is why they require strong mortals, because they could not oppose good spirits any other way. But it's not just about the spirits fighting; mortals are the prize to be won.*

If he could figure out how to move across the dimensions, push the evil spirit back into its own realm, it would become weak enough that Rifun could defeat it.

He continued his study for several days before returning to Earth. He did not need to wait long for Julianna to contact him.

"Is there a problem?" she wondered.

He explained what he'd learned so far, about the dimensions and the spirits.

"Well, it's good to know you haven't been idle, because Cassius sure hasn't," she told him.

"The demon inside Cassius knows I'm getting close, maybe thinks I know more than I do, or that I can do more than I can. Either way, it's getting ready to kill him, and probably me, too, and as many others as possible," Rifun said. "He's cut me out of his plans, as far as making them, but I don't think he's going to brush me off."

"He'll put you front and center as a human shield," Julianna stated.

"A very undesirable position, let me assure you. I did that once." He rolled his right shoulder for emphasis.

"And you thinking pushing him into the in-between dimension will have an impact? Evil spirit or not, he is still a very strong man. I don't fancy being trapped in here with him."

"You wouldn't." He sighed. "I would."

"I don't follow."

"In the Authored Book *Wolf Pack,* Anagalisgi traded places with Adahi who was trapped. I could trade places with you, put me and him on the same plane and get you out. The idea would be that I kill the evil spirit. Even if I failed, he would still be trapped there."

"Yes, but would the evil spirit?"

In spite of her disdain for his beliefs, the question sounded genuine, and it gave him pause. Finally, "I don't know. But it's the best plan I've got."

She hummed a sigh. "Well, it's more than what I've got. And we won't have much time to bat it around, either. Cassius has been busy. I was just hoping for you to show up when you did."

"Has something happened here?"

"I'll spare you Cassius' gloating. He's kidnapped a couple of Tommen's friends."

Surprise was less prominent than confusion in Rifun's mind as he said, "He...kidnapped a couple of Tommen's friends? What kind of plan is that? What is he up to?"

"I'm sure I don't know, but it can't be good."

"Do you know where he's taken them?"

"Some cave in the mountains. Do you want me to take you to them, or are you going to look for Cassius?"

Rifun considered this for only half a moment. "Take me to the boys, at least so I know the condition of our sudden hostages."

He Banded long enough to steal a car and get out of town. When he released the Band, Julianna gave him directions to the cave, getting as close as possible with the vehicle before having to hike the last couple miles to a cave where Cassius was just exiting.

"Good, you're here," the dark-skinned man said, brushing dust and dirt from his hands. He held out one hand. "Give me the phone."

"What are you doing?" Rifun asked, not handing over the device.

"Leverage. You want Tommen, I want the journal. Take his friends, we get both. Once we have Tommen, Walter will hand over Lily to save him, we kill Lily."

It wasn't the worst plan Rifun had ever heard, but it still wasn't very smart.

Cassius took an aggressive step forward, hand still out. "Give me the fucking phone."

"You're going to make a ransom call," Rifun stated, not moving.

"I'm not ordering pizza."

Rifun nodded. "Let me make the call. I'm a little more personable."

Cassius studied him for a long, tense minute. Finally he nodded, though his posture said he wasn't going anywhere and would be silently critiquing the call.

Rifun's first call was to Tadashi. While the phone was ringing, he looked at Cassius. "Go get the boys. Proof of life goes a long way."

Tadashi picked up, saving Rifun from Cassius' sneering. "What?"

"I need a favor," Rifun said.

"I need a paycheck."

"How much to hack a phone and put some kind of recording device on it for phone calls?"

"Phone calls are already recorded, dipshit. The government says they don't allow it, but they do because they benefit—"

"Spare me the political lecture. I need to record a phone call and have it accessible later to the other party."

Tadashi sighed. "What's the number?"

Rifun gave it to him. There followed about ninety seconds of intense keyboard strikes and mouse clicks. Then, "Give it about sixty seconds and it'll be ready."

"Good. You'll get your payment shortly."

He hung up before Tadashi could say anything, turning to see Cassius emerging from the cave. He had two teenage boys in tow, Banded so they would not resist, directed by a Gravity track so there was less fumbling inside the cave.

"Are you intentionally exposing them?" Rifun inquired.

Cassius shrugged. "Maybe. We're not exactly swamped with new recruits these days. Now make the call."

Rifun hesitated for half a second, then dialed Tommen's phone. As soon as the call connected, the phone was snatched from his hand. Rifun turned to see Cassius donning a Disguise of him.

"You're right," Cassius said in Rifun's voice. "You are more personable. But I am willing to do what is necessary."

With one menacing hand on the back of one of the boys' heads, Cassius-as-Rifun started to talk on the phone.

9 | Ìyàwó

West Virginia, 2013

Negotiation

This was the necessary thing, Cassius told himself. The necessary thing and his plan besides. What's more, it was time to drag Rifun into his own game, put some responsibility on him, force him to think on his feet rather than sit back in an endless stream of useless meetings.

Posing as Rifun, Cassius made arrangements to swap Tommen's friends for the Book of Abilities at a nearby airport. He wasn't going to go to the meeting as Rifun. No, they would go together as themselves. He wanted to see how Rifun would try and talk his way out of this one. Bets that he couldn't. It was all going to go straight to hell, regardless of whatever flowery, staged monologue he could come up with.

Still Cassius could find no rest. Although little of excitement had happened, other than what he created himself, he couldn't help but feel very much like a small mouse in a room full of cats, but all the cats were invisible. He smelled them, felt them, knew they were ready to pounce. He just didn't know when. The dragon was amused by this turn of events, but it wasn't enough to stave off his death.

He silently resolved that once they got the Book of Abilities, he was going to destroy it. Water had done little to it, but what about fire? Or maybe he would just use Matter to reach into it and disintegrate it entirely. Whatever it took, he was going to destroy it. The others, too, eventually, but the Book of Abilities was probably the most dangerous.

He never should have dictated it.

He never should have dealt with the spirits.

He should have died when the Timekeeper killed him.

But if the dragon was going to kill him anyway, might as well try to undo what he could. Julianna was already sealed in another dimension, which was less satisfying than killing her but it would have to do. Destroy the journals to unravel the Cult. Kill Rifun because he was an annoying, cowardly prick. Then go after Isthim, Misik, and take down as many Borelians as he possibly could before they inevitably slew him.

Sounded like a hell of a way to go.

With the ransom call finished, Cassius returned the boys to the cave, again using a Fast Band to confuse them and Gravity to move them.

"What the fuck is this?" one shrieked when he released the Band. "What the fuck—?!"

Cassius used Sound to mute the boys while they flailed in their bonds and blubbered their confusion. He left the cave, navigating a short tunnel to the outside where he unexpectedly encountered a Grunjor. It was a monstrous alien made of a special type of stone which, when infused with some kind of plasma and other methods unknown to outsiders, became sentient. Upon creation, a Grunjor only needed to be assigned a name and a task. Many races considered Grunjor to be a bit slow and uneducated, and how or why they had elected to side with the Cult was beyond Cassius. Or maybe it was just this one that had agreed.

"To keep the boys inside, in the event they do somehow go snooping," Rifun explained. He stood some fifteen feet away, Isthim beside him, currently orange. Tadashi was the unexpected guest, looking rather pissed off as he dared to push past Cassius into the cave. Once he was inside, the Grunjor placed himself in the tunnel opening, then appeared to dismantle itself stone by stone until it filled the whole tunnel. Only the warmth emanating from the stones gave any indication that it was not part of the surrounding landscape.

"And Tadashi?" Cassius wondered.

"Get rid of any electronics on them, so they can't be tracked. And a bit of a babysitter, as we all will be once this impromptu meeting is over." Rifun's expression said this wasn't up for debate.

"Why? Negotiation is tomorrow. The Grunjor is keeping them inside."

"Even so. They are collateral damage, and we don't need more charges than we already have. I understand you don't care, but I'm trying to keep us out of any unnecessary conflicts."

Cassius opened his mouth to speak, but Rifun beat him to it. "We trade the boys for the journal and leave."

"And bring Tommen with us if we have to. If you want to obsess over something, I'm going to give it to you just so I don't have to listen to you—"

"It would provide opportunities," Isthim interrupted, looking annoyed. Her expression softened only a touch as she turned her attention to Rifun. "He is too close to Time through his father, and we're still not certain about Micaiah's allegiances. With all of this going on, it's unlikely any of them will be willing to sit down for a talk."

"We make him follow us," Cassius cut in. "If he is your chosen one, he'll be a great asset, I'm sure. If not, well, it will send a message to the Time industry through Owain and the Akarin through Micaiah."

"We can't just tie him up and hold him forever," Rifun said flatly. He put up a hand. "Just long enough for him to see that we are not the threat. We are trying to fix the threat."

"Now you're thinking. Give us a good look at the character of his dad, too. See if Owain Fforidd really is a changed man."

Rifun sighed and pinched the bridge of his ugly nose. "Fine. Under one condition." He lowered his hand and looked at Cassius. "I don't want you interacting with Tommen. We don't need you scaring him off. Worse, we don't need any honor fights breaking out and you severely injuring or killing him."

"I'll do my best."

Actually, Cassius was kind of hoping to provoke a small fight, to make up for the pitiful excuse of a tussle at the boat launch. He could use that as a bit of a needle, he supposed, see what kind of rage he could drum up in the kid.

He wasn't right in the head, and he knew it, and he hated it. The dragon spirit laughed or sneered in his mind and he could hear it with all the clarity of the nearby birdsong. As they walked to the cave where the Grunjor allowed them passage, the others were having their own thoughts about the situation, while he was stuck with laughter and noise.

It was trying to distract him, drive him insane so he couldn't fight back when it finally struck the killing blow. What was infuriating was that it was working.

He paused before entering the cave, staring at the odd rock formation that was somehow a sentient being. What did it want? Why was it here? Where were its eyes and how did it do...this? How did it dismantle itself? Did it breathe? He looked inside the tunnel where the others had disappeared, back outside where a brisk wind rattled tree branches nearly devoid of leaves.

Maybe this wasn't such a good idea. Maybe he should kill the boys, send a real message. Maybe he should set them loose in the forest somewhere and see how long it took them to make their way to any kind of civilization, if they did. Maybe he should kidnap Tommen now and add to the negotiations tomorrow. Maybe he should kill everyone in that cave and see if the Grunjor couldn't somehow displace some rocks to make it look like a cave-in had crushed them. Or he could rapidly advance Time, decay them as he had Doug.

Should he tell the Akarin about the situation? Probably not. They would only be confused about it. Why was the Cult so focused on a couple of Unengaged humans? As for Tommen, he had shown no innate Akari talents that would bolster some insane theory that he was the Chivalrous Welshman. If anyone in the Akarin cared, it would be Micaiah, and he was already involved.

Cassius walked away from the cave a few steps. The Grunjor paused for a few moments, then reassembled itself into the tunnel's entrance, sealing it once more.

He didn't know what he was doing. He felt like a caged animal being tortured. He knew his time was short. He was trying to fight, but he just didn't know how. If he tried anything, the evil spirit was just going to kill him. It was going to kill him anyway. Did he dare try to take a knife to his own face, try to carve out the bullet? Using the Akari would be too delicate, too involved, but a sharp blade might work just fine. Of course, how foolish would he look, stabbing a knife under his eye socket? On the other hand, he wasn't going to entrust such a thing to anyone else. They'd just stick the knife in him and be done with it.

In a moment of odd clarity, he found himself hating Rifun even more. The man had been physically tortured for years yet had done nothing to try and save himself. At least he, Cassius, was trying. He just wasn't quite ready to go to the final extreme.

Kill Rifun, leave Julianna, kill Isthim and Misik, then see how many Borelians he could take down before they finally got him. If it came right down to it, that was how he intended to go. The dragon might even get a good laugh out of it, maybe place bets like some sort of sporting event.

Cassius hated that the dragon laughed at that and made a sound that was somewhere between a gurgle and a purr. He also hated that he knew that sound meant it was considering such a thing.

"Three hundred years and it's only come to this," Cassius grumbled.

A sound interrupted his grouchy trance, and it took a moment for him to realize it was Doug's phone, still in his pocket from whatever chore he'd last needed the phone with him. The caller ID said Micaiah. He really didn't want to talk to him, but his only other option right now was sitting in a small cave with Rifun and the others. Donning a Disguise, Cassius answered.

"Micaiah!"

"The Cult has kidnapped two of Tommen's friends," Micaiah blurted. "They're holding them hostage in exchange for the Book of Abilities."

Unprepared for the sudden jump into conversation, Cassius-as-Doug was unable to find words for several seconds. He hoped it was simply passed off as processing such information and already coming up with some kind of plan. Ultimately, all he could manage was, "Tell me what you know about the situation."

Precious little, other than what had been relayed to him about the ransom phone call.

"Do you know anything about where the Cult might be keeping them?" Cassius-as-Doug inquired.

"My guess would be wherever their secret lair is. It was suggested that it might be a cave, but that's Earth-side police talk."

"Those who wouldn't normally think to look on other planets, I understand. And I might agree, it is most likely their secret lair, except wouldn't that expose them to Time?"

"Judging by the way Tommen and Walt said they sound, they're already exposed but the Cult isn't doing much to assuage any fears."

"Keeps them paralyzed, easy to control. So why did you call me?" Cassius-as-Doug puffed out his chest a bit, even if Micaiah couldn't see. "Are you looking for me to show up tomorrow and heroically save the day? You said it was at the airport, right? We could make it a grand show for anyone in the terminal!"

Micaiah's tone was unimpressed. "Hangar 4 is nowhere near the terminal; they'd never see anything." There was some shuffling noise in the background. "I'm going to keep an eye on things, find an adjacent rooftop and do a little unauthorized sniping if I have to. With any luck, this will all go smoothly, but I can't believe that Rifun wants Tommen there just for kicks."

"It is a little suspect, I will admit," Cassius-as-Doug agreed. "Luckily for you, I may have managed to recruit a little help. In spite of all my persuasive words of grandeur, it's not that they care about Tommen so much as they think they're doing me a favor by helping you. You're not the most popular, I understand, but most people will do anything for me."

"Right. Keep telling yourself that. So long as you don't mind me telling Micah that I rounded up the help."

"He's going, too? You, Micah, Tommen, who's going to run the shop?"

"Micah, but he is going to be the one to call in the help. I think the rest of us might be a bit busy, and cell signal is notoriously poor inside Bands."

"There is that, yes. All right, well, I will let my heroic help know of the situation and try to get them coordinated so they can be ready at a moment's notice. I'll call you when they're ready."

"Thanks, Doug." It was more of a formal reflex than any real gratitude, Cassius thought, augmented by the abrupt end of the call.

The grinding of stone indicated the Grunjor's movement, and a moment later, Rifun appeared, though he kept a respectful distance, out of arm's reach.

"Did you think I'd wandered off?" Cassius wondered, not looking at Rifun as he shed his Disguise. "Gone to kidnap more children?"

"The thought crossed my mind," Rifun said. "Maybe you decided to add Tommen to this mix. Maybe you decided to kill him outright. Maybe you decided to go after Walter in some perceived vengeance."

If Cassius wanted to be honest, he didn't know what he wanted to do right now. It was like, at one point in the distant past, he had viewed the horizon and every possibility between him and the end of the earth. But now, he had reached the end of the earth, and it was a broom closet he couldn't get out of. There were no more possibilities, no great future, nothing but darkness and dying alone. He couldn't see anything, couldn't plan. The plans he made, he later couldn't recall why he'd thought of them, or thought them good.

The fact that he was aware of the situation did nothing to comfort him as he feared the day when that would no longer be the case. He had been accused of being a savage, a beast, a less than, and for many years he had embraced the moniker. Now he was afraid he was about to learn what it really meant.

"I like having a stage," he told Rifun, turning to face him hoping he did not convey any of his fear. "You enjoy the stage, don't you?"

"As an actor, yes."

Cassius spread his arms. "So act the part, like I did on the phone." He let his arms fall to his sides. "When did you start blanching at killing? Your line of morality is very convenient and not exactly stationary."

"I do what is necessary, no more, no less." Rifun gestured toward the cave. "This is unnecessary."

"Necessity also seems to be very convenient. If you do something, it's necessary. If I do something, it's unnecessary. Well, let me tell you something. Tomorrow afternoon, you're going to have to go out on that stage in front of a lot of men with guns and act a certain part. And it will be necessary for you to act that way."

Rifun's expression was hard. "So I've discovered. I also have a hunch that the men with guns will be the least of my worries."

Cassius did not reply to that, instead suggesting, "The boys might do better to sleep things off in a Band. Makes the nightmare go by faster, don't you think?"

"It's one way to stave off motion sickness while on a plane, yes."

"Good. Let's get to it, then."

He pushed past Rifun, heading for the cave. The Grunjor disassembled without complaint, or words of any kind. Did they even have speech capabilities? Cassius wasn't sure. Honestly, he didn't care, but he couldn't help but look back once they were inside the cave to watch the rock beast reassemble itself into the shape of the opening.

"He doesn't look like much, I admit," Rifun said, "but when a Grunjor starts moving, I advise you to get out of the way."

The boys weren't the only ones who were going to need a Slow Band to get them through the night. Cassius was going to need one, too, or else he was going to end up murdering everyone. He mentally paused and wondered if there was a downside to that, any reason not to. Kill Rifun, leave Julianna, kill Isthim and Misik and see how many Borelians it took to bring him down.

As far as Cassius was concerned, then, the night passed fairly uneventfully. Most of them were not on a regular Earth cycle, as far as sleep. The boys slept through the night, or they appeared to. It was morning before the others laid down.

Cassius watched them, stared at Rifun as he slept. How easy would it be to cut his throat? Would he be able to heal it before he bled out, or would he only do to himself as they had done to the two women? What if Cassius just snipped off his ponytail, a warning of what could have been? No. Kill him or don't. A warning would only make future attempts more difficult.

He should. Rifun and Isthim, prone before him. Tadashi, so there were no witnesses. Well, no witnesses of consequence. And what the hell, kill the boys, too. The Grunjor, well, Cassius wasn't sure how to kill stone, but he suspected it had to do with the magic plasma or whatever it was that gave it sentience.

Cassius entertained the idea for a good hour or more, walking over to Rifun several times, knife in hand. He would only get one shot. He had to do it fast enough and with enough creative Banding on his part that any Reflexive Bands would be rendered useless.

He did note one strange thing, that sleeping on a thin sleeping bag on stone, Rifun was still rigid, ready for action, and had not tossed, turned, or rolled over even once. Unless the man enjoyed bedsores, there was no way he could sleep like that. Just how aware was he?

One shot. Cassius found a comfortable grip on his knife and raised the blade. Careful not to make any noise, he swept the blade down in a straight line toward Rifun's neck, using Bands of his own to try and get around any Reflexive Bands Rifun might suddenly throw up, and invoking Gravity to ensure a heavy strike.

An eighth of an inch before it touched skin, the metal super-oxidized, turning to rust flakes that fluttered away harmlessly. Rifun's hand shot out and grabbed Cassius' wrist. With the strength of a weight lifter and the flexibility of a gymnast, Rifun launched himself off the floor from a supine position, slamming into Cassius and driving him to the ground. Cassius' head hit the stone and momentarily dazed him. When he recovered, he found Rifun on his chest, using Gravity to augment his own weight even as he paralyzed Cassius and held the knife to his throat.

"I wondered how long it would take," Rifun hissed.

"Why put yourself at risk, then?" Cassius sneered back. "Why fall asleep?"

"Spend a few years on the front lines. Spend a few decades in prison. Tell me how well you sleep. As for why, I'm here to protect those boys."

"From me."

"That's right."

Cassius chuckled humorlessly. "You seem to enjoy this little paralysis trick, but you still won't kill me."

"Because it's not you I'm trying to kill."

Now he laughed aloud. "The dragon? You want to kill the dragon? Better men than you have tried. And while you try and try, the dragon will continue to rampage. Through me or anyone else. So you might want to consider killing me and saving yourself the hassle." He laughed again, but he couldn't be sure it was even himself laughing. "Let me put it this way, the dragon is going after Tommen. He is your Chivalrous Welshman. So you can ignore him and try to keep me away, but the dragon has no shortage of minions to go after him while you're occupied.

Or you can kidnap him to try and protect him, but damn yourself in the process as you break every rule of morality you've set for yourself."

The look of uncertainty that crossed Rifun's face was one that Cassius had been waiting for years to see, that deep realization of just what he was dealing with.

"You have a part to play today," Cassius went on, unsure who was speaking. "Unfortunately for you, there is no script, no direction. Because this is the fucking battlefield, not the stage."

Rifun gave him a look and retracted the knife. "If that's the case, then I'm the ranking officer here, and I expect to be addressed as *adjudant-chef* or simply *monsieur*. If you want to get on my good side, you might try *tompoko* or *andriamatoa*."

"Fuck you. You lost every war you fought in."

Rifun stood. "I haven't lost until I'm dead."

He pocketed the knife and released the paralysis. Cassius twitched violently until he was almost in seizure. Only once he had calmed down did the Band drop.

The day passed similarly to the night, and it was early afternoon before Isthim and Tadashi were awake. Rifun checked the cell phone.

"Time to go."

The boys had sunk into a sullen, disbelieving silence and put up no resistance as they were marched out of the cave.

"Tadashi, do you have the keys?" Rifun asked once they were outside.

"Why are we taking the van?" Cassius complained. "Just open a portal."

"We will, with the van. It's just putting ourselves out there a little more, frustrating the authorities when they are unable to track us, yet we can navigate through places with the tightest of security."

It was also the least traumatic mode of transportation for the boys, Cassius realized when they climbed in the van. They might question how they had traveled so quickly from the cave to the airport, but they would not necessarily be directly subjected to the portal, the visual part of it.

This consideration was revoked, however, once they actually got to the airport. They were not going to drive out onto the tarmac and navigate their way to the hangar. Instead, they were going to park like civilized people and walk out to the hangar. Because they just had to do everything the hard way.

But it did give them a chance to look around and assess the situation, see what the police were doing. Walter and Tommen were there in the hangar, as promised, standing in the wide entrance of the hangar like sitting ducks in Kevlar vests, a SWAT Team just out of sight. Also as promised, Micaiah was there, perched on a large mechanical contraption that had something to do with the plane being repaired.

They headed to one of the plane's wheels. Before Rifun could drop the Band, Cassius spoke. "You know your part?"

Rifun gave him an annoyed look. "I thought we discussed this earlier, *soldat*. I am the ranking officer, you address me as *adjudant-chef* or *monsieur*, and I give the orders."

"As an Admiral, I outrank both of you," Isthim threw in casually.

"No one asked you," Rifun said. "Now then, let me go and start things off on the right foot, hm?"

He dropped the Band before anyone could say anything more, and the first person to speak was Walter.

"Two-thirty," he murmured.

"And you never fail to disappoint, Walter," Rifun said, using Sound so that his voice echoed around the room, coming from everywhere and nowhere. He strode out from behind the jet wheel, an actor going out on stage to play his part. As if to make a point of it, perhaps emulate the swinging of stage curtains, he flashed a regular Time Band, the colors flowing for just a second, just enough to be noticed and draw attention to himself.

"I'm disappointed, Walter," Rifun said. "You seem to lack faith in me. The gun, the Kevlar, the team waiting outside, why, I might have thought that you didn't trust me. But here I am at two-thirty, true to my word. Now then, prove that you are also a man of your word and show me that you brought what I asked for."

Fucking hell, the man was not a soldier. There was no way he could have ever fought a battle, never mind actually led men into or through one. And if he had, no wonder his wars failed.

"I will show you the boys, and you will see that we have not harmed a single hair on their chinny chin chins," Rifun was saying.

He needed to figure out a new strategy. As last night—or this morning— proved, a direct assault on Rifun, even in his sleep, wasn't going to cut it, and Rifun loved his paralysis trick too much. Could he outright Harvest him? Was the touch of death faster than a Reflex Band? Or would he have to go the coward's route and try to poison him? No. If he was too paranoid to sleep, he was probably checking every scrap of food and drink he ingested.

Nevertheless, they marched the boys out where Walter and Tommen could see them.

"And here we are," Rifun said amiably, extending an arm for dramatic effect.

"Eric! Varad!" Tommen called.

Maybe it was hearing a friend's voice, but something about being addressed snapped whatever trance the boys had been in, and they immediately began freaking out, as if just realizing that they had traveled a fair distance in a short time. There was a good amount of poorly-used profanity in their screaming, and Cassius had a mind to shoot them and be done with it. He had the shotgun he'd stowed in the van, so why not? Kill the boys, kill Rifun, leave Julianna, kill Isthim and Misik... And he might as well kill Walter and Tommen, too. Walter for escaping him years ago, Tommen because he was some chosen one of the Author and the dragon didn't like him.

"You exposed them to Time," Walter stated incredulously.

Rifun shrugged. "Yes, I did. I only said I did not harm them. And I did not."

"How much exposure?"

"Oh, a Band here, a Band there."

By now the boys were blubbering their confusion. Cassius sighed and looked around. His attention on the conversation was minimal, only because he knew nothing relevant was actually being said. He kept an ear on it just enough to fish for key phrases, but it felt like forever before he caught one.

"You've proven you're a man of your word and you haven't harmed them," Walter said, sounding very diplomatic. "Now let them go."

"You know, Walter, I like you. I really do," Rifun told him. "Always admired you and what you did for your brother and your kid here. So, we've established that we're both men of our words. That's lovely. I have the boys, you have the journal. So I suggest you cooperate and hand over the journal, let's say...now."

Actually, Cassius was more surprised that Rifun didn't hand over the boys first. Of course, if he had, Cassius might have had something to say about it, and it wasn't going to be pretty.

"The journal is an object," Walter said. "You have two lives resting in your hands. Release the boys first."

A heavy silence draped itself over the hangar, or maybe that was the shadow of the dragon. Cassius stared at the back of Rifun's head. He couldn't see where his head injury was specifically, but removing his head entirely was one way to sidestep that problem.

"See, the problem is, Walter, you're right. The journal is just an object. And your number one priority is human life." Rifun started walking toward Walter. He Banded briefly, himself only, then continued. "You seem to have deduced that Tommen is very important in this situation also, or you would not have given the journal to him for safekeeping. But love and hate seem to be your two greatest weaknesses, Walter." Now he was only a couple feet away. "So I will ask again. Hand over the journal."

Another silence as Walter weighed his options.

"I propose a compromise," Walter said at last.

Unfortunately, his Band only encompassed himself, Tommen, and Rifun, so Cassius missed anything interesting that was said. But then, how likely was it that it would be interesting at all? Negotiations, compromise, give-and-take, it was all so...tedious. Just take it. Take what you want. Fight for it.

Of course, the one time he didn't force his way into the Band and the proceedings, and something interesting did happen, for the next thing he knew, when the Band dropped, Tadashi had moved. He stood beside Rifun, Micaiah on his knees in front of him. He'd been beaten and was shaking and spitting blood. Tadashi held a gun to the back of his head.

"He's a fighter," Tadashi said. "Just didn't fight hard enough."

Cassius was more irritated that Rifun had asked Tadashi to subdue Micaiah and not him. Why not let him go after Micaiah and let Tadashi babysit these brats?

"Now I have three lives before me," Rifun said. "Where is the other one?"

Walter was fighting to maintain composure. "He didn't come."

Tadashi chambered a round.

Micaiah spat some blood. "He didn't come." His voice was shaking.

"Call him," Rifun ordered. "Call off your dogs. Then we'll go to the Wheel."

Walter glared at Rifun for a moment, tried to read his face, his body language. Tadashi pressed the gun harder against Micaiah's head. Finally Walter fished out his phone and dialed Micah.

"Micah," Walter said. "It's Walt."

"Speakerphone, please," Rifun said pleasantly.

Walter did so. "You're on speakerphone."

"What's going on? Did you get Eric and Varad back?" Micah asked.

"Here's the deal, Micah," Rifun said. "I have your brother here, and he's not doing so well. But as it is, he can still make a full recovery."

"Is that Rifun?"

"Now then, I know you have allies in the Wheel who are more than happy to try and arrest me if I set foot there—"

"I swear, if you harm a single hair on his head, I'm going to—"

Tadashi rolled his eyes, lifted the gun, and fired it into the air.

"Micaiah!" Micah screamed.

"I'm f-fine," Micaiah said. "He shot in the air."

Tadashi put the gun back where it was at Micaiah's head.

Rifun huffed irritably and continued. "As I was saying, I know you have allies. Walter here is proposing that we meet in the Wheel in order to do our little exchange. So, here is what is not going to happen. You, Micah, are not going to go into the Wheel to forewarn your allies and so have a rallying force waiting for me. And if you don't want the next bullet to end up buried in your brother's brain, you are going to agree to it in the next te—"

"All right!" Micah interrupted. "All right. I won't go." He sighed. "Sorry, Walt."

"I don't blame you," Walter told him, though Cassius could hear the disappointment.

"I am holding your brother to your word, Lieutenant." Then he nodded and Walter hung up, slowly putting the phone back in his pocket. "Now then, what were you saying about that little trip to the Wheel?"

Walter glared at him. "Me and Tommen and the journal. You and one of your friends, and the boys. We go in, do the exchange, and get out. No one need be harmed."

Rifun glanced at Micaiah. "A little late for that, wouldn't you say?" He made a motion and the rest of the group stepped forward. Isthim and the Grunjor kept the boys under control. Cassius lagged behind as Doug's phone buzzed in his pocket. That would be Micah, telling him to call off the rescue mission. Funny thing, Cassius had never actually put one together. The buzzing stopped, the call going to voicemail. He'd listen to it later, listen to the younger twin sweat, maybe blubber something about Micaiah being in trouble and not wanting to cause any more trouble than necessary.

"I will go," Rifun was saying. "As a show of good faith, I'll even go alone." He looked at Tadashi. Not Cassius. "If I am not the first one back through the portal, kill him." Tadashi nodded. "Captain?"

Walter sighed but nodded and took a step back. It took some effort, but he conjured a portal there in the hangar. Rifun went toward the portal and then paused. He gave Walter a stunned look. "Why, Walter, I just realized. Taking dear Eric and Varad into the Wheel will all but guarantee sufficient Time exposure that they will have to be trained. Are you up for taking on two more Apprentices?"

Opening portals was no easy task, and the most Walter could do was grunt and give Rifun a look. Rifun simply made a gesture and looked at Tommen. "After you, Tommen."

The problem with portals to the Wheel, was that, if the portal remained open, all time back home stopped. Or it just moved very fast in the Wheel. Rifun, Tommen, Walter, and the boys could have been in there for five minutes or five hours or five days, even. All the rest of them saw was the sudden appearance of the Wheel in a door-sized hole in the air as the portal opened. Then the five of them went through, disappeared, and then reappeared just as quickly. Or rather, Rifun reappeared, dragging Tommen by his bulletproof vest. In his other hand was his revolver and he was shouting orders.

The Grunjor leapt forward to scoop up Tommen protectively as it raced across the tarmac. Once he was free of his burden, Rifun lifted his revolver and got off several haphazard shots at the SWAT Team that was just starting to come around the corner, weapons raised.

Cassius did not bother to aim; that wasn't what a shotgun was for, especially when the first two slugs were all buckshot. It didn't do a lot of damage, but it caused enough confusion to buy them time to duck behind a baggage train, the Akari doing more to keep the bullets at bay than the paper-thin cars. The Grunjor set Tommen on the ground, still using its stony body to shield him.

"Oh, I always love a good shootout," Rifun said, twisting and standing just long enough to get in a couple haphazard shots. He sat back down to reload. "But, we are on a schedule. Donojok, stay here and help Tadashi and Cassius. Isthim, get Tommen to a safe place and wait for me there."

Isthim did not look pleased about being turned away from a fight, but she obeyed without question. As she grabbed Tommen and started running, the Grunjor, Donojok, stood with a roar, lifted the baggage train like a toy, and threw it at the SWAT Team. The cops scattered, one of them shouting into a radio. The train burst apart, the individual cars tumbling in all directions, the driving vehicle skidding across the tarmac in a spray of slush and sparks.

Cassius raised his shotgun again, now loaded with regular twelve gauge slugs, but before he could pull the trigger, Rifun grabbed his arm and leaned in close. "Don't kill anyone."

"Why?" He pulled the trigger and watched as one of the cops, still reeling from his flight from an escaped train car, only just managed to flop out of the way.

"Because that's not why we're here."

Cassius wrested his arm away and fired off the second round. "No, but they're here to kill us. Adjust plans accordingly."

The two of them jumped a good three feet apart as several weapons discharged at once, the police still shouting in terrified confusion.

"We should get out of here!" Tadashi yelled, Donojok providing some protection as he emptied his rifles.

Cassius still took the time to reload. Donojok provided flanking cover on one side, Tadashi the other. Rifun led the way and Cassius brought up the rear, running backwards, blasting his shotgun at any cops who got too close.

The cops gave up the chase once they perceived there might be too many civilians around, but they needn't have worried, Cassius thought. Rifun would not allow any harm to come to the poor, poor civilians. As it was, those poor, poor civilians were probably too busy demanding to know why their flight was delayed or canceled to notice the troupe of criminals running around the building trying to outrun a SWAT Team.

They reached the van and piled inside, Tadashi in the driver's seat, Cassius in the passenger seat, the rest in the back, the whole vehicle rocking violently as Donojok scrunched his way in amid the others.

"Well, I was about to say we all got away without a scratch," Rifun said with some resignation.

"It was a wound of his own doing," Isthim informed him.

There was a pause. Then, from Rifun, "Well, it's not deep, and it's not bad. Good news is, I think you're going to live."

"Where's my dad?" Tommen whimpered.

"Oh, he'll be fine. He has no idea what's just occurred, I reckon."

"What happens now?"

"Rifun, we should go before Captain Forbes finds us here," Tadashi said, putting his hand on the key.

"Excellent," Rifun said.

At least the man didn't make them stop and pay for their time in the lot, Cassius thought as Tadashi skipped over one curb, ignored the gates, crashed through a fence, and hopped back down onto the road, several cars honking irritably. Once they were not in any immediate danger of colliding with car, pedestrian, or solid object, Tadashi Banded the van. Driving was much smoother after that, though they still had to dodge all the suddenly-stationary vehicles on the road.

"Back to the same cave?" Tadashi asked as Rifun made his way forward to look between the seats.

"Might as well," Rifun answered. "Not like we can't relocate if we have to."

"I'm surprised," Cassius said. "Risky move, grabbing Tommen and starting a shootout like that. He could have been hurt."

"As I said, I'm trying to keep him out of harm's way, which means I'm going to need you to stay away from him."

"You want to bring a guest into our home and then tell me I can't welcome him? Even I know that's rude."

"You have made it perfectly clear that you don't want to wait around and babysit, and I am not going to force you. I expect we will be keeping Tommen for a few more days than his friends, and I wouldn't want to put any undue strain on you."

"Fuck you."

"So who is going to babysit him?" Tadashi asked, his expression saying he had a pretty good idea of the answer.

"I am charging you and Isthim with such a task, although I expect I will be there for a good amount of time also, in the event you have to leave for errands." The last part was dripping with sarcasm.

Tadashi was not amused. "I'm a hacker, a spider, not a babysitter. I can't even bring my setup with me because there is zero signal in that stupid cave. Overnight gig, fine, but I'm not doing some extended camping trip."

"You can and you will. The world will survive without you for a few days, believe me."

"Then I expect to get paid. I'm losing a lot of money, and I have debts to pay."

"Loan sharks are your problem, and I don't think they're of as much consequence as you would have me believe. If you haven't been studying up on Time or the Akari, that's your own fault."

Before Tadashi could argue, Cassius spoke up. "You do the babysitting so I don't have to, and I take care of anyone you're indebted to. How does that sound?"

The Japanese kid's expression turned contemplative. "Sounds like the better offer here. I'll get you a list."

Cassius glanced back at Rifun. "You will notice, then, that violence does solve some problems."

"I never said it didn't," Rifun told him coolly. "I simply argue your assertion that violence is the answer to every problem."

"Hang on, gonna get crazy here," Tadashi announced.

Their exit was not a complete log jam, but there were not a few protests from the back seat as Tadashi darted around the Time-stopped vehicles like a madman, weaving in and out of lanes, riding the shoulder a short distance, and nearly taking off a mirror when he got close to the concrete guards.

"If you could refrain from killing us, that would be the ideal," Rifun said from the backseat, though his words were not the most malicious. When Cassius looked back, the man was kneeling on the floor, skin milky white, staring at nothing. Cassius might have found this amusing had his own stomach not been roiling also.

"We should be good now," Tadashi announced, laughing darkly. "Traffic appears to have thinned out some."

"If you want revenge on him for being an asshole, fine," Cassius told him, "but don't piss off the one who's ready and willing to kill your enemies for you."

Tadashi just laughed again and shook his head, then intentionally swerved hard around another vehicle.

After that, things went smoothly. By the time they got out of the van, a short hike from the cave, it was almost as if it had never happened. No one was especially happy, but at least no one was sick.

Donojok carried a limp Tommen up the trail with no more difficulty than any of the rest of them might had have if they'd been carrying paper bags. When they reached the mouth of the cave, the unconscious teenager was handed off to Rifun who stalked inside without a word. Isthim and Tadashi followed, Isthim appearing rather bored of the whole endeavor, Tadashi still smirking from his antics on the road. Cassius loitered outside a minute, then decided that Rifun probably wasn't too keen on a fight at the moment and headed inside.

"How long are you really planning on keeping him?" Tadashi was asking, beating Cassius to the question as he walked into the small chamber.

"At least three days, just to make his father sweat a little," Rifun answered, "and to ensure that we have ample time to talk."

"I already told you he's your fabled Chivalrous Welshman," Cassius said. "We've already established that he has no Akari abilities to speak of."

"Which means he has no idea what's going on or the danger he is in. He needs to be warned and given a fighting chance."

"Well that's a polite way of saying you're going to train him to kill me."

"That sort of training would require many years, and I don't think you have that long."

Cassius ground his teeth but could not actually deny it. Meanwhile, Tadashi just looked confused and Isthim appeared infuriatingly thoughtful.

"And if we don't teach him now, he will not understand our plans moving forward with the elections," Rifun added.

If it was intended to soften the blow of Cassius' impending demise, it fell far short. Instead he just turned and said, "I guess I'll be checking in on the Akarin, then, and see if they've roused from their placid slumber."

He left the cave before anyone could respond. He barely remembered to don his Doug Disguise before heading to the Akarin fortress.

He wasted no time, storming his way up to the meeting rooms, and he made sure everyone along the way knew he was unhappy. It didn't occur to him until he was three feet from kicking down a door that if any of the council were moved by this event and contacted Micaiah, Micaiah would be forced to wonder just how Doug had found out when he hadn't contacted him. To Cassius' knowledge, he was the only one Micaiah was in contact with. On the other hand, Aklaq was a bit of a spiteful bitch. He might be able to say that Aklaq had told someone and he heard it from them, the fast-moving grapevine.

He would figure it out later, he thought, almost beating the door off its hinges in his rage. Unfortunately, this was not a full council meeting and only a handful of members were even present. Worse, it didn't even appear to be a formal meeting, but merely a convenient locale in which to trade gossip. As if there were really a difference.

"We have a problem!" Cassius-as-Doug announced loudly, almost shouting.

"Where is everyone?!"

"Not here," one of the other members sighed. "What's the problem now?"

"One of our members has been directly assaulted by the Cult, another has been kidnapped, and—"

"When was this?" another councilman inquired, mildly interested.

"Just a couple hours ago."

"And who was attacked? Who was taken?"

"Micaiah Durvin was the one attacked," Cassius-as-Doug reported. At the name, the other council members relaxed their slightly intrigued, not quite hostile, posture. Oh, it was only one of the little people, not one of the council. Cassius continued, "And Tommen Forbes was the one taken."

"Tommen Forbes?" the first inquired. "I don't recognize the name."

That wasn't surprising in the least, for multiple reasons, but even the benefit of the doubt was stretched thin here as Cassius said, "The Chivalrous Welshman. From the Books?"

The level of outrage at the initial announcement, hardly threatening to begin with, evaporated to something just above active interest. Not willing to let the momentum die, Cassius cut off any councilman who tried to speak.

"How long are we just going to sit here and let the Cult do whatever they want?! We sit by as they plot against the Time industry. We sit by as they grow an army! Now they have attacked one member and taken another!" He continued speaking over several sputtering protests. "And don't tell me that we can't know for sure that he's the Chivalrous Welshman. Does that really matter? Do we only care about people of standing and importance? The elections are coming up and we seem to be the only ones entirely unconcerned about what may happen!"

"Everything that has happened before will happen again," one councilman said sagely.

"Everything," Cassius-as-Doug stated. "Not everyone. And it is the everyone that we should be concerned about. How does it look if we do not even lift a finger to help?"

"If this was the same incident, then it sounds like Micaiah Durvin and Tommen Forbes have some history," another reasoned. "We may deduce, then, that this so-called Chivalrous Welshman is not powerful enough to save himself, which means he has little or no strength in the Akari, nor has he seen fit to introduce himself to us. All of the others of the Books have seen fit to do that much at least. And Micaiah clearly has not seen fit to bring him here. Therefore, he is unlikely to be the Chivalrous Welshman."

Cassius-as-Doug nodded emphatically. "All right, you say that Tommen didn't have the power to save himself, therefore he can't be the Chivalrous Welshman." He slammed his fist on the table. "Well we do have the power but refuse to use it! Can we conclude, then, that we are not Akarin?! Do we have any real advantage over him?! At least Micaiah tried to save him!"

Something happened, then, and Cassius could only describe it as a vision. He saw spirits of smoke and shadow, very much like the dragon in appearance, but more ethereal, and of different shapes and sizes. They surrounded the councilmen, as flighty as fog yet as strong as steel.

"Build up their defenses," the dragon hissed in his ear. "Make them impenetrable."

Pride was the name of this gang. Pride reinforced by Sloth. Cassius almost smiled. Rifun was worried about him bringing harm to Tommen, but there were plenty of enemies to go around, many of them disguised as friends.

Drown the Akarin, then. Drown them in their own pride, their own stupid certainty that no harm would ever come to them. Build the walls that would be their prison. Drown the Akarin, kill Rifun, leave Julianna, kill Isthim and Misik...

By the time he was done berating them, the only thing that had changed was the stranglehold the evil spirits had on the Akarin council members. Though there were only half a dozen of them present, it would leech out and spread among the others. That was the power of gossip and shared indignation. How dare he question them! How dare he call them out!

He hoped his expression was sufficiently frustrated when he left, because he actually felt like laughing. If the Cult ever did get around to actually trying to wipe out the Akarin, it would be a piece of cake.

He returned to Earth, just outside the cave. The Grunjor started dismantling itself, but Cassius put a hand up. The Grunjor did not understand this gesture and continued to take itself apart just enough that Cassius could go inside. Cassius just shook his head and moved off several yards.

Checking Doug's phone, he found a missed call from Micaiah. There was no message left, but even if there were, Cassius called him back anyway.

"I heard," Cassius-as-Doug began as soon as Micaiah picked up.

"Good, then I don't have to explain that part."

"We should start by —"

"We're going scorched earth, Doug," Micaiah cut in. "But not on Earth, and not in the Akarin."

"Well, I just got done with the Akarin council and probably would have spent my time better at a casino. But if you're not doing anything on Earth, and you're not going before the Akarin council, what are you doing?"

"If we can't wake the gatekeepers, we have to warn the victims. We're going all out, just telling everyone that Cassius is the Missing Zero Hour, back for revenge, and he's got the Cult of the Akari with him. All of this craziness lately, especially what just happened, it's not hard to get people riled up. What makes it even better, is telling everyone that they have a hacker with them who is poised to sabotage the election results."

"How do you know that?" Cassius wouldn't say he wasn't alarmed, but he was also genuinely curious.

"Unrelated pursuit of one Runner turned up a hideout of Tadashi Hajiku, another Runner, and he appears to be in league with the Cult as well. Given his skill with computers, why wouldn't they do something like that?"

Cassius-as-Doug grunted an agreement. "I see your point. Keep me informed of your progress. I might have to lend my loud mouth to this as well."

He hung up and hurried toward the cave, shedding his Disguise. He was two steps from the mouth when he ran into Rifun who was on his way out. Rifun held a paper out to him.

"Tadashi's list," Rifun reported.

Cassius took it and glanced over it. A dozen names or so, a few underlined or circled or both. He wondered if any of them had been the one to lead the Timekeepers to his lair.

"While you're doing that, I'm going to run some errands," Rifun told him.

"Seeing how I've been banished from the clubhouse, when and where should we regroup?" Cassius asked, intentionally focusing on the paper.

"Be back here in three days. That should be sufficient time to break down some of Walter's tougher barriers."

Cassius nodded, turned, and started walking away. Three days to kill twelve people? Not even a challenge. Time to see what other mischief he could come up with.

Conversation

"Somehow...the twins have managed to do more damage to our plans than the entirety of the Akarin," Rifun mused distastefully. "They may have even managed to do more damage than we have done ourselves."

He and Cassius, in Disguise, stood in the Wheel Archives, leaning against a wall, simply watching the goings-on around them and, more importantly, across the open atrium. With some help from the Archive secretaries, the Grandfathers were combing through the section dealing with any and all Hands and Hand candidates throughout all history of the Wheel. Some had migrated into general Time Agent records, though there were a few billion of those and might take at least a few minutes to peruse.

"This is why you kill your enemies," Cassius growled. "You don't coddle them. You don't play around with them. At best, you get one chance to recruit them. After that, you maneuver them into submission as quickly as possible and then kill them."

"I'm flattered, then, that it took so long for you to decide to kill me," Rifun commented casually.

"Where are Isthim and Misik? Why are the Grandfathers still here?"

"Interestingly enough, this little snafu is providing some exceptional opportunities for them to finalize their plans for the elections. With all the information they're poring over, they know which Grandfathers will be loyal, which ones must be dealt with. They're compiling a list of all past Hands still living, to get rid of them. And they may or may not be investigating some of the floor plans of the Seat of the Hands, to find any and all possible escape routes and secret hideaways."

Cassius folded his arms. "I assume they're also collecting all of the information being turned up about me."

"And your...four hundred aliases that you planted?" Rifun raised a brow.

"I figured it would keep them busy, and it is. But they're also collecting information about you, too. You know that, right?"

Rifun shifted his stance but did not reply.

"As much as we're going to try and take over the Wheel and the Time industry on Inauguration Day, the Borelians still have it out for us," Cassius reminded him. "They still intend to enslave us."

"They intend for us to enslave ourselves," Rifun corrected.

"We should kill them. Come Inauguration Day, all hell breaks loose, take advantage of the chaos to be rid of them."

"Don't think that thought hasn't crossed my mind. However, in the interest of not having them turn on us immediately, I was thinking something along the lines of...controlled opposition and manipulation. I don't think you would have any reservations about acting in such capacity again." When Cassius gave him a look that was half annoyed and half confused, he clarified, "We take over the Wheel, let things settle down. Then you start taking out the Borelians, but frame other resistance groups that will undoubtedly crop up. Your primary scapegoat should obviously be—"

"The Akarin," Cassius finished. "Frame them, the Borelians go after them, weakens both sides for us."

"Exactly. I think that is when your masquerading as Doug will pay off the most. I know you're not much for theatrics, but you will get to have your big reveal and stun the audience when they realize who they've actually been dealing with."

Cassius grinned but said nothing.

The two of them moved to new positions, separated by several rows of Glass tablets but still within general sight of the working Grandfathers. Because of their Disguises, they had been unwilling to risk the blood sample needed to acquire the chips required to read the information in the tablets. The Akari allowed them to understand others, making the translators unnecessary, and they were counting on the sheer volume of portal traffic to bury their comings and goings.

Even so, Rifun was debating how much of a risk it would really be to grab a chip and see what kind of information the Archives contained about various dimensions. He doubted they would have much on how to build one, at least not mechanically, but even understanding how they worked might be beneficial. Maybe some of the Scientifically Superior races utilized interdimensional travel and he could study their methods and theories. As it was, the best he had was what he had gotten from the Book of Abilities, any observations he might have gleaned from Anagalisgi's Book, though it had been a while since he'd read it, and half a dozen failed attempts outside the cave.

He made a few casual laps around the area. Was there a way he could use Electricity to view the information in the tablets? Probably not, because the chips themselves were what took "fluid coding" (whatever that was) and attached it to a language. The chip told the tablet which species the reader was, which planet they were most likely from, and gave the patron a list of languages to choose from. He would need to find another human from Earth and steal their chip in order to use the tablets.

Cassius tracked him down. If he thought he was acting casually, well, he wasn't much of an actor. "I'm leaving. Think I'll head to the fortress and see what they're up to. Maybe I can prod some opposition, call on Micaiah's allies and have them ready for the ever-looming 'something.' "

"Reasonable," Rifun told him. "I'm going to keep an eye on things here for a little longer, then go back to the cave."

"Enjoy camping."

His farewell was more snarky than sincere and his departure was not as subtle as Rifun would have preferred, with heavy footsteps, vocalized displeasure, and a few "accidental" bumps into the rows. The Grandfathers appeared too consumed with their work to notice, although they possessed infinitely more self-control and probably took note of him anyway. The good thing was that Cassius maintained his Disguise. Assuming he could keep it together long enough to get out of the Wheel, everything would probably be fine.

Rifun weighed the likelihood of him coming to Cassius' defense if something did happen. The man did not need defending per se, but what would his own role be if there were an incident here? Thinking about it, maybe he should get back to Earth and avoid such a situation. He wasn't going to be able to read the tablets, the Grandfathers were hardly entertainment, and time was ticking.

He left the Archives, perhaps the only quiet area remaining in the Wheel. Outside, in the marketplaces, panic buying was in full swing. Prices always went up around election time, as no one was really sure what would happen with new Hands and any new or changed laws that might come from them. Now, though, with the threat ranging from the revenge of an undead Zero Hour to another Dispersal—and Rifun couldn't say that either of those prospects was entirely untrue—people were desperate to stock up on Time. For some, the notion was ridiculous; Bortans already boasted an average lifespan of three centuries. For others, it was entirely feasible; the Minitine had been intentionally introduced to Time, and their average lifespan had gone from approximately nine years to over one hundred, thanks to regular use of Time Capsules. (It did not change their natural lifespans, but with common use among the populace, they had, like all those afflicted with slowed aging, artificially inflated their years.)

He remained very cognizant of his Disguise, keeping it as tight as possible, constantly fixing all the little blemishes that might pop up in the hustle and bustle of the markets. Incidental touches were of little consequence, but anything too forceful could expose him, assuming anyone was paying close attention.

Still, he made it to the portal room without incident and returned to Earth, thirty feet from the mouth of the cave where Isthim and Tadashi still babysat Tommen. He shed his Disguise. At his appearance, Donojok started disassembling himself. Rifun put up a hand.

"Not necessary," he told the rock alien. "Thank you for the consideration."

Donojok paused, then put himself back the way he was, blocking the cave. No one quite understood the Grunjor, but even they appreciated common courtesies.

"Cassius is out on a mission, and I expect to be gone for several hours," Rifun told him. "As always keep an eye on things, and warn those inside of any mischief."

Donojok did not respond. From what Rifun understood about his species, when he was in such a disassembled form, his consciousness was somehow linked with the surrounding landscape, giving him a greater range of earthen sensibilities. He could see and hear deep into the earth and for at least a hundred yards in any direction, but doing so cost his ability to verbally communicate. Rifun just assumed the rock alien agreed, turned, and headed into the trees.

He did not need to go far, just slid down an embankment and followed a seasonal riverbed about thirty yards to a small clearing. The clearing itself was unnecessary, but it helped to cut down on surprises.

He'd been using this place to practice dimensional travel, separating the dimensions, and even trying to fashion a dimension of his own. The problem was that he was a three-dimensional being, limited by Time and, to a lesser extent in this context, Space. Trying to get into a dimension where Time was more malleable and maybe even capable of moving backwards as easily as forwards, that was a little tougher.

Anagalisgi lived and walked among the spirits. He had sacrificed himself to rescue a friend. Julianna had also become trapped in the in-between dimension, although she had yet to report any spirits of any alignment. Were they in two separate dimensions, then? In *Alpha Wolf*, Anagalisgi claimed he had not died, but he could only be taken at his word. Would he know if he had died since he had, perhaps, died in such an unconventional way? Maybe he should investigate things from the Krydik's point of view at some point.

He first went to the shrine he had erected in the northeast section of the clearing and bowed to pray. When attempting to enter someone's house, it was only polite to knock. He also wanted to be sure he was going to be greeted by good spirits and not malevolent demons. Yes, he was going through all this hassle in order to kill a demon, but when it came to training and experiments, he wanted as few distractions as possible. When he was finished, he stood and headed to the center of the clearing.

The greatest success he'd seen so far had started with a portal. This made some sense, seeing how getting trapped in a portal while traversing dimensions was the most common way of falling into the in-between dimension. Of course, this also made it incredibly difficult to do his experiments because portals were notoriously difficult to hold by oneself, and he was not entirely sure how he might utilize the technology of the Wheel to hold it open yet remain on this side of it. The simple answer was to enlist the help of someone else, have them construct the portal, but he wasn't keen on alerting the Hands to such activities. Nor was he certain what effect such experiments might have on the Wheel, and he really didn't want to blow it up.

So it was that the best he could do was open a portal to somewhere, most often a remote area of Madagascar. Once it was as stable as he could get it, he would get as close as possible without actually going through and study it.

Portals did not appear to have spatial dimension, despite being of common doorway size and having to deal with the extreme discomfort of the passage. Anything Rifun had managed to read about them tended to favor one of two opinions: either portal dimensions were based in Space at an infinitesimally small calculation, so they might be likened to a Mobius loop; or they were actually based in Time, and so were more closely related to a Klein bottle. There were a scattering of other opinions and theories, but those were the two most popular.

Rifun had done many hours of research on both concepts and had decided that both theories were true. When looking at it from a purely secular point of view, yes, it seemed to favor the Mobius loop, twisting space and condensing it into a physical doorway to get from point A to point B. The discomfort one felt was the simple, physical transversal of this singular plane, becoming disoriented as a traveler twisted through the black hole and the Core of the Wheel and then reoriented in his destination. And yet, when one considered the existence of other dimensions, especially ones greater than three dimensions, the singular Mobius loop quickly evolved into a Klein bottle, multiple loops glued together. But because Klein bottles could not be seen in static, three-dimensional space, one had to consider Time as part of the natural equation. The mortal beings were running around on their singular, three-dimensional loop, while the spirits were traversing an entirely different plane where Time was as tangible as water or earth. Somehow, he needed to cross that boundary between the loop and the bottle.

Even as he thought it, he had a minor epiphany. Two loops made a bottle. Once that happened, the boundary vanished. The spirits were here all the time. There was never not a bottle. There was no wall, only a small fence, enough to keep three-dimensional beings in but not enough to break the bottle. And that infinitesimally small space that a portal took up was the gap in that fence, a hole just big enough for someone to possibly get a peek into that fourth dimension. This was the nature of the Land In Between, the balancing point between dimensions.

He released the portal he'd been holding, as much to relieve himself and minimize the possibility of a migraine as think about all of these things that were now starting to make tangible sense.

It was no real trouble getting from this dimension into the in-between dimension. Two-dimensional things could be embedded in three-dimensional space, but three-dimensional things could not be embedded in two-dimensional space except that they shed some property of their third dimension. Similarly, three-dimensional things could be embedded in four-dimensional space, but four-dimensional things could not be embedded in three-dimensional space except that they gave up that fourth dimensional property.

Julianna, as a three-dimensional being, had no trouble getting into the in-between dimension, and she could even bring other objects into the dimension with her. However, she lost her normal Time and Akari abilities because they were not naturally attuned to the extra fourth dimension. But she had picked up several abilities that were so attuned, such as the ability to nearly teleport and to view events of the past.

The spirits, both good and evil, as four-dimensional beings, then, had to give up that fourth property of Time, the ability to be anywhere at any time, when they visited mortals. And they became bound by the rules of three dimensions. As Lalao had said, the evil spirits were naturally very weak. They would gladly give up that fourth property because it meant a fairer fight for them. Seeing how mortals were the prize to be won, there was even greater incentive for the evil spirits to try and trick and kill mortals and for the good spirits to try and stop them.

Excited now, Rifun opened another portal and approached it from an angle. Kneeling, he slowly moved his head around it, looking for the exact spot the manifold vanished. There were no edges. There were no boundaries. Everything was a single surface that could be molded without changing the fundamental properties of the thing, which meant he should be able to reach inside that tiny dimensional space of a portal and pull it inside out.

It was a sudden change in the portal that caused him to jump back a good four feet. He wasn't even sure what he was watching initially. Studying the spot for a moment, he realized that a part of the portal was missing, like taking a circular piece out of the spot where he'd been trying to find the manifold's boundary. But if he was right, it wasn't a circle, it was actually a sphere, because a sphere also had no boundary. The only indication he had that this spherical area even existed, aside from the absence of the portal, was a distortion so subtle it made Akari Band distortions look as obvious as Time Band distortions. The only reason he noticed the distortion was because of the juxtaposition with the absence of the portal. Compared to the surrounding landscape, however, it was basically invisible. He hoped this was a true thing and not simply his injured brain missing something.

The sphere was about the size of a basketball. After staring at it for a few more seconds and being fairly confident it wasn't really doing anything, Rifun approached it once more. Now that it was started, he had no trouble making it bigger. He refrained from covering the portal entirely, although trying to hold an oddly-shaped portal was proving to be a hundred times harder than holding a standard shape portal.

With sweat snaking down his neck and face and a drum starting to pound in his head, he tried his first real experiment. Using a small pocketknife, he gave himself a cut on the hand. He put his hand inside the sphere. He knew when he crossed the threshold from three-dimensional space into four-dimensional, which gave him some hope. When he went to heal his hand, whether by Akari or Time, he could not. He pulled his hand out of the sphere and had no troubles healing it. He put his hand back in and snapped his fingers several times. He heard nothing. And yet, why could he still see it? It didn't make sense, but the fact that he had gotten this far was quite exciting.

He withdrew his hand and shrunk the sphere, stuffing it back into the in-between dimension. Then he let the portal collapse and made his way to a nearby tree to sit and rest.

It worked. He'd managed to turn a portal inside out. He'd crossed a boundary that did not technically exist.

He straightened where he sat against the tree. Of course, even Julianna could pull things into the dimension with her, and the majority of him had remained safely in his location on his three-dimensional Mobius loop, which was likely the reason he could still see his hand even if he couldn't heal it or hear the snap. What if he put something inside the sphere, wholly and intentionally, and then tried to get it out? That would probably be his next experiment. If he could do that, he would not only have a way to rescue Julianna from the Land In Between, but it might just erase that terrible tagline, "From Which No One Has Ever Returned."

After a few minutes, he stood and stretched. Well, that would be an experiment for another day. He needed to sleep on it a little, process everything he'd done and learned. Actually, first he needed a bath and a change of clothes. He was the one babysitting Tommen tonight and he wasn't fond of sleeping in his own sweat.

An hour or so later, with the sun painting colors on the western sky, Donojok disassembled himself to let Isthim and Tadashi out and Rifun in.

"No change," Tadashi reported flippantly, not even stopping for courtesies as he opened a portal and disappeared.

"The wardens appear in worse spirits than the inmates it seems," Rifun observed.

"He's more excited about the work you have him doing in the elections," Isthim told him. "So am I. One child cannot be worth more than these elections and our plans for them."

"I understand your reservations, I really do. My people are also a traditionally collectivist society. The people over the man. But that does not mean that an individual is entirely unimportant, for the group is comprised entirely of individuals. And he is an individual who has been chosen by the Author and gifted with his own Books, even if they don't exist yet. Myself and Cassius, Tommen, Micaiah, Aklaq, we are a group of chosen individuals. We have to work together as best we can. And it is no coincidence that we are all in the same place at the same time."

Isthim hesitated for a moment, then nodded. "Fine."

"It won't be much longer, I promise," Rifun told her. "We'll offload Tommen before Christmas, this way he can have a lovely holiday with friends and family. We take over the Wheel at the elections, then come back for...negotiations with the Time industry and the Akarin. But from a much stronger position."

"A solid enough plan on paper. Now let's carry it out."

Rifun held out an arm. "I've got this watch. You do what you need to."

They parted ways. Once Rifun was inside the cave, Donojok again assembled himself into the mouth, cutting off all but a sliver of outside light. The only other light to be had was from a small fire in the cave where they were keeping Tommen.

The teenager was still awake, sitting by the fire, though he seemed to have caught on that they meant him no harm, and he did not react to Rifun's appearance except to simply glance up and note it.

Rifun grabbed some sticks from the pile and added them to the fire. An air current running through this cave did a mediocre job of clearing out the smoke, probably due to Donojok blocking the exit. But they weren't suffocating, and an occasional invocation of the Akari to push the smoke out did wonders. With the fire tended, Rifun sat down and got comfortable.

"I read about you," he said, looking at Tommen. "The boy everyone called crazy because he thought he was from the nineteenth century."

"Yeah," Tommen murmured.

"Walked out of the old salt cave clutching a journal he had found. Swore it was 1855. Medics thought he'd just been knocked silly by the car. Well, you probably were knocked silly, but still you maintained it was 1855."

"Concussed, confused, uneducated, autistic, and probably a dozen more labels and diagnoses, I'm sure."

Tommen did not look at him, but his expression spoke volumes.

"If you could go back in time, would you?" Rifun wondered.

Tommen shrugged. "As I am? I guess. Go back and stop myself? I don't know."

"Worried about paradoxes and whatnot? Going back to kill your grandfather and such?"

"Kind of, I guess. But if I could go back as I am, well, it's only a little time lost, right? And hey, I'd have a lot of knowledge to bring back. If I went back, literally turned back time, I mean...it's like rewinding a movie. Rewind it all you want, go back as far as you want, it's always going to happen the same way. I'm always going to go into that cave."

Rifun nodded. "Interesting way to put it."

Tommen gave him a look. "Let me guess, this Akari that you've been babbling about can turn back time, too?"

"It only accesses the properties of the universe already available to us." Rifun straightened a leg. "You're a smart kid. You like science?"

"That's a broad question. Science encompasses everything from theoretical thermonuclear astrophysics to veterinary medicine."

"I'll take that as a yes. The science I refer to is a bit of a blend of physics and mathematics. Have you heard of a Mobius loop?" Tommen shook his head. "Have you ever taken a strip of paper and looped it to itself, but given it one twist so that it becomes one continuous path?"

"I did that when I used to make paper garland for Christmas. I thought it was just something cool."

"Well, that is a Mobius loop, a non-orientable surface that makes it impossible to distinguish clockwise and counterclockwise. You can walk the entirety of the surface and never actually have to cross a boundary, an edge."

Tommen shrugged in that teenager way of not wanting to show too much interest. "Cool."

"If you put two Mobius loops together, edge-to-edge, you get a Klein bottle, or a 3D representation of one as they do not actually exist in our space, our dimension. In order for one to truly exist, they must be viewed in a space where Time is a tangible dimension."

"Why the hell are you out kidnapping random teenagers if you're so smart? Or are you just saying things to make yourself look smart so you can try to strike up a conversation with me?"

"I admit, I'm not an expert," Rifun said, shrugging. "If I were, and with the abilities the Akari affords, well, I wouldn't mind going back and changing a few things in my life."

"So how does this imaginary bottle work?"

Rifun held out a hand as if cupping a ball. "Imagine a sphere. You can put your finger on any point on that sphere and you will always be touching the same surface of that sphere without crossing any boundaries. If that sphere were malleable—" He pretended to push on the ball. "—you could mold and shape it in any way and it would, mathematically, be the exact same object. If you were to add Time as a dimension—"

"You could go to any point in time on that object, mold it and shape it, and it would be the same mathematical shape," Tommen finished.

"Exactly." Rifun lowered his hand. "Some have postulated that the shape of the universe is that of a Klein bottle, but we, as three-dimensional beings, cannot actively perceive it as such. Those species with relatively short lifespans, such as humans, are at an even greater disadvantage. We only see the sphere."

"Some people say that our reality is a simulation," Tommen countered. "Everything around us, just computer programs. Our consciousness, AI algorithms. Maybe we're trapped in pods like The Matrix. Maybe we don't even really exist."

"Just words on a page," Rifun quipped.

"A little more sophisticated than that, but yeah, basically."

"And what if it were discovered that such is true, that we are just computer programs created at the whim of some cosmic programmer?"

Tommen opened his mouth as if to speak, thought a moment, shut it, shrugged again, shifted position, then said, "I don't know."

Rifun grinned. "Come on. You must have some opinion. What if there is an omniscient god out there, it's just not the one everyone thought?"

The teenager gave him a sarcastic look. "Then I guess a lot of computer programs are going to delete themselves while some computer programs are going to group together to try and delete other computer programs."

Rifun laughed. "That's one way to look at it, I suppose."

A silence settled over them, though it only lasted for a few minutes.

"What would you go back and change?" Tommen asked. "If you could tap into this Klein bottle?"

Rifun nodded slowly. "I think I would make better choices regarding my family life. I would better spend my energy on worthwhile pursuits rather than getting so wrapped up in petty fights with people who would never respect me, no matter what I did or didn't do."

Tommen scoffed. "I know what that's like."

"Unfortunately, everything we have done and had done to us has brought us to this time, these moments. And seeing how we are three-dimensional beings, we cannot simply change places on this Klein bottle that may or may not even exist."

"But as Time Agents, we do bend Time. It is tangible to us."

"Only in the barest of senses." Rifun shifted position. "I expect that, one day, if humanity were to become a real part of the Time industry, more work might be put into such dynamics of the universe."

"Why would that make a difference, if there are already hundreds or thousands of other species who are Scientifically Advancing and Engaged, or better?" Tommen made a flippant gesture. "Humanity isn't the end-all of knowledge; we're not the saviors of the universe."

No, just its demise, Rifun thought, considering both Cassius and the Tacagans. Instead of this, he said, "True enough, I suppose."

Tommen spit a laugh and, staring intently at the fire, said, "I mean, if your Akari is so great and mystical that you have to hide in a cave and put a babysitter on one dumb teenager...well...it doesn't look good for you." He dared a couple glances at Rifun, trying to gauge his reaction.

Rifun just grinned. The kid had spirit. If only he understood what he was up against. With any luck, he wouldn't have to find out the hard way. "I don't expect you to, but just believe me when I say that being here really is your best option at the moment."

If things went well, then within the next week, Cassius would be dead, Julianna would be free of the in-between dimension, and he could focus on the elections and taking over the Wheel. Once that was secure, then he could worry about the Borelians. He just needed a little more practice with this whole dimension thing, turning it inside out or however one wanted to describe what he'd done with the portal earlier.

In the morning, he would get a hold of Julianna and see if she was up to some experimenting. He didn't necessarily feel comfortable pulling her out before Cassius was dead, but if he could guarantee or even give her a strong hope of escape, well, it would lighten the load, say it that way. He would try that, then see about Cassius. If he could make this opening or forming or splitting of dimensions more reliable, he might actually have a shot at killing this evil spirit inside Cassius. Or, if the spirit was just using Cassius as a hideaway to run from good spirits, putting it back in its own dimension might attract the attention of the good spirits to come and finish it off. If he himself didn't have to do any real fighting, that would be great.

The following morning, once Isthim had returned — unhappy about babysitting detail and doing it as a prescribed duty only — Rifun returned to the clearing. As always, he prayed first. When he stood, he called Julianna.

Rifun did not fully understand how Tadashi got the technology to work, only that it utilized the Energy of the dimension, perhaps the same Energy that kept the two dimensions separated. What would happen if he put the phone inside the sphere?

Despite trying to keep things as simple and succinct as possible, he knew the majority of it went over her head. Still, the prospect of escaping from the in-between dimension held a certain urgent appeal and she agreed to take part in a small experiment.

"Take something from this dimension into that dimension," Rifun instructed. "A rock, a stick, nothing fancy. Place it here on this flat stone. I'm going to make an attempt. The first step will just be seeing the object."

"All right," Julianna said, her voice indicating some physical effort. "I've found a good size rock here. I am placing it...on the stone. It's sitting on this sort of darker splotch here in the middle."

"Perfect. And just so there are no complications, I'm going to hang up first."

"Understandable."

He ended the call without ceremony and turned his attention to the flat stone where the alleged rock sat, just out of reach in another dimension. Taking a breath, he began.

Start with what he knew. Step one, portal. He opened it in the area he believed the rock to be. Step two, find the infinitesimally small threshold, the boundary between dimensions. Step three, reach inside and bring the dimension out to be remolded.

Just from the nearly-invisible sphere ballooning out of the portal, he knew he succeeded at recreating his efforts from the previous day. Unfortunately, no matter how big he managed to make the sphere, he was unable to see the rock. Even putting his hand inside the sphere, he could not feel it. He still had no desire to put his whole body in there lest he be unable to leave, and he dropped everything.

A minute later, his phone rang.

"What did it look like on your side?" he wondered.

"It was...quite noticeable," she began. She fumbled through several nonstarters "It was like...looking at a ball, but as if it had been turned inside out. And there was color to it."

"Color?"

"Yes. Rather vivid color."

"It's nearly invisible on this side."

"I can only report, Rifun. I don't understand."

"I know." Believe me, I know. "Did you see my hand at all? I didn't see or feel the rock."

He could imagine her shrugging. "Of course I saw your hand. Nothing spectacular happened if that's what you're asking."

"I don't need spectacular. Mundane will do. Now let's try it in reverse."

Again he hung up. This time he found a rock and placed it on the stone, in a different spot than where she said she put her rock. Portal, sphere, make sure the rock was completely within the sphere, then let it all go.

The rock vanished.

Thirty seconds later, the phone rang.

"It's easy to get in. Quite a bit harder to get out," Julianna sighed.

"So I'm noticing," Rifun mused. "It gives me something to think about anyway."

"Well, you might want to think fast, because time is short and Isthim doesn't look happy."

Rifun turned and hung up when he saw Isthim crossing the clearing, heading toward him.

"Something wrong?" he wondered.

"How long is this going to go on?" she asked testily. "Prisoners and hostages are only useful if we use them. We have gotten past the fear and psychological torture and we are entering the retaliation phase. The police will be looking for us."

"My dear, they already are," Rifun told her.

"We end this. Or I end him."

"I'm guessing you don't mean Cassius."

Isthim lashed out at him. He dodged swiftly and took a few steps back, hands up in light surrender. "All right. I'll get the ball rolling, but it will still be a couple of days. I'm trying out a few experiments."

He explained what he was doing. At the very least, it replaced the irritation on Isthim's face with intrigue.

"Fine," she said at last. "But we have other work to do."

He made a gesture and she led the way back to the mouth of the cave. She ducked inside to retrieve Tommen while Rifun dialed a number. The line rang...and rang...and rang. For a moment, Rifun was worried no one was going to answer. Then, "Tommen Forbes' phone."

"Oh, good, for a second I wondered if something awful had happened to you, Walter," Rifun greeted. He paused a second to see if the man would speak. When he didn't, Rifun needled him a little. "After all, Christmas season, missing loved ones, it can make things very gloomy and depressing."

"Rifun," Walter acknowledged stiffly.

"Ah, so he does speak. But not much. Which means he is keeping a tight lid on his words, for vile they are as they race around his mind."

"What do you want, Rifun? Terms, I expect."

"You know, Walter, I have to say I am very impressed by your determination and your resourcefulness. You found every clue we set out for you to find, and even a few we thought were very well-hidden. But your detective brain sleuthed them out. More than that, you managed to do some very serious damage to our political campaign. I am both impressed and very, very annoyed."

"Where is my son?"

"Your son, you call him? I think not."

"Where is he?"

Rifun waved a hand though Walter could not see. "Safe and sound, I assure you. But where he is, is not—"

"I want to talk to him."

Rifun glanced toward the cave where Isthim held Tommen fast. Just playing a part, he thought. Kidnapper. Captor. All because Cassius was too happy to play the role of murderer. Still he nodded once and held the phone to Tommen's ear.

"Dad?!" Tommen asked.

Rifun could hear Walter on the other end, stoic determination melting into blubbering relief. "Tommen?! Oh, thank God. Are you all right?"

Tommen shrugged uselessly. "Yeah, I'm fine. I mean, as good as I can be. I don't know where I am. I mean, I'm in a cave. I haven't been outside since, I don't know, a long time it feels like."

"Tommen, listen, just—"

Rifun removed the phone and got back on the line. "There is your proof of life."

"What do you want, Rifun?" Walter asked, obviously struggling to keep his voice calm.

"As you well know, this message is being recorded thanks to an app we had installed on Tommen's phone. So, just like the first time, I expect this message to be played to anyone and everyone you deem necessary for the operation to rescue your dear boy, which I know you are already formulating in your mind.

"Now, this is how it is going to work. Today is Friday. Monday afternoon, at three o'clock, we will be at the shipping docks on the east side of town. One of the ships is going to be conveniently late to pick up its load, but provide us ample time to negotiate." He glanced at Isthim and made a gesture. She nodded once. It would be taken care of. He turned his attention back to the phone. "We already have the journal. Now we just need Lily Guile. Bring her to Warehouse 8 at exactly three p.m. to trade for your precious son. If you are not there by three-oh-five, your son, you, and everyone involved in your little rescue operation will die. And you've already seen Cassius' handiwork."

"If your goal was Lily and the journal, why get me and Tommen involved like you have?" Walter wondered.

Rifun chuckled, if only because he couldn't believe this was happening. Why had the Author brought him here to meet them so early, before they were even useful Akari-bearers? How was this, kidnapping teenage boys with few or no Time abilities, going to help him kill the dragon, rescue Julianna, and take back the Wheel for the Akari-bearers? This was absurd. The best he could manage at the moment was, "Oh, dear Walter, you already know the answer to that question. And one more thing. I expect that Tommen might have a few questions for you once you are reunited. I won't tell you them now, of course, I'll leave that for a father-son discussion. Perhaps Monday night, after all this is over, when you two have dinner together. That is your plan, isn't it, Walter? To have dinner with your son Monday night?"

He could hear the man grinding his teeth. "That's one plan, yes."

"Excellent." Rifun looked at Isthim again. "So I will leave the reservations where they stand. Dinner for two, seven o'clock, at a lovely little Italian restaurant. You know the one. Already paid, too, with dessert and gratuity." Isthim rolled her eyes but silently agreed.

"I expect it will be very nice," Walter growled.

"Wonderful. Then we have come to an understanding. Half the battle is already over, Walter. Now you just need to deliver the goods. Monday at three, Warehouse 8. Oh, and one last little detail I forgot to mention. You are not to mention or play this message for anyone or start rallying your team until Sunday. And believe me, Walter, if you do...we'll know. And the same consequences will ensue as if you are late. Enjoy your weekend."

Rifun hung up and stared at the phone, resisting the urge to throw it at the rock face and smash it to smithereens. What the hell was this? He needed to figure out a way to get the evil spirit out of Cassius. He had imagined that it would come to something like this. A direct assault was unlikely to work, but if he could use a chaotic situation, like a hostage negotiation or a likely shootout with police, maybe he could make something work.

He returned to the clearing, trying experiment after experiment. He lost track of time except to note when the sun was up and when it wasn't. He may have slept a bit, but even then it was restless, dreamless. He could access the in-between dimension just fine, it was just a matter of getting back out. Was there a way he could push Cassius in and kill him and the evil spirit while still in this dimension? He didn't see why not. He could push a rock into the dimension and he could fire a bullet at the rock with expected effect, all of it apparently in the in-between dimension.

A bullet would kill a man no matter where he was, but would it have any effect on the evil spirit? Sadly, no. He would need a ritual of some form. Considering that tomorrow—or he thought it was tomorrow—was the day they were supposed to do this exchange, he didn't have a lot of time to come up with something, gather any needed ingredients or make sacrifices.

He needed to be proactive about this.

Despite being very mountainous, it was surprisingly difficult to find anyone with goats in the area. Americans loved their cows, it seemed. But goats were not entirely unknown, and he found a small farm where several small goats were nibbling on some green table scraps.

He wouldn't say he actually inquired about the goat that he Banded and stole, but he left a little bit of cash (that he took from someone else seeing how he had no American currency on him presently) under the milk pail in the milking shed. Despite only being maybe fifty pounds, the critter panicked after going through a portal, throwing its horned head around and catching Rifun in the jaw once.

Carefully, Rifun set the goat down, keeping hold of its nylon collar. It jumped a few times but soon stood quietly, looking around and bleating. Rifun walked it over to the shrine and knelt beside the goat to pray. He made the prayer longer than normal, if only because soft words seemed to calm the agitated caprine. When he was finished, he stood, took a knife, and cut the goat's throat. The animal opened its mouth to cry, but only blood came out. Its legs started to wobble. Finally the front legs gave out, followed by the rear. It twitched some, then went still.

"You think tomorrow is going to go that bad?"

Rifun turned to see Cassius approaching.

"Isthim told you," Rifun guessed.

"Well, you had disappeared, so someone had to. Unless you wanted me to skip this little party?" Cassius' expression was mildly accusing.

"I didn't expect I would be able to keep you away."

Cassius gestured to the dead goat and the blood pooling around the shrine. "As I said, you expect it to go poorly for us?"

"Asking for help never hurt anyone."

Cassius barked a laugh. "That's a lie and you know it. You look at me and plot my death. Because I asked for help."

Rifun kept an even tone. "I'm asking for a different kind of help."

Cassius shook his head. "Your gods are the same as mine."

"I assure you, they are not."

"They are," he insisted. "They just use you for nicer things."

Rifun sighed. "Why are you here?"

"Just making sure you're still alive. Making sure you're going to show up tomorrow."

"I didn't think you'd want me there."

"I don't. But we all have a role to play, including you. You are there to be the face of things, the nice guy."

"The fall guy, you mean."

Cassius made a broad, mocking gesture. "This was your idea. You wanted to fuck around with a teenager and his fugitive father. The Borelians are obviously more concerned about the Wheel and the elections. I don't give a shit either way except this seems to be something exciting and there's a lot of death involved. But don't pretend like you're just being tossed about by fate. You chose to do this. You want to."

"No, actually I don't."

The dark-skinned man pointed to his face. "Do you have a kill switch in your face? Is some demon spirit holding an ax to your throat, or maybe to your head? No? Then you chose this because you want it. You think it will accomplish something. Now see it through and don't fuck it up."

With that, Cassius stalked off, muttering to himself. Rifun just watched him go, feeling conflicted. He'd been out here all day, or more than a day, alone. Experimenting, trying, failing, praying. Finally he decided to make an offering and ask for guidance, and this was what he got. Was that his answer? No, it couldn't be. His ancestors were not the same as Cassius' demons. That made no sense. He was trying to destroy the demon. If they were one and the same...they wouldn't destroy each other. It just couldn't happen.

No. The spirits had heard his prayer and the demons had come to confuse and discourage him. Tomorrow, they would probably try to kill him, via Cassius, the police, or some other means. He would have to get the jump on them. They expected him to be cowardly and defensive, so he would have to go with an offensive play. Hit them hard and fast, go straight for the top. None of this circling and prowling and stalking.

He returned to his chambers in the officers building, hoping to rest well in the peace and quiet before all the excitement, but he just lay there, staring into the void. He had no dreams, no visions, just confusion and uncertainty swirling around in his head and heart. It should not have gotten to this point. Fate was fixed, it was always going to come to this. He had the ability to choose. Why would he choose this? What was he going to do now? What was he going to do with Tommen? Taking people hostage was not the best way to make friends. Try to make allies of the other chosen ones of the Author, and this was what happened. Send Micaiah to a Time Trial, kidnap Tommen and hold him for ransom.

He had to get rid of the demon inside Cassius, and probably Cassius himself.

Then the fog of evil would clear and maybe he could salvage the situation. If this were to end up in a Book, and he had no reason to think it wouldn't, he could use it to explain the situation. Reparations or penance of some form may be in order, true, but it would be a better starting point than a mass murderer and a race of slavers. And he didn't know what he was going to do about the Borelians.

Rifun figured he must have gotten some sleep, but he woke in the most dreadful mood. He didn't like the chill in the room. He didn't like the stone. He didn't want to open a portal back to Earth. He didn't want to do anything. He was going to kill a demon today, and the fact that he hadn't done it sooner really pissed him off.

He let out a breath, trying to find some calm, got annoyed by the idea of calm, and got out of bed. Was this how Cassius woke up every morning, with a pressing desire to kill everyone who talked to him? Was that just how he went through life? Was that natural, or was there a demon lurking about him, Rifun, right now, trying to really screw things up? Where were his ancestors? Were the evil spirits really that powerful?

He had only himself to blame, he figured, freshening himself up before returning to Earth. He had allowed this. He had delayed action, refused to act, and this evil spirit had gone from a minor nuisance to a cosmic terror.

He stormed into the cave just as soon as Donojok gave him enough space. His sudden flamboyancy caught everyone inside off-guard and everyone was suddenly scrambling to pack up.

"Let's move it!" he snarled. "Places to be, things to do, people to kill!"

For as much as they whined about how long this was taking and they hated babysitting duty, Rifun might have expected them to be waiting at the door for his arrival. Instead, the nicest way to describe them right now was confused.

He could only hope that the demon inside Cassius was just as confused.

This ended today.

Charleston, 2013

Excitation

kokumbo

Demons could be such braggarts. Cassius had a vague memory of a preacher saying something about, "When the demons stop lying and start attacking, that's how you know you've got them on the run."

It didn't make much sense back then. Truthfully, it didn't make a whole hell of a lot of sense now, but Cassius thought he might have gleaned a bit of meaning, or perhaps a more realistic version of it. The dragon was no longer playing games, no longer promising death and glory, because it no longer had to. The game was up. Cassius was marching toward his death, and there was no escaping it. Just as he had marched Richard to the gallows, Richard dumbly believing that he would be rescued at the last moment, so Cassius was just coming to realize, in that half a second before his neck snapped, that no one was coming to save him, not even himself. He was going to die.

And as Cassius had taken the bag off Richard's head so he could see everything one last time — under the guise of ensuring the crowd saw "his" face so they wouldn't notice when he was "swapped out" for someone else — now the dragon was showing him a few things, showing him the fruits of his labor and some of the mysteries beyond time and fate.

There were only two sides. There had only ever been two sides. Shadows and Whites. Evil and good. Black and white. There was no multi-faceted complexity; mortals had invented those to make themselves feel better. At the core of everything, there were only two.

The same spirits that drove Cassius also drove Rifun. They were never fighting each other, not really. They were dolls in different hands of the same child. Not dolls, puppets. That child had a game he wanted to play, an outcome he was fighting for, and he would use whichever puppets would get him closer to that goal, with no concern for the puppet itself. At the end of the day, the puppet was going back in the box, so what did it matter?

In a way, it made things easier. Fuck everything. Stop trying to keep the tool in perfect working order when it was only destined to be burned. Use him to smash and crash and cause as much destruction as possible. A shootout with police sounded like a hell of a way to go, and a bullet in the face would be entirely plausible. Maybe they would figure that Walter had done it and he would get a medal. How poetic.

It was a bit of a surreal experience, even for him, climbing in the van, knowing that he probably wasn't going to come back from this. The hand of death did not feel so heavy when one did not struggle to keep it at bay.

The ride to the shipping yard was less than pleasant. Roads in West Virginia were narrow and winding, and their condition ranged from rutted and falling off the hillside to brand new construction with the smell of fresh asphalt still in the air. Cornering was a nightmare and no one paid attention to the lines. Even with Rifun Banding to make traffic a minimal issue, there was more than one occasion where Tadashi was surprised by a car in the middle of the road on a blind corner and had to make a sudden, jarring course correction. The congestion of the freeway, even weaving through lanes, was preferable by far.

The shipping yard itself was impressive, if disgustingly industrial. A dingy fence ran the perimeter, chainlink in some spots, sheet metal in others, all of it in some state of disrepair. A row of warehouses sat against the easternmost section of fence, huge, looming beasts in the rapidly darkening light, casting long shadows of their own. A handful of other warehouses littered the yard, a testament to the previous boundaries of a growing business. But other than these few anchors, the shipping containers were what really mattered. Dozens of them, hundreds, thousands, Cassius didn't know. He just knew that they made a good maze. The little river freighter that was supposed to have taken a good number of these containers was quietly sitting at the dock.

Tadashi slammed the brakes, throwing everyone forward. "We're here." He glanced back. "Cops have got this place locked down, all the warehouses, no personnel."

Cassius got out of the van and peered through the fence. Indeed, that was how things appeared. He saw no shipping workers, but, Banding to look around and get a more intimate feel for the situation, there were a good number of cops around. He returned to the van where Rifun had a similar Band around himself and the others, excluding Tommen.

"Looks like we have three teams out there," Cassius said, cutting off whoever was speaking. "Two on the ground—one pretending to be sneaky—and one team of three snipers."

"Snipers are to be expected," Rifun said firmly. "That doesn't change how we're doing things." He started gesturing around. "Donojok will still act as our heavy. He's impervious to bullets, he can do whatever he wants, draw their attention away from us, shield us when he can. Tadashi will draw the fire from the snipers. Isthim is going after Lily Guile."

"But—!"

"She will bring Lily into the warehouse for you, Cassius. That's all after the shooting starts. Before then, I want you and her to disable the backup ground team."

"Why only them?" Tadashi asked, his tone bordering on whining. "Why not the snipers, too? Why not all of them?"

"It's only a threat, a warning. We are here for one purpose, to exchange Tommen for Lily Guile. We don't need to kill everyone here just because they exist and they are here. We act on a much larger, more consequential stage. These peanuts mean nothing." Cassius glared at Rifun, but the man pretended not to notice. "However, do not think that I am ordering you not to defend yourselves. This will turn ugly; I can almost guarantee it. And because I am tired of playing games and don't want to do this again, we are not leaving without Lily Guile, dead or alive."

It was something, anyway. Cassius just hoped he got to be the one to deliver the killing blow before the dragon killed him.

"I will keep Tommen with me," Rifun dithered on. "I'm the least likely to accidentally kill him, I think. He's only here for moral support anyway, and to keep us from getting shot on sight."

"How will we know when to leave?" Tadashi wondered. "If we're not here to kill everyone, how will we know when Lily has been captured?"

"I expect the cops will let you know one way or another. Otherwise, stay close to Warehouse 8 and watch for Isthim."

"Me?" she questioned.

Rifun gave her a look. "You're bright pink, dear, and you change colors. I think you will be the most obvious target to follow."

Her expression turned annoyed, but she couldn't deny the logic.

Rifun looked around the group. "Any other questions, comments, concerns?"

Cassius knew from the man's tone that the inquiry was intended to be rhetorical, but he piped up with, "And if and when everything goes straight to shit?"

Their gazes met. "We don't need Tommen and we're not leaving without Lily Guile. Stay close to Warehouse 8 and watch for Isthim. You may interpret those instructions as you see fit, but there is no reason for this to be a bloodbath."

Tadashi opened his mouth for another whine. "So why don't we just—?"

Rifun dropped the Band, twisting it with a bit of Force so as to shut Tadashi up. The man glared at Rifun for a second, then went back to inspecting his rifles.

Cassius looked around a moment. This place was a dump. What a place to die. But he would do it. And he would do it with flare. Fuck Rifun's orders about not wanting a bloodbath. He turned his face toward the setting sun.

Let the bloodbath begin.

"Are we set?" Rifun asked, looking at his watch.

"Ready," Isthim reported, rolling her neck as best she could with her horns the way they were.

"When you are," Tadashi replied, keeping a rifle in either hand, pointed up.

"Ready," Donojok said, his tone difficult to judge.

Rifun looked at Cassius who smiled. "Always ready."

"Excellent. And so the mighty foes entered on stage to meet the great heroes of lore."

If there was any upside to being sent out with Isthim to take care of the backup team, he wouldn't have to listen to whatever bullshit Rifun was going to spew at the officers. Granted, he much preferred it when everyone knew what he was up to, but sneaking around would be a nice challenge before the real bloodbath.

Tadashi set out to scout the perimeter and identify the snipers. Rifun took Tommen into the facility, the teenager putting up very little resistance. Isthim turned and stalked off, using Gravity to get over the fence. Cassius followed.

"You and Rifun are pretty close, right?" he asked, using Sound to muffle their voices and steps, just in case the Band itself wasn't enough. "Joined at the hip, if I recall."

"What do you want?" Isthim sighed, cutting into the last word.

"What the hell is he doing here? Sure, the man's an actor, loves his stage and his monologues, but he's also a fucking coward. He sets up a standoff, doesn't want anyone to die—"

Isthim did not slow, but she looked at him. "He's trying to kill you."

Cassius blinked. "He's had plenty of opportunities. Has he pulled his little paralysis trick on you yet, or does that ruin the pleasure?"

"Maybe it was a poor choice of words. He is trying to kill the dragon. Your flesh just happens to be in the way."

Not surprising. Cassius could tell the dragon was not concerned in the least, but he himself was still very confused, and he was sure this reflected on his face. "And what does that have to do with all of this?"

They rounded a corner, heading down another aisle of containers, this one where the primary team was preparing to meet with Rifun.

"Lately he's been working on traversing the dimensions. His excuse is that he's trying to free Julianna. Really, he's trying to break into the spirit world. If he can do that, he may be able to actually do some damage."

"Is that a fact? Do people do this often?"

Her look was such that Cassius wondered if he might not die by her hand instead of a hail of bullets.

Kill Rifun, Isthim, leave Julianna...

"Few people have done it on the scale that he is attempting, but those who do manage it are often powerful enough to do considerable damage."

Cassius blinked. As they turned another corner, finally coming upon the backup police team, he identified his current emotion as confusion, but also confusion regarding his confusion. Only a fool thought there was nothing "beyond." No gods, no spirits, nothing but atoms and mathematics and chance. And yet, it was still odd to see Isthim speaking of such things, even knowing she was an undercover priestess of death. Or perhaps it was just odd to think of the spirit world as a tangible place that people could travel to. Didn't that defeat the purpose of all-powerful gods and spirits? Even Rifun's ancestor worship drew the line at life and death, right?

Still safely in his Band so that all else appeared still, he walked up to one of the officers and, after Isthim gave them a good tap with a bare hand, cut his throat. Once time resumed, all of the men would collapse from Borelian poison and bleed out within minutes. One moment they stood here, weapons at the ready, armor protecting everything but the most essential parts of the body, and the next, they were gushing blood.

"Judging by your tone," Cassius said, cutting another throat, "you're not too thrilled about Rifun's experiments."

"As a priestess of Tujor, I take great interest in his attempts to cross such a threshold. However, I disapprove of his plans."

He gave her a look, not paying attention as he cut the last man's throat, wincing as he nicked his own hand. "Why? Tujor is death itself, isn't he? Even if he is a real spirit, a real being, he is still death. You think Rifun is going to kill death? Or are you just upset that your lover is racing toward his doom?"

Isthim matched his look. "Hardly."

"Liar."

"Borelians are the chosen agents of Tujor."

Cassius rolled his eyes, though he was more sarcastic than offended. "Gee, never heard that one before."

She became flustered. Truthfully, he found it hilarious. "Whether or not Rifun chooses to engage Tujor and die by his claws, he still has the potential to severely upset things."

" 'Things' as in, you might not be the chosen ones anymore? You might not be the favorite child?" He made a vague gesture. "Well then, stop him. Maybe not right here, right now, but the next time you visit him or he visits you for a little romp, just touch him and be done with it."

Still flustered, Isthim tried to gather her composure with a huffed sigh and a mild, "The potential here is too great. To learn how to access the spirit world would be invaluable."

"Ah. Let him break down the door, you feed him to the guard dogs and then help yourselves to the goods."

"In a crude sense, I suppose."

Cassius nodded. He glanced at the dead men of the backup police team. They were still standing, but dead nonetheless. "You go ahead. I'll be a minute."

Isthim rolled her eyes, but turned and stalked off.

It actually wasn't the dead men around him that got him excited. Rather, it was a new thought that had popped into his head, or perhaps it was planted there by the dragon. Tujor was the Borelian god of death. Rifun's spirits were his ancestors, who were, one would hope, dead. He was trying to break into the spirit world, effectively breaking into death. The dragon spirit was going to kill Cassius. If and when Rifun did manage to break into the spirit world of death, what if he, Cassius, was there to meet him? Being dead, the man couldn't kill him, right?

Ooh, that was a lovely thought. The look on Rifun's face as he entered the domain of Hell and Death and the first thing he sees is Cassius. Fuck, that might even make this whole death thing with the bullet in his face worth it. Kill everyone here, go to Hell, wait for Rifun to show up. That would be absolutely marvelous.

After satisfying himself, Cassius navigated his way back through the maze and found a relatively safe perch from which to observe the happenings. Fuck everyone here. He was going to die, and then he was going to kill Rifun. In that order. Why not see what the man was up to, what insane, convoluted scheme he had cooked up? Isthim had implied that he intended to do such work here, use the chaos of the shootout to break into the spirit world and kill him, kill the dragon. This might be fun to watch.

He did not initially spot the others. When he finally dropped the Band, it was a minute before he spied them walking out of the warehouse. It appeared that Rifun was keeping Tommen close, as promised. Close enough to hold a gun to his head, in fact, and use him as a human shield. He did realize that they weren't dealing with stage props, right? If he wasn't careful, he might hurt someone. Cassius snickered to himself.

Now then, about that portal to the netherworld...Cassius couldn't imagine that it would be anything subtle, but dismissing it as a possibility entirely would only bite him in the ass.

He saw several Bands pop up, Time Bands, likely from Walter or Tommen, colors flashing brilliantly for those who could see them. He wondered what was being said. Well, he could have broken into the Bands and used Sound to find out, but he didn't feel like it. He didn't care one way or the other; he was just waiting for the shooting to start.

Let's see...who to go after first? He looked down at the men who fancied themselves heroes, arrayed amid the cargo containers, each with his own target picked out in the event things went south. There were a couple women with them, he saw. Maybe one of them. Fuck Rifun and his morals. If Cassius was going to die, well, he could get off one last time, right? If he had to settle for the team he just killed, he would, but maybe he would try to know a woman one last time. And he would take it by force, an excitement that even Isthim could not fully replicate.

One was a bigger woman with a nice, full chest. Cassius wasn't overly enthused by fat women, but this one, judging by what he could see amid all the armor, appeared to be just big. Scandinavian heritage, maybe. She would be a fighter. He liked that.

The other woman, even with her heavy armor, was a mousy little thing with stringy hair sticking out from a bun. Thin, but not in the most pleasing way. He would overpower her in a second, and he probably wouldn't even need to use any abilities to do so. That alone held some measure of intrigue.

He considered the area, the layout of the containers. The people below were still talking. When did the shooting start? Or was it, by some terrible irony, actually possible that this could go smoothly? Rifun was a smooth talker; was it possible he somehow convinced the police to give up Lily, or convince her to give herself up to save Tommen?

Several firearms discharged at once. Cassius leapt to his feet. Another firearm went off. Rifun doubled over, dropping his revolver. Walter rushed forward and grabbed Tommen, dragged him back to safety. Isthim and Tadashi protected Rifun as he stumbled back and went to a knee. The police officers maintained a wall between the Cult and Walter, Tommen, and Lily.

Everything stood perfectly still.

Cassius leaned forward and peered down at Rifun. He could see the man wasn't dead, but that was a lot of blood on the ground. He appeared to be wrapping something around his arm or hand. What had happened that someone had taken him by surprise? He had anticipated an attack literally in his sleep; wakefulness should have made him all but invincible in that regard.

Movement in his peripheral caused him to look away. He didn't see anything and might have dismissed it, except the dragon nudged him forward. Sighing, he Banded, turned, and started walking along the top of the container.

The thing about being in a Band and everyone else being slowed down or stopped completely, was that motion became very noticeable. Someone else was up here.

Like a hound that had finally found a scent, the dragon dropped the other end of the leash and let Cassius go to work. He started by tracing where he believed the movement to have originated from. Looking back at the negotiations below, he had a hunch that this was the person who had managed to injure Rifun as there appeared to be a direct line of fire from here to where he'd been standing on the ground.

There weren't too many ways to get the jump on Rifun. If Cassius hadn't just witnessed one, he might have thought there was no way. The list of suspects, then, was pretty short.

He wasn't sure if it was the dragon or his own reflexes that helped him dodge the bullet before it could be buried in his brain. When he turned, he only just managed to evade a heavy-fisted blow from Micaiah. Before he could reach out and Harvest the man at a touch, Micaiah used Force to whip himself around and put a good ten feet between them.

"Surprised to find you up here," Micaiah said. "Thought for sure you'd be down where the action is."

"I'm here to make sure there is action," Cassius told him.

He did not give the Irishman a chance to speak before launching himself at him, running up and using a little Force of his own to really throw his fist through the air. Micaiah dodged. He was unable to get in a physical counter, but he was able to knock Cassius off balance by introducing a new Force from a different direction. Cassius stumbled to one side, away from the scene on the ground, reaching for Gravity so he didn't fall off the stack of containers.

He'd only just gotten a Gravity track established when Micaiah sliced through it with one of his own. The competing forces fractured and the resulting boom was like being inside of a thunderclap. Dazed, Cassius tumbled to the ground. He wasn't sure how he didn't break into a thousand pieces, though he was not uninjured.

He knew instinctively that there was danger nearby. A rapid succession of popping noises told him that much. Pain lanced through his body as he struggled to his feet. Head still cloudy, he tried to get his bearings, but all he saw were shipping containers. Shipping containers everywhere.

Cassius flinched as the container behind him shifted, and he shuffled out of the way, wincing in pain and spinning to watch the top container. The whole stack shifted but did not fall.

Keeping an eye on the top container, Cassius Felt inside himself. Some broken bones, minor concussion, but nothing horrible. Nothing the Akari couldn't fix, assuming he had the concentration to use it. The best he could do for the moment was setting the bones and giving them a week or two of healing time, but he was by no means "healed." When he shifted his gaze downward, he saw Micaiah about twenty feet away, apparently doing the same thing.

Grinning, Cassius ran toward Micaiah, using Sound to muffle his steps as best he could. But with his head still fuzzy, his trajectory was by no means straight, and he was willing to bet that his use of Sound was embarrassingly amateur. Later he would reflect that everything he did in those first ten minutes after falling off the container was amateur, including his trip and fall into Micaiah who suddenly vanished like fog.

What the—? His muddled mind could not initially make sense of it. Then it occurred to him: Imprint. Micaiah had captured a tiny moment in time where he had been healing himself and left it on display for Cassius while he went...where? Cassius looked around, ducking several times as he expected a fist or a club or a bullet to make its way toward him in his distraction. Nothing came. He was alone in this particular area, although there did seem to be some excitement going on somewhere. A lot of shouting, a lot of gun fire. But where had Micaiah gone?

He would be going after Tommen, Cassius reasoned, trying to save him or get him out of the area. Or maybe he would go after Rifun, try to kill him. If that was the case, Cassius might just go and offer to lend a hand.

He used Gravity to get to the top of the containers for a bird's eye view. From what he could see, Tadashi had lured some officers and the snipers in one direction, and Donojok was fighting dangerously close to the river (could such an alien even swim?). He did not see Isthim or Rifun, but the trail of blood led into the warehouse. Looking around the back side of the building, Cassius spotted Micaiah skulking around the perimeter.

Although the worst of his dizziness was clearing up, Cassius refrained from Banding as he made his way down to the warehouse. He was not trying to be sneaky, but he was still caught off-guard when Micaiah spoke to him without reacting to his approach.

"What the hell has Rifun done?" he wondered, his voice a mixture of awe and fear. He reached out and touched the side of the warehouse. If Cassius' attention had not been drawn to something amiss, he never would have noticed the slightest distortion around the man's hand where he rested it against the sheet metal. Micaiah moved his hand back and forth inside the distortion, pulled it out, touched it again. "It's not a portal exactly. It's like...a quasi-dimension."

"A what?" Cassius asked dumbly.

Micaiah backed up suddenly, as if realizing some horrifying truth. "I think he's tried to turn a portal inside out. I've heard theories about..." He shook his head and took another step back, then another.

Annoyed, and admittedly a little curious, Cassius strode up to the building.

He reached out and touched it, hoping he looked more confident than he felt. It could be a trick, a way to distract him.

Touching the distortion, however, was not a trick. Nothing changed that he could see, but he could feel something. Something wasn't right. Using Touch, he checked inside himself, his bones and tissue. There was no damage. There was nothing physically wrong with him. But he could still feel it, deep down, in the way the hair on his arms and neck stood on end. Rifun had done something here. Pulling a portal inside out, Cassius didn't know, but he had done something.

He wanted everyone to stay close, but likely he wanted Cassius in particular to walk into the warehouse. Whatever he had done, it had to do with his plan to kill the dragon.

On the one hand, if Rifun was injured, now might be a good time to take him out instead. Cassius didn't need the dragon to be a better fighter.

On the other hand, if Rifun had already booby-trapped the warehouse in this way, what else might he have done?

Cassius looked around, but no one was nearby. The gunfire was starting to taper off, and Micaiah had vanished. Where would he go now? Surely not to the Wheel. The Akarin, then. He would want to report on this. Even as he thought it, Doug's phone in Cassius' pocket rang.

Cassius Banded and left the area, not releasing the Band until he was a good two or three miles from the scene. Then he donned his Doug Disguise and answered the call.

"Micaiah! How are things in your neck of the woods?!" he inquired boisterously, knowing the grin in his voice was genuine for both himself and Doug. "Any new developments from the elections?"

"Doug, you and I both know how to collapse portals," Micaiah began, sounding mildly winded, "but do you know anything about turning them inside out?"

"Inside out?" Cassius-as-Doug echoed. "I'm sure I've heard and studied plenty of theories, but I can't recall that I've ever actually attempted such a thing. I've never considered it necessary, why? You want to turn the Wheel inside out?"

He intended it as a joke, even as the line of thought suddenly made itself known.

"Listen, I told you that Rifun kidnapped Tommen. Well, his idea of giving him back apparently involved turning an area the size of, say, an industrial warehouse, into a quasi-dimension, turning a portal inside out."

"Are you trapped inside?"

"No. I didn't go in. I don't know that I could. It doesn't feel right, Doug. I'm afraid that those who are inside will become trapped."

Cassius-as-Doug shifted his stance. "Surely that which can be turned inside out can also be turned right side out again?"

"I don't know!" Micaiah cried. "I just watched theoretical physics become a very tangible problem, and I don't know what to do about it."

Cassius-as-Doug sighed. "Has anything actually happened? Do I need to come take a look? What's going on?"

"I don't know," he repeated.

"Well, when you know, let me know. But I guess I'll make my way that way and see if I can—"

"No. Go to the Akarin council and let them know. If Rifun can do this, who knows how he might try to apply it after whatever he's going to do with the elections?"

"Sounds like a rather nebulous fear or scheme, but I suppose it can't hurt."

Cassius could imagine Micaiah shrugging. "They're not going to hate you any less for telling or not telling them."

"True. Keep me updated. I might still swing by and see what in the universe you're talking about."

"Fair enough."

Micaiah hung up without ceremony, leaving Cassius free to burst into laughter. It tapered off awkwardly as he considered his present situation. He had fully expected to run into a shootout and die in a hail of bullets. Instead, he was two and a half miles from the scene, talking on the phone, and the dragon was oddly okay with that. It hadn't said or done anything while at the shipping yard, nor when he investigated the warehouse and this "quasi-dimension" Micaiah had babbled about, nor even now while talking on the phone. Had it abandoned him, expecting him to die? Did it want him to live? What were its goals? Had, perhaps, the "quasi-dimension" affected the dragon in some way when Cassius touched it? Was there some merit to the idea of using the dimension to gain an advantage over the evil spirit and defeat it?

After a minute or two, Cassius returned to the shipping yard, stopping when he was a good half mile away, looking at it from the hillside across the river.

Things had changed. Something had happened. Ambulances and fire trucks had appeared, and the place was lit up brilliantly with flashing lights of all different colors. He could not discern individual motions, but he knew well enough the sight of chaos and trying to contain it, clean it up. Two ambulances pulled out of the drive into traffic, sirens wailing.

So, mission accomplished. Even if Rifun's little plan to destroy the dragon hadn't panned out, it appeared as though they had managed to acquire Lily anyway, if not kill her. All in all, a productive day.

He wouldn't say he wasn't a little upset about not having a more active role, but maybe the others would have left Lily alive so he could have the pleasure of killing her. He returned to the officers building to find out. To his surprise, he found Isthim and Misik in conference, but no sign of Rifun.

"All right, where's Lily?" Cassius asked as he burst into the room, rubbing his hands together. "Show me the money, show me the prize we won today."

Neither of the Borelians' expressions was especially promising.

"What?" he wondered. "What happened?"

"Lily is dead," Isthim said evenly. "Or so we believe. There were other, perhaps more pressing, matters that arose."

"What, Rifun got a little too ambitious and managed to summon some demons instead of slay them?"

"Rifun has suffered the loss of a couple of fingers. I took him to a sympathetic Time Agent at a hospital."

Cassius blinked. He heard her words, but it took a few seconds for the meaning to really sink in. Then, "I'm sorry, what?" Isthim opened her mouth to speak, but he cut her off. "You can't guarantee Lily is dead, and you...didn't bring her here so I could make sure of it. And Rifun, who has demonstrated his unwillingness to die multiple times, somehow lost a couple of fingers and is now at the hospital. Is that right?"

Isthim shrugged. "If it makes you feel any better, Walter Forbes is dead. Or he will be, as I poisoned him."

Cassius slapped a hand on the table. "Are you fucking joking?! We had this in the bag! We—had—this!"

"Not something you have to tell us," Misik informed him distastefully.

"This is bullshit!" Cassius raged. He slapped the table again and turned away. "This whole fucking thing is bullshit."

"Maybe you would be willing to discuss the next phase of the plan, then. And I'm not necessarily referring to Rifun's plans for the Wheel."

Cassius sighed. "You're talking about the plan to enslave the Cult, take us to some new colony or slave world to farm for you, and some bullshit that I'm going to be the head slave over all of them."

The Borelians did not speak, but he could imagine them exchanging glances. Maybe they Banded so they could have some private conversation. After a moment, he turned back around to face them. "After I killed my master, I swore that I would never be anyone's slave ever again. Except, somehow, I have never not been a slave. Whether it is to some asinine cause, the politics of the Wheel, or your stupid fucking dragon, I have always been jerked around, poked and prodded like a bull in the arena." He shifted his stance. "Unfortunately, the stupid fucking dragon has a little piece of leverage over me that I can't do anything about."

He sighed again and leaned forward, both arms out to support him. "If I must be a slave, I will not be a slave to incompetent fools. I was prepared—" He slapped the table. "—to die today! But it didn't happen. Instead—"

"It is quite impossible to fight stupid," Misik cut in. "But it is very easy to manipulate and conquer." He made a vague gesture. "How do you think we ended up here?"

Grudgingly, Cassius met his gaze. "What's the plan?"

"Rifun being incapacitated for a short time will make this easier and faster, so we expect you to act accordingly."

Cassius looked at Isthim. "So that's why you took him to a hospital instead of healing him yourself."

Isthim shrugged. "I was too unfamiliar with human anatomy—"

"We both know that's a lie."

"—and he was losing too much blood. I was concerned."

"Also a lie."

"Anyway," Misik said loudly. "We have, according to your standard calendar, roughly three weeks until the elections in the Wheel. Isthim has been preparing the Grandfathers for the coup which will take place at the inauguration of the new Hands and the passing of the mantle. This way we have both old and new Hands in the same place at the same time. We expect there will be opposition, some violent. There will be bloodshed, which I am certain you have no quarrel with. We will deal with the violence. If Rifun recovers and is present for the operation, he may direct the Cult in the more humane aspect of taking prisoners.

"We will need some kind of work force to keep the Wheel running, new secretaries as it were, under our direction. Once we have sorted out the most useful ones in this regard, the rest will be sent to our new farming colony."

"So you get the Cult and the bulk of the Time Agent officers," Cassius stated. "They're required to be present for the inauguration."

"Yes. And with Rifun's experiments in dimensional technology—" Isthim's expression was knowing. "—I am certain that our scientists will be able to rapidly improve our external Suppression devices, to prevent the Time Agents from leaving."

"What about the Akari-bearers?"

"Leave the details to us," Misik answered. Can't give the slave the information he would need to overthrow his master, after all. "Your job in all of this is simple enforcement. Nothing flashy, nothing complicated. If someone doesn't fall in line, kill them. We're going to have a large enough pool that we can, indeed, afford to lose some. We must lose some, in fact. The survival instinct dictates that people will do whatever is necessary to avoid pain and suffering. Make sure they are exposed to plenty of both."

"Is the survival instinct the same across thousands of species?" Cassius wondered.

"Among sentient beings, yes, because they have spent far too much time cultivating sentimentality and self-esteem. You may notice that all the species that are involved in Time are bound by universal greed as well, which was one of the reasons the Cult got this ambitious in the first place."

Cassius considered this for a long moment, then nodded. "And what should I do in the meantime? We have three weeks, like you said."

"There are two avenues we can explore," Isthim said. "Whichever one the Akarin are attempting, do it twice as well. The first avenue is that of chaotic fatigue. The mind can only process fear and danger for so long before it must do two things: let go of the fear or die from it. If the Akarin are trying to get people excited and riled up about what could happen, go in and make them twice as afraid. Don't do any big displays or shows of force, but just enough that, by the time the elections come around, the people are so up tight from hearing about this fabled apocalypse that when it comes...well, it will make the initial culling that much easier.

"The second avenue is total suppression. If the Akarin are telling people to stay calm and consider things logically, make sure there is nothing for anyone to find. Perfect radio silence. No words, no hype, no acts of subtlety or aggression. People will prepare for nothing, and they will be caught off-guard when the coup hits. It makes the initial takeover much smoother with less violence, but it can draw out the later logistics."

"Why not do the opposite of the Akarin?" Cassius wondered. "Confuse people to the point they don't know which way is up?"

Isthim shrugged. "It will result in the chaotic fatigue, the first avenue. However, it will also highlight the Akarin in a way we do not want. We cannot afford the binary relationship. This is a matter of sabotaging their efforts and discrediting them."

"They're already discredited. Granted, not as much as the Cult, but—"

"You can never discredit someone enough in matters of politics," Misik told him. "Character assassination is only the beginning."

Cassius scoffed. "Well, at least you guys sound like you have a better long-term plan. Or a long-term plan at all."

"Given that you have been masquerading as Doug Templeton for some time, it should be no trouble for you to ascertain the Akarin's intentions," Isthim said.

He scoffed again. "What intentions? Their only intentions are to sit on their fat asses and worry about finance and by-laws and petty bickering." He thought about Micaiah reporting on Rifun's attempts at turning a dimension inside out. "But I suppose I'll go take a look anyway, just to be sure."

"It would be the prudent thing to do," Misik commented, his tone just this side of a threat.

Cassius left the room without being dismissed, first returning to his chambers. He did not hear the dragon say anything, but he got the distinct impression of being told that he was being a good little puppet. Cassius ground his teeth as he made several laps around the room.

He hated this. He hated not feeling in control of himself. He hated not having a say over his own life. After how many years of being threatened with the bullet in his face, he had gone to the shipping yard fully intending to die, and yet the dragon had denied him that. What a sick joke. Maybe he should just throw himself in front of a train. Or from a height. Or get on a spaceship and jump into space.

He knew that doing so would only take him straight into the dragon's claws, but the dragon couldn't kill him twice, right? Death could not die, not if it was supposed to be eternal torment. The dragon would have no power to control him through this mortal wound. Of course, who knew what greater power it had in its own realm?

Maybe he should talk to Rifun about that separation of dimensions or whatever the fuck he was working on.

Cassius stopped pacing, donning his Doug Disguise, and headed to the Akarin fortress. As expected, nothing had changed. There was no panic, no gathering army, no rallying cry. The most he saw were a few groups of people meeting together as if going out to lunch. Even on the upper floors, around the meeting rooms, there was nothing. He didn't even make it to a meeting room before another council member spotted him and moved to intercept.

"Whatever you've come to say, you can save it," the man — or Cassius thought it was a man — began. "Micaiah Durvin has already informed us of the Cult's recent developments."

"And we are going to do...what?" Cassius-as-Doug inquired, a bit of acid in his voice. "We can't just sit back and wait for them to figure out how to dismantle the universe before we act."

"Dismantling the universe would only end badly for them, but your hyperbole is noted."

There was no nearby table or wall to hit, but this did not stop Cassius from making a frustrated gesture. "Damn it, man! Are we really going to do nothing? Is that our policy? Play the fiddle while Rome burns?" At the council member's confused expression, he added, "Are we going to celebrate our own demise?"

"Our demise? Surely not." The councilman shifted his stance. "Think of it this way. The Cult is weaker than us. The Time industry is weaker than them. It would be bad form for us to take over and remake the Time industry —"

"So we let the Cult do it, then take over the Cult and the Time industry. Just use the Cult as a hired hitman." Cassius-as-Doug looked around. There were plenty of people milling about within earshot, yet not one of them seemed to react to the admission. He turned his attention back to the councilman. "The Cult took over the Wheel once before —"

"Allegedly. There is no record of such a thing happening other than a handful of accounts, of which yours is conveniently among them."

"And the testimonies of millions across the universe mean nothing?"

"Everyone loves to blame someone for the mismanagement of things, and conspiracy theories abound."

That memory wipe by the Borelians was incredibly effective, but also incredibly annoying. "Tell me —" He couldn't think of his name. " — sir, what is our purpose? Why are we here? Why do we do what we do, why are we gifted with the Akari?"

Such a simple question, and yet it seemed to genuinely confuse the man, catch him off guard. In a bid to save face, the best could manage was, "Why do you ask? Have you, perhaps, forgotten? Because it seems as though you are the only one who has any issue with how things are done around here."

"I'm not the only one, just the most vocal."

The councilman was undeterred, and his change in stance and tone suggested the conversation was over. "We are keeping an eye on things. As for this experimentation with the dimensions, it is uncorroborated."

"You don't trust Micaiah?"

"His report stems from a situation in which he is too closely involved."

"You don't believe Tommen Forbes is the Chivalrous Welshman?"

"If he is, the Author protects her own. He'll be fine. And this only proves that the dimensional experimentation is but a facade and we remain superior in our philosophies and abilities. Now, I have duties to attend to at home. Good day."

The councilman left without further ado or any real concern.

So that was it. The Akarin were perfectly fine with the Cult taking over the Wheel because it meant they didn't have to get their hands dirty. Then, if things got a little out of hand, then they might step in, kick out the Cult like an unwanted tenant, and take the Wheel for themselves. How quaint.

He returned to the officers building. Misik and Isthim were still speaking, and the papers and small computers laid out over the table suggested they were deep into their planning. They looked up as he entered the room.

"The Akarin aren't going to do shit," he said and relayed his conversation.

"Not until things go poorly and we start rounding people up," Misik mused, less enthusiastic than Cassius thought he should be. "If they are able to give aid to the slaves, then sheer numbers are not in our favor. Given that the first slaves will be the Time Agent officers, firepower will be evenly-matched at best."

"Then what do you suggest?" Cassius demanded.

"I suggest you mind your place," the general said hotly. "This is no longer your operation. You have your role, a simple one as befits your simple mind and status." He made a gesture. "Now get out and let us work. We will let you know when you are needed."

Cassius almost attacked the man, then refrained at the last second, instead turning and leaving the room. Time to talk to Rifun.

Expectation

Rifun got in the van in a dreadful mood, and being packed in with Donojok, Isthim, and Tommen was not on his list of how to make things better.

To sum it up, he just didn't want to be here. Like a bratty teenager, he didn't want to be here, he didn't want to do this, and he wanted to go home. On the other hand, he had to do something about the demon inside Cassius. The chaos of the almost inevitable shootout would provide excellent cover to separate the dimensions.

Rifun had discovered that it was a tad easier to turn the dimension inside out and hold it if there was some physical boundary to it. Maybe there was some science behind it or maybe it was purely psychological, he didn't know for sure. But the way he figured it, if he could do it inside the warehouse and get Cassius inside, it might at least contain whatever evil spirit indwelled the man long enough for Rifun to dispatch it.

He opened up his revolver and started removing the bullets to inspect them and the gun.

He'd given great thought to the ritual he would have to perform, spent a great deal of time praying at his shrine. He was uncertain about the answers he had received, but decided not to question them, not with so much at stake and such a small window of opportunity.

"So, this is how it's going to work," he told Tommen, still looking at the bullets and not the teenager, "I'm expecting Walter to bring in every gun he's got. But for the negotiating part, it'll just be me and you, Tommen. And since I know you want this to go over smoothly, I expect you to cooperate fully. Like I told him Friday night, he asked for proof of life, and he got proof of life. He did not specify in which condition this life need be, which gives me the freedom to beat you within an inch of it, if I'm feeling like an honest, decent man. If I'm not, well, I can just kill you outright. Follow so far?"

Tommen nodded silently, eyes huge.

Rifun started reloading his revolver. "Good. Now, there are some things I'm going to have you say. And you're going to say them exactly as I tell you to. I'm also going to do a few things which, if you flinch, will kill you. It's in your best interest then—" He whipped the gun around and shot at the floor of the van between Tommen's feet. Tommen jumped and fell out of his seat. "—to not flinch."

"What the fuck is going on back there?!" Tadashi demanded.

"Nothing!" Rifun said.

Fear, the spirits had told him. Specifically, the fear of death. The dragon would be drawn to it, irresistible bait. The greater the smell, the greater the draw. Rifun was too broken to fear death anymore. The police still maintained a fear of death, though they battled it as part of their daily routine. The sixteen year old in his possession had never experienced such fear, so his would be the strongest. Then, once Tommen was good and afraid, turn the dimension inside out and lure the dragon inside. Its attraction to that fear, from a chosen one of the Author no less, would distract it long enough for Rifun to strike.

The spirits had been silent about just how he was supposed to strike and kill the dragon. Maybe things would be such that a physical blade would work, that being in the other dimension would infuse it with some lethal spiritual properties as well. Maybe he would receive further instruction at that time. Maybe he would be inspired by something in the environment. Whatever it was, he could only hope it worked, because he was not going to get a second chance at this.

"We're here," Tadashi said, bringing the van to a rather violent stop. "Cops have got this place locked down, all the warehouses, no personnel."

"Wonderful," Rifun said, grinning. He looked at Tommen. "So it will be just us two, like an old Western showdown. What do you think of that?"

The shipping yard was industrial, shabby, a bit piecemeal in its construction, as one might expect from a growing business. The small freighter sat quietly at the dock, all the cargo containers that were intended for it and other vessels stacked high, packing the yard, providing a lovely maze to run around in. As reported, all workers had been evacuated to make room for the police who now littered the area.

Rifun Banded everyone except Tommen and handed out instructions, trying to make it as clear as possible that this wasn't intended to be a massacre. They were going out on stage for a performance. Perform correctly and they would get the response they desired, that is, Lily Guile. That was the only reason they were here.

Still, he had no illusions. This was going to turn ugly. Someone, or multiple someones, were going to die today. There was no getting around that, whether it was Lily Guile or the police or Lily Guile and the police.

"Don't fuck this up," Cassius growled as he turned and walked away, quickening a step or two to catch up with Isthim.

The irony was that Cassius was the one most likely to send things careening into open flame, Rifun thought, dropping the Band and grabbing Tommen. He did not enjoy what he was going to have to do, but telling himself that this was just a performance on a stage made it more bearable. He had to kill the dragon, and to do that, he needed to incite a copious amount of fear, specifically the fear of death. He himself held no such fear anymore; it had all been transformed into faith. That Tommen was also a chosen one of the Author was no coincidence and would surely only help him in this endeavor. The teenager with the fear needed to lure the dragon into a trap, Rifun with the faith needed to kill the dragon. A perfect team.

They headed to the warehouse in question. Still keeping Tommen close, Rifun studied the building. Industrial grade steel pole building, from the looks of things, although the frame and sheet metal were aluminum, not steel. This close to the river and in this climate, it was unlikely that the pillars were sunk especially deep; they would be relying on the poured concrete inside and asphalt outside to hold everything together. The interior was not overly cluttered, and the catwalk above looked sturdy enough.

He received no inspiration for any rituals or paraphernalia placement. Perhaps this really would be physical only, once they traversed the dimensions into the spirit world. He had no way of knowing; this was all entirely new to him, uncharted waters.

He decided to wait to open the portal until things went south. Although the distortion was only slight to his eyes, he didn't know what it might look like to the spirits. Better to wait until it was distracted with the action and the fear smell.

Isthim approached, looking about as happy as she always did.

"Where's Cassius?" Rifun inquired.

"Celebrating his victory over the backup team," she reported dryly.

Rifun sighed and gave her a look. "So he killed them."

"We sent a message."

He shook his head. "Damn it, that's what we have him for!" He gave Tommen a brief shake. "We're not here for the police or so Cassius can get off. We are here for Lily Guile!" He released Tommen and made a couple paces. Then, "You had better hope this goes the way we want otherwise, because I do not want to have to deal with anymore of this shit around here."

"You're the one who wanted to play games," Isthim hissed defensively.

"I've been trying to kill a demon, what do you expect me to do? Rush headlong into the fight and die, or do as much as I can to learn about it and how to dispatch it?"

He didn't like the look she got. "One man's demon is another man's angel. I suggest you consider whose god you're trying to kill."

It was the closest she ever got to an explicit threat, but Rifun suddenly felt very alone in this standoff. He no longer wanted to be the lead actor out front, because he wasn't sure he could trust the supporting actors behind him. The dragon might indwell Cassius, but it had clearly brought some combatants of its own to this fight. Maybe he should open the portal now.

Tadashi and Donojok approached. Tadashi somehow managed to look less excited than Isthim. Donojok remained as expressionless as ever.

"All right," Rifun said. "Let's get this over with."

In one fluid motion, he grabbed Tommen, spun him around, held him close, and had a revolver to his head. He had no real intention of using it, but the kid didn't know that. It was all about the fear. Now if only he had some similar protection for his backside.

The four of them left the cover of the warehouse, approaching a line of police officers who had apparently just figured out that their backup team—Bravo Team, he heard them called—was no longer responding on the radio.

"Negative, sir," a radio voice squawked. "I only have a visual on Alpha Team."

"Oh, don't worry about Bravo Team," Rifun said loudly, announcing their presence. All attention turned from the radios to the sudden standoff. Rifun went on, feel every eye on him, just like a stage, but not in a way he liked. "Ah, so glad you could make it. Now then, I have something of yours, and you have something of mine. Let's talk."

Walter tipped his head toward his radio. "Standish, keep an eye on Pink. Everyone else, do not let her touch you. She favors contact poisons that will kill you."

"Ah, so you have done your research," Rifun said. "I must say, Walter, you certainly know how to do your homework and pull together bits and pieces of information into some wildly accurate theories. Do you know what I'm thinking right now?"

"You're probably trying to stall for time, give your goons there a chance to size us up and pick their targets so that when this all goes south, all you have to do is give the signal."

"My goons. Why, how very...1980's of you. Please, Walter, if we're going to compare balls, at least let's do so like civilized men. 'Pink' as you called her is Isthim Borelian. My Oriental compadre over there is Tadashi Hajiku. And that's Donojok hiding back there in the shadows." He went on before Walter had a chance to speak more. "No need to introduce your team. I've already researched everyone in the department so I would know who the options were for who you might bring. So I know everyone you brought and everyone you left behind." He grinned. "I even know the names of everyone on your 'Bravo Team.' And my, you should have seen their faces when I whispered their names as they went down."

With luck, it would increase the fear in the officers and Tommen, but it might also confuse the evil spirits, just a touch. Why was he taking credit for something he didn't do, something he'd specifically ordered them not to do? Of course, he still didn't see Cassius, which was becoming a tad worrisome.

"Where is Cassius?" Walter asked, trying to keep things calm.

I don't know, and you're not the only one worried about it. "He couldn't make it, unfortunately. Meetings to attend and so forth. You know how politics can be. Just me and you, old boy."

"Why me? Why single me out?"

Rifun Banded the two of them so they could talk. He made it extra tight and powerful, not only to show off a little and demonstrate just what they were dealing with — and maybe discourage Walter from trying to play the hero — but maybe to get the dragon's attention, that something was going on here.

"At first, it was simply an opportunity," Rifun answered. "It gave me the chance to snub my nose at Earth-side and Time-side cops. Then Cassius told me who you were, both in relation to him and in relation to your so-called son. After that, I thought it would be great fun to see what it would take to get you to tell dear Tommen the truth."

"No," Walter told him solemnly. "There would be no point to telling him now.

It would change nothing except the trust we have with each other."

"Perhaps." Rifun shrugged. "Then once we got our hands on the journal, we started doing a little digging, and the last two weeks of observation were especially enlightening as we observed Tommen. Were you ever aware he has the potential to become an Akari-bearer?"

The man's change in disposition was noticeable, and not in a good way. Rifun knew what he was going to say almost before he said it. "The Akari is a myth, Rifun. It's like the Holy Grail, and the so-called Akari-bearers the Knights Templar. Perhaps once it was a real, tangible object, but it has become so steeped in myth and legend that it doesn't exist like you think it does."

So much for civilized discussion. If only he understood what was about to happen. "The Akari is real, Walter. Richard laid it all out."

"Why did you need the original journal and not the copies?" Walter inquired, trying to bring things back to what he obviously perceived as a more sane topic.

"There are abilities even you have not learned yet, dear Walter, things available only to Wardens, Dominion Timekeepers...and Akari-bearers."

"And Richard was...?"

"Warden, naturally. Granted, he lost his mind while he was an Akari-bearer, but the words in his journal ring true, and we have found no cause to doubt him."

"All right," Walter conceded. "You have the original journal. What does that have to do with kidnapping Tommen and murdering Lily?"

Rifun scoffed. "Killing Lily is purely political; I'm sure you and your Lieutenants worked out that much."

"Put Cassius back in power, create a new Dispersal, ensure your reign as some sort of Time Kings."

"Kidnapping Tommen was originally just a clever ploy to get what we wanted. Then when we discovered his potential, we also discovered that this path has always been decided, long before we consciously chose it."

Walter sighed deliberately, shifted his stance, and looked around at the two sides gathered, both appearing frozen in time, bored of the topic and trying to take command of the conversation. "We could sit in this Band and chat all day, but there is still a situation going on here, one that does really involve more than just me and you. So then, why don't we get out of this Band and get this show on the road? So, what are you going to tell the normal mortals gathered here about the reason why you singled out me and, by default as evidenced here, my son?"

Hard-headed fool, Rifun thought. Tommen was a chosen one of the Author, and he was stuck with a bunch of agnostics. Maybe it was a good thing Rifun was forcibly introducing him to the Akari, otherwise who knew how long it would have taken him to discover everything out there?

He dropped the Band with no less force than he had constructed it, just to see Walter flinch. "Because you are just too interesting of a person, Walter. You and your precious son both. As I said before, I have something you want, and you have something I want. So, you can obviously see that I've brought dear Tommen here relatively safe and mostly unharmed." He shrugged. "Now then, where is Lily Guile?"

Now it was all on the police, and they took a long moment to think things through. What were his intentions? Would he shoot on sight? What if they didn't do as he asked? Didn't any of the snipers have a shot?

Finally, Walter nodded to a female officer. A silent conversation happened, but she went to the police car and opened the door.

Lily Guile physically looked the same, but her demeanor was anything but ordinary. Here was another dose of fear to add to the pot. Now where was Cassius? Where was the dragon? How much fear would it take to be irresistible bait? She went to stand just behind Walter, her expression saying she didn't want to look at Rifun but she also didn't want to look away.

"No, no," Rifun said, flicking his gun hand. "Out in front where I can see you."

"She stays here," Walter said.

"How are we supposed to do a hostage exchange then?" Rifun inquired innocently.

"Lily is not our hostage, nor will she be yours."

Rifun nodded slowly. "Ah, so you expected that you would leave here today with both of them alive, somehow negotiating their release, put me in jail, and retire to bed as the hero of the day?" He frowned, a bit disappointed, but a little refreshed by the man's optimism. "I see. Unfortunately, Walter, that is not why I came here."

"I know why you came here, to kill her. And you are using my son to do it. I don't appreciate that."

"Maybe not, but it's working, isn't it? That's what really brought you here today. I can see it in your eyes, Walt, that you would do anything to get your boy back. And why not? But I can see it in your eyes. I can see it. You're wondering if you could get away with turning over Lily. What if the rest of Alpha Team suddenly dropped dead just as mysteriously as Bravo Team? You trade Lily for Tommen, I inflict some wounds on you so it's not too obvious, and you still get to play hero of the day."

He could see Walter's expression shift, just enough to know that he'd hit something. The man Banded, just the two of them.

"Did you actually kill Bravo Team?" Walter asked.

"Why do you question me? Don't you know my handiwork?" With any luck, Walter would think it over and realize he was dealing with two different entities here.

"Pink Borelians. What can they do?"

"Proximity will make anyone compliant. A brief touch will simply knock them unconscious for a day or two. That's not to say some didn't die, but I needed drama more than I needed blood, much to Cassius' dismay. But as I said, he has more important things to do today." *Like avoiding death, on today of all days.*

"Don't kill my team," Walter pleaded. "Knock them out. This fight is between us and us only. Leave them out of it and let's discuss things freely."

"Freely in a Band or in Base Time makes no difference to me, Walter," Rifun told him.

"Then knock them out anyway. Have your gloat."

"I might just do that anyway, except it's more fun when they futilely fight back. And you are still withholding Lily from me."

Walter let out a breath. "You want Lily out of the elections, right?"

"I want her out of Time completely, and I want to make a severe point of it."

"Knock her out, too. Mock up some blood or moulage or whatever. Take pictures. Make it appear that she's dead. Show your little band of followers. I'll make sure she doesn't interfere ever again."

"Cute, and I admire your creativity at trying to reach a compromise. But there are a couple problems with that plan. First, I didn't promise my 'followers' as you call them, mere pictures. I promised them a body that they would be able to touch and gorge upon if they so chose." He hadn't, but at this point, they would accept nothing less. "Second, we both know Lily too well to think that she'll just go into Time Witness Protection and never come out again. Sure, she might do that for a year or two, but her personality won't allow her to stay down for long. Eventually, she'll rear her ugly head again, and, with her resources and cash lying around, she'll be back and as powerful as ever."

"What about..." Walter closed his eyes. "What about breaking her clock? I know there are degrees of breaking. She doesn't have to be a Time vegetable, just crippled to the point where she can't use her Time abilities, but can still basically function in normal life."

It wasn't a bad idea, but they were in too deep for that. More to the point, he was in too deep. He no longer had allies around him, just pack members who hadn't killed him yet. Walter seemed to pick up on this notion as he dropped his Band.

"I'm sorry, Walter, but there is no other option here for me," Rifun said.

"Why not?" Walter asked diplomatically. "If Cassius isn't here to hold you, why don't we talk? Is he forcing you to do this under some kind of duress? What does he have on you, or what has he promised you?"

The fear clearly wasn't enough, nor was the use of the Akari. Well, if he couldn't get the dragon's attention, maybe he could at least get Cassius out here, assuming he was even still in the yard. What if the dragon did know what was going on and had spirited Cassius away in order to avoid the whole thing?

He leaned over and whispered in Tommen's ear, telling him to repeat it verbatim. Maybe if Tommen was the one who said Cassius' name, he would appear, just out of curiosity.

"Tommen, what is he telling you?" Walter asked cautiously.

Tommen swallowed nervously as Rifun stopped speaking. He took a steadying breath and said finally, "He says that Cassius has promised him great things and that they've extended this offer to me, to rise higher than any other human."

"What does that mean?"

Rifun leaned and started whispering again.

"Send Lily forward two steps, and find out," Tommen repeated.

Another moment of uncertainty among the officers. Walter glanced at an older officer beside him. A silent conversation happened in about the space of a blink. Then Walter and Lily stepped forward. Rifun opened his mouth, but Walter cut him off. "You did not order me to stay back."

Rifun nodded once. "And so I did not. My mistake."

He Banded then, just him and Lily.

"You've certainly gone to great lengths to kill me," Lily began before Rifun could open his mouth. Her words were strong, but her posture was not. "I'm sure you have Cassius just lying in wait, ready for some signal to pop up and cut out my throat."

"There is that option," Rifun said mildly. "Or, you could be noble, willingly trade yourself for Tommen, and I will make it as painless as I can."

She shrugged, still weak and afraid. "It's a tempting offer."

"I'm here for other business, Lily. This is just a side stop."

"If that were true, I would have expected to be offed, dumped in a ditch, and you go on your merry way." Now her posture morphed into something a little more confident. "The reason you haven't is because this is a big deal. The Time industry doesn't give two shits about Earth or humans. And it's not threatened by your little cult. You're weak and pathetic, which is why you're posturing so huge. Because your dicks are tiny." She shook her head. "I'm not going to sacrifice myself because there is no reason to. It's not noble, it's cowardly. And Walter is going to kick your ass."

The annoyance of the day that Rifun had woken up with only amplified. He gave her a look. "Too bad you won't be around to see it."

He dropped the Band and looked at Walter.

"Obviously, Walter, you care for your son," Rifun said. "But tell me, Lily, do you also care for young Tommen?"

"He's a good kid," Lily replied, her voice small as she seemed to be processing what was about to happen. What she had just allowed to happen. "I don't want to see him hurt."

"But your pride and arrogance and sense of self-preservation just won't quite let you sacrifice yourself for him, now will it? And why should it? Most people need a push, a moment of a split-second decision where they know they can and should be the hero. Average people can be heroes, after all. So then, Lily, what would it take to make you sacrifice yourself? Or, better yet, Walter, what would it take for you to sacrifice Lily for the sake of your child?"

In the next one billionth of a second, several things happened at once.

First, Rifun pulled the trigger on his revolver, which was still pointed directly at Tommen's head, pressed almost up against his temple. He had a hold on the Force of the bullet, although it was perhaps the first thing to test his abilities in that area.

Second, Walter mentally leaped forward with a Time Band, the strength almost blinding, like looking into the sun. He arrested the bullet, though he was struggling almost as much as Rifun with his Force.

Third, one of the snipers discharged his weapon. A Reflex Band informed Rifun of that, slowing Time so he could see and judge the distance and trajectory. Not letting go of Tommen or his revolver, Rifun leaned back just enough that the bullet whizzed by. He could feel the heat as it went past, but no harm came to him.

He looked at Walter, slowly letting the Band melt away. "So, Walter, how long are you going to hold that Band? How long until the force of the bullet breaks through your shield? How much—?"

There was a point, right at the cusp of the dissolution of a Band, when even a Reflex Band couldn't save him. It was an infinitesimally small moment in time, far too small for any normal combatant to take advantage of. But for those of great skill in Time or the Akari, it could be exploited, like breaking the surface tension of water, turning certain death into a soaking plunge. And so it was.

Another weapon discharged with God-like timing. Pain ripped through Rifun, and he could not immediately consciously identify its source. All he knew was that his hand flinched and his gun clattered to the ground. He tried to hold fast to Tommen, pawing at the still-nebulous pain in his hand, but then his hostage was taken from his grasp and he stumbled backwards.

Memories of Antsrinana Bay filled his mind, and his shoulder started to ache for no good reason. When he opened his eyes, he half-expected to see the jungle battlefield. Any number of nameless skirmishes from the Uprising added themselves to the confusing mix, and at the moment, he had no physical sight to fight against these images. His nose was suddenly awash in the stench of burning bodies, though some rational part of his mind knew it was impossible. He wasn't there. He wasn't there. He was there. He wasn't. He was.

Survival instinct kicked in and he recovered enough clarity to at least think about himself and his immediate needs. The worst pain was his hand. He had only a fraction of a second of useful sight with about every other blink, but he managed to discern that he was missing two of his fingers on his right hand, his index and middle fingers. His thumb was still technically attached, but it wasn't held on by much and he was pouring blood.

Tourniquet. He needed a tourniquet. Had to stop the bleeding. The bulletproof vest he'd taken from Tommen had had a handful of emergency medical supplies.

Groping around under his shirt with his off hand, he fumbled with zippers and velcro, finally feeling what he believed to be the appropriate shape of a packaged tourniquet and pulling it out. He ripped the package open with his teeth and started binding his hand and wrist. Most of it had to be done by feel as he vision was slow to return. It wasn't the best job, but hopefully it would get him out of here.

He seriously considered fleeing. Isthim and the others would ensure Lily died, but he was in no shape to fight just now, and he certainly wasn't going to be able to fight a demon. Looking around, blinking through sweat and occasional blindness, Rifun spotted Cassius on top of the cargo containers, though he couldn't see what he was doing. He'd done it. He'd lured the dragon to this place. Whether it was fear, the Akari, talking about Cassius, gunshots, the dragon was here. Or maybe it was lured by the smell of his blood. Whatever the reason, it was here, and he had planned to kill it. The tourniquet, though poor, made itself known as the blood to the rest of his hand began to slow and his hand started turning colors.

Slowly, he stood and returned to the group. Isthim and Tadashi had stood between him and the police in a tense standoff.

"That," Rifun said, addressing Walter but unable to conjure up anything in the neighborhood of threatening, "was a very nice trick. I have to say, I am impressed. And you even accomplished what you set out to do today, that is, win your son back and not have to sacrifice dearest Lily to do it."

"You have the right to remain silent," Walter told him firmly. "Anything you say can and will be used against you in a court of law. You have the right to an attorney. If you cannot afford one, one will be provided to you by the courts."

"I'm sorry, did I say I was surrendering?" Rifun interrupted. "Because I don't recall that bit. See, you set out to accomplish a goal, and you did. The problem is, I also set out to accomplish a goal, and I haven't done that yet. And most unfortunately for you, your son, and your entire team—not to mention Lily—I really can't leave until I've also accomplished my goals for the day. So, for as much as I admire your cunning, I'm afraid we're still not done here." He stepped back and Tadashi and Isthim filled the gap. "I'm sorry, Walter, but...I really need to kill Lily." He addressed the others. "At your leisure."

Isthim and Tadashi jumped into action. Donojok was not so graceful, but he was like a rockslide—pun intended. Once he got going, it was tough to make him stop. Rifun didn't know where Cassius was or what he was doing, but if he was here, he wasn't going to pass up the chance for carnage.

As for himself, he was going to have to retreat. He wasn't here to kill the officers, and the others were more than capable of killing Lily.

The pain had spread from his hand up his arm straight to his head. His head felt like a brick and a balloon at the same time as he stumbled his way into the warehouse. Once there, he found some cover and knelt, as much to contain his head as fix the tourniquet. He was no longer hemorrhaging, but he was still bleeding.

He looked up at the sound of footsteps and his head rewarded him with the threat of vomit. Still he saw it was Isthim with both Tommen and Lily in tow.

"I don't suppose you grabbed my fingers out there?" he asked, voice choked. He turned his attention back to his wrist where he was still fumbling with the tourniquet and a cloth binding for the open wounds. "I would hate to leave them behind; I have need of them."

"We'll worry about them later," Isthim declared. "Right now, we have bigger things to worry about. Walter will be coming for his child."

Rifun chanced a look up at her. "So let him have him. We have Lily."

Isthim shoved Tommen toward Rifun whose best move was to awkwardly fall to one side on his hip. He lost his grip on the tourniquet but snatched it back up and pulled tight once more. Isthim grabbed Lily and stalked off, deeper into the warehouse.

If he fled, Isthim or Cassius or all of them would hunt him down and kill him for a coward. If he stayed, the dragon was going to kill him one way or another, whether it was via Isthim or Cassius, or literally if he managed to split the dimensions.

He finished the tourniquet and the cloth binding and stood, head still sloshing. As he did, he noticed the large bay doors of the warehouse start to close. Well, at least this time, when he didn't show up to meet Lalao, he really would have died fighting evil spirits.

Tommen, frozen in fear, had not tried to run. Rifun took him by the arm and headed into the warehouse, going the direction Isthim and Lily had disappeared down, using Sound to muffle their movements.

They found Isthim standing over Lily who was tied to a chair, her posture limp as if dead.

"Great," Rifun said wistfully, making a vague gesture. "That's done. Now what?"

"You tell me," Isthim said, although her tone was a challenge, not a request for instruction.

Sighing, Rifun found another metal folding chair and pushed Tommen into it. He found some dirty straps to bind and gag the teenager. Then he stepped back and prepared to do the impossible.

His hand was numb, felt like a balloon filled with too much water. His arm was throbbing. His shoulder ached something fierce. His head hurt. He had become the irresistible bait, it seemed.

He opened a portal, and momentarily felt as though his head had exploded. He might have thrown up, he wasn't sure. But he knelt on the ground for some stability, found the boundary between dimensions, reached, and pulled. And kept pulling. And kept pulling. He pulled until the entire warehouse was encompassed within this quasi-dimension. It felt weak. It felt brittle. Like him right now. It wasn't going to last long. Neither was he.

He had discovered that when he inverted the portal, he could feel large objects become enveloped in the new dimension. He felt the cargo containers and the warehouse itself, naturally. He could feel the forklift at the far end of the building and the stack of folding chairs nearby. He could also feel himself, Isthim, Tommen, Lily, and someone else. Walter. Rifun grinned for no good reason, then used Sound to project his voice. Maybe if he kept talking he could focus a little more on the situation and less on his physical predicament.

"You know, Walter, I admire you. I really do." He paused, unprepared for just how much energy it took to talk right now. "I have to admit, though, I've never understood why criminals demand that an officer come alone, or maybe a parent or lover come alone with no cops. Believe me when I say this is much more exciting."

"Yeah?" Walter said, audible only because of Rifun's use of Sound. "Then why did you run and bring me in here alone?"

Rifun almost said, "I didn't," but pain and dizziness kept his mouth shut. He could feel Isthim watching him. If he went down, would she help him or kill him?

"Three shots," he began again, ignoring Walter's question. "One from a sniper, one from your Lieutenant. But where did the third one come from, I wonder?"

"I had a shot and I took it." He sounded very smug about that, Rifun thought.

"Pretty risky to shoot at me while I was still holding your son."

"It was a calculated risk."

"The same one you made when you broke out of Beaumaris Gaol, I presume? You're a very lucky man, Walter. Have you ever thought about what might happen when your luck runs out?"

"Then I expect I'll have to order some more."

"Well, that might be easier than ordering me a new hand." Rifun looked at his hand, now purple, completely numb.

Somewhere in the darkness, Walter spoke up. "Forgive me if I can't muster up enough sympathy to be concerned."

Rifun gritted his teeth, closed his eyes. "I should be able to keep my ring and pinkie fingers, my thumb if I'm lucky. But the other two are completely toast. They're gone. Nothing left for them."

"If it keeps you from pointing a gun at my son's head ever again, I don't feel sorry in the least."

Rifun managed an almost inaudible, wheezing croak of a laugh. "Oh, come now, Walter. Surely you know better than that. Dominant hands only matter in writing and long-distance target shooting. At close range, either hand will do. What is it they say, 'close enough for horseshoes, hand grenades, and nuclear war' ?"

Walter did not respond to that, or if he did, Rifun did not hear him. His whole arm was numb now, his shoulder screaming bloody murder, his neck stiff as a board. He was dizzy and a bit nauseous, and he didn't trust Isthim to help if something happened. He had to stay upright, at least long enough to get rid of Walter and get some help.

And how did he expect to get rid of Walter? There was no reason to kill him, except maybe that he was trying to kill them. There was a good chance, however, that Isthim wouldn't let him leave the warehouse alive, if only to make a point to Rifun.

The lights came on. Rifun got to his feet. He briefly wondered if it might not be better to be blind in this moment, so he didn't have to look at anything and make his nausea worse. His musings were cut short at the appearance of the man himself, his back to them for the moment as he strategically swept the warehouse.

"Congratulations, Walter," Rifun said.

The man jumped and whirled around. His gaze went to Rifun, then to Lily and Tommen, both still bound and gagged in their respective chairs.

"We couldn't have them giving away our position all the time," Isthim purred, covering for Rifun's fault. "It would take all the fun out of the game."

"Some game," Walter said grudgingly.

"But isn't everything about this a game?" Rifun said, trying to recover. "Lily here buys votes like a game of Monopoly. You hunt us down like a game of Clue. And poor Tommen just gets caught up as the Monkey in the Middle."

"Let them go, Rifun," Walter ordered. "There is nowhere to run."

"Oh, you are referring to your dearest Lieutenants and the Hands and candidates they bribed and manipulated into helping you? Well, Isthim already took care of one and the other couldn't get in here if he tried. And even if he did, he would be in no better situation than you are now, Walter. Because whether it is you or a hundred of you, I still hold the gun." He indicated his revolver, now resting awkwardly in his left hand. At close range, right or left didn't matter, but he wasn't especially intent on using it at all right now.

"Well, as soon as my guys take care of your goons, they'll be in here, and they'll not only take off your other hand, but they'll take off your head as well. Unless you surrender."

"Ah, so noble of you, Walter. Always offering a way out even for the worst offenders. Is this because you're a nice guy, or because of some sense of guilt that you escaped when no one else did?"

"Not my problem and we're a hundred years removed from it," Walter informed him firmly. "Try again."

A stab of pain tore into Rifun's head. He gritted his teeth, determined not to go down, not here, not now. This needed to end fast. Where was Cassius? "So, you've put the past behind you, have you? Time to move on, start new, turn over a new leaf as it were? So, instead of being a convicted murderer, you've gone to the other side, become a cop. What better way to run from your old life than with a completely new one? And yet, you've still held onto your old life, but he didn't even know it. So, Walter, before your son dies, why not turn over a new leaf with him, huh? Why not tell him who you really are?"

"Tommen..." he began, and trailed off.

"Dad..." Tommen said, his voice pleading.

Walter closed his eyes. He looked at Rifun. "No. I will not let you manipulate me or him with this bullshit! He is my son!" He took a step forward. Rifun, a bit surprised by his sudden bravado, took a step back, reaching for Gravity so he didn't stumble to his seat. "And you will not take him from me."

Rifun glanced at his hand. It was useless to him. The tourniquet had been effective and the gauze and cloth had done well to soak up the remaining blood, but he was of no mind to fight anyone or anything. Was Cassius or the dragon coming? How was he going to pull that off? He glanced at Isthim and nodded. She was going to kill Walter, but there was no getting away from death here.

She charged.

"Did you know," Rifun said, "that about forty percent of Borelians are what translates to in English as bitoxic. Not as impressive as bisexual in my opinion, but I digress. They have the ability to change color and so toxicity. Normally these toxicities are closely related, sort of like colors on the color wheel—blue and green, red and orange, and so on.

"But there are other Borelians called *vodrak* Borelians, or, as I call them, Vorelians. Only one in every million Borelians is a *vodrak*, able to change and move through the entire Borelian spectrum of color and toxicity, some colors which we can't even perceive and so don't have names for." He indicated Isthim, who still advanced on Walter. "Isthim is one such Vorelian. She was one of the most feared Borelian Fleet Generals, becoming so feared in fact, that her own people tried to imprison her for fear of what she might do."

Rifun chuckled. "Oh, and get this. She's a Harvester. Only an Intervention Harvester, true, but she'll kill you and then get paid for all the years you had left. And Tommen will be right here watching."

Isthim did not need to hurry as she moved, always in such a way that whatever fight they had would be within Tommen's line of sight. If she had sustained any wounds from the earlier fighting, they were now either healed or she was able to work through them as she moved from color to color to color.

"Dad," Tommen said weakly.

"It's all right, Tommen, I'll just be a few minutes longer than expected," Walter told him, trying to sound confident, like this was what he did everyday.

Then Tommen found a streak of courage as he began speaking. "Dad, blue is for the respiratory system, yellow for the circulatory." His voice was awkward, as if trying to speak around hearing loss. "White is for sexual pleasure and red is for the five senses. Green is for your clo—"

Rifun shoved the gag back in his mouth, if only because the sound was too loud and it annoyed him. He might have used Sound to muffle everything, but it was part of his ability to keep an eye on things and stay grounded.

Walter lasted longer against Isthim than he expected, and he respected the man for it. He was no rookie boxer. He was also no spry young man anymore. He was old, tired. He was going to die if he didn't get out of here. Rifun was going to lose a lot more than his hand if he didn't get help either.

"Lily is already dead, Walter," Rifun said, hoping to entice him to leave. "You gain nothing by fighting Isthim, and you have everything to lose. Why not just tell Tommen the truth?"

"Because you made him deaf, firing your gun at close range like that," Walter spat. "And even so, I'm not giving you the satisfaction."

"Cute excuse when it's a couple of high school girls, but we're grown men with some very high stakes. Can't you set aside your pride just this once?"

"I might ask the same of you." Walter almost missed the last word as he leapt back to avoid a blow from Isthim.

The veteran cop was able to get in a few good blows of his own, which Rifun could see only enraged Isthim. This was no longer just about proving a point to Rifun; now it was a matter of pride. She could not be beaten. She would not. There was no longer any chance for mercy for Walter.

"You see why I like her," Rifun commented.

"I'm beginning to get an idea," Walter admitted.

"But, we're on a timetable. Wrap it up, darling."

Isthim barely looked at him, but she nodded. What happened next took barely four Base Seconds, but it may as well have been four years for as well as Rifun felt. In the end, he Banded Isthim to give her a boost, and she charged through it like an arrow, augmenting her blow with Force, knocking Walter back against a stack of containers. The one on top crashed to the ground, kicking up a massive dust cloud.

Rifun walked over, taking his revolver from its holster. He'd maintained the current of his bad mood throughout the day, but now, with this injury, he was done. He was in some wretched pain and he was tired of this whole fiasco. This was not how things were supposed to go today. He pointed the gun at Walter who was just getting his head back together after the concussive force. He noted that Isthim had removed the man's vest.

"This has taken entirely too long," Rifun said coldly. Isthim came over and opened the revolver, removing the bullets and rubbing them with the poisonous oils on her fingers before reloading. "Cassius tells me I'm indecisive. Says I can't decide whether to do things straight arrow or play games with my targets. Maybe so. He also says that one day it will be the death of me. Again, maybe so."

"Isn't the bad guy's monologue supposed to be where he reveals his overarching evil schemes and tells me how feeble I am?" Walter asked, his gaze still fixed on the barrel of the revolver.

"Maybe," Rifun conceded. "Today is certainly a day for possibilities. But like I've told Tommen and the boys and now you, if I tell you my evil schemes and you somehow survive, then I only shoot myself in the foot. The risk isn't worth it."

"Well, like you said, at close range, dominant hand shouldn't matter. Or are you really that bad of a shot? Is that why you got Cassius to do the killing, because you either don't know how or are otherwise unwilling to get your hands dirty for the sake of an evil scheme?"

Rifun chuckled. "I like you, Walter, I really do. And I admire you. Facing death with such cool certainty and still finding it in you to come up with some witty, smart ass remarks. But you're right, what is a monologue without evil schemes but simply the bad guy talking for the sake of hearing his own voice?" He pulled back the hammer. It wasn't necessary, dramatic only. "Goodbye, Walter."

He fired.

If Isthim hadn't poisoned the bullets, Rifun could have strategically shot him so as to incapacitate him, knock him out, but still make a recovery in the end. But because of the poison, the best he could hope for was a swift, clean death. Painless, even. But the man was relentless, trying to Band and wiggle his way out. One shot turned into three, and none of them were the swift, painless death he might have hoped for. Except Rifun himself was running out of time and had to get going. Cassius wasn't coming, but more police probably were.

He passed by Tommen on the way out, untying the teenager's bonds, sparing a moment to watch him run to his father's aid. Then they were moving again. Four steps in, a wave of nausea took Rifun to a knee.

"Undo what you have done," Isthim commanded, hardly the voice or words of a concerned friend.

Rifun didn't know how, but he managed to put the inverted dimension back in its box, though it cost him everything but his life. With Isthim's help, he got back to the van, vomiting once before getting in the back and lying down on the floor.

The next thing he knew, he was being shaken awake and told to get out. He did so, the right side of his body barely functioning. He managed to discern the entrance to a hospital, big red signs marked "Emergency" directing him where to go. The doors slid open. Then his face met the floor.

kokumbo

"If you didn't want visitors, all you had to do was say so," Cassius said, folding his arms but feeling no real malice.

Actually, seeing Rifun laid up in bed was pretty damn satisfying. His right hand was bound tightly, though not in a cast per se, with pins sticking out of the stumps where his index and middle fingers used to be, and even more pins sticking out of his thumb. From what Cassius could see, he was not still under the influence of any drugs; he was just straight up depressed.

"I've told you twice to get out," Rifun whined, his expression a mixture of pain and annoyance but his tone barely getting over the threshold of a grumpy mumble.

"Are you going to make me?" Cassius wondered snidely. He made a vague gesture. "Why not just heal yourself? Can't the Akari grow you some new fingers? At the very least, get through whatever pity party bullshit you've got going on. Heal over the stumps and let's get going."

"I don't think you understand the process of human development in utero," Rifun said, his tone now well into the realm of rambling. "There is so much that has to go right at specific times just so we can have functioning fingers..." He lifted his arm and studied the spot where he could now see through his hand. "I wouldn't know where to begin right this second, and I don't know that I could do it later once it has healed. Maybe I can. But it will have to wait until I'm in a better mind, I think."

Cassius made a sarcastic motion. "Oh. Sorry. I didn't mean to intrude. Maybe I'll just tell Isthim to put off the enslavement, reschedule it for a time when you're 'in a better mind.' That make you feel better?"

"I would rather not be enslaved."

"Neither would I! Now snap the fuck out of it and let's come up with something!"

A shadow of Rifun's self returned as he said, "If you ever wanted a chance to invent and direct a plan without my interference, now would be that opportunity."

"The Borelians and the Grandfathers are going to wait until the inauguration, when the outgoing and incoming Hands are all in one spot. Then they're going to lock down the Seat, probably lock down the entire Wheel. They say they don't want a total massacre, but we know there will be violence. Is there any way we can turn the violence against them and get rid of the Borelians instead?"

Rifun sighed. His analytical mind and need for planning and control—and meetings, God help them—would not let him bathe in pity for long, and especially not when there was a problem to be solved. Still, that train was slow to leave the station.

"I know you wanted to kill me," Cassius said. "You laid that trap at the warehouse for me, not Walter."

"For the dragon, yes." Reluctantly, Rifun sat up and swung his legs over the edge of the bed, his movements awkward and exaggerated as he deliberately kept his right arm out of the way. "I will admit, I am a bit surprised to have woken up from the surgery—although I reportedly had a very nasty reaction to the medication, multiple seizures, which spooks me a little. But once again, I am surprisingly alive." His expression was a question as he looked at Cassius.

"I may have had some murderous intentions when I went to the hospital looking for you," Cassius admitted, shrugging. "I didn't find you there, figured you were fine. Came back here, expecting all to be well. Instead I find...this." He made a flippant gesture to compliment his sneer.

"As I said, this is your opportunity to implement a plan all by yourself."

Cassius ground his teeth. "I can't. The Borelians are still the dragon's chosen favorites. It won't plot against itself. This will have to be a forceful, physical break."

"Weren't you the one who said that my gods are the same as your gods? They won't plot against each other."

"As I said, a physical break."

Rifun shook his head. "Without the spirits, of any alignment, men are but weak, frail, flesh puppets. We as ourselves would never survive their wars. In that regard, our better option would be to make peace with the Akarin—"

"What?!" Cassius hissed.

Rifun put up a hand, his left hand. "Make peace with the Akarin, once again unite under the banner of the Author. We drive out the Borelians from our ranks and the greater Time industry."

Cassius took several menacing steps forward. "You yourself abandoned the idea of peace or reconciliation with the Akarin, declared it a lost cause. Even I, as Doug with his big mouth and obnoxious personality, can't get them to care about anything. What do you mean you want to make peace?" He continued before Rifun could speak. "Either of us goes there suing for peace, it will only confirm the Akarin suspicions that we are all talk and no action, that we are not the threat we proclaim to be." Still he went on, talking over the syllables that emerged from Rifun's throat. "We are literally begging people to take us seriously. Alliances are not the way to do that, not now. But if we, ourselves, were to take out the Borelians —"

"The Borelians," Rifun cut in forcefully. "Which ones? Just the ones in our army? There's only a dozen or so; go for it on your own, you can do it. The Grandfathers? A few more, yes, that might be a problem for one man. Or do you mean their entire civilization? The problem with the Borelians is that attacking one is attacking them all." He sighed. "We are already enslaved in every way but the physical chains." He lifted his right hand, winced, lowered it, raised his left hand and rubbed his face, his normal personality warring with his self-pity. "In that line of thought, the better option might be to conquer the Akarin instead. Subjugate them, force them to fight." He groaned. "But we don't have the time to plan out that kind of assault, not before the elections. And especially not without the Borelians knowing, damn Isthim."

Cassius nodded, took a step back, and spread his arms wide. "We're about to conquer the fucking Time industry. Again. Subjugate the Time Agents; all of the officers are going to be at the inauguration. Force them to fight."

Rifun paused, his demeanor saying that he was considering this almost against his will. Even Cassius could see the man wanted to go back to bed, but his mind would not let him.

"If we play this as 'the Borelians made us do it,' then we come off as their slaves already, their bitches doing their dirty work. As you said, we're already begging people to take us seriously. If we come in as the underdog, we will have no allies. If our amazing Akari power can't stop the Borelians, having some weakling Time Agents, even officers, with us won't mean much. All the Borelians have to do is Suppress them all anyway. But if we take control of the situation and frame this as our idea, our power —"

"And if our next target is the Borelians, some might listen," Cassius finished.

"Exactly. The Borelians are coming for the Time industry, so we endeavor to beat them to it."

"That's great, except the Grandfathers are carrying the bulk of the violence. Most of the Grandfathers are Borelians."

Rifun rubbed his face again. "Let me think on it some." He stood. "I think I need to walk around a little, get some fresh air."

Cassius got out of his way as he made his way to the door, still a tad unsteady on his feet. "Good. You still stink of iodine."

Rifun gave him a look over his shoulder. "You don't even know what iodine smells like."

"I do now."

The man was in no mood to argue and left his chambers silently, Cassius trailing as far as the doorway out of the officers building.

If the Borelians were good at anything, it was organization, and Isthim had organized the Cult well. Cassius hadn't been around enough to know what she was telling them to make them so eager to move out and conquer the Time industry, but he bet it wasn't the promise of a glorious future of enslavement and torture to the point of death.

Maybe he should go to the Wheel, see if he still held any power as the Missing Zero Hour or if the secretaries had rooted out every alias he had ever used. Isthim had said something about safeguarding his identity, but there had always been some tension between the secretaries and the Grandfathers. If any of the secretaries caught on and actually figured out what was going, what he had done, well, they could still do a lot of damage before the Grandfathers got to them.

He first returned to Earth, so if anyone did manage to track his portal, it wouldn't lead them right to the base. From there he went to the Wheel, delighted to see that he was shrouded as the Zero Hour. Good, so he hadn't been found out. He retained his virtually unlimited access to anything in the Wheel, including the other Hands. Things might get a little awkward if he ran into the "official" Zero Hour—assuming they hadn't been quietly demoted in the system—but he would deal with that if it came up.

A short tour through the marketplaces showed intense anxiety bordering on mass psychosis, but it was all quiet, a rip current rather than a frothing tide. It was the anxious walk before the actual chase, prey trying to get to safety as quickly as possible without igniting the predator's chase instinct.

Then he heard it. A hushed conversation between a couple of merchants, heard only through Sound in the din of the marketplace.

"There was an assassination attempt on the Harvester Lily Guile," one merchant whispered.

Assassination attempt. The first word was pleasing. The second was not.

Attempt.

"There have been many of those; what makes this one different?" the second merchant wondered, slightly skeptical.

"She escaped the Grandfathers themselves," the first hissed urgently.

"The Grandfathers? Are you sure?"

"Right through the claws of a Borelian."

"How?"

"I don't know. I know she's a Human, though, like the False Zero Hour. And the other leaders of the Cult of the Akari, if the rumors are true."

The second merchant made a sound of displeasure. "You think maybe the Humans and the Borelians, or—"

He cut himself off as Cassius, shrouded as the Zero Hour, approached. Although he seemed to have something more akin to scales than skin, the merchant appeared to go pale nonetheless.

"Perhaps you have some information about the situation?" Cassius inquired. "Something real and tangible? The Grandfathers don't like it when someone escapes their justice."

The merchants stared at him for a long moment. Finally the first one stuttered, "O-o-only rumors. N-nothing more."

Neither one offered up anything more, even as they had to be wondering if they were going to be turned over to the Grandfathers themselves. Let them see how easy it was to escape a Borelian.

"For your sake, they better be rumors only," Cassius threatened, then turned and stalked off.

They had to be. Word had gotten around about Lily's death and the telephone game took it from there. There were probably hundreds of wild stories about what happened. Maybe the dragon factored in, in some way. Maybe she rode off on the dragon. Maybe Isthim rode in on the dragon. Maybe there was some insane rumor about an epic and entirely impossible fight happening. That was how rumors worked; every party added some new layer of embellishment in order to make themselves look more "in the know" about what happened, or else to spruce up an otherwise boring report. Yes. That was all this was. After all, merchants had the most to lose from Lily's death, so of course they would concoct some daring escape or resurrection of their monetary savior. If and when it was confirmed that Lily was indeed dead, the panic would incite a metaphorical, if not literal, riot among the Merchants.

The Hands wouldn't be much better off, he thought, making his way to the Seat. The amount of money Lily dumped into the elections and the personal pockets of the Hands and Hand candidates was nothing to sneeze at, and its absence would be greatly noticed.

So, yes, they were just rumors. Lily understood these implications, this chain reaction that would occur if she were to die. If she were still alive, she would have to make some kind of appearance in order to reassure everyone that she was fine and business could carry on as normal. Not only that, but she would make a grand show of it, just to snub him, Cassius, and the rest of the Cult. Yes, Lily was most definitely dead. Besides, Isthim had been the one to kill her, and he would trust her to do the job far more thoroughly than Rifun.

Cassius wasn't overly interested in the day-to-day goings-on of the Wheel. Petitions were rote and petty, everyone bothering God with insignificant prayers to do well on a math test or smite the person who cut them off in traffic. It was only made worse when he considered that the Zero Hour didn't even vote except in case of a tie. With fifty regular Hands, the vote rarely even got close to a tie. Oftentimes, there were about ten or eleven interested Hands who really made a voting decision, and the rest went along with whoever they were allied to in that moment.

Still, he sat for a handful of cases, trying to get the feel of things. Were people really still worried about their dull grievances and slights to their oh-so-important pride? Or were they focused on more important things, like the security of the elections, the stability of the Time industry, and the future of the universe as a whole?

As it turned out, dull grievances and the oh-so-important pride were far more important than simple matters of existence. Who cared about the possibility of an intergalactic economic collapse and military coup when some tax loophole allowed a merchant to charge one extra turn for a Time Capsule of a particular grade?

Good grief, spirits good and evil, these people deserved to die like no one had deserved it before.

Then, just when he was ready to call it a day and walk out, the gate opened and the next petitioner walked in. He walked in, gawking like an idiot, like everyone did when they saw the Seat for the first time or it had been a while. Once his eyes had drunk their fill, he turned to face the Hands.

"Tommen Forbes," Cassius stated.

Normally one of the other Hands was in charge of keeping the cases straight, taking the notes from the secretaries, but in this case, Cassius couldn't help but speak. His one saving grace was that the acoustics of the Seat were such that the voice would be difficult to pin down as his.

Tommen stood there like an idiot for a moment longer, perhaps trying to make sense of it all, perhaps trying to figure out if the Zero Hour before him was Cassius.

"Great Hands of Time and Lord Zero Hour," Tommen greeted, his words strong though his posture denoted heaps of anxiety. "I come before you, Lord Zero Hour, overseer of the government. I come before you, Hand of Scientifically Advanced and Openly Engaged Civilizations. I come before you, Hand of Scientifically Advanced and Reserved Civilizations. I come before you, Hand of Scientifically Advanced and Unengaged Civilizations. Hand of Scientifically Advancing and Openly Engaged Civilizations."

Fifty-one Hands, each with his own title. Such introductions were incredibly tedious and often hurried through or overlooked entirely—especially for those who spent half the day before the Hands making petitions—but the kid was determined to get through them, butter up each and every Hand so as to curry favor.

The first twenty-one titles were easy. While the teenager stumbled through the last thirty, Cassius took the time to actually look through the notes of the case. Ha! He was here to strike a bargain. Well now, this was more exciting than some dull grievance.

"Timekeeper Tommen Forbes, you do yourself and your mentor credit with your knowledge, formality, and acknowledgment of tradition," Cassius said once Tommen was done with the titles. "You come before us now with a case that we may hear and act upon. You wish to ask a favor of the Hands and strike a bargain."

"I do."

"What do you ask of us?"

"Good Hands, in recent weeks on my world, my father, mentor, and Timekeeper Captain Walter Forbes had been pursuing two very dangerous Runners, Cassius Hand and Rifun Ndolo, whom I believe you are familiar with." He paused, perhaps looking for a reaction to the names. Cassius remained still. "He sought them out adamantly with the help of his Lieutenants, using every resource he had available to him on Earth and in Time." He paused again, maybe searching for words. "I myself was captured by these Runners and held for two weeks." Another pause. Clearly the kid wasn't a public speaker, but then, neither was Cassius. "Captain Forbes pursued them all the more and eventually confronted them, but Cassius and Rifun were not working alone." Yet another pause, perhaps an attempt at dramatic effect, except everyone already knew he and Rifun weren't working alone. "Among their helpers was a *vodrak* Borelian named Isthim." Still pausing, proud of information that everyone else already knew or was unimportant. "Rifun, being too cowardly to face Captain Forbes himself, sent Isthim to fight him instead." Even a teenager could see Rifun was a coward. "In the end, Isthim was unable to kill Captain Forbes by herself." Well of course Tommen was going to make his dad look as good as possible. On the other hand, Owain Fforidd had always been a formidable opponent; he may have actually proven a challenge for Isthim. "Instead, she poisoned the weapon that Rifun used to attempt to kill Captain Forbes. And Rifun and all his helpers got away."

Tommen stood there for a moment, studying the Hands, as if waiting for some cue. When none came, he continued, "Captain Forbes was rescued and taken to a medical facility where his major physical wounds were treated. However, the poison that Isthim used to taint Rifun's weapon found its way into his bloodstream. He's dying." He shifted uncomfortably, straightened, and finally got to the real point of his argument. "I have been told and read many times that there is no cure for Borelian poison, or if there is, they keep it under heavy guard. But just yesterday, my people made their annual celebration of gift-giving, and when we presented Captain Forbes with his gifts, a friend of mine who is a Harvester confirmed that his countdown reversed."

A Harvester friend? Well, there were plenty of Harvesters on Earth, but in Region Four, District Four—No. It wasn't Lily. If she were alive, she would be the one before them. She had the experience and the attitude to deal with them. They wouldn't send this puny teenager to argue in a court of law. They called in some other Harvester to help.

"It was not a large reversal," Tommen was saying, "only a few seconds, but for a few seconds, Captain Forbes was able to fight the poison that invades his system. It can be done.

"My world is scientifically advancing, but unengaged. The doctors treat him the best they can, but with no knowledge of Borelians or their poisons. One of their treatments unwittingly undid the small progress that was made and even made Captain Forbes worse. My friend who is a Harvester says he went from six days to four days to live." He tried to put on a tough face. "I have been told, and I have seen that Cassius and Rifun are very powerful Time Agents, a Triage Harvester and a Warden Timekeeper. And they have a powerful ally in a *vodrak* Borelian. This concerns everyone, regardless of any rumors. They are not the average Runner who may be pursued and turned over to the Grandfathers. They are cunning and bloodthirsty and may go after whomever they please with little or no resistance. And a *vodrak* Borelian will be immune to even the greatest torture the Grandfathers may inflict upon them."

Cassius was glad the shrouds masked his face as well, or his smile would have given everything away. How naive this child was.

"My proposal is a simple yet profitable one," Tommen continued. "You, Great Hands and Lord Zero Hour, are very powerful, and your influence reaches to the ends of the universe to civilizations untouched. I want only one thing. I want the antidote to the Borelian poison. I cannot say which poison she used as she is a vodrak and it was poor light when the incident occurred. Perhaps the acquisition of the antidotes will shed light on which one I need.

"I realize this sounds a steep proposal as the Borelians are willing to kill to keep the antidotes secret. But they also cast out Isthim because she was so volatile that even her own war-like race feared her. Now look what she has the power to do. I propose that the Hands—and perhaps the Grandfathers may be interested— devote all resources to the pursuit and capture of the *vodrak* Borelian Isthim— Cassius and Rifun being mere extras. The Hands will turn her over to the Borelians so they may dispense their own justice in exchange for the antidotes to each of their poisons.

"Now, you have an excellent opportunity to expand your market. People all over the universe will pay anything for a little extra Time, minutes, seconds, all precious. Borelian poisons transcend Time, making all those Time Capsules in the marketplaces and the auctions utterly worthless. How much more would someone pay for that antidote if they needed it? I have no doubt that once you get your hands on one antidote, you will find a way to make more and make money from it.

"And not only do you open a new market, but you hold the Borelians hostage to their own terror. They consider themselves superior, invincible, what wouldn't they give to remain that way and not have those antidotes distributed? What could you make them do? What could you make the Grandfathers do, since they rely on the Borelians for their staff?"

Cassius Banded and laughed. And laughed. And coughed. And laughed some more. Cassius had never been one to really appreciate comedy, but this kid was gold. Absolutely priceless. How incredibly ignorant he was of the situation. No doubt Micaiah had helped him prepare for this speech, which only betrayed even his limited knowledge of the situation. Damn, that memory erasure had really done a number on him. Or maybe Cassius just knew too much about the situation. Whatever the case... He giggled again before finally regaining his composure and dropping the Band.

"And you expect that we would just hand over a vial of the antidote to you?" he asked, trying to keep the smile out of his voice. "Why?"

Tommen smirked. "Because it was my idea. All the rest goes to you, but I only want the one. Because after all, if you had this idea yourselves, I have little doubt it would have been done already."

Cocky bastard, Cassius would give him that. But then, what teenager wasn't?

"You expect us to simply divert all available resources to hunt down Isthim?" another Hand inquired.

"Yes, I do, seeing how simply sending in three Timekeeping officers and twenty men of the local policing force was already inadequate."

"You said that Captain Forbes has approximately four days to live," a third Hand said. "Have you any idea where they might be, where we should send our forces to look?"

"I do not," Tommen admitted.

"What makes you think the Borelians will trade the antidotes for Isthim?" another asked.

"Because they know how dangerous she is. That was why they sent her away in the first place—or lost her in pursuit—either way to their shame. They cannot afford to simply let her go a second time. She once told me that only the highest officers are engaged in Time, so they understand the higher stakes if she is not dealt with. And the only way to deal with her is to execute her."

"We cannot simply let her go either," someone else pointed out. "They would call our bluff."

"Then don't bluff."

"Are you suggesting we actually let her go?"

"Set it up however you want to falsely release and then recapture her, enough to unsettle the Borelians and make them believe that you would do it, that you would release her again into the larger universe, into Time."

Naive, ignorant, arrogant, had Rifun somehow turned Tommen into his protege while in that cave?

"Your proposal is a unique and perplexing one, Tommen Forbes," he said, cutting off the hearing. "We will take your story and your proposal under advisement and retire to deliberate."

"That is all I can ask," Tommen replied.

The Hands stood and shuffled out of their seats and into the deliberation room. This part was not always necessary—especially for those who spent half the day in the Seat pleading petitions—but this time it felt necessary.

Tommen was not the first one to come asking about the antidote to Borelian poison; most often it was friends or relatives of those who had suffered at the hands of the Borelian Grandfathers. Normally such proposals were rejected without much, if any, entertainment or pretext of discussion. This one might have been, too, if not for Cassius' curiosity and the hushed chaos surrounding Lily's death.

Despite the lengthy, tedious introductions and formalities that some petitioners went through, the Hands observed no such rituals among themselves. Well, most didn't. Most were too sick of hearing such adulation to want to burn others' ears with it, although there were a few who never seemed to tire of the constant praise, however sarcastic it was at times.

"Why are we even bothering discussing this insane idea?" one Hand asked, at the same time another Hand remarked, "His idea is rather cunning and may be just the excuse we need to pull off such a maneuver."

"He's not the first to suggest such a thing," another pointed out. "What makes this time different?"

And so the arguing began.

"It is the beginning of an actual plan, and it goes after two known enemies of the industry."

"The Cult of the Akari, sure, but the Borelians? Are they really an enemy?"

"The Borelians are an enemy to all."

"Individual species, yes, but to the business? Do they plot against us in some way?"

"They control the Grandfathers."

"And what's wrong with that?" the Hand of the Grandfathers wondered. "They are an effective species to use to enforce the Laws of Time. Laws which we and past Hands have legislated. Are we going to bar them from such service because they are doing what they are good at?"

"And what's that? Torture and slavery?"

"We hold no such reservations about other powerful species," another Hand mused. "Even those whose technological capabilities rival our own, we do not exclude from engaging in legal business. Nor do we seek to overpower others based on simple biology."

Now there was a lie, Cassius thought. It was rare that the Hands felt so threatened, but the difference was that the Borelians had the means, both biological and technological, to fight back and hold their ground.

"But if we are a business, we should enforce laws only related to business. The simple Laws of Time, as they were in the beginning. I don't think anyone here can say that they have never used the Grandfathers for more personal uses, roughing up a rival, imprisoning a candidate who threatens a seat in the next election."

"But if we are a business," another Hand echoed sarcastically, "then this is just another product or service that we can offer. There are plenty of species who sell their technology and art and medicine in the wares marketplace."

"The Borelians would never stand for it. You know what happened the last time the Hands tried something like that."

"We didn't try it; we simply didn't stop it."

"And so triggered a war and a Rebuild."

"Coincidence only."

"You're willing to test that assumption?"

"I say we let him die," someone cut in, oddly echoing Cassius' thoughts. "We have no reason to humor this—not even an Apprentice Timekeeper, a probationary—and try to meet some arbitrary deadline. The Borelians are a threat any day on the calendar. There are plenty of people who have been killed or crippled by Borelian poison. We have enough problems of our own to worry about."

"He didn't even have a good lead to give us," another Hand agreed.

"We can't just dismiss him," a third Hand protested. "Helping him could help others. It's the right thing to do."

There were some sighs, a few murmurs, and probably a lot of eye rolling; with the shrouds it was hard to tell. Hands with morals didn't tend to get more than one term, if they made it that long.

The arguments continued, sides were taken. Those who wanted to pursue Tommen's idea favored expanded business opportunities and keeping the Borelians in check (and there was some weak voice about being morally correct or something). Those who rejected the notion thought it too risky to cross the Borelians or else it would be a poor business venture. It was good to keep a few predators around; it kept the prey on their toes. Still there were a few who wanted to publicly reject the idea and privately pursue it later, maybe after the elections.

It was all about business. Tommen was never mentioned, Walter only obliquely referenced once. Nevertheless, when all was said and done, the Hands were at a stunning tied vote. Such a thing almost never happened, had never happened while Cassius cared to show up for these meetings.

Die, Owain, Cassius thought as he cast his vote. *Die like you should have all those decades ago.*

They signaled the Bat that a verdict had been rendered, then filed out of the deliberation room. A minute or two later, the gate opened and Tommen walked back into the Coliseum.

"Timekeeper Tommen Forbes," Cassius began before anyone could steal the honor of delivering the bad news.

"Great Hands of Time and Lord Zero Hour, I thank you for taking the time to hear my case and for the time spent in deliberation. I hope all arguments were constructive and a consensus was made in fair and just due order." He was trying so hard.

Cassius grinned because he knew the teenager couldn't see it. "And we, the Hands of Time and the Zero Hour, thank you for your time as well, for the time spent before the lower courts, as well as your forethought in your case and proposal, your patience in waiting for our deliberations, and your participation in the courts as a whole. Our arguments were few but severe, yet our deliberations were swift. But in the end, we believe justice, reason, and common sense have prevailed."

Fucking hell, he sounded like Rifun. But in this instance, watching Tommen squirm in anticipation like an anxious lover, he was all right with that.

"Your proposal was a unique one, cunning and deliberate," he went on. "No doubt you as a human are considered brilliant and persuasive among your people, a leader with a satin voice." Maybe that was a bit over the top, but now he was just having fun. "It is not easy to come before us and speak, let alone deliver such a...controversial case." He shifted his stance. "What you have proposed, many of the Hands would stand to gain from. Arguments were severe on both sides. Verdicts are made from a majority vote of the Hands. As Zero Hour, I am tasked with presiding and do not vote unless there is a tie vote that cannot be resolved. I have not needed to cast a vote in nine years, and today I have needed."

Technically, it was true that Cassius himself hadn't needed to cast a vote in nine years. Now, considering most of those years were actually many decades ago, and whether the other, real Zero Hour had voted at any more recent time, he could not say.

"And so, in the case proposal brought by Timekeeper Tommen Forbes, bringing to light the circumstances of Captain Forbes' health as well as proposing the capture of the Borelian Isthim and the trade and distribution of Borelian antidotes, we, the Hands of Time and the Zero Hour..." He paused to much better effect than Tommen. "Reject your proposal."

Cassius Banded so he could savor the moment as the anticipation gave way to that look of stark horror. They weren't going to help him. They weren't going to help and his dad was going to die.

"If I may beg the Hands for an explanation?" Tommen asked, his tone suggesting he hadn't fully processed the news quite yet.

"We are aware of the circumstances of Captain Forbes' ailment," Cassius began, trying not to give too much away. "And while we are sympathetic, not only for the impending loss of your captain but your father as well, incidents with Runners happen every day. They are not always as powerful as Rifun and Cassius, but neither are they always without loss. As for the method of your proposal, while the pursuit and capture of Isthim—with the potential 'consolation prize' of Cassius and Rifun—would represent a significant victory for the Hands and Timekeepers...that is why the Hands have Timekeepers. It is up to the next Captain of District Four to be more judicious with his pursuit and attack, and learn from Captain Forbes' mistakes.

"Furthermore, it is the judgment of the Hands that the gamble of trading Isthim for the antidotes is too much risk for the safety of everyone involved. The Borelians are violent, war-like, and extremely unpredictable. They are as likely to accept Isthim back with honors as much as execute her, which would put her in a position of potential retaliation." The problem was that they already had accepted her back and they were in the process of retaliation. "And even if they did agree to execute her, there is no guarantee they would hand over the antidotes. Furthermore, they are well-documented to kill or make slaves of anyone who tries to steal or concoct their antidotes."

Cassius took a breath and continued to channel his inner Rifun. "As to the proposal of opening up a new industry focused on the antidotes, the price that the antidotes must be held at in order to both maintain demand and maintain control over the Borelians would limit the market and so outweigh the cost of efficiency, assuming we held the market ourselves. We were most intrigued, however, about your proposal to control the Grandfathers. While it is true that they rely on the Borelians for staff, there is no strife between the Hands and the Grandfathers to warrant such a binding."

It was a lie and everyone knew it, even Tommen down there, but that was the magic of playing politics. "We appreciate your loyalty to your Captain and your love for your father. We appreciate the forethought you put into your proposal and your desire to see that everyone benefits, and the industry—and indeed the universe—is rid of a grave evil."

"Then what's the problem?" Tommen cut in, temper flaring, flattering formalities forgotten. "Why won't you help?"

"To speak candidly, Tommen Forbes," another Hand said, "and with your pardon, Lord Zero Hour—" Cassius nodded. He was done here. "—even if we did agree to help, what do you think are the odds of us finding and capturing Isthim within the four days that your father has left to live? If it were that easy to find and capture her, you think she might not have already been captured by now, before all this began? Furthermore, the Borelians are no real threat to humans. The

Borelians terrorize other systems and other planets with far greater force and brutality. On some worlds, people would rather die trying to steal or develop an antidote than be captured and sold into slavery. Once, a small black market did crop up, but the only thing that remains of it now are the stories of how it was destroyed. And it was not a beautiful thing to behold."

"Well-spoken," Cassius said. "So you see, Tommen Forbes, it is a brilliant plan on paper and in speech, but in practice, it is wildly impractical and even deadly."

"Is there nothing you can suggest?" he wondered, the realization just now starting to kick in. "Are there no survivors who can share their secrets? The Harvester can attest to him gaining ground, before our doctors bungled it all up. There must be a way."

"There are survivors," Cassius admitted, "but they are slaves, far out of the reach of Time and inaccessible to most everyone else anyway. We are sorry, Tommen Forbes, but the Borelian poisons are unique toxins, and they alone hold the key to unlocking the antidotes."

With that, the verdict was rendered, and they went through the process of explaining which Hand voted which way. It wasn't necessary, but with all the other formalities they'd had to suffer through in this case, he might as well rub it in just a little more. Finally he closed with, "This case, being of Timekeeper Tommen Forbes inquiring of an antidote for his dying captain and proposal to the Hands for the capture and ransom of the Borelian Runner Isthim, is closed, having been rejected by a vote of twenty-six to twenty-five. This case may not be reopened or appealed, and a case may not be brought against it again in these circumstances. I, the Zero Hour, thank the Hands for their time and prudence in this matter, and thank Tommen Forbes for his time and forethought in his case. This will be the last case we will hear today, and we will reconvene for another session in due time."

And that was that. They filed out of the Coliseum and dispersed. Cassius went straight to the portal room and left the Wheel. Just as soon as he was recovered on the other side, he burst into laughter. He laughed himself all the way back to the Ruins of Meroian and the officers' building. Anyone who saw him must have thought him mad, but he didn't care. Isthim regarded him with some suspicion.

"Just what is so hilarious?" she demanded testily after he'd laughed for three straight minutes in her presence, most of it forced just for the pleasure of her irritation.

"I've come to appreciate what you and Rifun enjoy about psychological torture," he told her.

"Yes, the laughter of a madman can be agonizing." He couldn't decide how sarcastic she was being, but it mattered little. "Exactly what has prompted this psychological breakdown into perpetual hilarity?"

He bit off a giggle and sighed, giving her a look. "I still don't understand your fondness for big words, however."

"Then use simple ones to explain what is going on," she snapped.

So he explained what had happened, from Tommen going before the Hands, to Cassius rejecting the proposal by oh so narrow of a vote. He described the look of anguish that crossed the teenager's face as he realized what it all meant.

Isthim might have been more impressed if she hadn't been so annoyed to begin with. At the moment, the best Cassius was going to get out of her was mild interest, a single nod, and, "An interesting development, considering how spineless he was during the event. But he is no longer our concern."

Her tone suggested something much different. Tommen had just become more important, not to the Cult, but to the Borelians. He may not have committed the sin of seeking out or concocting an antidote to their toxins, but he had suggested it. He had attempted to persuade others and even succeeded with a few of his audience. *If any man even thinks about stopping the Borelians, he is guilty of the punishment,* Cassius mused.

He changed the subject. "Funny how things go well when Rifun gets out of the way."

Her expression said she was not going to change the subject, but neither was she going to discuss it with him. Instead, she took her leave and stalked off, probably to find Misik.

Well, he seemed to have a bunch of free time all of a sudden. Lily was dead, Owain was going to die, and the Akarin were going to sip tea all the way to the executioner's block. Maybe it was time to make good on his stalking and the paranoia he had instilled in at least a few Akarin members. He'd created a hit list. Maybe it was time to start knocking off hits.

He returned to Earth, one face among many in the bustling chaos of New York City. It wasn't difficult to swipe food here and there, just enough to nibble on while he considered his list and made his plans.

His stalking of the people on his list revealed that most of them were of mediocre to average talent, Journeyman or Master to compare them to Time ranks.

Those who were still part of Time had even worse abilities, Apprentices and Journeymen, only one Master among them. Not much of a challenge for Cassius. If he visited them Disguised as Doug, it might be even easier.

But he had to send a message. He no longer believed that the Akarin could be roused from their catatonic state into anything resembling action, but he wanted to make it slightly more meaningful than just another killing spree.

He could remove their throats, make sure everyone knew it was him. Maybe he would end up on national news as some terrifying serial killer. If he did it fast enough, where he couldn't possibly have traveled so fast by conventional means, maybe they would claim there were a bunch of copycats, or else an organized network of psychopaths or terrorists with a sickening signature. That would be fun. And, hell, it was Christmas Day. Such a slaughter would be terribly memorable and scar people, whole families, for years.

Maybe he could do a few today, a few over New Year's, and a few right before the elections in the Wheel. Keep them guessing. Let them realize that their passivity was only weakness, and he would not be stopped. It was impossible to kill him with kindness. Isthim had said something about complimenting the Akarin response—or maybe opposing it?—in order to discredit them. If the Cult was going to take over anyway, and if the Borelians were going to go on their own power trip, what did it really matter? Were a few more days of mind games really going to make that much of a difference in the grand scheme of things?

Who to go after first? Maybe he should kill Walter, just to get it over with, beat Tommen psychologically bloody twice in one day. That sounded like a good place to start. Then he'd go after Micaiah and then the others.

He knew he wouldn't be able to walk around Charleston as he was, so he Disguised himself as a nurse to get into the hospital. It smelled of bleach and iodine and sterile water and sickness and despair and death. Any Christmas cheer ended with the decorations, a sober reminder to any walking the halls that things were not supposed to be this way, not today. As if the universe cared about man-made holidays.

He snaked his way to Intensive Care. He might have hoped that every patient was catatonic enough that he could just peek in and leave—and he could have, if he'd thought to Band, which he hadn't. Instead, although the first room was empty, the second room he was flagged down by three little kids all huddled around a man thick with bandages.

Cassius could have ducked out, ignored them entirely, except he was fairly certain this was one of the officers who had been there.

"Daddy wants water!" one of the kids blurted before the man could speak.

Cassius took the out, nodding once, turning on his heel, and leaving the room. He'd come back for the officer once he'd taken care of the Akarin targets.

That was not the only officer in ICU. One was indeed catatonic, at risk of going brain dead. Another was in an induced coma while he recovered from what should have been a fatal neck wound. Cassius didn't recognize the man, but he recognized his handiwork. This had been one of the backup team members; obviously he'd botched the job if the man hadn't died instantly. Well, just another one on the list for when Cassius got back from his current kill list.

Finally he found Walter's room. But it was not Walter that drew his attention.

Lily looked up from where she sat at his bedside. She wore no makeup and her face was blotchy from crying and worrying. For a moment, one could almost picture her as a human being. She stared at Cassius, Disguised as a nurse. Finally she made a motion and said, "What? Are you going to do something?" Another gesture. "He's still alive."

"How are you alive?" The words came out of Cassius' mouth before he could stop them.

Her expression cycled through several compositions: resignation, as if she fully intended to answer the question; confusion, as to why a hospital nurse was asking such a question; realization, that this nurse might not be who she thought it was, helped in no small part by Cassius shedding the Disguise and Banding the two of them.

"Your pet bitch might know a lot about death, but she doesn't know a lot about practical jokes," Lily said, standing and taking one step back for every one Cassius took forward until she hit the wall. "Taking all those years I've skimmed and stolen, dragging them down into myself as if to make a Time Capsule out of them, bringing myself to within one second of natural death, leaving the residue of some terrible disease I've taken from the infants, she thought she scared me to death, watched my clock count down and never expected to have to verify it. Arrogant bitch."

Cassius approached until he was breathing on her. "Looks like I'm here to finish the job, hm?"

"You didn't know I was alive. You came here to kill Walter." She shrugged.

"Probably the others, too."

"And finish a job Isthim failed to do. Oh, that will burn her," Cassius chuckled and grinned, "and I'm going to enjoy it."

"If you're going to kill me, then do it. But don't kill Walter. He'll die in his own time."

He grinned wider, enjoyed watching her shrink even as she tried to put on a strong face. She even closed her eyes, waiting for the moment when her throat suddenly disappeared. Finally, Cassius took a step back.

"You're right," he said. "I'm not here to kill you. Not yet. And maybe I'll even give Walter and the others a few more days, too."

"You're not that merciful," Lily said, daring to open her eyes, though her breathing was still shallow. "You're not that smart, either. Who are you going to kill?"

"If I told you, you'd warn them."

"Because anyone could escape you anyway." Her intent was perhaps more hostile than her delivery. This was the fear he had been looking for.

He nodded and turned to leave. "Make sure you keep that in mind, in case you get any ideas about warning people."

He put Lily out of the Band, then held it until he was a fair distance from the hospital. There he dropped the Band and opened a portal back to the officers building. First he would inform Isthim of her fuck up, if only to see her expression when she learned of such humiliating failure. Then he would get back to his regular hit list. Once that was complete, he would return for the officers, Walter, and, finally, Lily Guile.

Remediation

Vulnerability was Rifun's biggest fear. When it came right down to it, he was afraid of being utterly vulnerable. Sleep was a vulnerability, but also a frustrating biological necessity. He had, however, learned how to sleep lightly and react to any perceived threat while he slept, this reflex most often tested by Cassius.

Drugged vulnerability was a yawning abyss of terror. Not only was he at the mercy of others, but he was chemically inhibited from reacting in any meaningful way. He didn't care if it had been necessary for surgery, it was still extremely terrifying. What made it even worse was having a reaction to those chemicals, not knowing what was going on, and having a very real fear and chance of having been poisoned. While the doctor overseeing his care was a Time Agent who understood what was going on and how things really happened, it didn't help that this doctor was also a tad questionable in his morals. He had a fascination with injuries and pain that was too reminisce of the callousness of Rifun's torturers.

But if he wanted care for his hand without getting found out, he had to see this doctor.

"I take it there's been no luck on your magical Akari regrowing fingers," Dr. Haunstein said, unwrapping the last layer of bandages.

"No," Rifun admitted, his eyes glued to the gore. He knew it wasn't bad, that Banding had given the wound sites several extra days to heal up, yet his mind was locked into two simultaneous thoughts: first, that something should be there and wasn't; second, a reminder that this was the present day and he was fine, and there were no prison guards here.

The doctor took Rifun's right hand in one of his and slowly removed the pins from the stumps; Rifun could feel them slide out of his flesh and it made his skin crawl. "And no further seizures?"

"No."

"Good. Just a reaction to the antibiotics, then." He put the pins aside and picked up a pen. "I'll make a note." He gently turned Rifun's hand over and back again, inspecting the stumps, the stitches, and the thumb which was still pinned in place. "The important thing is that your thumb appears to be healing up. Come back in a few days and I'll take the pins out."

"Why not just Band it?" Rifun wondered, watching the doctor reach for fresh bandages.

Haunstein picked at the end of a roll of gauze. "We mortal beings are temporal, linear creatures. We are set in this plane of time and exist in this plane. It is inherently unnatural for us to jump from plane to plane, faster or slower, whatever the case may be." He found the edge, put a small gauze pad over the stumps, then began wrapping, over the stumps, around the hand, gentle around the thumb, and back again. "While Banding is a useful tool, we exist in a certain plane, a certain frequency, and that plane is where we heal the best because it is our natural temporal climate, so to speak. A fish may swim from one depth to another because it can, but there is a certain depth where it is healthy, where it is home. Time is no different."

"But if I were to find a way to regrow my fingers, you wouldn't question the miracle."

The doctor sighed and taped the gauze. "No, I wouldn't." He let Rifun have his hand back. "I suppose that will be your homework assignment, hm? Regrow your fingers. Prove me wrong."

Rifun scowled as he stood and left the doctor's home with barely a thank you, returning to the Caves of Meroian and making his way to the officers building. He was still a bit out of sorts with everything going on, with most of his attention still focused on his missing fingers. He recalled in the aftermath of World War II and the Uprising, amputees would swear by all the gods and spirits that they still had limbs, and that they still had pain in those limbs. Rifun had never understood how one could feel such real pain from something that wasn't there. It wasn't even a spiritual matter, but a physical one.

Now he understood. He would drum his fingers in regular pattern, feel his index and middle fingers move in proper rhythm, but there was no sound and he couldn't feel the pressure of them actually tapping the table. It was a truly dreadful feeling.

So he was a little unprepared for Isthim to intercept him in the officers building and tell him something or other about Cassius threatening Lily—whose not-death had enraged Isthim—and how Tommen and one of the Hands had gone on a rescue mission for Walter and something-something the man was now up and walking around, cured of Borelian poison, but everyone here was angry and no one really wanted to wait for the elections to make a move.

"I don't care if Tommen is one of your special ones," Isthim was saying. Her vocal assist and the grating noises coming from it were doing nothing for the headache that had sprouted in Rifun's brain. "After the mess he left in the Wheel, the Grandfathers will—"

"Oh, save your energy," he told her, not in the mood to hear it. "Tommen is one person. Lily is one person. We're here for the Time industry itself, the Wheel itself. Just because you got bested by a couple of slaves doesn't mean—"

Reflex saved him more than conscious thought as she made to strike him. Instinctively, he put his right arm up to defend himself but was forced to dodge instead, twisting to protect his wounded hand. Isthim made no further move, though her anger was apparent.

"You and Cassius are working on that Akarin hit list," Rifun stated. "I applaud your use of Lily to get it done, especially since Tadashi seems to have deserted. You two focus on the hit list and tracking down Tadashi, I will go have a chat with Tommen. Maybe I can smooth things over a little in that arena."

It was the last thing he wanted to do, honestly, but it might be his last opportunity before the elections.

He was a bit behind on his information on Tommen, but it didn't take much to figure out that he was staying with the Durvin twins while his dad was in the hospital. The house was mostly dark when he stepped through the portal into the living room, though he noted the light in the bathroom. With his head still pounding, Rifun made his way to the couch and sat there, relaxing in the dark.

Lily Guile was alive. She'd given Isthim the slip. Despite every feral instinct telling her to kill Lily in the most abjectly cruel fashion imaginable—and Rifun could imagine a variety of torturous horrors—Isthim had instead sent several agents to intimidate her and recruit her into helping Cassius knock off his Akarin hit list in exchange for her life and potentially surviving the coming coup. He wouldn't let her, of course, but he was finally getting the fear he had been craving.

Meanwhile, Tommen and one of the Hands had run off in search of a cure for Borelian poison. A futile gesture by all accounts, but it was, as they say, the thought that counts. And Borelians couldn't abide the thought of someone even trying to cure their poisons. They might have even captured Tommen, too, if not for some help from Assim Foyez. Once a Regional Manager, Foyez now lived in western Canada on the border with Alaska, apparently terrified that the Cult was going to find him. Rifun didn't intend to kill the man necessarily, but there might be words later, once he was done here.

The bathroom light turned off, the door opened, and Tommen strode out with shaky purpose, trying to hold everything together but terrified of being too late. He didn't look around. Didn't even realize there was an intruder in the house.

"Hello, Tommen," Rifun said.

The teenager just about went through the roof. Rifun leaned forward, flicked on a lamp, then stood and approached.

"Off to save your father?" he inquired. "How sweet."

"How did you get in here?" Tommen asked, his voice wavering.

"How did you?" Rifun shrugged. "I'm a Warden, same as Foyez. All I needed were the coordinates."

"Why are you here?"

"You know, you've caused a lot of trouble for me lately." Rifun held up his right hand to show the missing fingers. "The thumb was able to be saved, albeit just barely. The other two?" He shook his head. "Toast. Or sausages, whichever you prefer."

"You did that to yourself."

"By holding you hostage? Dear boy, did you ever really think I was going to kill you? You, who are an Akari-bearer? You're far too valuable for that."

"Well then, it was a pretty convincing act. And I don't buy that Akari bullshit either."

"Of course you don't. Not yet. But you will. As will Foyez. As will Micaiah."

Tommen shook his head, mildly afraid yet unimpressed. "What is it you want? Cassius wants to be the Zero Hour, King of Time or some shit. What do you want? To terrorize people?"

"Think of me as his right hand. Or his puppet master, whichever you prefer. And that reminds me, you caused quite a bit of trouble in the Wheel today, too. Now, not only are the Hands and Grandfathers out for you, but several dozen Merchants are, too. Including one very angry Urdhei who claims you completely overturned his booth and wasted probably four years' worth of Time Capsules."

"I'll be more careful next time," Tommen said through gritted teeth.

"Oh, I'm sure you will. After all, you really won't have much of a choice."

"What do you mean?" His expression said he had a good idea where this was going.

"As of this moment, if you ever set foot in the Wheel again, you will be arrested on the spot and taken away to have your clock broken." Rifun was not one hundred percent certain of this, but if Isthim's swing at him was any indication, it was a pretty good hunch.

"On what charges?"

"Treason, of course. You openly admitted to conspiracy to overthrow the Grandfathers and bribing the Hands to help you do it." Rifun shrugged. "You're a Runner by all accounts, and a very dangerous one." He fake-gasped. "Why, what about your review coming up? You braved both hell and high water to save your father and mentor, and you lost everything to do it."

"It was worth it," Tommen informed him coldly.

Rifun pursed his lips. "Hm, the appropriate response would have been more like, 'Good golly gosh, Rifun, whatever shall I do?'" He raised his eyebrows to cue Tommen, but Tommen wasn't playing along. Rifun sighed and rolled his eyes. "Kids these days, no respect for their elders." He tilted his head. "Oh no, Rifun, whatever shall I do if I'm considered a Runner and can't—?"

"Just skip it," Tommen cut in. "I assume you're going to say that you have some sort of bargaining chip, a way to make sure I can go back to the Wheel without being arrested?"

"Oh, better than that. I can not only make sure you can go back to the Wheel, but I can ensure that, barring egregious error and incompetence, you will pass your review with flying colors."

"Yeah? Lily can do the same thing."

"If your review were after the elections, maybe. But not before. Not now, with her influence at an all-time low. Only I can help you."

That much, at least, was pretty true. The Hands and the Grandfathers weren't going to help him. Lily wasn't. Isthim wasn't. Cassius definitely wasn't. Walter, assuming he even lived, had good intentions, but he was only a Time Agent. The Akarin couldn't be made to care about literally anything right now. Micaiah, maybe, if he survived Cassius' hit list.

Tommen stared at him, studied him. He wanted to say any number of terrible thing which Rifun probably deserved. He wanted a way out, some bit of leverage.

He couldn't find any.

"Sticks and stones, Tommen," Rifun goaded, trying to wrap this up as his head pounded. "Listening never killed anyone."

"Fine," Tommen growled. "You clear me of all charges and get me through my review. What do I owe you?"

"First, a little gratitude would be nice. I don't think you realize the kind of favor I'm doing you. I'll even sweeten the deal a little by saying you don't owe me anything until after your review." He grew serious. "You will get a sign from me. Foyez may have told you about them, but they are unmistakable nonetheless. When you get these signs, you are to see me for special training, above and beyond what Walter can teach you in the Arena."

"Special training?" Tommen wondered.

"Akari training."

Tommen blinked and shook his head. "What? You want me to study...what, comparative religion? Are you trying to make me a member of your cult or something?" He shook his head and took a step back. "No. I'll give up Time before I become a fanatic...terrorist."

He turned as if to leave, but Rifun spoke again. "Did I mention that there are consequences for not accepting my offer?"

"I said I'll give up Time," Tommen told him. "I'll never go back to the Wheel, fail my review, live life as the little probationary Timekeeper that couldn't."

"That much is a given, not a consequence. The consequences I'm talking about are much more...consequential."

He chose a simple manipulation of Matter, similar to activating a seasonal allergy response. It took but half a second for Tommen's upper and lower sinuses to become gunked up, slimy, stuffy. Then he took that extra mucus and shifted it, changed it, turned it into straight water. Tommen went to his knees, spitting up water and coughing, desperate for relief. Rifun allowed everything to go back to rights.

Isthim will do a hundred times worse if you try to cross her, he thought. *Listen to me and avoid her. I can't let you fall into that.*

He got down beside Tommen. "Walter has probably told you that the Akari is a myth. Sifura might have told you that its power has degraded over time to little pieces here and there. But I assure you, it is no myth, and it is far more powerful than anyone realizes. It can do things that should not be done."

"What did you do to me?" Tommen whispered between coughs and gasps.

"Here is your first lesson, free of charge. Consider it more of a riddle to be solved. In order for someone to wield Time, they have to be exposed to it in sufficient quantity. For you, it was making a century-and-a-half leap into the future. In order for someone to wield the Akari, it has to be within them, part of them. What am I?"

"What kind of stupid riddle is that?"

"To wield Time, Time must be given to him. To wield the Akari, the Akari must be within him. What am I?"

"That makes no sense; you've already solved for all the variables. Unless you're talking about 'him' in which case it's whoever both wields Time and has the Akari."

"As I said, it's a riddle to be solved. I suggest you think about it between now and your next lesson."

Tommen sat back on his heels while Rifun stood. "What do I have to do?"

"Go now, and save your father. I know you have the antidote in your bag. Hug, cry, do what you have to do. When you go to the Wheel next, you will be clear of all charges and will pass your review with flying colors to the joy of all attending. At some point in the very near future, I will send you a sign, and you will meet me for your next lesson in the Akari."

"Just one lesson."

"No, of course not. It's an ongoing thing."

"For two favors?"

"Two very big favors, unless you consider cleaning out the garage and saving your dad's life equal favors."

"Fine. How long, or how many lessons do I have to take?"

Rifun chuckled. "Dear boy, by the time you will have worked off your favors, you won't want to stop meeting for lessons. And, just to make things interesting, you are not to tell anyone about this. Not your dad, not your Lieutenants, no one. Because I will know. And if you do, well, you know the phrase 'dropping like flies,' don't you?"

If he got the chance, Rifun considered warning Tommen about what was coming, the full story, the full plan. Isthim did not believe in the Authored Books, not really. She served Tujor. She served death. She would kill Tommen without a second thought. He couldn't let that happen. But right now, the kid just wanted to save his father. Rifun sighed inwardly and wished he'd had a father figure he cared about so much.

"Is there anything else you wanted while you're here? Cup of coffee, a shoe shine?" Tommen asked snidely. "Or am I free to go?"

"You're on my leash now, Tommen. You are most certainly not free to go. But if you are asking whether I am done talking and you can go to the hospital to save your dying father, then yes, by all means, you are free to go."

Tommen started to go, but stopped as Rifun interrupted him once again. "And just in case you get any funny ideas about trying to outwit me...here's a little reminder to take with you. Don't worry, it'll wear off."

He wouldn't realize it until he got somewhere with better light, but Rifun had temporarily healed the genes controlling his color-blindness. He could see in full color, though he didn't know it yet. It was possible to correct it fully, but that would take more time than they had at the moment.

Right now, Tommen was off to save his father. Maybe Rifun should have volunteered to open a portal directly to the hospital, but in the moment, Tommen wanted nothing to do with Rifun, and Rifun just wanted to go back to bed to sleep off his headache that was quickly evolving into a migraine.

He lay on the bed, on top of the blankets despite the natural chill that the fire in the hearth hadn't quite chased away yet. Sleep had been difficult for him for many decades now, but worrying about an injured hand wasn't helping anything. To make matters worse, the door to his chambers opened and Isthim walked in.

"We're not enslaved yet," Rifun sighed. "You can't give me orders."

"Maybe I should," Isthim said, her tone difficult to determine. She stopped at the end of the bed on his side. "This pitiful depression is annoying, useless, and unproductive."

"Pointing it out isn't making it any better."

"Have you found nothing to heal your fingers?"

"No, not yet. I've been trying to pay attention to the healing of my thumb—" He lazily lifted his arm a few inches and let it flop down. "—but I've yet to come up with a plan to regrow flesh in a truly restorative manner that does not leave me with useless appendages."

"Until you do, it may be prudent to turn your attention to other matters that do not require the use of your fingers, such as meeting with our allies to ensure their participation in the upcoming coup."

Rifun forced a laugh. "Well, it's good to know things are back on schedule and you didn't launch a revolution without me."

Isthim's expression was difficult to read, but he couldn't deny a twinge of fear as she took a couple steps forward. For a moment, he was afraid she was going to grab his injured hand and do something terrible. When she reached, he jerked his hand back. She stared at him, her intentions unclear, polydactyl hand hovering just over the spot where his hand had been a second before. Then she continued reaching, and he saw her skin change color from pink to white.

He poorly stifled a groan as she undid the front of his pants, the gas or the oils of her skin making him ridiculously hard. Her tone was all business, but that hardly mattered.

"I understand your preferential dexterity is that of your right hand," she said, "but I never thought your left hand was entirely incompetent. Given that all other needs have been met, I can only conclude that this is what you require."

Everyone knew about the gas and the oils being effective and deadly, but now Rifun was forced to consider the potency of saliva as well. This consideration took a back seat to his demonstration of the dexterity of his left hand as he grabbed her horn and shifted his hips. He knew she wasn't happy, but this was her idea after all.

If Isthim lacked anything, it was a bedside manner and the ability to make pillow talk. Going into it, she had been all business. The act itself had been rote and mechanical on her part, relying exclusively on the influence of her toxins to chemically more than physically satisfy him. And afterwards, she straightened, swallowed, mentioned something about being more focused on meetings and what needed to be done, then turned to leave.

In spite of his exhaustion, Rifun rolled onto one said and called after her. She stopped and looked back at him.

"You know, if this is how you motivate all your slaves, it might not be such a bad thing," he told her.

She scowled and left in a huff.

Oddly enough, it had also cured his migraine, or reduced it to little more than a minor throb easily ignored.

He waited a few seconds after her departure before deciding to get out of bed. He had to finesse his use of the Akari to get his pants back to rights. He told himself that things would be easier once the pins came out of his thumb, which they would, but then he was still presented with the problem of the reduction of his available dexterity to manage things like buttons and zippers. And, according to Isthim, other things.

Yes, he probably should get going to meet with their allies and give them final instructions for their specific roles in the coup. The Turitians, the Korin, the Grunjor—dodging a bullet there because of the rescue of Donojok from the bottom of the Kanawha River—and half a dozen others. Maybe he would warn them of the Borelians' treachery and vile plans. They could take the Wheel and then immediately turn around and depose the Borelians. It was a long shot, but he might still give them the courtesy of a warning. Worst case scenario, everyone backed out, the coup was a bust, Isthim and Misik got mad, and enslaved the Cult anyway. Either scenario ended in slavery.

But first, he had an apology to make.

Tomas was more upset that Rifun had missed his weekly lunch with Lalao than Lalao herself was, especially when she saw his hand. At the sight of the bandages and missing fingers, she snatched his arm, marched him to her kitchen table, sat him down, and started fussing. Somehow she managed to twist and turn his hand every which way with more exaggeration than the doctor, yet with half the pain, if any at all.

"I attempted to fight the demon," he told her. "I'm lucky this is all I lost."

"And the demon got away?" Lalao wondered.

"I didn't kill it. Honestly, I don't think I even scratched it. It remains inside Cassius, still controlling him."

"Has it tried to come after you since?"

"No. I find it somewhat surprising, but then, why would it have to hurry, now that it knows how weak I am against it?"

Lalao frowned. "Well, that is concerning, yes." She set his hand, compressed and wrinkly from constant bandages, on the table and stood. "I think we might have to eat inside today. What do you want?"

"*Vary amin anana* is fine."

"Oh, don't be modest. What do you really want?"

He grinned. "*Henakisoa ritra*, if you can manage it."

She waved a hand. "Of course I can."

Rifun did not miss Tomas' expression from where he sat in one of the chairs in the living room. It was one that said even her own son did not get so much consideration about what he wanted to eat.

Henakisoa ritra was strips of beef, in this case sirloin, that was dried, then cooked in thick tomato sauce bordering on paste. Leafy greens were added and cooked down, though some people also added more hearty vegetables like carrots or potatoes. Herbs and spices topped off the flavor profile. The beef was served along with the vegetables, the tomato sauce spooned out as a type of gravy.

It was the first thing he'd eaten since waking up in the hospital, partly out of depression because of having to try and eat left-handed, and partly because he'd been a bit leery of eating while any medications were still in his system. This, however, was a welcome first meal. The meat was tender enough that he could cut it with a fork, even if he did have to be more conscious of his hand-to-mouth coordination.

"What now?" Lalao wondered, a few bites in. "The demon won't wait forever. You must have learned something that will help you next time."

"I have to relearn how to eat and dress myself," he told her, mildly indicating his fork as he stabbed a piece of meat. "I don't know what now."

"You can't wait too long."

"I know that."

Her expression was stern. "Don't get short with me."

He sighed and resisted the urge to sulk. "I don't know. I learned that it is apparently impossible to bait the demon into a trap. It's too smart for that. Anything I do, I have to do spontaneously; I can't pre-plan too much."

"Hm..." She slid the tines of her fork under some limp spinach. "Or perhaps you should begin your preparations far in advance so that they no longer look like preparations, but simply the way things are. Normal."

Rifun considered this, buying time to think simply by putting food in his mouth and chewing slowly. He didn't have that much time to do what she suggested, a couple weeks at most. Granted, there was enough going on, enough excitement, that a lot of things weren't normal, but even the suddenness and abnormality of the shipping yard incident hadn't been enough to cover up the smell of a trap.

Another thought occurred to him, something he'd learned while in the army, training under French commanders. It was the Five Rings philosophy, *Be master of all, partial to none. In this way, you will never be caught at a disadvantage.*

He didn't need to come up with anything new or elaborate. He had no time to master something new, only to call on what he knew already. He knew a thing or two about the Akari and its history. He knew about the Books and the Author. He was no master of inverting portals and turning dimensions inside out, but he did know a little bit about the nexus of time and space, where all the dimensions converged. It was one place where he could see what others couldn't, because of his head injury. Because he was made different.

He blinked back to the present moment where Lalao was grinning at him.

"What?"

"You have this look like you've just had an epiphany."

"I think so. I think I have an idea."

She nodded and stabbed the last bit of beef on her plate. "Good."

He blinked. "Good?"

"Isn't it?" She took her bite, chewed, swallowed. "If you have something figured out, then we can move on to other topics."

"Ah. You mean topics such as, Tomas' silent griping that you don't ask for his culinary opinions nearly as often as you do mine?"

Tomas, who had helped himself to a plate of food and returned to his chair, looked up, curious, but said nothing.

Lalao hesitated, chasing the last few greens around her plate, using them to mop up the last of the sauce. "Oh, it's not so much that I ask your opinions, it's just..."

"You treat me how you did his father." Rifun looked at Tomas.

Tomas did not look at Rifun, but he did speak. "I knew you were a friend. A very good friend, powerful in the spirits, as she has tried to describe you."

"But there are some things she says or does that she said or did to another man."

Now the youngest son looked up, ignoring Rifun to address his mother. "I want you to be happy. But a family is more than one person, and such things affect the whole family."

Lalao was at a loss for words, but Rifun wasn't. "Tomas, I haven't come to take your mother away or pretend to be your father. That door closed on us many years ago. But that doesn't mean we don't care for each other."

There was no miraculous smoothing of the situation or forging of bonds between them. Tomas did not respond to him and Lalao appeared suddenly shy and self-conscious. Rifun let out a breath, stood, and muttered something about needing to get going.

He had just stepped onto the sidewalk when the front door opened again and Lalao called to him.

"Should I expect you for lunch at the normal time and place?" she asked awkwardly.

He nodded. "I'd like that."

She motioned for him to approach, and he did so. She gently took his injured hand in hers, minding his thumb. "I'll have to take another look at this, too, make sure it's healing right. Maybe I'll see if I can't find some kind of protection charm and put it on a bracelet for you."

"So I don't lose any more fingers?"

"Or anything else." She raised one hand and tenderly traced the burn wounds around his neck, where his French captors had once fired a chain and then tried to strangle him. The scars were normally hidden by a hoodie or scarf, but Madagascar was too hot for such nonsense, especially in the middle of summer.

"I'll see you for lunch," he promised, putting one hand over hers. "At least one more before I do anything else crazy."

"Don't leave me again," she scolded him, though her attempted tease fell flat.

He desperately wanted to kiss her, just like he had that one night when they were together. If her expression was any indication, she was feeling the same. But they were both very aware of Tomas just inside the house, probably watching though neither of them dared to look and find out. In the end, the most he allowed himself was to kiss her forehead and give her a hug.

"I'll see you in a few days," he told her, trying to sound encouraging as he let her go and departed.

Maybe a few days of political negotiations and alliances would do him some good.

Briefly he wondered if he might somehow get away with an older Disguise, like the one he had used to deceive the family so many years ago. Could he and Lalao still have a future together, however brief on her part? How would he make it work? Lalao knew he didn't age, and Tomas had already seen him as a young man.

He didn't want to walk into any negotiations distracted, but the Turitians were not known for dropping everything to meet with foreign diplomats, especially ones with whom they were conspiring to overthrow the Hands of Time. Rifun found himself mulling over Lalao more than political treaties while he waited, though he managed to shake off the majority of the distraction once he was finally on his way to meet with Queen Aronet and the others.

"Welcome, Rifun Ndolo," Commander Dira greeted. A ballet of gestures was exchanged among those gathered. "It pleases us to see you are recovering from your unfortunate accident."

Rifun self-consciously glanced at his hand, the pins sticking out of his thumb like a deformed claw. "I thank you for your concern, Commander. I expect I will be fully healed within the next few days."

"Does this accident have any bearing on our plans moving forward?" Queen Aronet inquired directly. "What of Cassius? He still lives."

He shook his head and made a gesture, minding his hand. "No. Although we failed to accomplish what we set out to do, it was a minor goal only, one that will be easily dealt with at the inauguration. As for Cassius, in order to avoid the appearance of internal assassination, it was decided that the best course of action will be to disguise his demise within the chaos of the coup." And that was as far as he got in his planning.

"There have been concerns that the Cult of the Akari is...fragile," one of the lords stated, performing a gesture of humble honesty with no intent of insult, a kind of request to confirm or deny an allegation. "Fragile, and indecisive. Chasing shadows of imaginary enemies or impossible dreams." He made a minor motion, his eyes flitting to Rifun's hand.

"I might share such misgivings if we had not already done this once before," Rifun reminded them, refuting the lord's gesture with one of his own. "We did it once. We can do it again. This time, we are ready for the burden we expect to take on. And getting rid of Cassius will stabilize that foundation."

"Good," Aronet mused, making a motion that the outsider guides referred to as "stoic discipline." "Because it is unlikely that we will get a third chance. The other families are restless, anxious. If we do not establish our own dominance in the markets you have promised, we will be challenged heavily."

"Am I correct to assume that the markets you speak of are not merely the Time marketplaces, but the market of information the Scouts provide?"

A gesture of affirmation. "You are correct."

"An understandable fear. The Scouts themselves do not appreciate such frequent and drastic changes in upper management. Once we take hold, we will not lose it."

"A bold statement," another lord said with a gesture of contemplation.

Rifun made a motion known as "stern resolve." "Leaders who are fearful and indecisive rarely lead long, or else they lead men smaller than themselves with no fight or ambition or accomplishments to speak of."

A gesture of acquiescence, with no words spoken.

"Then there are the men who attempt to ally themselves with the Borelians," the first lord said pointedly, his gesture augmenting his distaste. "I find it hard to believe that they are letting someone else run the show so to speak."

"There have been many objections from my men about fighting beside them," Dira commented. "They will do as I command, but I will not deny my own misgivings. I don't want to lose quality fighting men to slavery."

"No one does," Rifun acknowledged. "And I would be remiss if I did not disclose that there has been tension in the Cult over the same points. It is a problem that I inherited when I joined the Cult, and I have been considering ways to rectify such an egregious error."

"Given what we're about to do, I assume you have come up with something, perhaps within this coup?" Aronet's tone might have resembled a question, but her accompanying gesture was not.

Rifun nodded and made a similar motion they would understand. "The Borelians do not take slights lightly. To attack one is to attack them all. Their biological toxins are only part of the reason they have been so successful in their conquest and enslavement campaigns. Due to certain recent events outside of the Cult, I have reason to believe they will be coming after my own people in the near future.

"The Wheel of Time is the nexus of our physical universe, all of time and space and dimensions twisting through the Core of the Wheel. But there is more to the universe beyond the physical, and it is from this place that the Borelians have derived the greatest effect for their campaigns."

"They're religious," one lord stated flatly. "Everyone lays claim to a god or devil being for or against them when it suits them."

"I have seen this devil," Rifun informed him, meeting him head on, making a gesture to match. "I have fought this devil, and this is what it cost me." He pointedly displayed his hand. "What it only cost me, thankfully." He looked around at the rest of them, deliberately meeting each gaze. "There is more out there. To deny this is no more or less than petty, childish ignorance, the desire to know everything, yet put a limit on what can be known. Now, whether this being is a true devil or spirit or god or some creature beyond our three-dimensional comprehension, it does not matter. What matters is that this creature is the true powerhouse behind the Borelians. And I mean to reach through the Core of the Wheel to take it out. But I cannot deny that the Borelians as the Grandfathers are what will win us the Wheel initially."

Glances were exchanged.

"A dangerous game," Dira mused. "A balancing act of the most consequential kind."

"Why not use the Core of the Wheel to take over the Wheel?" a lady inquired. "It seems this would be a more efficient use of time and resources."

Rifun made a "gentle letdown" motion. "You cannot simply remove all of the supports from a structure and expect it to remain standing. Building as an art is laborious and costly, in time and resources. This is why Rebuilds of the Wheel are so significant. It must be done with precision so as not to cause the whole thing to implode, which would have repercussions throughout the entire universe. This precision, however, would only alert everyone to mischief, thus costing us time, resources, and the element of surprise. Taking the Wheel itself, then using the Core to reach beyond the Wheel is far more feasible."

He had no way to really know this, of course. He had seen the Core of the Wheel only a few times, had only learned about the inverting of portals in the last couple weeks, and probably wouldn't have a lot of time to practice anything more in the lead-up to the elections. He would be working solely on guidance from the spirits.

"Can we continue to count on your support?" he asked directly.

"You can," Aronet and Dira confirmed.

"Good. Your place will remain in the portal room, preventing escape as much as possible."

A good battle plan was like a marble statue, Rifun thought as they hashed out some details. Simple blocking came first, achieving the general shape of the thing the artist wished to carve. Then came the rough shapes and lines, and finally the fine details. But, work too much, strip away too much stone, and the whole thing became an ugly distortion, and cut stone could not—traditionally—be replaced.

He promised to return on Election Day for final numbers and last-minute adjustments, then departed.

He held similar meetings with the Korin, the Grunjor, and a dozen other allies over the course of approximately two and a half weeks. Most of them, if they had pledged an alliance even after a forty year absence, were still perfectly fine with what was going on. A few got cold feet and denied ever making an agreement in the first place. It was too close to the coup for Rifun to care at the moment, but he mentally noted who the deniers were.

He reported his work to Isthim who was in charge of coordinating the attack itself. While she was good at her work, she looked no happier for it.

"And what is today's catastrophe?" Rifun inquired of her when he delivered his last report to an icy wall.

"Tadashi and his helpers were supposed to be the ones getting into the election computer of the Wheel," she grumbled. "It was easier and safer to infiltrate from the outside rather than trying to recruit secretaries to do the same."

"Ah. Well, it won't matter much come the morning, will it? That's the wonderful thing about mandatory attendance at the inauguration."

She gave him a look. "He was also supposed to log the identity of everyone who came through the portal room, that way we would know if anyone escaped."

He nodded. "That would be helpful, yes. But we are too close to the finish line to worry about such minor details. Keep looking forward. We have the means and the opportunity to take the Wheel. And that is what we shall do."

He left before she could complain about anything else. One last thing before he wanted to do before engaging in this insanity — actually two things, the first being one last lunch with Lalao, just in case; the second being checking in on Tommen.

Walter lived. Somehow, whatever cure Tommen and Sifura had found on her world had worked to cure Walter of the Borelian poison, even as he was knocking at death's door. If any of them showed up to the inauguration, assuming they lived through the initial violence, Isthim was not going to make their lives pleasant. Sifura was a Hand and would have to be there. Walter, as an officer, would also normally have to be there. Rifun couldn't do much about Sifura, but maybe he could dissuade the Forbeses.

Arriving in Charleston, it was just about time for school to get out. By the time he made it to South Charleston High School, that was exactly what was going on, although not the only thing. Rifun was using a Band in order to conceal himself from prying eyes and ubiquitous surveillance. There was no reason anyone else should be moving except they were also in a Band.

Jogging up to the bus area where hundreds of students were frozen on their way to their respective yellow chariots, Rifun could only breathe a prayer of thanks to the ancestors for getting him here in time.

Tadashi had Tommen on his heels, exhausted, defenseless, just waiting for a knife to the heart. A short distance away, a Runner Rifun vaguely knew as Kyle Malargos was unable to keep up with Tadashi's Bands which were much stronger than his. A little birdie had told Rifun that Kyle was keeping an eye on Tommen at Walter's behest, except the man appeared to be less eagle and more chickadee.

Annoyed, Rifun approached Tadashi from behind, drew his revolver, and fired. Tadashi's head exploded, dead before he could comprehend it. A moment after his body collapsed, Tommen also fell over onto the cold sidewalk. Rifun holstered his gun and went to kneel beside the teenager, pulling his head onto his lap.

"Now, now, Tommen, you're safe," Rifun cooed. He stroked the boy's cheek and moved his hair back behind his ears as best he could, revealing hearing aids. From Rifun's gun going off next to his head? He knew a moment of regreat. The teenager's face was spattered with Tadashi's blood and he had a few minor scratches, but otherwise he appeared physically all right.

"How do you feel?"

"*Dw i ddim yn teimlo'n dda,*" Tommen whispered. (I don't feel so good.)

"No, I wouldn't expect so after the hell Tadashi put you through."

Using Feel, Rifun determined he had a minor concussion, but nothing life-threatening.

"*Merdu chi siarad.*" (You can talk.) He lifted his arm and tapped a hearing aid.

"Perhaps," Rifun acknowledged, "and yet, here I am, saving your life. You know I would never let any harm come to you, at least, not knowingly or intentionally. Lucky for you I just happened to be passing by or poor Kyle wouldn't have lasted much longer and you'd both be dead."

But Tommen's expression had changed. "*Ydy'chi siarad Cymraeg?*" (You speak Welsh?)

"*Ydw.*" (I do.) He paused. "How often do men wish for more time to pursue something? More time to travel the world or learn a skill or do anything at all? We have the time, Tommen. And I use it to my advantage. With you and your father-uncle on equal terms now, I figured that there ought to be no secrets among us. *Agus labhraim Gaeilge, má cheap tú aon smaointe cliste.*" (And I speak Irish, in case you got any clever ideas.)

Just one of the many frivolous hobbies Rifun had pursued while laid up with his injured hand. Sure, he might negotiate politics during the day, but it was always the worst in the morning, when he went to do something out of pure habit, felt his fingers move, and yet they were not there. Even just now, he'd instinctively reached for his revolver with his right hand, had to consciously switch to his left. He'd needed something to occupy his mind, push away the pain.

Tommen groaned and sat up, shivering. With Rifun's help, he got to his feet and looked around. His gaze naturally settled on Tadashi, not wanting to see, unable to look away.

"Why did you help me?" he asked deliberately.

"After all I went through to keep you alive and make sure you passed your Apprentice review, you think I was going to let this idiot kill you?" Rifun kicked Tadashi's shoe. "After he made his grand departure, he went and joined some other political group, thought he was going to use them to outwit me at my own game. As I said, I take care of my own."

"Why were you here? Really?"

"Just checking up on some things, making sure everything is in order for the elections tomorrow."

"Handing out Uncle Sam fliers, I'm sure."

"You never know. And he got my interest, too." He indicated Kyle, safely outside the Band.

"Who is he?" Tommen wondered.

"Name is Kyle Malargos, from District Eight." Rifun folded his arms. "Apprentice who decided he wanted to take a few years to himself and use Time to couch-surf and see the world from a homeless person's point of view, I suppose."

"What is he to you?"

Nothing, really. Just another unwitting agent of the spirits, of the Author, sent to protect her chosen ones from the madness of those like Tadashi.

"What are you going to do to him?" Tommen asked.

"You think I'm going to kill him? The person who intervened and saved my young pupil's life from the knife of my estranged former companion? Absolutely not! If your dad wants to put a bodyguard on you, he is more than welcome to."

"As long as it doesn't interfere with your interests."

"Well, there is that." Rifun shrugged. "At any rate, we should probably get this mess cleaned up before releasing the Band. Having a body suddenly appear on school property, well, we both know how that one goes, don't we?"

Tommen agreed, albeit reluctantly. No doubt, as he helped Rifun, he was having a number of flashbacks to the warehouse. Rifun could sympathize. There was no reason he couldn't have done this all himself, but the boy had been blooded. There was no going back now; time to make the boy a man.

"I know that was probably tiring and difficult for you," Rifun said gently. "Your dad is on his way. Get some good sleep tonight, and don't worry about tomorrow. Except for that part where you have an Economics test. You can fake all the degrees you want, but it's a good idea to have some smarts to back them up."

With that friendly advice, Rifun turned and started walking away.

"Where are you going?" Tommen asked after him.

Rifun turned but just continued to walk backwards. "As I said, I was just passing by. I have other things to do today, as I'm sure you do. You go to work or go home, and I plan for election victories. Everyone has their priorities."

It wasn't until he returned to the officers building that he considered he hadn't actually told Tommen to tell his dad to stay home. Before he could decide whether to go back, Isthim approached, walking up the steps behind him, saying something about a final meeting. He said nothing to that, just followed her inside.

"Tadashi is dead," Rifun reported, walking in the meeting room. "I made sure of that myself."

"At least we won't have to worry about him working against us," Misik commented, "not that he was much of a threat to begin with."

"Time's up," Isthim snapped. "The elections are here and we're moving out."

Election

In the original plans, made before the catastrophe at the shipping yard, Tadashi and a few of his equally-questionable, computer-savvy friends were supposed to "hack" into the Wheel computer systems and run the elections from the outside. Tadashi often bragged that he could do it without the secretaries ever finding out, frequently hinted that he'd done it before.

Well, that asshole was dead now, which only created more leg work for the rest of them.

The good news was that Cassius maintained his forged identity as the Zero Hour, which gave him access to the Wheel secretaries.

For as much as people liked to blame the Hands for things going poorly in the Time industry, or maybe outside forces like the Cult when things went sideways, the secretaries were the real power behind the curtain. They were the ones who maintained records of laws and decisions from the Hands, and it was amazing how old laws might suddenly pop up again just in time to prosecute someone who spoke ill to or of a secretary. Or a new law might not be formally and officially in the system yet, thereby sparing someone from prosecution, and the fact that it was a secretary's friend who was dodging the judicial bullet was entirely coincidental.

It was the secretaries who maintained the records of who was even a Hand. If any of them really wanted to get Cassius out of the system, revoke his shrouded privileges and expose him to the universe, they could do it. The fact that they hadn't said that he still had some support among them. There were those who had benefited from singular, if tyrannical, rule.

The secretaries worked in every part of the Wheel. They were not shrouded like the Hands or the Grandfathers, but they wore the symbol of the secretaries in some fashion that they were comfortable with, typically according to local fashion back home. This might be a simple lapel pin, some kind of embroidery on an article of clothing, even tattoos. Many secretaries also sported the symbol of the department they worked in, the Archives, the Seat, the Judgment Wing, and so on.

The secretaries he sought today were not found in the Judgment Wing where the elections were in full chaotic roar. Those ones were only the face of things, entering and cross-referencing information about the officers who were voting, and generally keeping the sheep moving in an orderly line. The ones down below, working in the Archives, they were the ones tallying the votes. Unlike what one might find on Earth—dozens or hundreds of people hunched over tiny keyboards staring into massive screens only inches from their face—the system in the Wheel more resembled a very large switchboard setup, the entire election system broken down into hundreds of individualized components, allegedly so no one race or one system could affect any other.

Elections were pretty much the same across the universe, Cassius found. There were those who genuinely believed that elections were honest and their vote could make all the difference. There were others who believed it was entirely for show, and the only reason they showed up was duress from the Grandfathers and Hands.

The truth was, uninterestingly enough, elections and voting really fell somewhere in the middle. Cheating never occurred at the beginning of an election. If the sheep wanted to vote their way to the butcher, there was no need to rig anything, and they truly had only themselves to blame in the end. Like Richard going to the gallows, it had been all his idea. Cassius was happy to carry it out, but the blame fell squarely on Richard's shoulders for his own demise. And there were a few consequential races where the sheep were indeed voting the butcher into office. There was no need to expend time and energy rigging those outcomes.

None of these elections mattered, really, except as certain favors that Rifun had promised. If a certain candidate won his certain race, he would pledge his army or whatever to the Cult cause in the coup. Whether these candidates understood that things were going to be very different under Cult rule and the Hands as everyone knew them would be gone, Cassius did not know. Nor did he care much. That was their problem.

Even the secretaries who were allegedly allied with them were nervous when Cassius, shrouded as the Zero Hour, appeared in their little hidey-hole, secreted away in a bunker-like chamber in the Archives. It was not illegal per se for him to be there, but it could be seen as suspicious. Not that the Grandfathers were going to do anything about it.

"How are things going down here?" he inquired. "There have been plenty of threats made, have any been carried out?"

"Nothing physical," one secretary reported, not looking at him.

"I'm not concerned with the physical. The Grandfathers can deal with that well enough. How about the digital?"

"All is going according to plan," another told him, giving him what he interpreted as a knowing look. In a slightly less suspicious tone, he added, "No one has been down here but us. There have been no abnormalities in the system, and even if there were, we have ways of deterring any mischief."

Cassius could ask for an explanation, but he knew he would never understand it. There was a reason Rifun usually carried the phone while on Earth. Instead he asked, "I'm sure there has been mischief before, but what would it actually take to force a stop to the elections? Force a redo, I should say."

"Only a catastrophic failure of the Wheel itself." The secretary gestured broadly to the sea of lights, screens, switches, wires, chips, and other technological equipment. "This system is too complex and well-organized to be affected any other way. There are too many fail-safes and cutoff switches."

"You sound very confident in that."

"The only way to influence the elections like that, from the outside, would be to hit most or all of the systems all at once. That can't happen without us noticing and the system shutting down."

Cassius shrugged. "What if they decided to do it one or two at a time?"

"Even assuming the person or group knew what they were doing, what they were looking for, they would never get through enough of the system to affect anything. The information here is not collected or coded the same as it is in the Archives; this is entirely separate and proprietary. And even if they did, somehow, crack that code, all that is assuming that they know how to cover their tracks." He made a vague gesture to several other secretaries. "We have physical monitoring for just such an eventuality."

Cassius nodded, genuinely impressed. "How is it, then, that there are always accusations of cheating?"

Even for an alien, the secretary gave him a rather obvious look. "Who doesn't want to believe that their favorite candidate is the best choice and that everyone must love them, that if they ultimately lose, then some other candidate must have been a sore loser and a cheat? Please, we hear about it all the time. If we have any respite, it's knowing that we are rarely the target for such anger. You public figures are much easier to track down."

Smug bastard, but not untrue.

"We'll keep the elections rolling along smoothly," the secretary promised. "We always have. We always will. It is our only job."

As much as Cassius may have wanted to stick around and watch and see how the elections were actually rigged, what sort of computer mumbo-jargon had to be done to overturn this "impregnable" system, he also knew he wouldn't understand it, and it would probably be boring to watch anyway. There was no excitement in digital things. Flashing lights and patterns, everything flat and dull. Give him something physical, something truly manipulable. Give him flesh, and he would do more with it than any of these blind, hunchbacked hacks could do with their digital work.

He made his way out of the bunker chamber into the main hub of the secretaries' work area. There were other branches and corridors to numerous workplaces. A Scout walked by, flashy apparatus in hand, off to deliver some report from a new world he'd been, well, Scouting. Otherwise, the place was empty, everyone diligently working in their cubicles, anxious to see what became of these elections.

The staircase leading back up to the Archives was spiral, made of metal, and quite dark. Cassius navigated it with ease, appearing in an unpopulated section of the Archives. It was perhaps the only area of the Wheel not drenched in chaos. He debated using the Akari to force open a portal, then decided against it. His mere presence, mingling among the crowds, would probably spook a few people. Besides, he should probably have a similar conversation with the Grandfathers. At least there he knew everyone was on his side, or if they weren't, they were less likely to speak up about it.

The Judgment Wing, unfortunately, was where all of the voting was taking place, and the line of voters must have stretched halfway across the universe. All of the posted officers of all disciplines from every corner of the universe converging on a single spot to vote. If any group was at a disadvantage, it was the Merchants, on account of their non-linear advancement system, and the fact that their numbers were based on the economy and free market supply and demand; it was in their best business interest to keep the number of Merchants low, even though that reduced their overall voting power. Timekeepers and Harvesters were fairly linear in their advancement, posted offices arranged by District and Region and so on. If either of them wanted to increase their number of eligible voters, all they had to do was create more Districts, more Regions, more sections on whatever map was being divided up, and appoint officers to those positions. All of this could be done under the guise of increased Runner activity, greater need for more Harvesters and more protection needed for them, and so on.

It was astounding how many people got a sudden promotion in the months leading up to the elections. And then, later on, a fair chunk of those officers would "not work out" and be removed from active office, the nascent Districts merged once more until they suddenly reappeared in time for the next election. Attempts had been made to stop such practices, such as requiring that Districts exist for so many years before the officers were permitted to vote, but such laws were always shot down. After all, the posted officers themselves were usually veterans of the Time industry. Sure, the District might be new, but the officers were well-versed in the ways of things. Why discriminate against them for such a thing?

One thing that hadn't changed was that the Hands themselves were not permitted to vote. No one had ever seriously sought to change this. On the one hand, fifty-one votes weren't going to make that much of a difference. On the other hand, it sounded like a really good idea to the weak-minded, while freeing up corrupt Hands to pursue their means of rigging the elections without having to go through the actual voting process.

Thus the presence of the Zero Hour in the Judgment Wing caused a minor stir among those standing in line. What was going on? Was everything all right? Was there some mischief afoot? He could feel the shift in the crowd, but he ignored it as he headed down the corridor to the room with the three doors. All of the voters entered one door, which took them to what basically constituted a private voting booth. He entered another door which took him to the normal processing room for Runners. From there, it was a short jaunt to what one could consider the private offices of those in charge of the wing.

Isthim and Misik were both present, along with half a dozen others who Cassius vaguely recognized as having more practical authority over the Grandfathers. Only two of those six were Borelians, but the rest, he was assured, were loyal to their cause. He joined them at what would be considered a very large meeting table, not unlike the altar in the officers building.

"I just checked in with the secretaries down below," Cassius said. "So far, everything is on track."

"What does it matter if inauguration attendance is mandatory and we're going to kill everyone anyway?" one of the Grandfathers wondered.

"Making a show of it," Isthim replied, her words and posture an echo of Rifun. "If we can make things as they were surrounding the Dispersal, make it absolutely outrageous—"

"Then it will scare some into flight, and the rest will be armed to the teeth."

"Are you afraid of a challenge?" She gave the Grandfather a look. "The universe is a big place, and there are a lot of people in it. What these people do not understand is that the universe does not require their existence or consent in order to function. In fact, the existence of some is of detriment to the universe and other people. Those who come armed will be dealt with. Those who flee will be dealt with." She went on before anyone could protest. "This will not be accomplished all at once. We will take the Wheel, but opposition must be slowly devoured."

"Even a dead tree gives life to new roots," another Grandfather pointed out, "as your last failure proved."

Cassius was not the only one who did not appreciate being constantly reminded of past failures. Isthim did not even bother to Band or use any other external advantage as she walked up to the antagonizing Grandfather and struck him squarely in the face. She was not wearing gloves. The Grandfather went down, under a comatose-like influence from her toxins, giving her more than ample time and space to kneel, place her hand on his face, and, through some odd biological technique, actively use her deadly oils to manipulate his body and kill him. To bystanders, it looked like nothing more than her simply sitting there with her hand on his face. Cassius could only imagine the agony she put him through, and he wondered if his excitement was noticeable through his Zero Hour shroud.

Then Isthim stood and looked around at the others. "Does anyone else have anything to say? Would anyone else like to bring up past mistakes? Or shall we focus on our imminent victory instead?"

A few glances were exchanged as she reclaimed her spot.

"It wasn't difficult to convince the Hands of the need for extra security around the inauguration," one of the remaining Grandfathers said tentatively. When he was not attacked, he went on, more assertively, "We will have forty Grandfathers waiting for the previous Hands to exit the Seat."

"Fifty Hands but only forty Grandfathers?" Cassius wondered.

"Borelians have two hands," Misik stated, his tone unsettlingly sarcastic as he held up his hands for childish emphasis. "Forty will be more than enough."

Isthim, however, looked contemplative. She glanced at Misik. "I want Tarma Balijor with them. She has demonstrated skill with Disguise and optical and aural illusions. She will help cover up the massacre of the Hands while we remain in the Seat. People will be nervous, but we don't want to tip them off early."

Misik started to speak. "But Hursa Par—"

"Yes, and he can do his part to cover it up, but I want Balijor there as well. At least we don't have to worry about her loyalty if Partamikol gets cold feet."

To the Borelians, not the Cult, Cassius thought. Although if Partamikol was so questionable in his loyalty, why give him one of the more essential missions? Unfortunately for Cassius, he was not in the kind of company where he could voice such questions, if the body on the floor was any indication.

The Borelians ended up on a half hour tangent relating to house names, some of them pitching a fit that this Tarma Balijor should not be tasked with such a mission because of her house name being of a lesser class. Or something to that effect. Cassius internally rolled his eyes. Isthim and the others would bitch endlessly about how things needed to get done and stop stalling and make sure everything is ready to go, then spend those precious minutes on this kind of nonsense.

Eventually they came to some sort of agreement, though it was not lost on Cassius that this agreement was made without the woman in question being present. Well, it wasn't his problem. Maybe a little strife would work in the Cult's favor, something to exploit in order to stave off slavery. Unlikely, but he could hope, couldn't he? No. He didn't know what to hope for anymore, or if it was even worth it. He could feel the dragon laughing in his head.

All heads turned as the door opened. Cassius did not recognize the man, but the mystery was solved just as soon as the door shut and Rifun doffed his Disguise. He wore gloves in some vain, self-conscious attempt to conceal his missing fingers, but the lack of natural movement, or the unusual way the stiff leather fingers retained a singular, manufactured shape, was just as distracting. When he approached and put his hands on the table, there was something obviously wrong with the first two fingers of his right hand, the leather still in place in those fingers, hovering over the table even as the others pressed hard on the surface. Cassius was not the only one who took note of this, though if Rifun noticed how everyone took turns glancing at the glove and trying to pinpoint just what was off about it—for those who didn't know—he gave no indication. Or perhaps it was his demeanor that said he was deliberately ignoring such looks.

"Apologies for my tardiness," he began. "Had to deal with some minor allies who suddenly got very uppity in the price of their support."

"What changes have been made?" Isthim demanded.

"Well, most of them, like the Dosqine and the Kribit, their demanded price was honored. However, they have been moved to the outer area of the Coliseum. Greater glory and spoils to be had, of course." He shrugged. "If any of them live through the ordeal, they will have earned their pay. The Kribit especially, given their greatest warriors are no taller than my knee. We're not getting more than a hundred from each. Their help will be noted, but their loss is hardly something to mourn."

And yet, if asked to kill a man in cold blood, however necessary, Rifun would give himself an aneurysm from the stress of any social, political, and religious implications, Cassius thought.

"One hundred men from one hundred allies is ten thousand men," Misik pointed out, still with his unnerving sarcasm.

"Are you afraid of ten thousand midgets with needles for weapons and toothpicks for bones?"

The way he asked the question suggested it was almost genuine. Rifun was fishing for some specific answer or reaction.

Whatever Misik's problem was, it appeared to lower his mental capacity to anticipate a potential trap as he answered, "Ten thousand stinging insects can still incapacitate or kill."

Rifun's expression suggested it was exactly the answer he was looking for as he replied, "Well then we better hope the masses don't have bug spray."

"Does that really change anything we're doing?" Cassius interrupted. "Or do we need some committee meeting about it?"

Without looking at him, Rifun sighed and let his head drop. "It does not change what we are doing as a whole, nor what we are doing personally. There were other matters I had to attend to that are of lesser importance and irrelevant to anything going on in the Seat of the Hands, but if you like, I can recount them all and we'll be here for at least another hour."

"That won't be necessary," Isthim said before Cassius could speak. She gave Misik a look. "Our primary forces alone are more than enough to accomplish what we're looking to do. Everything else is simply to make it easier and faster."

"Has the Bat secured the Seat?" Rifun asked, looking at Cassius.

"And the Day," Cassius confirmed.

"How about the shroud?"

Cassius spread his arms, the perpetually modest shroud billowing wide around him. "I'm wearing it, aren't I?"

"You and one other. We need to be sure—"

"If he does show up, I'll take care of him myself."

"We can't have everyone seeing two Zero Hours in the same room at the same time. We can't have the other Hands seeing that either while we're milling about, waiting for our grand entrance."

Cassius sighed and now physically rolled his eyes. "Fine. I'll track him down and take care of him before the inauguration."

"That would be the ideal," Isthim commented.

Rifun nodded. "And by the time it even got to the Grandfathers for a more serious investigation—assuming a body is found in good time, we will already be in power and can make it disappear with no repercussions."

Cassius was barely paying attention as he was already moving toward the door.

"Where are you going?" Rifun asked.

"I'm going to take care of our duplicate Zero Hour problem," Cassius said acidly. "It's much more exciting and productive than standing around here."

He left before anyone could stop him, and no one gave chase. He made his way out of the Judgment Wing, through the endless line of people still waiting to fulfill their compulsory voting requirement. How many of them would have showed up if it wasn't mandatory? How many officers would go to the inauguration if such absence would not be punished?

The others were afraid of the two of them being seen together at the inauguration, but the risk was the same, or perhaps greater, even now during voting. He probably should have done this a while ago, but like everything else, no one seemed to be able to make up their fucking mind about what was going on, who was doing what, who was supposed to live or die and when. If anyone decided now that the current "official" Zero Hour needed to live for some reason, well, too late. A decision had been made and Cassius was running with it.

His first stop was the Archives just so he could find out who the "official" Zero

Hour even was. He didn't really pay attention to things like that, normally. He had the power he needed; the rest of them didn't matter. Of course, this was bad practice as far as assassinations went. He found the name and celestial origin of the Zero Hour easily enough, but he had only a limited time to figure out where the man was currently. Was he having breakfast in his personal residence? Out on vacation three thousand miles or lightyears away? Here in the Wheel somewhere? There was no good way to ask these questions of anyone familiar with Time. Unfortunately, Zarib M'adul Dolpil'ish came from a civilization that was Openly Engaged. There were probably very few reasons why any outsider should be asking for him on Election Day, and none of them were good. And if another Zero Hour were looking for him, well, that definitely wasn't good.

To further the misfortune, Zarib's species, Forizian, was not exactly humanoid. Although upright in posture, their mode of propulsion more closely resembled some kind of propeller, at least, that was what Cassius was getting out of it, looking at the picture. He might be able to pull off a standing Disguise, just watching from some dark corner, but he would never be able to move in it.

Light, then, make himself invisible, or close enough. It was difficult to hold while moving, but better than a poor Disguise. Or, he could just Band, pull himself out of Base Time into a faster plane of Time, the oldest trick in the book. Since Akari Bands were invisible, even the Openly Engaged Forizians would not detect him.

Now he just had to find the bastard. The coordinates for Forx were 3-2-6-1-4, and Zarib himself hailed from Region Nine, District Seven. There was no guarantee that he was home, but it was as good a place to start as any.

Cassius grabbed a translator on his way out of the Wheel. It was not for the translating part, for he did not anticipate needing that, but for the atmospheric shell it would generate around him. This way he would have a comfortable Earth atmosphere to sustain him, in the event Forx was less than hospitable. There were limits to the shell—he couldn't jump out into deep space with it, and it could only overcome so much toxicity—but it was generally compatible among most planets, at least for a little while.

Whether it was the planet itself or just the region, Cassius did not know. All he knew was that when he stepped through his portal to Forx, to Region Nine, District Seven, the outskirts of a major city which he assumed would be a safe location for an outsider to drop in, the translator's atmospheric shell, whatever it was that determined when and how to activate and keep him safe, must have malfunctioned in its humidity sensors. He did not feel as though he were drowning, but the air was much thicker, much wetter, worse than tropical. Even casual walking felt like more of a chore than he was accustomed to. Was the gravity different here, heavier? What was this resistance? Looking around, the indigenous population propelled themselves to and fro with no more trouble than a fish in water, and here he was, slogging through invisible muck. He might have to Band just to keep up with his target.

He was not the only outsider around, nor was he the only outsider having trouble, so at least he had that going for him, that he wasn't attracting much attention with his difficulties. Still, this was a set of problems he had not anticipated having to deal with.

The prevailing architectural style seemed to be squat buildings that were annoyingly long and narrow, very much like the shotgun houses of the American South. The only reason Cassius was able to make this connection was because he'd seen many such houses; otherwise, they were just long, narrow, squat houses. It would probably be very easy to kill someone because he wasn't trying to make his way up to another floor and then back down. It would be a simple case of run right through, shoot on the fly, and never have to turn a corner as he escaped out the other side.

With the streets as narrow as the buildings, Cassius wondered if it wouldn't be smarter to just open a portal wherever he needed to go. He wasn't going to sneak up on anybody, and he certainly wasn't making a quick getaway.

He didn't even know where Zarib was. Sure, he'd found the man's hometown, but that didn't mean much. Did he dare risk just asking one of the locals? Surely the Zero Hour would be known among his own people if they were Openly Engaged, right? Did he work an equally important job at home? Would Cassius find him among the governing leadership of the town? Or the region? Or the country? Or did he decide that being Zero Hour was tough enough, he would just live comfortably on his salary and not work at home? Would Forizian culture allow for such a thing?

Cassius didn't know. He didn't care much either. But he was in a bit of a crunch and didn't have the time or ability to find everything that would be good to know. He should have done this a long time ago. Fucking bureaucracy.

Maybe his first goal should be to figure out just what was going on with the air that it was slowing him down so significantly. He didn't know how to go about this exactly, without returning to the Wheel. More information he probably should have investigated. It was entirely possible, to compare different planets using the Glass tablets in the Archives. But he hadn't been interested in the detailed information, just whether or not the atmosphere was generally tolerable and if a translator could stave off any outlying negative effects for a short period of time.

Maybe he should go to the Archives and look this up. No, it would just waste time. What time? Time stopped when a portal opened to the Wheel. The Forizians were Openly Engaged, so it wasn't as though he couldn't find some out-of-the-way place to open a portal. But would it actually get him any closer to his goal? It wasn't as though he didn't have options when it came to killing Zarib and getting away with it.

Cassius continued navigating his way along the sidewalks. They weren't so crowded that it was difficult to get through, but there was certainly noticeable congestion. There were separate lanes for those who had difficulty traversing the thicker atmosphere (or whatever the problem was) so as to keep regular traffic moving, which only frustrated Cassius more as innumerable Forizians and several other species zoomed by effortlessly.

There really weren't any dark, narrow alleys in this city; there did not appear to be any real difference between front doors and back doors and any path of navigation was free to traverse with little or no regard for community standards or privacy. Trash was not tucked away to rot and attract vermin, but moved swiftly from the door to a trash collecting vehicle that moved slowly down the road. The vehicle did not appear to ever actually stop, but moved at a slow enough pace that any home or business owner would have approximately two minutes to run out and meet it without having to give chase.

Personal vehicles did not appear to exist here. Foot, or rather, propeller traffic was the primary modicum of travel, with the center lanes between sidewalks reserved for the trash vehicles and larger public transportation. There also did not appear to be any personally-powered vehicles — scooters, bicycles and the like. Even as he thought it, Cassius watched some vehicular abomination go flying past him in the fast lane, piloted by a single Forizian though he did not stop to ponder its machinations.

There was nowhere to really stop and watch and consider what he needed to do. He had no real leads. Zarib could be just around the corner or in a city a thousand miles away or in another galaxy entirely. Looking around at the decorations on the buildings or the bus-like apparatus chugging down the vehicular lane, he saw no political advertisements. Sure, he didn't read their language, but from the pictures he saw, most of it appeared to be tourism-based. Visit this place, see that thing, buy this trinket. None of the imagery appeared to scream, "Vote for me!"

He didn't see too much of Time at all, either. He didn't see it used anywhere, people hoping to get someplace just a little bit faster. He didn't see any advertisements for Time Capsules, though surely an ambitious and successful Merchant would want to gain or maintain some notoriety in his hometown. Instead, there were charming and decorative storefronts with an array of displays and samples; small cafes where the open-air seating was inside the building where the roof was intentionally cut out of the center of that particular space; and micro-parks about every thousand feet where people could sit down, touch grass, and throw a coin into a wishing fountain (or whatever comparable frivolous superstition the Forizians observed here).

Maybe Cassius was just in the wrong part of town. This was turning out to be the tourist trap filled with starry-eyed tourists and the idiots who catered to them. All that mattered here was the present moment and the number of trinkets and memorabilia one could acquire in that moment. There was nothing serious or essential about any of this. Zarib would be nowhere near this place.

But how much time did he really want to spend searching? Did he really want to ask about the Zero Hour's whereabouts? Well, the average person on the street probably wouldn't think too much about it. Surely such an important figure wouldn't even entertain an interruption from every layman on the street, never mind one who said that someone asked a question about him. Whoop-de-fucking-do, people probably asked simple questions about him all the time. And it was Election Day, after all. Maybe there was a way to salvage the situation. After all, who didn't enjoy complaining about politicians?

He stopped in a bookstore, or he believed them to be books. They had individual pages, though the binding was strange. Bookish people were always so snobby, believing themselves to be more educated or better informed than plebeians who did not read. Surely they would have an endless wealth of correct opinions on all things, including local and galactic politicians.

The Akari as much as the translator brought the words to his ears from the store attendant. "Can I help you find something?"

"What do you think of Zarib M'adul Dolpil'ish?" Cassius inquired bluntly.

The attendant stared at him, expression foreign. Cassius noted that the two patrons in the store inclined their heads or turned their bodies slightly in their direction but never actually looked up from their investigations of the shelves. Ah, yes, political gossip rules all. Though the attendant was long with his answer, Cassius just assumed this was from being startled by the question. Considering that a foreigner was making the inquiry, he was probably trying to ascertain Cassius' body language and intentions.

"You're speaking of the Zero Hour?" the attendant inquired.

"He's the only one I know of. What do you think of him?" Cassius tried to lighten up his demeanor a little. "Come on, he's on his way out of office. There must be something you want to brag about him, being one of your own."

One of the patrons made an incredulous sound, similar to a scoff. When he realized he was caught, he made some gesture of embarrassment and said, with a twinge of snobbish self-righteousness, "Dolpil'ish may live in the Zorpal region, but he's from Adul, though he'd like to deny it." The man's tone said that Adul was probably not part of polite society, at least according to him. "He's brought far too much Adul influence here."

"He's the Zero Hour," Cassius stated. "What does that have to do with here?"

"M'adul Dolpil'ish," the attendant said, apparently forcibly correcting the patron over proper address, "was made High Governor seven years ago." He gave a pointed look to the patron. "Because of how well he'd done as Zero Hour."

The patron rolled his eyes and shifted his stance as if he'd like to come over and start a real argument but was just barely restraining himself. The second patron was still pretending to read, though her demeanor was less inflamed.

The attendant looked at Cassius. "Home politics aside, Forx has been honored to have a Forizian as Zero Hour. It's done a lot of good here, brought us new alliances, smoothed over minor disagreements—"

"Started at least two wars," the antagonistic patron threw in venomously.

"Maybe I should come back later," Cassius suggested. He had the information he needed.

"It's fine," the attendant said, making a flippant gesture that did not seem to go over well with the patron. "Politics is never an easy subject here."

"It's not easy where I'm from either," Cassius said, backing away. "Maybe I'll come back in a few hours."

And he left, pausing just long enough to turn and watch the attendant and the patron finally start a real argument, now that the outsider was gone. He grinned, turned, and continued moving down the sidewalk.

Zero Hour in Time, High Governor at home. Well, that simultaneously narrowed and expanded the possibilities for where the man could be. Narrowed, because he was unlikely to be working some mundane office job or running menial errands. Expanded, because he could be out meeting with other heads of state, going over some treaty details that might change once he was no longer the Zero Hour and could no longer leverage the final authority of the universe for or against certain people.

Fucking hell. How was Cassius supposed to find out where he was or where he was going to be?

It was about another twenty minutes of aimlessly wandering through an increasingly ridiculous tourist district before he considered that he did know where Zarib M'adul Dolpil'ish was going to be. He was going to be at the inauguration, and he was going to be there early so as to avoid crowds and do whatever he needed to do with the rest of the outgoing Hands.

Well, this had been a phenomenal waste of time. On the other hand, it beat being a lackey for Rifun or Isthim. He wasn't going to go report back to them about his failure. If he could help it, he wasn't going to see them at all until the inauguration.

He returned to the Wheel, busy as ever as last-minute voters scrambled to wait in line for several hours, or that was how it appeared to him. He bypassed all of this and made for the Seat of the Hands. A few ambitious officers were already claiming seats, but otherwise the whole place was largely devoid of life, perhaps the only day off the secretaries who attended the Seat would see until the next election. And even then, there were still chores to be taken care of.

The Bat and the Day, ever loyal, were preparing for the inauguration in the inner track, just outside the main arena where petitions were normally entertained. The Bat anticipated him first, its large ears turning ever so slightly to track his movements while the Day swung its long neck around to watch him.

"I need a favor," Cassius stated.

"Favors are unnecessary," the Bat said. "We follow your orders."

"Shut the fuck up. You follow the dragon's orders."

The expression that twisted the Bat's face might have been likened to a smile, though Cassius decided he didn't want to consider it at the moment. The hideous mess of a face that became the Day was even less flattering.

"I'm not going to hunt Zarib M'adul Dolpil'ish across the universe trying to stick a knife in his back and escape before his guards catch me. It's too much work when I could just let him come to me." Cassius pointed to a room within sight. "I'm going to hang out in there until the inauguration. When Dolpil'ish shows up, bring him to me there so I can kill him. Then we won't have two Zero Hours running around confusing everyone and starting a panic before it's time."

"It will be done," the Bat replied smoothly, though its tone was tinged with just a hint of amusement.

"I assume Isthim and Misik have already told you the rest of the plan after the old Hands are dismissed?"

"They have," the Day confirmed.

"Good. Let's not fuck it up, hm?"

Cassius stomped off before either could reply.

He entered the room he'd pointed to and sat down on the floor in a heap. Universal utilitarianism left much to desire when it came to interior decoration. The only thing that could feasibly satisfy everyone—or almost everyone—was a plain box with small bump outs that could be interpreted as seating or maybe a table. Cassius wanted a chair. Actually, he wanted a bed. Something soft. In theory, there was a way to make anything anyone could ever want, similar to how Cassius had come across something called a 3D printer on Earth. Why couldn't these rooms come equipped with such a thing? At the very least, he found himself wishing to be able to remove his cloak, wad it up to use as a pillow or just a thin cushion between him and the floor.

They had better not fuck this up this time. Once they got control of the Wheel, they needed to fucking hold it and fucking eliminate every threat against it. No treaties, no tiptoes, no trying to plan for a century down the road. Right fucking here, right fucking now. All that mattered. Someone had a problem with the way things were done? Beat them within an inch of their lives or sell them into Borelian slavery. Kill them if Rifun really insisted on mercy.

Maybe that was a way Cassius could stave off his own slavery. Fuck Rifun and the others; they could go die in some prison camp for all he cared. But him, he could hunt down dissenters. He could act as Calis Cutthroat once more, heartless mercenary, bane of the Gentleman Killers and the Tacagans and anyone who got between him and his target. He could probably go places the regular Borelian hunters couldn't. Everyone knew to fear the Borelians, and they weren't overly interested in subtlety like Disguises. True, he wasn't the best at social niceties himself, but he was better than them by a mile.

Maybe he should kill Rifun in the chaos once their plan was put into motion. Who was really going to know? And if they did know, who was going to do anything about it? In such pandemonium, the only thing that mattered was the three foot radius around you. Who was in the immediate vicinity and were they a threat? Whatever was going on across the room didn't matter, didn't even exist. There was only the here and now, life and death. As it should be.

Cassius figured he must have slept at some point because the next thing he knew, his head was a tad cloudy and his position had changed. Slowly, he stood, stretched, and looked around. Nothing had changed. He couldn't have slept long, then. Or else he'd managed to sleep through an entire revolution. If that was the case, he was probably going to be mad enough to start a second one.

The door opened and the Bat walked in, followed by a cloaked figured identical to Cassius, or how he appeared to outsiders.

"Ah, so this is the newly-elected Zero Hour?" Zarib M'adul Dolpil'ish inquired.

Outside the Bat and the Day, few had any idea of the behind-the-scenes work that went into the inauguration. Just by his tone, Cassius could tell Zarib wanted to be optimistic and welcoming to his apparent replacement, though he was evidently confused because this wasn't what he had done when he took office.

Cassius approached, trying to appear as non-threatening as possible. "No."

With the speed and dexterity of a cat, Cassius whipped a knife from his belt and buried it in the man's chest cavity, hoping there was a heart in there somewhere. Zarib put up no resistance, just made a strangled sound of surprise and slumped to the ground. The knife, deep in his chest, was hidden by his cloak, programmed to hide any and all holes that might cause someone to catch a glimpse of what lay beneath, the wearer's true identity. Even the blood was hidden, with nary a stain to indicate any sort of foul play.

Cassius looked at the Bat who was entirely unmoved. "He can probably stay here until later cleanup." The Bat just dipped its head once. "Now then, let's go take over the Wheel. Again. And let's fucking do it right this time."

"You're anxious, Rivotra," Lalao observed, "and I don't think it has to do with Tomas."

Rifun shook his head as he nervously stirred his tea, the sugar now well dissolved. "I have another opportunity to go after the dragon spirit." He intentionally moved his right hand to awkwardly tap on the table. "I hope my reservations can be understood, if not forgiven."

"Of course. Just like your courage to try again anyway is both respected and admired."

She clearly meant it as encouragement, but he could only sigh, still staring at his cup of tea, the pastry beside it only half-nibbled. "The dragon won't be alone. It will have help from like creatures called the Bat and the Day."

"Bat I understand, but...Day?"

He shrugged. "It's just how they're called." He gave her a serious look. "I have watched these creatures die horrible deaths and be resurrected. The power they wield is nearly unimaginable."

Now Lalao frowned. "Personally, I would take it as a compliment. That the dragon thinks it needs help in order to keep itself alive and defeat you."

Rifun laughed, more at the absurdity than the humor. "Then it knows more than I do about what happened—or didn't happen—at our last encounter."

She took a sip of her drink. "Do you think it possible that you did hurt the dragon in some way, but your own injuries prevented you from seeing it?"

"I don't see how, but I also don't remember a lot about what happened. I was too distracted."

"Exactly. So who is to say? Maybe that is why it needs friends this time."

"Maybe, but if I don't remember what I did—" He cut himself off.

The only thing he had done was invert the portal. What if it had hurt the dragon? What if Cassius, therefore the dragon, had crossed that threshold and been harmed? Could that be why Cassius hadn't shown up to ensure Lily's death?

Was the dragon wounded? How exactly did the Bat and the Day play into this dynamic? What would happen if they were taken down to the Core? Would they even go, or would it cause harm?

He could feel Lalao's grin. "You see? You just need to talk it out."

"Plans are wonderful until they're executed," he told her. "But you're not wrong." His gaze wandered back to his hand, the nubs aching even as he could feel the pads of his invisible fingers pressing on the table.

"Perhaps once you slay the dragon, you can retrieve your fingers from its belly," Lalao suggested. "Just as the spirits restored your sight, so they will restore your body."

He nodded, not looking at her. "Maybe." It would be a nice reward. Forget fame and fortune; he just wanted his fingers back.

"I'm guessing this endeavor is happening soon, or else you wouldn't have come so soon after our last lunch," she guessed.

Another nod. "In less than twelve hours is my window of opportunity, and I expect that window won't last more than an hour." He managed an awkward smile. "I wanted to make sure I saw you before I left. With any luck, I'll be back soon and you can chastise me about being so hopeless and uncertain."

She laughed. "Knowing what I know, what you have told me, and seeing what has befallen you so far, I think I shall be glad just to see you again. Shall I plan on lunch tomorrow, then?"

He shook his head. "No, no. If I win, I think I shall be too tired to want to do anything for a few days. We'll meet next week, as usual."

She picked up her drink and made a half-toast gesture. "Sounds like a plan."

They spoke of other things, comparatively minor things. Silly things, even. Family matters, births, deaths, marriages, the farm. Lalao had told the family of Rifun's reappearance, although such a claim was met with some understandable skepticism, considering that Rivotra Andilan was supposedly dead and buried. His "son" Fan, perhaps, but then there was the question of his age. No, he must be the next generation, Fan's son now. That was how the rest of the family explained it to themselves, but Lalao knew, and that was all that mattered.

He took her home, as per usual, Tomas meeting them at the door like a mildly disapproving father. Lalao stated that she would see him again next week, and he tried to meet her cheerful attitude with some like rebuttal. He wished them both good day and departed, praying as loudly as he silently could that he would indeed see her next week. Not only that, but he wanted to regale her with a lively, heroic tale of dragon-slaying and universe-saving. He didn't want to just leave her standing, waiting for him in the darkness, watching the days go by and wondering what had happened to him. Last time, she had lived an entire life without him. If it happened again, she may die without ever knowing what had become of him. He couldn't do that to her.

He'd originally intended to go back to Sadurnon and see about any final preparations from that end. At the last second, he chose to go to the Wheel instead. He had thought that maybe things would be a little too tense, maybe he didn't want to walk into that powder keg.

But despite the devastating injury he'd sustained, there had been a silver lining, a blessing in disguise that manifested while he was laid up in bed: the ability to take time and reflect on himself, his actions, his beliefs. Ironically, studying foreign languages helped in this endeavor because it forced him to learn new ways of expressing familiar concepts.

Courage, for instance. Few normal people would accuse him of cowardice. Sure, he wasn't fearless, but he had seen plenty of combat, led men into battle, led them on suicide missions even and still returned alive. And yet, Cassius frequently berated him for indecision and cowardice. Now then, there was the fact that some men were never satisfied with anything but action, and even the slightest bit of planning and forethought was viewed as hesitation and cowardice.

And yet, Rifun had another thought. It wasn't Cassius calling him a coward. It was the dragon taunting him. Taunt him with such accusations, aim for one of two responses: meek acceptance of the accusations, causing him to stop planning altogether; or desperate, stupid action in some vain attempt to prove that he wasn't a coward. And if Rifun wanted to be honest, he had succumbed to both outcomes. He had become so paralyzed with fear that he used his planning as an excuse for inaction. Then, when he did make plans, they were rash and foolish and cost everyone far too dearly. Not only himself, but the rest of the Cult as they gave time and resources to what became a lost cause; as well as Tommen, who was largely innocent of all of these shenanigans; Micaiah who could not possibly fathom what was going on here; Walter and Micah who, like the rest of the Time industry, was about to undergo a cosmic shift and they knew not why. By allowing himself to be subtly manipulated in such a way, Rifun had condemned men to death.

Whatever the dragon had planned once the Wheel was under Cult control—or perhaps Borelian control—it was going to be a lot worse than a few dead cops and a couple missing fingers.

If he had to go through all this trouble to have a chance against the dragon, he couldn't expect average people, or even average Time Agents to carry any weight. Especially if he intended to go to the Core of the Wheel, they wouldn't be able to handle it; they would kill themselves.

The bustling activity of the elections was dying down, voting nearly closed. The Wheel itself was still busy, but hardly the chaos from earlier. Rifun had no trouble getting to the Archives and making his way to the staircase that led down into an employees only section. With all of the attention focused on the voting chamber where the votes were tallied and manipulated, Rifun had no trouble turning his attention to the corridor that, through some magic or technology, was invisible to most psyches.

He knew he had forgotten much of what he had experienced the last time he had been here, but walking down the corridor now was like stepping into an old pair of shoes, assuming those shoes were cold, wet, and filled with spiders that may or may not be poisonous. Another thought occurred to him as he advanced into the darkness: would he remember any plans he made here? If he forgot the magnificence of the Core itself, would he also forget any of his plans for practical usage of the Core against the dragon?

It was enough to give him pause anyway. After a minute, he continued on. He would take that risk. He would take the dragon's risk that he would remember his plans and he would be able to execute them.

Framing it that way made it much easier to bear as he continued down the hall, the dread creeping up on him like slowly rising water. When he hit the spiral staircase that led to the Core, he took a breath and plunged himself into the thick, murky water. Not literally, of course, thankfully. Still, it felt a chore to breathe as he descended. Just one foot in front of the other. Step, step, step. Ignore every stab of fear that said he was going to stumble into the torture chamber. Step, step, step. He was in the Wheel of Time, the nexus of Creation; there was no reason he should be hearing screams or smelling burning bodies.

He needed to focus. How was he going to get the dragon down here? Was it also affected by this crushing darkness? Rifun couldn't come up with any reason why it shouldn't be. If the Core was designed and put in place by the Author, why shouldn't she want to protect it from the likes of the dragon and those who served it? But then, why make it just as difficult for Builders and those who served her? Would he have this much difficulty getting through this darkness if and when he did lure the dragon this way? If so, why?

Could there be some merit to Cassius' statement that their gods were the same? No. He dismissed that idea as swiftly as it entered his head. Rifun desired the betterment of the universe. Cassius wanted to watch it burn. They were not the same. They were on opposite ends of that tugging rope.

One rope with enough length can hang at both ends, a small voice whispered, causing an involuntary shiver as he took yet another step.

Although his memory was hazy, he still retained enough to remember the sudden drop at the bottom of the stairs, even though he couldn't see it. Instead of falling to the bottom, he used a Gravity track to gently lower himself to the platform overlooking the Core of the Wheel.

It was just as magnificent as before, even to his addled eyes. At once solid, at once gas, at once waves, at once a perfect sphere, at once the strings of an impossible instrument, at once perfectly silent, at once thrumming with the base energy of the universe, all of the black holes and dimensions and every physical particle of Creation, twisting through the eye of an infinitesimally tiny needle. Perhaps this was what also controlled the aging of the universe, and once every atom had slipped through that needle, then the end would come.

Mortal beings were too enraptured by the Core to stand it for very long before killing themselves in order to reach it, at once a mile away and at once within arm's reach. Even Rifun would not claim to be immune to its effects, whatever protection his head injury afforded him. It was not only visual; there was a spiritual element to this as well, as if his soul were also being threaded through that needle.

How did spiritual beings react to this? Was there some extra element known only to them because of their nature? When Time was a tangible dimension to them, what more did they see and feel when they looked over the edge? And if this was some essence of the Author, how would the dragon react to it? Would it be overpowered by the magnificence? Would it become enraged?

Another thought occurred to Rifun, his thoughts now like freshly sharpened knives. What if the dragon wanted to come here? What if the blackness, the darkness, the difficulty in getting here, what if it had some compounding effect on evil spirits, to keep them out? What if Rifun's bait was just the invitation it needed to cross an otherwise impenetrable threshold?

But then, did that not play into the idea that Rifun's spirits were the same as Cassius' spirits, that they should both have difficulty reaching this place? That couldn't be right, could it? He couldn't recall any mention of Akarin Builders having no difficulty getting here—although they were the only ones reported to have survived this encounter. He couldn't be an agent of evil spirits and be able to stand here like a Builder. And he couldn't be a Builder if he were an agent of evil spirits. Right?

That did not solve the problem of whether the dragon was supposed to be here. And, really, if normal mortal beings who weren't Builders came here and committed suicide, it might just be a case where Cassius threw himself over the edge, died, and the dragon moved on to another host, exactly as if Rifun had killed Cassius in any other way.

His first reaction to that, oddly enough, was that it was so terribly anti-climactic. He wanted to give Lalao a grand tale of battle and heroics and a stunning victory. A loss was not something he liked to admit, but at least there was some circumstance around the warehouse, actions and reactions and reasons. Bringing Cassius here with the intent of fighting the dragon, only to watch him throw himself to his death and the dragon quietly slink off into the universe...that wasn't much of a story. And it was a lot of wasted time and energy to achieve the same result as just killing the man in his sleep.

Was there any way to be absolutely sure? Rifun wanted to get this done as quickly as possible, using the chaos of the initial takeover as cover, but he didn't want to screw it up.

He couldn't let himself be paralyzed into inaction and so let the dragon run rampant, but he also couldn't let himself get baited into a foolish plan that would only blow up in his face. Was this a warning from the Author that this wouldn't go as planned, or doubt from evil spirits to try and dissuade him from the only plan that might actually work? Could evil spirits survive in this place with the Core, the essence of the Author? If not, then it only stood to reason that this was a quiet caution impressed upon him.

Rifun looked around. Physically, it didn't look like much, just an enormous room with only a single platform and a bottomless pit filled with the nexus of Creation and all the twisting dimensions, but what havoc could the dragon wreak in this place? What if, like some spirits, the dragon needed to be invited into this place? What would happen if Rifun did just that? What if the dragon would not be weakened here, but enormously strengthened? What would happen if evil had unfettered access to every particle of universe at one time?

He backed away from the railing overlooking the Core. Just as well he came here to think things through before carrying out this plan, or things could have gone sideways in a devastating way.

But what did he do now? Was it even possible to invert a portal inside the Wheel? How did the in-between dimension work here when all of the dimensions ultimately twisted into one another in the Core?

Another thought occurred to him. Builders could manipulate the Wheel through the Core. If the dragon couldn't come here, what if Rifun stayed here and used the Core to manipulate the Wheel to destroy the dragon? If he had access to all of the dimensions through the Core, there was nowhere the dragon could hide. Of course, without knowing exactly how Building worked—he knew theory but not practical application as it concerned the Wheel—he didn't want to risk everyone else in the Wheel, especially in the chaos of the coup for which he was still expected to be present. He might have to wait for the initial chaos to settle down, maybe wait until Cassius went off alone somewhere. He would probably want to torture at least a few prisoners. Rifun would destroy the dragon, kill Cassius, and put the poor tortured soul out of their misery all at once.

He used a Gravity track to return to the stairs and ascend into the blackness. There was no resistance when leaving, though he could feel the memories of the Core slipping away. He remembered some fear about not recalling any plans he made while in the Core's presence, but, at the moment, those fears seemed to be unfounded. Use the Core to manipulate the Wheel to destroy the dragon. Any details he had made to support this plan seemed to be fading, but the foundation of the plan remained.

He had no intentions of revealing his plan to anyone. Cassius, for obvious reasons. Isthim or any of the Borelians, because he didn't want any of them even thinking about how to use the Core to their own advantage. Actually, once he took care of the dragon, maybe he would see about going after them next, rid the universe of two evils in one day.

He had little trouble returning to the Archives, though it appeared as though he had spent more time in the Core than intended. Had he lost track of time, or was it some strange time warping feature of the Core? Whatever the case, either the coup had not yet begun, or else it had already come and gone, though he found that unlikely.

Heading to the Seat of the Hands, it had not yet begun. Indeed, even the inauguration had not yet begun. At his arrival, however, the Bat approached.

"This way," it commanded.

Rifun did not argue as he followed the Bat through the Wheel to the inner track just outside the gate where old Hands and newly-elected candidates were milling about. At a glance he could tell not all of them had arrived yet. Cassius was nowhere to be seen. Rifun made as if to slow and join the group, but the Bat made a motion for him to keep following.

About thirty yards from the milling group, the Bat opened a door to what would normally be a waiting room for those who came to petition the Hands for various matters. Now it was the meeting place for their band of revolutionaries.

"Cassius was elected Zero Hour, but he will be walking out as the current Zero Hour," Isthim began, jumping into the conversation. "Anyone looking for a fight over how the elections were handled is going to attack what they believe is the newly-elected Zero Hour. Because Cassius cannot play both roles, and to throw off any such ravenous hounds, you, Rifun, will walk out as Cassius as the newly-elected Zero Hour."

"Bait," Rifun said simply.

"Of a sort."

"Lovely."

"All you need to do is exactly what is expected of a new Hand greeting an old," Cassius told him. "I will take care of the rest."

"He will announce us," Isthim clarified. "Not explicitly, rather, he will be our cue to move."

"Oh, good. I hate it when villains announce their intentions," Rifun hissed sarcastically. "Makes it far too easy to resist them and fight back."

Her expression was not amused, and she ignored the comment. "Once all of the Hands and candidates have walked out, Misik and I will leave here to direct the Grandfathers as planned. Are there any concerns or changes that must be made known now for the good of the people?"

Rifun looked at Cassius. "Has there been any movement from the Akarin?"

Cassius waved a hand and scoffed. "They don't give a shit. If anything, they want this to happen just so they can tell any survivors 'I told you so.' Then they might come out and pretend to oppose us. If they don't, I'll force them through controlled opposition."

"Sounds promising," Isthim commented dryly. "Anything else? Anyone else? The Akarin are not the only ones likely to oppose us. Few others have a real chance, but they can be a nuisance."

"Nothing that stands out," Misik reported. "We've already planned for pockets of resistance, perhaps a few stronger campaigns, nothing we've not dealt with before."

"We" referring to the Borelians, not the Cult, Rifun figured. He would have to get down to the Core as quickly as possible once the initial confusion subsided. Or maybe that would be his goal once the fighting started, using the chaos to his advantage and cover his escape. He couldn't allow the Borelians to sink their claws into this kind of power.

The meeting ended abruptly, Cassius storming out of the room after some comment from Isthim or Misik, Rifun did not know. He himself said some banal departing pleasantry and followed, hoping it looked somewhat natural rather than anxious.

As soon as they stepped out of the room and casually rejoined the rest of the group which had swelled in number, the two of them did not know each other. They could not express any more familiarity than business associates, if that. They certainly couldn't be in cahoots with one another. Or rather, that's what Rifun told himself. Looking around at the others, there was plenty of undue familiarity. Some of it may have been unique to species and culture, but even then, some of it appeared just a little too friendly, even for politicians, Rifun thought. Maybe that was just him.

He looked as the gate barring the tunnel to the center arena started opening. It made no sound, neither grunt nor grind nor tiny squeak, as it lifted, propelled by ancient, physical mechanisms currently controlled by the Day. Rifun was more acquainted with the Bat, so it was a bit odd to watch this fourteen foot tall giraffe-peacock abomination hefting the wheel over and over to lift the gate. When it was open, the Bat walked out to begin the ceremonies. When it was through, the gate closed again.

The Day then went to work arranging the old Hands, pairing them neatly with Cassius at the very back. At a certain point in the Bat's opening speech, they would walk out into the bright light to face the ravenous mob, and split off in opposite directions with the Zero Hour landing in the center of the line.

Rifun did not expect to hear the Bat's speech over the din of conversation both in the track and out in the Seat, but he did.

"Timekeepers! Harvesters! Merchants!" Despite its normally calm demeanor, the Bat had no trouble making itself heard. "You have endured eleven years of submission to the same Hands of Time. You have cast your votes and let your voices be heard, whom you want as your Hands and your leaders. We begin today by shedding the old leadership to make way for those whom you have chosen to take their place."

The Bat was a creature of few words, but it knew how to make those words count, and word choice was not lost on Rifun. There was too much emphasis on the people's decision. The people's elections, the people's votes, the people's choice. And yet, there was some truth to it, even with the rigging. The people had been content with the ways of evil. They loved to complain about it more than they loved to do anything about it. As long as the evil was in place, there was an abstract evil to blame, and every so often, bread crumbs might make their way to the floor. And most importantly, lesser evils could be gotten away with because they were, comparatively speaking, very minor. If things were good, if leaders were just, then it only emphasized the wrongdoings of the people who liked to believe themselves special and that their wrongs were justified or just "not that bad." And spirits forbid that someone they didn't like be successful under a fair law.

The Day opened the gate once more and the line of Hands shuffled their way out.

So, yes, the people had chosen this. Maybe not these people; these were just the poor souls who were finally reaping what their predecessors had sown. Although, there was a case to be made that it was their fault, Rifun thought. It had only been forty years or so since the Cult was last deposed. The Time industry could have at least made an effort to better itself afterwards. Meddling from the Borelians probably made any such attempts difficult at best, so Rifun was willing to give some benefit of the doubt.

"Hands of Time!" the Bat bellowed. "We shall begin the oath of leaving office."

This was easily one of the dullest points of the inauguration. Rifun was forced to wonder why no Council of Hands had ever made an honest effort to shorten the ceremonies. Was there some ancient law in place that said this was how things had to be done? Were the majority of Hands really that conceited about being sworn into office? What would happen if this whole hullabaloo was just the new Hands coming out, the Bat telling the crowd that these were the new Hands, shrouding them, and then leaving? Five minutes, done and over with.

The oath was intended to bind the Hands to their word and any decisions they had made while serving. It looked good for the peons, made them think that the Hands might still be held accountable for their actions once they were no longer Hands. This was hardly the case, often thanks to the secretaries and their background manipulation.

"And now! We begin the unshrouding!"

Ah, yes. The second-most boring part. Instead of just having each Hand remove his own shroud, there was a big to-do over dramatically pulling the hood off each one. What could have taken fifteen seconds instead took at least fifteen minutes. And the Zero Hour wasn't even included; there was a separate ceremony for that.

On the other hand, it took about that much time for the Day to organize the rest of them into similar lines, two columns of Hand-candidates with Rifun at the end, masquerading as the Zero Hour-elect.

"These Hands!" the Bat went on once all fifty normal Hands were finished. "These are the Hands who have served you for the last eleven years! They have taken their ending oath of office, and now they will turn over their power to the new Hands whom you have chosen!"

Again with the emphasis on choice, Rifun thought, watching the Day return to the wheel to begin hefting the gate once more. When it was open, the lines began moving, through the corridor into the Seat.

Sometimes Rifun wondered if anyone really appreciated what the Coliseum represented, at least to humans. To some species, perhaps the one who had decided this is what the Seat should look like in this iteration, maybe it was a grand place of high society and political grandeur. Maybe some saw it as a regular sports arena. Humans couldn't be the only ones to whom it meant death at the hands of psychopaths and sycophants.

The Hand candidates split off as those before them had, so that by the end, they stood in two lines, the old Hand facing his new counterpart. In the middle, Rifun faced Cassius, still in his shroud, waiting for a separate ceremony.

"The Hand of Scientifically Superior and Openly Engaged Civilizations!" the Bat announced from somewhere down the line.

The named Hand removed his cloak—what technology allowed for this and at what time it was allowed, Rifun did not know—and draped it over his replacement. The technology that made it so the cloak was absolute and entirely unwavering also made it so it could conform to any body size and shape. Although Cassius had mentioned on a couple occasions that the cloak was real and tangible against his skin, Rifun still thought there was more technology than tailoring behind it.

Again, what should have taken just a few minutes lasted over an hour. Rifun shifted position uncomfortably. Would there be time for a bathroom break before the fighting started?

"The power of the Hands has been transferred!" the Bat said at last. "Look upon your new Council of Hands!"

The overall aura of the crowd was, quite frankly, bored. No one wanted to be here. In a way, it only helped the Cult's cause. Everyone had been expecting something massive to happen right away. Here they were, two or three hours in, and nothing had happened. Maybe everything would be all right. The perfect false sense of security.

"The final transfer of power," the Bat announced, standing some distance away from Cassius to address the crowd, "is that of the Zero Hour! The Zero Hour is the leader of leaders, the Hand whose only job is to oversee the Hands and govern without bias! The Zero Hour is the final voice in votes and matters of state, voting only when the Hands are unable to reach their own conclusions! The Zero Hour is the ultimate and final authority figure, the champion of Time and its interests, bearing upon his shoulders the awesome weight of the universe!"

For as bored as Rifun was, he almost didn't want anything to happen right now. Get this bullshit done and over with, go home, take a nap to recover his motivation, then come back in the morning with an army.

His wavering determination snapped back in place. The Bat had said something he didn't catch—didn't matter anyway, really—and moved to stand behind Cassius. Now it was happening. For the others, this was the moment of triumph. For him, this was going to be his chance to get to the Core and stop them. He couldn't help but grin.

"Behold, your Zero Hour who has governed you for the last eleven years!"

The Bat reached as it to remove Cassius' hood, but Cassius stepped out of the way, out of line. Rifun followed suit to stand beside him.

Any remaining chatter or conversation in the Seat abruptly ceased. The coals of anxiety were slowly stoked back to life, more so as Cassius moved to stand center stage, removing his hood as he did so.

"Many of you were expecting to see a familiar transition of power," he said. His words dripped acid, his annoyance with these pointless ceremonies bubbling into rage within an active pressure cooker whose lid was about to be removed by force. "Many of you were expecting to hear the same familiar words that have been spoken from one Zero Hour to the next as he hands over his cloak.

"I know that you were told—by your Lieutenants, by your Physicians, whoever told you today that the elections for the Zero Hour had been rigged in such a way that it didn't matter how you voted because they got rearranged anyway. For many of you, this came as a shock. And now you sit here wondering what's going to happen. Was it done with the Zero Hour-elect's knowledge? Was it a scheme, a scam, a ploy? What fiendish powers are behind this? Could there be some truth behind the rumors of a False Zero Hour?"

Was there some cue Cassius was initiating, or waiting for? The man hated speeches, was dying for action. Rifun discreetly scanned the crowd, noted several coveys of Grandfathers or secretaries. Was he trying to buy time for something?

"All during the elections, you heard about a False Zero Hour, one who was masquerading as the highest authority in the land with no one to rein him in. You heard tales of Calis Cutthroat being this enemy, this False Zero Hour." He paused dramatically. "I. Am. He."

English was not Rifun's first language, or even his second, and although he was reasonably skilled, he would not consider himself natively fluent. And in those few heartbeats between the cue to chaos and the chaos itself, Rifun found himself unreasonably distracted by whether or not Cassius' incredible statement was grammatically correct.

Then the crowd began to move, helped along by sudden pockets of violence centered on those groups of Grandfathers or secretaries he had noted. The rest of the Hands, old and new, panicked. The majority of them took off for the small gate from which they had all emerged. The Bat covered them, as if trying to help them escape when really it was just herding them into the slaughterhouse. The few Hands that did not run that way turned on Cassius. With a flourish, he swept his Zero Hour cloak aside and turned to engage them, all his pent-up rage finally able to be spent.

Rifun did not stick around to attack or defend the man; he had little doubt that Cassius could physically defend himself however he needed to. Instead, he made his way toward the same small gate the Hands had. Around him, the majority of those in the crowd were simply acting on animal instinct to flee. As the orderly line got bottlenecked at the large gates and then at the portal leading to the Wheel, flight turned to fight. Even in the best of intentions from the non-violent, not a few patrons were knocked over the edge of the last row of seats, falling two to three stories to their death. As he drew nearer to the tunnel from which he had emerged, he could hear the last sounds of blood and battle.

The gate was still up and the floor at the far end of the tunnel was littered with bodies. Not wishing to have his head chopped off as soon as he entered the inner track, he called out, "Incoming!"

Not trusting his allies anyway, he still used a Band to dart through the last twenty feet.

A few less than fifty Hands, forty Grandfathers, and the Bat. It hadn't been a battle, say it that way. Rifun did not linger, did his best to block out as much as he could as he turned and mentally mapped a way out of the Coliseum with as little known resistance as possible.

"Where are you going?" the Bat asked, catching up to him. It did not stop him, though Rifun had a deep spiritual sense that the Bat, whatever its connection to the dragon, knew his intentions.

"I'm getting out of the Coliseum, for one," Rifun told it. "It's a bloodbath in there, or it will be. There will be more room to maneuver outside, catch any escapees, cut off the portals."

It wanted to stop him. Rifun could see that in its beady little eyes. It wanted to, so badly. Then it came up with an excuse.

"The Grandfathers have positioned themselves so as to slay any who exit the Seat portal, and the surrounding portals after that. It would be unwise to attempt to leave."

"They will be using Time to their advantage. A few may even use the Akari. But I have the advantage of Building. I'll be fine." Assuming their intentions were honest and they backed down once they realized who he was. On the other hand, they could take the opportunity to cut him down and claim fog of war.

"The gates are about to come down," the Bat pressed. "If there are any trapped within the Seat whom you desire to save, now would be the time."

The creature said it in such a way that gave Rifun pause. It knew there was someone, or multiple someones, in the Seat whom he was concerned for. Tommen, or perhaps Walter or Micaiah. Of course Walter and Micaiah, and Micah, too, for they were posted officers. They were required to be here.

Frustrated, Rifun whirled around and stalked back to the tunnel leading into the Seat. He would get Walter and the twins safely into the Judgment Wing—though they wouldn't see it as such—and then head to the Core. By then, the trigger-happy Grandfathers should be calmed down enough to give him some safe passage. And in the cooldown following battle, it might be his best chance at destroying the dragon and the rest, while they absorbed the blood from the sacrifices.

He ran into Cassius just inside the Seat. He had replaced his cloak, though the hood remained down, and he had the look of a man who had just finished warming up and was now ready for some grueling physical work. He even grinned when he recognized Rifun.

"See, this is how you do it," he said breathily, bouncing on his toes.

"We can't just kill everyone in the universe," Rifun told him. "Come on."

He headed for a narrow stairway leading into the stadium seats. Normally it was hidden away, like a maintenance access, but it had been ripped open for this special occasion, likely in the panic of everyone trying to get to where they believed safety to be.

"We're not killing everyone in the universe, just the ones with the power and authority to come against us," Cassius said. "The officers, the Hands and Grandfathers and secretaries who wouldn't support us." They found a spot out of the way of the throng of panicked aliens. On the opposite side of the Seat, a small squad of Grandfathers and other co-conspirators waited patiently. Cassius pointed to an alien in the crowd below. "He's a liar." He pointed to another alien. "He's a cheat." Another point. "He used Time to kill his girlfriend."

"You know this, do you?" Rifun wondered, raising a brow. "Everyone lies. Everyone cheats." He shifted his stance. "Not everyone kills their significant other, true, but—"

"Prepare to meet thy God," Cassius cut in. "Today is a day of judgment."

With some help from nearby Grandfathers as well as the Bat, the panic calmed into an uneasy tension, a fire burning low before another splash of kerosene.

"You all came here today expecting—hoping that you could hear some fancy, familiar, empty, lying words that would let you know that everything was going to be okay; everything was going to stay exactly the same," Cassius began, sneering. "Well, things are not going to stay the same. Things are going to change, and we're going to start doing things my way. But if you're going to clean house, first you have to...clean house."

This was not Cassius talking, Rifun knew. This was the dragon speaking. Although he suspected that the dragon had held power in the Wheel for a long time, playing with dozens or hundreds of small puppets was undoubtedly quit tiring. Now it was consolidating its power into only a handful of players. And, in the end, to one.

The large gates that provided a quick, direct exit from the Seat to the outside, came crashing down. For those trapped in any of the tracks that ran around the Seat, loyal guards took care of them. For those unfortunate enough to be close to the innermost gate, loyal guards took care of them, too. The Grandfathers and co-conspirators on the opposite side of the Seat in the stands also turned on each other, the last of the disloyal weeded out after the traitors no doubt expected they were finally safe and free to carry out any resistance from within.

Everyone flocked to the center of the Seat. Some huddled down, praying to their gods and waiting for the end. Some took up defensive positions, challenging the guards either verbally or silently. Guards and Grandfathers surrounded the group but made no further violent motion. Instead, the small gate opened and a host of secretaries came to collect the dead.

"We're still not done," Cassius said coolly once the bodies had been cleared. "That was just the easiest and fastest way to weed some of you out. The second way is going to take some time, but it is not productive to keep you here. Therefore, I am implementing martial law within the Wheel of Time and across the entire Time industry, to all civilizations, from Scientifically Superior and Openly Engaged, to Scientifically Primitive and Unengaged. I am the final authority in Time. Rifun may also speak with my name and my power. But from now until this mess is cleaned up and I have instituted a new order, only the Grandfathers and the chosen Hands have authoritarian power. The Merchants do not. The Scouts do not. The Harvesters do not. And the Timekeepers especially do not have power.

"And so, I, Cassius the Zero Hour, shall send you all to the Judgment Wing, to the prison to be held until your trials where the Grandfathers will determine your loyalty and your usefulness to me. Take them away."

Cassius the Zero Hour, hardly. This was the dragon, plain and simple.

But, the dragon had also just ordered everyone to be taken away to the Judgment Wing, which meant that the Grandfathers probably weren't going to be hacking and slicing at everyone who walked through a portal. With the dragon no doubt basking in its own glory at this victory, now was the time to strike. Unfortunately, Cassius wasn't done talking, though his volume had dropped, his audience limited to Rifun.

"That's how you do it, Rifun. That's how you win."

"Only day one," Rifun cautioned. "Winning is something you have to do every day."

"So now that you're my adviser, I can expect more of these sagely tidbits of wisdom."

"I expect so."

Cassius, no, the dragon regarded him for a moment. "So, how's your pet project coming?"

"Better than I expected, given the circumstances," Rifun answered. "Tadashi going off the deep end certainly didn't help things, but the situation was salvaged."

"I don't see why you want to pursue this. We have the journal. We have the power. It's not smart to take on pupils in the middle of this. How many of them have officers in this mess? Tommen alone, his father and Lieutenants are here. Sentencing them to death is not going to win his heart. And he's already defied you multiple times. Cut your losses, and get rid of him."

"Is that an order?"

"Do I need to make it one? You can't kill them and keep Tommen, but you can't let them live either. You've created a no-win situation."

Rifun ran his tongue over his teeth. "Oh, I can think of a few ways to make this a win-win scenario for everyone involved. I just won't be able to prosecute them as fast as the others; they may have to be held a while."

Cassius snorted indignantly. "Your games got you in trouble last time; why do you think you'll fare any better a second time?"

"Because I've made some modifications to my game. And if it doesn't work, I still have the option to kill them all."

That was assuming they didn't kill themselves first. It was a fine line with Walter, after all. The man could run into a shootout or a domestic abuse situation, and it didn't seem to faze him one bit. But get him in a dark room with virtually no light, and the man turned into little more than a fearful child. Unlike fearful children, however, fearful adults were capable of seeing reason, as long as the end goal was not only freedom, but freedom of their own choosing.

What would Walter give so he could see the light of day again? Rifun had no interest in his house, his car, his turns, or any other worldly goods. Would Walter be willing to give up his free will? His soul? Would he be willing to give up his son in exchange for the one thing he held most dear? He'd already proven that he would die for his son, but that had been in a heat of the moment situation, when they'd both been in danger. Now it was time to test those limits. Just how selfish was Walter Forbes?

But that was a problem for another day, once the bigger threat had been taken care of.

"Where are you going?" Cassius asked as Rifun moved to leave.

"Searching all the nooks and crannies and little hidey-holes for anyone who slipped through the lines," Rifun lied smoothly, slowing to turn but not stopping. "Yes, I'm sure Isthim has her Grandfathers going out in packs, but one silent man may find what ten noisy soldiers miss."

He kept moving. He couldn't let anyone stop him. Not Cassius, not the Bat, not Isthim. He did a cursory glance through the Coliseum, jogging around each track once, but found nothing. The secretaries were eerily efficient in their removal of the bodies.

He left the Coliseum, then, deliberately ignoring the line of prisoners being marched to the Judgment Wing. They weren't in chains, but Rifun could still hear the high-pitched clatter of metal, half-expected to see each man wielding a pickax.

It wouldn't be long, he told himself. This really was the kinder option. Once he got Cassius out of the way, once he got rid of the Borelian scourge, then he could begin to implement logical, needed, professional reforms. And if he could use the Akari to manipulate the Core to execute such goals, it would be a grand launching point to introduce everyone to the Akari, to the Author, and get them to read the journals and ask questions. Darkness before the dawn and all that.

The stillness of the Archives now was enough to make his skin crawl. He had no doubt that there were people who were hiding in the farthest reaches of the place, tucked between aisles, maybe even hiding in the shelving if they were small enough. They were not his problem right now, and if they were hiding here, they probably weren't looking to mount a massive resistance.

He reached the staircase that led down into the secretaries' work area, the hub of many corridors. Curious, he poked his head into the chamber where the election system had been humming away just a day before. Now it was quiet and there were but two secretaries in the room. He noted blood on the floor.

"Is there a problem?" one of the secretaries inquired, his demeanor conveying sincerity. He was wiping down a knife.

"If there were, I wouldn't be down here," Rifun replied. "I take it there are no problems down here."

The secretary made a last wipe of his blade and made a show of inspecting it in the light. "Not anymore."

"Let me know if that changes."

He ducked out of the room with two grunts of affirmation at his back and made for the invisible corridor of darkness. As he navigated the shadows, he couldn't help but wonder if the dread was the normal effect of the corridor, or his own fear. He chastised himself for it; he couldn't afford fear now. Fear and doubt would only cloud his judgment and make him unworthy of this power. He may be inexperienced, but the Author would guide him. Right? He was doing her work, being rid of the dragon, being rid of the Bat and the Day, being rid of the Borelians. Why wouldn't she help him?

In spite of his urgency, or perhaps because of it, it was no easier to navigate the spiral staircase down to the Core, and he almost forgot to count the steps. As it was, he couldn't be sure that he hadn't missed a couple, and he slowed as he neared the bottom. Then, once his foot found empty air, he used Gravity to lower himself to the platform.

Nothing down here had changed. There were no bodies, no secretaries, no spirits good or evil. Well, none that were obvious. And the secretaries would never be able to handle the awesome power of the Core. And there would be no bodies if they flung themselves over the side of the platform. Another prickle of unease rippled through Rifun's skin as he faced the Core.

He had done this before. He had touched the Core, been enveloped in its life, its spirit. Before, he had gotten lost, lost himself and years of time. He didn't want to lose years. He couldn't afford to simply explore. He was here for a purpose. Once that purpose was met and the universe was safe, then he would come back and explore more, learn more, maybe even lose himself again.

Staring at the Core now, he couldn't help but want to lose himself, let himself be drawn into the womb of Creation once more.

He took a moment to bow and pray, asking for guidance, wisdom, and a heavy dose of grace and mercy. He ended his prayer and stood with some trepidation. Hazy memories came into focus as he reached out to touch the Core. It was a sentient thing. It would know and understand his intentions, his will.

As soon as he thought it, he touched the Core, like *The Creation of Adam*, creature reaching out to its Creator.

He blacked out. He did not feel pain, nor sleep, nor the impossible cosmic expansion of the mind and all knowledge of the universe sifting through his tiny, mortal brain. If he had to liken it to anything, it was as though his vision had simply ceased. This applied to all of his senses, but it was his vision that was most noticeable and most frightening to him. He retained only an awareness of self, but nothing more, for what must have been at least two minutes.

Then it returned, like a light suddenly turning on. There was nothing gradual, but neither was there any pain or discomfort in the experience. Something had been, and then it wasn't, and then it was again. He was on his back, on the platform, staring up at a vast, empty darkness. He had all of his senses, he was self-aware, and like before, he felt no pain.

Pain, and an assortment of other, minor discomforts, returned to him as he sat up. The Core remained exactly where and how it was. Rifun had no recollection of actually touching it or doing anything with it or through it. It certainly hadn't drawn him into it like last time. And why not? Was it a one-time-only experience? Had he done something wrong? Had he forgotten to do something? Or had he done something but he wasn't permitted to remember it for some reason, as most memories were rendered hazy upon leaving the Core?

He stood, mildly disturbed by this unusual turn of events. What was he to make of this? How normal was this experience? Who could he ask who didn't probably want to kill him on sight?

He approached the railing again, staring at the Core. He reached out as if to touch it again. Like a knife, an impression of warning cut through his mind, and he withdrew his hand. An old warning from Andrianary floated through his brain. *The more we try to impose our will on the spirits, the less our will aligns with theirs, and the greater the consequences.*

Was the destruction of the dragon and the Borelians not the will of the spirits? Had something truly happened and he was now denied the memory? How much time had passed?

He backed away from the railing and crept toward the stairs.

ꝁꝋꝁꝰꝲꝰꝋ

Killing everyone in the universe was looking more appealing by the minute, and he knew just who he would start with.

Whatever Rifun had said about going to look for stragglers, he obviously hadn't done it. Cassius had spotted the man emerging from the Archives—far too soon from his departure to have been able to sweep the entirety of the place—white as a fucking bedsheet and trembling ever so slightly. He looked around the room, noted the many prisoners being led to the Judgment Wing, and actually seemed to calm down. Then he noticed Cassius and appeared to get nervous for a moment. Cassius was no expert on body language, other than whether someone was likely to attack, so he couldn't name all the different expressions and postures the man cycled through across the room.

Once things got settled down with the prisoners, Cassius was going to kill him. Fucking hell, the man just wasn't fit for the job. Everyone could see it. Maybe he could spark some small, foolhardy rebellion, use the chaos as cover. Maybe he should make a spectacle of it in front of the prisoners, let them know just who was in charge and not even the other Cult leaders were safe from his wrath. Yes, that sounded much better. The rebellions might be better for covering assassinations of the Borelians.

Anyway, it didn't take half a day for Rifun to set up shop in the Seat of the Hands. With the Borelians as the enforcers and the secretaries, he set up what amounted to an unemployment line. Once it was running under Isthim's watchful eye, he stepped out. Cassius tracked him as far as the closest bathroom and waited.

Rifun startled when he emerged and found Cassius standing right there.

"What the fuck is this?" Cassius demanded. "Unemployment? Welfare? Are we handing out loaves of bread?"

"The Wheel didn't run by itself. It took an army of secretaries for maintenance and upkeep," Rifun told him. "Well, most of those secretaries are dead now, and I don't think the killings or the suicides are at an end. We will need to replace those we've lost."

Cassius studied the man. Finally, "And it gives Isthim a headcount for the new slave colony they intend to populate with us. You're just making her job that much easier, aren't you? She must have jerked you off good this last time; was she in heat again?"

"The Borelians did not invent war tactics and strategies, they just know how to exploit them well. A census and forced labor is hardly anything diabolical in itself." He went to put up his right hand, caught himself, raised his left. "I understand your concerns. I had the same thoughts."

"Are we even going to execute anyone? A few of the old Hands got away, and a few more than a handful managed to escape the Wheel before the Grandfathers locked it down. And I'm sure we have plenty of disgruntled opponents in the asylum who would never yield to us."

"Yes, I imagine there will be executions. But we can't execute those we don't know we have."

"Well, we got Walter and Micaiah. Can we execute them?"

"What about Micah and Tommen?"

"No sign, living or dead."

Rifun shook his head. "We can't execute Walter and Micaiah. As long as they live, they're bait."

Cassius made an incredulous gesture. "So what? So fucking what? We rule, Rifun. We have the Wheel. And I consider the threat of Borelian slavery a little higher priority than any of your pet projects."

"Unless they give us physical cause to execute them, or unless they commit suicide in the asylum, they will remain alive." His tone left no room for argument.

But proof of life did not specify in what condition the life need be, Cassius thought, walking away before he said something really stupid. He should just kill Rifun, except he'd already decided to make it a spectacle. He would have to work on coordinating that. Maybe he could get the Bat and the Day to help him. Maybe he should put Rifun in a Time Trial. That would be fun.

He headed to the Judgment Wing and demanded Walter be brought to him in one of the interrogation rooms.

The fun thing about cells in the asylum was that they could be modified just like a Band, to move faster or slower at will relative to the rest of Time. He'd been going by about every hour or so since Walter had been locked up and adjusting the thermostat so-to-speak, listening to the wails from inside. From what he could discern, Walter had spent four months in prison in about twelve hours.

The interrogation rooms were nothing special, basically just bare stone rooms. While Walter was being retrieved, he had a table with shackle mounts and some candles brought in, arranging everything so it resembled what he remembered about Beaumaris Gaol.

He retreated so Walter could be brought in first. Let him sit and sweat for a few minutes. Oh, who was he kidding? The man had been sitting for four months and Cassius was trying to recover from a sour mood. It was time to raise a little personal hell.

So Cassius sauntered into the room and plopped down at the table across from Walter. The man looked and smelled atrocious. Thin, pale, sickly, unwashed, unkempt. He looked almost as bad as he had in Beaumaris Gaol.

"Good morning, Walter," Cassius greeted sarcastically, unable to suppress a grin.

"Is it?" Walter wondered. "It's hard to tell."

"You know, I've been waiting for this moment for a long time."

"How long have I been down?"

"By Base Time? Only about twelve hours. But I had a little fun adjusting the cell Time; it's as easy as changing the thermostat. You've been down about four months." He shifted position. "I have to say, I expected you to break a lot sooner than that, given your history. And from what I'm gathering, you haven't actually been broken yet."

"Are you going to send me back until I do?" Walter's expression did not change as much as Cassius expected it to. Perhaps he had run out of fear.

"No. It was more of an experiment. I listened to you rant and scream and wail. Prisoners do that when they still have hope, you know. Even if they're sad or angry, they will scream because of the agony. They go silent when all hope has left them, when they have no resolve left but to die. You haven't quite reached that point yet, but it's no matter."

Pause.

Cassius shifted again. "Do you know who I am?"

"Cassius," Walter answered. "Calis Cutthroat. Sorry to say I don't know your real name, but I know you were one of the gaolers at Beaumaris."

"Yes. Mi Chin figured that one out." He didn't know why he said that. He didn't even know if it was true. Maybe to try and brush it off himself. "You know, I remember you, Walter. I remember the day you first walked into your cell. I remember the day you were sent out to be sunk. And how you escaped. You disgust me. You were a drunkard, a fighter, given the world and you squandered it. You left your wife and child to die and then murdered those who had once been so good to you. And yet you still seem to think that by seeking out your little brother's son and raising him as your own that you are somehow vindicated of all responsibility."

"You can talk," Walter cut in. "You who murdered countless innocents for your own disguises."

Cassius grinned. "I wasn't done." Beat. "You've lived on both sides of the law, Walter. Earth-side, you are the law. But that law cannot help you here. But I can."

"Oh, so we're going for good cop, bad cop. You need two for that, don't you?"

Cassius laughed. "Rifun was right. Sarcastic to the last." He sighed. "But it doesn't have to be the last. The Hands were corrupt and everyone knew it. Everyone saw that something like this would happen; all that needed to happen was for someone to push the big red button. Now we have the opportunity to build something flawless."

"All men are flawed," Walter told him nobly. "And as such, anything they build will be flawed."

"Ah, still clinging to that old religion? I can respect that, but know this: mankind, the entirety of the universe, with Time and the Akari, is on its way to perfection. We need only provide the cornerstone for it. Provide the cornerstone and the building falls into place. You have a spot in this kingdom, Walter.

"Think about it: No more corruption. No more changing laws based on the whims of the Hands and the bribes of the elite. Absolute law. Laws that can be enforced. If there is a law, you enforce it without worrying about whether this Hand or that Hand will seek retaliation."

"Instead I have to worry about all the black laws that I don't know about and whether you will come after me for perceived offenses, coupled with evidence you will manufacture. I'm not an idiot; I know how the communists work."

"A clear conscience is a good way to get to sleep, but it offers no hope for the dead," Cassius said irritably. "I am offering you a way out, a way to stay alive and do the job you've always wanted to do as a Timekeeper. Why can't you see that? You die, you lose your life, no one will notice or even remember that you existed. Stay alive and you will be known. Not as a drunkard, a fighter, a shame to the family. But as a good Timekeeper, a keeper of the peace in the Time industry."

If Cassius could get some definitive declaration from Walter that he was not interested in joining them and would rather die, Rifun would have to see it as a lost cause and give permission to execute him. He was close. He could feel it.

Walter grinned. "Tommen's alive. And you don't have him."

"I don't—"

"You promised to kill everyone who actively opposed you. I have no doubt that you've been making good on that promise while I've been down, but that's the only reason you would be sitting here talking to me and offering me a way out. As long as I'm alive, you know that Tommen and the others will come for me. You want to use me as bait." Walter shifted, flinching in pain. "But you don't need Tommen. All you want is power. Which Rifun promised you. He's the real mastermind here. You put on the show to attract all the attention and let Rifun work his magic in the background, is that how this works? Rifun wants Tommen for his psycho Akari cult, God only knows why, and you want power. So he comes up with a plan to get what you both want. Am I correct to assume that Rifun is somehow sifting through all your prisoners to look for more apprentices for his cult? Or—?"

Cassius didn't need to Band in order to strike Walter, but it was necessary in order to remove the man's manacles and still be able to get in the first strike. Walter went back on the floor, the wind knocked out of him, clearly dazed. When his senses came back enough for him to try and sit up, Cassius kicked him in the back so that he pitched to his front. A moment later, he gingerly tried to get up again. Cassius grabbed him and hauled him to a chair where he slowly sat down.

"So, we're going to try that again. Hi, my name is Cassius."

"Walter. Pleased to make your acquaintance."

"Do you know who I am?"

"You were a gaoler at Beaumaris Gaol."

"And who am I now?"

"The Zero Hour."

"Very good. Who are you?"

"A prisoner."

"You are a prisoner right now. But you can become more. I have the power to elevate you, Walter. You can be a Timekeeper again, and not just a lowly Captain on some insignificant planet. You can work here, in the Wheel, or anywhere you choose. You can make a difference, be the officer you always wanted to be."

Walter chuckled. "Power...is only your ambition. It's true, I enjoy being a cop and a Timekeeper, but being an officer was never my ultimate ambition. My only ambition for the last almost hundred years has simply been to find my nephew and be a good father to him." He spit some blood on the table as if to make a point. "You may kill me, but at least I will not die in shame before my son. And when I'm dead, you and Rifun will have lost him forever, too."

Just the admission Cassius needed. Walter would rather die, and Cassius would rather kill him. Excellent. But just in case, he needed to make it about more than just Walter's pride, and he had learned a few things while masquerading as Doug.

"You know, being king isn't easy," Cassius said. "There's a lot of work that goes into ruling a kingdom. I know where your boy is hiding; he's not that good at it, and your other little Lieutenant isn't very good at protecting him. But being king —and with Rifun also busy—I can't just go and get him myself. And it takes a special talent to be able to get through the dampening field in the portal room, so almost all of my Timekeepers and Grandfathers are out right now, too. But there is another weapon I have at my disposal, one that was banned over a thousand years ago along with the last Cult of the Akari. Do you know what they are?"

"Can't say as I do."

"As with all bad translations, their name is not as fearsome as anything I might have come up with, but they are called Trackers. In years past, when relations were better, the Akarin used to send them out to track down wily Time Agents. They're like bloodhounds, able to track down even week-old Time wakes from an uncoordinated Apprentice. Nice, strong Lieutenants? Well, might as well hang a steak around your neck and release the hounds. It is also said that they can track down those who bear the Akari, which your boy just reeks of, according to Rifun."

"If you train them to track down Bigfoot, you might win more converts to your cause," Walter said sarcastically.

But Cassius was beyond amusement now. "They'll find your son, and they will bring him to me. Unless you agree to my terms and work for me."

Walter shook his head. "No. I taught my boy better than that, and I know he would expect nothing less from me. You are going to have to kill me first."

Perfect.

"Very well then. We'll see just how much like you your son is." He made a motion and six guards entered the room. Two of them seized Walter and hauled him to his feet while Cassius addressed the other four. "Send out the Trackers. Bring me the boy." To Walter's guards, "Take him back to his cell. He'll be in the next round of executions."

Walter was hauled away dramatically. Cassius remained in the room for a long moment while the other four guards also departed. The man was willing to die, Cassius was willing to kill him. Sounded like a match made in heaven, or more likely hell.

He stayed there for a good ten minutes. Was he waiting for something? No, not really. Was he thinking about anything? No, not especially. But as he made to stand and leave, the door opened and another guard walked in.

"Rifun's here. And he has friends."

"Well that's a shock," Cassius said. "I didn't know anyone found him interesting enough to call him a friend." When the guard did not reply, he sighed and asked, "Where is he?"

The next interrogation room over, apparently. Walking in the door, Cassius did not immediately recognize either of the two people with Rifun. The man couldn't have been over twenty-one with baggy clothes, blond dreadlocks, and the overall demeanor of a teenager who tried to play it tough but had no real propensity for violence or true rebellion. The female was of some Hispanic or mixed Hispanic origin, slender, pretty, dressed for a hot day at the beach and not stomping around recent battlegrounds. Their biggest tell, however, was that they were clean. Nervous, yes, but they did not have the same disheveled look that everyone else from the coup did. Either they had indeed been hiding, or they'd gotten in by some other means.

While the two intruders got their bearings, Rifun Banded himself and Cassius. "Tried to get in under Walter's and Micaiah's names."

"Get in?" Cassius questioned, looking at the pair. "Not much of a rescue party."

"Spies, more likely."

"Disposable."

Cassius broke out of the Band and turned his attention to the man and woman.

"So, the rescue party arrives. Please, have a seat."

The pair sat without question. Cassius and Rifun took their own seats more casually.

"I have to say, I expected more, but maybe I expect too much."

"Ah, but we are being rude," Rifun interrupted. "We haven't been properly introduced. You may know me, I am Rifun Ndolo. My counterpart here is Cassius."

"Kyle."

"Jenna."

"Tell me, Kyle, Jenna, how did you get here? I put a dampening field over the portal room. You are the first ones to break in."

"The same way Micah and Tommen broke out," Kyle told him with a hint of sarcasm. "Your dampening field isn't impermeable."

Cassius grinned. "No. Indeed it is not." He shifted in his seat. "So, Micah and Tommen are alive and well, are they?"

"All they want is for Walter and Micaiah to come home," Jenna said anxiously. "They don't care about Time, and Earth isn't significant. Just send them home and they'll be fine with not interfering with anything else."

"I like you, Jenna. Searching for a soft spot, hoping to strike a bargain perhaps. There's just one problem: we have no emotions to play. We're giving people new life assignments and killing those who refuse to go along in there, in case you haven't noticed. We're burning down the world so we can be kings of the ashes and build our own kingdom. You're right, two insignificant people from an insignificant planet shouldn't mean much. But if we start with the mercy now, where will it end? We'll be weak. We'll be overthrown."

"And we might have even let them go, if they didn't represent such a significant investment to us," Rifun went on. "Tommen is of particular interest to me. I've lost him, though. And he won't come back if I don't have something to lure him here."

"His dad," Kyle stated. "You're sick."

"Be that as it may, it's business."

"I am curious, though," Cassius said. "Portals cannot stay open while the dampening field is in place. How were you intending on getting back?"

"We were going to free Walter and Micaiah, and Micaiah would open a portal back home," Jenna said.

"Ah, such a noble plan," Rifun sighed. "And you were hoping to find them before you were set to be executed, correct?" Kyle and Jenna glanced at each other. "Do you even know where they are?"

"No," Kyle admitted.

"Are they even still alive?" Jenna asked quietly.

"They are," Cassius confirmed. "For the moment. Though they are due to be taken out momentarily, I believe. I don't think they'll take mundane assignments and subservience to us very well."

"You know, this is all very special," Rifun said, slapping the table and causing their guests to jump. "I think Walt and Micaiah ought to know how close they were to freedom. I say we send these two with them and they can all go together."

"That is an idea," Cassius mused. "Send them out, then. And send word ahead that I am going to oversee this one personally."

Cassius motioned for guards and he and Rifun stood.

"Can I ask one question?" Jenna blurted. The two of them paused and turned. "I came here for someone else, too. Her name is Janice Riley. She's a—"

"Dear, do you know how many people have been through today?" Rifun cut in. "I can't keep track of them all. Besides, you'll be joining her soon enough. Or if she's still alive, just wait a little while and she'll come to you."

And the two of them left the intruders to the guards.

Once they were well separated from each other, Cassius paused. Rifun walked a couple steps more before glancing back.

"Now can we start the executions?" Cassius asked.

Rifun stopped.

"This isn't going to be the only rescue attempt, for Micaiah or otherwise," Cassius went on. "Eventually, we're going to have resistance and rebellion to deal with. If we don't set a precedent now—"

"We will be seen as weak, I know," Rifun admitted. "But do we want a kingdom built on blood?"

"Name one just kingdom that has as indomitable power as any of the unjust ones. You yourself said we're burning down the universe to be kings of the ashes."

"To your first point, the Akarin, if they care to use it. And I assume these 'unjust' kingdoms you are referring to are the Borelians and possibly the Time industry. One of them we have just overthrown."

"With blood."

Rifun sighed and shifted his stance uncomfortably. "The French overpowered my people with blood. My people overthrew them with blood. The French returned and overpowered us again with blood. But even when they had us defeated, they continued to engage in such heinous cruelty—"

"I've read your part of the Book," Cassius cut in.

"I will not be my own worst enemy. I use fire to cleanse, to cauterize the wounds inflicted by so many corrupt Hands over so many years. We must burn it down in order to start anew. But cauterization and healing hurts, and there is more to our kingdom than me and you. These are living, sentient people. Yes, some must be taught a hard lesson—"

"But no discipline at all is worse than harsh discipline. The only reason you are even having this dilemma is because of whatever the fuck you believe about Tommen being some chosen one, and Micaiah said mean things to you a few years ago. We have a dozen others lined up for execution, but you don't bat an eye because they're not special." Cassius continued before Rifun could speak. "You may not want a kingdom of blood, but do you want to be accused of favoritism? That's not very fair and just, is it? You want everyone here to believe in the Author and learn the Akari? Great. How about we start by supernatural rescue from execution? If the Author really cares, she'll rescue them. Otherwise, we make a grand and just point about crossing us."

Rifun frowned, obviously conflicted.

"Walter already told me he'd rather die than serve," Cassius pressed. "He—"

"Of course he would tell you that," Rifun sighed. "You have shown no inclination to honor any other means or end." He paused. "Let me talk to Micaiah first. Maybe I can get him to talk, maybe I can convince him to serve. If not, I will pass the death sentence myself."

"I'll get things ready in the Pit."

Rifun hadn't been moving, yet he seemed to suddenly hit the brakes. "The what?"

"The Bat showed me. After you left to do whatever you did, he took me to a new part of the Wheel. Well, it's not new, not really. It was simply cut off at some point in the past. The Bat asked what we did to reopen it, reconnect it to the rest of the Wheel. I told it I didn't know."

"Show me."

He was unusually forceful about it, Cassius thought, but he obliged anyway. It was like uncovering a secret cellar in the Coliseum, and what lay beneath was about as cheery.

It looked very much like the Coliseum, and Cassius wondered if it didn't change to be an echo of whatever was up above. The difference was, this was not the Coliseum in its heyday, but a thousand years later, dark, crumbling, full of monsters and ghosts of the damned who were executed in the most brutal fashion. The structure was not built of marble or metal, but simple black stone, and left to rot. Even the use of Light appeared limited, as if something in the stone absorbed a fraction of the intensity, like a slow leak. Unlike the Seat of the Hands where one entered from the ground level, here they entered from the top, the door depositing them onto the top of the coliseum-like structure where they would have to make their way down into the gladiator's arena.

"The Bat said this was the original Judgment Wing, in a time when justice was a little swifter and a little harsher. True laws and punishment rather than flexible rules and minor jail time."

"As good a place as any to hold an execution, I suppose," Rifun mused. "And it will keep the floor of the Seat clean."

Even in the dim light, Cassius could see the man had again gone pale.

"Prepare this place," he said at last. "I will speak to Micaiah."

He departed, perhaps a little too hastily in Cassius' opinion. Once he was gone, Cassius waited a minute or two before moving, just to make sure he was really gone. As he started down, a shadow briefly overcame him. He looked up to see the Bat approaching, eventually falling more or less in step.

"It's about time," the Bat said. "When training animals, there is only a short window of time to dispense punishment for wrong action."

"I'm surprised he agreed to it at all, but I'm not complaining," Cassius grumbled. "But we should probably get this place ready as quick as possible so he doesn't have the opportunity to change his mind."

"His obsession with the Authored Books and those within is disconcerting," the Bat mused with perhaps the most conversational tone and expression it had ever displayed, "but it can work to our advantage."

"You don't believe in the Authored Books, then. Think they're fiction?"

"Just because the people exist and the events happened does not make them true, nor does it excuse any hidden agendas by the Author."

"That doesn't make any sense."

They continued their descent among the ruinous stadium seating.

"One man's story is one man's story. Just because he does not lie does not mean he is telling the truth."

"Is there a third option?"

A Gravity track saw them—Cassius, anyway, as the Bat just glided down menacingly—to the safest-looking part of the floor.

"Reality," the Bat said. "There is truth. There are lies. And there is reality, the all-encompassing state of things. For those like us, reality is what we make it."

"Wouldn't truth be reality, or reality, truth?" He scoffed and shook his head. This philosophical bullshit was Rifun's business. He didn't get it. He was here to execute people violently with much blood and gore and screaming, not bore them to death with lectures and debate.

"Mortals create their own bubbles of reality based on what they understand is truth. A man claims another man offended him. The other man did not intend to offend and did not know his actions would cause offense and so he carries on. This is the truth of the second man. The truth of the first man is that he was offended, regardless of intent. Thus, both men create his own reality based on flawed truths."

"Then what is reality?"

The Bat regarded him. "You are too small of a creature to understand."

Cassius bristled. "And you're some all-powerful god to punish me for sins I don't know I have committed?"

Now the Bat's expression turned bemused. "Knowing you, if you were aware of such sins, you would seek to commit twice as many once you had learned what they were." It began circling him, wings extended just enough as if to create a barrier but not so much they were fully extended. "You are a small creature, bound to three dimensions and having only the slightest understanding of the fourth. Yet you have no ambition to understand it. Rifun has greater understanding of the fourth, though even he only scratches the surface because his mind could not handle more. And yet, he lacks any tangible ambition. The wars which should have strengthened him have only made him weak."

"Is that your truth, or reality?" Cassius leered, keeping one eye on the Bat and one eye elsewhere just in case it had help, like the Day.

The Bat did not grin so much as reveal it had fangs and was lightly amused by the comment. "If I thought you had the capacity in that small ape brain of yours to comprehend the reality surrounding you two, I might let you have a glimpse."

"If speaking to the dragon isn't enough to—"

"Ha! The dragon. A limited, three-dimensional form to accommodate a small mind. And words...spoken one at a time with predetermined sounds and double-meanings. You only prove reality with your foolishness."

Cassius continued to watch the Bat stalk around him in circles. "Why did you come here? To mock me? To bait me? If you want to kill me, let's just get this over with and fight it out in this limited third dimension."

He got in a low stance. His first strike would set the stage for the fight. He would have to go for a wing, period; he could not let the Bat get airborne. Gravity, then, and just crush it. No, too quick. Enough Gravity to prevent it from flying, maybe crush just its wings. Then they could have a real fight, and Cassius would gain a real victory. And this time, he wouldn't resurrect the creature.

The Bat continued to circle and stare for a long moment. Cassius was just calculating his strike time when it stopped and folded its wings in where it normally kept them, using them almost like a cloak. "As great a pleasure as that would be, there is still one more mission for you to fulfill."

"Just one?" Cassius wondered, still in fighting stance.

His whole being suddenly seemed to shift, like a mental change. He'd accepted his death for a long time, expected it on many occasions. Something about this nightmare creature telling him he had but one more mission, one more use in this universe, not only made it a little more real, but strangely terrifying. He chanced a look around the crumbling coliseum, somehow envisioning the seats filled with Shadows, creatures of smoke and shadow and sometimes lightning. A never-ending battle, one he would always lose.

"Just one," the Bat confirmed, again looking rather self-satisfied, as if sensing his anxiety and thoughts. "And it will become apparent to you very, very shortly."

Not two breaths after he spoke, the whole room shook. It was very reminisce of the time Cassius was sabotaging the gravitational balancers in the Wheel. This room was not the epicenter, but it was close enough to notice.

"What was that?" he wondered, looking around, ignoring the Bat.

"Go find out," the Bat told him. "I will prepare this place for the time to come."

Unable to resist a snarl of frustration, Cassius whirled and ran for the exit, using Gravity to deliver him directly to the door at the top of the structure. Except there was no door. A few prisoners had already arrived and were looking around, confused as they staggered to their feet. Several shrank back when they saw him, but he didn't care about them right now. Where was the fucking portal out of here?

The prisoners had to have come from somewhere, and he was certain the portal had been right here. There was the rock that had been immediately to the right—or had it been to the left? No, it must have been right because there was the crumbled bit of floor that was uncomfortably close to the portal. You could break an ankle just walking into this place.

Now there was nothing here. The top of the coliseum just kept going around, framed in by black stone that was slowly sucking away any light that remained from whatever source kept the room perpetually dim. Or maybe the black stone was emanating its own kind of sickly light. But what did it matter when the only door in and out of the this place was gone?

Cassius racked his brain, thinking back on his days of sabotaging the Wheel. Gravitational balancers were his main thing, but that didn't mean he didn't collapse a few portals, too, usually by accident. He didn't think he'd ever been part of reestablishing those portals, but then, he also didn't think he'd actually orphaned any rooms. He didn't know there were any orphan rooms in the Wheel, certainly nothing of this magnitude. Had he known this Pit was here, he would have utilized it with some prejudice. He could have made his prisoners fight to the death with the promise of the victor being freed. Hell, he had five prisoners right here he could do just that. Maybe have them fight the Bat and if any of them lived, he'd let them go.

Maybe he would do that. It wasn't as though it would take long for the Bat to shred them to ribbons, just long enough to be entertained and distract him from the worst of his rage over whatever the hell had happened.

The prisoners were still looking at him, fearfully awaiting whatever fate he had planned. None of them were especially imposing creatures. Two were humanoid, one resembling an insect, two of them too strange and yet too boring to bother describing since he was only going to send them to die.

"So, this is all he sends me," Cassius huffed, trying to salvage the situation and not appear as confounded as the rest of them. "That's all right, it's just a test group, I suppose." He shifted his stance. "As you can see, the portal is gone. You're all locked in here. With me. And the Bat. I know you've been through a lot in the last day or so, and you know you've been sent here to die." When no one argued, he went on, "That need not be the case." He gestured into the coliseum. "Down there is the Bat, the same Bat you all know and love. Anyone who can kill it can walk out of here a free man."

The prisoners dared glance at each other, then around the room as if expecting the Bat to come flying up at them in a fury. It didn't happen. Cassius wasn't actually sure where the Bat was, but seeing how it wasn't up here on top or in the stands, the pit itself was the last place he could think of. Did this coliseum have the same tracks outside the arena that the Seat of the Hands did? This could be fun.

None of the prisoners really jumped on the prospect of freedom, perhaps expecting a trap. Cassius pressed a little harder, "You're not getting out of here unless you do. The door is closed, portal's gone. So either you try to win your freedom, or the Bat kills you anyway. Your choice."

It was a hulking beast of an alien who moved first, slogging off across the stone like a Neanderthal with all the grace and subtlety of an earthquake. Gradually, the rest of them followed, slinking down the rows of seats, watching for the Bat.

Speaking of Neanderthals, Cassius thought, he wondered how many Tacagans had gotten trapped in the Wheel. What must they be thinking right now? They must be seething, having been outwitted by a couple of lesser humans. No doubt they were already conjuring up plans and threats and bribes, desiring to free themselves, desiring to regain some control and power in the Wheel.

Below, a high-pitched scream would have shattered any glass in the area before being abruptly cut off.

He should find the Tacagans and put them up against the Bat next. Maybe he would even instruct the Bat to let them think they were winning. Maybe it would be up to the task of dying and being resurrected again. Cassius was not fooled; the Bat and the Day had some connection to the Shadows, more than just enamored mortals who foolishly desired knowledge. This was something far deeper, far more destructive. Surely it would make the Tacagans fully aware of their atheistic foolishness just before they died, far too late to reconcile themselves with any gods.

Now there was a roar, but it was one of pain, not necessarily death.

Cassius picked his way down the stands, sitting on the bottom row where he could see the carnage play out. One of the competitors did indeed lie dead. It looked like it had been ripped in half, not the best way to go. The hulking beast alien had been grievously wounded, perhaps a punctured artery. It still limped around, made tired swings, but it was dumping blood everywhere from a leg wound. The Bat didn't even pay it any mind when it finally collapsed and started twitching in agonized death throes, still pulsing blood, creating a slippery, dangerous mess on the floor.

The humanoid aliens were remarkably agile, and the insect alien might have actually been able to move faster than the Bat, though it appeared considerably weaker. Like any annoying insect, it would dart in, slash at the Bat to get its attention, then dart out before the Bat could retaliate. In that moment of distraction, the humanoids ran up to deliver several blows of their own.

But fisticuffs were not enough to fell the Bat, only enrage it, and the Bat was no rookie combatant. Its three assailants knew what Cassius knew—don't let the Bat get in the air—but their effort at keeping the Bat on the ground cost them time, options, and stamina. They couldn't keep this up all day, and the only thing they'd managed to do so far was annoy it. One of the humanoids had an opportunity to pick up what may have been a sharp rock, but it did little more than scratch the Bat's leathery hide.

The Bat swung around, lashing out with its massive wings. In the split-second as its opponents jumped back, the Bat leaped forward, away from them, and, with a mighty pump of its wings, got into the air.

One humanoid was dead within three seconds, and Cassius was a little offended it took that long. Both humanoids might have been taken out at the same time except the insect alien managed to distract the Bat enough that its followup strike missed the second one.

The Bat went after the insect first, and it took Cassius a moment to figure out why when the humanoid would be the easier target. He was betting on the two of them working together. If the insect was the only one in the arena, it would spend all its time simply fleeing, and it had demonstrated well that it was faster than the Bat. But if it did anything to try and help the humanoid, it would have to get close to the Bat. It would have to get within striking distance.

And it did. And the Bat struck, a clean slice from the claw at the tip of its wing taking off the insect's mandibled head. The humanoid stopped short of whatever it was doing, giving the Bat ample time to do the same thing to it on the backswing.

The Bat, on the far side of the arena from where Cassius sat, did not give any sort of victory cry or any indication at all that it knew it had won and reveled in it. Rather, it spread its wings and took to the air once more, approaching Cassius and stopping just in front of him, still hovering over the open arena. If Cassius was right, the Bat was using overly-dramatic wing beats to try and emphasize his power. But he had already told Cassius there was only one mission left before his death, so the intimidation somehow meant significantly less.

"This is not why I am here," the Bat said, clearly annoyed.

"We are here to execute prisoners, no?" Cassius wondered innocently. "I never thought they would actually defeat you. I'm surprised it took that long, honestly."

"Execute. Not battle for your entertainment."

Cassius made a gesture toward the area where the portal used to be. "Looks like we're stuck here for a few minutes. Why not have some fun? You've been around so long, been there and done that a thousand times over, it's like you don't enjoy yourself anymore."

"The constitution of my personal enjoyment is not your concern. The execution of prisoners is. And I would suggest that it be carried out as swiftly and efficiently as possible so the Wheel may be secured in like manner so we do not lose it yet again."

Cassius reiterated his gesture. "You open the door, I bring you prisoners." He lowered his arm and leaned back as far as he dared on the open seat. "And maybe leave those five down there; don't clean them up. Adds a nice touch of hopelessness. I imagine it's the most recent decor this place has had in a very long time."

The Bat snorted through its narrow nasal passages. "One last mission."

Was the dragon immune to criticism from its underlings? Was it possible that the Bat and the Day got so fed up with Cassius that they petitioned the dragon to let them kill him? It was something to consider as the Bat flew up to the spot where the portal used to be, stopped, and waited.

It was no great intellectual feat to consider how a room within the Wheel might become orphaned, though the list of people who could pull off such a thing was rather short. Rifun was one of those people. Had he trapped them in here intentionally, maybe hoping the Bat would kill Cassius? It would keep his hands clean, and the Bat would be one of the few entities in the universe who might be able to pull it off in combat. But if Rifun was all concerned about demons and evil spirits and such, was the Bat really the right choice for the job? Was it possible for evil spirits to harm each other? He couldn't imagine they couldn't or wouldn't, but he had the backing of the dragon. No evil spirit would dare go against the dragon, would it?

Thankfully, he didn't get an answer.

A minute later, new light filtered into the room as a portal opened up and the Day ducked inside, meeting the Bat. Cassius sighed, got to his feet, and slowly made his way toward them. He noted, half a moment before they noticed him, that between themselves, they spoke a unique language, one the translator or the Akari could not—or would not—discern. And yet, part of him, the part that was enslaved to the dragon and had just a sliver of understanding of the nature of the Shadows, knew that this was a primordial language of darkness and evil. This was the dragon's tongue rendered within the limitations of a three-dimensional plane where concepts had to be conveyed by pitiful words.

Then, as soon as his mind registered this, the two dark servants noticed him and effortlessly switched to a language which was readily interpreted in his ears and mind.

"So what happened?" Cassius demanded. "Someone put up some resistance, did they?" He went on before either could speak. "I told Rifun, we should have started executions earlier to make a statement. But no, we had to be nice first."

"Four have escaped," the Day told him sharply. "All of them human."

Unimpressed, Cassius shifted his stance dramatically. "Hm...would their names happen to be Walter, Micaiah, Kyle, and Jenna?"

"We should go after them," the Bat growled in a rare display of raw emotion.

"Reinforcements have already been sent," the Day said, its tone difficult to determine, though it appeared to be annoyed in some fashion. "Our work is here."

The Bat grumbled something under its breath in the primordial tongue.

"Given the earthquake we experienced in here," Cassius cut in, "I'm guessing it wasn't a clean, sneaky getaway."

"The portal room has been orphaned," the Day reported.

Cassius shrugged. "So reconnect it. You reconnected this place."

"This room is an end, a place of death and despair. This door is a one-way door, more often than not."

"Let me guess. Because of the nature of the portal room, connecting energies from across the entire universe, it's a little more complicated and a little more difficult. And I'll bet that the dampening field isn't going to make it any easier."

"You are correct."

Cassius frowned. "Are you going to tell me that in all the history of the Wheel, all the wars and all the bullshit, that something like this has never happened before? Are we honestly stuck here?"

"Only petty Time Agents," the Bat said disdainfully. "The weak and the small-minded."

"But not Akari-bearers like us."

"No, not us."

"Great. Now that no one can escape, should make executions a little easier, I think. And we can talk about reestablishing a connection later."

The Bat and the Day glanced at each other in silent deliberation.

"Yes," the Bat said at last, regaining its normal, passive composure. "That is one way to frame it."

"Excellent." Cassius gave the Bat a pointed look. "And since you were just lecturing me on the short timeframe of punishing animals, I think now is the perfect time to start executing people and doling out punishment for attempted coup and-or escape. What say you?"

The Bat made a gesture of affirmation, not unlike a nod. "I will await the prisoners here." It looked more at the Day as it said, "Bring them to me."

The Day did not say anything, just ducked back out the room, Cassius following.

Reentering the Wheel proper, Cassius was momentarily stunned by the destruction. It really was just like when he sabotaged the gravitational balancers, except the gravity of the room remained unaffected. If they had been affected, the dispersal pattern of bodies and decor would look different, Cassius thought. As it was, the pattern more closely resembled a bomb blast, where the point of origin was the portal to the Pit.

"I'm guessing Micaiah is the one who started it," he said, looking around while still keeping pace with the Day. "Walter is no Akari-bearer, and I doubt the other two are. Or if they are, if they're the best the Akarin have to offer, well, it's no wonder we've subjected them so easily time and again."

"Subverted, not subjected," the Day stated distastefully.

"Well, I think that's going to be our next objective, once we get things cleaned up here. Deal with all these minor inconveniences, button up the Wheel, then go after the Akarin. One last mission, right?"

It was difficult to ascertain the Day's demeanor from its expression when its head was seven feet or more above Cassius. "The one called the Bat prefers threats, to instill fear beforehand. I prefer simple, swift action."

"Spoiled your plans to kill me, huh?"

The Day did not reply and they entered the Judgment Wing, which was in some disarray concerning personnel, though it had not been so affected by the blast.

Cassius went on. "Although I've always wondered. You two have been around a long time. I understand that you're Shadows, or else very closely linked to them. What would happen if you were to die, or your physical body? If you were torn apart by wild animals, for instance. What would happen?"

"I care not for religion." The way it spoke was evasive. It didn't even believe its own words; this was a rehearsed response.

"I'm not asking for truth," Cassius told it smartly. "I'm asking for reality."

The Day made a sound that resembled a chuckle, except it seemed to reverberate up and down its long throat. "You must be close to cull if the Bat gave you that lecture."

"Close to cull? Not close to death?"

"You are already dead," the Day informed him. "You are walking dead, a reanimated corpse for the use and whim of the one."

"If that is so, then the dragon has only itself to blame for how useless I apparently am."

Many species throughout the universe preferred to use a hand, paw, or other similar appendage when striking a foe. Even the Day had its many prehensile vines. In this instance, however, it decided that a full blow from its head was necessary to convey its mood, and it was a bit like being hit by a wrecking ball. Cassius was lifted clean off his feet and sent airborne, slamming into the wall with more force than he thought possible as his head snapped back and stars exploded in his vision.

He crumpled to the ground, dazed for a long moment. When he got his bearings, the Day was nowhere to be seen.

With his head still dizzy, the best Cassius could do was severe irritation. Fine, so he was being discarded by the dragon as useless after one last mission. That was no excuse to be treated like shit beforehand.

Should he head to the asylum and see if the Day needed assistance bringing up prisoners for execution? No, he would either be treated like dirt in front of prisoners who should rightly fear him, or he would be thrown in with them. Better to retreat to the Pit with the Bat and help with the executions. After all, he was better at the action than the politics.

Grudgingly, he left the Judgment Wing. If anyone knew what had happened, they wisely said nothing. He paid no one any attention, just stalked his way through to the portal. He couldn't have been dazed for too long, as everything looked exactly as it had just a moment ago when they came through.

If he was relieved by anything, it was that no executions had taken place without his knowledge or attendance. The five bodies remained in the arena where they had fallen, and the Bat had gotten things cleaned up a bit, brought a little charm back to the ancient ruins, somehow made them look fearsome again rather than just tired in their old age.

"All right, the Day is bringing prisoners," Cassius said, again making his way down the rows of seats. "Let's get this over with as quick as possible. Execute the prisoners, reconnect the portal room, destroy the Akarin. You think we can get that done in a reasonable amount of time?"

The Bat did not reply, nor did it slow in its attempt to move what looked like the remains of a pillar.

"You think we can trick Rifun into coming down here and execute him, too?" Cassius went on, using Gravity to lower himself into the arena. "How is it that I, who has done so fucking much for this cause, I'm the one being taken out first?"

"You are the short-term tool," the Bat said apathetically, straightening the pillar. "One to be used and driven hard and disposed of. He is the long-term tool, the one to be guided, used gently, and then discarded with a single snap of one of its pieces."

Before Cassius could say anything, some noise captured their attention, and they looked up to see a line of prisoners being marched in. Cassius looked at the Bat who simply said, "No."

"Come on," Cassius goaded.

"Swift and precise, as you just stated."

Cassius shrugged. "Fine, have it your way. What do you do for fun?"

The Bat did not reply. After a minute or two, Cassius went out to meet the prisoners, and he was delighted to see that the one at the front of the line was Lily Guile.

Elusion

After interrogating Micaiah and getting a less than optimistic response, Rifun was tidying up an office space in the Judgment Wing—thinking he might call this one his own—when the whole room shook like the outer waves of an earthquake. If he hadn't already had everything on the floor in various piles, some things might have gotten knocked off the walls or ceiling, but it didn't feel heavy enough to rattle anything structurally, assuming that were even possible in the Wheel.

Curious, Rifun left the office and followed the trail of disgruntled and panicking personnel back through the Judgment Wing. Stepping through the portal into the main hub of activity, he came across a scene that at once put him in mind of a bomb blast. The pattern of destruction looked correct for such a thing, but it was the smell that really set him on edge. The piss and shit of the dead, and the blood just starting to congeal. Give it an hour and the stench of everything mixing together, especially in such quantity, would be unbearable.

Guards and Grandfathers were running to and fro, many in a daze, knocked silly from the concussive force or else dealing with some form of shock from various wounds. For all of this, however, there did not appear to be any immediate threat. There was no fighting that he saw, no attacking force, and no aftershocks.

With that knowledge, his mind shifted to assisting the wounded. If there was anything the Wheel didn't have, it was a medical clinic. No one wanted to be responsible for understanding the anatomy of every species in the universe, and no one wanted to be the one who got it wrong. Even so, they couldn't be allowed to wander about, potentially hurting themselves more or harming others in their confusion.

He commandeered the Food Court for triage and holding purposes and got a few cognizant individuals to take over operations. He'd no sooner taken two steps away from the individuals when the room shook, sending several people into a blind panic. It was like the wave that went through the office, suggesting that this second blast was elsewhere in the Wheel. But where?

As he crossed the room to a portal picked at random, it dawned on him what else looked off about the hub. He slowed and came to a stop, the activity around him a little more coordinated now. One of the portals was missing, and it happened to be the one leading to the Pit. It was also appeared to be the epicenter of the blast in this room. What happened? Had there been some kind of mechanical malfunction? Had Cassius tried to sabotage the balancers again? The portal itself?

"Faharoa!"

He turned, searching for the voice. A Grandfather came limping up to him.

"What happened?" Rifun demanded.

"Several prisoners have escaped," the Grandfather reported. Whatever the cloak was hiding for injuries, the person's voice clearly made up for with forced professionalism. "They did something to the portal to the Pit, and they've just sabotaged the one to the portal room itself. It's become orphaned. Two Grandfathers dead, many more Grandfathers and guards injured. And you see what's happened here."

Rifun gave the Grandfather a look. "These escaped prisoners...they wouldn't happen to include one Micaiah Durvin, would they?"

"I don't have that information, sir, I was told to report the situation."

Rifun grunted and moved past the Grandfather toward another portal he knew would lead him toward the portal room. The Wheel was basically empty since everyone had been rounded up for reassignment, interrogation, and imprisonment. This made it much easier to follow the path the pursuers had taken after the escapees. It was even easier once a stream of wounded began trickling through, likely on their way back to report what had happened or get new orders.

He gave each one a glancing-over as he walked by but otherwise told them to head to the Food Court. Most acknowledged him in some limited fashion, others were too dazed to walk straight and he wondered whether they even understood his words. A couple he had to physically assist and he called over several uninjured or lesser wounded to take them. Then he waved over a few more to take the two bodies, no small feat considering they were Borelians and the oils were still fresh enough to have some toxicity to them.

Eventually he got everyone cleared out, on their way to the Food Court. He continued on his way until he came to the spot in the Wheel that should have led to the portal room. Now it was just a bare wall in an empty room. He touched

Light, altered it, trying to cast shadows, change colors, anything that might reveal something merely invisible. Nothing. Sound, Gravity, Force, all of it coming back empty. Finally, he put his hand out...and touched a bare wall. There was no illusion, no trick. The portal was gone. The portal room was orphaned, detached from the Wheel, as the Pit had been.

Micaiah had done this. There was no doubt in Rifun's mind about that. He couldn't even blame the man, really. Being taken out for execution, Rifun would fight for his freedom, too. There was even some inherent nobility in saving one's friends as well.

Unfortunately, it also complicated things. Micaiah didn't understand what was happening here. He was thinking too personally. Yes, it was personal inasmuch as they were all ones chosen by the Author. Except that alone should have elevated their understanding and cooperation in this situation. They should be working together now to bring the Akari to the people. More importantly, they had to work together to destroy the dragon.

But the Akarin didn't want that. They wanted to whine and complain and sit back on the sidelines playing poor me. They had become lazy as it concerned real action, but who knew what they could inspire with whatever twisted words Micaiah would speak to them of what had happened? Micaiah could tell them anything, that the Cult was amassing an army and getting ready to invade the entire universe. He could tell them that the Cult was reforming the Wheel itself in some way, turning it into a fortified fortress, or perhaps the prison of the universe for any opposition.

None of this was true, but without the ability to navigate between the Wheel and the universe, isolation would only breed paranoia, and that was true for both sides.

He turned at movement in his peripheral, but it was only the Day.

"The Pit was reconnected once," Rifun stated, looking back at the blank wall. "I think I did it when I touched the Core this last time, but I don't remember. Is there another way to reconnect orphaned rooms?"

"I have reconnected the Pit," the Day informed him. "Operations are returning to normal." Executions had begun. "But the Pit is a dead end, serving a singular purpose and having little bearing on the energies of the universe. The portal room is not so simple."

"No, of course not."

"It will require manipulation of the Core." The acid in the Day's voice was palpable.

Rifun frowned. "Manipulation of the Core requires a Builder. With exception of myself, all Builders are Akarin. It may stand to reason that no one wanted this particular room to be orphaned, but it could not have been an impossibility within their thinking. Therefore, either portals built by the Akari will still work, or else Micaiah just condemned us all to death."

The Day said nothing.

"This may actually work in our favor. Time Agents will not be able to get in, which means we have no fear of resistance or retaliation from ninety-nine percent of the universe. Anyone who does want to get in or out will be forced to learn the Akari. In here, we have the advantage and can start teaching. Obviously we won't teach portals first thing—though higher ranks will likely figure it out on their own—but it is a unique opportunity." He shifted his stance. "The problem lies on the outside. I don't expect the Akarin to attack, but that doesn't mean they can't poison the well."

"So do you want access, or not?"

Rifun mulled over the question, still staring at a blank wall. After a minute, he replied, "No. Not yet. There is still much chaos going on around the universe, I imagine. There will be fear and speculation, not all of it unwarranted. And there will be reflex desires, many of them rather inhospitable to us. Shouting only produces one more voice lost in the cacophony.

"Instead, we must improve ourselves here. As before, we must make life better so that our detractors ultimately look like fools. We will rebuild the Wheel, repurpose it. We will educate." He cut himself off and looked up at the Day. "How loyal are you to the Grandfathers? Do you hold any love for the Borelians?"

"I hold no loyalty or love for either," the Day replied.

Rifun got an odd sensation, then, that the Day was telling the truth, but that didn't bode well for the Cult either way. Pushing the sensation aside, Rifun nodded and said, "Good. Because the Borelians are also trapped outside the walls as it were. Isthim and Misik and the few enthusiastic members are here, true, but their civilization won't come marching in to enslave us. Nor can they reasonably send us off to slavery, not so kindly as they have planned, anyway."

"What is our next move, then?" The Day sounded a bit annoyed.

"Continue the executions for the rest of today. If nothing else, we do need to make that point. We must first show the stick. We are capable of violent justice, and we will carry it out against those who would violently oppose us. Tomorrow we bring the carrot, the deal for those who do not violently oppose us, and especially those who are willing to listen and learn."

"How will this be done, exactly?"

"We will begin with the Book of Philosophy. Everyone already knows about Time, and most likely have preconceived notions about the Akari and what it can do. If we don't explain the history first, all we're doing is party tricks with a few cultish rules and slogans. History is important. They need to know and understand what the Wheel of Time is actually for, why it was made, where these abilities come from." Rifun nodded, mostly to himself. "Of the more compliant prisoners, those who could be taken for reassignment, we'll take them in groups of one hundred or so, educate them for about half an hour to start, then send them to start working and getting this place cleaned up."

The Day regarded him for a long moment as if waiting for further instruction. When none came, it made a gesture of affirmation—because ten feet was a long ways to nod—and departed. Rifun returned his attention to the spot where the portal was supposed to be.

Once, Rifun had taken a group of rebels to defend a small village deep in the southern jungle of Madagascar. The village was a little more adamant in its support of the rebels and had a cache of weapons that they had taken from a French military base. The containers of weapons were heavy steel with locks and keys.

The French attacked the village, and Rifun and the rebels were lined up to be questioned and shot, and not always in that order. One of the men tried to swallow the key to one of the containers but was shot before it could go all the way to his stomach. The French couldn't reach it through his mouth, so they opened him up, gutted him like an animal in front of everyone. To make a point of it, the French did not just remove the stomach and esophagus to retrieve the key. Instead, they intentionally broke his sternum and pried open his ribcage.

Opening a portal now was very much like that. Despite their best efforts to look strong and tough, the French had a blasted time opening the rib cage, even without the sternum. Once they did get it open, they removed the heart and lungs for all to see, then yanked out the esophagus like a giant worm to cut it open and get the key. Just as soon as the weapon container was open, Rifun made his move, invoking Time to give himself and the other rebels an advantage. The rebels ended up fleeing, but it wasn't much of a victory for the French.

The portal never really opened, not enough for Rifun to trust it, and he let it collapse. As he sat down on the ground, winded and sweaty, he was forced to wonder if Micaiah and the others had actually made it out or if they were trapped in an orphaned portal room. Being in an orphaned room with a dampening field, that couldn't be an easy task. If the rest had Akari abilities, maybe, but could Micaiah really do it alone?

A minute later, he stood. Well, even if they were trapped in there, they could sweat for a few days. Either they were naughty prisoners who were paying the price for attempting escape, or else they weren't here at all and he couldn't be worried about them personally right now. He had work to do. He had a kingdom to rule, a kingdom to save from the greater threat within. He headed back the way he'd come.

He wasn't fond of ordering blanket executions. He had sat on death row twice in his life; he knew the feeling of anxiously cherishing every day as his last. The Author had saved him from both occasions. There was a chance she had snatched Micaiah and the others from the same fate. But they were all chosen ones. They had Authored Books. They were special. What about everyone else? He'd read enough Books to know that the Author did not take the time to list every innocent bystander and his life story, give him a eulogy or even an obituary. They were just nameless masses, wrapped up in terms like "group" or "mass" or "thousands" or something of the sort. Considering how very different all of the chosen ones were —a psychotic necrophiliac from Africa, a wounded freedom fighter from Madagascar, Native Americans with their own issues, a Irishman who owned a bakery, a teenager with nothing to his name—what thread bound them together that they should have such favor? Only that they were human? Did the Author not care about the rest of the species in the universe?

This thought carried him through the Wheel back to the Archives and down to the corridor that led to the Core where he paused. Somehow, he had reconnected the Pit the first time, but he couldn't remember how. He didn't remember anything about his last trip to the Core other than it didn't go as planned. Would he remember it as he got closer?

He decided that his goal this time would be to simply understand the Wheel and how Building was utilized here. With the introduction of the Akari, there would be little and less use for Time and the marketplaces. He didn't necessarily want to get rid of those rooms, nor did he want to orphan them, but maybe he could repurpose them. Classrooms, training halls similar to the recreation areas in the Akarin fortress. The Seat of the Hands could stand to be scaled back as well. There was no reason for the people to fear their leaders. Reviews and petitions should be more of a discussion, not a looming judgment.

Speaking of judgment, Rifun thought as he started down the corridor into the darkness toward the spiral staircase, the Judgment Wing itself could use a little updating. It was functional, yes, but ruthlessly efficient. People were not machines to interpret input instructions in a singular way. With the disposal of Time and the Laws of Time, much of the Judgment Wing could become obsolete. Or repurposed.

He didn't have as much time as he would have liked to consider every little detail, and extending the executions all day just to buy him such time didn't sit well with him, but he couldn't come up with anything else. By definition, prisoners had escaped and the Wheel had been attacked. That demanded punishment unless they wanted it to happen again, potentially with worse results all around. A message needed to be sent regarding such violent dissent. And yet, starting tomorrow, Rifun was going to have to try and convince everyone that they desired peace and unity.

The French desired peace and unity, a small voice said in the back of his head as he descended the spiral staircase. *It was just their peace and unity they wanted, and damn those they stepped on and murdered to get there.*

But the Malagasy kings of old had peace and unity among the tribes, he fought back weakly.

Merina kings. Merina nobles. Second-class and slavery for everyone else. The Betsileo alone stood proud and independent, because to not do so was to subject themselves to the same fate.

People are different. That doesn't make them unequal.

There is no such thing as equality this side of the grave. Only in the ancestors and the razana is everyone truly equal, the force of life and the universe.

The Core of the Wheel.

He reached the platform without incident, went to the railing, and knelt to pray. He should have brought an offering, but he didn't have time to put one together. The Food Courts were still being used for the wounded, and he wanted to put a stop to the executions as soon as possible. He would bring an offering later, once those were cleaned up and proper education underway.

He finished praying and stood. He would not deny that a current of anxiety still tremored through his bones, but he couldn't let fear paralyze him. He was the most powerful living soul in the universe right now. The least he could do was try.

He reached out to touch the Core.

Assuming his memory of these events was reliable, each experience was different. The first time, he had been cocooned within the Core, and several years had passed. Last time, he had touched it and done something—at the very least, he had reconnected the Pit, though there was no evidence of anything beyond that single accomplishment—yet he remembered none of it. This time, it was like looking out at the vast and endless ocean and being given five drops of water to do with as he pleased. And yet, each of those drops was an ocean in itself, or a large lake anyway.

He got a certain sensation that this was a test. If he could be trusted with little, could he be trusted with much? He had begun in mere Time and so graduated to the Akari and finally Building. Now, within Building, there were more tiers of responsibility. Perhaps the portal to the Pit had been a single drop. Now he had five to work with. But what were they? What did he do with them? Examining them closely, he saw that they were more like strings, still connected to the greater instrument.

But these were not singular strings, he saw, but ropes made of many strands. Individually, they were nothing, they were weak. Together, they wove the fabric of the Wheel.

Touching one of these ropes put Rifun in mind of playing a harp, and he again lamented his missing fingers. Then he paused and considered. Where did the threads of Creation stop? The razana encompassed all things, living and dead. It was all part of the fabric of existence. If Builders could change the Wheel and alter things millions of miles away, why couldn't he recreate his fingers? Matter and Energy could be neither created nor destroyed, but for the size of his fingers, there had to be some innocuous exchange he could make, something he wouldn't be able to do on his own as he had been lazily attempting. Some small forest creature, for instance, one that was deformed and could never survive on its own. Of all the thousands of planets out there, one had to exist somewhere. Take that and reshape it into his fingers.

Except that was not what these five drops were for. That was not the song these five strings played. Any attempt to search out more or different strings resulted in that feeling one gets before touching a hot surface, the heat and primal instinct to withdraw. What he wanted, the Core would not allow him to do, not this time. That was a higher tier of responsibility, and he still had not even touched the five drops he had been given.

He returned his attention to the five strings and touched them, still oddly compelled to place his hands as if ready to play the harp. He had never played the harp, had only ever seen them from a distance in the orchestra pit of the theaters in France when he was acting. There was little doubt in his mind that he was doing it incorrectly, but he did not suspect that really mattered.

One of the good things about the Core was that it acted on his thoughts, not his ability to articulate them. Rifun normally considered himself a cultured, educated, articulate person, yet the Core had a way of doing away with all of his external capacities and cutting directly to his innermost being. He did not need to explain what he wanted, for it already knew.

This also proved to be one of the most frightening aspects of the Core. With common, limited words, he controlled the flow of information. Even body language and facial expressions could be crafted to be deceiving. The Core was not fooled. The razana was the power of the universe and the ancestors within knew him better than he knew himself.

But these strings were connected to different places in the Wheel, places which were, to his knowledge which was augmented by the metaphysical sense of the Core, unoccupied and undisturbed. He could change these places, make them what he wanted. And he did not have to try and describe the walls or the floor, gardens or balconies or interior decor. He had only to picture it. The strings at his fingertips vibrated ever so faintly. Was this Building? Was this touching and manipulating the Klein bottle?

Rifun almost was not aware that he had closed his eyes until he opened them. The string he had been manipulating melted back into the Core. As it did, he noticed something in the Core itself. There was something there, as if the Core had a core. But that could not be. The Core had no real limits; it only appeared so for the sanity of the Builders. And for as much as Rifun knew his mind had been fried and his memory wiped from his encounters here, he was fairly—fairly—certain that this thing, this dark spot on the sun, hadn't been there before.

As soon as he turned his attention to the thing, the rest of the strings vanished and the Core seemed to shift, like rolling over in bed and taking all the blankets. The thing vanished and it was like a protective wall went up. Rifun could not penetrate it, was unsure how to go about trying, but the more he tried, the more that danger sense pricked at him until he was quite literally shocked, as if he had stuck a fork in an outlet. Enough to hurt, enough to warn, and he knew that the next time wouldn't be so kind.

The euphoric daze of manipulating the Core subsided, and it hit Rifun that the dark spot in the Core was the key to the temple in Ancrath, the temple where the Book of Commands was hidden, trapped. It had to be. Had he discovered this before and forgotten? How would he know? Would he forget it again later? And why wouldn't the Core let him reach it? It must be a terrible thing to have, like a tumor. Could the Core feel pain?

Or could this be the end goal of the tests? If Builders hid the key in there, they were easily more experienced than him. They would make it difficult to remove, to stop the Cult from getting the journal back. Maybe the Core knew something he didn't. Maybe it wanted him to remove the key, but it was using these tests to strengthen his skills so he could. Yes, that made sense. It was not difficult to put a bullet in someone's body, but it required skill and precision and experience to remove it without making things worse.

Rifun reached out one more time, hoping he could convey his desire to go back to the strings he had been presented with but not touched. He assumed the Core understood because it did not electrocute him, but it still gave off the sense of danger and refused to open up or reproduce the strings for him. Could the raw power of the universe be moody? Now there was a thought. And why not? If it was the collective consciousness of the ancestors, the ancestors were people who had thoughts and dreams and moods.

But it appeared as though his work here today was done. He sighed, feeling a bit defeated. He'd come here wanting to do more in order to soften the blow of the coup and put the Akari on grand display, but he'd gotten distracted and blew his chance. How long did he have to wait to come back? An hour? A day? Longer?

Maybe he could take the time to see what it was that he'd changed, see if it really had worked as smoothly as he thought. Then when he returned, he could handle the other strings, and maybe more besides. Yes, that sounded like a productive use of time.

He headed to the spot on the platform under the stairs and cast one last look at the Core. It did not appear to budge from where it had rolled itself up, and yet it still pulsed freely with the energy of the universe. How strange a thing it was.

Gravity saw him up to the staircase, and he had no trouble returning to the Archives. At a casual glance, nothing appeared to have changed here. Outside the Archives, still nothing. But if he remembered correctly — and his memory of this last encounter was already fuzzy — he had done something to a lower marketplace in some distant part of the Wheel. Unoccupied, undisturbed, perfect for experimentation.

He took what might be considered a back way to said marketplace. He didn't want to be pinned down by someone needing something from him just because he was there, but he also didn't know if he could face watching the lines of prisoners as they were marched to their deaths. How many of them actually deserved it? How many of them had simply acted on instinct, the need to survive the fight? How many of them would like nothing more than to go home to a family and never return?

He passed through a portal into an empty room that had once been an intermediate marketplace. The Wheel was purely a construct. An artificial construct for artificial, if holy, purposes. The only indigenous aspect was that of the Akari, the original purpose and intent, which had been snuffed out. But there were no culturally inherent rules here. Rules had been created to usurp the power of the Akari and authority of the Author. The Cult intended to strip away those burdening rules.

And yet, were there not rules to using the Akari? Was that not the whole purpose of the Book of Commands, to make rules to live by? Or perhaps to discover the rules instead?

A line had been crossed, and they weren't going to come back from it. Was it this coup? The last? Rifun felt an icy tingle of fear creep up his spine. The Akarin would come for them. Not because they had any initiative or motivation, but because they were the only ones who could feasibly oppose the Cult, and the Author would not let this trespass go unpunished. Children needed discipline, yes, and this was too far.

That was why Rifun did not recall reopening the Pit, because it would make him culpable. But he was guilty of cowardice, of not trying hard enough to be rid of Cassius, the dragon, the Borelians, all of the evil that had so permeated the Cult from the beginning. The Core had shown him the key as the prize to be obtained, but he had become distracted by it and ignored the lesser skills he needed to get there.

He passed through another portal, another empty marketplace. Maybe he could turn this in his favor. The warehouse may have ultimately failed, but he'd been on the right track. He couldn't kill the dragon alone; he needed help. The problem was, all of his qualified help was either in league with the dragon in some way, or else physically opposed to him or the Cult. Maybe if he could lure the Akarin here, they would help him be rid of the dragon. Not directly, for they would be the Author's hand of punishment against the Cult, but maybe as a distraction. Like the warehouse, cause chaos, lure the dragon in, then strike. The warehouse had been isolated, giving away his intentions. He would have to face it in open combat.

Another shiver passed through him as he entered another abandoned marketplace. No, not abandoned. He had seen abandoned villages and marketplaces, and the eerie thing about those places was that they rarely looked truly abandoned. When immediate evacuation was ordered, people took only what they could carry, if that, and left everything else behind, making the place look like its occupants might actually return. Sometimes they did. Most times they didn't. This marketplace here was not abandoned; it was clean. Walls, floor, ceiling —these terms being relative in the Wheel—some market stands that weren't even decorated enough to look like stage props but rather as pristine as they might be on the showroom floor.

He needed to stop the executions. He needed to transform these into classrooms and places of study and recreation and life.

He finally passed through the portal that led to the marketplace he believed he had altered. And alter it he had. The Wheel had always been very dull and utilitarian, plain metal and glass and other materials he did not understand. No life, no decoration, just basic shapes and geometry to suit as many conceivable purposes as possible. The ultimate big box store.

Now there was life and history here. At the time, in the Core, he had been thinking about his time on stage, all the plays he had helped bring to life. However the Core had deciphered his thoughts, it had done so at a time when he was considering Shakespeare, or something from 1600's London. Cobblestone streets took patrons to market stalls made of wood and thatch. When Rifun touched each of these elements, they felt like the real thing even as he knew they couldn't possibly be those things. But why not? If the Core was the nexus of Creation, why wouldn't it know how to create wood or thatch or cobblestone?

It was still very geometric, in Rifun's opinion, but it was a start. Later he would return to the Core and see what he could do to spruce the place up, make it feel more real and less utilitarian with lipstick.

"What in the fuck in this?"

Rifun turned to see Cassius standing near a portal, looking around, expression mildly confused and disgusted.

"Doing some experimenting in the Core," Rifun told him. "Doing a little redecorating, make the place a little more inviting, and make it more suitable for the work we intend to do."

Cassius raised a brow and deliberately looked around. "What did you have in mind exactly to make this necessary?"

"Community, for one. Our work is not merely a business in service to greed. We must give people a sense of togetherness, and a communal setting goes a long way in establishing such a feeling."

"And what do you expect to sell?"

"There is no reason we could not expand the wares market, give people a chance to show off the goods of their home worlds. Other marketplaces will be turned into learning environments and recreational areas for Akari training. Honestly, Cassius, I understand you are a very practical, but you cannot say you have no sense of aesthetic or beauty."

"Actually I can, and I don't."

Rifun rolled his eyes then sighed. "Why are you here? Shouldn't you be decapitating something?"

Cassius shrugged and took a few lazy steps. "Took a break. Decided to see what sort of mischief you were up to."

"I see."

"And all I find is..." He made a vague, flippant gesture. "This."

"It's harder than it looks. The Core of the Wheel is not to be trifled with."

"Neither am I. Yet here we are."

RIfun shifted his stance. "If you're looking for something to do, I might have an idea."

Cassius paused, his posture still lackadaisical. "Oh? And what's that?"

"Return to the Akarin fortress — as Doug — and find out what they're up to. Are they even aware that this has happened, or are they completely catatonic?"

"Bets on catatonic." He went on before Rifun could speak. "Even if they're not, who cares? We have the Wheel. It's hard as hell to get in or out anyway, so they won't be invading any time soon. Can't you just relax and enjoy success?"

"I will enjoy my success when I achieve it. We have the Wheel, yes, but our enemies still surround us. Our isolation and the difficulty of coming and going may be the only thing standing between us and Borelian slavery right now."

"So why is that not a higher priority than seeing what those lazy Akarin slugs are up to?"

"We're not going to be isolated forever," Rifun said. "The Day, the Bat, someone else with great skill will reconnect the portal room and the dampening field will be lifted. It's just a matter of time."

"Yeah, okay."

"I'll take care of things here. If I take charge of the restoration and redecorating of the Wheel, I can probably buy us some time if needed. You go to the Akarin and see if they can't be prodded. If not now, they never will be, and we haven't lost much. But if they can, make a plan. Doug's an ass, but he's a smart ass."

"Engineer the plans for their destruction," Cassius concluded. "But get them to take out the Grandfathers and the Borelians first."

"Precisely."

"And when they turn on us?"

"We are already more powerful. This is simply the way to sort out all of our problems at the same time."

Cassius waved a hand. "Whatever." He sighed. "Fine. Sitting around here is boring as fuck anyway." He took a few steps away, then turned back. "As long as you don't fucking lose this place in the time I'm gone. Again."

"There are only two ways that could be done, and neither is subtle."

"The fact that there are ways tells me—"

"There are always ways, Cassius. Would you like to go and prevent one of those ways?"

Cassius angrily waved him off and continued walking away.

"If you do help the Akarin make plans, don't forget to tell the rest of us!" Rifun called after him.

He did not reply, and Rifun was left alone soon enough.

His first impulse was to return to the Core and see if he couldn't continue his

Rebuilding of the Wheel. Small changes here and there, learning the ropes, examining the individual pieces before putting them together in grand building plans. Still part of him thought that might not be the best idea. Until Cassius could confirm whether the Akarin were catatonic or mobilizing, he should probably err on the side of caution and the need to buy time. If he rushed in and mastered Rebuilding now, then he wouldn't be able to plead ignorance later. It would be easier to feign ignorance now, then jump in with a sudden epiphany and breakthrough in skills if he had to start making changes.

He left the altered marketplace, heading back toward the hub of activity. Yes. He would take some time away, think about what he had seen, what he had done, what changes he had already wrought. At least he had a good excuse for the next few days, that he wanted to ensure the safety of those who were trapped here with them. It might even give him an excuse to check every room and every portal for stability.

Things had greatly calmed down by the time he returned to the hub, the portal to the Pit still open, the Judgment Wing not far from it, the Food Court a fair distance from either. The Bat and the Day were conversing just outside the Pit portal. With Cassius hopefully on his way out to the Akarin fortress, the executions had been suspended for the time being. Rifun breathed a quiet sigh of relief at that and turned his attention to the Food Court.

With the initial chaos done and over, some people had come to discover that they were not actually injured. Any and all people requiring attention, therefore, had been condensed to maybe one quarter of a single venue, the Food Court of Minerals, one of the least-used courts. Simple mats were laid out for patients, and attending nurses used whatever they had on hand. Judging by the supplies gathered, someone here had been a secretary before the coup and knew where everything was stashed.

It was only the array of non-humanoid species that made the scene bearable, Rifun thought. These were not dying men, they were dying animals. Hunted animals, trophies. It was terrible to consider them in such a way, but it was the only way he could look at the scene objectively as he approached the command post.

The Hutch, normally overseeing the Judgment Wing, was now apparently in charge of this impromptu medical camp. It looked much happier for it as there did not appear to be any Grandfathers hovering over its shoulder. It came to a sort of nervous military attention as Rifun approached.

"Sir," the Hutch greeted anxiously.

"How are things here?" Rifun inquired. "Any lost?"

"Eight dead," the hamster-like alien reported. "Admiral Makijor already took the Borelian dead, but that still leaves three."

He nodded. "What species?"

The Hutch told him.

"Discern their identities, if you have not already. I will see to it that they are returned to their homes. If you have any access to those being executed, do the same. What of the injured?"

For a moment, the hamster appeared to struggle processing Rifun's apparent compassion for the dead. Then it's tiny eyes blinked rapidly and it remembered itself. "Sixty-three injured. Well, more were injured, but sixty-three needing attention."

"Anything life-threatening?"

"A few, maybe. For some, it's too soon to tell."

"By the time you do, it may be too late. But that is the pitfall of having such diverse species."

The Hutch said nothing.

Rifun looked out at the little camp. To his eyes, it almost appeared that there were more volunteers than patients. Enthusiastic to help their fellow man, er, alien? Or just looking for a way out of prison? Considering there were prisoners and guards here, it could be either. Rifun was willing to bet that there would be a few more deaths in the night, and it wouldn't be from the injuries sustained in this fiasco.

"I'll be back in the morning," Rifun told it. "Find the information on the dead."

"Yes sir."

This was Julianna's specialty, Rifun thought as he departed. She would be the one to tend to the sick and injured, to give reassurances and a hand to hold. She was the kind face of their operation which was what they really needed right now. Cassius and Isthim had fulfilled their military roles, now it was time to shift back into civilian life.

Rifun returned to the Judgment Wing, navigating the maze to the office he had claimed as his own. Because returning to civilian life was easy. Yes, just a flip of the switch and a man could shrug off every instinct that told him everyone wanted him dead, everything could conceal some sort of trap, and trust wasn't even part of the vocabulary, sometimes even among those you fought beside.

How long had it been? Well over fifty years as far as the rest of the world was concerned. For him, it was...ten years now? A little longer, maybe? With all the times he had jumped into the future, it could be difficult to keep track. Not that it mattered because it did not feel so long. A year or two, maybe three on a good day. When he had lunch with Lalao, he could almost realize it was a decade or more, that he hadn't just stumbled out of prison into a country still in tatters from the Uprising.

Dammit. Lalao. He still owed her a lunch. True, he'd pleaded a few days to recuperate, but what was he going to tell her? He had failed once more to kill the dragon? Another man of great power had slipped from his grasp and caused significant damage? This whole plan was an enormous sin against the Author? Exactly what kind of champion of the ancestors was he? He couldn't seem to do anything right.

He picked up a pen and a piece of paper—both unusually valuable commodities in a setting run by computers—and started writing. At least the pen no longer fell out of his left hand, but the words being produced looked worse than his first attempts in primary school. So many sentences, over and over again. *Voix ambiguë d'un cœur qui au zéphyr préfère les jattes de kiwis. Hetezo voankazo fotsy mangatsiaka lehibe dimy ao anaty akanjonao rahampitso.* Damn it all, he forgot how much he hated these pangrams, yet here he was. But he would take the pangrams over the Bible verses they had to write out equally ad nauseum. He could finagle to write with his right hand, but it caused such cramps.

He shouldn't hide from Lalao. That would be true cowardice. But how did he explain his ongoing failure? Maybe he should make an attempt to rescue Julianna. Maybe the Core could help with that in some way. Then at least he might be able to brag a little about having rescued someone, a damsel in distress as it were. Then at least he might have something to his name.

Voix ambiguë d'un cœur qui au zéphyr préfère les jattes de kiwis. Ambiguous voice of a heart which prefers kiwi bowls to a zephyr. Largely nonsense, but it used all of the letters.

Hetezo voankazo fotsy mangatsiaka lehibe dimy ao anaty akanjonao rahampitso. Cut five large frozen white fruits in your coat tomorrow. Grammatically correct, but still a bit strange. Why would you want to cut fruit in your coat? Don't ask questions, just practice the letters.

He finished the page on both sides and stared at it forlornly. Getting better, legible at least, but hardly the ruler-enforced perfection of his schooling. After a moment of savoring his disgust at his own handwriting, he balled up the paper, tossed it away, and stood. He would take a tour of the entire Wheel. If anyone asked, he was inspecting all the portals. And he would, because he was curious, and it might lend him some help when he finished and went to the Core to hopefully continue his exploration of the Core and Rebuilding. He did not intend to do any more Rebuilding today, just some learning and inspection. Maybe, if he was feeling ambitious, he would see what happened if he tried to turn a portal of the Wheel inside out.

When he was done with that, then he would check in with the Hutch and ensure the dead were returned to their homes. He could not ensure they were laid to rest as appropriate to their customs, but he would give them the best chance he could. And it could be that that would be his only boast in this endeavor, the only one he could relay to Lalao, anyway. Yes, he had failed to kill the dragon. Again. But at least he ensured the dead were laid to rest.

With any luck, their vengeful spirits would add to the razana and so increase his strength when he did finally face off against the dragon.

19 | Ṣàyẹ̀wò

Consideration

kokumbo

If Cassius had actually placed any monetary bets on the disposition of the Akarin, he would have lost spectacularly. In his own defense, it could just as easily have been the standard initial outrage over any upsetting political decision. As Rifun put it, rattling their sabers, but never actually drawing for a fight.

There were meetings. Lots of meetings. A nearly endless stream of them. Cassius-as-Doug didn't even bother trying to attend them all. If there were ten meetings, he would go to one, maybe two. Most of the time, half the meeting was spent solely on roll call and making sure everyone was "up to speed on things." Of course, real information was pitifully scarce, and the speculation was never consistent. At least until one meeting where an unexpected guest showed up.

"Aklaq!" Cassius-as-Doug announced as she walked in the door. "My goodness, woman, I haven't seen you around lately! We were starting to get worried! And Micaiah, too! Where is he?!"

The woman looked a bit haggard. She wasn't dirty or unkempt, but she had an air of exhaustion about her, as if she hadn't slept well for a while and maybe stopped doing anything more than the basic necessities for hygiene.

"Micaiah was in the Wheel when the Cult took over," she reported quietly. "He was being taken for execution when he managed to do a little damage and escape."

Cassius-as-Doug spread his arms wide in some sort of celebratory gesture. "Then I'm sure he has plenty of good intel for us, let us know what we're up against!"

Surprisingly, she shook her head and it was minute before she said, "He was injured in the escape. He lost part of his right leg."

"Lost? As in—"

"Amputated. He got to keep the knee, but that's all."

He shrugged. "I mean, it could be worse."

"It could, yes, but...he's not even talking to me much. Even Micah says he's a bit of a recluse."

He waved a hand. "It's only been a few days. I'm sure he'll come around."

"I'm sure he will," Aklaq sighed unconvincingly. "If you want anyone with motivation for revenge or just fighting spirit, he's got it. But now he's..."

"Having to deal with a severe physical disadvantage."

"Stated bluntly, yes."

He shifted his stance. Doug was not known to be a compassionate person. The whole concept seemed foreign to him. He weighed everything as being a tactical or strategic advantage or disadvantage. Cassius was not such a brilliant military mind, but at least he didn't have to pretend to really care about people.

"The good news," he went on, "I've heard rumors of small groups who are going to try and break into the Wheel, if for no other reason than to gather information. The more we know the better. Micaiah doesn't need to be with them."

"What do you mean by small groups?" Aklaq wondered, her tone and disposition suggesting she was not fully in the conversation.

"Small groups of Akarin and other affiliated factions who are tired of all these damn meetings and want to take action."

Aklaq shifted her stance. "That's great and all, but we can't have a bunch of freelancers running around doing whatever they want."

"Oh, I wholeheartedly agree. But you know how the Akarin council is. All talk. Talk, talk, talk. If we make no attempt to control them, what use are we as an organization? If we do make such an attempt, we better have either a reason to stop them or a goal for them to accomplish in order to expend their energy in the most efficient manner possible." *And expose their weaknesses.*

She just nodded, still not quite in it. "Makes sense."

"Did Micaiah say anything about Rifun or Cassius or the Hands or the Grandfathers or anyone in charge?"

"Not really, nothing concrete. Just blames them for everything."

"Well if he ever does feel like sharing information, he knows where we are."

"I'm sure he'll come around eventually." Her words were flat, devoid of any real present hope.

"Are we quite ready to begin the meeting?" one of the council members cut in irritably, as if he hadn't been having his own side conversation just a few minutes prior.

"Of course!" Cassius-as-Doug declared, turning his attention back to the prattling morons who were only considering action because disgruntled peons were pushing them toward it. "Let's begin, shall we?!"

"There are eleven teams that we know of," another councilman began. "The Faithful Akari-bearers, the Peaceful Akari-bearers, Author's Rite, and The Locked Word have the largest teams, and they are the ones most likely to succeed in any endeavor."

"If they work cooperatively, they might increase their chances," Cassius-as-Doug threw in.

"The Faithful Akari-bearers and Peaceful Akari-bearers will be working together, yes. Their goal is simply ascertaining the extent of any death or carnage, getting a count of the dead, estimating executions, and so on."

"How do they intend to do that?"

"I don't know."

"Might be beneficial to find out."

"We're going into this blind no matter what. We've had too much speculation and it's only doing us a disservice. If you know something concrete, please, share it." The councilman added distastefully, "Although I'm sure you would have by now and made sure everyone heard you."

"Oh, I'm happy to share everything I know. And what of the other two?"

"Author's Rite is only loosely affiliated with us. Some have suspected that their allegiances lie more with the Cult, or with their own brand of heresy. They are not disclosing their plans other than as simple information gathering. The Locked Word offered to assist and was strictly refused."

"So is Author's Rite even going to share what information they learn?" one councilman inquired.

"Unlikely," another mused. "It may be they are informing us of this nascent plan at all so that if something goes wrong, maybe someone will send a rescue team or we will know not to do what they did."

"How will we know what to not do if they don't tell us what they're doing?"

The councilman made a helpless gesture. "Ask them. We can't force them to go or not go, tell us or not."

And whose fault is that? Cassius wondered silently.

"That's four of the teams," Aklaq said. "What about the other seven?"

"More willing to work together, but not necessarily with us. Nor are they forthcoming with the specifics of their plans."

"And what about us? Do we have a plan?"

"Not as such. Not yet."

"Well why not? Common militaries have plans and strategies ready to deploy at a moment's notice." She went on before anyone could object. "I understand that we are not a standing army, but in seven or ten days or whatever, surely you must have thought of at least something?"

"Some plans were in the works, yes. But, with all of these teams intent on gathering information, we have decided to put them off until the teams return with information. At this point, there is no bad intelligence."

He wasn't wrong, but all Cassius could think was, *Too little, too late.* The Akarin had sat on their hands for too long, and even now, in the middle of this crisis, they were finding every excuse not to take action. Not enough information. Other teams were getting information. Assuming those teams found anything and lived to tell about it, then the council would no doubt be very troubled and very concerned about said information and stall by saying that they needed to consider things very carefully and not make any rash decisions. If the deadly sin of Sloth had a following, the Akarin would be its more ardent devotees.

He suffered through the rest of the meeting and made sure to catch up to Aklaq when they were finally dismissed.

"Keep me apprised of Micaiah's situation, won't you?" he inquired. "He's a good fighter, good leader. We'll need him for a future fight, I'm sure."

Aklaq laughed humorlessly. "Well, by the time this lot gets around to doing anything, never mind fighting, I'm sure Micaiah will be leaps and bounds ahead of them."

"Pun intended, right?"

She just sighed.

"Well, after gathering my own intelligence on 'this lot' over the last few days, I think I'm going to be working on a few plans of my own. Let me know if you want to get in on them!"

She gave some sigh or guttural sound of assent but spoke no words. Cassius-as-Doug let her go and strode away, a short man on top of the world.

A few steps in, he paused. He couldn't hold a Disguise while unconscious. If anyone came looking for Doug with some important news, they wouldn't find him in the middle of the night. Should he go back to the Wheel? What about the Cult's hideout on Sadurnon? There were a few lingering units, just in case things hadn't gone entirely as planned, but otherwise it was pretty empty.

The ruins seemed to be his best bet for a little shut-eye. He'd go back to the Wheel in the morning with this scant news of reconnaissance teams, assuming the flies hadn't already been swatted by then. Assuming they broke into the Wheel at all.

Getting out of the Wheel had been hard enough. Getting back in, even with his great power and a good night's rest, was significantly more difficult. He hadn't been aiming for any particular room of the Wheel, and whether this helped or hurt him he didn't know. It probably didn't matter. He just knew that his first concern when he clawed his way back to consciousness was whether he'd fallen into the Land In Between like Julianna. What would that look like in the Wheel? How would that even work? She claimed it was impossible to traverse portals while in the dimension, so did that mean he would be stuck in the same room forever? Fucking hell, if that were the case, he'd just kill himself.

Such was not the case as he drunkenly stumbled through the first portal he found. It took him a minute to recall where he was—every room looked the same without the Merchants around hawking Time Capsules—but once he figured it out, it was short work to find his way to the Judgment Wing. There he ran into Rifun who was apparently just leaving to go do some errand or another.

"You look like hell," Rifun observed in greeting. "I take it things didn't go well?"

"There are eleven teams going to attempt to break into this place," Cassius informed him. "They claim it is only to gather intelligence, but I have my doubts."

Rifun frowned. "I see. What do you know of these teams? What are their plans specifically?"

Cassius shrugged. "That I can't say. None of them are from the Akarin themselves, only their smaller allies and affiliated groups. They're only telling the Akarin about the plans to be polite, and in case they need a rescue. Otherwise, they're not too keen on helping the Akarin at all."

Rifun nodded. "Good to know the cost of their sloth remains high. What can you tell me?"

Not enough to justify the air used to explain it. A few were working together, a few weren't, a few had questionable loyalties. Their first hurdle was just getting in, and they'd take it from there.

"It's not much, but we should not ignore the possibility of infiltration," Rifun decided, his gaze turning inward. "I'll have the guards start making patrols, let them know what's going on. The Akarin and like groups are the greatest threat, but by no means the only one. We should anticipate that other groups will attempt similar feats. The Tacagans, the Psiaco, and others with great technology and a fiendish loyalty to Time." He turned his attention back to Cassius. "Stick with the Akarin, keep an eye on their plans and any others they get wind of."

"I also got another bit of news you might find intriguing. Micaiah and the others made it out of the Wheel. In the process, Micaiah was injured and lost his leg."

The news seemed to genuinely shock Rifun and cause him a small bit of distress. "What?"

Cassius smirked. "I talked to Aklaq. She says he got to keep the knee, but he's become a bit of a recluse."

"Can't imagine why," Rifun said flatly, his expression turning mildly accusatory.

"I didn't do it," Cassius defended. "Anyway, just thought you might like to know, in case that somehow figures into your magnificent plans for the Author's 'chosen ones' or whatever."

He walked away before Rifun could speak, either to chastise him or go into some anxious monologue. He was not eager to open a portal anywhere so soon; instead he took the opportunity to head to the Pit where he found the Bat. The mysterious creature did not appear busy, but then, it never did, and yet it accomplished so much.

"Finished all the executions?" Cassius wondered.

"Other than a few specific incidents, executions have been suspended," the Bat reported, sounding a bit annoyed.

"Rifun felt guilty, is that it?"

The Bat grumbled in a rather unsettling manner. "Regretfully so."

Cassius shifted his stance. "All the regime changes, all the coups and attempted coups, and you just follow along, pleading your allegiance to the Wheel. What makes this so special that you start showing emotion?"

For a long moment, Cassius foresaw two possibilities: the Bat would answer him, or the Bat would eat him. In the end, it chose the former. "Opposition."

"What the hell does that mean? Of course people are going to try to oppose us."

The Bat sneered at him. "Fleshy, three-dimensional creature, still cannot grasp that which you have witnessed and experienced for yourself."

"The Shadows? Fine. And I'm guessing you're referring to the Whites or whatever they're called? Who cares about them? They're as timid as the Akarin. All bark, no bite. We might have been a little slow on the execution, true, but we took a chance. And it has paid off."

"Sly, not timid."

"I told you, we got this. I'm hanging around the Akarin, probably doing the same thing you're complaining about the Whites doing. Imitation, infiltration. I'll be able to tell us if there are any real threats coming."

The Bat made a sound that in any other animal might have been a snort, but in its oddly-shaped nose came off as more of a nasally popping sound not quite a sneeze. "You have one more task. Then your time is up. And I will be glad for it."

It was amazing what it took to get honest answers from people, Cassius thought as he exited the Pit. When a man was leaving his job, he told his coworkers and his boss everything he really thought about them, all the things he couldn't say before because he valued money and "cohesion." When someone else was leaving, especially someone that no one else liked, it was like a license to breathe a sigh of relief and to freely abuse that person on their way out. Just some of the many reasons why the nine-to-five had never appealed to Cassius.

Although he was curious what Rifun was doing with the prisoners if he wasn't executing them, Cassius decided that it might be better if he didn't know. One more task, as the Bat had stated. Whether that involved masquerading as Doug, he did not know, but it was the only task he cared about at the moment. At the very least, it seemed to finally be paying off now that the Akarin — or their affiliates, anyway — were doing something.

Eventually he returned to the fortress, still avoiding meetings as much as he could while trying to keep an ear out for the success or failure of the recon teams.

As it turned out, their failure was not so interesting as having broken in and been repelled by Rifun's patrols. Instead, it merely amounted to the simple inability to break in. Everyone was so accustomed to just stopping at the portal room and letting the technology of the Wheel take over that they didn't know how to do anything else. Because of the nature of the Wheel, no one was quite sure how to feel it out, either. Even if the teams were aware that the Wheel was the focal point of all black holes, there was a difference between knowing that and knowing how to overcome it to feel out the Wheel to open a direct portal.

This anti-climax and subsequent void of intelligence confused some and emboldened others. Soon enough there were truly organized teams who routinely attempted to break in. A couple even succeeded, though the patrols took them out to a man so no information could be returned. As far as the rest of the teams were concerned, those teams that disappeared probably did something wrong and landed themselves in the in-between dimension. Maybe some did. Who could say for sure?

Cassius gave Rifun updates when he could, when he thought there might be some credence to a threat. But as one week passed into two, then three, then four, and the isolation of the Wheel still held, the reports became less and less frequent, and less and less exciting. People were starting to adapt to life without the Time industry. For the majority of people, it was a good change, once the withdrawal symptoms wore off. From what Cassius heard around the water cooler at the fortress, some species were setting up their own, smaller industries, tailored to their own species, like the Psiaco with their Time Academies, but the authority stopped with the Gatekeeper; it did not continue up and up to the Hands. Among the Akarin, some wondered if they shouldn't encourage something similar with the Akari.

The Cult was hidden away, brooding in their castle. No one could get in to see what they were doing. At the same time, the Cult was isolated and had made very few moves to attack from that castle. True, Cassius had sent out some Trackers to hunt down specific Time Agents and deliver them to Rifun—the man had gone from military leader to headmaster of a school in whiplash time—but other than that, everything was just sitting tight.

Bad enough Cassius-as-Doug had to talk to Micaiah's twin brother and try to explain things. Doug might have been a teacher, but Cassius was not. His only saving grace was Doug's repulsive, flamboyant personality and Micah's massive skepticism. He was more hurt that Micaiah had never told him about the Akari than he was eager to learn it.

Soon enough, Cassius found himself sitting in Doug's house—the new owners at work—wondering where it all went wrong. Where was the hostile takeover, the huge battle, the ultimate victory, the subjugation of the universe? They had started out so well with the takeover of the Wheel. Now what? Rifun was trying to run a school or some shit, believing everyone could be loved and rehabilitated to death. No doubt Isthim and the Borelians wanted to press forward with their new slave colony, but their current position was preventing such a thing. So why didn't Rifun take out the Borelians? If they couldn't move people out, then they themselves couldn't escape. Surely there was a way to do such a thing. He was Mr. All-Powerful-Master-Builder-of-the-Universe after all.

He startled as Doug's phone rang. The caller ID was familiar but not marked. Sighing, he donned his Doug Disguise and answered.

"Doug Templeton."

"Doug, it's Cai and Kayla."

"You're not naked in a hotel room, are you?"

"Just ignore any weird sounds you hear; you're on speakerphone."

Micaiah coughed to badly cover up a laugh.

"Duly noted. Micaiah, how are you doing? Haven't heard from you since your...escape. I expect a full report."

"It'll have to wait a bit," Micaiah said. "But I'm doing all right."

"Good, good. Hey, your brother has the potential to be as great as you, once he gets over his shock and fear and all the things that normally accompany an eye-opening." He didn't even know if that was true and he hoped they didn't ask about any progress Micah was making.

"I don't doubt it, but that's not why we're calling."

"Well, I'm sure Aklaq's filled you in on a lot, but I'll just reiterate that no one is coming in or going out."

"She told me, but that's not it either."

"Don't keep me in suspense, guys, out with it."

"We have a plan to get into the Wheel and depose the Cult."

"You and everyone else, but all right, let's hear it. Let me tell you, though, that if I can't come up with something, no one can." That sounded about right for Doug.

"I'm going to go to the Wheel and demand a Time Trial."

Even Cassius was stunned into silence for a minute. Micaiah let him have the moment. Finally Cassius-as-Doug asked, "Haven't you already been through one Time Trial in your life? With both legs? How'd that go?"

"It's not about the Trial. I don't expect to even get to that point. We do expect that Rifun and Cassius will be attracted to the sport and will want to or have to be present. We smuggle in a gun in Disguise, go before the Grandfathers or the Hands or however they're running things these days. When Rifun and Cassius show up, shoot them before the Trial even has a chance to get underway. Then we can open a portal for the rest of the Akarin to come in and fight and liberate the Wheel."

He ran over some of the finer details of the plan which he had apparently been thinking about for a couple weeks, including Disguising others as Tommen and Walter, enough to bait Rifun into accepting the proposal without actually endangering the pair.

"You came up with this all on your own?" Cassius-as-Doug wondered.

"Yes sir," Micaiah confirmed.

"Has anyone told you how idiotic this sounds? It's a suicide mission, you know that."

"That's why we're asking for your input, Doug," Aklaq said, her tone grudging. "Help us make it not a suicide mission. Everyone comes home."

"In one piece," Micaiah added.

"Oh, I understand that," Cassius-as-Doug chuckled. "Okay, well, it sounds like you weren't idle in your downtime. Good to hear. Listen, why don't you let me chew on this for a while, see if I can't come up with something a little more likely to succeed and a little more likely to get everyone home alive and in one piece as you said."

"How are things going?" Aklaq asked. "Has there been any news at all out of the Wheel?"

"Tighter than a Ziploc bag, sorry to say. We've had reports of Tracker attacks across all Divisions, but only when Time was used. Akari-bearers seem to be largely unaffected."

"What are the Trackers doing?"

"Those that aren't killed by their targets? Some targets are killed outright, usually explained away as a dog or bear attack or what have you. Others disappear. One Merchant was attacked when he was having dinner with his wife. Tracker was unconcerned with the wife, got its jaws around the Merchant and they just vanished."

"Vanished?"

"That's how the wife described it. Vanished. I can't tell you much more than that because I don't know more than that. The only thing we can assume is that they go back to the Wheel." Not for execution or anything so dramatic, just to go to fucking school.

"Any pattern to who dies and who vanishes?" Micaiah wondered.

"Nothing we've been able to determine so far, but without access to the Archives and other Wheel databases, we're working on pre-coup information, and public information at that. What nasty little lists Cassius and Rifun kept, they likely kept to themselves."

"Imagine so."

"Listen, I'll let you get back to your date night, and I'll contact you if we come up with anything."

"Thanks, Doug," Aklaq said politely and hung up.

Ask and ye shall receive, Cassius thought darkly, standing and stretching. This would certainly make things interesting. Then he had an even darker thought. What if he didn't tell Rifun about this? What if he let Micaiah surprise Rifun with the challenge, let Rifun walk into it blindly, see if Micaiah could actually pull it off and kill him? As for Cassius? Well, he could maintain his Doug facade, maybe even join them in their little revolution, and stab them in the back once Rifun was dead.

Of course, part of the plan was dependent on Doug motivating the rest of the Akarin. Well, not the Akarin, for most of the grunts were pretty well motivated. It was getting the council to go along with it. Or maybe he wouldn't bother with them. Motivate the people alone, let their overwhelming will dictate what they did. Let the mob rule. Let the mob throw themselves into the fire of revolution and liberation. Let the Grandfathers and the guards and the Cult forces kill them.

Except the Akarin grunts were fairly skilled. They could prove to be a small challenge for the Cult. This needed to be decisive victory. No more piddling around with the rules of war or wiping memories. Absolute destruction, utter annihilation. No terms, no quarter, nothing. But in order to achieve that, he needed to inform Rifun of the situation. Or maybe Isthim. But Isthim would tell Rifun, so he should probably just bring them both in on it at the same time.

Well, he didn't have to go running off right away like an eager puppy. He could sit on it for a few days, do some thinking or pretend to. Pretend to have difficulty with the council, difficulty with the grunts. How far could he stretch the trust Micaiah had in Doug, or Doug's tactical mind? Could he really come up with a plan or part of a plan that would see Micaiah's demise, all the while telling him to "trust the plan" that everything would work out? Well, Micaiah was kind of doing that on his own by even coming up with a Time Trial as a viable option.

Another thought occurred to Cassius. This was likely some knee-jerk reaction from Micaiah—all pun intended—over his imprisonment and subsequent loss of his leg. He was doing this for revenge, not revolution, however much he said otherwise. Cassius couldn't let this sit for too long, then, lest Micaiah's rage cool too much, to the point where he realized he couldn't fight as well as he thought.

Or Cassius could ignore Micaiah as a key player. If the man backed out, send someone else in as the sacrificial lamb, carry out the plan regardless. There were bound to be stragglers after the fight. A few Trackers would clean them up, Cassius was sure. Whether it was in battle or afterwards, total annihilation was total annihilation.

He waited a few days at least, just in case anyone else called with any more brilliant ideas, but none did. The Akarin teams continued to fruitlessly throw themselves at a metaphorical brick wall, and there were no reports of successful breaches from any other groups. Everything remained in the holding pattern, and it would remain there until Cassius decided otherwise.

His low tolerance for the politics of the Akarin and his general lust for battle saw him back to the Wheel in just over a week. Although Rifun had set up several classes to teach the Akari, he himself was not an instructor. Instead, he was down in his office in the Judgment Wing. Actually, Cassius was surprised it still looked like the old Judgment Wing and he hadn't changed it into some school dormitory or something equally soft.

He had, however, been hard at work transforming his office. Cassius had seen one very similar to it, once, in Europe back in the day. Plush, opulent, rich, complete with stone hearth fireplace. Was it real fire in there, or some facsimile generated by the Wheel? He didn't care enough to find out. The desk that Rifun sat behind was just as fancy as the rest of the room.

"Tapping into your French heritage with this remodel, eh?" Cassius began.

"Only a fool ignores the pleasurable aesthetic simply because its origins are distasteful," Rifun informed him. He appeared to be concentrating on writing something, not looking up until the last word was written. "What now? More overly confident assailants coming to rob us in the night?"

Cassius shook his head. "Better."

Rifun shifted in his seat. "Oh? A real threat?"

Cassius shrugged. "I don't know about a threat, but it is an opportunity." He relayed the conversation he'd had with Micaiah and Aklaq, finishing with, "If we don't take this opportunity, then we deserve to lose."

Except for an occasional clarifying question, Rifun had been silent. Now he appeared thoughtful.

"They didn't mention you at all, did they? Gave no indication that they suspected Doug wasn't Doug?"

Cassius shook his head. "Everything I heard said they wanted Doug's great tactical mind, not necessarily him. That's how I've been able to pull off this charade, remember?"

"I've not forgotten, trust me. In fact, I'm still amazed you have pulled it off at all." Rifun shifted in his seat. "And with this proposal, it would be a grand reveal, for there is no way I foresee being able to continue such a charade."

"We shouldn't have to," Cassius insisted. "No more tiptoeing around, no more games, no more facades. We are here. One battle, one victory, winner takes all."

Rifun blinked. "It's like you have no idea how war actually works."

"Two people, one winner, one loser. That's a fight. Why does adding a few more people make a difference? Not crushing our enemies is the reason we had such trouble getting where we are."

"And yet, we are here regardless." Rifun stood. "We are not fighting people, Cassius. We are fighting ideas—"

"If I have an idea in my head, an idea no one else has, killing me kills that idea. If ten people have an idea to rob me, killing those ten people eliminates that idea. There is literally no difference."

Cassius could see that Rifun did his best not to outright sigh. "I suppose it depends on who we work for. You work for yourself, regardless of the dragon's involvement. Your goal is yourself. Your victory, your glory. I work for the spirits, the ancestors. They have given me the power of the razana for that end. Blatant mass murder is not my first method of—"

"Your dead power the universe. So why not make more dead?"

"It is the attitudes of the dead that steer things here and there. If they lived well, were loved and respected and esteemed in their families and communities, the razana is a force for much good. If they were disrespected, murdered, slandered, the razana quickly turns dark and malicious."

Cassius rolled his eyes. "Shite, I should have known better than to ask."

"I work to educate the people, bring them into a greater understanding of the universe. This isolation proves an excellent opportunity in its own right."

"Are you at least training them to fight? You said it yourself, our enemies will come. And it sounds like they are definitely trying."

"Instruction thus far has been of our history, through the Book of Philosophy. It takes but twenty-eight days to change someone's mind when inundated with an idea. Some have reached this threshold, others are close. Granted, our classes are very small groups compared to the population of the universe, but it is a start. There has been minimal instruction in the Akari version of skills they may already possess, such as Banding.

"As for what you suggest, it has already occurred to me. Seeing how you appear to have some leeway with this Time Trial idea, give me ninety days if you can. That will bring in plenty of ideological recruits, and most of them will have some ability to help us."

Cassius spread his arms wide with some mild sarcasm. "Finally! Something is going to be done!" He let his arms drop. "And the total annihilation? It's not going to be more than what we could pack into the Coliseum."

"It would be, I assure you. And no, we cannot issue blanket execution on the Akarin."

Now Cassius slammed a fist on the desk. "Every. Man. Woman. Child. Everyone! That is how it was done in the old days!"

"And how much has been lost because of it?!" Rifun countered testily. "Your humanity, maybe?" Cassius blinked. "Your own people sold you into slavery, Kokumbo. Because they were conquered. Every man—woman—child—taken at some point. Children lured away from their mothers." Rifun let that hang there. "That is the price of absolutes."

Cassius mentally scrambled for something to latch onto. "By your admission, is fate not fixed? Is that not an absolute?"

"Then what are you worried about? Either we will win or we won't, and so it always was and is and will be." Rifun leaned back against the desk. "I will give thought to the Time Trial and how we may rig things in our favor. I will also begin considering our defenses. If there is to be a total annihilation, it will be the Borelians to face such a heavy hand."

"Well," Cassius scoffed. "It's something."

"It's the best solution I have to that problem. If we can make it look like they perished in a large, bloody battle for the Wheel, the chances of the Council of Ancrath or the Great Admirals of the Fleet declaring war on us are...minimal at best."

"Better than being carted off to a slave colony of our own making, I guess."

"Worst case, it buys us time and it cuts off the direct route they had clearly been planning."

Cassius nodded. Then, "So how does Isthim feel about all of this? I haven't seen her around much. Or did she go running back home to her...well, I don't think it would be a comfortable bed, but her own bed anyway."

"That is where she and Misik spend most of their time, yes. They haven't come up with a reason for us to move from the Wheel into their new colony. As I said, this isolation works well for us in more than one respect."

"So she left you."

"Excuse me?"

Cassius sighed dramatically. "I'm sorry to hear it. But you know how it goes. Women will always go back to their abusers, no matter how wonderfully you treat them."

Rifun smirked. "What does that say about you, then, that she's gone with Misik and not you? Is your kink not weird enough or rough enough for her?" He laughed as Cassius was at a loss for words. "Don't feel bad. There are still a few white Borelians wandering around here as Grandfathers if you really need it. At least two of them are female."

"Just...work on the plan!" Cassius sputtered.

He turned and stormed off before Rifun could say more. Cassius couldn't recall the last time he had felt so humiliated. And insulted!

His people were strong! Proud! They were the warriors! They were the conquerors! There was no way they could have been conquered. Tricked, maybe, but not...it couldn't be. Cassius tried to bring that day to mind, when he was taken so long ago. But it had been centuries, and he couldn't remember anything about Africa, or his specific home. Anything he did recall was rote knowledge from the Authored Book. Had it said that his own people or a neighboring people had captured and sold him to white slavers? No, that couldn't be right.

No, Rifun was trying to throw him off. Trying to save his own skin, buy time so Cassius wouldn't kill him. But this only made Cassius resolve all the more firmly that Rifun was going to die in this upcoming battle. Rifun wanted to be rid of the Borelians, well, Cassius wanted to get rid of Rifun. Hell, get rid of everything and everyone. No more Borelians, no more Akarin, no more Cult. No more Akari for that matter. Strip everything down to primal nature, just as the

Time industry had done. Oh, they pretended to be noble, more evolved perhaps, but noble savagery was just greed. And the Hands of the Time industry had been the gods of greed.

Burn it all down. For cleansing. For punishment.

Whether it was luck or providence that he ran into a white Borelian, he did not care. He did not even bother with some tired proposition as he simply used Gravity to grab hold and take it to a hidden corner. He couldn't even say that he felt any more satisfied than the chemical reaction in his brain said he was. Oh it felt breathlessly wonderful as it always did, but hardly satisfying, and he left in the same mood he had come.

He would motivate the Akarin. He would raise up an army so fearsome it would be a threat to the Cult and the Borelians. He would concoct a plan so malevolent that the only logical outcome was the total annihilation of everyone and everything, even the Wheel itself.

He veered off his already destination-less course and headed to the Pit to speak to the Bat. It was about as enthusiastic as the last time Cassius had seen it, skulking around in an empty Pit.

"You're immortal, right?" Cassius began. Before the Bat could answer, he added, "I don't give a shit about what I did to you last time, resurrected you or whatever. You yourself are immortal. I don't know what bet you lost that you have the form you do, but at your core, you're a Shadow. You and the Day."

The Bat studied him for a long moment. "Sometimes it is too inefficient to simply whisper in the ear of a pawn; no matter what, we always fight the free will and the primal instincts. Sometimes, direct enforcement is required."

"The real power behind the throne. Point is, you've been holding back."

"What do you want?"

Cassius explained everything that had happened so far, from Micaiah's plan to his conversation with Rifun. He finished, "I'm going to get the Akarin riled up and ready to march on this place with their full force. Every member, man, woman, and child. If the Borelians can be persuaded to do the same, by all means. And we'll all meet here for the final battle for mastery of the universe." He chuckled humorlessly. "One last task: destroy the universe."

The Bat made a sound whose intent was impossible to determine, but it didn't attack him, so Cassius considered that a good thing.

"I realize it's a lofty goal," he went on. "And, let's be honest, it's probably impossible, at least the way I envision it. But I do intend to bring the Akarin here for a battle. There will be blood and chaos. And whether we win or lose or something else happens, I want you to personally ensure that Rifun dies, even if you have to do it yourself. And I don't think it will be a matter of just cutting his throat. Cut his throat, cut off his head, dismember his body, and burn it all until there is nothing left. Then Band the bone and ash until it is nothing more than dust molecules in the air and then send those molecules into the frozen vacuum of space, heading directly for a star so that—"

"Your point is taken," the Bat interrupted, now looking a tad annoyed. It turned away briefly, but Cassius was fairly certain it fully intended him to hear its next words. "Unlike you, he seems to understand that flesh is fleeting and inconsequential; it is what lies beyond that we must kill. To kill what lies beyond, we must use methods from beyond this fleshy world." It looked back at him. "Was there anything else, or are you going to posture some more?"

Cassius blinked. Then, "I'll let you know when the Akarin plan to attack. Be ready. And tell the Day what's going on."

The Bat said nothing, instead returning to whatever it was doing, lurking about in the gloom of the Pit. It was shaping up so it no longer looked like old, crumbling ruins, but had the shadowy gleam of a newly-built dungeon. No, not dungeon. This was not a place for men to sit and rot; this was where they came to bleed their false hope of survival into the black stone.

He left the Pit and started in the direction of the portal room. Halfway there, he stopped. There was no portal room. Damn force of habit. At some point, when Cassius came to report on some minor plan by the Akarin to get into the Wheel, Rifun had mentioned something about taking the opportunity to break up the singular portal room into multiple rooms. This way, it would be easier for species who weren't Engaged to access the Wheel without having to walk all the way from the back of the room.

Assuming everything worked the way it used to, thus making portal travel slightly easier, it would also allow for multiple entry points and escape routes. Even Cassius questioned the wisdom of this. If Rifun was smart, he'd hold off on such a project until the Wheel was completely secured and the Akarin vanquished. Yet by Cassius' own orders, Rifun wasn't going to last that long. Hm...

Truthfully, he didn't expect to survive the encounter either. One last task, and this was it. Even if he did somehow survive, the Bat would probably just kill him outright. Or the dragon. Hadn't heard from that bastard in a while. And why should he? He was useless. When sliding down a steep slope, there was no further need to push. He would reach the bottom and the dragon would release its hold on the bullet in his face.

So it was no concern of his what became of the Wheel, the Cult, the Akarin, the Borelians, any of them.

What would happen if he blew his cover early? What if he walked right into the Akarin fortress, right into one of the council meetings, dropped his Doug Disguise, and started killing? How long would he last? How long would they? Would it cripple the underlings? Would that push them into a blind rage and presumptuous assault on the Wheel?

Or what if he went and killed all the Borelians in the Wheel, both those like Isthim and Misik who had trained in the Akari and those who were simply fulfilling their roles as Grandfathers? How long would it be before the Council or the Admirals or the Holy Men found out? How would they know it was the Cult and not some uprising of prisoners? Would it matter to them? And how did they expect to launch and assault on the Wheel? Without Isthim and the others who had the advantage of the Akari to aid their portals, the Borelians would have as much luck as the Tacagans, or any other race with incredible technology.

He rubbed his eyes. He should get some rest before going to the fortress again. He shook his head. No, he had to get this ball rolling. The faster he came up with a plan, and the sooner he got the Akarin to agree to and implement it, the better. No more politics, no more lurking and skulking, no more talk. Talk was no longer an option, and thank whomever for that.

He pulled his Doug Disguise over himself like a wet rubber suit and pried open a portal to the Akarin fortress. If he had eaten anything recently, he might have given it up as he went to all fours in the portal room of the fortress. He should have taken at least a short nap before coming here. Wasn't as though the council was that inclined to action. Couldn't sleep here because he couldn't hold a Disguise while unconscious. He would have to make this quick. Plop down the plan, let them argue, get in a few comments of his own, and leave.

Pulling himself to his feet, Cassius double-checked his Disguise, then entered the main atrium. He approached the large stone staircase and looked up. His headache was bad enough, but now the nausea started to creep in. If he went up, he wouldn't be coming back down for a while, not unless he wanted to tumble down dozens of flights of stairs and either lose his Disguise or kill himself. What an unexciting way to go.

The sooner he got this moving, the sooner it could be put into action, the sooner the universe would cease to exist.

Who said he didn't have lofty goals?

The Wheel of Time, 2014

Proposition

They're here."

Rifun looked up from his desk. "Finally."

A few weeks, maybe a month. This was what Rifun might have expected when Cassius said there was a plan in the works. Three months later, now well into May or almost June, if his calculations were correct, Rifun had begun to wonder whether there would be any resistance if the Akarin did ever come calling. Sure, he'd asked for ninety days, but he never actually thought he'd get it.

He followed the Bat, who had been the messenger, as far as the main hub, then continued on alone. Perhaps it was the change in aesthetics that kept people sane. He had become more proficient and more comfortable with Building and had certainly spruced up the place. Barren, boring rooms were now decorated with stone and gardens and beautiful things. Some marketplaces had been converted into classrooms, though with the arrival of Micaiah, presumably to carry out this plan, they were now being evacuated so everyone could prepare for impending battle.

He had also experimented with portals, turning them inside out, or trying to. The sphere was familiar enough, but when he dared to put a hand, then a head through, he discovered that it led directly to the Core. Unfortunately, it was a direct shot to the endless abyss surrounding the Core and not the convenient platform off to one side.

However proficient he was, and whatever insights his experiments had given him, Rifun had always made sure to pretend to stumble on the portal rooms. He had divided the main portal room into several smaller rooms. The theory was that Engaged species could have permanent portals open and it would not inconvenience more fleeting, Unengaged species who simply came and went as the need arose. Unfortunately, for reasons that were stumping even his brilliant mind, he just couldn't get portals to reliably open, not like they used to, and it was too dangerous. Or that was what he told the Borelians and the Bat and the Day, anyway. He could tell they were starting to question him, either his abilities or his honesty. He didn't like being called a liar and having his integrity questioned, but he liked not being in Borelian slavery more.

There were no permanent doors or portals into the portal rooms, but it was easy enough to do since he had established anchor points on either side. He found Micaiah in the second room he checked, held down by a Tracker. The Trackers had been invaluable in bringing skilled Time Agents to the Wheel for Akari training, and a few had been kept here for the sole purpose of alerting them if anyone broke into the Wheel. At Rifun's appearance, the Tracker got off Micaiah, and he stood.

"Well, it's about time you stopped by," Rifun said. "We were beginning to worry about you." His gaze dropped to Micaiah's leg. Yes, it really was gone, cut off at the knee. "It looks like we have more in common than I expected. We really must sit down and catch up on old times."

"I'm here to—"

Rifun held up a hand. He wore a glove, not because he didn't think everyone knew about his missing fingers, but to conceal the results of his failed attempts to regrow them. At this point, he was just trying to get them back to the way they were before his experiments. "Now, now, you don't just walk into someone's house and start chit-chatting away. You say hello, take your shoes off, ask them how they are, and suggest that you go and sit in the living room or at the kitchen table. So, we've already said our hellos. I would tell you to take your shoes off, but that might be in poor taste." He saw Micaiah shift uncomfortably, expression irritated. "We can see visually how each other has fared recently. All that's left is to retire to another room and speak privately."

"Yeah? What did you have in mind?"

Rifun took Micaiah on a roundabout tour of the Wheel, showing off all the changes. Cobblestone streets and medieval towns, pleasant gardens, opulent mansions, marketplaces and classrooms. Most of the people had been evacuated by now, but some still lingered, most of them uninterested in the Akari but still willing to work without issue. They cleaned and tidied and reported any Building discrepancies in need of repair.

Their tour took them at last to the Judgment Wing. There, Micaiah was given a stamp which would allow him to go into the deeper Judgment Wing, but not out. Then it was a short walk down the hall where Rifun bypassed the holding cells and the formalities and instead took Micaiah straight to a judge. In the past, this would have been Gatekeepers, Wardens, and Dominion Timekeepers, but for the moment, it was a Grandfather.

"Everyone knows what you've done," Micaiah said, gesturing to the Grandfather. "Why do you still bother with the shrouds?"

"Small changes," Rifun told him, depositing him in the testimony box and stepping off to the side. "One thing at a time. We're in no rush. Have to make sure we do everything right the first time, right?"

Micaiah said nothing.

"Micaiah Durvin, Lieutenant Timekeeper, Quadrant One, Parsec Eleven, Sector Five, System Four, Planet Thirty-Eight, Region Four, District Four," the Grandfather recited, reading the information off a panel which had been transmitted from the stamp on Micaiah's hand.

"That is correct," Micaiah confirmed.

"You have been brought before this court, charged with treason. This carries a mandatory death sentence. Warden, do you have any thoughts?"

"Just one," Rifun said, stepping forward. He looked at Micaiah. "Why come back? Earth is such an insignificant place; you could have lived for a good decade or more before I came. You have a life, and a twin brother to look after. Why do you come here to your death?"

"I didn't come here to go to my death," Micaiah informed him. "I came to make a bargain."

Rifun grinned. Exactly as planned. "Ah. So the noble Micaiah Durvin does it again, able and willing to sacrifice what's left of him in order to protect those he loves. Some might say you have a Messiah complex."

"I demand a Time Trial."

Rifun paused and pretended to be stunned by such a bold declaration. Somewhere, a wandering thought said that people underestimated the value of taking even a few acting classes, and here he was, a professional actor.

Micaiah went on. "If I win, you leave Earth alone in whatever grand scheme of yours you have planned. Like you said, Earth is insignificant anyway. It would make no real difference whether we're Engaged or not."

Rifun folded his arms. That was the best excuse he could come up with? "And if and when you lose?"

"You've already pronounced me dead. So you get me, my Stake, and my

Testimonies."

"Who do you expect to call?"

"Micah will stand as my Stake. Walter, Tommen, and Doug will come as my Testimonies."

Even if Rifun didn't have an in through Cassius, the bait was so perfect that anyone could see this was a trap of some form. Time to press his hand a little. "I'll meet your bargain, and I'll even raise you."

"What more could you want?" Micaiah asked warily.

Rifun chuckled. "I want to know that this was a group effort and that you are all truly willing to sacrifice yourselves. If and when you lose, Doug will have his clock broken, Tommen and Micah will become my Apprentices, and you and Walter will be my personal servants. You will have your clocks broken in that you will never be able to use Time again, and you will swear a holy vow that you will serve me faithfully with no thought of treachery for the rest of your days." When Micaiah hesitated, he went on. "It's easy to die for a cause. It's much harder to live with the failure."

"Speaking from experience?"

"If you would have asked me six months ago, I might have said yes." He shifted his stance. "At any rate, we will need time to consider your proposal. As I am sure that you are tired and wish to get off your feet, I will allow you to do so. I'll even let you have your own cell. With recent housecleaning, quite a few have opened up."

Micaiah was taken away and Rifun returned to his office, but he found himself rather unsatisfied. Maybe this was akin to being so familiar with the machinations of stage and theater that it was impossible to enjoy anything while sitting with the audience. He understood the effects, the trap doors, the cues and lines. Everything was going precisely how they planned, because they had both planned it, even if Micaiah was unaware of the treachery. After a while, Rifun asked that Micaiah be brought to his office. Time to go off-script.

A couple guards brought Micaiah to the office, and Rifun went to meet him where he was ogling the decor.

"Do you like it?" Rifun asked. "The room?"

"It's an improvement," Micaiah answered diplomatically.

"I designed and built it myself. Much better than doom and gloom from a medieval dungeon torture chamber, wouldn't you agree?"

"Guess that depends on who you ask. Regardless if I'm thrown in a black cell or put up in a luxury resort, I'm still going to a Time Trial."

"Yes, this is true. And while you may think me a cruel, heartless bastard, I do try to make my guests comfortable. As such, I am offering you this one opportunity for last meal rights. Anything you want, from an olive with the pit still in, to a six-course gourmet meal from ten different worlds."

Micaiah raised a brow. "You mean there are still cooks left?"

"Time does many wonderful things, but we are still only human, are we not? You think we've been stuck in here for six months with no food?" Rifun grinned. "As I said, I am trying to be nice and offer you some sort of dignity."

"Rather macabre to be compared to dignity, isn't it? The last meal you expect I'm going to eat while in this universe. 'Dignity' does not even begin to describe it."

"Call it what you will, but either the next words out of your mouth are your order, or you can go back to the black cells with no food at all."

He told Rifun his meal order.

"Ah, and you'd like it just how your mother used to make it, right?" Rifun said pleasantly, nodding at a guard who ducked out of the room.

"No one could make it like she did," Micaiah informed him. "Not even me, not even Micah."

"Oh, I'm sure you can and do, but it's the psychology of it."

"So you brought me here to discuss the psychology of home-cooked, childhood meals?"

"Of course not." Rifun took a seat behind the desk and motioned for Micaiah to sit also. "I am here because you interest me."

"I believe you said something similar when we first met. Problem is, I know who you are now."

"Yes, but you have not yet answered one question to my satisfaction. Why did you come back? You demand a Time Trial, knowing that the success rate overall is only about thirty percent, and the rate for humans is only two percent. More than that, you are so new to your disability that you can barely fend off a Tracker. What in the galaxy is going through your mind right now? It's not as if I killed your father or some similar, overtired story arc."

"No, but you are a cruel and evil dictator, you and Cassius both, guilty of crimes against the universe, who think they can somehow impose their own order into a universal system of chaos. If anyone has a Messiah complex, it's you two."

Rifun grinned. So simplistic and naive. "Do you think Cassius would have really gone for all the redecorating I've done around here? Do you think he ever cared for art and beauty the way I do? Do you honestly think he ever had a plan for after he became the Zero Hour with such absolute authority? He was a bottom-feeder who got lucky. He was lucky only because I made his luck for him, even if he didn't realize it. He was a bloodthirsty bastard, true, but he was also an unstoppable weapon."

That was more true than he wanted to admit. More than once, Rifun had gone to the Core with the intent of reaching through the universe to kill the dragon and smite Cassius. After a few dozen sideways attempts, Rifun had at least managed to figure out how to focus on someone in the universe. He couldn't remember who he'd found, other than it wasn't Cassius. He also couldn't remember just what he'd found, but he knew it went beyond the three-dimensional material world. Coming from a regular person, it had been frightening.

"I always thought he was crazy, going on about the Akari," he went on, trying to keep himself in the present moment. "Until he demonstrated its power. Then, I knew I had to have it. It was impossible to work around him, so I decided to work through him. His little stunt through the Time Portal the first time threw things off, but with Julianna also out of the way, it created the perfect mixture of chaos needed to create the Dispersal. That was when I really tested him, sending him to slaughter as many adversaries as he could."

"And keeping him in as the Zero Hour gave you access to every aspect of Time," Micaiah said.

"Oh yes. When he told me about the journal, I knew that was our key to power. So we returned to the cave, but it was nowhere to be found."

"When you came back out, it was modern day. Since it was almost election time, you had to keep Cassius in the system, but Lily figured out that there was one Hand where it shouldn't have been. And you tried to kill her."

"She's dead now, though, so what does it really matter?"

"Cassius is dead, too, isn't he?"

Cassius was long dead. When Rifun had dared return to the Core and search him out one more time, somehow sending himself through that fourth dimension of the universe, he had found what should have been Cassius. But there was nothing. Just an empty, rotting husk. And the thing inside... Not even the memory-dampening inherent to the Core could make him forget the glowing eyes, the teeth, the claws, the black fire. And he hadn't returned to the Core since.

Rifun simply leaned back in his seat, using his professional acting skills to keep him calm in the eyes of his prisoner. "As I said, did he ever strike you as a Victorian kind of person?"

Micaiah shifted uncomfortably. "But here's one thing I don't understand. I thought you weren't normally given to monologues."

"When it reveals my evil schemes for the future. I have done nothing more than simply recite the past."

"So what is to prevent me from killing you here and now?"

"For the simple fact that you couldn't if you tried."

And he did try. Rifun would give him credit for putting up a valiant effort. In the end, Micaiah was left bruised and bloody and slightly disoriented, lying on the floor with no motivation to move. Rifun, kneeling with one knee on Micaiah's chest, stood and brushed his long hair out of his face. He took a step back and made a motion. A guard hauled Micaiah to his feet with one arm and set down his meal on the desk with the other.

"For the sake of your brother and your friends," Rifun said, "I hope you do a lot better than that at your trial." He looked at the guard. "Take him to the black cells."

Micaiah was taken away. Rifun glanced at the meal on the desk. Well, no reason to let it go to waste, and it did look appetizing. He was three bites in when the Bat entered the room.

"The summons have been sent," it reported. "All goes according to plan."

"Of course it does," Rifun said, "because it's barely begun. He is only the narrator, the lead-in, at this point. The show doesn't begin until the trial itself. Have you made those changes we talked about?"

"They are in effect."

"Good." He leaned back in his chair. "I am not sorry about not watching the event, but it is too bad I'm going to miss the big reveal." He took another bite, stared at the food and sighed. "I do feel a bit guilty about this, though. He was looking forward to it. Well, maybe before he goes out."

The Bat said nothing.

"In the morning, then, I suppose."

According to Cassius, the Akarin expected all of this to take place very quickly, between Micaiah breaking into the Wheel and when they were called to fight. They expected Rifun and Cassius to jump on the trial like starving dogs on a bone. But Rifun now made them wait, at least a day or two. On the one hand, it might make them nervous. On the other hand, it might make them complacent. Either one benefited him. The only way it might go sour is if the Akarin or one of their allies got too anxious about it and decided to attack early.

No such thing happened, however, and the following morning, Rifun headed to Micaiah's cell, breakfast tray in hand.

The black cells were, as one might expect, very dark. Throwing open the door and letting a bunch of light in, then, was enough to stun Micaiah and prevent any clever attacks.

"Room service," Rifun said sarcastically.

"You're feeding me?" Micaiah wondered, standing and limping toward him, in obvious pain, making sure to stand just out of arm's reach, suspiciously taking the tray which was held out to him.

"Time Trials are amusing, but only when the Accused actually tries to put up a fight and thinks he has a chance. There is more to be gained by an aspiring actor doing his best to win the stage, than a meager criminal sewn into the skin of a lamb and fed helplessly to the lions."

"I guess that's supposed to be an assurance that it isn't poisoned." He took a few steps back to sit and eat.

"If it had been up to Cassius, he would have killed you and sent out the summons to your friends to draw them here and kill them, too. No one would know, after all, what really happened. As far as anyone else would know, you'd simply failed the Time Trial and been subsequently executed. As for me, however, I am a man of my word."

"Here to strike a bargain with your dying and desperate prisoner, bringing food as a peace offering?" Micaiah sneered.

"I am not here to strike a bargain. I am the one holding all the cards. You brought the bargain to me, and what a bargain it is. I will admit, however, that I did have similar thoughts, especially when you named your Testimonies. You have already rejected me. Doug surely would, too. Tommen and your brother are the prizes to be won here, and your brother, I think it is safe to assume, slips from my grasp more and more with each passing day.

"But none of them would agree to anything if you were dead before the Time Trial even began. If they're going to agree to any bargain, best do it when they must honor a fair and square loss, hm? Besides, you may have guessed that life in the Wheel currently is very boring. I need the spectacle."

"How long have I been here?"

Rifun picked a bit of dirt from under his nails. "A day, perhaps. Maybe more. You're lucky that the Executioner's Block with the Pit was already constructed when you arrived, or else you might have been sitting here quite a while. As it is, you will be the first to test it out in such a fashion."

"The Executioner's Block?"

"A far more efficient model of governing, I think. Rather than taking up valuable time and space in the Coliseum, or the Theater as it is now called, simply make it a separate sport for those who enjoy such things, and leave the politics to those who care. Things are getting back on track quite nicely, I think. As I said, you will be the first to test out the new model. I'm quite excited."

"Thrilled, I'm sure." Micaiah finished the meager meal and set the tray aside. "So, the Day and the Bat are still around?"

"Oh yes, they are. You needn't worry yourself about that. Many things have changed around here, but your Time Trial will proceed just as all Time Trials have proceeded in the past." The man wanted to react to that statement. He was dying for a comment or a smirk, Rifun could tell. "You have six hours until your trial. Regretfully, we have yet to fill the prison chaplain's position, so you'll have to make peace with God by yourself."

"I'm not worried," Micaiah said.

"Ah, banking on that 'Greater love has no man' and all that? Tell me how that works out for you."

"You first."

It was the closest Micaiah got to admitting there was some plan afoot, as if anyone couldn't have guessed that already. Rifun left the man to the darkness and made for the main hub where the Bat had assembled a dozen guards.

"Are the others here already?" Rifun inquired. His real fear was that the Bat and the guards were here for him.

"Cassius sent a message that they are on their way," the Bat reported.

"No doubt going over last-minute details, ensuring everyone knows what they're supposed to do and what certain code words mean. I admire their tenacity and their confidence, I really do. But for all that, everything is ready on our end, correct?"

"The board is set. We need only the pieces."

"Your word choice is not lost on me, and it is a tad disturbing. But your point is taken. Very well, we shall wait for them to arrive."

To everyone's chagrin, it was almost an hour before they received the notice that there were intruders in one of the portal rooms, and Rifun was more than ready to get this mess over with. He led the guards through the Wheel and opened a portal into the room, the light momentarily stunning the occupants, giving Rifun a chance to examine and Test them.

Doug Templeton, Cassius in Disguise, as expected. Tommen Forbes, being played by Aklaq White Bear, also known as Kayla Durvin, Micaiah's wife. Well, that was sweet, wasn't it? And Walter Forbes, a facade for a man called Junior who was so riddled with cancer and disease that the last thing he could do in this life was go down in a blaze of glory. How noble.

And Micah, the ever-loyal younger twin brother. Except for the part where he wasn't. In Testing the rest of the group, he suddenly found himself staring at a fifth impostor. This was Micaiah, the lankier frame and in tact leg fading away into muscular bulk and a prosthetic. So, they had switched places. Because right now, Micah was the better fighter.

The moment of stunning light passed.

"Sorry we're late," Rifun said, entirely unapologetic. "Got a little caught up in the construction and rebuilding and whatnot. Moving things around, it tends to get confusing. You understand, right? It's a bit like moving into a new house, or even just remodeling. Wouldn't you agree, Walter?"

"I suppose," Junior-as-Walter answered cautiously.

"I have to admit, I'm a little surprised you showed up. After all, Akari-bearers aren't typically of the 'greater good' mindset. Micaiah came here to turn himself in and he offers me exactly what he knows I would want. But did he tell you that?"

"He's gambling the world," Cassius-as-Doug said pompously.

"He's gambling your lives. To save the world. It sounds noble and yet, I am forced to wonder if there is some ulterior motive. What's really going on in that collective head of yours? One Akari-bearer in custody, one whom I have pursued for decades, one who has only recently discovered his potential, one who has yet to believe, and one who still thinks it's a myth. Quite an entourage. Of course, I might expect some sort of failed assassination attempt or coup, but this is hardly the force I expected to deliver the blow."

"Akari-bearers aren't exactly the violent type either," Cassius-as-Doug told him. "You must have missed that day of class."

"Ah, such wit. I love it. And I'm sure I will also love whatever little plan you have for this trial later on. As you might expect, we don't get a lot of excitement around here these days. With that said, let's continue, shall we? Things to do, people to kill, planets to conquer."

Rifun turned. One of the guards lowered its voice. "Should we check them for weapons?"

"Check them for weapons? What for? Even if they do have a small arsenal hidden under their shirts, they'll never get very far. Or are you saying that your entire force is unable to handle five meager humans? Of course, look what happened the last time. Shall I call in a few more hands so we can get them safely to the Time Trial?"

"No, sir."

"That's what I thought," Rifun said coldly. "Bring them."

He gave the group a tour of the Wheel, much like had done with Micaiah. Instead of taking them to the Judgment Wing, he took them directly to the Pit. They walked around the rim of the structure to a staircase that would take them down into the arena. The Bat waited for them at the bottom of the stairs.

"The Bat?" Junior-as-Walter wondered anxiously.

"Of course," Rifun said, matter-of-fact. "Who else would I trust with such a job?"

"I didn't think you trusted anyone," Cassius-as-Doug said.

Rifun couldn't decide if his irritation was with the Doug facade or Cassius directly. "And I never thought you capable of loving anyone but yourself. But I digress."

That got the man a little flustered, and Rifun moved on. "So, this is how things are going to work from now until the trial actually begins. You will be taken to your own special holding cells to wait. Someone will be by to properly process you. I'm still working out the finer details of all the paperwork involved, so you will have to be patient. It is highly advisable that you answer all questions thoroughly and honestly.

"When everything is in place, you will be escorted from your holding cells to the appropriate place in the Pit. There will be the introductions, formalities, all that fun stuff that we all love to hate. I've thought about keeping it for nostalgia purposes, but I might scrap it after today. We'll see how things go. Then, after the formalities, we'll discuss how the trial is to proceed." Rifun gave "Micah" a look. "I don't know how much your brother told you about how Time Trials work, but just know that it will do you no good now."

He left the Bat to its duties and left the Pit.

Cassius had given him all the information about their little scheme, except for the part where the twins had switched places. Probably they hadn't told anyone. But it made sense. Micah was the better fighter now, having two good legs. And Micaiah was rumored to be a better shot, no doubt so he could take out him, Rifun, and Cassius. But was there more to it? Maybe he could poke and prod a little, see if he couldn't get the younger twin to let something slip.

He found a nearby secretary and sent orders ahead. By the time he reached his office, Micah-as-Micaiah would already be on his way. Indeed, Rifun had barely settled into one of the comfortable chairs in the room when the door opened. It was only a cook, delivering a tray of food to the desk. A minute later, Micah-as-Micaiah walked in.

Rifun watched him in the reflection from an object on the mantle. The room was impressive, yes, and the man couldn't help but stare. The only thing missing was the light haze of cigar smoke in the air.

"Cassius was the smoker, not I," Rifun said. He stood. "Though he preferred a pipe."

"Having second thoughts about killing him, are we?" Micah-as-Micaiah wondered.

Rifun went to his desk, sat down, and made a motion. "Please. Eat. I insist."

"Is it going to kill me?"

"Only one way to find out."

He was hesitant at first, but then his stomach won out and he was ravenous in his consumption.

"That's more like it," Rifun said. "Now I don't feel so bad about discussing business."

Micah-as-Micaiah swallowed. "What kind of business?"

"The business of your—how shall I say?—rescue? Conspiracy? I'm really not sure what to call it other than clever. In a normal Time Trial, it might have even worked."

His expression wavered. "This is a Time Trial, isn't it? Isn't the whole point of it to fight for my freedom?"

"Of course. According to some specific parameters. Your Testimonies, for example."

"What about them?"

"You named Tommen and Walter as your Testimonies, two of them anyway."

"Yes?"

"Except, they're not the ones who showed up. But they looked like them. It took me a little time to go back to the journal and do some research, but I think I found what they were doing. It's called a Disguise, isn't it?"

There it was. Micah was too new. He had no idea the real history between Micaiah and Rifun. He didn't know how any of this worked, not really. The best he could manage was, "I've heard of it."

"The one Disguised as Walter is Michael Junior, another rather prominent Akari-bearer, though a bit difficult to work with, am I right?"

"That's the nice way of putting it."

"Yes, it's too bad about his diagnosis. I'll bet that's why you chose him. He's dying anyway, so what difference does it make if it's today or a year from today?

"And then there was the other one. I found it a little hard to believe, but apparently it's a woman impersonating Tommen, did you know that? Aklaq White Bear. A decent Akari-bearer, true, and quite a looker, I must say. Though I have to ask, why bring her along?"

"Too few sixteen year old boys in the ranks; she was the only volunteer who could get Tommen's Disguise to fit her frame properly."

"Ah, so there are limits to it. A good thing to know. I shall have to write such an addendum when I am finished translating Richard's journal."

Micah-as-Micaiah tried to turn the subject away from things he did not understand. "What are you going to do to them?"

Rifun let him have his change of subject. "So far, I haven't done anything. The secretaries did their job processing them for the trial and brought the discrepancies to me for review." A lie, but oh well. "Needless to say, there has been something of a rain delay in the trial proceedings, but you brought that on yourself." He folded his hands together. "I thought of a number of things I could do. I could kill them, maim them, inflict other bodily harm upon them. I could throw them in the black cells, inflict some psychological harm on them. I could take you out to them, kill you in front of them, inflict some psychological harm on them and send them home, having made my point. Really, there are a number of things I could do, so I'll just leave most of it up to your imagination. But, do you know what I am going to do?"

"Clearly not."

"Yes, that's right, you've been locked up, haven't you?" He smirked. "I have decided that, in light of this rather irritating turn of events, I am going to do...nothing."

Micah-as-Micaiah raised a brow. "Nothing?"

"Let me rephrase, I am not going to expose them or harm them in any way thus far. Such a clever plan, one that might have slipped me by if I hadn't changed the rules of the trial just that little bit. I want to see how it's going to play out. Can they really pull off their Disguises and make me truly believe that they are who they pretend to be?"

"It's worked so far."

"Indeed. However, I cannot let this go completely unpunished. So we're going to change the stakes a little." He noted the man's discomfort and grinned. "Look at the wheels turning already. What am I going to ask, and how can he counter? How can he negotiate so that there is as little loss of life as possible? I like that. All right, here are the new terms. If you win, Earth remains insignificant and cut off from Time for good. Time, Akari, all of it, sealed off forever. You and your brother—and Doug, since he surprisingly appears to be the only honest Testimony this time around—return home. Mike and Kayla, however, stay here with me."

"No. They go home, too," Micah-as-Micaiah said firmly. "If Earth is to be sealed off, they will be of little threat to you."

"I have to punish them somehow. Besides, Mike is going to die anyway. Or is it that dear Kayla means something to you, but because you don't want to be thought of as playing favorites, you include Mike only as a courtesy?" While this would make sense for Micaiah to want to defend his wife, Rifun couldn't help but wonder if Micah might not be a little jealous. "Oh, now this does add a new layer to the game. All right, I won't make them stay here. But I'll tell you what will happen. Mike gets his clock broken up to the point where he's a drooling idiot. He won't even know he's dead until he's dead."

"And Kayla?"

Rifun leaned forward in his chair, resting his arms on the desk. "I get to fuck her in front of everyone. What's more, Isthim is going to be there. As a vodrak, she is capable of pushing all Borelian poisons, including the one for sexual arousal and stimulation. I'm going to fuck your girlfriend, and she's going to like it."

It was more of a taunt than a real threat. Rifun was no rapist. Still, it had the desired effect. And just like before, Micaiah—or Micah—was easy to put down.

"Those are the terms for if you win," Rifun stated. "Wait until you hear what happens when I win."

Micah spit at him, missed. Rifun blinked and dramatically wiped his face, his expression unreadable. Then his fist flashed out and caught Micah-as-Micaiah in the jaw. And he was speaking again. "When I win, you—and Walter still—are going to be my servant lackeys. I'm not going to break your clocks beyond your inability to perceive time because I want you to experience and remember everything you've done and failed at. Doug I haven't decided if I'm going to kill or make him a clock-broken lackey. Tommen and Micah are going to be my Akari Apprentices. Mike, I might just put him out of his misery. Throw him in the ring with the Bat, perhaps. And as for your girlfriend, well, fuck her enough times and eventually, maybe I won't need Isthim's influence."

He motioned for a guard who came to restrain Micah-as-Micaiah. Rifun couldn't help but admire the switch. Most Disguises were physically given away upon touch, but the twins had the advantage here. Even the differences in physique were slight enough that the rest of their shared genes just kind of blurred the discrepancies. Rifun might have been able to kick his leg and expose the prosthetic, but he would let them have their secret for now.

"Take him to the Pit," Rifun ordered the guard. "Lock him in the holding cell and retrieve the Day. When the First Grandfather arrives, begin the trial, whether I'm there or not."

"What are you going to be doing?" Micah-as-Micaiah hissed. "Hiding?"

"Being the master of the universe is a lot of work. You might have an idea of what it's like, running your own business. Managing personnel, overseeing supplies, advertising and reaching out to all your customers, it's hard work. I have a few deadlines to meet, so I'm going to go and get a little work done, then come and watch the end of the trial."

Rifun made a small motion, and the guard turned, jerking his captive along with him.

And just like that, the office was quiet. For as keen as he was about saving his own skin and not being assassinated, and for as much as he desired any excuse to not be at the Time Trial, Rifun was also unenthusiastic about not being there just to see how things were going. Maybe he could go in Disguise, just for a few minutes. No, he shouldn't tempt fate.

He wasn't even particularly worried about Micaiah and his band of merry men, or the Akarin. His greater fear was either the Bat or the Borelians. Or both of them together, wouldn't that be a nightmare? Isthim had come to his bed a few times over the last few months, though the ensuing pillow talk was less than cozy. She knew that he knew, and she just wanted to know when he was going to open the door for a new slave colony. The inquiries were almost polite at first, when he was still experimenting with the Building. Now, with the portal rooms divided, even feigned affection had dwindled to little more than rote duty just hovering over the first levels of hostility.

He'd set up a shrine in one corner of the room. There were no cardinal directions in the Wheel, so he could not definitively say it was in the northeast corner, but neither could he be accused of placing it in the southwest corner. There he bowed to pray.

People made many small choices every day, but in the end, fate was fixed. For most people. People who were not him. All of the threads converged on this point, but he could step outside of the moment and change it. His verbal prayers tapered off into silent ones, then slowly transitioned into quiet meditation. If the Seat of the Hands, now Rebuilt as an adapted recreation of a Malagasy village with an added amphitheater, were not such a target for any invading or defending forces, he might have gone there to pray instead. Granted, he himself was a pretty hot target for the Akarin, but it was harder to break into the Judgment Wing. He had also created a small portal room off this main office for just such emergencies.

His heart nearly stopped as the door opened, though it was hardly anything malicious.

"Faharoa." Sounded like a secretary. "The First Grandfather requires guidance."

Rifun sat up and twisted around to look but did not stand. "In what way?"

"The Accused of the Trial is performing poorly—"

"She wants to know if she has permission to give a mercy killing?" When the secretary did not reply, he sighed. "Offer the Accused one chance at surrender. He knows the bargain we made. The First Grandfather will oversee its execution if he accepts. Otherwise, the Accused may continue the Trial as is." It started to leave, but he called it back. "On your way out, tell the Hutch to bring out the stand. He'll know what that means."

The secretary made some gesture of affirmation, then ducked out as quietly as it had come.

The Akarin had come to kill him. They had concocted this entire ridiculous scheme around him being present at the Time Trial. He and Cassius had done everything they could to thwart such plans, but they still needed the Akarin to blow their cover and sacrifice the element of surprise. Give them a decoy to shoot, let them be the ones to initiate battle. They were still alone in the Pit with a host of Grandfathers. Even if the Grandfathers turned on each other, the Borelians versus non-Borelians, there was still a sizeable enough force to take care of five little humans, to say nothing of the Bat and the Day.

After another moment of consideration, he stood and stretched. It wouldn't be long now. Micah or Micaiah couldn't be doing too well. Even if they were feigning fatigue or injury in order to entice Rifun to come to the Pit, they couldn't keep up the fighting forever. And that was just against the Bat and the Day. Start a fight with the whole of the Cult, well, what were they expected to do? Run away, their part was done?

Rifun made several laps of the room. Give it a few minutes, and then...

"Faharoa!" The guard's voice carried through the wall even before the door was flung wide open. "Faharoa, the Accused and his entourage have rebelled! Fighting has broken out!"

"And now we separate the loyalists from the traitors," Rifun stated calmly. He made a motion. "Come with me."

Fighting may have broken out in the Pit, but the rest of the Wheel was still eerily calm. Months of planning, figuring out who was who, where their loyalties truly lay, what abilities they might possess, and arranging for certain people to be in certain places. Rifun did not believe in blanket executions, and Cassius' absence had given him plenty of time and ability to sift through the Cult ranks and everyone who had been captured during the coup.

By the end of the day, their numbers might be fewer, but their loyalty would be unbreakable.

He sent the guard ahead to gather more forces and clear the way into the Pit. By the time he arrived, fighting had come to a standstill. Bodies littered the ground here and there, Grandfathers and secretaries and guards. He spied Micaiah and Aklaq and the rest of the merry men, even Cassius, still in his Doug Disguise, just waiting for the cue.

"My, my, my, what have we here?" Rifun wondered casually, looking around. "I knew Time Trials were exciting, but I never imagined they could get this exciting. We really should do this more often, I think. But then, that isn't what you hoped to accomplish here, is it, Micaiah?" He looked at him. "Micah? You and all your little friends came here for the sole purpose of assassinating me and bringing my empire to a glorious end."

"That was the idea, yes," Aklaq said matter-of-factly.

"Had we the time, I would be interested to know what you take me for. An overconfident fool, perhaps? Do you think I haven't anticipated that such attempts might come to pass? Do you think that some haven't already tried to kill me with no obvious success?"

"You ever think that you talk too much?" Micah told him.

"Ah, yes, I have always been given to monologues. But if a monologue conveys no information—such as a dastardly scheme or vile threats—is it still a monologue, or just a man talking to himself? If so, does that make me the fool regardless? But I digress. Your little revolution was fun and interesting to watch, and it told me who my dissenters are, so if they will kindly remove all shrouds and other disguises?"

Grudgingly, false and turncoat Grandfathers, guards, and secretaries removed all remaining evidence of their disguises and get-ups.

"That's better," Rifun said. "Makes it much easier when you know who you're trying to kill and can see them. So then, this is how this is going to play out. I already gave you one chance to surrender. Clearly, you have no such interest. Similarly, I have no reason to think you won't try this ever again, or that friends and family will not attempt something similar if I send you home alive, even with your clocks broken. Therefore, these guards and Grandfathers here, they will be coming down to kill you all. And I am going to end this madness once and for all."

"There will always be more," Cassius-as-Doug cut in, though it was hard to tell who was really speaking.

"Perhaps. But not today." Rifun took a step back and let the Grandfathers advance. "At your leisure."

He left the Pit.

That was the cue for "Doug" to open the portal for the Akarin forces to break in and run right into an ambush. In the initial chaos, there would be plenty of deaths from friendly fire. Fighting would become too congested for the Pit and it would spread through the rest of the Wheel.

Rifun had asked for the live capture of Micaiah and Aklaq, though this was a dubious proposition at best. They would be brought to the Judgment Wing where they would go with him to the Arhives and either aid him in killing the dragon or die trying.

Rifun was just about to enter the Judgment Wing when something hit him in the back. It was not a blow as from a fist or a weapon, or anything physical. Rather, this was more like a pulse that reverberated through him. A shadow seemed to darken the room though the light remained constant. He turned just in time to see smoke billowing out of the portal to the Pit. Even with, or perhaps because of, his odd vision, he knew it was not ordinary smoke. This was formed by shadow and laced with lightning. It was nebulous and yet carried a distinct form. It had limits as it wafted out of the Pit, a singular entity rather than something continuous as from fire.

The billow turned, as if by conscious will, and Rifun could have sworn there were eyes within the shadow, piercing red. He had seen those eyes before, when he used the Core to try and find Cassius. His heart seized with fear and he squeezed his eyes shut.

"Not quite."

Rifun nearly came out of his skin as something spoke behind him, and yet he found himself paralyzed with terror, too afraid to look at the beast or do much more than tilt his chin up as if to avoid the sulfurous breath.

"Not quite," it repeated. "You know I am not killed so easily. And a puppet cannot kill its master."

"I'm coming for you," Rifun said, searching his mind for any scrap of courage and will to even look at the dragon, never mind what he thought he was going to do to wound it, much less kill it. He could feel its looming presence, a far too big creature in a far too small space.

The dragon hissed something like a laugh, making Rifun gag on more sulfur. "Here I am."

Like a rubber band snapping, Rifun whirled around, fist flying wildly like an amateur boxer but meeting only empty air.

"I'll be waiting," a faint hiss echoed.

The lingering shadow vanished, the light in the room seeming to return to normal, if indeed it had ever changed. No one in the vicinity seemed to have noticed anything amiss, and more and more fighting was spilling into the area.

He jumped again as something grabbed his arm. He spun around and just caught himself before he struck Isthim.

"Cassius is dead," she told him.

"I know," he found himself saying. "And the Bat or the Day, too, right?"

"The Day." She sounded surprised that he knew.

"Good. Two down, one to go."

She grunted, but they were suddenly separated by some large, disgruntled alien. It appeared to be focusing more on Isthim at the moment.

Another wave of fear gripped Rifun and he hurried into the Judgment Wing. He wasn't sure why other than that was the plan. But there was no plan now. Cassius was dead. But the dragon wasn't. Worse, the dragon had come right up to him, stood right behind him, taunted him, and he had frozen. He couldn't even look at the thing, never mind fight it. He flexed his hand, emotions swinging from aggravated frustration that demanded physicality to release, to knee-knocking fear that wanted only to run and hide.

In the end, with the battle raging just outside the Judgment Wing, he retreated deeper into the wing, all the way back to his office. He was not afraid necessarily, though he was, but more frustrated. At himself.

The dragon had gotten away. Cassius was dead. But it was a physical death at the hands of physical men with physical weapons. It had done nothing to stop the real horror controlling him. It was like curing a disease by killing the patient. Now the dragon was going to disappear, find someone new to inhabit and wreak havoc, and come for him. It had said that it would be waiting, but Rifun wasn't going to play that game. He needed to bring the dragon into his playing field, his advantage. Except he had done exactly that. He had every advantage here. He'd had the dragon right there. And he'd frozen. He should be going to the Core now, to search for the ethereal dragon before it could indwell someone else. But just the thought was enough to stop his heart, and he continued on his current path.

He retreated to his office and poured himself a drink. If there was any good news, it was that without Cassius and the evils of the dragon, he could expect an easier victory. The dragon could not augment Cassius' ruthlessness, nor assist the Borelians. The Author was the only thing left, and she would sweep away the Borelians and the Akarin and forever cement the Cult as the Akari authority in the universe.

He wanted to believe this, but it could not overpower the more deeply-rooted belief that the Cult had crossed a line here, and this was their undoing. Then the Bat entered the room, and he knew that any hope of a Cult victory was gone. He stood from his chair and turned. Just by the look on the creature's face, Rifun knew what was about to happen.

"Have we won?" he inquired innocently.

"Hardly. The Akarin are too numerous, too powerful. Your playthings are on their way here. Isthim will attempt to hold them off."

Playthings. Like Cassius, the Bat did not understand the art of strategy, blackmail, or mercy. Or entertainment. He would have just killed Micaiah and the others and been done with it. Like he was about to try with Rifun.

Rifun sat back down, still keeping an eye on the Bat in the reflection from the mantle. "Well then, I won't deny them their prize." He grabbed his drink, his second only, untouched for...how long now? "Would you like to be present for it? Or are you just going to kill me and be done with it?"

"Your petty factions mean nothing to me." The Bat could move heavily when it wanted to, and now it did so deliberately, approaching Rifun's shrine. "Your petty gods are nothing." It turned to face him. "Your gods and Cassius' gods are all the same."

"Yes, he told me something similar. But if that were the case, why fight me?"

Before the Bat could answer, the door opened again and Micaiah and Aklaq barged in.

"Okay, we're here," Micaiah said, breathing heavily. "Now where is Rifun?"

"Oh, don't worry about me," Rifun said. "Though if you'd done any sort of preliminary search of the room, you might have noticed me." He leaned forward to set his glass on the table, still untouched. "I'd wondered how long it would take you to beat your way in here. Do you want to know what I came up with?"

Micaiah took a step forward. "Rifun Ndolo, for the charges for treason against the Hands of Time—"

"Three hours, forty-one minutes, and twenty-two seconds." Really he just made that up. He had no idea. "I must say, it is a bit disappointing. Personally, I was betting more on an hour, maybe two if the fighting got really bad. But really, I expected more from you, especially since Banding is fully within your capabilities."

"—and crimes against the universe, including coup, holocaust, unlawful imprisonment and enslavement, unauthorized used of Time, and misrepresentation of the Akari—"

" 'Misrepresentation of the Akari'? I beg to differ, and I had no idea that was a crime recognizable by the Laws of Time."

"—I, Micaiah Durvin, Lieutenant Timekeeper from Quadrant One, Parsec Eleven, Sector Five, System Four, Planet Thirty-Eight, Region Four, District Four, and Core Akari-bearer, hereby arrest you. Seeing how there seems to be a lack of proper justice system and due process—"

"And the fact that the Grandfathers work for me anyway."

"—and because I'm sure no one will put up too much of an objection, I will also act as judge, jury...and executioner. Rifun Ndolo, I sentence you to die."

The Bat took that moment to move, crashing into Micaiah like a truck.

"I'm sorry," Rifun said, "but did I say that I was ready to surrender? You and Walter have worked together for far too long, I think; you're starting to act like him. It's not bad until you start to look like him, but this is pretty darn close." He cautiously approached, keeping one eye on the Bat. "You know, this is all starting to look very familiar. Where have I seen this before? Ah, yes, the warehouse. Except it was Walter beneath my shoe instead of you."

"I was thinking the same thing," Micaiah said.

"Oh, good, so we both know what's going to happen."

"You're going to send one of your minions to distract us while you get away, or that's what you're going to try to do."

"Tell me, have you ever heard the definition of insanity? It's where you keep doing something the same way over and over again, expecting a different result each time. My problem last time came only when I did not stick around to make sure that Walter died. Between you and me, though, I'm glad he didn't. He's too much fun. You, however, I have no problem with killing."

Rifun got within six feet of them and stopped. "So, here's how this is going to work. I'm going to go into the next room—"

Micaiah made a sudden move then, trying to Band and get in a strike. Rifun saw the knife and quickly countered, breaking Micaiah's wrist, taking the knife, twisting the man around, and stabbing him. He wiggled enough to avoid a spine shot, but kidneys were still a vital organ. He made a small noise and sank to his knees when Rifun released him. Micah knelt beside him.

" 'Tis but a scratch," Micaiah said hoarsely, sitting back on his seat.

Micah went after Rifun, then, raising his arm to strike, but Rifun caught him easily and soon had him pinioned, cheek pressed against the wall.

"That was very rude," Rifun said. "From both of you. You interrupted me. Now then, as I was saying, I'm going to go into the next room. Things are going to get very violent and very messy, and I would just be in the way. You understand. You're going to be facing off against an old friend of yours. Too bad your brother got injured beforehand, because you could have really used him, I'm sure. So, I guess it'll just be you alone against the Bat."

"The Bat?" Micah huffed, trying to breathe as Rifun leaned heavy against him.

Rifun let the man go and turned to leave. There was every chance the Bat would aid them in coming after him instead, but maybe, just maybe, with that thought in their minds and their attention diverted, they would go after the Bat first and take its attention.

His gamble paid off. The Bat was quickly distracted by the twins and Aklaq, giving Rifun ample opportunity to slip into the side room which was just a small portal room for emergency exits. If this didn't qualify as an emergency, he didn't know what would.

Though it was a portal room, it still had the same elegant decorum as the rest of the office. He took half a moment to give it one last, longing look. As he clawed open a portal, first to Earth, then a second to the Ruins of Meroian, he couldn't help but wonder, *Why?*

kokumbo

Every move the Akarin planned, Cassius took back to Rifun and Isthim. Every time the Akarin installed a fail-safe to bolster the standing and chances of success of the twins and the others, Cassius, Rifun, and Isthim changed some aspect of the Time Trials to maneuver around it. It was perhaps the first time that planning something actually felt satisfying.

By the time he walked into the bakery the night they were supposed to launch their rescue mission, he felt on top of the world. Or the universe as the case may be. He barely bothered with formalities as he knocked on the door of the office and let himself inside. Micah and Aklaq sat at a small round table in one corner of the room.

"Evening, Micah, Kayla," he greeted.

"Doug," Micah acknowledged. Aklaq just nodded once, looking annoyed.

"I know I'm early, but I wanted to make sure we're all on the same page. Has anything new come about?" Not that there were likely to be any major changes at this point, but you never know.

"Well, Tommen's message was intercepted."

Cassius-as-Doug raised a brow. "By whom?"

"Tommen."

He turned to see the teenager standing just behind him. "Oh. So you know what's going on?"

"Vaguely," Tommen answered.

"He's not going," Micah clarified. "We were trying to keep him out of this entirely, but apparently we weren't thorough enough. Either way, neither he nor his dad are going to be part of this."

"I agree," Cassius-as-Doug said solemnly.

Tommen blinked and folded his arms. "No."

"What do you mean, no?"

"Tommen, I can see that you're a good kid and ready and willing to help in any capacity. But that's not going to happen, not here, not this time. You're going to stay here and wait for our return." Once everyone else was dead, Cassius was going to come back and murder Rifun's little pet.

"But—"

"That's final. I am the one in charge here, so you listen and report to me, got it?"

Tommen sighed and rolled his eyes. "Fine."

"Let me hear you say it."

"Yes, sir, I understand."

"Good."

They took a few minutes to go over what was expected of a Time Trial, and spent a few more minutes speculating all the ways it could have changed.

"We can only assume that Micaiah's trial is rigged to be completely unwinnable," Cassius-as-Doug said. It took every ounce of self-control, little though he had, to maintain a serious expression. "Or else, it's rigged in such a way that even if he does 'win' that he still won't really win, or walk away unharmed at least."

Aklaq and Micah murmured their agreement.

"And how exactly were you planning to kill Rifun?" Tommen folded his arms and shifted his stance.

"Element of surprise," Aklaq replied. "We smuggle the gun in using a Disguise. Stake and Testimonies are brought in first, then the Hands, Grandfathers, and the Accused. We have to expect that Rifun will be expecting some sort of assassination, escape, what-have-you, but maybe not so soon. As soon as Rifun enters the arena, as soon as Micah has a shot, he takes it."

"Sounds...risky."

"We only get one shot," Micah said. "After that, the jig is up, and we either make a hasty exit or else we're all dead. There is no middle ground."

"And it will likely only make it harder to get off any more attempts in the future," Cassius-as-Doug went on. "Fool me once, shame on you, and it'll be hell trying to get in a second chance."

Tommen nodded. "I could see that happening. You know, becoming difficult."

"No matter what, though," Aklaq said, "we're not leaving without Micaiah, or else we're going to die trying."

"So, that's it?"

"Were you expecting more?" Cassius-as-Doug wondered.

"I don't know, it's just..."

"Too straightforward for you? Were you expecting some stealthy spying, political intrigue, secret assassinations, and a quiet change of power? And maybe a few women in there, too?" When Tommen blushed, he went on. "Life isn't like the movies, Tommen, at least not all the time. Some things really are as simple as they sound."

They could be simpler, but those like Rifun insisted on making them difficult.

"So, does all this mean that you're going to lift the Suppression?" Tommen wondered.

Cassius-as-Doug nodded and did just that. Make the kid think he had a chance to escape when Cassius came for him later. Tommen's expression shifted into one he'd witnessed many times in the black cells, the light bursting into the room and the prisoner unsure what to do with it.

"You're a quick study," Micah told Tommen. "Don't forget that you're more apt to pick up things under pressure. If you do something you didn't know you could do, don't let yourself get stunned by it; it could cost you. Simply accept it and move on. Your life is at stake."

Tommen nodded. "I understand."

In the main room, the service bell dinged. Cassius thought the kid was going to go through the roof as he hurried out to deal with a customer.

"He wouldn't last two minutes," Cassius-as-Doug stated. "It's a good thing I'm going and he's not."

"He kept his head while we were escaping the Wheel," Micah said, "but I'm not disagreeing."

Aklaq frowned and stood. "I think I should have a word with him."

"About what?"

"Just to reassure him that we're coming back."

"Aklaq, we don't know that. What we're doing, it's a long shot."

"Maybe, but he still needs the assurance in the here and now."

"Well, tell him to make sure he takes the trash out. Just because I'm not here doesn't mean he can slack off."

She gave him a look and left the office, closing the door quietly behind her.

"Ready to get your brother back?" Cassius-as-Doug asked of Micah. "Or die trying, anyway?"

"No, but yes," Micah sighed.

Cassius-as-Doug nodded. "I wish my own brothers had been so willing to fight for me."

"I thought you only had one brother?"

That gave Cassius pause. How many brothers did Doug have? Were they even alive? He couldn't remember and tried to wave it off. "I speak as much of metaphorical brothers as blood ones. Brothers in arms."

"Oh."

The younger twin's mind was too focused on the impending trial to worry about such discrepancies and oddities. True, this impersonation wasn't intended to last past this trial, but Cassius didn't need to trip over the finish line.

Aklaq returned from whatever pep talk she gave Tommen. Not long after, the office door opened again and a man they all knew as Michael Junior walked in, Tommen trailing uncertainly.

"Junior, we were starting to get worried," Cassius-as-Doug said.

"I wouldn't have been late," was all the man said to that.

"Tommen, this is Mike Junior," Aklaq introduced. "He'll be impersonating your dad during the trial."

To make a point of it, Junior donned a perfect Disguise of Walter. Tommen went pale though he tried to play tough.

"Pleasure to meet you, Tommen," Junior-as-Walter said

"I'm not going to lie, that freaks me the fuck out. Is there any way to tell the difference?" Tommen asked.

"Mannerisms, mostly," Aklaq answered. "There are a few other ways to tell, but we can't go over them at this moment."

"Should have been here earlier," Micah told Junior. "Could have gone over the plan one more time."

Junior dropped the Disguise. "Yeah? You're one to talk. Little Johnny-Come-Lately over here." He shook his head. "Still don't get why your brother didn't bring you in on this sooner."

Before Micah could come back with a sharp reply, Aklaq stepped in. "It doesn't matter now. You volunteered to help us, Junior, so you can at least take this seriously—"

"I do," Junior protested.

"—and when we get Micaiah back, you can ask him why he chose to withhold information from Micah. Until then, we have a job to do."

The man sighed dramatically. "What time is the trial?"

"Nine-eleven," Cassius-as-Doug answered. "I'd be willing to bet he chose that time for a reason."

"Well, be that as it may, is there a bathroom around here I can use beforehand? Nothing worse than running into pants-pissing terror and actually pissing your pants."

Micah gave him brief directions and saw Junior out the door with a glare to his back. "Maybe take the stick out of his ass, too, while he's at it."

It was nine-ten before Junior returned to the office, to the chagrin of all others gathered.

"I wouldn't have been late," was all he said.

Aklaq rolled her eyes. Cassius-as-Doug put up a Band.

"Does anyone have any final questions?" he asked, a tad impatient. "Once we don our Disguises and step through the portal into the Wheel, that's it. No more talk, no more questions."

He waited about thirty seconds, then nodded solemnly. "Then may the Author write us each a happy ending."

He handed Micah the gun intended to kill Rifun, Disguised as a pocketknife. Inanimate objects were generally easier to Disguise than living things with constant bodily processes and were more forgiving in what it took to expose them. The Disguise probably would come off after being under Micah's sweaty arm for an hour or two, but that hardly mattered. Cassius knew what was going on, so did Rifun. They weren't doing anything that had not already been anticipated and preemptively countered.

"Here we go."

Cassius took over the majority of the portal, both because Doug would believe himself the strongest and most capable of doing so, and because he really was the strongest and most talented one here when it came to breaking into the Wheel. He'd only been doing it on a weekly or bi-weekly basis for several months now. He just had to make sure no one passed out and lost their Disguise. He and Rifun were aware of the plot, but there was no reason for the group to get caught, almost literally, with their pants down.

Then they were through. In those first few moments, standing there in the empty portal room, the first priority was the Disguises. They got only a few seconds to check themselves and each other and get their bearings before light spilled into the room and Rifun entered with a dozen armed guards. All exactly as planned.

Cassius had come up with the idea of having a guard suggest they be searched for weapons and Rifun shoot it down. The apparent display of arrogance or self-confidence would only bolster the group's hope that things would turn out well. The bigger they are and all that. Rifun had been hesitant. Even if he wasn't going to be there to actually get shot, he still worried about the panic the shot would cause. It was the cue for an attack. Regardless of this plot interception, the Akarin still had control over the situation, albeit just barely. He relented when Cassius made the point that if the weapon was found, it could spring the attack early if the rest of the group got aggressive with the guards in the portal room. It would be easy enough to kill the group, but they needed to get the Akarin in the Wheel, and this was the plan they were expecting to do just that.

They were not searched. The gun Disguised as a pocketknife was not found. The guards escorted them into the Wheel, Rifun at the head.

But, of course, Rifun couldn't just take them to the Pit for the trial. No, he had to play tour guide and show off his interior renovation. Good grief. If there was any chance of any of them surviving, Cassius might have suggested Rifun and Aklaq go into business together. He could build the exterior and she could design the interior. Match made in fucking heaven.

"Everyone in the universe would like to believe themselves special," Rifun was saying to some provocative comment someone had made. "—that somehow they will be the ones to make a difference. Somehow they will be the ones remembered. Battle is naturally bloody, coups no different. And there are plenty of pawns to go around. Those who survive may be useful, and use them I have. Others have been executed. It is the nature of war. And history is written by the victors."

"You are not the victor," Cassius-as-Doug cut in, "not unless the Author says so. And what fate awaits you if you are not the victor the Author intended?"

Rifun turned on him, stance rigid, gaze fixed. They locked eyes for a long moment. Rifun thought he meant to attack when really Cassius just wanted to move this along. They had a Time Trial to get to. Stop stalling and get this show on the road. After a minute or two of crackling tension, Rifun relaxed. He backed down from his threatening pose, but kept his gaze firmly locked on Cassius-as-

Doug. "If your body and your abilities are as strong as your convictions and as quick as your tongue, you may have a shot at surviving the trial to come."

That goes both ways, Cassius thought. But it got them moving anyway.

"What was that?" Micah hissed seriously. "You could have gotten us killed before we even got started."

Before Cassius could answer, Rifun beat him to it. "Fear not, young Durvin. You were never in any danger. Yes, I considered ordering him beaten or some such thing, but then I decided that watching you struggle in vain in the Time Trial would be far more rewarding. And who knows, maybe I will be pleasantly surprised if you do manage to win and pull this off today. Things get boring quickly when they always go your way."

Cassius wasn't sure who his comment was intended for, but he got the feeling that it was him. If it was, he wasn't sure what "victories" or "everything going your way" was referring to. Their victories were few and far between, assuming they could even be called victories. They were lucky and enormously consequential, even fragile, not calculated and built upon smaller victories and so hedged against cataclysm caused by the most minor inconvenience. Fuck, he sounded like Rifun now. Or worse, Doug.

They reached the Pit, the darkness closing in around them like a blanket until it was little better than a partly-cloudy twilight. Micah, who had been a clumsy, nervous wreck the whole walk, tripped and stumbled multiple times walking around the rim to the staircase that would deliver them to the arena. Cassius looked around, trying to look serious and analytical. Doug would be looking for clues and advantages and weaknesses to exploit.

Except he and Rifun and Isthim had already prepared for such weaknesses. The Pit itself was its own physical deterrent, but just in case, they'd set up a system similar to the Judgment Wing. Cassius did not understand the technology, but only those with special stamps—which became embedded in the skin so they couldn't simply be wiped away—could pass through a force field. Some stamps permitted two-way passage, others only one-way. Not having a stamp, or a one-way trying to pass back through, would be electrocuted, if not fully incinerated.

The Bat was the one tasked with doling out the stamps and ushering them through the force field, through the tunnel, and into the arena. As one might expect, the group on Trial was given one-way stamps. They were not expected to survive, and this, in theory, prevented their escape. From the arena, the group was separated, each to his own cell. This was to prevent conspiracy among those on trial.

Every step the Akarin took with this plan, the Cult took care to take back two or even three more. From his vantage, Cassius could see Micah in a cell on the other side of the arena, though he could not say what he was doing, nor could he see the others. That also meant, however, that they could not see him.

It wasn't thirty seconds after his arrival in the cell that the door opened again and a secretary walked in. He did not know the species name off-hand. It was humanoid, covered in orange-ish fur, and its jaw jutted out and almost upward, as if it just dropped food down into a hole rather than bring it to a mouth to chew. It had four fat fingers and a tail that did not look like it belonged on this animal but had been stolen from somewhere else.

The thing offered him a translator, but Cassius waved it away. It looked uncertain but did not push. Instead it turned its attention to a digital tablet in its...hand? Paw?

"I am here to process you," it stated. "I will require your DNA."

Cassius-as-Doug grinned and held out a hand. "Let's start with that, then."

The secretary did not react as it prepared the tablet to receive a DNA sample. They rarely reacted, the secretaries. According to Rifun, many were just fine with resuming their normal duties, and some even enjoyed the change of pace and not having to cater to the whims of the Hands and the stupidity of the markets. Cassius could not say for sure, but he imagined this one here might be a tad nervous. The anxiety soon became more obvious as it took three different DNA samples.

A Disguise would trick the eye, make a few surface changes, but this simple type would not change who lay beneath. If the secretary had regular skin instead of fur, Cassius would have expected it to go completely white. As it was, the best it could do was wide eyes and an odd, low-tone sound coming from the hole that passed as a mouth.

Cassius-as-Doug put a finger to his lips. "We know what's going on here. We're in control. Do you understand?" The secretary nodded wordlessly and put its tablet away. "Good. Now then, go over to the Bat there, get the two-way stamp from it, and bring it here. You understand why."

The secretary nodded again and, still saying nothing, left the cell, somehow more lifeless and robotic than when it entered.

It was a while before it returned, wiping the one-way stamp off his hand with a special cloth that removed all the little digital bits that would set off the electrocution part of the force field.

"One of the other secretaries has been doing the same to the others," it said, not looking at him, instead fixing its gaze on the two-way stamp and carefully pressing it onto the back of his hand. "Are you all impostors?"

Yes, but not in the way this secretary thought. Cassius examined the new stamp. "No." He looked at the secretary. "But don't tell anyone."

"But that is dishonest. It is nearly treason."

"And it would be, if we didn't know about it."

The secretary was silent but still appeared anxious.

"Why don't you go out and make a list of all the secretaries doing it?" Cassius suggested. "And anyone else who is helping them? Once this Time Trial is over, we're going to be looking for such blatant sympathizers. Do you understand what I'm asking?" After a moment, the secretary nodded. "Good. Now then, I think that's all you need from me. Right? That's what I thought. Go on, now. Make that list, then find somewhere safe to sit and hide. If you manage to catch a moment with Faharoa, give him the list and maybe he'll even send you home. You don't want to be here for this."

Again, if the alien had normal skin, he would have expected it to be stark white. The best it could do was nod and stiffly exit the cell. Maybe it would make a list, maybe not. He didn't really care, and he didn't expect Rifun would either, honestly. Just as long as it didn't blab to the others about his Disguise, that was the important thing. So maybe they had overlooked a couple small details. Could they have overlooked anything else? Well, if they had, it obviously wasn't important.

And besides, it wasn't the end of the world if they could get in and out of here. That was just a buffer, an extra measure. Nothing about their plan hinged on the others not being able to escape the Pit because of the stamps and the force field. The frenzy of battle would do that well enough.

Another secretary came by for one last review before the Trial. If it knew of his Disguise, it gave no indication.

The cell door opened, and Cassius-as-Doug was led into the arena. When they had entered, it would have been too kind to call it a ghost town. Now it was packed, as one might have imagined the Roman Coliseum of old would have been at its peak, gladiators fighting wild beasts. The audience today was comprised of mostly Grandfathers, though there were a fair number of guards and a handful of secretaries. Most were Cult, but some were of questionable loyalty, and their actions today would force them to either choose a side or show their colors.

Four platforms had been erected in the arena. One was for Micah, the Stake, and the other three were for the Testimonies. Each one was roughly six by six feet, plain and boxy with little flourish, the same black stone as everything else. The Stake platform was a good ten feet high, while the rest were only about four feet high. Each one had similarly plain, boxy stairs leading to the top. At the top of each one was a chair and a manacle for their ankles. Cassius-as-Doug put up a slight bit of resistance, enough to be believable to the others, but nothing like he could have done. His manacle was different anyway, or it was supposed to be, easier to escape than the others once his cover was revealed.

It had been an oddly smooth collaboration between Cassius and Rifun to elevate the Stake's platform so high. If it had been kept low, there would have been no real chance to get off a clean shot at Rifun. In making it taller, however, it was taunting them, daring them to take the shot. Handing over the best shot possible on a silver platter and then snatching it away. Cassius-as-Doug glanced up at Micah to see if he had realized the shot he had, but Micah and the others were too busy trying to figure out something of a backup plan. This was not going the way they had wanted.

Before anyone could say anything, the Bat entered the arena. In the stands, where the Grandfathers waited, Isthim stood up from among them, the First Grandfather, and threw back her hood.

"This is the Time Trial of the Grandfathers and Faharoa Rifun versus Micaiah Durvin," she announced, her voice carrying across the entire Pit. "Bring forth the Accused."

From a spot opposite the Bat, the Day emerged, Micaiah limping badly before it. He looked awful, and Cassius wouldn't deny he was surprised by it. He had honestly expected Rifun to give him a luxury suite, catered gourmet meals or buffet, and maybe let him have an aromatic bath beforehand. As it was, he looked dirty, smelly, probably spent some time in the Judgment Wing, maybe been in a few fights already as a warm-up. He gimped his way to a marked spot and faced the Grandfathers.

"Your name," Isthim commanded.

"Micaiah Durvin."

He looked terrible, but his spirit appeared unbroken. A second later, an unearthly sound ripped through the air, startling even Cassius. Looking around, it appeared to have come from the Bat who took several menacing steps toward Micaiah. The Day did the same from the other side.

"Enough!" Isthim snapped. "What is the meaning of this?"

"The Akari has been used," the Day growled, and the Bat hissed in agreement.

"Has it?" Isthim did not seem impressed. "Well then, I imagine you are going to have your work cut out for you, a little challenge during combat. I would hate to see him lose too badly."

She carried on with whatever formalities and rote bullshit she and Rifun had cooked up, but Cassius did not pay it any mind. Instead, he focused on the Bat and the Day. Had it been an act, a way of intimidating Micaiah? They weren't stupid, they knew plenty about the Akari, what it was, how it was used. They'd been around for a very long time, it wasn't as though anything came as a real surprise to them. So why the overreaction? Cassius mentally shook his head. It had to be an act, some form of intimidation. Nothing else made any sense.

The rules of the Time Trial were announced, not that it mattered. Even when Isthim announced the players in this rigged game, she still used their Disguised names and titles. She still introduced Doug Templeton, Walter Forbes, and Tommen Forbes. Why bother? At this point, it seemed like everyone knew everyone else was a liar. Skip the questioning, skip the charade, go straight to the war.

"The terms of agreement of this Time Trial are as follows," Isthim went on. Cassius-as-Doug shifted his stance, curious to know what side bets were on the table. "If the Accused is successful in defending himself over the course of questioning to the satisfaction of the Grandfathers, he is free to return home, along with Micah Durvin, Doug Templeton, Walter Forbes, and Tommen Forbes. Their world, Earth, will be sealed off from the Time industry forever. They will have no further contact with any aspect of the Wheel or the Time industry, or any races involved therein.

"However, due to unforeseen circumstances regarding the summoning of the Testimonies, an addendum has been made to these terms. Should the Accused be successful, he will retain all rights to the aforementioned terms, however, Michael Junior and Aklaq White Bear, being Runners in Time and Master Akari-bearers, also of Earth, will be summoned here for punishment before being released with the Accused. Michael Junior will suffer clock breaking of the most severe form.

Aklaq White Bear will be brought before Faharoa Rifun where he will have his sexual pleasure with her before releasing her back home."

Isthim looked directly at Aklaq-as-Tommen as she said it. "If the Accused is unsuccessful, he and Walter Forbes will have their clocks broken unto an inability to wield Time, and they will remain as Lord Rifun's personal servants until the end of their days. Micah Durvin and Tommen Forbes will become Faharoa's willing Akari Apprentices, to be personally trained by him. Doug Templeton's punishment will be at the discretion of Lord Rifun, based on the proceedings of this trial.

"Also, pursuant to the aforementioned unforeseen circumstances, Michael Junior and Aklaq White Bear will be summoned for their punishment. Michael Junior will face off against the Bat in the Pit in single combat. Aklaq White Bear will be brought before Rifun to remain as his mistress of sexual pleasure. Do all agree to the terms?"

"No!" Aklaq-as-Tommen blurted, taking a step forward. For a second, she seemed to realize what she'd done, but she pressed on. "You can't treat women like that! She's done nothing wrong! She's innocent in this. You can't—"

"Hush!" Isthim barked. Aklaq-as-Tommen shut up. "The question was not one for you to answer, though I and the Faharoa admire your persistence and outspokenness." She shifted her stance. "Now then, if all parties are satisfied, then we may begin with the questioning."

Cassius would not deny that such terms amused him, at least as far as watching Junior get ripped apart by the Bat and the Day. It was Aklaq's punishment he couldn't figure out. Sure, Rifun might not be a virgin, but he wasn't a rapist. It was beneath him, or something else that had to do with morals. It had to be a taunt, something to upset Micaiah. Hell, it had almost gotten Aklaq to blow her cover.

Isthim finished whatever she was talking about and the first Grandfather stood to begin questioning.

"Micaiah Durvin, less than one year ago, you were caught snooping around the Archives looking for information related to the Dispersal, specifically high-ranking Timekeepers and Harvesters. Is this true?"

Micaiah glared at him. "It is."

"Who can corroborate?" The Grandfather glanced over the four of them.

"I can," Micah said. "I was with him."

For a moment, the Grandfather was silent. Then, "This answer is unsatisfactory."

An unsatisfactory answer meant a swift kick in the ass from the Bat. The Bat and the Day would alternate attacking as the unsatisfactory answers piled up. People were entirely correct in their observations that this was not a fair form of justice, but there was nothing they were going to do about it. Time Trials were voluntary, not mandatory. There was a reason they were considered last-ditch efforts at freedom.

Micaiah hadn't even picked himself up off the floor before the second Grandfather was asking its question.

"In that same time frame, it was reported that you sought information about Faharoa Rifun and the former Zero Hour Cassius, seeking to overthrow them. Is this true?"

Micaiah groaned as he stood, wobbly on his right leg. "No."

"Explain."

"Seeking to overthrow them would imply that they were already in power. I was trying to stop them from gaining power in the first place. Rifun was no longer a Hand, and Cassius was a Zero Hour by cheating."

Apparently no corroboration or explanation was necessary before the Grandfather declared, "The answer is unsatisfactory."

This time is was the Day who laid Micaiah flat on the ground.

This went on for some time. Micah and the others remained anxious, skeptical, on high alert. Micah was frequently looking at the empty spot where Rifun was supposed to be. Cassius, however, was growing bored. All right, they had their fun, now it was time to just kill everything. Micaiah was getting his ass beat, but if it went on too much longer, he was going to die here instead of in battle. Sure, he was going to die either way, but Cassius really wanted the joy of killing him.

A question was asked, the answer deemed unsatisfactory, and the Bat moved in for punishment. Micaiah did not put up much of a fight, and the Bat knocked his head hard against Junior-as-Walter's platform. Micaiah crumpled to the ground and did not move. Cassius moved as close as he could to the edge of his platform, the ankle chain alerting him to his limit.

A secretary approached and knelt to examine the older twin.

"He is alive," the secretary reported. "He is only unconscious."

Up above, Isthim sighed and folded her arms. For a long moment, she did not speak, as if deciding whether to continue this farce or simply declare failure. She should declare failure, Cassius thought. Rifun wasn't here, they didn't get their assassination chance, they would still be chained for a few minutes, giving ample time to kill them after bringing the Akarin army here for slaughter.

"Return him to his cell," Isthim decided finally, sounding none too pleased. "And the others. We will recess the trial for now; I must have a word with Faharoa Rifun."

So maybe there was still some coal of fondness between them, that she would ask for Rifun's opinion. How sweet. And how boring for the rest of them. At least until Micah, as soon as the secretary unlocked his ankle chain, bolted from the platform and ran to his brother. There was a small commotion, but Isthim allowed it.

As for the rest of them, they were marched back to their cells. Cassius-as-Doug made a few laps, then leaned against the wall where he believed he could not be seen by the others. It was tempting to shed his Disguise, but he didn't dare. He might not be Rifun, but he did have a small sense of the dramatic reveal.

No one came to him to offer food or drink. No one came to tell him of changes in plans or other tidbits of knowledge. When someone did finally come by, it was to take him back out to the platform so the trial could resume.

Micaiah had cleaned himself up a bit, but Cassius' attention was focused more on Rifun, now sitting in the stands beside Isthim. Cassius looked at the others. Did any of them have even an inkling to check for a Disguise? Even a stray thought that said there was a chance it could maybe possibly might be a trap? Nothing? At all? Had the Author truly abandoned the Akarin so completely that she couldn't even bother to whisper a faint warning? Just to be sure, Cassius used Test on Rifun. Sure enough, it was a decoy. He didn't know who it was, but it wasn't Rifun.

"The Accused, Micaiah Durvin, is awake and has recovered," Isthim announced. "Faharoa Rifun offered him a chance to surrender, but he has refused. He has elected to continue with this Time Trial and see it through to its end. Therefore, we will pick up exactly where we left off. Noble Grandfathers, you may continue your questioning."

A question was asked, the answer given and deemed unsatisfactory. The Day moved in. Cassius watched the Rifun decoy. Waited for the sudden snap of the neck and spray of blood. Micaiah went down, got back up. The next Grandfather rose to ask a question. Cassius-as-Doug looked at Micah. Micah gave just a slight shake of the head.

What was going on? Was Cassius going to have to do everything himself around here? Had they hatched some scheme in the recess time?

The second question, the second answer, the second fight. Still no shot. Cassius-as-Doug shifted anxiously. He was going to have to do it himself. He would, gladly, but could they at least pretend like they had come in here with a plan and were going to carry it out?

The third question came around. This time when the answer was deemed unsatisfactory, Micaiah called his Stake, Micah, to stand in for him.

So that was how they were going to play it, Cassius thought. Not a bad idea, really, give themselves a small advantage. It was just too bad they hadn't been smart enough to check for the last possible thwarting of the plan. A secretary went up to unlock Micah's ankle chain, but the man did not move.

"Micah Durvin, you have been called to stand in for the Accused," Isthim told him, sounding very annoyed.

He nodded. "I know. I heard you. There's just one little problem, though."

"And what's that?"

He scratched under his arm, reaching for the gun. "I'm not Micah Durvin."

Cassius watched in amazement as Micaiah Durvin shed his Disguise, the lanky form of the younger twin giving way to the muscle of the elder. At the same time, Junior and Aklaq also doffed their Disguises. Micaiah snatched the gun from its hiding place, aimed, and fired.

Now when had this happened? It had to be during the recess. But how? They wouldn't have been left alone and— Could it have been earlier? Could they have switched places even before the trial?

Cassius saw the decoy's head snap back and disappear into the sea of black shrouds at the same time the Pit erupted into chaos.

Everything began moving at once. Isthim screamed and knelt beside her fallen master decoy. The Bat and the Day advanced on Micah who scrambled onto Cassius' platform to get out of the way as much as possible. All around them in the Pit, Grandfathers, guards, secretaries, all stood up and started shouting, confused and outraged. What had just happened? Who did it? What was going on? What happened now? Who was going to stop this?

Micaiah took the opening to make a calculated leap from his platform onto Cassius'. It was less than perfect and he had all the grace of a bull. He made it, but he was too unaccustomed to his running leg and he fell, almost sliding right off the platform. He pulled himself up and looked ready to blow the chain on Cassius' ankle, but then a secretary appeared with a keyring. It freed Cassius and looked up at him.

"I will free them. You must flee."

"Don't worry," Cassius-as-Doug said. "We've got reinforcements coming."

"Well, they can show up at any time," Micah said, looking around nervously.

The confused crowd seemed to have gotten their heads together and now they began pouring down from the stadium seats. The internal battle had begun, loyalists and traitors fighting in a confused panic. The twins and the secretary moved to free Aklaq who was already working on her chain.

Cassius-as-Doug got to the ground and simply melted into the confusion. Give things here a minute or two to sort themselves out before bringing in the Akarin.

Perhaps the most interesting thing about the battle was the variety of weapons. Yes, yes, everyone had Time at least, many had some skill in the Akari thanks to Rifun's schooling, but there was just something about having a physical object in your hand to wield, even if it was just a stick. One guard had an ax-like weapon, another a spear. Some had firearms of one variety or another. All of them unnecessary, but fun.

Then there were the Grandfathers, many of whom were Borelians. Cassius quickly turned his attention to the four that were closing in on him. For the Borelians, every hand-held weapon was a ranged weapon, and these four did not have anything in hand.

So, someone else had been doing a little planning, too. He shouldn't be surprised, really. The Cult wanted to use the chaos to be rid of the Akarin. Why shouldn't Misik and Isthim have worked out some plan of their own to be rid of any threats and enslave the rest?

Cassius ducked as something in his peripheral flashed and got close to his head. In his moment of distraction, one of the Grandfathers lunged. His first instinct was to grapple, but he pulled himself up short at the last second. Instead, he reached for Force, extending the momentum of his swinging arm and pushing the four back a good ten feet.

A roaming tussle between a couple of secretaries got between them. Cassius waited patiently, intending to strike just as soon as they cleared. On the other side, Cassius watched Michael Junior jump one of the Grandfathers while it was distracted, stabbing or doing something so it went down. Its three friends turned on him and the man was soon lost in a pile of black shrouds.

When they straightened, only three were left. The tussling secretaries had moved on, and Cassius took the opportunity to strike. His arm was met with stony resistance from one Grandfather while the other two moved to flank. Cassius withdrew as quickly as he could, never taking his eyes off them, but soon found himself backed up against a wall.

The Grandfathers surrounded him. He still could not discern their colors and he hated how much energy it took to keep himself alert enough to ward off any side effects of Borelian gases.

Before any of them could make a move, Cassius was suddenly covered in blood, the center Grandfather's head splitting apart. Then, before the other two could react, they two were nearly cloven in two by an enormous ax wielded by none other than Aklaq. Micaiah jogged up beside her, his movements still awkward and limping.

He could go after her. Could go after them both. They'd been fighting, they were weak. He could. He should.

"Is Rifun dead?" he asked.

Micaiah shook his head. "No."

"He survived?"

"It wasn't even him. Rifun Disguised someone else to look like him. He was never here to begin with."

"Shit. So we still have to find him and kill him."

"Yes," Aklaq confirmed. "But it looks like we may have tipped off something of a civil war in here."

"It's hard to love a dictator," Cassius-as-Doug said. "I knew we had friends, but this surprises me. Still, Rifun has more of an army than this at his disposal. Battle's not over yet."

"That's what worries me," Micaiah agreed. "We have to find the others and get out of here."

"Junior is dead."

"What?" Aklaq wondered.

Doug nodded. "He was determined to go down in a blaze of glory. So he did. He went down under four Grandfathers; I saw it myself."

Micaiah shook his head. "I don't know whether he's a sorry bastard or a stupid one."

"Doesn't matter. He's a dead one now."

"What about Micah?"

"I haven't seen him."

"I have to find him." He looked at Aklaq. "Stay here and guard Doug."

"Last I saw, he was over there." Cassius-as-Doug pointed somewhere over by the cell of the Accused, unsure of the truth of his own words.

Micaiah took off in that direction.

He could kill Aklaq, while their backs were turned. Kill her, claim something else got her. Actually, why even bother with the ruse? Just kill her now. The initial fighting was dying down. Now was the time when he was expected to bring in the rest of the Akarin.

He didn't get a chance before two guards assailed them. Aklaq took them out easily enough, but it robbed Cassius of his chance to kill her. He didn't even get much of a chance to help the guards kill her. By the time it was over, the twins had returned.

"Good to see you're all right," Cassius-as-Doug forced himself to say.

"Is it over?" Micah asked, looked around. "Did we win?"

"We won this battle," Aklaq said suspiciously. "But if we didn't kill Rifun, there are a lot more to come in the near future."

There wasn't even enough time between her words and the following action for anyone to properly savor the irony as a new hoard of Grandfathers swarmed into the Pit. All activity came to an awkward, tense halt. Cassius looked up as Rifun walked out onto the platform where he and Isthim where supposed to have been sitting.

"My, my, my, what have we here?" he said casually.

Fucking hell, it was the middle of a battle and the man still found a way to get in a monologue. Well, he at least got the traitors to reveal themselves, removing shrouds and disguises and other means of tomfoolery. With Cult reinforcements now securely in place, Rifun left them to shooting the fish in the barrel.

"Don't worry, guys," Cassius-as-Doug said as the Grandfathers advanced. "Help is coming. We've been here long enough that I think I understand the spatial-temporal coordinates of this room."

"Then stop psycho-babbling and open a portal," Micah told him impatiently.

"Cover us," Aklaq told him.

They moved to the center of the Pit, Micah taking up a sword while Micaiah, Aklaq, and Cassius-as-Doug worked on opening a portal. Cassius pretended to have a difficult time locating the army and where they were waiting. He pretended it was a struggle to open the portal, forcing the other two to lend even more strength.

"Any time now guys," Micah said nervously.

Cassius waited just a moment longer before allowing the connection to be made. A tiny portal the size of a fist opened up. Another one was punched open. Then another and another. Finally the whole thing opened wide.

They jumped out of the way as a small army came barreling through the portal. There was no chance to warn them about friends this side of the portal, and a few of the helpful guards and Grandfathers were cut down in accidental friendly fire.

"Where were these guys before?" Micah asked.

"On reserve," Cassius-as-Doug lied. "If we could win with the force we had, great. If not, better to not show all our cards too soon."

"But you, sir—" Aklaq said, poking Micaiah. "—are still in trouble for throwing in that wild card."

Micaiah sighed. "Can we talk about this later, honey? We're kind of in the middle of a battlefield."

"That is very true," Cassius-as-Doug said, jumping out of the way as one entanglement got a little too close to him. They moved out of the way, trying to get toward a small open area where they might be able to speak. Aklaq was shuffled away in the chaos, but Cassius ignored her. "And we should seek shelter as soon as possible. Now that we have the coordinates—"

"No." Micaiah shook his head. "No, we're not running. We rallied this force, so we ought to be here fighting with them."

"We did our job—"

"No, we didn't," Micah interrupted. "Our job was to kill Rifun. In case you haven't noticed, he's still alive. We have to complete our mission."

Cassius-as-Doug sighed. The army was here. Cards were down. His purpose had been fulfilled. One last mission.

"Fine," he said, shedding his Disguise of Doug and drawing an ancient French rapier in one hand, pilfered from Rifun's fancy office, and his shotgun in the other. "Guess I'll just kill you here."

One last mission, one last roar onto the battlefield.

Cassius made as if to go after Micaiah first, then turned on Micah, aiming the shotgun in order to get him to jump out of the way and directly in line with the rapier. Micah skidded and twisted at the last second to avoid being skewered, but the blade still found skin, and blood blossomed from the wound.

Without hesitating, Cassius continued to move the rapier, catching Micaiah's pilfered sword and parrying so that the shot from his pilfered gun was equally useless. Then he jumped back so that the twins were suddenly facing each other.

Cassius shifted his stance as if he would charge both of them, then paused for half a second, his attention caught elsewhere. Aklaq was a short distance away, still fighting, but within a clear line of sight.

He raised the shotgun.

Clumsily, Micaiah leapt at him. Whatever attack he had planned, it didn't go well, but it got Cassius off-balance. The first shot went wide. The two of them stumbled to the side together. In the confusion, something sharp punctured flesh. Cassius snarled in pain, but it turned to a howl as they landed on the ground and the blade went deeper.

A lung, nothing more. Pull it out and he could heal. Except that was not the only wound he suffered. Slowly, slowly, the dragon was releasing its grip on the bullet in his face. Slowly, slowly, it tore at flesh under his eye, into his brain.

"All you Akari-bearers are cowards," Cassius burbled, blood bubbling up from his wounded lung, thoughts going cloudy.

"How long were you Disguised?" Micaiah demanded.

"Long enough." He couldn't breathe, and the world was going dark.

"Where is Rifun?"

"Long gone by now."

"Where is Doug?"

Cassius couldn't even be sure the next words were his. "Long gone. As you will be."

The world faded away, as did the pain.

Cassius picked himself up, but he was no longer in the Pit. He found himself instead in a black void, ankle-deep in something sticky. Blood. The air was not sweet oxygen, but copper.

Something moved. He did not need to wonder what it was.

There was no obvious light source in this void, and yet he could see the dragon as it approached, perhaps not in the light of anything else, but because its even more robust darkness signaled its presence by its absence.

"Three hundred years," Cassius said. "Three hundred years I served you."

The dragon drew near, circling him. It was already as big as an airplane, yet Cassius knew it could dwarf even that. "Does a fork serve a hand? Or a hand, a man? Or is each only a tool for a greater purpose? And when it has worn out, it is discarded."

"Three hundred years, and the best I ever got—"

Suddenly he was flying as if hit by a train. He felt everything in his body shatter, yet he knew with a sudden, terrifying certainty, that he could not die. He landed an unknown distance away, splashing in the endless lake of blood, now covered. Not just covered, but it was as if hands reached out to grab him and pull him in. All the hands of those he'd slain.

"Ungrateful speck!" the dragon hissed, approaching slowly, like a cat investigating some small prey. "You were given every desire."

Cassius got to his feet, still kicking off the last few bloody hands, his body still broken and in screaming torture. "Does a fork feel gratitude for having been used, plunged into all manner of fetid garbage and then stuck in the stinking, rotting mouth of a man? Does it feel gratitude for being washed? Or is it merely a tool? And is it the fork's fault for stabbing a man and causing him pain? Or is it the fault of the man who wields it?"

The dragon never gave him an answer, but there was an air of disinterest. Cassius jumped as more hands began clawing their way up his body, some of them beginning to form into heads, then bodies. They did not appear to seek to pull him down into the blood, but hold him in place. Cassius tried to fight it, but he was suddenly weak, weak like a newborn babe. His muscles atrophied, his body withered. The dragon circled him one more time before getting in a stance.

"My name is Kokumbo," he whispered, the last of his defiance leaking out of him. "This one shall not die."

The dragon rumbled a noise akin to a laugh. "This one...was never alive to begin with."

Then it opened its mouth, and the last thing Cassius knew was the searing agony of black fire.

The Caves of Meroian, 2014

Rifun sat at his desk in his chambers in the officers building in the Ruins of Meroian on Sadurnon. He stared at his shrine, but he made no move to pray. Specifically, his gaze was fixed on the Authored Books, laid out reverently amid the rest of the paraphernalia: animal bones, food, cloth, bundles of herbs and plants, and personal knick knacks.

How? Why? There was no earthly, physical reason for their loss. They had the numbers. They had the superior warriors. They had the Akari. They had the backing of the Author. They had the will to go and do things while the Akarin sat on their thumbs and bickered. They actually consulted the Author rather than some witless council. They had gone to great lengths to retrieve all of the journals.

The journals. Dictated by Cassius. But Cassius had been possessed by the dragon. The Borelians, who were not overly keen about any off-world religion and only fearfully tolerant of the Holy Men of War, had slowly come around to them, somewhat. So were they really the words to follow?

The door opened and Misik stormed in. Had Rifun been more uptight, he might have stood, expecting an attack. True, Misik was likely here to kill him out of revenge for Isthim who had perished in the battle, but Rifun wasn't going to give him the satisfaction of an anxious reaction.

"The last of our warriors have been accounted for," Misik reported. "Now what?"

Rifun gave him a cat's regard. "And here I thought you fancied yourself the one who was truly in control. Why don't you tell me? Or are you rethinking your slave colony idea?"

Misik got closer, his skin turning bright yellow. Blood and circulation. Rifun silently noted the most likely contact points. Misik opened his mouth as if to speak, thought better of it, closed his mouth, then opened his mouth again, but to say instead, "We have, at most, fifty thousand in the camp right now. Countless thousands more have fled to their homes. Even pretending that we lost no one, we are down to a fraction of what we left with."

"I am aware of the relationship between war and math, thank you."

"So what—?!"

"We sit," Rifun stated. "We lick our wounds and we wait for morning. Regardless of whatever brilliance you and I possess, whatever skill in whatever discipline, whatever plans we may concoct at this very moment, even we must rest. I'm sure you could come up with some great attack against the Akarin in the Wheel right now while they revel in their victory, but the fact is, our warriors could not handle such a thing. Not physically, not mentally. And if such an attack would not produce any meaningful victory or recuperation, then we only send them to the slaughter." He shook his head. "No. We wait."

"For how long?"

Rifun gave Misik a look. "Until I say. I am the only leader left. Cassius is dead, thank the ancestors. Isthim is dead, much to the chagrin of the Admirals and the Ul Ik Zol, I'm sure. Julianna is still trapped in the in-between dimension, but she was never much help in such matters anyway."

Misik took a step back and glared at him. "And do you have anything else to say, O Singular Lord of the Cult of the Akari?"

Rifun chanced a glance at the shrine behind Misik. "I think I'm going to go back to the Wheel. Disguised, of course. I want to see what they intend to do with the place. Cassius mentioned that the Akarin council had batted around a few ideas of what to do with the Wheel if they took it from us. Once I get the lay of the land, then an idea may strike me as to what to do next."

It pacified the cranky general for the moment and he left, still in a huff.

Rifun did not move for a long time, still staring at his shrine across the room, letting the fire in the hearth burn down some.

He had been given the power of the razana, the power to Build, to take down the dragon. And he had failed. Looking back, he understood his reasoning, but it just felt...foolish. He no longer had black wool over his eyes, but there appeared to remain a fine veil he could not fully penetrate. And now the dragon had gotten away. Where it would manifest, who its next victim would be, he did not know. And if he wanted to be honest, that frightened him.

What would his next move be? He didn't know, because he didn't understand. He knew he was still called to vanquish the dragon, but he would be lying if he said he didn't have doubts about the journals' ability to get him to that point. If the dragon dictated the journals, it wouldn't include information about how to kill it.

So where did he go? Back to the source. Richard was dead, but Julianna wasn't. She had been protected from all this chaos by being trapped in the in-between dimension. Now, with Cassius and Isthim out of the way at least, maybe it was time to seriously consider a rescue mission. Without those two looming over her shoulder, she might have greater insight into the journals and anything else her husband knew but could not write down because of Cassius and the dragon.

Yes. That sounded like a good first step. He didn't know where the dragon was, but while he had the time, he might as well spend it in preparation.

Rifun groaned and stretched, then got out of his chair to do more of the same. He stoked the fire a bit and knelt to say a brief prayer of protection at his shrine. The problem with being the only leader left, well, he was the only one. He was the only one standing between the Cult and the Borelians. Say one thing for Cassius, Rifun never doubted whose side the man was on when it came to slavery. But now that mountain had been toppled, leaving only Rifun.

He straightened and started working on a Disguise. No, he wasn't alone. Just as Julianna's isolation had protected her until this point when she was most needed, so Tommen Forbes' role had only just begun. Perhaps Rifun had misjudged the timing, certainly the methods, but now was the time to bring him in and prepare him for the battle ahead. Now that he had seen the evils of the universe, the darkness within Cassius, the apathy of the Akarin—understandably debatable at this point—Tommen might be a little more receptive to Rifun's training.

He created a few different Disguises, layering them like jackets. If he was somehow outed or there was chaos or shenanigans, he could slip from one to another for an easier escape. He wasn't fooled into thinking that there weren't a ton of people out looking for him. The first twenty-four hours after the battle had simply been hunkering down in the ruins, waiting for an impending attack that never came.

With his Disguises in place, he first headed to Earth, then to the Wheel, a much easier endeavor now that all of the dampening fields had been lifted. He wasn't sure whether to use Time or the Akari. He chose the Akari simply because it was less likely to draw suspicion right now, or so he hoped. Some of the returning soldiers had mentioned something about new elections, but Rifun had a hard time believing that. There was no way such a thing could be thrown together so quickly.

Entering the Wheel, apparently they had not only set up new elections, but they were already in the inauguration stage of things. Thousands of Time Agents and Akarin slowly made their way toward the Amphitheater. Looking around, everything appeared to have been cleaned up. No blood, no guts, no bodies. No Building, either, as all of his changes remained in tact. Cobblestone streets, lavish gardens, and, his favorite part, the sample of his homeland that now served as the Seat of the Hands.

Hard red clay provided a solid ground, but majestic mountains rose all around them in wonder. Lesser rooms and courts were little more than open grass canopies and huts, but greater courts were buildings made of red clay bricks. On the far side, a classic, Greek-style amphitheater served as the true Inner Seat. No longer secreted away, everyone would see and know the Hands. Or whomever the new governing body was.

There was plenty of speculation and confusion among those gathered. The Hands were dead or long gone. Sure, they'd all just held an election, but had it really meant anything? What had happened exactly? Stories and accounts were mixed and contradictory, and no one knew what to do. In this moment, then, the only thing to do...was nothing. As Rifun said, just sit and wait.

The secretary who walked out now was one who was well-known in the Seat, a dog-like anthromorph called a Lixon who could walk on its hind legs or down on all sixes with ease. It took a minute for it to get everyone's attention, but it wasted no time when it did.

"Welcome," the secretary began. "We are gathered here today to present to you the new Council of Hands, those who will govern the Wheel and the Laws of Time. A terrible tragedy has occurred here recently. And everyone is to blame. We allowed our greed to blind us to the corruption that flowed through the Wheel like blood. Those who spoke up, we struck down. In the midst of our petty pursuits, a single man was able to destroy everything we thought we knew."

The secretary looked around. "It does not matter whether you were a Dominion Timekeeper, a Triage Harvester, an Investor Merchant, anyone who worked closely with the Hands, or whether you were a Runner who actively opposed the Hands at every turn. We allowed the system to become corrupt and stay corrupt, creating a system where seats were bought and sold to the highest bidder, where those we commissioned to keep us safe were punished for doing just that. It is no secret that that system was on a constant cycle of war, but a wheel that spins while going downhill, still goes downhill.

"To that end, a new system has been put in place. It is no longer one man with one word that governs all. Rather, you will be governed by those who are one of you. Harvesters have no business with Timekeepers, and Scientifically Superior and Fully Engaged Civilizations have no business with Scientifically Primitive and Unengaged Civilizations. You will conduct your own affairs. There will, however, still be a Zero Hour. As before, the word of the Zero Hour is absolute, but it is not final.

"There are many changes that have yet to be disclosed, and to do so today would take more time than we would wish. Instead, we will name our new Hands. They will be the ones to pass down the information."

While the secretary began naming off the lesser offices—guards and secretaries and other positions, Rifun might have said he was almost hopeful. Sure, these could just be flowery words, or it might actually be a cause for real change. On the other hand, he thought with some resignation, the Dispersal had been far bigger and far bloodier, lasted a lot longer, and it had devolved quickly into the same bickering Hands. And yet, he couldn't deny that the Cult did have some small part in that. They had needed and used that chaos to make the takeover that much easier. If this did work out, then, even for a short time, maybe there was a future hope for peaceful resolution.

His hope was bolstered a little when it was announced that no position would be shrouded. Secrecy had been a major catalyst for the distrust and deception, but no longer. The people needed to see their leaders.

Then it was time for the Hands themselves to be named and introduced. They were all brought out at once, made to stand stage right. It was unclear whether their arrangement was intentional or simply haphazard depending on where they ended up. As the secretary named each one, the Hand would step out and swear the oath of office. When done, the secretary would thank them, and they would move back to stage right. No more fancy words or speeches, no empty promises or displays of grandeur.

When the Hands were done, the secretary announced that it was one of four who had been elected to replace the Bat and the Day. She was the Labrador, while the rest were the Pike, the Vornir, and the Mist. Each one was pointed out in turn, but Rifun could not see them well enough to commit them to memory. They were elected positions now, on offset rotations, so none could accumulate the power, influence, or treachery that the Bat and the Day had.

They all thought this was about politics and simple corruption. Did they never suspect the true nature of the Bat and the Day? Did they never wonder if there hadn't been something more?

Then the crowd was dismissed. The whole thing had taken maybe three hours, if that. Rifun almost didn't know what to do with the other nine hours he had mentally set aside, like what used to be required. It took him almost a full ten seconds to even move from his position. It was an odd sensation of freedom he had not expected to experience today.

He left the theater, retreating into the shadow of a brick building to simply watch the world go by. No catastrophes in this inauguration had defused a majority of the tension in the crowd, and they now more freely mingled. Some expressed hope for the future, others lamented the failures of the past. Some spoke or sang of those who died in the coup, and Rifun found himself oddly moved by it. It was good that he had put a stop to Cassius' endless executions, but he knew these people here would never see it that way. Maybe they would never know.

All they saw was a crazed group of aliens from across the universe wielding a power they had all been told was a myth. That group took over the castle, put up the drawbridge, and trapped everyone inside. That group had been a terror to the Time industry for decades, even centuries, all because of some books.

This wasn't how things were supposed to be, Rifun thought. Without Cassius, it might be a little easier to have a civil conversation with prospective members and allies.

Members like Tommen Forbes. Rifun spied the teenager a distance away, speaking with Walter, Micah, Micaiah, and Aklaq White Bear. Their demeanor was curious and pleasant, wondering at this new system of governance the Hands had concocted in so short a time, but their disposition was both alert and weary from being so for so long.

He needed to collect the third journal. All three of them needed to be re-examined and rewritten, properly. Richard was inspired by the Author, but his fear made him an easy target for the dragon to hold sway and speak new words, evil words, and twist the Author's intent. Julianna could work on the two the Cult possessed. The third would prove a little trickier to handle.

Locked away in a Borelian temple, the key hidden in the Core. With Misik hovering over him, no doubt reworking plans of his own to enslave the Cult, Rifun could not risk trying to recover the key himself, to say nothing of the matter of getting into that damned temple. And yet, for as many times as Rifun had been to the Core, had touched it, had moved across the universe through it, it would not give him access to the key.

Tommen. Tommen Forbes, just as he had suspected, was the key to this whole thing. He was the one standing at the nexus, the focal point of Time, the Akarin, and the Cult. Maybe the Cult had lost the Wheel because Tommen hadn't been here to play some important role. Even if that were the case, however, the first problem was that he was a teenager. A boisterous, rebellious teenager with no discipline. At sixteen, Rifun had run off to join a nationalist group and risk his life to free his people. Tommen couldn't drive, fawned after girls, and couldn't handle one bully at school. He would need discipline. Unfortunately, that only called to mind the fact that every encounter so far had not been the most pleasant. He would be resistant to Rifun and the Cult. At the same time, it might drive him to the Akarin, to the Builders, to be that link that Micaiah would not. If he agreed to help of his own accord, that would be the ideal. But even if he tried to run, there was only one place he could go. And if the Akarin sought to undermine Rifun, even then, they could only help him.

Yes, Rifun thought, nodding internally. The Author was still with him, still guiding him. He did not understand why things had to happen this way, but the flowers were beginning to blossom and would turn into fruit in time.

Tommen wandered away from the group. Rifun followed at a polite distance, circling him as he went to explore the larger area, past the village toward the surrounding jungle and the mountains beyond. Although it was a large area, for most species of human size or bigger, it was not possible to lose sight of the village area before reaching an invisible boundary. Rifun had intentionally made the Amphitheater larger than the Coliseum, so it wasn't as claustrophobic and so the scenery might help calm people down while they were waiting to meet in whatever court they were assigned. He'd also been sure to include environmental ambiance: a gentle breeze, birdsong, rustling in the bushes, movement of shadows.

Tommen found the outer wall but remained where he was, looking up into the trees, toward the mountains. Rifun stood several paces to his right.

"Beautiful, isn't it?" he began conversationally, not looking at the boy.

"It is," Tommen confirmed, looking at him. He nodded, perhaps at the clothes of the Disguise. "Kinda cold where you're from?"

"A bit chilly, yes. Is your home warm?"

"Getting there. I mean, it's nice, but it's not overly hot."

Rifun nodded absently. "You know, I miss this view. They say that young people are incapable of appreciating beauty and art. I'm quite a bit older now as you might imagine, but even as a young man, I could stare at this view for hours."

The teenager's tone turned suspicious. "And what view is that?"

Now Rifun looked at him and grinned, though he did not break the Disguise. "The view from my village on the north side. Where the more civilized Frenchmen came to spread their civilization and the seeds thereof."

Tommen turned and opened his mouth as if to call an alarm. Immediately Rifun was on him, closing off his windpipe so the best he could manage was a pitiful squeak. The sudden sensation paralyzed him so he could not run. Had he tried, well, Rifun could have easily fixed that, but he really didn't want to cause a scene. Right now, he just wanted the kid to listen.

"Did you really think that I would just go off and hide in some hole, waiting for the manhunts to find me? When you have the power to Disguise yourself as anyone and go anywhere, why wouldn't you? Cassius walked right into the Akarin base and stole their leadership. I am the most wanted man in the entire universe right now, and yet I can walk right into the inauguration of the new Hands. I can be anyone, go anywhere."

"Then go to Hell," Tommen rasped.

"And that's another thing. Did you think that because I am out of power that somehow our deal is null and void, and you owe me nothing? We have an agreement. I saved your dear daddy and saw you through your review. You owe me."

"Fuck off."

"The more you resist, the more painful it will be. I did warn you of 'dropping like flies,' didn't I?"

Standing there with only a minimal stream of air, Tommen slowly stopped struggling against forces he did not understand. After a moment, Rifun released the hold.

"The timeline may have changed," he went on. "The locale and overall manner of your new training may have changed. But our deal and your training have not changed. I will still send you a sign, when I am ready for you. If you don't respond, well, I don't think I have to try and prove my record to you. And in the future, dear daddy will be lucky to be any more than a vegetable, and Micaiah will be losing a lot more than just a leg. Do you understand?"

Tommen glared at him. "When are you going to give up?"

"I never give up. I always win." There wasn't much of a choice at this point.

"You lost your power."

"Temporarily, but I am still alive. The only thing that will stop me now is death."

"And what's to stop me from telling everyone that you're here and need to fucking die?"

"Because as soon as you open your mouth to do so, you'll be dead. And even if I decide to let you raise an alarm, by the time anyone notices and comes to investigate, I'll be long gone. So consider your actions carefully."

The kid was silent for a long moment, trying to come up with options, a way out. Then, "I'm going to tell them. You know I will."

Rifun grinned, donning another Disguise. "I would be heartbroken if you didn't. It makes the game that much more interesting, especially if you got the twins involved. I almost want to make it an order and tell you to tell them. What's that going to do to your little plan, hm?"

Tommen glanced up the hill toward the village where his father and the others were still talking.

"Don't forget," Rifun went on. He changed into another Disguise. "I can be anyone. And I can go anywhere. I'm like Santa Claus. I see you when you're sleeping; I know when you're awake. And I know if you've been bad or good, so you better do as I say or else more people are going to die."

"I don't think that's how the song goes."

"Perhaps, but do you doubt me?" Tommen did not reply. "Watch for my sign. And heed my warning. I think I'm being overly generous even giving you one."

He Banded and slipped away before the kid could raise an alarm. That didn't go as planned, but it started the ball rolling, anyway. Because of Cassius' treachery impersonating Doug, Rifun had no illusions that he would be able to go sneaking around the Akarin fortress any time soon, but if he could push Tommen that way, and bring him into the Cult, it might prove advantageous.

And if the kid turned out to be as bullheaded as Micaiah, well, he would just have to figure out something else. But that would be for later. Things were still too hot on his neck. He needed to lay low and work on something a little more innocuous, like rescuing Julianna.

As much as he wanted to go to the Archives, he returned to the ruins instead. Contrary to what his enemies believed, he wasn't much for giving speeches, not on the fly anyway. He preferred to have such things written down beforehand so he could practice and memorize. However, in accordance with the opinions of his enemies, and his friends, if he had any, was that he was a people person. He knew how to talk to people, even if they were of a completely foreign culture.

He didn't know how to talk to his people now. Oh, he meandered about the city and offered words of encouragement, but the best he could do was hope that he sounded more confident than he felt.

How did he explain their loss? They had every environmental advantage, with a Rebuilt Wheel and the Pit. They had every martial advantage, with superior numbers and the power of the Akari. They had every strategic and tactical advantage, knowing the entirety of the enemy's plan ahead of time and countering every point they could with at least two brilliant minds and one bloodthirsty mercenary. They had every spiritual advantage, between the Author's backing and Rifun being a Builder himself.

Yes, he might have had some semblance of a plan going forward, but how did he explain it? Sorry, the journals might be a teeny bit corrupt and need to be reviewed, and then we'll give it another go? Our greatest asset doesn't even have Akari abilities and he wants to see us dead? Might as well prepare the noose for the Cult and everything he had worked for, for years. No, he couldn't do that. Even if the journals needed revision, that was best done through the hands and mouths of "professional scholars" or, as luck would have it, one of the founders.

Julianna was his next goal. There could be no other. Anything requiring violence or overt operations would not be met well.

He made his way to the officers building and headed for his chambers. He needed to collect his notes on the in-between dimension and everything he had tried so far. Even if he had failed in trapping the dragon, there might be a way to utilize the techniques to rescue Julianna. He hadn't done as much research on the subject as he should have, being trapped in the Wheel of all places, with unlimited access to the Archives; he'd been focusing more on what information Cassius brought him, figuring out the Core and Building, and trying to keep everyone calm and orderly in isolation.

It was a good thing he'd kept everything here. He had intended to bring everything into the Wheel, to his lavish office, once the Wheel was again open for business. Had he brought it over sooner, he was sure nothing would have survived.

Mobius strip, Klein bottle, yes, everything appeared to be in order. Now if he could just sit and do some reading, dust off his memory, maybe some time away from this puzzle would prove enlightening.

He had no sooner sat down than Misik walked in, looking as cheerful as he had the last day or two. He bore a computer tablet of some form which he handed over with some disdainful resignation. Rifun gave him a look and gingerly took the tablet. The tablet itself was Borelian in origin, as one might expect, and it appeared as though Misik had already gone through the trouble of translating the words on the screen. Must be important information, then, if he was—

"War," Rifun stated.

"The Council of Ancrath, the Great Admirals of the Fleet, and the Ul Ik Zol voted unanimously," Misik reported.

Rifun set the tablet aside. The details hardly mattered. He looked up at the general. "You are forewarning me of this. Why? Or are you here to kill me and be done with it?"

"Separate orders. You are not mine to kill. The high priest of the Ul Ik Zol has claimed that honor."

"He flatters me. So when does he come to claim his prize? Or are you in it for the bounty?"

Misik's expression was stony. "Although the governing bodies would like to publicly parade you around Ancrath and enslave the whole of the Cult, the Council has decided that it is in Brelix's best interest and more efficient to go after humanity as a whole first. Therefore, I have been named as your warden. My job is to stay by your side and observe your comings and goings—"

"Keep track of me so when it's my turn to go up to the gallows, I can be found."

"Exactly."

"Why, though? Why go after humanity first? These orders made it sound like I'm the bigger prize, and I believe I saw Micaiah Durvin listed as well. Surely he is a good catch as well, to be named specifically."

The general's expression never changed. "Efficiency. The Cult and the Akarin have the capacity to meaningfully resist. Humans do not."

"The least effort for the greatest gain."

"Exactly."

Rifun leaned back in his seat. "Am I to expect a sudden influx of Borelian recruits into the ranks?"

"Unlikely. The Cult will fall, as will the Akarin. But you are the bigger prize, like Micaiah Durvin."

"I see. And what is to stop me from killing you right now, and all the other Borelians here?"

"The knowledge that the victory would be even shorter-lived than the one in the Wheel as the wrath of Brelix and Tujor came down upon the Cult."

He wasn't wrong. Rifun nodded slowly. "Fair point. But while your people are fierce, they are not stupid. It may be more efficient to go after Earth first, but it will take longer than a day or two. Are we to sit here staring at each other for weeks or months? Are you going to follow me to the bathroom and watch me pull my cock out to pee?"

"If I must."

"But those aren't your first orders, so long as I play nice, stick around the area, and don't tell the grunts what's going on."

Misik nodded sarcastically. "Exactly."

"I suppose we can manage some kind of understanding, then."

He could tell the general was instantly suspicious. He'd come here expecting, maybe even hoping for, a fight. But Rifun wasn't Cassius. He could play along for the time being. He did not expect Misik or the Borelians to keep such a distance for very long, but with any luck, it would be just long enough to figure a way out.

He handed the tablet back to Misik. "With you by my side, I find third-hand information to be insulting and unreliable. I'm sure you will tell me everything I need to know regarding our impending enslavement."

Misik's expression was unreadable as he took the tablet. He turned and made for the door. Before he could leave, Rifun called to him, and he looked back.

"While you're out and about, if you happen to run into a man by the name of Godwin Lore, send him to me, would you? Be careful about how you word it, though. He was an ardent supporter of Cassius. I would hate for there to be any incidents so soon after our defeat. We really don't need to fight amongst ourselves."

The general left without a word, but his expression said plenty.

Rifun shifted in his seat and looked down at his notes, but his mind was far from the scribbled epiphanies. He glanced back at the door, expecting to see prison bars.

He should have expected this. Misik had been unhappy for a long time now; this was simply the consequence of Cassius' decision to enlist Isthim's help coming to its full, poisonous fruition. But did it really have to feel like he was being kicked while he was down? Perhaps this was the new manifestation of the dragon. Now that it had left Cassius, it was free to return to its more faithful subjects and use them to root out the less faithful or the opposition.

Did he even have time to rescue Julianna now? Would it make a difference? Rewriting the journals would mean nothing if they were facing slavery. At the same time, what else could he do right now? Misik was on high alert, proud of his new position as warden. Rifun would have to learn the rules, then figure out how to exploit them.

He continued to stare at his notes, but there were no epiphanies, no breakthroughs.

It was an hour before Godwin Lore arrived at his door. He was human, white, sported the faintest of accents that could not be placed even as he spoke perfect English. He stood about five-eight with a quietly muscular build, brown hair kept short, face clean-shaven. Rifun did not know the man personally as he was rumored to spend more time with a smaller faction, but his reputation suggested he might be the man for the job.

"You sent for me?" he inquired from the doorway.

"Come in and shut the door," Rifun ordered. He stood as the man did so. "Godwin Lore, isn't it?"

"That's my name, sir."

"What do your friends call you?"

"Win, sir."

"Because you never lose?"

"I haven't so far."

"How are you faring, Win?"

"Sir?"

"Since the defeat in the Wheel. How are you faring?"

"I was not badly injured, and what wounds I did sustain were easily healed."

"Yes, that's good to hear, but what about you? Do you still believe in us, the

Cult, the journals, the Author?"

Now the man blinked. "Has someone questioned my loyalty?"

Rifun ignored the question. "How did Isthim treat you, under her command? Well, I hope?"

Win's voice was tight. "Strict but fair, I suppose."

Rifun grinned. "She's gone now, Win. Tell me what you really think. Permission to speak freely."

The man was still reserved, as if expecting a trap. "I cannot say I learned nothing, but I would not have chosen a Borelian as a commander."

"Nor would I," Rifun said. He meandered away a few steps. "And yet, here we are."

Win studied him. "Is everything all right, sir?"

"I asked you here for a couple of reasons. First, you're human. Call me biased, but I prefer to deal with my own kind. It also makes things a bit easier in other regards which we are about to discuss. Second, you are the only human who has managed to rise through Cult military ranks and even squeeze a compliment out of Isthim. What's your military background?"

"Slavic, sir. A slave mercenary for various caliphates in the ninth century."

Rifun folded his arms. "Really? That surprises me. Few human Time Agents live so long, for one reason or another."

"My training won't let me die, sir. Not easily."

"And what have you done with yourself in the past thousand years? Have you been a mercenary this whole time?"

"Off and on. Raised four families, or tried to."

"Not an easy thing with our lives. But what brings you here? Mercenaries aren't known for their loyalty to causes or ideologies, and I won't say that the Cult offers the most competitive wages."

"For a mercenary of my skill, no one can afford what I'm worth," Win said bluntly. "For a man of my lifespan and unique talents, money means very little. I take what I need, through steel or stealing if I must. But although my training does not allow me to die, it gives me no reason to live, either. The Cult has given me purpose. I was one of Richard's first followers. Well, once it grew to be more than a gaggle of clucking hens."

"Were you ever Akarin?"

"No, sir. I was little more than a curious passing Time Agent at the time."

Rifun nodded. "Then surely you are the perfect man for the job."

"What's that, sir?"

Rifun pulled on Sound, buffering the room. "Understand that this conversation does not leave this room."

"Yes, sir."

"Does the training you have received in any way resemble what you recall from Richard and Julianna's earliest lessons? The Book of Abilities, the Book of Philosophy, the Book of Commands. Do they match the manners of the Browns in those first days?"

Win's expression turned thoughtful. "I cannot give an honest answer to that, sir. If I recall correctly, everything about the journals and the so-called 'heresies' was new. Many were comparing them to the Akarin. I could not do such a thing as I only knew Time."

Rifun shifted his stance. "Maybe I should rephrase the question. Did anything Isthim or Cassius said or did contradict the journals? And did anything in the journals contradict the early teachings of Richard and Julianna?"

Win frowned and appeared to search his memory. Then, "I don't believe so, sir. To be honest, Richard and Julianna contradicted themselves often enough in the early days as they tried to iron out minor teachings. I attributed it to them simply being poor teachers; not everyone is cut out for instructing others." He added hastily, "Sir, what is this job?"

"Maybe I will explain the situation first," Rifun decided. "Some things I do not expect you to understand. In the realm beyond ours, the Whites are the servants of the Author. The Shadows serve a malevolent being simply called the dragon."

"I remember hearing such things from those who had been Akarin," Win said, "but there is very little about them in the Book of Philosophy."

"Cassius, to no shock, served the dragon. He is the one who dictated the journals to Richard."

"You think he coerced Richard into writing lies?"

"Not just lies, lies made using only the truth. We know the history, we have the abilities. We can manipulate the Akari just as well as the Akarin. I myself learned Building. All truth. But with some key component missing so that it is still a falsehood."

Win nodded slowly, his expression turning more resolute. "What's the job?"

Rifun let his arms drop and he took a few wandering steps. "We have two problems. First, Julianna remains trapped in the in-between dimension. We have crude means of communication, but our best man for the task decided to turn on us and I was forced to kill him." He reached his desk and leaned on it, staring at his scattered notes. "We need to get her out. Not only is she better at morale than I, but she is still our best source of information from the early days. I'm hoping that without Cassius' malevolent shadow hanging over her, we can figure out what those missing pieces are and clear up the truth of the journals." He sighed. "I believe that was part of the reason for our failure in the Wheel. We still lacked those pieces and the Author punished us for it, for going ahead with the lie, without the truth."

"And the second problem?"

Rifun straightened and turned to face Win who hadn't moved. "The Borelians have declared war. On humanity. On the Cult. General Misik has been designated as our so-called warden."

"Warden?"

"According to Misik, the Council of Ancrath has decided that it is more efficient to go after the human planets first because they don't have the means to resist like we do. The least effort for the most gain. Once that's done, they're coming for us."

Win nodded. "You want me to take out the Borelians in our ranks?"

"Not yet, but you're on the right track." Rifun folded his arms again and leaned back against the desk. "I'm under too much scrutiny. Misik is going to be watching my every move. No doubt he is already suspicious of our meeting, but he doesn't want to cause a panic in the Cult, doesn't want to spook the sheep on their way to slaughter.

"I'm going to work on a way of freeing Julianna from the in-between dimension. It's innocuous enough that Misik shouldn't question it too much. Ancestors know I've already been trying with no success."

"What do you want me to do, sir?"

"I have a few tasks for you. First, keep an eye on the Borelians in our ranks. They're secretive and tight-lipped, but I expect there will be some tell before the invasion. Believe me, I don't expect them to wait until every last human planet is enslaved before coming after us. They'll strike in the middle."

"Agreed, sir."

"If possible, recruit others to help. The Borelian god of death is just the dragon

Shadow by another name. Another stranglehold over Richard and Julianna in the early days, I'm sure. We need to be rid of the Borelians, but to do so openly would only guarantee an invasion."

"Understood, sir."

"I don't know if you know this, but the Book of Commands has been missing for some time. I will spare you the details and say that it is currently locked up in a temple on Brelix." Win visibly flinched. "Yes, that is a problem, I agree. What's worse, the key was hidden in the Core of the Wheel by the Akarin." Godwin opened his mouth to speak, but Rifun cut him off. "It's a very, very long story, one I'll not repeat today. I made several attempts to free it while we were in the Wheel, but to no avail. How ever their Builders did it, I did not have the time or skill to undo before we were ousted."

"Quite a conundrum."

"Yes, it is. I have a gamble I'm working to try and make things easier, but this new war and warden has made things harder."

"May I ask what the gamble is?"

Rifun studied the man for a moment. "What is your opinion of the Authored Books?"

"I couldn't say, sir, I've never read them."

"Well, the central figure of what I believe to be the central series is out walking around Charleston, West Virginia, right now."

Win shrugged. "So? Do you believe in the Books, sir?"

"Some believe the Books and the journals are contradictory. I say they are complimentary. Such is the conundrum of Cassius' dictation of lies using truth and all that we've already discussed. But I believe that Tommen Forbes is the key we need to open some of these doors."

"Do you want me to bring him here, sir?"

"Not yet. Not until I, or we, can better ascertain Misik's intentions here. But I do want to keep an eye on him. He is wandering around on a planet marked for enslavement, and is very close to Micaiah Durvin of the Akarin." Rifun shifted his stance. "My real hope is that the Akarin will be afraid that I will have gotten the key or some other dastardly thing—"

"And go after it themselves," Win finished. "Do the dirty work for you."

"Exactly. But I need the journal delivered here, not destroyed or turned over to the Akarin."

"Shall I use a Disguise and go to the Akarin—?"

Rifun shook his head. "No. Cassius was Disguised as Doug for almost a year. The Akarin will be too paranoid for that to work a second time. What I might have you do, though, is Disguise yourself as me so I have an alibi here and can go out from time to time and keep an eye on things."

"And if I'm caught?"

"You are under my orders. Any of the grunts have an issue, you may send them to me. You will face no repercussions from me, provided you don't take such liberty too far." He gave Win a look, then let it drop. "If Misik catches you, do whatever the situation calls for, be it talking or fighting your way out. I don't anticipate needing such a decoy often, but if the occasion arises, that is what I expect."

"Of course, sir."

"Any questions?"

"Just one. What do you expect will happen if the Borelians do invade, whether provoked or not?"

Rifun sighed. "I expect every man to fight like hell. I also expect that it will quickly devolve into every man for himself."

Win nodded. "That is what I also foresee."

"I can't make you the commander of the army and have you working for me in this capacity, not without being found out. But I expect you understand what I'm asking of you."

"Yes, sir."

"You are working for me personally. You will report to me personally. Is that understood?"

"Yes, sir."

"Good. You are dismissed."

Win snapped a salute and left without another word, a mercenary with a mission. Rifun watched him leave, then let the Sound barrier dissolve. He went to his desk and sat down, but he wasn't there for sixty seconds before he was pushing everything away and standing again. No time like the present to test the limits of a Borelian's patience.

As much as he did not want to risk Lalao's safety, the Borelians would probably come for Earth first. He wanted to see her. He needed to figure out a way to protect her.

It was not a day they had scheduled to meet. All the same, she was thrilled to have him visit her at home and quickly ushered him in. Tomas and his brothers were out and about, and it was just the two of them. Lalao soon had tea and rice on the stove.

"So, last time we had lunch—" Her tone was half-teasing and half-annoyed that their lunches had been cut back from once a week to about once every two or three weeks. "—you said something about getting ready to kill the dragon." She grabbed a couple of mugs. "I was so worried! And now here you are! I take it that means things went well? The dragon is dead?"

Rifun just sighed. Lalao frowned as she took the kettle, just starting to whistle, and made up two cups of tea. She set one in front of him and sat down. "The dragon...is dead, right? You wouldn't be alive if it wasn't."

"Well, let's just say things went from good to bad to worse..."

23 | Amelioration
Fianarantsoa, 2014

I was beginning to think you'd forgotten about me."

On a whim, Julianna had decided to go to Madagascar, to see if she might find Rifun stomping around his home territory. And she was right. She caught him walking down the street of a residential neighborhood, looking...pacified, as if he'd been in a foul mood but something had cheered him up. Not enough that he was in a good mood, just not in a bad one anymore.

It was nothing for her to reach inside a streetlamp and manipulate the Electricity within. Some flickering got Rifun's attention, and Morse code told him to call her.

"You can't tell me you're ignorant of everything that's happened in the Wheel," Rifun told her, slowing his walk.

"And with so much going on, were you not going to fill in the details?" she demanded.

He sighed, whatever emotional balm had been applied to his bad mood quickly melting in the tropical heat. "How much do you know? What have you heard?"

"A fair amount, I think. I was sticking around Charleston, keeping an eye on Tommen Forbes. I heard about the coup, and I heard something about the Wheel being cut off from the universe. There was very little after that, and some speculation that perhaps it had even been destroyed, that there was no more Wheel of Time to go to. Then I happened to run into Cassius—metaphorically speaking, of course—and learned about the infiltration you had going on, using Cassius, impersonating Doug, to be the middle man between—"

"If you know all this, then what are you asking of me?" Rifun cut in, stopping on the sidewalk. "Do you want a play-by-play of the battle? If you've been following Tommen Forbes around, then I can't imagine you didn't track down the twins afterwards, and you've probably already gotten the story. We lost, Julianna.

We lost the Wheel."

"And...what? You're just going to retire back to your family farm, call it a day, oops we tried and it didn't work out?"

"I'm testing a few things."

"We had the Wheel, Rifun. We can try again."

"Not right now we can't because we have bigger problems. The Borelians have declared war on humanity, the Cult, and the Akarin." He explained the details, resuming his walk. The street turned from a respectable construction of paved road and sidewalk into a less impressive dirt road with no discernible division between vehicle and pedestrian, or even vehicle and vehicle. When he finished the explanation, Rifun said, "I came here just to see what my limits might be with Misik, see what I can get away with, and get some breathing room in general."

"Does the rest of the Cult know?" Julianna wondered.

"No, and I don't plan on telling them just yet. I've brought in one other person —"

"Who?"

"Godwin Lore. He's going to be my eyes and ears while I play nice with the general."

"I've heard the name," Julianna offered. She couldn't bring a face to mind, but she got a battle or military feel from it. She didn't pay much attention to the soldiering side of things, so she couldn't say anything more.

"Mercenary by trade, excellent soldier."

Rifun was lucky he couldn't see her expressions or body language. "You would trust a mercenary? After Cassius? After lecturing me about Cassius?"

"Cassius was possessed of an evil spirit, and I think we can safely say he was an exception to a universal rule. I do not put all my faith in Godwin Lore, but I can't do nothing while the Borelians close in."

Julianna hummed a resigned agreement. "You're not wrong about Cassius— him being an exception, I mean. But mercenaries are not known for their loyalty to anything but money."

"His life and not being thrown into Borelian slavery is worth more than fleeting currency. He said so himself. As I said, he is but one avenue I am exploring." Rifun turned off the main road onto something Julianna could not rightly describe as a street, but something more akin to an alley or a cart path. It snaked its way through a couple rows of slum houses before narrowing into a game trail and vanishing into jungle that quickly grew very dense.

"Yes, well, I thought I was another avenue," Julianna huffed. She passed through anything solid, but still she twisted and turned, trying to avoid touching anything.

"I was busy running things in the Wheel." Rifun cut her off. "If you don't want a moment-by-moment recap, then let's move on to the problems of the present." He stopped in a small clearing where an old wooden bench had rotted past its usefulness. "The Borelians have it out for us and all of humanity, I'm boxed in, and you're still trapped in the Land In Between."

Julianna took an even breath, trying to stop it from turning into a sigh. "All right. Fine. I'm guessing you want me to keep an eye on Tommen still?"

"If possible, but I figure I will make a renewed effort to rescue you. We've been trying off and on for a while, and I think it's benign enough that Misik won't care much about it."

"Hm...I can't say that I've ever been called 'benign.' That's a new one. But your words and your tone tell me this wasn't your first priority, if the Borelians were not actively coming after us."

"It was in my top five list."

"That's lovely when that list includes doing laundry and washing dishes. Your other four projects on that list, I think, are a bit more involved than that."

"Listen, I've got Godwin working on other things, and I'm doing a few things, seeing what my limits are with Misik. Once I've figured out a few things, then we can start planning your escape."

"That's quite a few things."

"More than you know."

"You can fill me in. I have the time." She went on before he could speak. "And what of the journals? You were able to retrieve the Book of Abilities. Now what of the Book of Commands?"

Rifun shifted uncomfortably. "The journal itself..." He sighed. "It's locked away in a Borelian temple in Ancrath. The key was hidden in the Core of the Wheel by the Akarin."

For a long moment, Julianna couldn't process his words. She'd heard that it had been found, but it was being kept safely squirreled away until after the coup, to minimize the chances of it being lost. Again. Now, it was both safely squirreled away and lost. She blinked and shook her head. "Beg pardon, Rifun, I don't think I heard you correctly."

"Yes, you did." He made a noise. "I was trying to get into the Core of the Wheel. I was able to do a lot of things, make a lot of changes, but I wasn't able to get to the key before we were ousted."

"Even so, I doubt Misik is going to just let you walk in, grab it, and check it out for three weeks."

"On that we can agree."

"So how do you propose we get it back?" Julianna shifted her stance. "If there is any consolation, it's that it is the Book of Commands and not the Book of Abilities, but it is still necessary for our operation."

"That thought has crossed my mind as well."

"Amid other thoughts of how to get it back, I hope?"

"A few passing thoughts to that regard, yes."

"I sense hesitation." Now she wished he could see her expression and body language. "Rifun, it's normal to have doubts about our beliefs and destiny, especially in the wake of such defeat—"

"How much did Cassius coerce you and Richard?" he asked.

"I'm sorry?"

"Come now, Julianna, the man is finally dead. Isthim, too. If Cassius was possessed by an evil spirit, then his words cannot be relied upon. We maintained the facade that the spirits simply drove Cassius mad with their knowledge and wisdom, but I think even you know that isn't true. What did Cassius tell your husband to write, and what did Richard actually believe?"

Julianna could not find the words to answer right away, for she could not understand what he was asking. Was he questioning Cassius? Or Richard? "Rifun, what are you suggesting? That we've been teaching evil things? Are you Micaiah in Disguise, perhaps?"

Rifun sighed and made a point of covering the nubs of his missing fingers. He also vigorously rubbed his face for good measure. Any Disguise would have been revealed by such movements. Had something overtaken his mind, then?

"I looked to the journals, the Book of Abilities, for a way to be rid of Cassius' evil spirit," Rifun continued. "But if that evil spirit dictated the journals, it wouldn't have such information in there. Given the difficulty I had with Building...I suspect there is a lot more that's missing. From all the journals in their respective areas."

She considered this for a minute, occasionally stuttering a half-hearted response. Then, "You know Richard and I were Akarin, and we left because of the turmoil that ensued when the first Authored Book appeared. The Akarin were corrupt. Are corrupt. Richard was inspired to write, but he was no author. Like Moses and his speech impediment, Richard required a helper to interpret and dictate."

"If I remember correctly, Moses and Aaron were brothers with a common cause."

"The point is, Richard needed help."

"And Cassius' evil spirit...it just...doesn't bother you? After everything he put you through, you never once wondered if there might be something wrong with or missing from the journals?"

Julianna straightened with a huff. "Are you saying—?"

"I'm asking what Richard honestly believed. What you believed. Before Cassius got involved. I'm thinking we may need to slowly revise the journals, remove any evil Cassius slipped in, and add anything he left out because it went against the evil spirit."

She shook her head. "Rifun, you're a smart man. You believed in the journals even before you read them. And when you did, you learned so much! You became a Builder!"

"A Builder who could do everything except the two things that needed to be done: retrieve the key from the Core and defeat the dragon."

"We could not have predicted the key," Julianna defended flatly.

"The key is less important than the Core itself," Rifun said. "The Author showed me the Core, showed me what I would need to do. The journals gave me the guidance and abilities. But it just wasn't enough."

"Rifun, I don't know what you're asking."

He sighed. "I don't know how else to explain it, and I think I'm running out of time with Misik."

"Is he going to watch you sleep? Follow you to the bathroom?"

"Well, he hasn't posted a guard on me yet, and I don't want to tempt it."

"Fine. What do you expect me to do from here?"

Rifun nodded. "I think I was on to something with the separation of dimensions. If you can revisit any of the sites and see what they look like now, if there is any evidence, that might prove useful. If you are able to explore the mechanics of your so-called Traveling ability, that might help also. And keep watch over Tommen. I fully believe he still has a part to play, but I'll explain that later."

"All right, I'll do it. But you can't leave me in the dark for long periods of time and then get flustered when I ask for information."

"I'll be around as often as I can. If not me, I will send Godwin."

"The mercenary."

"You're in the in-between dimension; he can't touch you."

"I know that. I'm not worried about myself, not directly."

"Flattered, I'm sure." Rifun shifted his stance and straightened. "I'll be back as soon as I can, hopefully in the next few days, with better information."

"I will hold you to it."

He hung up, looked around, opened a portal to his chambers in the officers building, and disappeared, leaving Julianna alone. She paced back and forth a few times in the clearing that was slowly being reclaimed by the jungle. It may have been a park once, or an attempt at one. Now it was just something that used to be, a rotting memorial to better days, when people who knew what they were doing ruled the land.

If Julianna was thankful for anything in the in-between dimension, it was the ability to Walk, or Travel. All she had to do was turn in a direction, think of where she wanted to be, and start walking. Whether it was some residual manner of Time or a portal, she did not know, but she would be at her destination in just a few seconds, a few steps it felt like. All the convenience of a portal or a Band, without the actual, physical strain.

She wished she had someone she could order around, send to Charleston in her stead, but most fateful visitors ended up killing themselves once they realized there was no way out of this dimension. But she was growing weary of shadowing Americans. Loud, obnoxious, blinded by their own arrogance as if they single-handedly stood between Earth and evil. She was especially tired of following a teenage boy around. He had no social graces to speak of. His customer service at the bakery was mediocre at best and when in the kitchen, he kept his workspace as clean as his room. If not for the mandatory cleanup at the end of the night, the place would look and smell just as bad.

And he had no concept of how to court a woman. He was clumsy and inarticulate and had little to offer. Julianna found herself offended, not only by his girlfriend and her low standards, but by the girlfriend's father. Oh, he pretended to scrutinize Tommen, but how or why he agreed to let the two see each other was beyond her.

Was Rifun really sure that this uncouth, hormonal child was in any way favored by the Author? Micaiah was a bad enough choice, being an unruly, savage Irishman—at least he looked good—but Tommen? That was a tragic step down. And that was all assuming the Authored Books meant anything. If the Author placed her hope in the unlikely savages of the world—the Native Americans, the Irish, the Welsh, the Malagasy and the Africans—well, the Akarin were the payoff from that, and what a sad investment it had been.

Now her, Julianna, she was of pure English stock. Richard had just as fine a pedigree. Even when she was just a common Harvester she had Harvested only Englishmen so as not to contaminate herself. And the group that they started, the Cult of the Akari, had been the one to mobilize. They had been the ones to retake the Wheel from the corrupt Time industry. Julianna could not speak to precise movements or tactics as she had not been present at the ensuing overthrow, but the one common denominator she saw was that Rifun and Cassius had been left in charge. That was why the Author had punished them. They should have freed her before taking over. Then they would still be ruling in the Wheel.

But what could she expect from a couple of savage men, men from people who saw something they wanted and just took it, with no regard for others? Rifun she had held some hope for on account of his French parentage, except now she wondered whether he wasn't allowing the more superstitious and less noble part of himself take over.

This line of thought bothered her more than she thought it should as she kept an eye on Tommen Forbes. She did not follow him around like a prison guard, but she checked in on him a few times a day, watched for about an hour, then retreated to the more civilized parts of the world. Very little of interest happened, as near as she could tell. He went to school, went to work, went home. The school year ended and summer vacation began. Nothing changed except he started working a little more.

Bored, Julianna also checked in on the twins. At least Micaiah should have something more interesting to look in on, and she wasn't referring to the feral sex between him and his savage wife.

At least this endeavor proved more fruitful. Although she could not follow the twins to the Wheel, they were kind enough to hold a meeting about it afterwards in the bakery office. The Akari was now banned in the Wheel, all use and mention. It might frighten the plebeians after the recent traumatic ordeal involving the Cult and the Akarin and whatnot. They organized another meeting for the end of June to discuss it further with the larger Akarin community on Earth, or so she assumed.

It was two days before Rifun returned to Earth so she could call him and tell him the news.

"Unsurprising, really," was all he initially had to say about it. "At least we don't have to worry about hostilities on that front. Even if the Time industry is weak, they are still more numerous and annoying."

"Are you going to see about infiltrating the Akarin meeting?" Julianna wondered. "How are things with the Cult? Have you come up with any ideas regarding the Land In Between? Darn you, Rifun, but I don't hear from you often enough!"

"I've been more concerned with other things, like the Borelians."

"Are they taking members away into slavery?"

"Not yet, but they are preparing their first waves of mobilization against humanity. I think Misik is just trying to rub my nose in it, the way he talks about it. I think he wants to see what I'll do, if I'll try to tell anyone or come up with some counter."

"Is there anything I can do? What are their plans?"

He looked around as if expecting a Borelian to be standing there. "They're not going after Earth first. Too easy, too obvious, especially with me and you here. They're going after Treman and Trebald first."

"The twin colonies? Why them? Why not...why not Hlohi? They have the smallest population and the worst defenses." She added quickly, "Well, maybe not the worst defenses. They are still primal savages there, they will defend themselves. Aleis, then, for the worst defenses."

"Treman and Trebald are the closest to Earth in population and technology, just a couple decades behind. It's a test run." Rifun shifted his stance. "I don't know what you can do. The only thing I can think, since you can manipulate computers, get word to some Time Agent somewhere who can make contact and maybe give them some kind of warning."

Julianna nodded unnecessarily. "I can figure something out, I suppose."

"The good news is that, warden of the Cult or not, Misik is still a general, and his attention is now divided. The rest of the Borelians in our ranks are also more interested in the impending invasion and war than anything we're doing. I expect there will be a gap opening up for us to get you out of the in-between dimension."

"You have given it some thought, then?"

"I have. Did you visit the warehouse and any other sites of interest?"

"Honestly, no. I got distracted by other things."

"Well, do that. And while you're at it, visit Forbes Cave again and see if you can learn anything more about it from that side."

Julianna shifted her stance. "Rifun, I visited that place often enough when you were planning to retrieve the Book of Abilities."

"The Time Trap may have changed in forty years."

She rolled her eyes. "All right, fine. But you had better have something for me the next time you come here."

"I'll let you tell that to Misik."

"Please, Rifun, I'm sure he'll figure it out once I magically show up after so many decades of being gone."

"Permission and forgiveness."

"True."

"And what about you?" Rifun wondered.

"What about me?"

"Have you given any thought to my question earlier? Is there anything missing from the journals? Or some evil that has been added to them?"

Julianna sighed. "You do realize that such questions would cast doubt on their —on our legitimacy, right?"

"If the books were written by men, certainly." He did not sound concerned. "Only a fool denies the spirits. I simply wonder which spirits wrote the journals. I can't trust that Cassius' evil spirit did not omit essential elements of the Author and insert its own ideology."

"But would that not only prove that the Author is unable or unwilling to defend her people?"

"We are still human, Julianna, still subject to human whims and flaws. Peer pressure, for instance. And Cassius was a great tsunami of evil pressure. In the aftermath of the Akarin split, it would not surprise that your guard was down as you sought guidance from the Author."

"Rifun, the journals are fine," she cut in sharply. "They're fine. You just didn't have time to learn everything you needed to know. Cassius was too unpredictable. You had a bag full of tools but couldn't figure out the one you needed in time. I'm sorry. With him gone, no longer hovering over us as you said, you can take time to figure things out. And it sounds like you may have some ideas when it comes to freeing me. That in itself should be a worthy test, right?"

He still looked uncertain. Then, "I suppose. Some things should be prioritized more than others. For right now, you over the journals. The fate of humanity and the Cult over the journals."

"Excellent. Now then, figure something out."

She hung up before she said anything foolish.

How could such brilliance and such stupidity reside in a single man? Smart enough to survive under the thumb of the Borelians and use others to carry out clandestine operations in hopes of saving humanity, stupid enough to question his betters. He wasn't there in the beginning. He never knew Richard. Julianna was there. She knew. Her husband had been strong. He had conviction. He had conviction unto death. She had read and edited the journals herself. She had ensured their accuracy.

Or was Rifun assuming that she was just some less-than woman? That she was incapable of reading and editing and discerning for herself? Was he suggesting that she was too weak? She would not deny that she had been very afraid of Cassius, that she had run from him. But that was the point, wasn't it? She had run. She never gave in. She looked him in the eye and stole the journals, hid them away.

Frustrated, she left the area, returning to London and searching out a high-ranking Time Agent, specifically his computer. She was going to have a say in this. She was going to help save Treman and Trebald, and she was going to do a damn good job of it.

As it happened, she found the Doctorate Harvester for Earth (the equivalent of the Gatekeeper Timekeeper) sitting at his computer in his office in some swanky upscale building in downtown London. Reaching inside his computer, Julianna switched over to his email, opened up a new message, and started typing, manipulating the tiny electrical currents in the system to generate letters on the screen. The Harvester, a man by the name of James Wicke, just about shot through the window behind him as he violently pushed himself away from the desk.

"Good morning, Mr. Wicke," she wrote, hoping that politeness would win her a receptive audience. "This is not a cyber attack, nor a virus of any form. I am holding no files hostage, nor am I asking for any form of ransom. If you ask your IT department to trace this work or look for some external perpetrator, it will come up only as a malfunctioning computer."

"What the fuck?" Wicke said aloud, getting close and peering at the screen like an old man.

"You are the Doctorate Harvester for Earth. Therefore, you have some peer influence over other Doctorates, and maybe the Gatekeepers. The Borelians have declared war on humanity, although the declaration may not have been officially sent out yet. Their first target is not Earth, but Treman and Trebald. They need to be warned."

Wicke was still mesmerized by the letters popping up on the screen. "What the...? Who the fuck are y—? What's going on here?"

For a long moment, Julianna considered introducing herself and her relation to the Cult. Then she decided that might not go over very well. Wait until the threat was proven true, then let everyone know who it was that saved them. "My identity is not important. Only this information and the safety of the twin colonies. They must be warned."

Now Wicke blinked, and his expression turned from childish wonder to something serious. "Well, I don't know what's going on here right now, but with everything that's happened in the Wheel lately, I suppose we shouldn't discount the possibility of a Borelian attack." He shrugged helplessly. "I guess if you've got control over my keyboard, you probably have control over my camera and microphone, too. You'd have to, to have answered my question. You probably also know that I was up-jumped to this position, after our ranks were decimated. Truthfully, I'm barely more than a Master Harvester. But I appreciate the confidence you have in me. I will warn them."

"Thank you. Good luck."

"Although, if you can hack my computer, why not tell the Tremene and Trebaldi directly?"

The only thing Julianna could come up with was, "The Borelians go after communication systems first, to monitor their targets. This way is safer."

It could have been entirely true, for all she knew. Even if it wasn't, it was convincing enough. The man nodded. "Makes sense. All right, I'll see what I can do."

"Thank you."

Her mission complete, Julianna departed, feeling rather accomplished. There. She did it. She sent out a warning, or she mobilized someone else to do so. Briefly she considered finding a few other high-ranking Time Agents and attempting to get them to coordinate their efforts, then decided against it. That would be on Treman and Trebald to do; she was only sending out the messenger.

That was how a plan was supposed to go. Make plan, execute plan, accomplish a simple goal. Too many extra pieces only slowed things down and increased the likelihood of it all going to hell. Take over Wheel, hold Wheel. Why had that been so difficult, really? Because a couple of superstitious numbskulls had been in charge.

Next plan, then. Freeing her. Her part in this was, once again, examining Forbes Cave. She had already done so many times for various reasons, and somehow, Rifun thought this time was going to be different. Knowing no one would see, Julianna rolled her eyes as she Walked to the cave.

Still there, the giant boulder not quite blocking the entrance, a small chain with a pretty sign supposedly deterring curious passersby, a tarnished plaque detailing the history and dedication of the cave. Inside, the Time Trap still writhed like a living creature, ready to swallow the unwary and spit them out at some unknown point in the future. Nothing had changed, even in forty years.

"Sad, isn't it?"

Julianna looked, if only out of curiosity. The cave was technically off-limits to hikers ("toxic gases," the sign said) and the trail had been cut off years ago. Who was coming up here now?

It was a single man, Native American by appearance though he wore clothing that was as out of style as her own, and it was this that made her suspect he might actually be speaking to her.

"What is?" she inquired cautiously.

"The things that are going to happen." He walked up beside her on the right, about ten feet between them, hands behind his back, looking at the cave, looking mildly amused by the little warning sign. "But that for as much as they will change, the more things will stay the same."

"Who are you?" Julianna demanded. "And how are you speaking to me? I know everyone in this dimension, and there aren't very many, but your clothes suggest you've been here a while."

"You know who I am. I am the reason you are where you are." He put up a finger. "The reason, but not the cause."

"Anagalisgi."

"That's right."

She turned to face him fully. "You and your fucking brother ruined everything. The Akarin collapsed because of you. All of this, the split, the journals, this war between us, is because of you."

He gave her a sideways glance. "The reason. Not the cause." He turned to match her stance. "The Akarin were already falling away and in need of guidance. When that guidance came, they rebelled."

"A book about a savage people," Julianna hissed.

He was unmoved, countering, "From a savage race, according to some. My people or yours, we are still just savage humans. Why would the Author write a Book about any of us at all?"

"A prank by a couple of bleeding heart traitors."

"Nathan and Andrew."

"That's right. They divided the kingdom and the Akarin. And when we tried to set things right again, they took the journals and tried to divide us, too."

Anagalisgi snickered which only served to annoy her further. At her look, he shrugged and said, "I mean, you did fall for it. Bested by a traitor and a savage Irishman."

Julianna waved a hand and made an angry noise as she stormed off half a dozen steps. She whirled around. "Why are you here? To patronize me?"

"An attempt to warn you away from the path you are about to take. Although, I now see that this conversation is what perhaps steers you into it more completely, thus setting in motion the required sequence of events."

"I don't believe the Author favors you in any way, and I don't believe in your pagan soothsaying magic. Your demons can't see or influence the future."

"The Shadows have only an inkling of the future, yet they work their hardest to change it. They will steal, kill, and destroy, all to save their own skins and spite the Author if they can."

"And that is what I am trying to prevent. The Borelians are coming after humanity you know."

He shrugged again. "You are but a slave to them. A less than. A nobody. Why don't you fall in line, puny savage? Don't you know your place in the universe? They travel through space, we do not. They have natural biological advantages. We do not. Now sit down and listen to your betters."

Julianna straightened. "I never!"

"That's right. You never." He began casually walking toward her. "You never feel appreciated, never feel satisfied. You never take initiative because you never want to feel defeat. And as long as you let others do the work, you never feel responsible for such defeat even as you never appreciate the risks others take on your behalf."

She wanted to slap him. She wanted to punch him. As it was, the best she managed was a small, frustrated stomp, rather reminisce of a cranky toddler. "How dare you speak to me in such a way! When I am freed, all your evil demon spirits will be defeated!"

"That has already been taken care of," Anagalisgi said, still as calm as ever. "My nephew did that a hundred years ago. As for you, you were bound here by the word of the Author, not through some mystical means. The exit has always been there; it is the key that has been hidden until such time as the Author decreed."

"Do not blaspheme the Author on your tongue," she growled.

She paced back and forth several times. Anagalisgi was reputed to be a powerful sorcerer, and she wasn't sure she really wanted to test her abilities against his, not now. And she could never take him in physical combat.

"If I am trapped here by decree of the Author, if the exit is always there, why are you here then?" she countered. "What's keeping you here?"

"The love of family, the love of people. This is the task I have been given, to work with the Whites, to guide. I am here by choice."

Julianna shook her head. "A poor choice, then. Perhaps you are the reason I have been trapped here. You are the guardian holding the key. Well, if I have learned anything, it's that everyone pays attention to the lock. No one looks at the hinges. I will be free, and you will still be here. And when I am free of this place, I'm going to go after your nephew and kill him and his demonic consorts. Then I'll go after your whole people, your whole tribe, wipe them out of existence. And after that, every single one of the Author's so-called chosen ones from the Books."

Anagalisgi frowned. His demeanor shifted, as if he had known something would happen in spite of his best efforts, yet he made those efforts anyway. He looked Julianna in the eye, yet he did not seem to speak to her. "Yes, Sedagina. You will try. And you will fail, as you have failed over and over and over again. Because the end does not change."

"I will not listen to your poison words," Julianna declared. "I will be free and I will free the universe of the Akarin's heretical influence."

She turned to leave, but Anagalisgi spoke again. "Julianna." Sighing, she looked at him. "Cassius was slave to Sedagina. And you knew his feelings about being a slave. I know your feelings about being subservient. I expect Sedagina to introduce itself as Atsvsnoquisi and promise a great many glorious things. But know that you will always be its servant. And one day, you will see that Atsvsnoquisi and Sedagina were always the same and you are a slave."

"Seems to me that you are on a first-name basis with a whole host of devils. I'll get to them eventually. Maybe they'll disappear when your people do."

He just shook his head. "Names are trivial matters here, for the beast knows its identity well enough. After all, the Borelians call it Tujor."

Julianna glared at him and stalked off without another word. How she wished she could have recorded that conversation. If ever there was confirmation that the Authored Books were evil and misleading, this was it. Anagalisgi was no hero. He and his people worshiped devils. They fled Earth to work their dark magic in isolation, where no one could stop them. They had bewitched the Akarin. Perhaps they were responsible for Cassius' madness and his alleged consorting with demons.

No wonder Rifun had been unable to defeat the evil spirit. He had failed to factor in an entirely unique angle. Perhaps there was a kernel of truth in the Authored Books, but it was a seed of evil, rotten, poisonous fruit. The Krydik were evil demon-worshipers. They had corrupted the Akarin.

So then, what about the rest of the so-called chosen ones? Micaiah Durvin was a savage Irishman, but he had been raised Catholic and his current disposition was fairly ambiguous as far as she could tell. His wife, Aklaq, still practiced some savage spirituality from her homeland, but nothing to the extreme of Anagalisgi or the Krydik. Tommen Forbes, if he was a chosen one, was a professed atheist. Where did it all intersect? Or were they just the gullible parishioners, the Krydik the mysterious head of the cult? Wasn't that how it worked for the Masons and Freemasons, the grunts knew nothing while the highest officers dabbled in darker things?

She was right, then. It all had to go. Anagalisgi, the Krydik, the entire Akarin order. Of course, she would have to take some time to collect her thoughts and craft her speech. She couldn't just start her next phone call with Rifun saying that she wanted to commit mass genocide against one people and then go and wipe out one of the primary religious sects of the universe. She would have to sell the idea to him, let him know that it really was for the greater good that this would have to be done. Perhaps she should wait on such an argument until after her rescue, lest he have second thoughts about saving her at all.

She left the area of the cave and headed into town, intending to shadow Tommen. Of the so-called chosen ones, he was the greatest wild card right now, pledging allegiance to no faction other than Time, and that only because of rote duty, because of his Apprenticeship. That tie was not especially strong. He could be swayed in any other direction; they would just have to ensure it was the right one, before Micaiah convinced him to look too deep into the Akarin.

This time of day, he would probably be at the bakery, she figured. But when she arrived, she found only the twins and Walter. She might have left to look elsewhere, but decided to listen in on the conversation, just in case.

"What are you going to do with yourself?" the younger twin, Micah, was asking.

The bakery wasn't busy, just the three men at the counter and a couple sitting at a table across the room.

"I don't know," Walter mused, stuffing a couple napkins in the bag Micaiah handed him. "I might take a few days to enjoy it, not having to listen to him stomp around the house or turn his music up too loud."

"You're going to take a nap, is that it?" Micaiah said.

"Of course I am."

"And he's pretty far up there, isn't he?" Micah wondered. "Few hours, at least. No quick jaunts back home in the middle of the night."

"He says he understands." Walter's voice was sarcasm mixed with amusement. "We'll see how long it lasts."

"Four weeks is a long time. Up in...Whitewood?"

"Wellspring."

"Wellspring, right. Still, you think he can handle it? He's never been around kids before. At least, not like that."

Walter shrugged. "We'll see."

Wellspring? Kids? For four weeks? Julianna had trouble piecing it together until Micaiah went and removed a flyer from the bulletin board on the wall. She managed to jog over and sneak a look at it before he threw it in the trash. Eagle Eye Youth Summer Camp. Actually it was a help wanted ad, for a counselor assistant.

So, Tommen had left the bakery. Hm...maybe she should have been keeping a little closer eye on him because she had never gotten any indication that he was that dissatisfied with his job.

One advantage of the in-between dimension was the ability to look back in time, turn the clock back to see anything she wanted. She could not interact, but she could watch. Here, now, Walter and twins melted away, and she began to watch various moments from the bakery in the last week or two. Most of it was mundane, until she found a meeting between Tommen and the twins.

The twins had gotten in trouble with OSHA for making him manager. Too young, the inspector said. The twins' hands were tied, and Tommen had a small temper tantrum and quit to go work as a summer camp counselor. Well, that might make things a little bit easier, she thought. That meant he couldn't go running to the twins or his father for safety.

She found a map of the state in some tourist center and eventually managed to track down Wellspring. It was some dinky, no account speck on the map near Elkins. Something nearby caught her eye. There, just a few miles from the speck, "Krydik Tribal Grounds and Reservation."

Not separated. Spirited away. Micaiah knew that he and his wife and brother would be targets for the Cult, so they sent him to be among the Krydik, or their Earth offices anyway.

Julianna shook her head. She looked around to get her bearings, then turned in the direction of Wellspring and Walked there.

Like most towns in West Virginia, the homes and businesses were stacked on top of one another, parking was virtually non-existent, and garbage from the last flood littered the riverbanks up to the streets. Among the men, and even some of the women, wearing a shirt meant you were overdressed. Most people had a cigarette in hand or mouth, some with bottles or cans, many with obnoxious tattoos. But their cars were nice. Everything else was falling apart, but state law said the cars had to be nice and in tip-top condition. How quaint. And this place was what people in other states aspired to? Bloody hell, how did they ever win the revolution?

The summer camp was about ten miles outside of town and another three miles straight up a mountain. Because why not? Where else would you put such a thing? In the valley? Well, no, because then it would flood. Why the hell did people live in places like this? If not for the ability to Walk anywhere she needed to go, Julianna might have just given up. Rescue her first, then deal with Tommen and the Krydik.

Where the rest of the area was basically in shambles, the camp was remarkably modern and luxurious. An enormous log building served as the main hall with a full kitchen, a dining area that could be converted into a basketball court, and multiple classrooms off another hallway. A couple cinderblock buildings housed offices, the nurse's station, the camp store, as well as the laundry and showers. The cabins where the campers and counselors slept were log buildings filled with metal bunkbeds to sleep between twelve and twenty, depending on the cabin. Then there were outdoor basketball courts and other cleared areas for various games and activities. All of this on a huge slope so that just getting from one's bed to the dining hall was a major workout.

There were people here, whom Julianna guessed were the counselors, though it did not appear that there were any kids here yet. Judging by the cleaners and the trash bags everywhere, the counselors were preparing the camp, dusting off furniture, minor repairs, things of that nature.

It wasn't difficult to locate Tommen, cleaning the bathrooms, but it was the man he worked with that really got her attention. She might have said it was Anagalisgi, except this man was clearly interacting with the normal world. There was an undeniable familial resemblance, yet this was overshadowed by something more. More than just bottled trauma, it was almost like a righteous anger or determination.

Didn't matter, Julianna decided. He was Krydik, and that was enough.

She turned and was suddenly face-to-face with an enormous white wolf. Its hot breath stirred her hair. While she was momentarily paralyzed with fear, the wolf shouldered its way between her and the Krydik man. It kept one eye on her, but it also seemed to watch something beyond her. When she looked, she saw nothing and no one.

"The Whites are supposed to help people," she said, finally finding her voice. "Good people on righteous missions from the Author."

"And so we have," the wolf growled, still only half paying attention to her. "And so we will."

"I may not understand the nuances of how you move about in the dimensions, but he is the heretic here." She pointed at the man who stood from where he was fixing a sink pipe. He stretched and winced at some pain in his back. "Him and all of his people. Tearing the Akarin away with their 'Authored Books.' "

The wolf continued to bare its teeth, but Julianna was not convinced that it was aimed at her as it continued to glance at something she evidently could not see.

"I seek only to bring the Akari-bearers back together in unity and peace and restore the Akari to its rightful place and pure glory."

"And you will do so, one way or another," a familiar voice said. Anagalisgi appeared near the wolf. He walked up to it and put a hand gently on its back. "You have a chance to do many great things, and your goal will be fulfilled. Whether this is because or in spite of you, is up to you. Set aside your anger, your contempt for mortal men, and work to build this relationship you seek. Or pursue this road of treachery and death and watch as the walls close in on all sides, pressing hard against you until you fall."

Julianna glared at him, shaking her head. "More mysticism. More pagan nonsense. I will unify and spread the Akari."

"More mysticism, more human nonsense. Or is it, perhaps, the truth that matters? The message, not the messenger?"

More white wolves began to appear. She started backing up. "I will be free. And when I am, I will destroy your people. You're trapped here; you can't help them. And when they're all gone—" She pointed at him. "—I will come back for you specifically. Then we'll see who the Author really favors, who the Whites really should be supporting. Assuming you're actually Whites and not just Shadows in Disguise. I assume that's a thing."

"Wouldn't your journals tell you if that were the case?"

"I'm coming for you. But first, I'm coming for your kid here, whoever he is to you." She nodded. "I'm coming."

She turned and hurried away.

Rifun didn't know much about the Krydik. Even their last Authored Book ended with them being defeated at the end of the American Civil War. There was some mention of a child called Sabelu at the very end, but in the hundred-plus years since, nothing had come of the exiled peoples. Why Julianna was so uptight about them, he did not fully understand. Was it concerning that Tommen was working under one of them, possibly a cover by Micaiah to whisk him away for secret Akari training? Yes. Was it the most concerning matter on his plate right now? Well...no, not really.

He'd even impersonated Sabelu, also called Saul, a time or two, just for a few minutes, just to see if he were training Tommen secretly, but all evidence said otherwise. Was Sabelu even Akarin? He must have had some Akari abilities to still be alive at over a hundred years old, but he did not appear to be Akarin. But then, none of the Krydik were, to Rifun's knowledge. Again, not his highest priority.

At the same time, dragging Tommen away for some clandestine training seemed more feasible than breaking Julianna out of the in-between dimension. He had managed to sneak away to Forbes Cave a few times, still experimenting with inanimate objects, pushing them into the in-between dimension and then trying to get them back out. He did seem to be making progress. He couldn't describe exactly what the change was, but he was able to retrieve small objects: a book, a bowl, even a chair. But when he went to grab Julianna, he just couldn't do it. At best, it was a Chinese finger trap. At worst, the dimension itself seemed to want to pull him inside.

The Energy of the dimension was different. Rifun had a theory that maybe it operated on a principle of Energy being neither created nor destroyed. It had to exist in some kind of perfect equilibrium. Julianna had been part of the dimension long enough that she was part of that equilibrium. Her Energy—be it literal energy, as from heart and brain function, or metaphorical, as from her spirit, he did not know—could not be removed, only replaced.

If that were true, then even an animal should serve as a suitable replacement, a simple sacrifice, nothing uncommon for him. He just needed to find an acceptable animal—a goat or a cow should do it—and prepare the ceremony.

He looked up as his door opened. Any day now, Misik would barge in and attack him. He just knew it. But it was only Godwin.

"How did it go?" Rifun asked.

"Package delivered," Win reported. "Message sent."

"Details, Win. I can't not know what I've been out doing or saying."

"The kids were out in survival camp, or what passes as survival camp these days, I suppose." He shrugged and Rifun non-verbally agreed. "I gave Tommen his first Book, suggested he read it. He gave me lip so I demonstrated a few party tricks. The water in the lungs and the paralysis are your favorites, I believe."

"They're the ones he is most familiar with, yes."

"Anyway, he has his first Book. I fully expect he will tell the twins about it, if he hasn't already by this time. I also left a few more clues for him to find."

"Oh? Like what?"

"Reiterating your warning about 'dropping like flies' and whatnot, left for his dad to find. I also caused a little mayhem and destruction around the camp. Broken windows, busted doors, a cut gas line—"

"Why?" Rifun cut in. "What purpose does that serve?"

"Letting him know who's in charge. I didn't steal anything."

"Broken windows and doors, fine. You could have blown up half the camp with a cut gas line. Tommen is the only one there we're focused on. We don't need to kill a bunch of little kids."

Win appeared to consider his words, but his expression was unmoved. Rifun sighed. "Anything else?"

"Julianna called while I was there."

"Still obsessing over Sabelu and the Krydik?"

"She had me kill a wolf and leave it for Saul to find."

Rifun slapped a hand on the table. "Dammit, Lore, why?! For one, you're working for me, not her. For two, what purpose does it serve?!"

Win blinked. "She said she wanted to see if she couldn't provoke him to some kind of action that would reveal where the Krydik stand."

"On Hlohi, a million lightyears away. Who cares? If this is about the Borelian declaration of war, that is a horrendous way of trying to warn them or see if they need or want help. Otherwise, this is just her personal vendetta. And now I'm going to get blamed for this shit. Worse, I have to pretend like it was my idea." Win opened his mouth, but Rifun beat him to it. "Do shit like this again, and I will hand you over to the Borelians myself as a traitor. I'm not here to blow up children or destroy icons. Is that understood?"

"Yes, sir."

"Good."

Win shifted his stance. "What should I tell Julianna, if she confronts me about it or asks something else of me?"

"You are to refuse her request and refer her to me. At this point, all she can do is yell at you, at which point you refuse her request, refer her to me, and hang up the damn phone."

"Yes, sir."

"Good." Rifun shifted uncomfortably in his seat.

"Was there anything else you needed from me at this time, beyond standing orders?"

Rifun sighed, thought a moment, then shook his head. "No. I think you've done enough for the time being. I expect that within the next week or two, I will be making the first true attempt at freeing Julianna from the Land In Between. I suspect I shall need to keep my head low around Misik during this time, which includes my impostor. Standing orders remain, but you are free for your own pursuits for the time being."

"Thank you, sir."

"Dismissed."

The mercenary saluted and left the room.

By the ancestors... Rifun sighed and rubbed his face. He might have hoped that Win would be a little smarter than Cassius when it came to executing plans effectively. Next he was going to find the man had the same sick sexual fetishes. Was it a requirement for mercenaries or just the ones he knew? Where were the normal commoners he wanted to attract to the Cult, those who simply believed in something and wanted to defend it?

He slapped the desk again, less violently this time. Damn it.

He turned back to his notes but found his attention wandering. He needed to rescue Julianna, yes, but he would have to somehow repair what damage had been done at the camp. There had been no call for any of that, and it would only make

Tommen paranoid that the Cult was evil and Rifun was out to kill him.

Sighing, Rifun stood and went to his shrine. Julianna first. If he was correct in his energy assumptions, then that would be an easy rescue, relatively speaking. Do that, then maybe use her gentler demeanor to help him repair the bridge between him and Tommen. He bowed to pray, asking for guidance. He only wanted to make this attempt once. Maybe he should just go with the cow. It would have the most energy to give to replace what Julianna would leave behind, as compared to a goat or a chicken.

And yet, as he prayed, he knew it wouldn't be enough. A cow was only an animal. Part of creation, yes, but still an animal only. This was not merely about electrical activity in the heart and brain, this was about the soul. If he were rescuing a cow, he could use a cow. But he was rescuing a human. Furthermore, it had to be voluntary.

Why, though? he wondered silently. No one entered the in-between dimension willingly. Julianna hadn't when she got sucked in. And whoever went willingly would be trapped just as she was. That wasn't a rescue. It wasn't even a hostage exchange.

Human sacrifice. The thought was not his own. Room had to be made. One spirit slain so another could take its place.

The dragon, Rifun thought hopefully. Remove the dragon, rescue Julianna, bring her out in its place. *Now where is it?*

Saul Wolf. Sabelu.

Of the Krydik?

The very same.

Rifun opened his eyes and sat up. He'd just chastised Win about killing the wolf. That was going to be a tough pill to swallow. On the other hand...how would that make sense? The Krydik were the ones first written about by the Author. Was it possible the Authored Books were as heretical as Julianna believed? He thought over what he'd read in the Krydik's Books. Sabelu was mentioned only briefly at the end of the second Book, his life fought over. Was he a prophet of good, or possessed of an evil spirit? Well, Cassius had been alive at the time, but was it possible the Krydik priests had been looking ahead? Was it possible that the dragon had gone to Sabelu after Cassius?

It must have. Both priests had been right in their own way, it was just a matter of where they were looking in time. Maybe Sabelu was an excellent priest or prophet of his people, but his attunement to the spirits made him susceptible to the dragon's influence. Yes, that had to be it.

Rifun bowed again for a few moments, then stood.

If there was anything he didn't like about this, it was the massive lump of pride he was going to have to swallow when he told Win what he was going to do. Sometimes, there really was such a thing as instant karma.

He waited a day before summoning the mercenary.

"Change of plans?" Win inquired.

"Swallowing the pill of pride," Rifun admitted grudgingly. "I have been inquiring into the methods and rituals required for rescuing Julianna from the in-between dimension. Part of it involves a sacrifice. That sacrifice has been determined to be Sabelu, Saul Wolf."

"If you are apologizing for chewing me out over the wolf thing..."

"It was a warning, yes. To him, that his time was short. His time of being an impostor priest is coming to a rapid close. I see and understand that now. It doesn't excuse the cut gas line, but for the wolf incident..." He trailed off, silently choking on the pill as it went down.

"Apology accepted, sir." Rifun did not miss the tiny smirk on the mercenary's face. "When would you like the job done?"

"I must do it myself. It is my ritual to perform, my plan for rescue being conducted. I need you to buy me time here, be my alibi."

"Of course, sir. Shall I take out the Borelians at the same time?"

"Has their disposition changed any that you have noticed?"

"No, sir."

"Then no, not yet. That may change once Julianna reappears, if they figure out our little charade we've got going. Therefore, you are permitted to plan for the eventuality, but do not carry it out just yet."

"Understood, sir."

"We'll also have to move quickly on Tommen. Micaiah Durvin is his friend, which is a difficult enough bond to usurp. I believe Micaiah sent Tommen to the camp to train and be protected by Sabelu, believing Sabelu was still an Akari-bearer bound to the Author, not realizing that after Cassius' death, the dragon took possession of him. Tommen is in danger but none of them realize it yet. I will have to get to him and begin his training as soon as possible." Rifun noted Win's expression. "You look like you have something to say."

Win cleared his throat and shifted his stance. "Permission to speak freely?"

"Granted."

"What the hell are you talking about, sir? I am familiar with many different religions and I don't mean to step on anyone's beliefs—God knows I still struggle with the teachings of the Book of Philosophy some days—but what are you going on about, dragons and possession and whatnot?"

Rifun nodded. "The Whites are the spiritual servants of the Author. The Shadows oppose them, and their leader is the dragon. Cassius was a puppet of the dragon, but merely killing flesh will not kill the evil spirit within. Cassius was killed rather unceremoniously and the dragon got away. I have tracked it to Sabelu."

Godwin's expression was carefully neutral. "I see."

"I'm afraid I am not much of a teacher or else I would do a better job of explaining it."

"I understand, sir. I'm not much of a teacher either."

"The point is, I have a ritual to prepare for and a spirit to slay. Once that's done, I will rescue Julianna from the in-between dimension and begin Tommen's training. And somewhere in there, I suspect we will have to kill the Borelians."

"If I may, sir, how does killing Sabelu, or the dragon, help Julianna?"

"Creating a void in the razana that she must fill, that it will pull her out of the in-between dimension back into our dimension."

"Er, yes, sir."

Julianna was still a bit prickly about the idea, but they really might have to rewrite some portions of the journals so they made a little more sense.

"When do you plan to pull this off, sir?" Win inquired. "Seeing as you need an alibi."

"I will need some supplies for the ritual, but those I believe I can acquire without raising suspicion. I also believe that the required setup will not take a significant amount of time. The execution however..." Rifun thought it over. "It will be a few days, at least. Do you require some specific amount of time as notice?"

"No, sir."

"Then I will let you know. Dismissed."

As usual, the mercenary saluted and left.

It didn't take long to gather the necessary supplies for the ritual. Each morning, Rifun went to his shrine to pray, and the spirits revealed one more piece that he would need and how it would be used to bait and trap Sabelu and the dragon.

Rifun would be lying if he said he didn't feel just a tiny bit uneasy about the whole thing. Why had the spirits been silent on the matter so far? Why wait until now to show him these things? Why was it so important for Sabelu to be the one to die and not Cassius? If Cassius had been taken out in such a way, the Cult might still hold the Wheel. Was Sabelu perhaps a bad priest anyway and needed to be punished?

Still, he did as the spirits bade him, gathering the supplies and arranging them appropriately. The spot was a couple hours' hike from the campsite the children's camp used as their "survival camp." It did not appear especially significant to Rifun's eyes, but if this was where the spirits decreed, then he would do as they said. He finished setting everything up the same day the campers arrived at the campsite. Even if they stumbled across the area, it was highly unlikely they would notice his work. Unlike pop culture portrayals, Rifun did not need to dig pentagrams in the earth, fill them with blood, and light enough candles to burn down the forest. Simple paraphernalia in strategic spots and a few laps of the clearing while reciting prayers was all that was needed.

When he was done, he headed back to a place that was civilized enough to have cell reception and attempted to contact Julianna. It took some effort, but eventually they managed a connection.

"Are you ready to be free?" he asked.

"Lord, am I ever," she huffed. "You have a way?"

"I do. I don't expect you to understand, so I will simply tell you to go to Forbes Cave tomorrow and be ready. I will call you when I get there."

"Oh, lovely! And you're sure this will work?"

"As sure as I can be. Considering the preparation I've had to do, I believe so."

"Good. I will see you there tomorrow."

She hung up, sounding eager and excited.

He returned to the officers building for a night of fasting and prayer. Slay the dragon, rescue Julianna, begin Tommen's training—likely end up bringing him here for that—and start the Cult's gears turning towards being rid of the Borelians. He wasn't sure where the Akarin fit in yet, but he wasn't concerned with them at this point. Likely they'd retreated back into their little hole to hide. The lion had roared and attacked, but now it would retreat to its den, not to be roused for a while.

Slay the dragon, rescue Julianna, begin Tommen's training, move against the Borelians. He didn't understand why it had to be now with Sabelu rather than before with Cassius, but he would trust the wisdom of the spirits. He couldn't shake the feeling, the nagging at the very back of his mind, that something was wrong, but he would go along with it anyway. He couldn't let himself be bound by fear and indecision. The spirits had come through with the answers he had long sought. It was time to carry out the plan.

Slay the dragon, rescue Julianna, begin Tommen's training, move against the Borelians. After that, when the universe no longer had to fear the scourge that was the Borelians, well, the possibilities were limitless. With the slaying of the dragon, of Tujor, the Borelians would be crippled, or he liked to think so. Even if the majority did not believe in Tujor, not truly, the dragon still held subtle control over their society, had built them up as its own mortal empire and army. Yes, perhaps that was why they had been unable to keep hold of the Wheel. It would have caused a civil war among the Cult, and that would not look good for them or the Akari or the Author. Better to do this out of public view. Take care of one's own house first and all that.

Slay the dragon, rescue Julianna, begin Tommen's training, move against the Borelians.

By the time morning came around, Rifun was ready. He summoned Godwin to begin the Disguise deception, then returned to Earth, to the spot where he would lure and ambush the dragon.

It was a beautiful view, a rocky outcropping overlooking a magnificent valley. A herd of deer moved along the opposite side. Small songbirds twittered at each other as they hopped from branch to branch to the ground and back to the trees. A hawk glided lazily on the overhead currents.

He took the time to pray and meditate, still keeping one eye open for Sabelu.

It was early afternoon when the man appeared, bow in hand. He walked right into the clearing, as Rifun knew he would. He paused, trapped by the ward Rifun's prayers had created. Rifun, hiding in a copse of trees among thick undergrowth and some fallen branches, began to sneak his way around behind Sabelu, one hand going to his revolver.

As he quietly slipped down the slope toward the clearing, Sabelu began speaking. Yet his conversation was not with Rifun. It would not surprise that a priest or prophet might be in tune with the spirits, but it admittedly bothered Rifun that this man might see the spirits and he could not. Or perhaps it was the dragon trying to distract him. Likely it knew of the ward, knew what had been done here.

"I was told a long time ago," Sabelu said to his invisible partner. "I came because it is necessary."

He stood with his back to Rifun, head up as if addressing a spirit in the trees. His posture and tone suggested that he truly believed he was speaking to something. Rifun drew his revolver, still sneaking forward.

"You fail to understand time," Sabelu said conversationally, his words edged with conviction. "You fail to understand destiny. You fail to understand love."

Rifun paused. What did evil spirits know of love beyond themselves? No, this had to be a trick.

Then the man's tone changed. Although he did not move his body, he addressed Rifun. "I know you're there. I know what you've come to do."

Overhead, the hawk let out a shrill scream. The hair on Rifun's arms prickled with unease. Something about this wasn't right. "Don't you want to face the one who's about to kill you?"

Was the dragon even here? Had it escaped already? Had Rifun missed some part of the ritual? Or was the dragon overconfident in its ability to survive and make it to another host?

"I am," Sabelu stated, not looking at Rifun though his words answered the question and spoke volumes more he did not understand. Sabelu turned his head just a little, speaking to Rifun. "Don't you want to know how and why you've been led here?"

This was a trick. A trap. Something wasn't right here.

No, the dragon was trying to confuse him. It was trying to escape even as Rifun hesitated.

Stop hesitating! Trust the spirits!

"I already know," Rifun said.

And he fired his revolver.

Sabelu did not Band, did not invoke the Akari or Time in any way, put up absolutely no resistance. He pitched forward without much ceremony, the bow bouncing from his hand. Rifun raced forward and grabbed the bow. The bow, likely infused with some kind of spiritual power. Kill the dragon with its own weapon. Rifun ripped the arrows out of Sabelu's quiver and, with one deficient hand, managed to stick all of them in his back, pinning him to the earth, draining the evil spirits into the ground to die.

He was tempted to take the bow, but at the last minute decided to leave it. The man had still been a prophet of his people, had probably led them well for many years. He would be buried with honors and may need it in his next life, however it appeared for them.

Rifun did not wait around for the man to die, but quickly opened a portal to Forbes Cave and stepped through. With this void of spiritual energy, the time to rescue Julianna was now. He whipped out his phone and had no trouble connecting with her.

"Are you ready?" he asked hastily.

"Absolutely!" she told him, almost scolded. "What do I need to do?"

"Go into the cave near the distortion. I will open a portal and pull you out. It will be difficult, but you cannot let go or give up."

"Of course not! I'm going in now."

The call dropped as soon as she went inside, but that was fine. He made his way to the entrance of the cave, easily bypassing the warning sign. Inside, the wild tapestry of Bands that constructed the Time Trap continued to twist and writhe, seemingly unchanged for two hundred years. He remained at the entrance, safely out of their reach, giving it a count of ten before beginning the rescue.

He opened a portal into one of the tunnels near the Ruins of Meroian. The blackness stood out against the menagerie of colors of Time. Though it was difficult to hold in its own right, it was almost like the Time Trap itself pulled against it, tried to dismantle it and pull it into the Trap, as if to fuel it. Gritting his teeth, Rifun reached into the infinitesimally small crease, that miniscule portion of the meeting between third and fourth dimension, and pulled the portal inside out.

He saw Julianna and reached for her. As his hand crossed the threshold into the in-between dimension, it was like his hand and arm were being degloved in fire. He froze, his throat closing, will wavering. His hand and arm looked fine. There was no visible damage. When he forced himself to move his fingers, they responded appropriately. There was no pain in the movement, only the existence.

Julianna, perhaps thinking he was unable to reach farther into the dimension, grabbed his hand. It was like being slapped with a frozen metal paddle. He startled, unable to return the grip. The Time Trap continued to pull on the portal. But it wasn't trying to take it apart. It was trying to amplify it. It was going to turn the whole place inside out. Rifun could feel the fire creeping up his arm, the chill of Julianna's hand.

At some point, he found his nerves and pulled.

Come on, he willed. *The sacrifice has been made. The void is open. She just needs to step into it.*

Julianna continued to pull on Rifun, as if unable to simply step out.

The Chinese finger trap strikes again, he thought. But he was close. So close. He put one last massive effort into simply yanking her out. The fire that seared his arm turned his muscles and his will to water. He lost his grip on her and the portal. He stumbled back, watching her face draw into an expression of disbelief as the portal righted itself and closed. Then he was falling backwards, tripped up on his own two feet. He didn't know if he lost consciousness before or after his head hit the ground.

When he came to, it was dark. Or he hoped it was merely dark and his vision hadn't gone out. Groaning, Rifun got his feet under him and managed to stand, briefly fighting the warning sign across the tiny cave entrance.

It was indeed nighttime, the crickets out in full force. Rifun put a hand to the back of his head which throbbed. He looked around. Nothing out of the ordinary, as far as he could tell. He put his hand on the boulder and pressed hard. Well, he was still in the correct dimension, so that was a plus. But he didn't see Julianna. As if on cue, the phone rang. He squinted at the bright screen and answered.

"Good, you're awake," she began. "Are you all right?"

"Just great," he said.

"We were so close this time! I just know we were!"

"That's great." He sighed. "I think so, too, but I'm not eager to try again tonight."

"I thought you said that the window of opportunity was limited? We have to try again!"

She wasn't wrong. He reluctantly agreed.

The second time it was midday before he recovered, but at least this time he had managed to avoid hitting his head and instead opened a portal back to his chambers so he could sleep in his own bed. Win took his leave without a word, and Rifun didn't argue. When he woke, the best he felt was functional, and he lay in bed for a lot longer than he knew was good for him.

What had gone wrong? Surely slaying the dragon should have greater consequences. Even if he had been entirely unable to open a portal and turn it inside out, it would have been something more than just the usual. Had the dragon gotten away again? How? He had followed the spirits' instructions to the letter. Except, perhaps, for not hesitating. Still, he should have had a bigger, better opportunity. Sabelu hadn't even fought back. Hadn't even really looked at him. Something was missing. Again.

Slay the dragon, rescue Julianna, train Tommen, go after the Borelians.

Maybe he was doing this in the wrong order. He was almost there, could almost pull off the first two. Just not quite. Maybe he needed the help first. Sabelu was dead, and his loyalties had been questionable anyway. Micaiah was fully Akarin and couldn't be counted on. Aklaq went where he went, as could be expected. The only one left, then, who was a chosen one of the Author was Tommen.

He would have to train Tommen first and get him to help free Julianna. Unfortunately, it might be more stick than carrot at this point. Tommen's first Book didn't exactly paint him, Rifun, or the Cult in the best light, what with murder and kidnapping and ending with the attempted murder of his father. But time was running out, and the only thing he could do was try.

He waited until night when he could dream-walk to Tommen. There he could first assess the teenager's state of mind. Sabelu was not the easiest person to get along with, but that didn't mean the kid wasn't affected. But as he searched out Tommen to dream-walk to him, he found that he himself was being sought out.

Rifun found himself in a forest, and the first thing he saw was a huge wolf crashing into his chest. He didn't have time to react and went limp as he was driven to the ground. When the dust cleared, he saw the wolf had transformed into Tommen.

"So. You found me," Rifun said. Tommen wasn't off weeping in the corner. He was confused, and he was angry. Likely he did not understand how the dream-walk worked, perhaps dismissed it as some "hokey belief," but he had tapped into it nonetheless.

Rifun heaved the teenager off himself and stood. "If I didn't know better, I'd say someone else was training you besides me. I already killed Saul. So who is it?"

Tommen looked at his hands, at himself. "I don't know. I don't even know what this is. It's a dream, but...dreams aren't real."

Rifun conjured a staff in his hands. "It's as real as anything else. Does this feel real?" He swung the staff at Tommen and clocked him over the head.

Tommen stumbled to the side. "What the fuck?" He righted himself and dodged another blow. "I don't understand. Dreams aren't real. They're images and sequences conjured up in our own brains, the interactions of neurons in REM sleep. Nothing more. They're not messages or anything. And they certainly can't be manipulated by someone who's hundreds of miles away. Or even in the next bunk."

Rifun paused in his advance and lowered the staff. He studied Tommen. "So it is possible that you don't know. Would you like to learn?"

Tommen coughed, expression bewildered. "Are you fucking insane?! You beat me over the head with a stick, kill one mentor, threaten another, plus everything else that you've fucking done in the last year, and you still think I'm going to just waltz after you like an eager puppy?"

He didn't have time for the carrot, only the stick, though Rifun would not say he didn't have a little fun beating Tommen with the staff. It was like combat training all over again, only this time he was the instructor.

"You are weak because your mentors are weak," Rifun growled. "They teach you party tricks, and they expect that it will be enough. Did they never teach you anything like this?"

Tommen was bent over, hands on his knees, coughing and fighting to catch his breath, but he shook his head no, whispering hoarsely, "I don't even know what this is."

"I thought as much." Rifun took a few steps back. "When you wake up, meet me where the stony guardians protect a wooden throne."

He withdrew from Tommen's dream and quickly conjured a portal to the designated location. Really it was just a spot a little ways outside of camp where three unusual rocks surrounded an old tree stump. He might have hoped for a little more punctuality, but modern teenagers did not seem to understand the concept. Many hadn't even heard the word.

He picked an apple and sat on a nearby log. It was easily ten minutes or more before Tommen stumbled into the area, still in his clothes from the previous day, looking drowsy and annoyed.

"Okay. I'm here," he sighed grouchily. "No one else is. And if anyone finds me here, it better be a hot girl because that's about the only thing that's going to—"

"Hm...so much for chivalry," Rifun mused. Tommen jumped and whirled to face him. "Honestly, Tommen, why do you still tout your flag of chivalry? I mean, I think it's fairly obvious to everyone that you really want to sleep with your girlfriend, if you aren't already. Where's the chivalry in that? Given that chivalry was developed by Christian knights and the fact that your girlfriend is Catholic—or proclaims to be something of the sort—then either you should have your eyes gouged out for lust, or the two of you should get married so as not to burn with desire." He shrugged and tossed the apple core away. "Not that it matters to me; I'm simply pointing it out for your sake. After all, I would hate to think of the fate that awaits you if you are indeed wrong in your assessment of the afterlife."

Tommen blinked. "So, you dragged me out here in the middle of the night, interrupted my sleep, so you can lecture me on morality and religion?"

"Hm...in a sense I suppose." Rifun approached him casually. "See, you want everything to operate in a universe of logic, facts, mathematics, things that make universal sense. But there's one element that you are forgetting, something that is as universal as mathematics."

"And what is that?"

"Faith. I'm not talking about hokey beliefs and rain dances of some Pango Pango tribe running around naked on the African savanna. I'm talking about sheer, unadulterated faith."

"What are you talking about? The only kind of faith is hokey beliefs and everything else. It comes in a lot of different varieties around the world, but they're all the same thing."

Your gods and my gods are the same, Cassius echoed in his mind.

"No," Rifun said, as much to himself as Tommen. "There is more. It's the kind of faith that can move mountains."

"Yeah?" Tommen pointed to a nearby peak. "Tell it to move."

Rifun grinned. So predictable. "Cute. I will, however, point out that if I did so, it would cause a minor earthquake. Who knows what would happen to the camp then? And you running around out here doing who knows what? It's the kind of faith that can reach inside a person and manipulate their body to do whatever I want them to do."

Stick, not carrot, manipulating the water in Tommen's body to drown him, or come close to it. He needed to understand. He needed to learn. Ideological cohesion might have to go on the back burner for a little while. With Tommen choking, coughing, and sputtering on one knee, Rifun knelt before him. "It is the manipulation of atoms, of DNA, of the very fabric of the universe. It's not something you can do just by thinking about it. You have to believe you can do it. This is the secret of the Akari."

He released Tommen from his invisible drowning. Tommen dropped to all fours and spit up water for several minutes before finding enough air and enough strength to stand and breathe.

"Your days of being an untrained whelp are over," Rifun told him.

"Saul already gave me my first lesson," Tommen said. "He was starting to teach me about Imprinting and combat."

"Excellent. Then that is where we shall begin."

"What?"

It didn't take two seconds for Rifun to get Tommen on the ground, gasping for breath, bruises blossoming on his body and stomach. After a moment, he unsteadily got to his feet.

"Try to do the same to me," Rifun ordered.

"I won't do it," Tommen said. "I can't."

"I know you can't," Rifun chuckled. "That's why I am here to teach you."

Tommen shook his head. "You're smarter than that. You won't teach me how to beat you. You might teach me some techniques and try to have me beat up on others, but you'll always save the best cards for yourself, and you'll use those to beat up on me and keep me in line and remind me how weak I am. And of all that remains, there is nothing you can teach me that Micaiah can't also."

The dragon won't tell you how to beat it, a small voice whispered at the same time a twinge of a headache prodded his old injury. *The journals are flawed. Your gods and my gods are the same. They just use you for nicer things.*

Rifun raised a brow. "You know, you're shaping up to be quite the actor yourself with your little monologues. And you are quite the detective with all your deductions. You're right, of course. Micaiah could teach you many things, I'm sure. Even his brother might show you a magic trick or two. Any one of the Akarin could probably get you trained within reason. But they lack the final piece of the puzzle, the one that unlocks that final level of power."

The teenager did not look impressed. "Okay. I'll bite. What is that?"

"The journal. Richard's journal. While the Akarin squabbled and feuded over old teachings, he wrote the manual on the Akari. All the information in one spot, straight from the Author. Start to finish, it details everything."

"Then what about the books? You yourself gave me one."

Rifun shrugged. "Oh, they're interesting tales, to be sure. Good to read, good to study, but limited and incomplete in their usefulness. And they're not even fully correct. Nor are they originals, but just copies! We'll go over that part at a later date. The point is, I can teach you the Akari from start to finish, with none of these...substitute teachers or reluctant teachers or any of that."

Tommen blinked and shook his head. "You think that after everything you've done to me so far that I'm going to just drop everything and sit at your feet because you make a pretty speech?"

"Fine. Don't ask me. There are plenty of other groups out there who have been delighted to have Richard's journal found and brought to them. But, as I've said before, we have a deal. You owe me."

"I don't owe you anything."

"Don't you? And what makes you think that?" Stick, not carrot. Tommen was tired of the attempts at persuasion and Rifun didn't have the time. "Actually, no, skip that. I know what you're going to say. You're just going to cite duress or some such thing. Maybe I'll rephrase the question: what is stopping me from turning you over to the Hands or the Grandfathers? After all, you said it yourself, you're training in the Akari. All I have to do is get someone to claim that you were trying to get them to 'convert' from Time to the Akari as it were, and there you go. Instant prison time, if not worse. Or, there is that whole bit about the Borelians declaring war on humans. I know you were personally listed on the declaration of war, and I bet your name is still running around in some circles. I'm sure I could find someone to take you in."

Tommen was verbally silent, but his body language was loud. He was looking for something. Anything. Finally, "All right. I'll see your deal and raise you one more."

Rifun raised a brow, intrigued. "Very well. Let's hear your offer."

"You want to teach me and have me as your student? Then cut the shit. Teach me something right here, right now. Something useful. Something I can take home with me, or back to the cabin as it were."

"I tried that already. You refused."

"Teach me something that doesn't involve getting my ass kicked. I can't go back to my cabin looking like I've been out wrestling bears all night."

Rifun nodded. Let it be Tommen's idea, then. "Baby steps then. All right. Why don't we start with something your daddy would be teaching you had you stayed home this summer? Pinpoint Banding for example. Your face looks simply awful."

"No thanks to you."

"And perhaps there will be a lesson in gratitude while we're at it."

Tommen cringed as if expecting some retaliation, but Rifun continued, "All right. Show me your best Band. Let's go with a Fast Band."

He was poor in skill but a quick study. By the time Rifun got done with him that evening, he could Band, Pinpoint Band, and Double Band, all using the Akari. He first used it to heal his face and body.

"Now, was that so hard?" Rifun asked once they were about done.

"No, it wasn't," Tommen admitted, studying the Band he was currently working on.

"Shame no one taught you that little trick," Rifun commented, picking at some dirt under his fingernails. "It's very easy, as you've just admitted. Would have been nothing for Micaiah to teach you before you left."

Tommen dropped the Band. "I know what you're doing. You can cut the crap."

Rifun shrugged, unconcerned. "I'm only saying—"

"I know what you're saying. What's next?"

Just rehashing everything he'd learned. He needed to learn a lot and learn it fast, but it was still possible to overstudy. Still, Rifun liked the enthusiasm. If he could keep up the pace and the strength, they just might be able to work together.

"Time isn't bad," Rifun said. "It has its limited uses. But mostly it's just for practice. You can see the difference in the colors, can't you?"

Tommen gave him a look. "I'm red-green color-blind, not monochromatic. Yes, I can tell the difference. One is blue, the other is yellow." He paused. "That thing you did before. To fix my color-blindness. Can you show me how to do that?"

"In time. Baby steps."

"What about that water trick you seem so fond of?"

"Oh, the drowning? That's a little more advanced, sorry to say."

"You know, your sales pitch for new converts isn't very good. If it's not threats, it's too advanced."

"Ha! Still with the sense of humor, even under duress. It must run in the family."

Tommen dropped his Bands and faced Rifun. "Tell me something, though. In the warehouse. If my dad had confessed. To being my uncle, to being a murderer locked up in prison, all of that. Would you have spared him?"

Rifun did a sweeping bow. "I am a man of my word, child. If I say I will spare someone, then I will spare him. If I say I will kill someone, rest assured, death is coming."

"So then who was the note intended for? The one with the flies on my bedroom door?"

"Who indeed?"

"That's not an answer."

Rifun grinned. "Call it a warning. And as you have seen, one has already fallen. Saul is dead."

"And the others? Would that be my dad, the twins, someone else?"

"Tell me, Tommen, is that what you want to know? Because I think you already know that answer. What's really on your mind?"

Tommen searched his face, looking for anything, but finding nothing. Finally he relented. "What would it take to get you to spare them?"

"Ah, so the truth comes out. He wants to be the protector, the hero, the real man. What must he do to ensure the safety of his family and friends? Concealing the truth and withdrawing to become a hermit is very Hollywood, I will give you that. But, it is a multi-billion dollar industry. In real life, however, it is as simple as this: If you continue to train under me and be my student, I will let your father et al live. I make no guarantees as to their safety concerning the war with the Borelians and anything else that may arise, but I assure you that they will not die by my hand or on my order."

"As long as I train under you," Tommen sighed.

"Exactly."

"Is there an end date on this contract?"

"Of course not. As I said before, pretty soon, you won't want to leave."

"I have my doubts."

"One more thing before you go," Rifun said, stalking up behind Tommen as he headed for the cabin. He leaned in close and whispered, "I'm almost certain that you intend to report on this to your little friends. Whether this was a predetermined plan to get close to me and learn my movements, or just something you intend to do on your own, I don't care. You are not to report any of this. Not what I have taught you, not even that we have met. Nothing. I'm adding that as the fine print to our agreement."

"Let me guess. You want me to report their movements to you, though."

"I have enough moles without having to worry about a turncoat like you. I wouldn't trust you with something like that, not at this point. You're too questionable. Given time, maybe. But not now. And if you break our agreement, and you do tell your little friends, well, there are always more flies, aren't there?"

Tommen grunted. He made to leave, but once more, Rifun held him back, saying, "And just something to keep in mind. You're one of those flies, too."

"What happened to keeping your word and sparing those you say you will spare?"

"It only means I won't kill you. But Borelian slavery is still a very viable option. Something to consider."

He let Tommen go, watching him disappear into the trees, heading for the cabin.

Tommen still wasn't quite connecting the pieces. As much as Rifun would love to lay it all out for him, that wouldn't go over well. People could accept answers and conclusions that they themselves deduced. The more outlandish the conclusion, the more they needed to work it out for themselves. This was true across the board, from government conspiracies to matters of religion. Rifun could give him pieces, but Tommen had to put them together. Like Godwin standing there with that glazed look in his eyes when Rifun tried to explain the dragon's possession of Cassius, the truth could not always be so plainly laid out.

Stick, not carrot, Rifun reminded himself.

He returned to the officers building, relieved Win of his impostor assignment for the time being, and laid low for a few days, going over everything that had happened. Sabelu was dead, but it did not seem to have made much of an impact. Something still felt off about that, more than just the apparent failure to kill the dragon. It was more than just hesitation, something was wrong about that whole encounter.

He had been so close to freeing Julianna. But that back-breaking straw remained, as obstinate as ever. He wasn't even sure what that straw was, that last threshold he could not overcome. Did it have something to do with the fire and ice sensations? Was that a normal thing, or was it some kind of response to his deeper fears?

After a few days, he slipped away to have breakfast with Lalao at her home. He might not be able to explain everything, but he might be able to bounce some ideas off her. If nothing else, he wanted to see a friendly face and hear news of home and family.

"I performed the rituals as the spirits described," he lamented. "I laid the paraphernalia, I said the prayers. The dragon walked right into the trap. It should not have been able to escape, but..."

"But...?" she pressed, scooping some more rice onto his plate.

"I'm...I'm not convinced it was the dragon."

"Did it look like one?"

"It was still possessing a man, so it was hard to say."

"Did it sound like one?"

"Well...no. The man asked if I wanted to know why I was there."

"Did it act like one?"

Rifun felt a rock of dread form in his gut. "No. He never once tried to defend himself." He shifted in his seat. "Did I murder an innocent man?"

"The spirits would not have directed you in such an elaborate ritual for nothing," Lalao told him, face and tone gentle. "It may not have been the dragon you trapped, but a lesser evil spirit. Perhaps this was just the preparation you needed for a confrontation with the dragon. Not only preparation, but confidence."

He thought about this for a moment, then nodded. "Yes. That does make sense. It also means I still don't know where the dragon itself is." He made a sound like a half-sigh. "But why not direct me in this way earlier? Why not give me the ritual and this practice run sooner?"

Lalao shrugged. "I do not pretend to know the ways of the spirits and the ancestors. Such is fate."

He nodded, though he didn't feel entirely confident, and he couldn't shake the little pebble that remained in his stomach that said he actually murdered someone.

Before he could say anything more, the cell phone rang. Lalao gave him a disapproving look as he answered and excused himself.

"Yes, Julianna, where are you?"

"I'm at the summer camp in West Virginia." Her tone was not pleased.

"What time is it there? It must be the middle of the night."

"It is."

"So what's wrong?" If it was so bad, why couldn't she just volunteer the information to begin with?

"The camp's on fire. The whole mountain and forest is on fire."

Rifun blinked. Then, "I'll be right there."

He hung up and hurried back to Lalao.

"Something wrong?" she wondered, glancing at his food which he'd hardly touched.

"Um...something's on fire. Something important."

"Oh, goodness! Is there anything I can do to help?"

"Pray that it's only something physical and not my hopes and dreams, too."

25 | Pyrolyzation
Wellspring, 2014

Fire was one of the few things that was volatile across dimensions, and Julianna made sure to steer clear of the camp once it was obvious that the fire was most definitely out of control. She watched from the safety of another slope, upwind from the fire. Every so often there was a small explosion, likely a propane tank. From what she could see, judging by the buses coming and going, all the campers had made it out and were being shuttled down to the town. After a while, she headed that way herself.

Emergency personnel staged in a small park, babysitting the campers until parents could come get them. Some were crying, others quiet, a few laughing at some joke only they understood. She didn't see Tommen anywhere, but then, maybe Walter or one of the twins had Banded to come get him as quickly as possible. As much as she might have wanted to chase after him and keep an eye on him, she had a sneaking suspicion that he was going to be spending a long time in bed to start and then a day or two at home just to clear his head. He was safe for the time being.

She answered her phone when it rang, looking for Rifun but not seeing him.

"Yes?" she wondered.

"Go and investigate Tommen's house," Rifun ordered.

"Whatever for? If he's home—"

"If—he's home. I want to make sure he didn't just do something incredibly stupid."

"Like what?"

"Like blow himself into the Land In Between."

"What are you talking about?"

He sighed. "I decided to use the fire as a teaching moment, introduce him to Energy. I intended to send him back to the rescue crews, but I think he may have gone off and tried to do some experimenting on his own."

Julianna shifted her stance. "That's surprising. On your part, I mean. Getting close to such an inferno."

"Don't think I wasn't sweating, believe me. But it was a unique opportunity. I think he may have gotten cocky."

"A sixteen year old getting cocky? Now who does that sound like?"

"I'm sure I wouldn't know. Just go take a look, would you? See if he somehow opened a portal back home, see what Walter is up to, maybe the twins. We can't lose track of him."

"All right, I'll go take a look," Julianna told him. "I will let you know what I find."

As it turned out, not much. Tommen was not home, nor any other place Julianna would expect to be safe and familiar for him: the bakery, the twins' house, his school. Both twins were accounted for, as well as Aklaq; none of them had any clue of Tommen's whereabouts or any mischief at the camp at all. She tracked down Walter, speeding his way north, looking more annoyed than worried. Just couldn't leave that boy alone for ten minutes.

On return to the staging area and listening to some conversations from those in charge, it became clear that someone was missing. By the time Walter arrived, it was confirmed to be Tommen. Last anyone knew, he had wandered off to find a wayward camper. The camper had been found, swore Tommen was right behind him, and then he just vanished. Well, Rifun admitted to taking him aside to teach him something. But then what? Looking up the mountain where the fire was slowly dwindling thanks to efforts of fire crews and some helpful rain, Julianna debated her chances of safely walking up there and looking around.

She called Rifun back.

"Did you find him?" Rifun asked. "He's not in the camp."

"Not at home, not with the twins, not with Walter," Julianna reported. "The only place I haven't looked is the camp, but I'm a bit leery of getting close to fire while in this dimension."

"It's pretty well out by now, but I understand. Maybe check the nearest hospital; if he did hurt himself, he might have ended up there."

It was a good idea, but it proved as fruitful as every other search so far.

"The camp is the only place left for you to look," Rifun told her. "Search crews are heading up there now, including Walter, so I don't think I would be very welcome."

"No, I don't expect so. But it's dark and I don't think he's going anywhere.

Meet me there in the morning."

He reluctantly agreed and hung up.

Julianna made a few paces. Rifun had once mentioned something about Tommen helping him to free her, but what if he was now trapped in this dimension with her? How was that going to work? He hadn't shown himself to be uniquely talented in anything, so it wasn't as though he were bringing some missing piece of the puzzle to the table. There were no missing pieces, not in the way Rifun seemed to think. So how did he expect Tommen to help anyway? Just because there was some book written about him?

She deliberately pushed that line of thought aside. She would worry about that later, once it had been proven that Tommen could or couldn't help. That idea wouldn't be entertained until they found Tommen, and she could not search well in the dark. She tried anyway, but with no success.

She spent the night in the town. In the morning, she was greeted, not by Rifun, but by Micah and Aklaq in a pickup with a couple of Trackers. Not a bad idea, she thought. The ugly beasts were used to hunting down Time. If Tommen was still primarily using Time, he probably reached for that first once his fire experiment, whatever it was, went wrong. Curious, Julianna hitched a ride in the truck and headed up to the camp.

The problem with the in-between dimension, or one of the many problems, was that she was unable to observe anything that went on in a Band. There was no way Micah and Aklaq were going to be able to parade the Trackers around the camp, not with the search and rescue teams out and about. They parked on a narrow pull off and got out of the truck. Julianna followed suit, wondering how much she was going to be able to see and hear. As it turned out, not much. As soon as they put up a Fast Band, they were as invisible to Julianna as they would be if she had been a normal person standing in Base Time.

And then they were back.

"Do Trackers get treats or something?" Micah wondered when they got the Trackers lifted back into the bed. Aklaq closed the tailgate, but opened the window. "I mean, how do we reward them for a job well done? Or do you think they understand, or what? I mean, they did a good job, and we might use them in the future."

"I don't know," Aklaq admitted. "Maybe we can find something for them later. Maybe pick up a package of hamburger at the store or something on the way out."

The rest of the conversation was completely benign. If they had found anything, it obviously wasn't enough to expound on here, nor call off the search.

Julianna did not join them on the ride back to town. She already knew there would be nothing for her there. Instead, she made her way to the command post, looked around at the teams and the work they had spread out. After a minute or two there, she headed up and over the hill into the camp. From what she had seen, the Trackers had had hooves. No deer would be coming this way, so it wasn't difficult to locate hoof prints in the muddy, ashen ground, though the trail made little and less sense. Here and there, circling trees and rocks all the way to the edge of the camp.

Maybe the Trackers had been untrained. Or maybe the handlers were. It was an idea, true, but what good did it do when a handler didn't understand what the dog was trying to say?

Frustrated, she started back up the slope. Once she got to the top of the hill, she would call Rifun and —

There he was. Tommen Forbes. Standing right in the middle of the camp. Well, not literally, but there he was in broad daylight. He looked terrible, probably smelled worse up close, and was obviously injured, heavily favoring his left side. Julianna blinked, momentarily unsure what to do. If he was here, considering all of the search and rescue going on around them, then that meant he was definitely in the Land In Between.

He was almost kneeling on the ground, hovering just enough so he wouldn't get his pants any dirtier than they already were, not that he could. He was examining the Tracker prints in the dirt.

"Now what came through here?" he wondered aloud.

Julianna answered before she could think twice. "They used Trackers to try and find you."

The teenager jumped and twisted around to face her, his wounded arm flinging out awkwardly in a bid to stay safe. She saw that his coat sleeve had melted into his skin, and the wild movements were ripping open watery burn blisters.

"What? Wait. You...can see me?" Tommen asked.

"Did you think you were alone here?" she retorted.

"I don't know. I don't know where 'here' is. I mean, I have an idea, I think, but...I don't know. Am I dead?"

She grinned and shook her head. "You are in the in-between dimension. The Land In Between, from which no one has ever returned."

"How did I get here?"

"The way almost all creatures get here. They opened a portal, but it collapsed on them halfway through."

"But I didn't open a portal. I don't know how to open portals."

"Ah, but you did. And you do. Portals are a manipulation of Energy. You tried to put out the fire by manipulating the Energy rather than the Matter. I suppose I don't need to tell you now that Energy is very unstable and very finicky. When it backfired on you and caused the explosion, it was enough to tear open a portal. Likely you were subconsciously trying to save yourself, reaching for a place where you felt safe and wanted to go. Home, for instance. But the concussive force of the explosion knocked you out before you got all the way through the portal, and it sent you here instead." She didn't know how she knew this, only that she did, and it was right.

Tommen looked around at the trees and the burned landscape, then at her. "Who are you?"

"Ah, of course. Introductions. I am Julianna Brown."

"Julianna Brown. I've heard that name before."

"I expect you have. Richard was my husband; he wrote the Akari journal."

Tommen took a step back. "What did you say?"

She sighed. "Please, Tommen, let me explain—"

"How do you know my name?"

"I know quite a bit about you."

"And how do you know what I did here? The only other person here was Rifun."

"If you would rein in your paranoia for just a few minutes, I could explain a few things," Julianna said irritably. She took a breath. "Richard was my husband and a great Akari-bearer. He wrote down the words of the Author herself as a manual for mastering the Akari. For good. But there were those who would try to use it for evil. Cassius was one such man. He had my husband imprisoned, sentenced to die unless the journal was turned over to him. I searched for it and found it, but Cassius did not release Richard as promised. So I broke into the prison and stole it back."

Not entirely untrue, she supposed. Besides, it wasn't as though anyone held any love or sympathy for Cassius, even in death.

"I fled to America, but Cassius was like a mad dog. Once he got his mind fixed on something..." She shook her head. "Anyway, I had heard stories of the Time Portal, and I hoped to use it to escape. Cassius followed me in, but he did not see me hide the journal in the old miner's bones. He attacked me and tried to kill me, but I managed to escape. I got out of the cave and did my best to hide in the chaos of World War II. That was where I Harvested an old friend of yours, Lily Guile."

"Hardly a friend," Tommen said.

"Anyway, I Harvested her and trained her a bit. Then the Dispersal of '63 came around, and Cassius had returned, madder than ever. He pursued me again. I returned to the cave to look for the journal, but it was gone. Cassius followed me again. Cassius and Rifun, actually. This time, they caught me and cut up my face as you see here. Before they could kill me, I opened a portal and tried to escape, but it closed on me. I've been stuck here ever since.

"Once I was here and learned how to move around here, I eventually discovered the whereabouts of my husband's journal. You had found it, an innocent little boy who almost stumbled into the hands of a killer.

"When Cassius and Rifun turned up again and started going after Lily, I took an interest in things once more. I watched her, to be sure, to make sure nothing happened to her. But I also began to take an interest in you. You are an extraordinary young man with great talent, great potential."

"Rifun said something similar," Tommen said flatly.

Julianna frowned. "Tommen, you cannot base everything you encounter on the actions of a single person. Your encounter with Rifun cast a very long shadow over the Akari, true. But your encounter with Micaiah and the Akarin opened your mind to new possibilities."

"Yeah, like Matter and Energy and—no. Wait. Rifun did that." Tommen shifted his stance. "So you claim to be Akarin, then."

She shook her head. "No. Perhaps at one time, but when Richard began journaling and writing the words of the Author, I saw that the Akarin were flawed and greedy, self-serving in the most despicable ways. Not all of them, certainly. Some were very good. But as a whole, they had fallen, succumbed to the same lust that drives the Time industry through its constant cycles of war and peace."

Rifun wasn't here, he didn't need to know about her blatant lies. Besides, he still believed in the Authored Books. If Tommen really was some great Akari-bearer, now might be the best chance she had of steering him away from such foolish thoughts. Not only that, but she needed to conjure up some sympathy for herself. Oh, woe is she, poor damsel in distress trapped in another dimension. Play on the chivalry he professed to observe. If Tommen knew she had played a heavy hand in things, considering the influence Micaiah and the Akarin held over him, he might not agree to help free her. Carrot first, stick if necessary.

"I've learned to use this dimension," she went on, "make it work for me. I'll show you a few tricks, too, about getting around. But overall, I keep...I keep an eye on things in certain places and certain people. I noticed when you and Rifun started dabbling in Matter and Energy, and I came to investigate. Regardless, first we need to do something about your arm."

From fingertip to shoulder and part of his side and neck were fried to varying degrees of severity. Great Akari-bearer or not, he was still human, and he couldn't help her escape if he was too sick or dead. It also meant that they would have to make an attempt here very soon. She could only do so much for him and he was already toeing the line with infection.

She stole supplies from one of the paramedics' vehicles and used them to wrap Tommen's arm properly. His arm was already infected, but it would help. Now then, how to motivate him to invent a way out? Tell him there wasn't one. Teenagers loved to rebel and prove others wrong, especially adults. She got him started with Walking through the dimension and watching past events, then returned to the camp where she pilfered more supplies for his arm.

"Why doesn't the trap go both ways?" he asked, taking the bag.

"Because that's what the Author has decreed. I don't know." She took a step back. "Those supplies should last you a couple days. I expect you will have at least a basic understanding on the Walking and the time travel by then, so we might see each other again soon. Otherwise, welcome to the Land In Between. Hope you enjoy your stay because you don't have much of a choice."

She left him then, retreating to a city an unknown distance away so she could call Rifun.

"I found him," she said.

"So he is in the in-between dimension," Rifun stated.

"Yes, and badly injured. We're going to have to make some kind of attempt in the next few days, assuming we have that long."

Rifun spat a word neither English nor French but still very clearly profane.

"I've given him the basics of moving about this dimension. I'm working on trying to curry favor and sympathy, with and for me if nothing else."

"The Chivalrous Welshman must be chivalrous to damsels in distress," Rifun mused, his tone still sour.

"That's what I was thinking, too."

"Well, do whatever you have to. We need to get both of you out of there."

"Really? I'd forgotten."

He hung up.

Julianna pocketed the phone. She didn't know what he expected her to do. She wasn't sure he knew what he expected. What specifically did he think Tommen was going to be able to do? Everyone in the world could "want" her out of the in-between dimension, but happy thoughts weren't going to be enough. Tommen was already significantly less powerful than Rifun, and that was on the outside of this dimension. What was he going to do from within?

Unless... Yes. Micaiah would happily let her rot in here, but he wouldn't leave Tommen alone in here with her. Assuming they hadn't already figured out what happened to him, they would have to learn. The easiest way to learn would be if Tommen told them himself. He was a teenager; he had his phone. If it hadn't been destroyed in the fire, he could use it to call out. Even if it had been destroyed, Julianna could just swipe one from the primary dimension and hope Tommen at least had his father's phone number memorized.

It was no surprise to find Tommen in Wales, watching his father as a young man in a grimy prison, a violent criminal who had brutally murdered half a dozen men. As much as she might turn her nose up at Walter, she couldn't help but pity Tommen. For years, his dad had been his hero. Now he knew. He not only knew, but here he was, staring at the cold, dark, stone fortress.

He ran. He did not Walk or Travel, just ran away from the scene, letting the years fall away. Julianna calmly followed until he stopped and turned. He startled at her presence.

"Shit, don't scare me like that." He put a hand to his chest.

"It's hard, isn't it?" she said. "To watch and see the way things were, how different they are from the things you knew."

"I don't know what you mean."

She ignored his comment. "I saw your dad once, you know. In passing. I was on my way into the prison to deliver my husband's journal to Cassius. Your dad had faked his death and was being carted out. I didn't know it was him until I got stuck here and could review my life, see where I had gone and what I had done wrong." She studied him. "I know why you're doing this, and don't tell me it has to do with a history lesson."

"I admit, I was curious."

"Do you know how many times people have tried to break out of here?"

"Do you know how many times Einstein failed to invent the light bulb?"

"Ten thousand and one, I'm sure. But sheer determination and mind-over-matter philosophies will not give men the ability to read minds or use telekinetic abilities. Positive thinking has never stopped the executioner's blade from swinging. Willing something to be true does not make it so. A child who innocently yet sincerely believes that he is a kangaroo will not miraculously grow a tail and a pouch."

"Maybe, but that doesn't mean that it can't happen, or that I won't be the one to accomplish this breakout. After all, men can't breathe underwater or in space, and yet we go there with the help of equipment. So it might not be mind-over-matter, only the sheer determination to build something to bust out first and drag me along with it."

There it was, the rebellious teenager.

Julianna nodded. "All right. Fine. Like I said, I can't stop you. The only way you're going to learn is to learn."

"So will you teach me?" Tommen asked.

"I will teach you. But on one condition. If you find a way out, then take me with you."

"Deal."

Men were easy to manipulate.

His phone and charger appeared to still be functioning, though they had to cross back to the States so he could use a plug. Julianna led the way, choosing a house at random.

"If you can plug it in, you can steal the electricity," she explained, gesturing to an outlet. "The neat thing about the dimensions is that the boundaries are almost exclusively in the realm of Energy. Well, what is electricity but Energy? The two play nice with each other, and the transfer is almost seamless. It takes longer to charge because of the barrier, and I don't know how long you intend to wait, but having some is better than having none, I figure. Go ahead and try it out."

He did so. As promised, his phone flickered to life after a moment. Also as promised, it took a few more hours than it normally would, though the reasons for this were both varied and mysterious.

"Thank you," he said sincerely, still adjusting his hearing aids.

"Oh, don't thank me just yet," she told him. "We still have a lot of work to do."

"Okay. I'll catch up in a minute. I want to see if I can't get my phone to charge a little more."

She shrugged and headed outside. If she was right, the first thing he would try was 9-1-1.

It didn't take fifteen minutes for the police to show up, and another half hour for Micah and Aklaq to appear. Julianna remained at a respectful distance so as to not get in the way while Tommen floated around, no doubt trying to get their attention, while still keeping an eye on the situation overall.

As expected, the police didn't find anything, nor Micah and Aklaq when they brought the Trackers back. The homeowner was left feeling bewildered and violated. And although Tommen had been unable to get anyone's attention no matter how much he yelled or what he did, the whole encounter had gotten him thinking. Finally, he gave up and left the house. Julianna went to meet him, their paths crossing at the end of the block.

"So, I assume—" she began.

"You're bullshitting me," Tommen stated.

She straightened. "I beg your pardon?"

"There's something you're not telling me. I don't know what it is—about this dimension, about Time or Energy or whatever—but I can say that you are a very bad liar. Okay, I was able to get my phone to ping to dispatch and get cops out here looking for me. Now, if I can do that within half a day of landing in this dimension, do you think it will take me long to figure out how to bust out of here?"

Julianna merely raised a brow. "Even prisoners can call out to the outside. That doesn't mean that they are free to leave whenever they wish."

"Even so, there's something you're not telling me. I want to know what it is."

"You wouldn't be interested."

"Why not?"

"As far as you're concerned, it's all magic and hocus pocus."

"I believe what I can see. Tell me what I see."

"Which would you rather learn, the big picture or the details? I was going to show you the individual parts, the details first. You seem to insist that you only need to see the greater machine in order to understand how it works."

"It would be nice to have a map of the maze I'm running around in."

She sighed and pretended to think it over. "You're in the in-between dimension. Some call it the dream lands, spirit lands, whatever. There is a lot of mythology surrounding it because there are some who understand how to move within it or manipulate it. In the real world, we call them ghosts or phantoms if they make apparitional appearances. Some try to speak through others, and are called demons or bad spirits. Still others go a different route and have learned to walk in people's dreams.

"The in-between dimension, regardless of all the mortal mythology that has shrouded it, is the land of the Akari. It's the only thing that works here. Time is nothing. It has no power, no jurisdiction. Even in the real world, it is a diluted, poisoned misrepresentation of the Akari." She paused. She knew the words she spoke were true, yet she could not say how she knew them. She turned her attention back to Tommen. "You have a gift, Tommen. You're quick to challenge, true, but you are also very quick to learn. Who knows? Maybe you will be the one to find a way out of this awful place."

"Well, the only way we're going to find that out is if you teach me everything you know. Then maybe my modern, invincible, stupid teenage mind can come up with something."

So malleable, these mortals. "Very well, then. Come with me."

He followed her down the street. "Where are we going?"

"The best place to learn anything is in the field, where you can use what you learn immediately. For you, that means going home."

Walking was far less traumatic than portals for getting from place to place. Julianna had often wondered whether she had learned enough about the mechanism that she could somehow apply it back in the primary dimension, or what she could do to learn more about it. For now, though, it simply saw them to a hilltop overlooking Charleston.

"I know Rifun already told you some of this, but I'll give you a little better explanation," Julianna said. "The Time industry is concerned with only one aspect of the universe, and that is Time, as you may have guessed. Matter encompasses the observable, physical universe. Solid, liquid, gas, plasma, all those basic things you learned in Chemistry. Atoms and molecules and the things they build. Every civilization out there has their own Matter industry, but most just call it commerce or trade. All those people down there in Charleston? They deal in Matter every day. Iron is turned into steel. Wood is shaped into tools and furniture. People trade the Matter of dollars for the Matter of clothes, food, whatever they want. Sometimes they trade Matter for Energy when they pay for their electricity.

"Energy, as far as the Akari and manipulating said Energy is concerned, is fickle and dangerous, as you have experienced yourself. It is used to open portals between dimensions, but it is also used as a barrier to keep those dimensions separate. The ensuing paradox is how we end up with the in-between dimension, a way to store and regulate the Energy.

"Time is the only thing left which all creatures in the universe crave, which the Hands of Time learned to manipulate, monetize, and monopolize to put themselves in power. They watered it down to make it accessible to anyone and everyone. But in order to keep the masses in line and keep them from discovering the true power which they could wield, they demonized the Akari and made it a hated thing, if it could be acknowledged at all. By now, most Time Agents understand it only as a myth."

She paused and faced Tommen. "That is the big picture. Everything we do with the Akari falls into one of those three categories."

Tommen looked around. "My dad was one of those who thought the Akari was a myth, and he could do some pretty scary shit, or so I was always told. If that's the watered down stuff, then what's the real thing?"

"That is what I am going to teach you."

They ended up at a small diner where she snatched a burger for him to munch on while she regaled him with the tale of Richard writing the journals and how Cassius messed it all up. It wasn't a lie exactly. If Cassius hadn't been driven mad by his own teachings—his less evolved brain too primitive to fully understand the grand, universal concepts he was espousing—things really might have been better. Why he had been chosen, Julianna did not know. Perhaps anyone would have gone mad, but Cassius was simply convenient and more expendable than the betters of the human race. Who could say for sure?

If Tommen struggled with anything, it was faith. He had pushed away any notion of God for a long time, though his girlfriend was slowly opening him up to the idea once more. The problem for Julianna was that only his so-called Authored Book was even tempting any ideas as they related to Time or the Akari. How could she expect to fight against the heretical author of the Authored Books and say that he or she was wrong, when that author had just handed Tommen his own biography of sorts? How did she explain that this adventure was wrong when it very clearly wasn't? It was lies built on truth. Like the news media, everything they said might be objectively true, but that didn't mean they weren't still lying.

She gave him the Book of Philosophy to read at home. Word of mouth could only go so far before one had to examine the source material. If he compared it to the scribbles in his so-called book, she was confident he would make the right choice.

But what if he didn't, a voice wondered. Just as she was trying to use his naturally rebellious teenage nature to compel him to break out of this dimension, what if he also used it against her? It wasn't as though he didn't have a reason to want to break out, but if she played too hard-to-get as it were, he might get suspicious. Suspicion without guidance could lead to the wrong conclusions, especially if he went time traveling.

You need to keep a better eye on him. The carrot is only good for so long before the animal gets pushy. Use the stick early and often, make them value the carrot. If you can, do not stop at the belief that the stick is good. Make them crave the stick and fear the carrot.

That would have to wait until after they escaped the dimension. Right now she was relying on charity and sympathy to persuade the self-proclaimed Chivalrous Welshman to take her with him if and when he escaped. There was a good chance Micaiah and the Akarin would have to get involved, and it would be Tommen's word that ultimately freed her.

No, she resolved. *It will be my word that frees me. He will be the driver, and I the passenger. The client. I will tell him where to go.*

Julianna pondered the situation as she left the diner herself and started Traveling to the spots Rifun was most likely to visit if he had the chance. She did not find him, but that was little surprise. She tried calling, but the result was the same. After a while, she returned to Charleston. Her expectation was to simply find Tommen quietly reading Richard's journal before bed, or at least have it nearby and bookmarked while he slept. She Traveled to a point near the house and walked the rest of the way. She didn't want to disturb him, just observe.

What she observed was not him sleeping, but trying to break out of the dimension with the help of his dad and one of the twins. She circled around to another side of the house, looking in through one of Tommen's bedroom windows.

They opened the portal directly around him, she noted, immediately encasing him in the inside-out bubble that Rifun had created. But why did that work?

Just a moment later, the alarm bells were going off in her mind. She couldn't let him escape! Not without her!

The attempt ultimately failed, but it looked more effective than what she and Rifun had been trying. No doubt they would try it again just as soon as they could. She would have to stay close. It looked like everyone was going to wander off to bed for a while, so she had some time to let Rifun know what had happened.

But the man still wasn't around to call and inform. She again checked his usual haunts and a few other likely places, but he just wasn't around now that she really needed him.

Eventually she returned to Tommen's house. It was daytime now, but he was in bed. He looked a wreck. His arm and bandages looked messy, he was paler than usual, and his overall disposition suggested he hadn't slept well. He probably wouldn't be trying another escape attempt in the very near future, but the fact that he had tried without her was annoying. The fact that he looked so bad suggested the attempt had somehow exacerbated his injuries and any infection, which meant he would need medical care. What a perfect role for her to step into.

At the moment, though, she was incredibly annoyed.

"So, how did it go?" she asked, clapping her hands together once to shrill effect.

Tommen startled awake, then relaxed and put a pillow over his eyes. "Listen, I'm not feeling very good right now, so if we can talk later, that would be great."

"Would that be before or after you die? Your wounds are infected, and a little headache medicine isn't going to make it better. I'm no expert, but if I had to hazard a guess, I'd say you're going septic."

Tommen moved his pillow and rubbed his eyes. "That doesn't sound pleasant."

"It means you are going to die very quickly if something isn't done."

"Great! So tell me what I have to do!" He groaned as if his outburst had provoked some pain.

"Do you think you can come with me to the hospital?"

"Great, so you're a doctor now, too?"

Julianna approached him, forcing her own tone to soften. "Tommen, I saw what you and your dad tried to do. I saw what you did to try and escape. I think it will work, but it won't work for either of us if you're dead or too weak to go through the portal. I need to keep you alive. You're my best hope of escape. I've been here a long time and I've learned some things. And to your point, yes, I was a nurse once. If you want to try to escape again tomorrow, you're going to need your strength. It may not be a cure, but it will tide you over. Come on."

He fumbled his way out of bed and managed to follow her to the hospital. She ducked into one of the private offices and began perusing the selection of books and binders. Tommen was unsteady on his feet by the door.

"What is septic, anyway?" he mumbled.

"Sepsis is a blood infection that moves very quickly," she answered. She moved her hands over and through each book. It was a strange sensation, one she'd not felt before in previous situations, but it was as if she could sense the material inside and find just what she needed. "Your blood vessels dilate and blood starts leaking out of your vessels, causing low blood pressure and low blood volume. It messes with your heart and your entire circulatory system."

"Fuck."

"Yes, well, it's not fun. Give me a minute to find something, but the best thing you can do for yourself right now is stay conscious."

She found the book she needed, pulled it into the dimension, and started reading. It was not an easy find, but she found what she believed she needed. She bade Tommen sit while she went to get an IV, drugs, and various supplies to redress his burns. He was not so lethargic that he was unhelpful, but it was still concerning.

You know how to escape now, a voice said. *You don't need him.*

I will take all the help I can get at this point.

If Rifun is so fixated on him being a chosen one of the Author, the best way to prove him wrong is to escape without the boy and maybe let him die.

It might break Rifun of his stupid fixation, but I can't just murder someone like that. He's injured and in pain.

She finished up her work and sat down in a chair a short distance away. "Now then, I heard what you did earlier this afternoon."

"How is it that you're never around, but you know what I'm doing all the time?"

"Quite frankly, you never don't advertise yourself."

"Oh. Guess that makes sense." Tommen shifted uncomfortably in his seat. "So do you have any insights about it?"

"Well, it looked like it almost worked," Julianna said plainly. "I don't know if your dad and your friend just didn't have enough strength by themselves or whether you were too weak because of your infection or what."

"Problem with that, though," Tommen said, "is that if that's the case, these meds better work. Otherwise, we're only going to get maybe one or two chances a day until I'm dead. The entire Akarin force could be keeping that portal open, but if I can't go through, it's useless."

"I agree, which is why we're here." She nodded and stood. "Stay here. I'm going to do some more snooping around this hospital, see if I can't find anything else that could be of help to you."

"I'll be here."

Her second sweep of the hospital turned up another patient with sepsis, and she paused to watch the nurses and doctors work. This patient was in far worse shape, the doctors not holding out much hope of a recovery. Knowing that, she felt less guilty about stealing the medicines they had lined up for him. She gathered them up, plus a few more syringes and antibiotics just in case, and returned to Tommen who was sitting at the desk.

"Good news," she said. "Someone else in the ER has sepsis, too. Well, it's not good news for him, but it's good for you. I watched them for a little bit and took notes. What I did grab so far was all good, but these might be of some use, too."

Tommen nodded, looking better but still not well. "Okay. Listen, I might have an idea of how to make it easier on everyone when we try to bust out tomorrow."

She dumped the supplies on the table. "I'm listening."

"So, last Christmas, Rifun kidnapped me and lured me and my dad into this warehouse in a shipping yard east of town. Micaiah was supposed to help, but he said he couldn't because the warehouse had been turned into some kind of quasi-dimension. It existed in the same realm as us and could be seen, but he couldn't break into it. I don't know the details.

"My idea is this: What if someone tried that again? Turned someplace into a quasi-dimension or whatever, and got one step closer to us?" He indicated the phone on the desk. I brought this phone in here and made a call. Okay, there is no way I brought the entire phone system into this dimension, which means there has to be a cut-off somewhere. If the others step into a quasi-dimension and throw us a life ring as it were, they might be able to pull us out."

She went to the table and chose a syringe. As she pushed it into the IV line, Tommen asked, "Is there any way you can think of where it could work?"

Julianna paused and sighed. "The time of the great Builders is gone, when men could construct stable dimensions and bend them to their will, almost as if they were God." She tossed the empty syringe away and went back to her buffet of medicine. "These days, men build quasi-dimensions and call themselves great. There are few in the universe with such mastery of the Akari and the elements of the universe and its dimensions."

Tommen hesitated for half a second before saying, "What about Rifun?" When she stopped, he went on, "I know you don't like him. I'm not too fond of him either. But he's the only one I know of who might have that kind of power and control. He built that quasi-dimension around the warehouse and he completely redecorated the Wheel. He turned *Star Trek* into *Shakespeare*. I don't know about you, but he might actually be our best bet for help from the outside. In that area of expertise," he added quickly.

It was a long moment before Julianna put down the syringe she was holding and turned to face him. "You would suggest an alliance with the man who took over the Time industry, enslaved millions, almost killed your father, almost killed you, and even now seeks to recruit you as his Apprentice?"

"I'm not happy about it either, believe me. Listen, when I'm done here, I'll go to Micaiah and ask if any Akarin have similar abilities. Whatever infighting they have going on, I'd still rather ask them than Rifun."

She snorted. "I would rather escape by our own means."

"Micah and Micaiah are Akarin and they're our best chance at getting out the way we tried this afternoon! Whatever your beef is with the Akarin, take it outside this dimension. But first, we actually have to get out of this dimension. You might just have to accept their help. In the same way that we might have to accept Rifun's help if he is most qualified. Okay, if I'm sepsis—"

"Septic."

"Whatever. If I'm as sick as you say I am, I can't be picky about who my doctor is." He noted her expression. "We have to get out of here. All other concerns are secondary."

They stared at each other for a few seconds. Could it really be that easy? Was he seriously just offering himself on a silver platter? Surely he had to know that asking for Rifun's help would incur some unspoken debt.

Men are easy to manipulate.

"So what's your plan, then? Where are we going after this?" she inquired.

"First we're going to the shipping yard. I want to check out the warehouse.

Even though it was last Christmas, I want to see if, being in this dimension, we can see anything unusual about it because it was once a quasi-dimension."

She raised a brow. "Like what?"

"I don't know. That's just the sort of smart stuff that someone on *Star Trek* might say. I have no fucking idea what I'm looking for."

"Well, neither do I, but that's not to say that something isn't there. If there is, we can investigate. If there isn't, well, we haven't wasted a lot of time. Walking does wonders."

He nodded and took another bite of salad. "And if I haven't said it lately, thank you for helping me."

"Helping me get out of here is all the thanks I'll need."

Their investigation of the shipping yard proved as fruitful as every previous investigation she had done. Still, it was Tommen's idea and he was going to try and pull in the Akarin to help. Who knew? It might be enough.

Eventually she took him home—with another load of medication from the hospital—and sent him to bed. She wouldn't say she was not a bit fatigued herself, but she still had to make another round and try to contact Rifun.

This time she was able to locate him, running around Madagascar, one of the cities with a ridiculously long name that he typically shortened just to Fianar. She called him.

"To what do I owe the pleasure?" he greeted sarcastically.

"Tommen has a plan to escape tomorrow and he's calling in the Akarin. But he also wants you there," she reported. "Seeing how you are the current leading expert in quasi-dimensions."

"Oh I am? I must have missed the crowning ceremony."

"Don't let it go to your head."

"Am I correct to assume that the quasi-dimension in question is in a certain shipping yard?"

"It is."

"When does he expect this rescue to take place?"

"Tomorrow is all I know. I'm going to keep an eye on him and let you know when those wheels start turning."

"Good." He looked around at the sky. "Judging by the time here, my guess is he is currently in bed sleeping."

"Heading that way, yes. I might suggest you take a quick nap yourself, just in case he tries to communicate with you."

Rifun frowned. "I don't know that he will be able to get through from that dimension, even if he did know what he was doing."

"As I said, take a nap."

He sighed. "I don't know about you, but I operate on a slightly different timezone. Even jumping back and forth from here to Sadurnon can be detrimental and confusing. Point is, I just woke up."

Julianna gave him a look though he couldn't see. "So get a cup of warm milk, roll over, and go back to sleep."

"Is Tommen still unwell?"

"Worse, he's septic. I got him a pharmacy's worth of drugs and he has shown improvement, but he needs real care, whether in a hospital or someone skilled in the Akari."

He grunted. "I see. Rescue cannot come too soon, then. But it also means he should sleep well tonight. I will take care of a few errands here, then return to Sadurnon and attempt a nap so I may speak with him."

She nodded. "Good. And while I know how things have been going so far, might I suggest using honey instead of vinegar? Slapping him around won't make the sepsis go away and he is already well-motivated to make his escape."

"This I understand."

"Good. I will keep you apprised of the situation, provided you are here."

"I am doing my best. Keeping a low profile seems to be paying off; Misik and the others are more concerned with goings-on at home and do not seem to feel the need to keep us— and by us, I mean me—under constant lockdown. Once you and Tommen are free, we can move forward with the next phase of our plans."

Julianna shifted her stance. "Who is 'our'?"

"It will be easier to explain when you are free and we can discuss things openly. Tone I detect, but body language is somewhat lacking."

"You're blind, what does body language matter to you?"

"Ha! I like you. But even the blind can hear body language to a certain extent. But we're getting off track. I will attempt to visit and speak with Tommen, and I will let you know how that goes. You keep an eye on him, but also keep an eye on Micaiah and Aklaq, see what they come up with from the Akarin. I expect they may want to pull in some Builders."

"Maybe Nathan and Andrew will reveal themselves," Julianna said. "Then we might get some answers from them as well."

"What answers? They hoodwinked you and got hoodwinked themselves by the Ururian." He shrugged. "I will call back or visit you if something surfaces, and I expect you to do the same."

Julianna nodded as she lied, "I will."

The Caves of Meroian, 2014

Extraction

So, I heard you wanted to talk to me."

Rifun was in fact able to connect with Tommen while he slept and now walked in his dream. It was a sickly fever dream he could tell; it was too empty to be a true dream from restful REM sleep.

"You've made a lot of progress since getting sucked into the in-between dimension," Rifun said, walking right up to Tommen to stand face-to-face. "Maybe this was just the kick in the ass you needed to start actually learning."

"That dimension you built at the warehouse, can you recreate that?" Tommen asked.

Honey, not vinegar, Rifun told himself. *I need him to learn, but I don't need him doing stupid shit like this. He'll get himself killed long before the dragon has a chance.* "Why would I want to do that? More importantly, why would you want me to do that?"

Tommen explained the idea of using a quasi-dimension at the warehouse. "Micaiah doesn't know how to do it, and he's not sure of anyone who does. But I know you can do it. Obviously, I've seen you do it."

"So you're asking me for help, to get you out of a mess which you put yourself in?"

Tommen grudgingly answered, "Yes. Will you help me? Please?"

"He even remembered his manners," Rifun smirked. "Just for that, I will help you. And because I know the circumstances are difficult, I will even let it be its own reward and I won't ask anything for it. This time. Don't go getting any ideas that I'm a charitable person."

Tommen shook his head. "Never cross my mind. But I do wonder what the price of information is."

Rifun shifted his stance. "Oh, now things are getting interesting. What kind of information?"

"Who is Julianna?"

Rifun raised a brow. "Julianna? Well, I suppose it's not surprising that you've met her given where you are and all."

"Is she as evil as Micaiah seems to think?"

"As the Akarin seems to think, you mean. The Akarin blame her for the rise of the Cult and the dissent within their own ranks. Of course they're going to paint her as an evil sorceress of sorts."

"Were you her Apprentice once? How are you two affiliated?"

"Affiliation is one way to put it, I suppose. She and Cassius were affiliated long before I was involved. The deal was that she would give him the journal and he wouldn't execute her husband. You know how that turned out."

"I know that she tried to make a power play," Tommen cut in. "I saw it. In the time travel. Cassius was the Zero Hour and he was going to release Richard in order to win the loyalty of his followers and overtake the Akarin. Julianna looked like she was a partner in the whole thing."

Rifun sighed. *The journals are flawed. They were dictated by an evil spirit, not the Author.* "It wasn't a power play. It was a peace play. It's the same one Micaiah is trying to make by using Aklaq to bring in District Nine in the war against the Borelians. Just as he is attempting to unify all the human colonies, so Julianna was trying to unify Akarin and the Time industry. But that wasn't going to happen as long as the Akarin were corrupt and dissolving. Richard wanted to stop the dissent by bringing everyone together under the words of the Author, not some so-called novels full of pithy mistakes and needless errors. Suffice to say, it didn't work. The Akarin were still too powerful. Everything went to hell from there.

"When it failed, Cassius—a power-hungry, blood-thirsty bastard as you well remember—sought to destroy Julianna. He chased her into the old mine the first time where she stashed the journal that you found. When he came out, I picked him up. He told me about the Akarin and the journal, the words of the Author. He was sure Julianna still had the journal. My interest was solely in the journal. His was seek and destroy. I didn't find the journal, but he found Julianna. She escaped death, but not before he'd cut up her face."

"And when you came out, you just started murdering women in your quest for the journal," Tommen stated. "I don't believe you're entirely innocent."

"Did I say I was?"

"Why should I trust anything you just said?"

"Because if you had a better source of information, you wouldn't be asking me in the first place. In the same way you went to Micaiah first to ask about rebuilding that dimension."

Tommen sighed. "If you show up there tomorrow with them, they'll kill you on the spot."

Rifun barked a laugh. "Ha! I'd like to see them try. Honestly, Tommen, I really wish you would have a little more faith in me."

"Why should I? You're the one who left me to my own devices and now look where I am."

"Perhaps, but as you like to remind everyone, you're not a child who needs to be supervised all the time. You're an adult, capable of making your own decisions and acting on your own. Which you most certainly did."

"I had no fucking clue what I was doing!"

"And whose fault is that?"

Tommen snorted and looked away and sighed. "Okay, fine. Just get me the fuck out of here. Can you do that?"

"I make no guarantees on anything. The in-between dimension is a fickle beast, or so I hear."

"And one more thing. How did you know I wanted to talk to you?"

"You project your dream-walking intentions as badly as your fistfight moves. Subtlety was never your strong suit."

"Fine. Okay, so, sorry, I lied. One last thing. Can you not kill anyone, if you do show up to help with this?"

Rifun raised a brow. "Your terms are steep. I shall simply say this: I will not initiate a fight, but I will not allow myself to be taken in. I will act only in self-defense."

"Fine. You guys can deal with that one. But I'm not going to have a second horror show at that shipping yard."

"I do not wish such a thing either. After all, we are all coming together with the intent of freeing you from your miserable prison."

"Well, don't sing kum-bah-yah too loud or you'll overload my hearing aids."

"Ha! Always such wit. I admire that about you. Was there anything else you'd like to talk about during this therapy session?"

"You said your help was free. What's the price of the information?"

Rifun folded his arms. "See, that's the surprising thing. I don't know. I haven't decided. Every encounter thus far has been me approaching you, and usually only when I want to teach you something and get something in return. This is the first time you have reached out to me." He smiled and looked at Tommen. "Maybe we'll just call that square, then."

He left Tommen's dream and soon woke up from a nap that had been several hours in the making. If he hadn't needed to speak to Tommen, he wouldn't have bothered as he now felt worse than he had when he woke up from regular sleep not much longer before. Traveling back to Earth a little while later didn't make him feel any better.

He wasn't on Earth for two minutes before his phone rang. No surprise, it was Julianna.

"Has something happened?" he inquired, not in much of a mood for conversation.

"Tommen attempted an escape without me," she reported coldly.

"Was he holding another girl's hand, too? I just talked to him." He rubbed his eyes. "You only said attempt, which means it failed."

"It did, yes. But now he's on the run."

Rifun didn't even have the energy to sigh. "What do you mean? There is only so far he can go."

Julianna made several frustrated, unintelligible noises. "I think I may have spooked him a little, or else he did more time traveling here than I realized and came to some wrong conclusions. I don't know if you've realized just how paranoid he can be."

"Well he can't go far for very long. He does still require rescue. It's either rescue or death at this point. Stick around the twins or his father. I have a feeling that they're going to try and change something." He shifted his stance. "It will root out our relationship, however much you may be trying to distance yourself from me in hopes of being rescued, but I think we may have to go with vinegar and the stick over honeyed carrots."

"You may lose him over that, you know." She sounded oddly smug about it. "What will you do then?"

"My first priority is rescue. Let me know what they change."

He hung up.

Tommen was still a chosen one of the Author. Rifun couldn't lose him to a life of ignorance, missing out on the other half of the Author's philosophy because he was either completely lost—disregarding the Akari completely—or else clung solely to his Books like a petulant child of the Akarin. *The journals were dictated by an evil spirit, not the Author.*

The problem was that Tommen was fairly insignificant in and of himself. He was not uniquely talented in any way. The only reason he was special was because he had Authored Books. Julianna didn't ascribe any authority or authenticity to them, so in her eyes, Tommen was expendable. As far as she was concerned, he was worth something only in this matter, to help her escape.

And then what? When do you become expendable?

She has no military mind. Her expertise is that of humanitarian efforts and history and quiet, learned things. I am the military mind, the planner, the one who keeps things running. Without Cassius and Isthim, we might actually get something accomplished.

His hunch proved to be correct, and Julianna later relayed that the rescue attempt had been moved from the shipping yard to Forbes Cave. She gave him the time and said she would be waiting for him. No mention of Tommen was made.

The change of location made sense. Forbes Cave and the Time Trap were more powerful entities than the warehouse, and Rifun could fully appreciate that Tommen might experience some distress over returning to that area. Probably Walter would, too, as Rifun heard his voice as he walked up the trail toward the cave. Walter, Micaiah, not a stretch to think Micah and Aklaq were also present.

"Tommen, if you're here, you should have no trouble hijacking my phone and poking out some kind of message," Walter said.

There was a moment of silence, then Micah asked, "So what should we do?"

"You should turn and welcome the one who is going to save our beloved friend," Rifun said, announcing his presence.

All four of them had their weapons trained on him before he could take another step, but he continued to advance, largely unconcerned.

"What are you doing here?" Micaiah demanded.

"Tommen asked me to be here," Rifun answered. "Seeing how I am the most powerful one here, it seemed only logical. And the thing he asked me to do, well, only I can do it."

"We're not building any quasi-dimensions here," Walter told him. "So you can —"

Everyone hit the ground as a shot was fired. Everyone, that is, except Aklaq, who fired, and Rifun, who casually stepped forward to face her eye-to-eye. He chuckled. "I admit, that was both unexpected and yet so tragically predictable. Did you think I came unprepared?" He lifted his shirt to reveal his bulletproof vest. It had blocked not only Aklaq's shot, but the ones from the warehouse as well. "See, Tommen also asked me not to kill anyone tonight. To the best of my ability, I intend to uphold that promise as well."

Micaiah took a step forward and put his gun to Rifun's head. "Block this, motherfucker."

It was not the first time someone had put a gun to his head, nor the first time Rifun had faced Micaiah. Most people expected the first move to be to knock the gun itself away. Rarely were they prepared for a sudden, sharp jab into the armpit first. The only reason he really got away with it was because of the ability to Band. Armpit, floating rib, elbow, wrist, knee. With Micaiah's stance, no doubt the same one he had developed out of habit over the past several decades, it was nothing for Rifun to take him out right at his prosthetic, collapsing him into a heap on the ground. He knocked the pistol away and drew his revolver. Micaiah stared up at him for a full second, as if trying to figure out what had happened and what options he had, expression badly covering any pain from the blow to his leg.

"We could do this all night," Rifun said, sighing and holstering his weapon. "But it would only produce dead bodies and no Tommen."

"Tommen, did you ask him to be here?" Walter wondered, holstering his gun and looking at his phone. A second later he read aloud, "Yes."

Rifun nodded once. "There you go."

Grudgingly, Micah and Aklaq lowered their weapons.

"Fine. You're here," Micah said. "What do you plan to do?"

"If you're not building a quasi-dimension—which I guessed as soon as I heard the locale was moved here, away from the shipping yard—then that means you intend to exploit the dimensional weakness here in the cave. But if a whole troupe of Akarin couldn't sustain the portal to get Tommen out, what makes you think I would make a difference?"

"It's not opening the portal that's the problem," Aklaq told him, glaring at him. "It's getting him out. There's some kind of force in the dimension that's holding him back and tried to take Walter in with him."

"I see. And are you hoping that I will be able to overpower this force, or are you hoping to use me as bait to swap places with Tommen, rescuing him and sealing me inside the in-between dimension?"

"*Ní cuma an dara rogha leath-olc,*" Micah hissed to Micaiah. (The second option doesn't sound half-bad.)

"*Chuala mé sin,*" Rifun informed them. (I heard that.)

"So, how do we go about doing this without jumping a century into the future?" Walter was saying. "Regardless of whether there is or isn't an eye to this storm, we still have to cross the storm in order to get there." He looked at his phone again and read, "Not from this side. Time doesn't work here. I can walk right into that cave and the Time Trap won't touch me."

"Can you open a portal, though?" Aklaq asked.

More from Tommen. "Well, no. But you guys can. If I can find a weak spot in the trap, you guys can open the portal. Rifun can separate the dimensions, and Dad should be able to pull me right out."

"It's a nice theory," Micaiah said, "but how is it any different than anything else we've tried?"

"Because this time you have me," Rifun chipped in. "And on the other side, you have Julianna. We can meet halfway and widen the hole in the barrier, enough to get them out."

"No. Julianna is not coming out."

"Why not? She's a human being, too. And she's been trapped in there far longer than Tommen has."

"She will only cause chaos and disorder."

"By that, you mean she will unite the scattered and sometimes misguided followers of the Cult. You're just jealous because the Akarin have no such leader to do the same since he was accused of murder and imprisoned. You just keep dividing."

"I already lived through your reign of terror." Micaiah indicated his leg. "I have no desire to see hers, too."

"You get Tommen, I get Julianna. Those are my terms."

None of them liked those terms, and there was more to-do about whether they needed Rifun at all.

"Tommen comes out first," Micah said. He went on before Rifun could speak. "We've already tried and failed. If we're able to rescue them now, it's only because Rifun helped, which means he can do whatever he needs to in order to get Julianna out, with or without us. But we're not going to leave Tommen trapped in there. He comes out first."

"I would never abandon my Apprentice," Rifun informed him. "You seem to think I have not been looking for ways to free him also. I am insulted. And to think

I felt honored to be asked to be here."

"Well, don't get cocky," Micaiah growled. "They're still trapped in there." The group of five moved just inside the cave, facing the darkness and the Time Trap within. "Ready, Tommen?"

Walter's phone pinged as Tommen typed out, "Getting in position. I'll help as much as I can."

"We'll give them until a count of fifteen to choose their spot," Micaiah said. "After that, we give it everything we got. Tommen first."

It was more like thirty seconds, but Rifun wasn't going to argue.

"Okay, Tommen, we gave you a little longer than a fifteen count," Micaiah said. "Hopefully you've found the best possible spot. Here's what's going to happen. We're going to open a very broad and very weak portal to start, at least until we find your exact location. It is advised that you stand together so we can reach both of you. Then the portal is going to close. Be ready because once we locate you, we're going to throw everything we have into opening another, stronger portal, just like we've been doing. Once we get the portal open and as stable as it can get, Rifun is going to do his best to separate the dimensions and figure out what it is that's holding you in there. After he's subdued it, destroyed it, whatever, he is going to be the one to come grab you and pull you out. I hope you're ready because here we go."

It did not matter where the group intended for the portals to open, for the Time Trap itself seemed to steal the Energy and prevent it from going to that place. It quickly became very obvious how Julianna had gotten sucked into the dimension in the first place, Rifun reflected. At the same time, it was also providing the best avenue for reaching her strength on the other side, homing in on it until he discerned their location and pointed it out.

"Tommen comes out first," Walter repeated, straightening. "We can kill each other when this is over."

"Gladly," Aklaq growled, her gaze never leaving Rifun.

"All right, Tommen, this is the big one," Micah said. "We're going to give it everything we got. If you see an opening, take it."

Then came the intentional portal, about fifteen feet away. As the portal opened, Rifun saw the colorful Bands twist and bend, the in-between dimension sucking the Energy into itself, providing a clear path for him to approach Tommen who appeared frozen in place, unable to move. He grabbed Tommen roughly, hauled him out of the in-between dimension and toward his father's waiting arms.

Next was Julianna. Rifun held a hand out to her which she took delicately. She gritted her teeth as she stepped into the real world once more, but it still appeared to be a strenuous endeavor.

"No!" Tommen cried suddenly.

In his teenage brain, he probably thought himself some kind of hero, going to vanquish some evil villains into the depths of a netherworld prison. When he got close enough, Rifun turned and drove his palms into Tommen's shoulders. The kid crumpled to his knees, then tried to rise, twist, and grapple Rifun about the waist. But Rifun was no lightweight, and he could feel the sickness within Tommen. He folded around the teenager in a somewhat uncomfortable and mildly provocative position, holding Tommen's head in his abdomen and groin area. He stayed that way for a moment. When the teenager began flailing, he grabbed him by the shoulders, making sure to dig in as much as possible on the boy's injured left arm.

"Maybe a few more days in the dimension will teach you a little lesson in gratitude," Rifun said simply.

He pushed Tommen backwards, then, into the portal. He stumbled and fell, but just before Rifun could fully grasp Julianna and lead her out into the real world, Tommen stood and pulled her back, grasping her hair and yanking.

Julianna fell back. Rifun, annoyed and exhausted from this endeavor, backed up and let the portal close.

"What the fuck was that?!" Aklaq demanded.

"If Tommen thinks he's going to play the hero," Rifun panted, sweating and weak, "then he's going to learn that...actions have consequences...even for the hero. He can sit in the dimension for a little while longer and...think about his actions."

"He's wounded and sick. He needs help. And how is another day of 'thinking about his actions' going to sway him to your point of view, which is really what you want?"

"Because he will have little choice."

As he spoke, Rifun meandered his way out of the cave, essentially letting the curtain fall back into place and allowing the Time Trap to go back to the way it was. A moment later, the younger twin spoke, and it was not unreasonable to think a gun was involved in some way.

"You're going to get Tommen back for us," Micah said. "Whatever you need to do to get Julianna out, well, you know the secret now. You don't need us for it."

Rifun grinned and turned to face them. "You think we needed you for any of this? It was never about you. You are the ones who have failed to learn the secret of rescuing someone from the in-between dimension." He put up a hand before anyone could speak. "Don't worry, I'll spare you the suspense. It's about Tommen. But I knew he wouldn't come out for me alone. He would only come out for you. Really, I was just trying to kill two birds with one stone in the most humane way possible by going along with this dog and pony show. But, seeing how this all just turned out, I'm thinking I may need to use more drastic measures."

More guns were drawn.

"And what measures would those be?" Walter asked.

"Walter, Walter, Walter. Have you learned nothing from me, in all the time we've known each other? Why should I tell you my plan? Obviously, your guns don't mean much except as a means to comfort yourself that you have them, and your abilities in both Time and the Akari are inferior to my own. Therefore, you have nothing to threaten me with." Rifun shifted his stance and did a dramatic, sweeping bow as best he could with the bulletproof vest. "I have kept my promises tonight so far. I have assisted in the attempted rescue of young Tommen, and you're all still alive. You are free to mark this day on your calendars as the day Rifun Ndolo spared your lives." He straightened. "But know that those promises end here. If anyone attempts to follow or stop me in any way, then I make no promises on what may happen next."

With another, stiffer bow, he turned and left.

Once out of sight of the cave and those still hanging around it, Rifun made a short portal jump to a random, secluded area on the other side of Charleston. Then he just stood for a few minutes, going over everything that had just happened.

Tommen and Julianna had both been freed, or right on the cusp of freedom. Rifun had even humored them and brought Tommen out first. Then the kid had to play hero and, perhaps on Micaiah's orders or perhaps not, attempt to seal both him, Rifun, and Julianna in the in-between dimension. Did they not understand how much effort had gone into this rescue? How had they not experienced the same resistance that he and Julianna had with the Chinese finger trap? What had really changed from one rescue to the next? Only Tommen. His presence had changed something, made it so the two of them could be rescued.

Maybe it hadn't been the smartest idea to push Tommen back in. Rifun would admit that, especially since they were now right back where they started but with far less honey and far more vinegar. There would be no more carrot, only stick. Unfortunately, Julianna would be the driver of things now, being a spiteful woman. Rifun could only hope that she managed to stay on Tommen so that even if Micaiah led the next rescue effort, she would have a chance of getting free if Rifun couldn't be there.

Fucking hell, he didn't have time for this. He didn't—have *time* for this. Damn it!

It was tempting to return to Sadurnon for a few hours, but there was too much riding on this now. He couldn't just leave in case Julianna called and needed something, or if there was a narrow window of opportunity for another escape attempt.

So as to not cause himself more problems than necessary, Rifun refrained from using portals to travel anywhere, although he did use a Disguise to take a walk around town, killing time and cooling his head. It was a few hours before he noted someone following him. He continued a casual walk for a few blocks before ducking into an alley, using Light to hide himself while he slipped into a hiding spot about halfway down.

The tail followed. He paused when he did not immediately spot his quarry, but continued nonetheless. Rifun waited until he was a few steps past him before sliding out of hiding, grabbing the man, and putting him in a choke hold. The man was surprisingly calm about the whole thing.

"Who sent you?" Rifun hissed.

"It's me, sir."

Rifun let go. "Fucking hell, Godwin. I could have killed you."

Godwin took a few steps away and turned, dropping his Disguise. "Well, it would have been an interesting fight, anyway. Personally, I was gambling on you wanting information, if I were an Akarin assassin, for instance. My bet turned out to be well-placed."

Rifun grunted. "All right, so what do you have for me? Is Misik upset at my absence?"

"I don't think Misik even knows you're gone," Win said dismissively. "If he does, he doesn't care. No, but I got word of what happened."

"By what means?"

"Akarin means. Moles, spies, turncoats, all the fun things. Bit of a fire drill going on, sounds like, the Akarin racing to rescue Tommen before we do."

"Good to know, but Julianna hasn't contacted me."

"No, but I contacted her. She filled me in on the details."

Rifun gave him a look. "What did I tell you about working for her?"

Win matched his look. "Quite frankly, I don't give two shits about her. She's a weak, whimpering woman." He shifted his stance. "Anyway, I put a few bugs in ears, got balls rolling, et cetera, called in some fast favors." He paused. "Couple weeks ago, there was a drone strike in Egypt, the Americans burning down castles to kill a few rats in the kitchen. Timekeeper in the area pulled a nearby building, a church, into a quasi-dimension to save it. Like I said, I pulled some strings and favors. You'll have a full power detail waiting at the church in a few hours, ready to lend strength to rescue Tommen—and Julianna, too. She managed to subdue Tommen, and she'll have him there."

"How did she do that?" Rifun wondered.

Win shrugged. "Knocked him over the head, she said." He pulled a small package from a pocket and handed it to him. "I also managed to put a little something together to make it so you and Julianna can communicate more freely, on an open line as it were, without needing to tie up a hand with a phone."

"That would be most handy." Rifun looked over the device. It did not look especially involved, some small pieces and wires attached to the phone, but he wasn't going to mess with it now if it was working.

"It may also benefit you to know that I did this while masquerading as you," Win went on.

Rifun carefully pocketed the phone and assorted accessories. "You flatter me, but why?"

"Loyalty, sir. There is too much instability in the Cult right now, especially in management. The underlings need to see a leader. No one will follow a Borelian, and Julianna is, as I said, weak."

"And what about you?"

"I'm no leader, sir. Not like that. But I can support a good leader."

"Am I a good leader?"

"I believe so, sir."

Rifun considered this for a moment, then nodded. "Thank you."

Now Win handed him a piece of paper. "Coordinates of the church in question, sir. I will return to the camp and present an alibi."

"Good." Rifun pocketed the note. "I don't expect this to take too much longer.

And when I get back, I'd like to know more about these Akarin spies of yours."

"Of course, sir."

Win returned to Sadurnon while Rifun studied the coordinates. Egypt, huh?

The last time Rifun was in north Africa, he'd been on his way to France. It had been only a short encounter, but little good had come from it. He could only hope this turned out differently.

Humidity quickly turned arid as he stepped into a hot Egyptian morning. He wasn't entirely sure where he was, somewhere outside a city, ancient walls still standing, large swaths of scaffolding speaking to restoration attempts and archaeological studies even as vehicles motored their way here and there in a haze of dust and exhaust.

Rifun was not out of place as he walked through the streets, at least by appearance. It would be his lack of language that would give him away. Oh, the Akari might translate, yes, but, like movie dubs, there would still be the discrepancy between the words his lips formed and the ones that reached the listener's ears.

He used the GPS on the phone to take him to the coordinates Win had written, not that it would have been difficult to find. The area was still taped off for a block in every direction, and the only thing still standing amid broken stone and twisted steel was an otherwise unassuming building. This church was, by appearance, nothing more than perhaps a large estate or maybe a small meeting center. There were no large crosses or ichthus, nothing to designate it as the site of a holy gathering.

Rifun Banded to get inside, past the odd military patrol still wandering around, looking bored. The inside of the place wasn't any more extravagant. It might have been, without the interruption of a drone, but by now, most of the plants had withered away. There were a few cracks in the walls where the building had clearly been shaken before being saved in a quasi-dimension, but otherwise, it appeared sound.

"So then, who did this?" Rifun wondered aloud.

"I did."

Rifun turned to see Assim Foyez. Once the Gatekeeper of Earth, now just a humble Captain in Region Four. He appeared from another room. He did not approach Rifun, but preferred to lean against a table at the front of the room, perhaps the makeshift altar. He folded his arms.

"You're a bit far from home, aren't you?" Rifun wondered. "Either Iran or Region Four."

Foyez shrugged. "I get around. Just as you keep an eye on your homeland, so do I. I keep an eye on the region, even from afar. I may not have appreciated being kidnapped by a Tracker and dragged to the Wheel for a few months of schooling, but I won't deny that your classes were informative. I was one of your biggest advocates before the new Hands to simply get the Akari and assorted groups merely banned rather than hunted down."

Rifun made a vague gesture. "And this? You couldn't have known about the drone strike. Even so, why save the church and not the mosque? Last I checked, you're still Muslim."

Foyez shrugged again. "I have my contacts. By the time I got here, when I Banded, the drone had already penetrated the mosque. I could not handle that kind of Energy, to redirect it, not without potentially blowing up the entire city. Even so, the mosque was empty. But this church, there were worshipers here. I grabbed what I could and held it. As it turns out, one of the worshipers, a true Copt, was a Timekeeper. I couldn't even tell you what we did, only that we did it, and the church was saved."

"And you've been skulking around here for two weeks?" Rifun raised a brow.

"Micaiah contacted me about Tommen, explained what happened, wanted me to keep an eye out for him. I agreed. I also listened to what he said about the previous rescue attempt. This place...it was a logical assumption. My gamble has paid off, it seems."

"And you're here to...do what, exactly? Even if you did advocate on our behalf, to my knowledge, you haven't been around the Cult for any further instruction. Unless you've gone to the Akarin?"

He shook his head. "No. It was good to learn, but I've no such lasting interest. Time is already toeing the line of blasphemy. I don't know that I could rightly do more. Really, I'm here to rescue Tommen. I don't know what I did before, but I figure I can at least lend some strength."

Rifun studied him for a long moment. This was too coincidental. He Tested the man just to be sure, and it really was Assim Foyez. Well, Rifun wasn't worried about the man trying to kill anyone, especially if he was only casually interested in the Akari. And he really couldn't turn down a helping hand, even if it was just lending strength. With any luck, this would be the last rescue attempt, the one that actually worked. More hands, lighter work.

"Fine," he said at last. "But we have some more assistance on the way, and we have to wait for Julianna to make contact."

"Fair enough," Foyez agreed. "If it's all the same to you, I might use a Disguise as well, so as not to stir up any questions from Julianna."

Rifun hesitated, then nodded. He didn't want to deal with her obsessive objections either. Rescue, then worry. He found a chair and sat to wait. Foyez did the same, ten feet away.

Godwin's help arrived about twenty minutes later, five Arab-looking men, only one with enough English skills to confirm that they were there to help. They didn't know exactly what was going on, but they had strength to lend as Timekeepers and a debt to pay to Godwin.

That conversation had barely finished before Julianna called.

"We're heading to a church in—" she began.

"I know," Rifun cut in. "I'm here with help."

"We'll be there shortly. Keep this line open."

It wasn't two minutes before Tommen's voice came over the line. "Where are we?"

"It's a church, not that I would expect you to know that," Rifun answered. "Next door to this church was a mosque. A couple weeks ago, American intelligence determined that a terrorist cell was in the area and using the mosque next door as a training ground or radicalization center, whatever you want to call it. A drone strike was ordered. Foolishly, it happened on a Sunday, not a Friday. But then, what do you expect from American intelligence, anyway?

"One of the Copts here is a Timekeeper. He pulled the church into a quasi-dimension in order to save the people inside. The Energy from the blast rocked the building and there is some minor damage as the Energy was absorbed and expelled, balancing out as it always does, but no one inside the church died. Some called it a miracle from God. I'm sure there were mass conversions around the world because of it. But for us, it provides enough scar tissue to use as a gateway, like we did in West Virginia."

There was a pause. Then, "How the hell do you know we're here? Or where I am? Or what I'm saying?"

Julianna chuckled. Rifun imagined her showing off the device Godwin had cobbled together, or gotten someone else to cobble. "It's the Middle East. There is no shortage of military equipment lying around. Rifun was able to take your huge, clunky design and reduce it down into what amounts to a wire tap."

Sighing, Rifun stood. "But at any rate, we have business to take care of. Now then, if you would kindly take your place at the altar."

"Don't try anything funny," Julianna growled, likely to Tommen.

"Can I try something sad?" Tommen wondered stupidly. "Or joyful? Or smart? Or any of that?"

He barked out a cry of pain then, and a moment later, Julianna said, "We're ready."

Just like last time, Rifun opened a portal around Julianna and Tommen, the six helpers lending strength. It was poor strength, given that they were Timekeepers only—Foyez was the most knowledgeable of the goings-on and he seemed to be the weakest of the group—but it was better than nothing. Dimensions ripped open and the visage of the dimensional prisoners appeared.

Rifun was actually surprised that Julianna let Tommen go first, but maybe that was just to test the waters, make sure this wasn't some kind of trick.

Julianna looked ready to make her move when suddenly there was a shout and Assim Foyez made a move. Startled, Rifun's concentration wavered. He whirled around to see Foyez shed his Disguise and lunge for Julianna. Julianna grabbed Tommen close like a shield, but Foyez barreled into them both, driving them back into the in-between dimension.

"Run, Tommen Forbes!" Foyez shouted.

Rifun, still exhausted from the first try, plus the portal travel, plus this second try, and stunned from this turn of events, lost control of the portal now. It collapsed, trapping the three of them inside. For a long moment, he just stared at the spot where it had been open, where Tommen had walked through, where Julianna had prepared to walk through. There was nothing there now, and there was only unintelligible noise coming from the open line.

"What?!" he cried, mostly out of sheer frustration. He turned to one of the Arab Timekeepers who looked just as exhausted and twice as bewildered. He made a universal motion and the Timekeeper meekly surrendered a small handgun.

Rifun turned back toward the altar. Some of the noise on the line had died down, but it was impossible to say where the trio was. Then all went quiet.

"Great," Tommen panted after a second. "We got her. Now what do we do with her?"

"There is only one thing we can do," Foyez said. "We must kill her."

"Ki—what? Why? Okay, scratch that. I get it. But...I mean, heat of battle is one thing. It just feels like cold blood now."

Foyez's tone turned incredulous. "It's only been fifteen seconds since she was trying to choke you."

"I know, I know. But I'm not called the Chivalrous Welshman for nothing."

"Little fucker," Julianna growled.

"Nope. Sorry. Still a virgin."

"What would you do, then?" Foyez asked. "She knows how to escape. It would only take one more person to accidentally fall in here and she has another conduit. She will not stop. Rifun will not stop. We must end this now."

"You want to end this?" Julianna said. "Fine. Let's end it. Forward and to your left a step."

Rifun made the motion and held out the gun. It disappeared from his hand into the in-between dimension. There were two shots and the sound of something hitting the ground. Fearing she had killed Tommen, Rifun opened his mouth to speak, but she was already talking.

"Now it's your turn."

"No," Rifun said quickly.

"Excuse me? No? He has caused nothing but trouble. He is worthless."

"He is my Apprentice. I am training him. How do you think he got here?"

There was a long pause. Rifun wasn't even sure which "he" he was actually referring to. With any luck, she had dispatched Foyez. He should have expected some kind of treachery, really. It had been way too coincidental for him to be here, whether or not he had "contacts" and whatever the rest of his story was.

"Do you have the strength for one more attempt at opening a portal and separating the dimensions?" Julianna asked, voice tight.

"I do," Rifun answered.

"And your men. Are the rest of them really who they claim to be? No more surprises today."

"Give me two minutes to make sure."

Rifun went to the Timekeepers who had gathered, a huddle of frightened, tired mice. He intended to give them a little pep talk, but when Julianna started speaking, he decided to let her spite work for him this time.

"We're going to do this again," she said. The English-speaking man did his best to translate. "If I'm not walking free within the hour, I don't care what Rifun says about you. You are going to die. Is that understood?"

The Arab men nodded vigorously even as Tommen said, "In my defense, I had no idea about Foyez."

"Do you understand?" she demanded again.

"Yes, ma'am."

"Good." A pause, then, "Are we ready?"

Sighing, Rifun nodded and motioned for the men to take their positions and ready themselves. He only had one more try in him today. He was exhausted.

Just before he could open the portal, Julianna shrieked something in the realm of "No! You little bastard!"

"What's going on?" Rifun asked, more tired than annoyed by this point.

There was no reply and the open line went dead. Rifun sighed and walked up to the altar, little more than a fancy dining room table. He put his hands out to lean against it, waited a moment for some kind of reply. When there was none, he slammed his fist on the table.

"Damn you, woman!"

One or more of the Arab Timekeepers shuffled awkwardly and cleared his throat. Rifun sighed and turned to face the English-speaking one. "You are free to go. I don't think we'll be making any more attempts today. You may consider your favor paid."

One of the Timekeepers said something which the interpreter relayed to Rifun. "Our attempts were unsuccessful; we cannot in good conscience consider the debt paid." More speaking. "And you are not our debt holder, so you cannot free us from such debt."

Rifun nodded. "If that is your will, I will respect it. Take it up with Godwin." He straightened and stretched. "But we're not going to be doing this again today. Go home, or wherever, get some rest. Be ready to be called upon again, perhaps as early as tomorrow."

The men acknowledged and thanked him and left the building, talking amongst themselves.

Rifun returned his attention to the table that served as an altar and stayed there for a good amount of time. Most of the time he stared at the table itself, studying the grain and groove of the wood and the carvings along the outer edge. It was nothing especially fancy or intricate. In the United States, it probably would have passed through several garage sales by now. In Madagascar, it might be considered an important family possession or heirloom type piece. Here in Egypt, it served as an altar to God.

His gaze flicked up, where a cup of wine and loaf of bread might have sat during service, a candle on either side, maybe some other religious paraphernalia, now cleaned out by fleeing parishioners or opportunistic thieves.

Tommen had no trouble being rescued. His rescue had been completed once already, nearly a second time as well, within a week of his arrival in the in-between dimension. Julianna had waited over forty years with no real progress. There was only so much anyone could attribute to easier communication through more advanced technology. There was only so much anyone could attribute to Tommen being a chosen one of the Author. If Tommen's ease of escape was because he was chosen, then Julianna's difficulty could be similarly attributed to not being chosen. But if she wasn't chosen, adding into Rifun's suspicions that the journals were not entirely accurate or complete on account of Cassius and the dragon...

He jumped as the phone rang. Sighing, he answered it technologically only, not even bothering with a greeting.

"Where are you?" Julianna demanded.

"Still in the church," he said flatly, "seeing how you did not give me the courtesy of—"

"Meet me at Forbes Cave."

Click.

He didn't have to, he thought. Not today. He didn't really want to. Aside from being tired, and another portal jump was not going to help that, there was something more he needed to work through. Something wasn't adding up.

He rubbed his face. He needed sleep before he did another rescue attempt.

Naturally, this delay greatly displeased Julianna, and she made sure he knew it. Every time he tried to mute the phone while she ranted, she simply had to reach in, manipulate the electricity or the motherboard, and unmute it. Somehow, the only thing Rifun could think was, *How was Richard married to this woman, and could he have gone to Beaumaris Gaol and his death willingly?*

With Godwin as the middleman, Rifun brought the Arab Timekeepers to Forbes Cave to pay off their debt, or try to anyway. Somehow it ended up being on them who had to act as the "conduit" to free Julianna, at the cost of himself. Why it had to be this way, no one seemed able to explain. Why would Tommen have been able to come out with her, but no one else could? Even sending all of the Arabs into the in-between dimension and attempting a similar rescue could not reproduce such results; one of them always remained trapped.

Julianna gave them some flippant advice about the dimension, suggested they return to the church in Egypt to continue their attempts and experiments, but otherwise showed no sympathy whatsoever for their plight.

"Good to see you, too," Rifun told her as she began walking away down the slope.

She glanced back at him. "Oh, I am grateful to be free, believe me. There is no better feeling in the universe. To touch grass as it was meant to be touched and felt is a wondrous thing. Although, having to watch out for solid objects like trees and rocks and doors, that is a bit inconvenient after so long of not needing to worry about such things."

"The plight of us mere mortals," Win murmured sarcastically.

"But I am glad to be free. I think I will return to Sadurnon first, dust off my chambers, sweep out the spiders, and get some sleep. Then we can proceed with the plan."

It was the closest Rifun or Win got to a thank you as she simply conjured a portal and departed, not even bothering to hold the door open for them as it were. Reluctantly, Rifun conjured a portal for the mere mortals, straight to his chambers in the officers building.

"What is the next phase of the plan, sir?" Win asked uncertainly.

Rifun rubbed his eyes. "I get the feeling she's going to tell us."

"You really think it was a good idea to bring her back?"

"It seemed like a good idea at the time. Maybe she'll settle down after a few days. After all, she hasn't been able to leave Earth in years, hasn't had proper conversations or interactions."

Win still looked unsure. "If you say so, sir."

"Besides, we still have to rescue Tommen, or get to him quickly if the Akarin manage his rescue."

"Of course, sir."

"Tell me about your Akarin spies."

"A necessity, sir, after they tried to plant some within our ranks."

"And how were they rooted out?"

"I discovered that your Authored Books had gone missing, sir. Replaced by gibberish copies. So I sent some spies of my own to swap them back. Now we have the originals and the Akarin have the gibberish copies. They don't read the things anyway, so—"

"Obviously they do if they knew enough to plant fakes," Rifun said.

"At any rate, sir, they were low-level, superficial cover spies. They fled with only minimal prodding from my own men."

"Low-level or not, they know where we are. They know the location of our base of operations."

"Well...yes. But we know the location of the Akarin fortress."

"Something they can easily change because portals there are opened exclusively by feel, not coordinates. We have no such luxury. If none of them were smart enough to get the coordinates of this place, it really wouldn't take much."

"Agreed, sir."

Rifun sat and leaned back. "We're facing two enemies right now, Win: the Borelians and the Akarin. The Borelians have the reputation, the intelligence, and sheer firepower. If not the Akari, then their biotoxins and physical weaponry, combined with some Time prowess, makes them a formidable foe. The Akarin don't have the reputation or the intelligence, but they have skill and they have one solid victory against us. The Borelians are currently distracted by their war on humanity, their attention still on Treman and Trebald. The Akarin have no such distraction except for themselves and their ever-splintering leadership."

"In my opinion, sir, the Borelians are the bigger threat," Win offered. "They are here, among us, now. As much as they will happily enslave us themselves, they would have no trouble calling upon allies in Time to attack, overwhelm us with sheer numbers. The Akarin have no such advantage."

Rifun chuckled. "Neither do we. Many of our allies have backed off since our failure in the Wheel, to say nothing of that declaration of war was made public and I was specifically named."

Win nodded. "Well, our own distraction of freeing Julianna and Tommen is no longer a distraction. We may tout it as a victory among the underlings to boost morale, but we can't just sit here without some plan going forward."

"You think I don't know that?" Rifun shook his head. "Spread the word of Julianna's rescue. If you can convince her to make a few public appearances, do that. Boost morale, as you said. Give it a day or two. Then we'll see about the rest of the plan."

The mercenary saluted and left the room.

It was nice to have someone to whom he could delegate work. It meant he could get in a decent sleep after several days of dealing with a cantankerous woman and her inability to woo and control one teenage boy for a few days.

He didn't know how long he slept, but when he woke, he would say that he did feel better, more prepared to take on either the Borelians or the Akarin. But as he sat up and swung his legs over the side of the bed, the door opened and Julianna glided in. She appeared to have benefited from a full night's rest in her own bed as well. Her face still left much to be desired, but the rest of her looked lively.

"Been out making speeches, have you?" Rifun wondered. "Boosting the morale of all those who awaited your return?"

"And those who desired some kind of victory over our most recent defeat," she said, her voice much lighter than it had been the last day or so.

"Well, we still don't know about Tommen. I know you don't—"

"Oh, Tommen was rescued." She waved a hand dismissively. "The one they call Chandler, Anagalisgi, he had some part in it, I think."

Rifun nodded once. "All right, so we rescued both of you. I would call that a victory, yes."

She barked a laugh that was decidedly more venomous than Rifun was comfortable with. "Oh, I'm not talking about that, although it is one more victory we can brag about in the past few days."

Rifun raised a brow. "What did I miss?"

She grinned grotesquely. "I killed Micaiah Durvin."

27 | Marination
The Caves of Meroian, 2014

"Y"ou do realize you've just declared war on the Akarin, right?" Rifun inquired.

"That's the point," Julianna informed him coldly. "He's been the biggest pain in the arse since he joined the Akarin." He opened his mouth to speak, but she cut him off. "I am done with this, Rifun. No more negotiations, no more alliances, no more back-and-forth cat-and-mouse pretending like we can somehow still be allies, or distant cousins. They are fractured already, and with Micaiah's murder, it will only further the disarray. Now we move in for the kill."

He had pulled together some clothes for the day and now stood near his desk while Julianna remained near the door which was closed.

"In case you haven't noticed, the Borelians are still here. They are still intent on enslaving us. You think they are going to let us mobilize to anything without repercussions? If anything, we need to take them out first. We can't strike the hornet's nest while we're preparing to attack an alligator and expect the hornets to not respond."

"We move against the Borelians, it will cost us dearly, in both time, energy, and manpower. I am not ignorant of this. The Akarin would use it to their advantage to take us from behind."

Rifun barked a laugh. "The Akarin are so rarely roused to action, you think they would be smart enough to do something like that? If they're in civil war, they're not looking for external strategic advantages."

"They are the easier target," Julianna insisted. "They are the only ones to defeat us so far. Take them out, it sends a message at the very least. Then we can set our sights on the Borelians if we so choose."

"Choose? That's a funny word to describe our options, considering we don't have any."

"It will also cement our superiority. Richard's journals must triumph over the Authored Books."

Rifun raised a brow. "Oh they must? Or else what?"

She glared at him. "Do you doubt?"

He sighed. "The Authored Books may be flawed, but they are not useless. I have Authored Books, you know that. They are reasonably accurate. The journals are the technical manuals, the textbooks, the edicts, however you want to phrase it. The Authored Books are the stories of our daily lives, the context in which the Akari is used." He made a motion. "There is textbook knowledge, and there is real world application. There is no reason for them to be mutually exclusive." He shifted his stance. "The only thing of consequence that I doubt is the completeness of the journals."

He's lying, a voice told her.

"Cassius was controlled by a malevolent spirit," he went on. "That spirit is not going to gift us the information on how to defeat it, and it wasn't. It is still out there somewhere. I have spent months, even years, trying to divine a way of defeating this evil spirit."

She raised a brow, unimpressed. "And?"

He faltered, just a little. "I was...misled. Not by the ancestors or the razana, but by the evil spirits themselves. They pulled a fast one on me, I think."

He doubts. It was his own fault he was unsuccessful. He has divided loyalties.

She shrugged and folded her arms. "All right, then. What do you say is our next move? Now that Cassius isn't here like a stick of lit dynamite and Isthim isn't leading you around by your cock—" She noted his expression. "—what is our next viable, efficient, level-headed move to bolster the Cult?"

For a long moment, Rifun was silent. Then, "That depends. Are you going to be a new stick of lit dynamite? Going out and murdering a man isn't something that just anyone can do on a whim."

"As I said, he's been a pain in the arse for a while."

"You were planning it for a while, then. Watching his every move, his routines, his habits. Even I can respect that the list of people who could get the jump on him is very short. I would expect my name on that list, but not yours. So why not include the rest of us on your plans to declare war?"

She sighed dramatically. "Because I am so very fed up with being treated as second-class. I am tired of my ideas not being given equal weight. Yes, I am forcing the issue."

"Because you're a woman? Or because you have no experience in any of the areas you're messing with?" Rifun made a motion. "Please, enlighten me. What do you know of warfare? Troop movements? Resource management? Strategy? Espionage? Infiltration? Tactics? Traps? When is the last time you even mediated a dispute between two parties? You took Tommen hostage, wanted to kill him, and you just killed both Foyez and Micaiah. Now tell me how that helps us?"

She glared at him. "Right now it's revealing your own cowardice. You haven't answered the question. What is our next move?"

Rifun growled and paced a few times. "On the one hand, I don't want the one who deliberately caused the problem to be in charge of the solution. On the other hand, I almost want to have you lead this endeavor just to see where it is you think we're going and how. The only reason I don't is because we still have the Borelians hovering over our shoulder! And now we're going to have the Akarin knocking on our door!"

"Not if they can't be roused to action, as you stated earlier. And even if they can be bothered, they don't know where we are, and I hear you've been very diligent about keeping spies out. Or...is that no longer the case? With Tommen and all?"

"Tommen has not been brought here. What few training sessions we've had have all been on Earth."

"Looks like you'll have to start making some decisions on that, then, too. Earth, a target for the Borelians. The Akarin fortress, where he will no doubt be heavily indoctrinated against us. Or here. But you will have the Akarin as an enemy anyway." She added, "Forget Tommen for a moment; it's time for you to choose a side, Rifun."

She could see his mind working, mulling over his options.

"Fine," he said after a long silence. "I will see what we have to work with against the Akarin. We have some low-level spies among them; I will see what intelligence they have for us. But I want something from you in return."

"Stay out of your way?" she inquired lightly, if sarcastically.

"Isolation clearly hasn't been good for you. I can't say I don't understand to some degree. You do your best work when you are involved with humanitarian efforts and helping people, boosting morale through kind, feminine ways. Do that and let me handle the finer points of war."

"I will not be pushed to the side. I am an original leader! I spent years in the in-between dimension, watching the past, looking over all of the first meetings, the first writings of the journals."

"Then perhaps it would benefit to work on a system of such education. I was working on that in the Wheel, but discipline in such endeavors has...decreased since our defeat. Reinstate journal studies, create tiers of classes, ensure that what the instructors are teaching is true and correct."

Julianna blinked, then nodded. "I will. But I do not want to be kept out of the loop. I want to know when we are attacking the Akarin. Whether or not I am involved, it is an important thing to know."

"Fair enough," Rifun conceded. "And if I may make a suggestion?"

"What's that?"

"Never forget that the Borelians are out for our heads. I suggest you find one or two people you trust with sensitive work, maybe someone who is willing to act as a decoy, as Godwin Lore does for me."

She dipped her head. "A sensible suggestion. And how is Mr. Lore working out for you?"

He spread his arms. "I'm still here, aren't I?"

"Of course." She huffed a sigh. "Well then, I suppose I should start catching up on what I've missed. I know all about the goings-on of Earth, but my knowledge of Sadurnon and Cult activities is depressingly limited."

He did not stop her, and she returned to her chambers, still warming up after a forty-year absence. She had already cleaned the room once, but she cleaned it a second time just to be sure. She never thought she would be so grateful to clean something, to be able to touch a hard surface and affect what was on it, to leave a finger trail in the dust. Just seeing her reflection in the mirror was a godsend she never knew she needed.

Deprivation only proves the depths of the heart, what one truly cherishes.

Julianna silently agreed, still mesmerized by her ability to write and doodle in the dust.

Rifun understood this once, but years have softened the sharpness of that blade. You are merely helping to restore his edge. The blade never thanks the whetstone, but it is still an important tool.

She nodded absently. With Cassius and Isthim gone, maybe now they could get some real work done. Defeat the Akarin, push back the Borelians, retake the Wheel (yet again), finally establish the empire they had been dreaming of and preparing for. And to do that, she needed to get the education back up and running. But the Borelians wouldn't want such widespread education. Uneducated slaves were easier to control, especially when it came to the Akari. Rifun had to try and maneuver them into battle preparedness without somehow tipping off the Borelians, or aggravating them too much, but that didn't mean that she was entirely in the clear. She was an original leader after all, still a high profile target for mischief.

A decoy, as he had suggested. But she wasn't going to just pick out some lovely maiden to wash linens while she was away. She would need someone who could, perhaps, act as an advisor, both to herself and Rifun, who knew what was going on. Rifun seemed to have found such a one in Godwin, so why shouldn't she do the same?

She wiped the dust clean, smoothed her dress and her hair, and walked through the officers building. General Misik was nowhere to be seen, but there were four or five other Borelians meandering about, their activities more akin to prison guards than officers with their own duties.

Don't worry about them. Be as a dog, be forgotten, and go where you will.

She didn't like the idea of being relegated to being an animal, but the principle was sound; no one questioned her or even acknowledged her beyond a glance. Despite her desire for real conversation, she would save it for the more normal mortal beings in the ruins proper.

Leaving the officers building, she was momentarily stunned by how lively the city was. And what a city! No longer crumbling ruins, but ruins in the midst of restoration, even completely restored in some places. For a moment, she was almost worried that her help and advice on such humanitarian efforts would not be necessary. Then she decided that she would advise on the projects anyway. They needed her help and she needed to get back into things.

They will listen to you. They must.

Godwin had taken her on a tour of the ruins when she first returned, but it was a different feel now, less of a staged parade and more of daily life. Perhaps that was what stunned her, that the Cult was still so active even in her absence.

Now then, to find a decoy...

The ruins had divided by military rank while under Isthim's rule, and it appeared that Rifun had not deemed it necessary to change that. This made it easier for her to locate the higher ranking soldiers, though she was not familiar with any of them, not enough to ask them to be a decoy or some such thing.

"You lost, ma'am?"

She turned at a familiar voice. Godwin approached, looking mildly curious. He was a good-looking man, five-eight or five-ten, white, brown hair, brown eyes, Slavic features, physically fit to the point where even most casual clothes couldn't hide or downplay it.

"Ah, just the man I was looking for." He wasn't, but it seemed as good a place as any to start. "Walk with me."

He did so, though his enthusiasm was notably lacking.

"Rifun has advised that I take an...advisor, such as you are to him," she began, trying to be casual in her search for Borelians in the vicinity. "Now, Rifun may very well be able to handle himself, but I have no physical advantages. I think it may be prudent for me to have an advisor who is as skilled in physicality as in the Akari."

"I only work for one leader at a time," Godwin informed her. "And, to be blunt, I like him more."

His loyalties are questionable.

"I am not trying to steal you away, sir, but I do think you know the people better than I do at this point in time. Maybe you have some...recommendations?"

"No one is coming to mind just now, but I can ask around. I know there were a few who were more than thrilled to have you back."

"And what about you? Do you regret playing a part in my rescue?"

"I was one of your first followers, ma'am. I am glad to see you returned. I just avoid treating anyone like an icon or a god. Or goddess, as the case may be."

He's a mercenary, what do you expect?

"I mean no disrespect, ma'am," he went on. "I've just seen too much to get so excited for anything."

"Of course. Time does tend to erode the extremes of our emotions. I do request, however, that you do not take long in your inquiries. In light of some recent developments among the Akarin, our own time may be short and decoys may be necessary."

The man's expression turned curious once more, but he dipped his head. "Of course, ma'am."

"I suggest you go talk to Rifun for this latest update. It may concern you."

He nodded once more and took his leave, jogging up the steps of the officers building. He was easy on the eyes, she couldn't deny. But his loyalties... He was loyal to Rifun, it seemed, and Rifun was loyal to...what? The truth, he claimed, except he still yearned to find meaning in the Authored Books, believing himself special in some way Julianna did not understand. Perhaps it was his French side desiring to break free of his Malagasy side and going about it all the wrong way. And he was going to take poor Godwin with him.

Or maybe not. Maybe this little push that she had given him, to move against the Akarin, would be just what he needed to truly define his beliefs and loyalties. Most everyone liked to believe himself the sharpest knife in the drawer, but some needed a few more runs through the sharpener.

It took a few days, maybe a week, but Godwin found a couple of skilled Akari-bearer soldiers who were more than willing to serve her personally. Neither was human, but both were humanoid.

Torbak Martin was a Bardin from the planet Bari, Quadrant Two, Parsec Two, Sector Eleven, System Four, Planet Seven. He was just a head taller than her, almost human in his general shape, but with a face that made her own look angelic, as if he had an unfortunate run-in with a rock slide. His skin was a nearly luminescent green, almost yellow, and entirely unflattering. He was more than ecstatic to be honored with her request for a personal bodyguard and possible decoy and wasted no time in telling her that there was nothing he would not do for her, even going so far as to inform her that he had researched and confirmed the compatibility of their individual sexual features if she so desired.

She did not, but she said only that she would take it into consideration. As long as he could fight and lead, and use a Disguise to be able to pass as her, she could use him. He assured her he could and promised to one day demonstrate such strength and loyalty. For now, the best he could do was demonstrate the Disguise which was, short of the nuances of her personality, flawless.

Drinjin uh Ersik, an Ardan from Ardo, Quadrant One, Parsec Two, Sector Nine, System Thirteen, Planet Two, was less interested in Disguises and pretending to do her work and more interested in keeping her safe. He had a quiet yet severe reverence for the journals and for Richard, one that spoke of true and honest loyalty. She spoke and he listened. He did not argue or try to inject his own ideas or judge hers. He listened and did as he was told. From what she could discern, his given, individual name was, in fact, "uh." Drinjin was a family name detailing their traditional profession or trade, and Ersik was their ancestral region. However, it was considered an insult to use the given name out of context, or at all, really; he could not be referred to as anything less than Drinjin Ersik, but "uh" was added only if there might be some confusion, which there wouldn't be because there were no other Ardan in the Cult that Julianna was aware of.

Only once she approved of her decoys did she begin to understand the gravity of the situation. Rifun was generally more suited to war, and as the only remaining leader for a long time, it was not unexpected for him to need to meet with higher soldiers like Godwin. But for her to go walking around with a couple of bodyguards, that attracted a tad bit more attention from Misik and the Borelians. She had to turn her first attempt at getting them into the officers building into something of a scripted interview of how things had gone while she was away. A few hours later she managed to get them in without the Borelians noticing. She took them to Rifun.

"Your decoys?" he wondered, giving them a brief glance as they walked in the door.

"Recommended by Mr. Lore, yes," she confirmed.

Rifun nodded. "Wait a moment. I'll go get him."

He left the room. Julianna took a moment to look around. She did not rummage, but she did a thorough visual scan, ending up at his shrine.

"Something you're looking for?" Torbak asked.

"I don't know," she admitted. "For as long as I've known him, and for as much time as I spent in his wretched country trying to understand his culture, he is a hard man to figure out. His obsession with spirituality goes beyond mere devotion or even thorough education. I fear it is turning into paranoia, even extremism."

Before any of them could say more, the door opened and Rifun walked in, Godwin following. Rifun put up a Sound barrier as they assembled in a loose circle.

"So, the ragtag band of resistance heroes holds its first official meeting," Rifun mused. "How quaint."

"And what are we meeting about, exactly?" Julianna wondered.

"The Borelians have already mobilized against humanity, as we've heard, going after Treman and Trebald. We can't do anything about that at this point, but it only buys us time for so long. We need to act, save ourselves first."

"We can't take on their entire civilization," Drinjin uh Ersik stated in a near-baritone.

"Nor am I suggesting such a thing."

Rifun made a gesture and Godwin took over. "It's a risky move, but it may give us the cover we need. Julianna has effectively declared war on the Akarin, if you didn't hear." He gave her a look. "Between what's happened in the Wheel, now Micaiah's death, and their own fractured leadership, we can turn this to our advantage. Take the fight to the Akarin, conquer them, assimilate them into our ranks."

"They would never allow it," Torbak said incredulously. "We would get in their fortress and they would just blow it up."

"They're too cowardly for that," Rifun stated, but something about his posture said that he was weighing the actual likelihood of such a thing and wondering if that risk was worth it. He shifted his stance.

"And how does that help us with the Borelians?" Drinjin uh Ersik inquired. "If they are intent on coming after us, they will not allow us to mobilize in any form."

"Unless they think it is to their benefit," Godwin told him. "Tacagans are human, too, however much they deny it. They have the technological capability to resist the Borelians, maybe even repel them entirely. But they can't stop the Akari. If we can make the Borelians believe that the Cult is willing to help them go after the Tacagans, we can train and mobilize, allegedly, to that end."

"Our real target," Rifun continued, "as Godwin as stated, is the Akarin in their own fortress. Before we leave here to attack, Godwin and I will ensure that Misik and all Borelians in our ranks are dead. We attack the Akarin, win for we have no other choice, and take over the fortress. The fortress is safer and more easily defended. If and when the Borelians figure out what happened, they will have some choices to make. And we will be in a better position to plan offensively or defensively as the situation demands."

"And what if the Borelians don't believe us, that we want to help them go against the Tacagans?" Julianna wondered.

"Then we will have to come up with a new plan, probably something along the lines of killing the Borelians that are here and going straight into conquering the Akarin. It's not the ideal, but it may be the only." Rifun made a motion. "Personally, I think they will accept our alleged help. They know our history with the Tacagans and the Gentleman Killers. If we can make them believe that we are so naive as to still consider the Borelians allies and that we are somehow taking out a common foe, well...Sometimes it pays to act like the idiot others think you are."

"Why go to the Akarin fortress?" Torbak asked. "Take it over once they're defeated, fine, but why not draw them out, bring them to our home field? You just said the fortress is easily defended."

"Too precarious to coordinate. Besides that, how are we going to entice them in? If they want to destroy us, they don't need to interfere with the Borelian declaration of war. We don't have the ability to go after the Wheel again at this moment. Anything else, attack anyone else, the Akarin won't do much more than yell at us not to do that. And there needs to be as little time gap between the deaths of Misik and the others and the battle itself."

"If we're pretending to assist the Borelians with an attack on Tacaga, won't they notice when we don't?" Julianna wondered.

Rifun shrugged. "And suddenly the Akarin got wind of what we were doing and tried to intervene. We defended ourselves. After all, the Tacagans love the Wheel and the Time industry. Without them, who knows what the Hands of Time will do? How will they survive without their Tacagan overlords?!" His expression was tangible sarcasm, then he lightened up a bit. "That's why we need to do this quickly." He paused, seeming to think through his words. "We should also understand that this is only putting us in a better position; it is not eliminating the real threat. I fully expect that we will have to confront the Borelians eventually. And as much as I hate to say it, that is a problem for future us, and first we have to make it to that point.

"The Cult has been going back and forth for years now. Unfortunately, we lost much of our momentum and now we're shifting to the back foot. If we don't do something, we are going to fall. Right into Borelian slavery."

"What are our roles, then?" Drinjin uh Ersik inquired.

"The first step will be testing the waters with Misik, seeing if we even can get into their good graces as it were." Rifun looked at Julianna. "Have you said anything to any of the Borelians about the Land In Between?"

She blinked. "Of course not. I've done my best to avoid them."

"Good. Gives us a little wiggle room to lie."

"About what?"

"We can't just walk up to Misik and offer to fight. We may as well announce our plans while we're at it. Right now, Misik thinks he has us cowed. We have to give the appearance of ingratiation, trying to buy favors or freedom. The Borelians actually have a word for such people, *kinilik*. Like dogs begging for scraps. If we lie and say something along the lines of how you learned that the Tacagans are planning something terrible—such as, say, offering up Earth, the parent planet of humans, to the Borelians in exchange for being spared, we have a reason to hate them and go after them, and the Borelians do, too."

"Why?" Torbak asked.

"For being self-righteous, slaving scum of the universe, the Borelians have a strange code of honor that they expect from themselves and their enemies," Godwin answered. "Offering up members of your own species in order to save your own skin is a terrible betrayal, greatly dishonorable. Such a person instantly becomes public enemy number one."

"It may even work to buy time for Treman and Trebald," Rifun commented thoughtfully. "If we do convince the Borelians about the Tacagans being traitorous bastards, the Borelians may turn their attention wholly on the Tacagans. Not only are they traitors, but with the Tacagans' advanced technology, it could end up being a longer, drawn-out affair."

"A lot of speculation," Drinjin uh Ersik stated.

"Less than you might think."

"Sometimes it pays to sleep with the enemy?" Julianna threw out.

"Just because it's true doesn't mean it needs to be said aloud," Rifun retorted, not looking at her. "And if you actually meant that, you might have said 'thank you' instead."

Drinjin uh Ersik shifted his stance and made an obvious noise akin to a sigh. "So what are we doing?"

It was Godwin who answered. "Once Rifun and Julianna have Misik's ear and-or approval of the Tacagan plan, the three of us will muster and mobilize. We can help them out by planting rumors of the Tacagans being aforementioned traitorous bastards. No, the underlings may not run to the Borelians with the knowledge, but if it comes up enough in casual conversation that the Borelians take notice, it may provide some subtle, social push for the Borelians to consider."

"As stoic as they proclaim to be, they are not immune to groupthink," Rifun added. "It is the basis of their entire culture; they can't just ignore the signals that tell them how to operate in every other situation."

Drinjin uh Ersik thought about this for a moment, then nodded.

"When did you expect to start this operation?" Julianna wondered.

He looked at her. "I expect our sudden meeting with Misik will buy time for these three to get out of the officers building without being questioned too heavily." He made a motion. "Now that you've been back in the real world for a few days and gotten caught up on the state of things, you wanted to warn me about something you heard or saw in the in-between dimension. I suggested we take it to the Borelians, ask if we can help in the eradication of the Tacagans."

"Does that not make us the same traitors we are accusing the Tacagans of being?"

"It simply makes us messengers. And, acting as agents of the Cult, not humanity, we are simply invoking the Cult's history with the Tacagans and the Gentleman Killers." He went on before she could protest. "We can't be any more wanted or bound for slavery than we already are. If you can come up with a perfectly safe and foolproof plan, I'm all ears."

He mocks you. Degrades you. He doesn't have a plan. He's just trying to save his own skin.

She said nothing.

"Good. If there are no further concerns for the good of the public, we will adjourn here, and Julianna and I will go put our necks on the chopping block."

He is weak. He is willing to sacrifice you, as he has sacrificed others for his iniquities.

Rifun straightened and made for the door, still holding the Sound barrier. He glanced at her expectantly.

His doubts make him uncertain. How can he fight for something he does not believe in? You will have to carry this. You still believe. Your faith will protect you and sway the Borelians.

She followed Rifun out of the room and down the hall. With any luck, Misik and the others would be out on some mission for their own people doing their own thing. There was no reason for them to be hanging around here if they truly believed the Cult was cowed and contained.

But there they were, in the meeting room, eight of them standing around the stained stone table that used to be an altar.

One of the fascinating things about Borelians was that their toxins could still affect each other. Like poisons and illness, tolerance had to be built up. Misik, as a yellow and gray bitoxic, was immune to his own toxins, but he could still be susceptible to the purple Borelian to his left, or the red one to his right. Of course, with his rank and age, he was probably immune to all of the toxins, but Julianna could imagine that childhood for a Borelian was a very confusing, tumultuous time as they were attacked and harmed by other children through no other means than simple existence.

Misik looked up as the two of them entered the room, careful not to touch anything. Whatever was being said suddenly ceased and all eyes were pinned on them.

"Can I help you?" he asked irritably. Julianna had an image of a father in an important meeting being interrupted by an interloper, even his own child.

Rifun hardly bothered with formalities. "News from the human front." He made a vague gesture toward Julianna. "A report on something she saw while in the in-between dimension."

"What do we care?" one of the Borelians hissed to Misik. "Unsubstantiated rumors at best."

Rifun continued, giving that Borelian a pointed look. "The Tacagans are making up a plan, hand over Earth in exchange for their own freedom, seeing how they continue to whine and complain about not actually being the same humans as the rest of humanity."

"And how do you know this?" another Borelian asked, looking at Julianna. "How did you learn this from another dimension?"

"The in-between dimension afforded me many unique opportunities," she began awkwardly. "I could Travel anywhere on Earth, view events from the past, eavesdrop on any meeting or conversation. A Tacagan envoy met with a group of Earth Time Agents, attempting to facilitate such surrender. An inside job. In theory, the Earth humans involved would be granted asylum on Tacaga." She shook her head. "It would never happen, but it worked for them in the moment."

A few of the Borelians glanced at each other, but their expressions and body language were less than convincing.

"Sounds like a human problem," Misik said at last, looking back at the computer tablets he had laid out before him.

"You're right," Rifun said, shrugging and slowly taking a few steps forward. "It is. A very big, very annoying problem. The Tacagans have always been a pain in the arse, for humanity, for the Cult, and the Time industry."

Misik looked up once more, his expression warning Rifun from getting too close to the altar. Julianna stepped up beside him.

"They would betray their own species to save themselves," she stated. "They already betrayed the Time industry when they took over and conjured up the Gentleman Killers to do their dirty work. The Gentleman Killers and not the Grandfathers."

Misik did not reply, but neither did he dismiss them.

"Last I understood, you were working on Treman and Trebald," Rifun continued. "Allow us to go after the Tacagans. Their over-reliance on Time has made them vulnerable to the Akari."

More glances among the Borelians. Finally Misik said, "I want proof of this conspiracy, not mere speculation from a mysterious dimension and unreliable source." He looked at Julianna.

Rifun agreed, and he and Julianna left the room. They returned to his chambers. The three advisors were gone.

"So, you're just going to sacrifice Treman and Trebald?" she wondered.

"I had to make this about our vengeance against the Tacagans, not saving humanity," Rifun sighed. "Misik wasn't going to allocate Borelian resources to the cause like I'd hoped, but I still had to make it convincing that this is an authentic vendetta. It is, just not for the same ends."

She studied him for a long moment. Then, "If we can conjure up enough convincing proof, he might just change his mind about the allocation of Borelian resources."

"Agreed."

"I'll have to move quickly, though. If I got all of this information from the in-between dimension where I could go where I wanted and eavesdrop on everything, I should know where to find that information again and procure it more substantially. And it might give me an excuse to have my decoys hanging around, watching my back, keeping me safe in case the Tacagans find out about this little scheme."

Rifun nodded. "Good thinking. Meanwhile, Win can manage his little spies in the Akarin and we can start formulating a plan of attack."

A brief compliment, as if your own plan means nothing. Then he just shifts back into his own plan. A Narcissist never sees his own shortcomings, and his failures are always someone else's fault.

"All things considered," Julianna mused, "this will mean framing people. The Tacagans I don't care about. But we will need Terran accomplices. Mi Chin would be the most logical—"

Rifun shook his head. "No, she isn't. She's in a position of power and it is still in her best interest to defend Earth. And for as smug as the Chinese might be about their own perceived racial perfection and global demographic domination, their genetic traits are not well-liked by the Tacagans. And if our imaginary traitors are looking for asylum, they would have to be able to blend in, or so the Tacagans would want them to believe."

Throwing out jargon like he thinks he knows what he's doing. Pretending to be educated, pretending like he knows more than you.

"We're looking for Time Agents who are either not in power or are low-level, Lieutenants and Captains. Skin color is less of a factor as the Tacagans utilize all kinds as environmental responses based on geographical location. What they want is athleticism and intelligence in equal, obscene amounts. Smart enough to invent great machines, strong enough to build them. So, a low-level Timekeeper officer who is strong and smart, unappreciated, undervalued, keeps up on current events —"

"Rifun, I'm looking for scapegoats, not a husband," Julianna said, only half-serious.

He gave her a look. "—wants to escape the Borelian invasion and doesn't care who he has to step on to do it, even if it means betraying the entire human race. And charismatic enough to recruit a few others to help him."

He describes himself. Too bad he can't be used for this little exercise.

Maybe for the next one.

"Seeing how the Wheel is a bit dangerous for us right now, I might have to use the regular Time Agent database on Earth," she mused.

"Do what you have to, and keep your bodyguards close," Rifun told her.

Extends a vote of trust, then yanks it away. He mocks your intelligence and baits a reaction.

"Of course. And what about you? Since we didn't get the pistol start like you had hoped, what will you be doing?"

"I am going to bring Tommen here and begin his real training. He needs discipline, so he doesn't go blowing himself into any other dimensions. Training him when apparently no one else would, well, maybe it will spark some gratitude and foster some loyalty toward us so he will more willingly help us, especially when it comes to things like retrieving the Book of Commands or defeating the evil dragon spirit."

Julianna folded her arms. "You still see something in him?"

"I do." He shifted his stance. "I went to Micaiah's funeral. Disguised, of course. Nice service, I guess, but far less exciting compared to what mine was, what I'm accustomed to. Afterwards, I visited Tommen, a dream-walk. He's agreed to train. Whatever else is going on here, I can't lose him."

"Why?" She put up a hand before he could respond. "You know what? Fine. He's a body to fight for us anyway. And maybe he will show some talent." She doubted it. "Just don't forget where your own loyalties ought to lie."

"I never forget."

He lies. He doubts. He is too obsessed with the Authored Books. He prefers them over the journals, fiction over the absolute word of the Author. Everything that is going on, and he still wants to hang on to his pet project. When the solidity of stone is perfectly and readily available, he clings to sand.

She left before she said anything out loud.

Her time in the in-between dimension had done her some good, she decided. It had not been the most pleasant and she had no desire to repeat it, but good things had come from it. She finally had a clarity of thought she had never experienced before, the ability to really articulate her frustrations. Just like fasting from food could break addictions and reset the body, so a fast of interaction and conversation appeared to have reset her mind.

And all the running around that he has ever done, spending years away from the Cult in some fanciful pursuit of family, it clouded his judgment. Even now, past all of that, he cannot live outside of his head and the things he thinks are and must be.

He may lead the army into battle, but you will be the one to steer the Cult.

Step one is framing some Timekeepers.

Although she had long since left the Time industry, there was something fiendishly enjoyable about doing such a thing. Timekeepers often accused Harvesters of being stuck-up, but they weren't the most humble Time Agents themselves. Julianna knew plenty of them who loved to take bribes and threaten the less fortunate with a quick trip to the Judgment Wing. And unless a Time Agent happened to be cross-trained, there was no way to try and run. Even if there was some cross-training, just slap a Runner label on someone and instant open season. Corruption at its finest.

Although only a verbal accusation had been made so far, with little interest in pursuit, Julianna took her bodyguards with her to Earth. Torbak was easy enough to Disguise, though Drinjin uh Ersik required a little work. Without the ability to simply enter any house at a whim and never get caught, she decided a library was the next best option. There she set her bodyguards on simple observation duty while she logged in to a computer and then the Time Agent database.

Smart and athletic and a low-level officer. Europe was a small continent, but it was competent enough to boast enough Time Agents to require three Regions and twelve Districts. That meant three Managers, twelve Captains, and twenty-four Lieutenants. Managers might be a little too high, she decided. She eliminated several Captains and Lieutenants for various reasons.

After about an hour, she leaned back in her chair and examined the list. Smart and athletic, all of them. She wouldn't deny that she thought a few of them were even handsome. But were they really traitors? Could a staunch and strictly-bred Brit really betray his homeland? Even the French and the Germans had such honor, and the Scandinavians had a proud, rich heritage that they would defend. Maybe the Spaniard. Yes, he looked like a devious fellow. And the Romanian, probably a traitorous, thieving gypsy anyway.

She picked a few more at random, enough to make it look like a credible conspiracy rather than just one or two disgruntled Timekeepers. Now then, time to invent the conspiracy. Unlike the Wheel and the Akarin, the Cult did not have the resources to allow its members to go dark and build new lives complete with perfectly forged paperwork to support a new, fake life. That did not mean that they were without resources, however.

She gathered up her bodyguards and left the library. It hadn't taken her two days to miss Traveling, the ability to just go anywhere on a whim, without the struggle of opening a portal. Honestly, if not for the isolation, she might have wished to return to the in-between dimension. On the other hand, what if people could be persuaded to move into the dimension instead? Go anywhere on a whim, view past events as they actually happened. But then, there would be a distinct lack of access to resources to be able to continue to build civilization. Was it possible to bring whole planets into the dimension?

Fanciful thoughts, born of childish whimsy. The dimension is a prison and should be used as such.

Not a bad idea, actually.

Eventually she got up the nerve to open a portal to a town in New York. Close enough to New York City for convenience, far enough away that the deep city-dwellers considered it "the country" despite being almost nothing of the sort.

Like Tadashi, Wade Smith had a knack for technology. But where Tadashi had specialized in computer hacking, Wade's skills trended toward forgeries, of both the paper and digital kind. Unlike Tadashi, Wade also operated a legitimate day business and was more inclined to open his door when someone knocked.

"Can I help you, Miss...us?" he wondered.

"Julianna Brown. Perhaps you've heard of me."

The man went pale. "I see." He took a step back to let the three of them inside. Once the door shut, Torbak and Drinjin uh Ersik shed their Disguises. Suddenly the large kitchen got a lot smaller. "Listen, if this is about Tadashi, we just worked together occasionally. He didn't like collaborations, but every so often he was forced to mingle with us plebeians."

She nodded. "I understand. We don't always get to choose our coworkers. But if you're that worried about your own guilt by association, I have a task for you to make up for it."

His gaze flickered to Drinjin uh Ersik. "And what's that?"

"You are a forger. I need some forgeries." She explained her idea. When he hesitated, she added, "I understand you don't claim solid ties to any single group, and that this could set you up to be classified as a Runner among the Time industry. Do this, not only are you doing your part to shield Earth from the Borelians, but you play a role in saving the Cult as well, which gives you somewhere to run if you ever encountered such a need. And who wouldn't like to paint a target on the Tacagans' backs?"

He still looked uncertain.

"Do you doubt your abilities?" she pressed.

"No, not at all," he told her. "I've seen my forgeries go to court and get upheld. But I do work on things like embezzlement, cheating spouses, employment or education records. One time I had a cop approach me, had a murder case that was pretty solid, but he just needed one last little link, just a couple text messages and an email. I wouldn't do it until he showed me the rest of his case; I wasn't going to condemn an innocent man."

"A noble cause, except we are talking about billions of lives lost if we don't."

"How can you be sure the Borelians will take the bait?"

"If they don't, then nothing has changed."

He sighed, paced a time or two, glanced again at Drinjin uh Ersik, then finally nodded. "All right. You're not wrong there; it only matters if they believe it."

She grinned. "And I'm sure you have ways of covering your tracks and your involvement, since you said you've seen your stuff go to court and pass."

Wade nodded again. "Yes, I do."

"Which means the only way anyone will ever know of your involvement is if you tell them. Or I tell them. And, of course, implicating you is implicating myself."

"All right, all right, I get it." He turned as if to head to an office or living room.

"Good. Now then, understand that this is a rush job, so we will be standing here until delivery."

He paused. Then, "I only ask two things: first, don't watch directly over my shoulder; second, don't drink my coffee. You can wait all you want, but it might be a while."

"How long do you expect it will take?"

"What you're looking for, going to be a few hours, probably the rest of the day. Wait here, wait elsewhere, I don't care."

Julianna dipped her head though he couldn't see. "Of course. You're a gracious host."

Instruction

The Borelians bought the forged evidence and agreed to allow the Cult to continue its military operations, provided all plans were run through Misik or one of his lieutenants first. Rifun agreed without a fight and immediately sent out orders to begin training.

It wasn't as though there hadn't been some training going on, between the defeat in the Wheel and the present moment, it just wasn't focused on battle or military strategy; everything was taught for minor, personal use, if at all. It didn't take Godwin a full day to turn that around.

With such heavy training underway, Rifun headed to Earth to collect Tommen. The teenager, slowly healing from extensive burns, appeared to have come to terms with the situation and his need for more formal training and discipline. If Rifun didn't have the Borelians hovering over his shoulder awaiting battle plans against the Tacagans, he would have trained Tommen himself. He should have, seeing how they were both chosen ones of the Author, and they'd had a couple sessions so far. Well, once the Borelians were taken care of and the Akarin subdued, then they would get back to their private tutoring. For now, he would have to make do with bootcamp like the rest of the new recruits.

"This is a military compound," Tommen stated as they entered the city, looking around as the Disguise opened up, turning crumbling ruins into a lively city.

"You're quick," Rifun said. "We're in the mid-level ghetto right now."

"Ghetto? I'm...not sure how to take that, actually. It feels kind of racist to say."

" 'Afovoany toby' is also acceptable. Calling each section a toby has become popular lately."

"Is that Paramilla...vorxian for 'ghetto'?"

"No. That is Malagasy for 'middle barracks.' "

"So everyone here speaks Malagasy?"

"Hardly. But when your commanding officer routinely yells at you in his language, some begin to pick up a few things. If there's any Earth language that most have a decent grasp of, it's English, the language of the journals, as is appropriate."

Tommen looked around at the alien creatures. "They can understand us right now?"

Rifun replied in Welsh. *"Wydd o trafferthu 'chti?"* (Does it bother you?)

"Yn bach." (A little.)

"Why? It's easier to make friends that way. Plus, you'll be at an advantage during training since you will already know what's going on and being said without needing it explained."

As he had done with the group in the Wheel, Rifun took Tommen on a roundabout, informal tour of the city.

"What's that building?" Tommen asked, pointing.

"That is the officers building," Rifun explained. "It's unlikely you will ever need to go there, unless, of course, you cause too much trouble."

"I don't understand the layout of this place. Where does one toby end and another begin?"

"You will learn more as you come here and continue your training. For now, all you need to know is where you will be staying."

"Staying? Whoa, wait, I have school tomorrow."

"Forgive me. My word choice was poor. This is where you will be coming to train."

Eventually they arrived at the vaovao toby, the new recruit barracks. Military attention was poor, with many of the recruits defaulting to whatever their culture determined was the proper way to greet a superior officer.

Then, a voice rang out above the din of activity. "Attention!"

The recruits scuttled along to an open area, bumping into each other and scrambling to impress Berkloff, their Korin commander. Rifun walked to the front of the group, Tommen trailing uncertainly.

"Faharoa," Berkloff greeted, making a proper salute. He turned his attention to the mess of recruits. "Is that how you greet your Faharoa? Despicable! Unacceptable!"

Before he could launch into a demeaning tirade, Rifun stopped him. "We're not here for long, I promise, certainly not longer than the punishment they will have to endure for their insolence. I have brought our newest recruit."

"What's his name?"

"Tommen Forbes, given name and family name."

"What are his abilities?"

"Paltry, but he's a quick study. He'll not be staying here with the others."

"Noted."

"I will bring him personally, so there is no need to worry."

"Very good, sir." The rhino man indicated Tommen's cast. "Is he weak?"

"Recovering from an accident, but he'll be fine." Now Rifun looked at Tommen. "This is Captain Berkloff. He is in charge of the new recruits. You will train under him. Any questions?"

"I don't think so?"

"You're in training now, so you will address your superiors appropriately," Berkloff growled.

Tommen was staring at the man's enormous, three-fingered hands covered in a kind of pseudo-keratin substance, but he still managed, "No, sir, I have no questions."

And just like that, he was inducted into the ranks. Rifun still would have preferred to train the kid himself, but circumstances just did not allow for such a thing right now. The best he was able to manage was retrieving Tommen for training every few days and then taking him home afterwards. In the time in between, he was cooking up bogus plans for attacking the Tacagans.

"It really wouldn't be difficult," Rifun was saying. He stood in the meeting room with Misik and three others. A crude map of Tacaga was laid out before them. "Their domed cities are perfect for a runaway greenhouse effect."

"It would take too long," one of the Borelians insisted. "That large of an area —"

"Only if you intend to attack at the same time," Rifun cut in. "Start a week or two weeks ahead of time. Right now, everything is working just swimmingly, so they have time to consider the declaration of war. We have to turn their attention inwards. A failure of their environmental regulation would pose a huge problem that they would have to solve in the immediate. Distract, then strike."

"Too weak," another Borelian said. "Such a system likely requires constant maintenance already, and because of their paranoid fear of the outside world, they likely already have plans in place in the event such a thing ever happened and became a real threat."

"Evacuation, yes, I agree. But a door once opened may be passed through from both sides. Now you see where I'm going?"

"It's not any slower than some of the methods we have already deployed, but it still feels far less effective," a third mused, bored.

Misik opened his mouth to speak but paused as the door opened, revealing the figure of Win. The mercenary made a motion.

"Excuse me, gentlemen," Rifun said and slipped out of the room, closing the door behind him and erecting a Sound barrier for good measure.

"What?" he asked.

"Julianna's kidnapped Micah Durvin," Win reported bluntly. "Rather, she had him kidnapped. Sent a Borelian to scope him out, knock him silly, and bring him here."

"Why?" Rifun hissed. He glanced down the corridor one way, then the other, toward his chambers, as if expecting the woman to appear at any moment, dragging Micah with her.

"My informant said Julianna mentioned something about continuing the charade with the Borelians."

"What the—? How?" He put up a hand. "Never mind. Where is he or she now?"

"Last I saw..." Win looked uncomfortable. "She was Disguised as you, taking him to the vaovao training yard."

"What?! And you didn't stop her?"

Rifun pushed past him and started down the hall. Win jogged up beside him.

"I judged the response from the Borelians too uncertain and potentially volatile," the mercenary said hastily. "We're working on a facade of unity. I confront Julianna and tell her she's wrong, the Borelians smell weakness and they strike."

Rifun slowed his walk just a touch. "And this was somehow intended to reinforce our charade of an alliance?"

"My informant couldn't get the whole story, sir, I'm sorry. That failure is on me."

"The failure is mine, that your informants have to be distracted by or dedicated to stupid shit like this."

He left the officers building and headed for the vaovao toby, though he ran into Julianna about two blocks from it. She walked with purpose, but with a half-smile on her face, as if pleased with herself but did not want to appear too joyful to outside viewers. She noted his approach and stopped, but her smug half-smile remained.

"What the hell are you doing?" Rifun demanded.

"I am merely testing the skill and loyalty of your favorite protege," she told him. "Or your pet, seeing how he has no real skills to speak of."

"The comradery and bonding of bootcamp will do that just fine without you giving him a reason to hate us, hate me! Why did you have to wear my face?!"

"Good cop, bad cop. You know how the game goes. You work on the skills, the discipline, the loyalty, the consequences. And when he gets stressed or hurt or overwhelmed, he comes to see me where I offer lovely, beautiful, feminine reassurance and soothing."

"If we're comparing apples to apples, you put a gun to his head, too."

"And your mother never slapped you a time or two? The point is, he needs an avenue of safety. I will be that avenue. I know the journals better than anyone, and I have more faith in them than you do. You may mold his body, but I will mold his mind. We'll see which one wins out."

"And how does kidnapping Micah Durvin help?" Rifun demanded. "Where is he?"

"On his way back to Earth." Her smile had faded, but the smugness remained.

"On his own two feet?"

"With a Borelian who is going to start carrying out some threats you seem unwilling to follow up on, and to test your faith and loyalty as well. Tommen Forbes, Micah Durvin, Walter Forbes, all of them so special to the Author, according to you. Well, let's see just how special they are."

Rifun met her gaze. "And if she does deliver them, if they do survive these threats and encounters, are you prepared to consider that the Authored Books are real and worth consideration in addition to your husband's journals?"

Finally she faltered. She shifted her stance, her expression becoming more serious. She did not respond and Rifun let the moment pass.

"Why use a Borelian at all?" Godwin asked. "Why not get one of your bodyguards to do it? The smaller one, Torbak, he would be much easier to Disguise and his loyalty is far less questionable."

"For as much as we may fear the retaliation of the Borelian civilization, there are only a handful of them actually running around here. I figure if we can keep them busy on mundane tasks as much as possible, the less chance there is that they might learn of our own planned treachery. Playing into the naive thought that we're still allies and maybe this can all be salvaged."

Rifun sighed but nodded. "Well, you're not wrong there. Still, kidnapping Micah? Right after murdering Micaiah? What the hell are you thinking?"

"As I said, I am testing loyalty. His loyalty. Your loyalty."

He bristled. "You have a lot of nerve."

"Good. At least one of us does."

"If you had spent even a day looking over my life, as you claimed to have been able to do in the in-between dimension, you might understand some of my hesitation."

"Your demons are your own," Julianna retorted. "Meanwhile, in the real world, we're fighting the Borelians and the Akarin."

"And ourselves, apparently," Rifun growled.

"Well, we can only fight one enemy at a time, and we've chosen the Akarin first." She made a vague gesture back toward the training grounds. "Once you take Tommen home, let me know and I will gather my bodyguards and we can convene for our next secret meeting."

And she departed. Rifun watched her go, Win by his side.

"You think it was a mistake to bring her back?" Win ventured.

"Absolutely," Rifun answered quickly. "She's going to be the death of me at this rate."

"In my experience, sir, women rarely make good leaders."

"Few people at all do, whatever we tell ourselves."

Win shifted his stance. "So what do we do about this one? She won't be the death of just you, sir, but all of us."

"Idle hands are the devil's playground, as the saying goes. She needs something to do."

"Last I checked, sir, she does a lot of work with our refugee camp we've got going on and tends to the sick and wounded in the infirmary. We'll have to send her to the kitchen if we want her to stay any more busy."

Rifun barked a laugh. "She'd kill all of us trying to poison a handful of Borelians."

Win made a noise and reluctantly nodded. "Aye, I could see it."

Rifun sighed. "Unfortunately, she may have to wait. I think Misik is up to something, and I think I know what."

"What's that, sir?"

"Halloween."

"Never heard of it, sir."

"All Hallow's Eve, or the Americanized version? Sugary candy by the truckload, everyone in costume?"

The mercenary nodded and took a breath. "Right."

"It's too perfect for them to pass up."

"What are you going to do, sir? That's not just Misik, that's the Borelian standing army. You can't stop them. You can't very well warn anyone; they'd never believe you."

Rifun sighed and folded his arms. "Maybe we can make our charade work for us a little more."

"How do you mean, sir?"

"Infiltration."

"Of the Akarin? My spies—"

"No, not the Akarin. The Tacagans. Get in their cities, get in their government. They have the technology we need, but they're too stuck up to want to share. Use our bogus attack plans as an excuse to get into the Tacagan government—most likely their ruling body of Governors—and start working their system. Find their sympathies, their technology, all of it."

Win nodded. "With the attack as an excuse, we wouldn't need to disguise the comings and goings of the operatives."

"Especially if I am that operative," Rifun agreed. At Win's look, he said, "If I'm successful, we get the information we need. What that information is, well, it differs between us and Misik. If I'm unsuccessful, if I'm found out, then little has changed. The Borelians are still going to attack, and the Cult remains an enemy of humanity and the universe."

"Low risk, high reward. In mercenary work, we call that a good day."

Rifun nodded and started walking, making his way back to the officers building. Misik and the rest barely acknowledged his return except to say, "How fortunate we are for you to grace us with your presence once again."

"Don't worry, I will be departing soon enough for Tacaga," Rifun told them smartly.

That at least got two of them to look up.

"Are you planning to attack?" one asked, his tone suggesting he thought Rifun was out of his mind.

"No. I'm going to infiltrate their government. Rather than speculating and hoping that what information we do find is accurate and not either an intentional underplay or woeful self-aggrandizing, I will go and see for myself what their capabilities are."

Now Misik looked at him. "The Tacagans are heavily reliant on genetic engineering and modification. A casual Disguise will not be enough and I don't believe you will have the time to effect any permanent changes."

"Planning something, are we? Halloween, for instance?" He met the general's gaze. "I'm not worried. And there is no risk to you, so what do you care if I am discovered? It's not as if they don't know that you have declared war on them, or that we are allied here. The only thing they will have to be surprised about is that we dared to try. And seeing how we are not strangers to such infiltration, they will be surprised that we have managed to do it again, in spite of any safeguards they have."

Misik thought about this for a long moment, then nodded. "Very well. But only you. More spies means more risk, especially in a society so heavily reliant on perfect genetics."

"My thoughts exactly. I will report my progress later."

The Borelians went back to their business, ignoring the servant who left the room. Rifun made a motion for Win to follow.

"Keep an eye on Julianna, whether you personally or through your spies. And if you hear anything about some stupid, cockamamie plan that she's cooking up, cut it off. Stop it, distract her from it, sabotage it, I don't care. I do not want to make a habit of worrying about a bunch of small fires popping up while I'm gone and having to put them out when I get back. The fact that I even have to ask you to babysit her offends me."

"I find it offensive myself, sir," Win admitted.

"Do you think it might improve once the Borelians are gone?"

The mercenary offered a half-hearted shrug. "A bit, perhaps, as stress can cause people to do strange and desperate things, especially in people unaccustomed to such stress, and the Borelians do invite a lot of stress. Even I cannot say that I am immune to it. But in my experience, sir, that same stress also reveals the true nature of a man. Or woman. What his concerns and priorities are, what he is willing to do to meet his basic needs."

"What need is met by murdering one man and kidnapping another to use as some sort of object lesson about loyalty?"

"Control. Power. Recognition. The same needs that you hope to meet by undermining the Borelians using the guise of gathering information about the Tacagans."

Rifun grunted. "You make a better bodyguard than philosopher."

"Sorry, sir."

"Don't worry about it. Go check on Julianna, make sure she isn't doing something else stupid. And see if you can't follow up on what she—or her Borelian compatriot—did with Micah. I'm going to take Tommen home and then head off to Tacaga."

They parted ways.

Vaovao training had concluded for the evening, and Rifun found Tommen mingling with a certain group of aliens he might potentially call friends.

"I hope I'm not interrupting after-class locker room gossip," Rifun said, approaching and hoping to appear non-threatening.

"Not really," Tommen said.

"Good. Let's get you home, then."

Rifun moved off and Tommen followed, fumbling with the cast that protected his burned arm.

"What did you do with Micah?" Tommen demanded once they were out of earshot of the others.

"He is safe and sound back on Earth, I assure you," Rifun answered. He continued before Tommen could speak. "Well, he's back on Earth, anyway. Safe and sound is a relative term, I suppose."

"What did you do to him? Okay, I'm sorry about the insubordination, but I really don't appreciate getting beaten up by Berkloff because he doesn't like my eye color or something."

Rifun did his best to evade the question. "No pain, no gain, as they say, but I do understand. You will simply have to improve—rapidly. As for Micah, he was merely a convenient object lesson at the time; his original purpose for this evening was something a little more...exciting. But don't worry; he has a pretty good chance of surviving the night."

"What did you do?" Tommen asked, more forcefully this time.

"And if I answered, what would you do about it? What could you do about it? One way or another, you would expose this whole operation and our little deal, and even if you had saved him, he would die anyway." *Damn you, Julianna.*

He delivered Tommen to his bedroom, then prepared for a trip to Tacaga. With a simple Qalik Disguise, Rifun went to the Wheel Archives.

He wasn't going to pussyfoot around with any lower officials; he was going straight to the top, the Governors themselves. Misik wasn't wrong when he said there was a very high chance of being found out with a casual Disguise. If the Tacagans had any advantage, it was their reliance on genetic engineering, constantly cataloging and analyzing everyone's DNA. His Disguise, therefore, would have to include as few changes as possible.

Of all the Governors, he decided the one called Toros would be his best bet. White skin, brown hair, brown eyes, same height, roughly the same weight, with minimal need for feature blending. Concerning the current fashion, casual, trick-of-the-eye changes would have to do until he could raid Toros' closet. It was easy to overlook, but clothing could be the most vulnerable part of a Disguise. Few people were in a habit of touching other people's faces, but clothes took a major beating throughout the day.

Being so fiercely loyal to Time, it took only minimal effort for Rifun to find Toros' most recent information concerning his residence. The Governors were even kind enough to provide a mailing address so any extra-terrestrial inquiries could more easily find their way to the appropriate destination. From there, it was a simple cross-reference to find where the man's home address was.

He found Toros' living arrangements in an apartment building near the primary governmental center. Actually, it was attached to the governmental center via two causeways: one walkway high in the air to dazzle the citizens below, and one escape tunnel for emergencies. And those were just the ones admitted to. Apparently, a certain incident a few decades ago had prompted the construction of new safety escape routes.

According to a calendar converter, it was approximately six o'clock in the evening in Lip. Rifun was willing to bet that even if the Governors used the same bank hours as Earth, Toros wouldn't be home for a while yet. Such was the nature of government bureaucracy. If he wasn't in some legislative session, he was probably at a late night cocktail party with his fellow Governors and maybe some minor officials.

The Hand Holding the Knife

It was a risk he was willing to take as he left the Wheel and headed to Tacaga.

The minor difficulty with which Rifun opened a portal into Toros' apartment suggested that there were designated portal areas where portals were allowed and expected to open. Maybe it was as specific as the lobby of every building, particular street corners, or train stations. He did not give it too much thought as he quickly assessed the situation.

His first task was to use Electricity to root out any cameras in the place and disable them, or at least freeze or fudge what they were recording. With that taken care of, he could browse relatively at leisure.

No wife or children, but that was expected. The Tacagans grew their humans —their genetically perfect definitely-not-Homo-sapiens—and had no need for bestial procreation. No procreation, no marriage, and Rifun wondered if the Tacagans had engineered out natural sexual desires. There were still male and female Tacagans, but without marriage and family, there was no need for—

Never mind. He was here to infiltrate and gather information. Who knew? Maybe they would have to attack the Tacagans one day. Self-righteous bastards. The important thing now was that the apartment was empty and he could snoop around a bit, get a feel for this infiltration.

Exterior Tacagan society was very efficient, very geometric. Everything had to be optimized. Interior design, however, was a little more permissive, and Toros' tastes ran toward what Rifun could only describe as a Greco-Egyptian aesthetic. Whether this was the current season's fashion or the man's more personal preference, Rifun could not say.

There were exactly four rooms in the apartment, and they were arranged in such a way that Rifun was sure was highly optimal for heating, cooling, time management, and guest entertainment. Bedroom, bathroom, living room, kitchen. The bedroom doubled as an office or study, Rifun saw, and he headed there first.

His first mission was finding suitable clothing. He tried to pick something that wasn't too flashy, like a dress uniform, but looked slightly more than casual. In the end, he judged the attire to be just short of a full suit and tie, as far as formality went. Truthfully, he wasn't entirely sure he was wearing it correctly, but at least it wouldn't get accidentally revealed as a Disguise.

With Toros still not home, Rifun sat down at the small desk near the bed. The desk immediately lit up with words and options and menu items. The Tacagan language was a blend of Ancient Greek and Latin, mixing letters, vocabulary, and grammar from both until it formed a singular language. Seeing how he was not currently in a bind looking for specific information, he was free to work out meanings in his own time and explore to see if he might happen upon anything.

He found the man's schedule, at least. Looked like he had a busy day today, booked up through the late hours. Same for the next few days. Which was good, because it meant Rifun could snoop around a little more and become more acquainted with the man's life. Of course, unlike Cassius fully impersonating Doug, Rifun only needed to pick up certain pieces of information and maybe go to a few meetings to glean what he couldn't find in rote documentation. Even still, he couldn't afford to be a complete ignoramus; he was a Governor, a head of state.

After poking around in the man's computer for a few hours, Rifun decided that was all he was going to do that evening. He was far more comfortable now than he had been, and he had a better idea of how to look for any information he needed. Besides, according to Toros' planner, he was on his last scheduled engagement, if not already finished. He would be home soon and probably want to just fall into bed. Rifun would oblige him for the time being.

He returned to Sadurnon without incident, shedding the DNA part of the Disguise and going to change into more comfortable clothing. While he was doing that, he also had to adjust his mental Circadian rhythm. Sitting in the dark in Toros' apartment, he might have been ready to go to bed himself. Now he was back in the ruins where it was only just becoming evening, judging by the decreasing din of activity.

Then he was out and about, looking around. He hadn't been approached by any Borelians about treason or slavery, and nothing appeared amiss. Godwin wasn't waiting around for his return to report some horrible news. Maybe he could hope for things to go well for once while he was away.

He hated having such a thought. For all his misgivings about Cassius, he had been right about a few things. Cult leadership was not what it should be.

So then, next move. He had the cover with the Tacagans, now what? He needed to gather information, both with the idea of attacking on behalf of the Borelians, the Cult, and humans everywhere, and with the idea of exploiting their wealth of technology to save the Cult and humanity from the Borelians. But if their real goal was the Akarin, then they would need some more information from there. And he had an idea of how to go about it.

The following morning, while the Borelians schemed away in the meeting room, Rifun brought together the little resistance council in his chambers.

"I have an in with the Tacagans," Rifun said, explaining the cover and the real plan. "But we need to test the waters with the Akarin, too."

"How is that?" Win wondered, at the same time Julianna sighed and said, "We go in and attack. Why do we care about their petty politics anymore?"

"It will tell us the overall strength of their army," Drinjin uh Ersik explained calmly. "Unified leadership, unified army. Fractured leadership, fractured army."

"One of them is infinitely easier to overrun, and yes, I am speaking from experience." Rifun gave her a look. He looked at Win. "Pick half a dozen vaovao and send them on a little terror mission to the fortress. No lengthy battle, no prisoners, no death if they can help it. Just cause mayhem, judge their response."

"Vaovao?" Torbak wondered.

"Use it for testing purposes, give them a chance to advance to afovoany," Rifun went on. "Testing their skills on enemies in the wild as it were, if the Borelians ask. It will let them fly under the radar, or that is the hope. They can bring their information to us afterwards. I don't think the Borelians are going to wait much longer to start launching larger attacks and even full-scale invasions, and that includes us as well. Send out the scouting party, maybe we'll make some show about it having been a bad idea, too dangerous, whatever. Then we begin testing the rest of the troops—from vaovao to ambany and officers—here in the ruins. I will continue to perpetuate this idea of going after the Tacagans. We must be ready to strike down the Borelians here and immediately move out to take out the Akarin."

"Perhaps we should discuss our goals with such an endeavor," Julianna suggested. "Are we eliminating them entirely?"

"Ideally, no," Rifun said evenly. "For reasons both philosophical and practical, we cannot simply commit mass murder like that."

"Philosophical, fine," Drinjin uh Ersik stated. "But the Akarin do still outnumber us. We cannot take them all prisoner or expect all of them to assimilate."

"Maybe not, but neither are we going to hold mass executions as a sick, ghostly homage to Cassius. If we can merely subjugate them, then when the Borelians do come after us for Misik and the others, well, petty differences in philosophy may have to wait a while." He went on before anyone could speak. "Once again, if anyone here has a foolproof plan that won't cost us any lives and will keep us perfectly safe from the Borelians, I'm all ears."

An awkward silence settled over them. This was not how things were supposed to go, but they were already in the rapids. They couldn't go back, they couldn't calm the river. The best they could do now was hope to survive and not crash on the rocks.

"All right then," Rifun said at last. "Win, you have your assignment."

The mercenary nodded and left the room.

"And the rest of us?" Julianna wondered.

"Drinjin uh Ersik and Torbak, I want you to start assessing the officers, all of them. Until we see how this episode with the vaovao scouts turns out, do it discreetly. Then, once they get back, we will transition into testing, assignment, and full tactical plans." He looked at Julianna. "You will coordinate the medics. Assess their skills, do your best to stockpile supplies. I understand medicinal requirements may be too varied to do well, but do what you can."

The three of them nodded and also departed. Rifun went to his shrine to pray, then headed out. He would collect Tommen for training, then cavort with the Borelians for a few minutes before heading off to Tacaga.

His plans stalled after collecting Tommen when he went to cavort with the Borelians and found only Misik in the meeting room. Rifun tried not to let his discomfort show as he looked around for any others.

"They're out running other errands," Misik stated.

"Yes, I suppose if you spend all your time plotting and planning, you don't get much time to go to the market," Rifun retorted. "Might as well make a day of it, get all your chores done at once."

"Your fascination with the human boy Tommen Forbes is not unnoticed by us. The others don't understand it, and even I know that it only has something to do with the Authored Books."

"What of it?"

They stared at each other for a long moment. Rifun knew, and he was suspecting that Misik knew that he knew.

"Is there any way to protect him?" Rifun asked.

"You can bring him here," Misik said, making a casual gesture, akin to a shrug. "I know Earth is Unengaged, but that is not my problem."

"And if I weren't able to bring him here?"

"As I said, not my problem."

Rifun tried to come up with something quick. It wasn't so much that he was fighting for Tommen alone, but trying to edge in some show of strength. "He may not be, no, but we, the Cult, are your problem. Tommen Forbes is a part of the Cult. He is in the vaovao grounds now as we speak. How would it be for him to suddenly be kidnapped or killed by you or your men?"

"It's not as if they don't know about the war on humanity." Misik's look was both casual and hungry, like a predator.

"Maybe, but as far as they are concerned, that war is a distant nothing, barely a headline except for me and you, really. Everything to us, nothing to them. Human Cult members start disappearing, especially if it becomes known that it was directly related to the war, well, fear is a terrible thing. Give a man just a reason to fear and all that. And what happens if fear turns to paranoia? Do you really want a mess on your hands here over one person?"

Misik glared at him. "Hardly one person, I think."

"Even so."

"I'll be sure to pass along your concerns."

"You do that. In the meantime, I will be doing something constructive, like going to Tacaga. In case anyone needs me."

He left before Misik could object, heading to his chambers to change into Toros' outfit.

He could bring Tommen here, yes. He didn't know how the teenager felt about Halloween, but life and limb should probably come before candy and costumes. And yet, he had a sneaking suspicion that Misik was going to come up with something to occupy Rifun during that time. Maybe there would be a fabricated emergency, or something else that demanded his undivided attention to where he wouldn't be able to retrieve Tommen.

Toros' clothes fit no better this time than they had previously, and Rifun spent a few minutes adjusting and readjusting. Nothing seemed to really make it any better, so he decided to just call it good enough. Maybe it was just body size and type. They were of a height, but the Tacagans had genetically re-engineering their muscles to be more efficient, stronger with less bulk. He and Toros might have been able to lift similar weights, but Toros did not have to work as hard for it, or so the theory went. Personally, Rifun wouldn't mind putting that to the test one day. The only muscle the Tacagans really worked on a daily basis was their mouths; did they have the strength to back it up?

According to what he found on Toros' computer that afternoon, there was a good chance that they did. A little disconcerting, but it only made the challenge all that more enticing. Well, maybe once they had dealt with the Borelians in the Cult and Rifun might be able to devote a little more time to helping humans against the Borelians at large.

There was very little that Rifun could not access from Toros' private computer. He had feared that there would be greatly sophisticated levels of security and complex decentralization that would drive him from place to place, each link in the chain at risk of being the weakest one and revealing his snooping. Such was not the case that he found. Could he be looking at incorrect information? Was he misinterpreting what he was reading, struggling through the Tacagan language? Or were the Tacagans so sure of themselves that they didn't believe anyone would ever make it this far?

Maybe the tug on the portal he had felt wasn't that of a portal station type area, but some kind of weak portal shield, like the dampening field they had used in the Wheel? A normal Time portal couldn't be opened here, but the Akari merely laughed and bypassed the whole thing. Well, he wasn't going to risk an alarm going off if he did try to open a Time portal here just to test out a minor theory.

The governor's busy schedule once again afforded Rifun plenty of time to peruse the computer system, becoming well acquainted by the end of the night. He might not have understood all the words, but he knew what most of the labels would do and what he could access. Getting into the heavier prose and technical material, that would require a little study. If he had any advantage, it was his fluency in French and skill in English giving him a mild inkling of some of the vocabulary. But, according to the schedule, he would have plenty of time over the next few weeks to learn and study.

He shut everything down at the end of the night and returned to the old Elif temple. No alarms were raised that he was aware of. He dropped his Toros Disguise, got out of the uncomfortable clothes, and went to collect Tommen.

On his way to the vaovao grounds, Rifun decided not to mention the Halloween plot yet. He'd given it a little thought while on Tacaga. This was a crime of opportunity. Why bother with small cities like Charleston when they could take advantage of places like New York City, Chicago, Detroit, or Los Angeles? If the Borelian army was anything like the French or Malagasy army, middle management—and even most upper management—couldn't suggest a maneuver based on some personal vendetta. Misik couldn't suggest Charleston just because he wanted to maybe possibly grab a single teenager just to spite Rifun.

Rifun couldn't decide how he felt about the slight easing of his conscience. A realistic analysis, or false security? His brooding thoughts were interrupted as Tommen came jogging up to him from the grounds.

"So eager to get home?" Rifun wondered. "I thought you would have enjoyed staying and bragging about your own combat adventures."

"I have to get home so I can get to school and keep my dad from wondering why I'm not home," Tommen informed him.

"That is very true. What else is on your mind? Did you learn anything?"

The kid had a look of minor hesitation. He had learned something. He wanted to brag about it. Doing so, however, might be an admission of gratitude for the training and an appreciation for group inclusion.

"I'm working on a Funnel Band," he said finally.

"Oh? And what does that mean?" Rifun could guess, but it wasn't anything he remembered from standard training.

"My arm is still too sensitive to really endure combat, but if I just Band it and try to cut off the pain, releasing the Band only sends all of the pain in a single rush. And it hurts."

"I understand, believe me."

"So, I've been working on a way to siphon off the pain, mix it in with the rest of my bodily processes going on and basically dilute it to the point where it no longer fires off as pain. It works when I think about it, but I can't do it in combat yet."

Rifun would admit he was impressed. Maybe a little formal training and group comradery was all he needed to unlock his talent as an Akari-bearer. "The fact that you have done it at all is good. The rest will take time, which is why you are here to train."

"What is the special mission that you're sending those guys out on?"

Rifun grinned. "Ah, the joys of learning English as a foreign language. Word choice is a sight to behold. You and I both understand that, better than some, though we are more practiced in the nuances. The word is not 'special' it is 'secret.' It's a secret mission. One they carry out, bring us the results—and by us, I mean myself and the other leaders—and we analyze those results. Once we have done that and made a constructive counteractive plan, then we will inform the rest of you. Sorry to say, my dear apprentice, but you are still the low man on the totem pole."

"I'm in the fourth row."

Which really didn't mean much in the grand scheme of things. "Yes, you are. But a vaovao still. Once you move up a little more, perhaps you will have a similar opportunity to advance into the afovoany with just as much flourish and flair. But it is all as circumstances permit."

He was getting there, but he still didn't quite have the skill to back up his bravado. At the next combat training, rather than go to Tacaga, Rifun stopped to watch him. His own faith in the journals was a little shaky, he would admit, but that was because of Cassius. Julianna's odd behavior wasn't the most encouraging either. He did still have faith in the Authored Books, but he was having trouble understanding. He was great. Cassius, if insane, had been exceptionally powerful. Micaiah had been great. Saul had been great. Tommen...he wasn't all that great at anything, really. Sure, he was advancing, but at best he was just mediocre. Another body in the mass, not another hero for them to aspire to.

Tommen went down again. Annoyed, Rifun made a motion. Berkloff called a halt to the individual trainings. The group might have assembled into formation, but Rifun walking into the middle of the grounds was apparently a universal gesture for forming the fight ring. Rifun looked at Tommen and motioned him out.

"You're certainly doing better than you were when you started," Rifun began, circling him, "but you're just not quite there. There's a threshold you have yet to cross, a door you have yet to walk through. Something is holding you back. What is it, I wonder? Strength or speed? Perhaps, but seeing how this is a group of mixed races, strength and speed will only take you so far. Cunning, perhaps? I don't think so, since you have discovered the point of weakness for most everyone here. So what is it?

"Ah, I know. It's your own weakness, your personal weakness. Pain. You've been trying so hard to protect yourself from pain that you've sacrificed any chance you have at winning. That's great when you're here, but out there, they don't care.

"Pain is your weakness, Tommen Forbes. That may seem to be true for everyone; after all, no one truly enjoys their own pain. But you fear it. You're like all children of the twenty-first century first world. You want to win, but you don't want to work for it. You would rather be a loser who feels no pain than a winner who took what was his. Do you think you would be able to go out and chop wood for the winter, or break a horse, or work the fields, or tame the forest? No. You're not like your pa. You're not strong. You're not anything. You're just a spoiled little seventeen year old brat who would rather call a mechanic than do the work himself."

Little could provoke a teenage boy more than an affront to his honor. Tommen rushed Rifun, and Rifun counted a good two seconds before he saw an actual plan formulate. He pulled up short from his rush as if in a feint, but done incorrectly, it drained his momentum instantly. As he tried to move to the side, Rifun simply put an arm out, grabbed Tommen around the midsection, lifted, and slammed him to the ground. The teenager was wiggling even as he was dazed, but he was unable to do anything before Rifun simply went down and curled his whole body around Tommen's head. The kid struggled and flailed for a minute. Only when he stopped struggling did Rifun release him, mildly telling him to stay down.

Rifun stood and looked around at those assembled. "Right now, you are only practicing, learning basic moves in a controlled setting. But one day, perhaps soon, you will no longer be facing each other. You will be facing those like Berkloff. Those like me. Except the goal will not be simple besting, but life or death. Continue to train and work hard, but never forget why you train."

He turned the class back over to Berkloff for the remainder of the session, but he still stayed to watch, keeping an eye on Tommen whose poor performance only enraged the Korin. But he stuck it out to the end. Another Korin said something to him. Rifun watched for just a moment before approaching. The Korin came to attention and was dismissed. Rifun turned his attention to Tommen.

"I imagine you are ready to go home and sleep all this off," Rifun said.

"More than you know," Tommen grumbled.

They moved across the training grounds toward the street that would take them to the gate out of the city.

"Now then, what did you learn?" Rifun asked.

Tommen sighed but answered grudgingly, "I don't need to let everything and everyone provoke me to a fight."

"Yes, there is that. Although you do seem to be doing better about it. Time was, all anyone had to do was look at you wrong. But that is not what I am referring to here."

"Then what are you referring to?"

"Sometimes—"

"Faharoa!"

They stopped and turned as someone came running up to them, an alien that was all limbs and rubbery, iridescent skin. It made some kind of attempt at a salute, but it did not look natural to the alien's physique.

"Speak!" Rifun barked.

"Faharoa, the special task force you assembled has returned with news."

"About time."

He followed the alien back to the officers building where the team waited.

"You're late," Rifun said. "What took so long?"

"Jitan was wounded and captured," one of them answered. "We had to go back for him."

"Where is he now?"

"Being healed. It was a near-fatal blow. The Akarin healed him enough so they could interrogate him, but it was poorly done."

Rifun sighed. "What is Berkloff teaching you guys?" He looked at each of them. "Tell me what you found."

"The Akarin are divided," another reported. "After the death of the leader Micaiah, his loyalists went to war with the traditional council. The loyalists control the sub-floors while the traditionalists control the upper levels. The main level may be seen as neutral territory."

"What are their numbers?"

"That is impossible to tell, but not more than us, or not by much if it is. Even during the secondary raid, when they understood they had a common and more powerful enemy, the Upper and Lower Akarin did not unite. Both times, many Akarin fled rather than stand and fight. They are tired and have no desire to see violence."

Rifun nodded once. "Excellent. If we can avoid bloodshed, then by all means. And the weary are always more open to new ideas than the bold."

"We should attack them now," someone else said. "Slaughter them. Then we will never have to worry about an uprising."

"Did I ask for your counsel?" Rifun let that hang there for a minute. Then, "Where is Julianna?"

He looked at the messenger who had not left. The messenger paused a moment, then, "Outside the wall, helping the camps."

Rifun did not move as he suddenly raised his voice and said, "Tommen."

Standing non-chalantly a short distance away and pretending to be uninterested, Tommen moved out of his hiding spot as Rifun turned. "Sir?"

"Find Julianna and bring her here."

Tommen darted off, but it was several minutes before he returned, Julianna in tow and looking entirely unconcerned. She spoke before Rifun could open his mouth. "I was busy working."

"Yes, well, while helping the unfortunate is a noble work, I am trying to stop the number of poor and impoverished refugees from growing," he retorted. "Our special task force has returned."

She hiked up her skirts again as she ascended a dozen steps to the first platform where they all stood. "This I see. And what do they have to say?"

"Good things, I hope." Rifun glanced over the team. "Give Julianna an account of what happened, what you just told me. I'll be back as soon as I take him home." He indicated Tommen.

"Don't be too long."

"I'll skip the lullaby tonight."

Rifun walked down the stairs, collecting the teenager on his way.

"You knew I was there," Tommen said meekly.

"I expected nothing less," Rifun told him. "I did not give you an order to stay, you thought it would be interesting, and I took no precaution to ensure the meeting was private. Honestly, I'm more surprised you didn't come up to the platform with me and interject yourself into the conversation. But I suppose we all need to indulge our little fantasies now and again."

"Fantasies?"

"That you're some sort of heroic spy who is going to conveniently overhear an important conversation so he can relay it to those whom it might offend. Good thing it's only a fantasy, or at least, I hope you don't believe that, because you're not very good at it."

"I was curious."

"Of course you were. I would be, too."

There was a moment of silence save for their walking.

"So the special task force," Tommen began.

"What about them?"

"You sent them to attack the Akarin."

"No, not attack. More of a raid. A little skirmish. Enough to get in the door, get a feel for things, ruffle a few feathers, see what they were up to, and get out."

Tommen hesitated just a moment, then, "Kayla was in the middle of that. She broke her hand."

"Did she?" Rifun wondered sarcastically. "Maybe I'll drop by the bakery one of these days and offer to sign her cast. Think that will make her feel better?"

They made it to the outer wall surrounding the city and passed the gates. The Disguise parted for the briefest of moments, then settled back into place, and the lively city crumbled into ruins. Rifun headed to the place designated for portals, but Tommen did not follow.

"Everything they said sounded like good news for you," the teenager said. "Divided Akarin, fewer numbers. I've been there myself a time or two, and there are a few spots where an invading army would have an advantage, and where the home team would be at an advantage, if they cared to use it. So one person got hurt. They got him back. Why get all snappy about it? Did I not fetch Julianna fast enough? Quite frankly, I'm in no position to tell her what to do, only that you wanted her."

Rifun couldn't stop a sigh from escaping.

Tommen shifted his stance. Then, "Or was that...not what you wanted?" He nodded slowly. "You weren't looking for an easy sweep. You wanted a battle, a real fight to be had. You want to feel justified in your attack, make it feel like self-defense, or something of the sort. Right now, with the Akarin divided, they're just a nuisance. Squabbling children. But if they're unified, if they fight back, you can justify it in your mind." He paused. "Is that what the French did to your people? Not all the Malagasy wanted to fight. They squabbled among themselves or just didn't care, making them easy prey for the 'more civilized Europeans.' Not even a fight to be had."

Fury shot through Rifun and crossed the distance between them in several long strides. "Open your mouth any wider, and next time, I will put my cock in there. Do you understand?"

"I understand," Tommen said quietly. "But I still have a question." Rifun rolled his eyes and took a step back. "If you're looking for a fair fight or a challenge from the Akarin, why did you murder those in the Wheel who could not fight back? Millions, gone. My dad almost one of them. You can't have it both ways, both victor and victim."

"The war is between the Cult and the Akarin," Rifun said sagely. He shook his head. "Time is but a side show, a distraction. Time Capsules and Auctions, it's all fluff. You and I know better."

"So you murder those you perceive as the tyrants, even if petty and beneath your power. But those you look upon as equals, as worthy opponents, those you want to conquer as fairly as possible. May the best man win."

"May the Author favor whom she will, and write us all happy endings," Rifun murmured.

He took Tommen home and reluctantly returned to Sadurnon.

He didn't want to admit it, but Tommen had been correct in some ways. He didn't want to just slaughter the Akarin. He wanted them to put up a fight, for their sake if no one else's. He didn't want to see them crash and burn as so many others apparently did. "Put up a fight!" he wanted to tell them. "Defend yourselves!" It wasn't only their honor they were defending, but the honor of the Author and the Authored Books.

Julianna had gathered everyone in his chambers for a meeting. Rifun joined them somewhat joylessly, making a gesture.

"All right. Tell us what you found."

29 | Preparation
The Caves of Meroian, 2014

G oodness, Rifun, what happened to you?"

Julianna was doing some work in the infirmary when Rifun walked in and helped himself to a chair, right side of his face smeared with blood. She couldn't decide whether he was simply annoyed or if he was expressing his pain as anger. What was more interesting was that he had the wound at all.

"Let's just say Misik and I had a little spat," he answered sharply, not flinching as she started to clean the blood and reveal the wound itself. "The good news is that he was yellow when he struck me. The better news is that I keep quick-clot close to hand."

"I'm guessing you had an argument about the Halloween attack," Julianna said, tossing some bloodied gauze in a small bin. "It's a wonder he didn't kill you outright."

"And the rest of the attacks on Earth, yes. And I'm sure he would have liked to kill me. But he still believes we are going to launch an attack on the Tacagans."

"That's going to be soon, I imagine. When it comes to the Borelians, well, I'm surprised Misik even gave you a warning."

The wound wasn't as bad as it looked. It didn't require stitches. The problem was that yellow Borelian toxins affected the heart and circulatory system. Even if temporary hemophilia was all Rifun had escaped with, it was going to be at least a few hours before it stopped bleeding, and the healing would be slower.

"I figure we can time our attack with the next major Borelian campaign on Earth," Rifun went on. "Halloween was a crime of opportunity, limited primarily to North America. Just like they've been using other local festivals and activities and even wars for smaller attacks. But next up, something that occurs all around the world—"

"Christmas," Julianna said. "Christmas and New Year's shortly after."

"Exactly. Any fool can see that it's too good for them to pass up. The way I see it, we trip them at the starting line. Take out Misik and the rest, take over the Akarin, shore up defenses in the fortress."

She held more gauze to the wound and instructed him to hold it there, which he did. She took a few steps back to look at him. "You are suggesting that we pivot from the Akarin directly to the Borelians?"

"Even you know better than that," he told her. "Are we really going to have a choice?"

She studied him for a long moment, then let out a breath. "No."

"If we're lucky, we can still pull this off where we can disguise their deaths as being casualties of the battle with the Akarin. That might buy us a tiny sliver of breathing room."

"And what excuse are you giving Misik for the delay? Christmas is observed on Earth, not Tacaga."

He removed the gauze and studied it as if he'd never seen blood before. "No, but as it happens, the Tacagan Governors have some big diplomatic soiree going on around the same time. A fairly juicy target in its own right, enough to make it plausible."

Julianna scowled and retrieved some more gauze as the wound continued to bleed. "But why wait so long at all? What is actually, honestly stopping us from attacking today? Or tomorrow? Or a few days from now?"

"Readiness, for one. We have a much smaller army, fewer allies, so we need to be as prepared as we can possibly be. Time Agents are grass. The Akarin will be trees. Even standing dead trees take some effort to fell." He took the new gauze as it was offered. "On top of that, it's a matter of simple physics, a body in motion. Are the Borelians attacking now? Yes, they are. But it is no different than any wars currently going on. I expect their upcoming plans for Christmas and New Year's are going to be much heavier."

She folded her arms. "Exactly. So what's the problem? What does that have to do with physics?"

"The Borelian machine isn't moving yet, not truly. Not in the heavy way I just mentioned. Therefore, it can still be turned in any direction, including ours. If we wait until the machine is moving and the direction cannot be easily changed, then we can trip it up and hope that it crushes itself, or at least does a fair amount of damage."

He's afraid. He's a coward. You could be thrown into slavery right now and he would still make excuses.

"I still don't understand," she said shortly, electing to bite her tongue.

"Interestingly enough, the only one complaining is you," Rifun mentioned casually. "The Borelians aren't known for fast warfare."

"That's because they have the time and firepower to spare. It's like saying that the rich never complain about the cost of food or fuel."

"They do, actually, but your point is noted." Again he took the gauze away from his face and looked at it.

"Would you stop that?" She grabbed his hand and put it back up to his cheek which was still bleeding. "Just keep it there for a while."

"I was seeing if there was anything different about it because Misik struck me."

"Can't you do that while it's still in your body?"

He shrugged. "Maybe."

"Then do it," she ordered. "Don't bleed all over the place if you don't have to."

A coward and a fool.

He made a humming sort of sound. "Well, seeing how it's only a minor cut, I suppose I don't need to take up space here." He stood. "Do not think, however, that we are entirely idle. In a few weeks, we are going to start testing through the ranks and placement for our assault. You should be there for the assessments."

Julianna nodded. "I will." She grabbed a few more gauze pads for him. "Here. For the next time you decide to study your blood."

He offered a mild thanks and departed.

Delaying this attack only gives you more time to make your own plans.

She nodded slightly to herself and went back to her work, cleaning up the infirmary. *He has played his part but overstayed his welcome. Now he is only holding us back.*

A lapse of faith is expected from time to time, but this has gone on far too long. Questioning one's beliefs in order to reinforce them is healthy. Questioning the journals should have brought growth. Instead, he now questions his questions. He is going adrift.

He can't even prove the greatness of the Authored Books now, not with Tommen as weak as he is. And I'll be sure to point that out in the assessment.

Expectations can be a good thing, but putting that much weight on such a boy is only going to destroy them both.

As Micaiah has been destroyed. And Saul. And now Tommen and soon Rifun. One by one, these so-called chosen ones will be disposed of and quickly fade away.

Exactly. One by one. We mustn't get ahead of ourselves.

Ha! At this rate, we can barely get started and moving, never mind ahead.

She finished up her chores and left the infirmary, making for the officers quarter. No one wanted to stay in the officers building with the Borelians around, so they had staked a claim to a particular nearby neighborhood instead.

When Rifun had told her to start gathering supplies, she had known at least a few days of hope and excitement. Maybe they were finally going to be doing something. Yes, yes, they had to keep everything under wraps from the Borelians, which might require a little more time than normal, but they would be doing something.

"And now here we are," she sighed aloud. She looked up at Drinjin uh Ersik. He had been standing in the street speaking to a couple of lesser officers, dismissing them when he saw her approach.

"We are here now, yes," he stated, obviously puzzled. "Is there something you need?"

"Do you know where Torbak Martin is?"

"On his home world currently, I believe. Shall I fetch him?"

She waved a hand. "No, I'm sure you can tell him later. Come, walk with me."

He fell in beside her as he had learned to do when acting as her bodyguard. She headed towards the underground lake.

"You come from a military background, don't you?" she began.

"Of course." His tone was neutral, perhaps hiding annoyance as if he thought she'd forgotten any of the many times he had proclaimed so.

"Would you say it is better to attack the Borelians now, while they are doing nothing, or wait until they are mobilized for some other endeavor or campaign?"

Drinjin uh Ersik made a sound Julianna had come to know as a thinking sound, sort of like a human "Hm..." It was a minute before he answered.

"Either one has its advantages. Attacking now would catch them off-guard, send them scrambling for a short time. Attacking later, if they are already engaged, would not only surprise them, but it would introduce a new enemy after they are already tired. And we may find an ally in those whom they were already attacking."

Julianna frowned. "You think Rifun is doing the right thing, then? Delaying our attack on the Akarin?"

"Testing of the lower ranks will begin soon. Has he invited you to it?"

"Yes, he has. But if we had begun testing sooner, maybe we could have prevented the Borelian attack on Earth." She went on before he could speak. "I understand you are not human and have little or no stake, but whether it was my people, your people, or someone else entirely, the fact remains that they are identical situations. We could have attacked as the Borelians were mobilizing, then gone to attack the Akarin. In your professional, military opinion, is or was there a good enough reason for the delay?"

Again he made the thinking sound.

"Please, Drinjin uh Ersik, you will not compromise yourself by agreeing or disagreeing," she pressed. "But with our situation as precarious as it is, we cannot afford mistakes. The next attack the Borelians have planned will be even bigger, and our action or inaction will be that much more consequential."

Drinjin uh Ersik made an affirmative gesture. "To utilize a phrase Faharoa has used before, I think we dodged a bullet."

Julianna nodded. "Yes. I had similar thoughts. No one thinks the Borelians are going to politely wait until they have finished enslaving humanity before they turn on us. Considering our request to mobilize ourselves under the guise of attacking the Tacagans, I was surprised they didn't do something."

"Seeing how it was the first major attack on Earth humans, they may have been focused more on testing their reaction and response," Drinjin uh Ersik offered.

"It would make sense. North America was the only continent they had not tested in some way. The rest of the world they had the excuse of war of one form or another. But now they know the reaction. And I suspect they will move against us at some point surrounding the upcoming attack. Unless we get to them first."

He made a sound of agreement.

They reached the lake. At one time, judging by the crumbled ruins, the wall might have extended out into the water, but no more. Julianna continued along the shore for a short distance before turning back onto a street.

"Tell me, Drinjin uh Ersik, what do you think of Rifun? As a soldier and a leader? Is he doing his best, or could he be doing more, doing better?"

"Considering the circumstances, I do not believe him to be doing poorly. We are not dead or in Borelian slavery. At the very least, he keeps busy and is not unaware of the situation we're in."

"But...?" she prompted. "Please, constructive feedback is welcome."

He still squirmed a little. "I do think he could do better. Although we will be moving into testing soon, I believe we have found the limit where caution turns into sloth."

She nodded thoughtfully. "And...do you believe he is committed to the Cult? He has expressed some belief in the Authored Books and seems unwilling to...really hurt the Akarin. At least to my eyes."

He made a gesture of agreement, like a nod. "It is noble to not want to repeat Cassius' foolish wrath, though it has been debated for many centuries across many cultures whether it is better to completely annihilate your enemies so they cannot take vengeance, or attempt to subjugate or ally with them so as to bolster your own resources."

"And in this instance, what do you think?"

"I think it depends on what comes after. Is there a reason we need an alliance with them, after everything that has happened?"

"Or are we wasting time and resources in order to keep a clear conscience, when it may end up costing more lives in the end?" Julianna finished.

"Yes."

She nodded thoughtfully and they walked in silence for several more minutes.

"Seeing how we are speaking of constructive feedback," Drinjin uh Ersik ventured, "may I offer some to you as well?"

Her first reaction, which she thankfully kept internal, was revulsion. No, she would never believe that she was perfect, but that someone so boldly suggested that she was imperfect was somehow rather revolting. Then the moment passed and she nodded. "Of course. By all means."

"Where Faharoa is slow to act, you are sometimes too rash, as in the case of murdering Micaiah Durvin, then using a Borelian to kidnap Micah Durvin. While these opposing traits might normally work well for the two of you to balance each other, our situation is, as you say, precarious. You are two extremes, but the situation demands a middle ground. You must slow down to see and weigh all options. He must learn to make the decision. Pull the trigger, to use another idiom."

"Of course. However, it would be useless, even counterproductive, to use Rifun as a means of improving myself in such a way. He has his own problems that he must work on, as you just said, and we are, perhaps, too connected in such a way to be of use to each other. I would rather have you and Torbak to hold me accountable for such things. You are already dedicated to me as my decoys and bodyguards; perhaps we may also include areas of self-improvement."

Drinjin uh Ersik said nothing, which she took to mean agreement.

"And what of Godwin Lore?" she went on. "What do you think of him?"

"A capable warrior, certainly. Strong, quick, decisive. A leader in his own way, but not to the scale of an army."

"A small band of warriors, maybe. Mercenaries."

"Exactly."

"But mercenaries are not known for their loyalty."

"I have heard no treacherous words, nor inferred any treasonous intentions from him, but that is not to say they do not exist in some fashion."

She gave him a look. "Very diplomatic of you."

"When Faharoa gives him a task, I have no doubt he will accomplish that task, or if he fails, it will not be without tremendous effort. So far as I have seen, he has every inclination to align himself with us and Faharoa, as a mercenary, as a soldier, as a human. I have not seen any inclination toward betrayal because no circumstances have arisen to challenge his loyalty."

She considered this for a long moment.

He is working for Rifun now, but what if a better offer came along?

Is this a problem for now or later? Is he a threat that can be ignored for the time being? Learn to prioritize.

"Well, with the Borelians hanging over us, I don't think we need to worry about him," she decided.

This time Drinjin uh Ersik grunted an agreement.

"And finally, what about Torbak?" she asked. "What do you think of him?"

Another grunting sound. "A good soldier, a good leader, but, perhaps, a bit blinded by...infatuation. For you. Noticeable before but nothing that ever got in the way. Unfortunately, his distant idol has suddenly gotten very near to him."

Julianna frowned. "Do you think this...infatuation puts others at risk? Has it potentially or actually compromised any of the tasks I have set before you and him?"

"On the one hand, this infatuation drives him to complete a task well, in order to please you. However, it has the side effect of possibly neglecting others he is working with or neglecting simple chores around the camp."

"Neglecting others, to make himself look better in some way, through ignorance or malice does not matter. Neglecting chores, because either he is daydreaming or else trying to make himself openly available to me."

"Yes."

She hummed a sigh. "I do not know his species or culture well enough to know how to discourage the fixation while encouraging the loyalty. But you have not indicated that it has become a serious problem, so it may have to wait until after we make our move." She added quickly, "Of course, you will let me know if this infatuation rises to a more dangerous level."

"I will."

"Excellent." She put her hands together. "Well, this has been an exciting and educational chat. I'm glad we could have it. I'm sure the information will be put to good use."

He made a sound. "If I may ask, what have others said about me?"

For a second, she was tempted to tell him that she did mind and he wasn't going to know. At the last moment, she opted for, "You are the first I've asked. I expect Torbak will be next, perhaps Mr. Lore if he's around."

She dismissed him before he could say more, then made her way toward the officers building.

He is loyal, and has done his job well.

He provided an honest assessment of his peers, but was still reluctant to speak against Rifun.

And why not? He doesn't know if I'm trying to set a trap for him, question his own resolve or abilities or loyalty.

Then that speaks only to your own inability to lay subtle traps, a skill that should be improved. And the best traps are laid, not through yourself, but through others.

Use Tommen to get to Rifun. Force him to choose.

Exactly. Step one has already come to pass. He flounders in his training. Step two is testing. Is he even good enough for battle?

Julianna knew he wasn't. Even considering his injured arm, he was still a bit whiny about combat, and he held no true love for the journals or the Cult. He barely tolerated them except that Rifun had basically roped him into service under threat of death.

He's wasting too much time on Tommen, Julianna thought. *Hopefully, the testing only proves how useless he is, Rifun will abandon that pet project, and we can move on with things that matter.*

So it was that she kept her mouth shut about such things over the next few weeks as they shifted their focus from training and the daily routine into testing. She avoided going to the vaovao grounds, avoided Tommen except when he was sent to help her care for the sick and refugees on charity days. She ignored Rifun's comments about Tommen, pretended it didn't bother her. All would be revealed in testing. There was no other choice, for the Borelians would be present as well. They wanted to know the abilities of their future slaves, after all, see who was a threat and who wasn't.

She took Drinjin uh Ersik's advice and stayed back, doing nothing rash or flamboyant. Even when it came time to clear the main hall in the officers building in preparation for testing, the most she did was watch and politely inquire as to which of the thirteen judging seats at the high dais was hers.

On the other hand, she mused, even if Tommen wasn't some magical chosen one, he could still be useful. Weak in body and mind, Rifun had already proven he could be easily coerced or manipulated. But why bother with him when she had high officers swooning over her, ready to carry out her will?

Because the Akarin would never listen to the swooning officers. But a potential turncoat is worth something to them. Water may be a solid wall when struck, yet a gentle entrance parts the waves. And a door, once opened, may be passed through both ways.

There was something there, some plan or bit of knowledge right at the edge of consciousness, but it wasn't coming to her while she watched the preparations in the main hall of the officers building. The Borelians did most of the work themselves, perhaps not trusting others to do it correctly or to their liking. Julianna wasn't sure what was so difficult about it. The bare room was enormous, four rows of seven pillars towering like giant sequoia trees, requiring ten or twenty average-size men to surround them holding hands. Each one was surrounded by braziers yet the stone never blackened from the fire leaping upwards. Large hearths with equally large fires lined the walls, providing both heat and light. At the front of the room, on the high dais, behind the long table where the judges sat—like the table in the meeting room, she suspected this, too, had once been an altar—an even larger hearth roared with flame, creating a foreboding, dramatic effect as well as tragic heat on the backs of the judges.

"So, what do you think?" Rifun wondered, walking up beside her. The wound on his cheek from General Misik had healed to a thin scar.

"I feel like you didn't have much input on the decorum," she answered, watching a couple Borelians move a large stone chair into position. This one looked fancier than the others, the carvings more exquisite.

"The ancient Elif weren't thinking about future renters when they built this place, no, but the Borelians are doing a marvelous job of returning it to its original intent."

"Blood sacrifice," Julianna stated distastefully. "To appease the gods that they might relent on the electrical storms on the surface." She turned to Rifun. "The ancient Elif did not understand the nature of their planet's weather, did not understand the nature of gods and men. But we do. We need to ensure that our sacrifices do not go to waste."

"Well, we have seventeen victims to present first, and they're not the most willing subjects," Rifun said quietly. "They have to go before anything or anyone else."

"Why not bring them into battle with us? They are a very powerful tool."

"One that Cassius tried to use and lost control of. No. Not an option anymore. If we can't stand on our own two feet without them, if we can't rely on the Akari and the Author, then we deserve to lose and be tossed into slavery." He went on before she could speak. "Furthermore, I expect presenting their heads to the Akarin will create a suitable shock to them."

"For what purpose?"

"An attempt at peace, an alliance."

Julianna drew a sharp breath and straightened, fixing him in a glare. "Peace?! Alliance?! Are you mad?!"

"They're not going to accept," Rifun told her easily. "I have no expectation that they will accept. They're too proud. But how does it look for the Akarin council to turn down an offer of peace in front of a divided people?"

She considered this for a moment, then nodded. "All right. I can't deny you may have a point."

"And while they're proud and divided, I have a special task for you to ensure their complete and unconditional surrender."

She studied him for a long moment, used Test to ensure it really was Rifun and not some Borelian in Disguise looking for treachery. The man before her was genuine, but where this sudden stroke of genius and malice came from, she could not say.

Before either could say more, one of the Borelians approached, this one gold for the manipulation of bones and the skeleton.

"We are ready to begin," it reported. "General Misik is on his way."

"Oh, is he?" Rifun wondered sarcastically. "I was worried."

The Borelian gave him an unreadable look and walked away.

"Is everything all right?" Julianna inquired of Rifun.

"By the ancestors, I cannot wait to be rid of these bastards," he whispered. "It takes everything in me to maintain the level of civility that I am, knowing their time is limited. Or ours is."

"Considering how...polite and...roundabout Africans are said to normally be, I expect that—"

"I am annoyed," he stated, a little louder. "I am frustrated. I am tired of the desk job and desire to be on the field of battle or the plane of peace."

She couldn't decide how much, if any, of this was theater for the benefit of the Borelians, but probably not much. Still, she nodded and also raised her voice to an appropriate level. "I understand. But that's the reason for this testing. Once everyone is through and we understand their abilities, then we may make our move against the Tacagans whenever you are ready."

He said nothing to that, just walked away, looking unhappy.

She looked around again, unable to ignore a certain prickle of unease that crawled across her skin. The fires were hot, yet there was a chill in the air. They were large and provided plenty of light for the room, yet the shadows appeared too large, too wild, as if they had a mind of their own, dancing from one fire to another, or perhaps trying to hide from them. Or maybe trying to attack the light.

Just Cassius casting long shadows after death, she told herself. *Whatever deals with the devil he made, they're long gone.*

Yet the Borelians remained, and she had to get uncomfortably close to them to get to her seat at the table. Hers was the farthest on the right, facing the room, the farthest from the Borelians. Meanwhile, Rifun had to sit next to General Misik in the middle, both of them pretending to still be allied, to still like each other. Did the grunts know about the fight between Rifun and Misik? Did they suspect anything amiss? Did they wonder how or why the alliance continued in spite of the Human-Borelian War?

She took her seat, unable to stop a few anxious glances toward the Borelians, glad when her view was finally blocked by the great Korin Berkloff. The rhino-man did not pay her any mind, just twitched a leathery ear once and made a grunting sound as he adjusted in the seat several times before finding some semblance of comfort.

"Day one," someone sighed, already bored of the engagement. "Acolyte one."

Wait, they were going through all of the members? As in, every last one of them? From the freshest greenhorn to the most seasoned veteran? There hadn't been any lower-level testing to make things easier? More efficient? Was Rifun or Misik fishing for something? Was each one trying to outlast the other? Or just annoy each other, see who would snap from boredom first?

Patience. In the excitement and the mundane. This gives ample time to plan and consider. There are only a few you care to see.

Not untrue, but she preferred to think while doing something. Tending wounds, caring for the refugees, cleaning, cooking, anything at all other than just sitting here watching test after test.

It was not entirely mundane as she occasionally asked for a demonstration of a particular skill, but it was by no means exciting. Testing a few might have yielded productive results, but as one turned into ten turned into fifty turned into a hundred, as one day turned into two and then three and beyond, it was tempting to simply pass everyone and let the nature of battle sort everything out.

They had started at the top of the chain and worked their way down. As the ambany turned into the afovoany and finally vaovao, the tests got faster and faster as there was less to demonstrate, less to prove, less to fail at. Sorry to say, but they just mattered less. They were the fodder that bought time and space for the more trained and more talented to do their work and win the battle.

This did not make the testing any less tedious, however, and not even Rifun could be roused to real interest when Tommen Forbes walked in. The teenager still gawked like a tourist at the architecture and decor, and he couldn't even take the testing seriously when he had the audacity to ask a question before beginning.

"You're listing everything that everyone goes through, citing how I already speak English and stuff, and how we're not learning Energy. Just because, well, to cover my ass, is there no testing on the journal?"

"That will be tested," Rifun told him blandly. "Don't worry about that. Now then, let's begin."

Julianna would not deny that Tommen had some skill in Time. He ought to, considering he'd been learning since he was ten, far earlier than the Time industry normally allowed humans to begin. But even though a tone deaf person could learn to play an instrument through sheer repetition and note reading, they would never have the creative instinct of someone who was naturally musically-inclined. His Funnel Band, designed to siphon the pain of his burned arm away from his body so it did not overwhelm him, was of some interest, but it was hobby tinkering only. Yes, it worked, when he had the time to sit down at the metaphorical desk and poke around with it. But when it came to instinct, battle, he was pathetic.

This deficiency was immutably proven when it came to Matter. Changing his eye color, manipulating the genes he already had, easy enough, one of the first tricks anyone learned. Identifying the composition of stone, more head knowledge of the various materials than skill with Matter. Splitting stone along those compositions, extracting a vein of gold or a cluster of crystals, well, there was that rote knowledge and repetition and tinkering. A skill of finesse, practiced on an inanimate object.

"Using only Time," Rifun said, "put out the fire around one of the pillars."

If Julianna noticed how Tommen froze at the suggestion, she knew the others certainly saw it. Swallowing, Tommen approached the pillar closest to his current position. Whether he was actually studying it or simply gathering his nerve, she could not say as he circled the pillar twice. He got in a position where he was three-quarters turned away from the table, perhaps so they couldn't see his fear.

The fire flared up for a moment, causing everyone to jump, then suddenly died down until it was out.

Truthfully, Julianna was more surprised he had been able to do it, in the sense of overcoming an obvious fear of fire. Did he fear the punishment if he didn't at least try? Was he trying to prove something to himself?

Nevertheless, he had done it. But all of it so far had been inanimate tinkering. Now an instructor aide was brought in. This aide was sickly and cancerous, though not yet dangerously so. She had volunteered to keep her sickness for the time being in order to help vaovao in their studies of Matter. All they had to do was use Touch to identify the location, size, and shape of the tumor within her body.

Tommen had the same reaction Julianna did when she heard about this particular test. It was shocking, appalling. This was borderline animal experimentation, if not illegal, at least unethical. They should use her to test the ambany abilities to heal the tumor. The aide refused and said such a test would have to wait until the tumor actually posed a danger to her.

After a moment, Tommen reached out a tentative hand, maybe expecting a trap of some form. But the aide did not flinch as he Touched her.

To Julianna's eyes, it was nothing especially exciting to watch. Just a human teenager petting a...dog-like alien. Then his stroking stopped and his curious expression went slack. She expected him to look up and tell them what they wanted to know. After two or three seconds, she knew he wasn't going to give such information. From watching other vaovaos and Rifun's explanation, he had found the creature's nervous system. Senses, thoughts, memories, all were starting to blend because he didn't know enough about how to protect himself.

Rifun stood and crossed the room. He grabbed Tommen and threw him away from the aide. The aide yelped and scurried off to a dark corner to regather herself, remember who and what she was. Meanwhile, Rifun stood over Tommen, offering a hand.

"What happened?" the teenager asked, taking the hand and drunkenly getting to his feet.

Rifun hopped back up the steps and resumed his place at the table. "We will discuss it later, for we have not the time here and now. We have one last part of the test to complete, the combat test."

Given what had just happened, fighting was the last thing on his mind.

Tommen glanced around the room. "I didn't hurt her, did I?"

"No, you didn't," Julianna replied gently. "And she holds no ill will for you." He wasn't the first vaovao to screw up that test.

He nodded. "Okay. So who am I supposed to be fighting?"

Beside Julianna, Berkloff stood. Tommen took a level breath. "Um...is that even fair?"

"Is combat fair?" Berkloff retorted, walking down to meet Tommen, heavy steps echoing menacingly in the enormous room. "Is your opponent always going to be evenly matched? You are looking for weaklings as much as the strong are looking for weaklings like you. I have found you on the battlefield, and you cannot run."

It wasn't even a competition, Julianna thought, and wet grass stood up to a scythe better than Tommen did to Berkloff. Even after the Korin—who had been in multiple such tests today and showed no signs of fatigue—returned to his seat, Tommen lay on the ground making pitiful squeaking noises and occasionally rolling here and there.

"Get up," Rifun commanded after a minute or two.

Tommen groaned as he did so, flinching at some pain in his ribs, perhaps broken. When he got around and sat up, his shoulder was obviously out. Gingerly, he got to his feet, favoring his ribs and cradling his arm to minimize movement in his busted shoulder.

"So, other than combat, how did I do?" Tommen asked in a small voice.

Berkloff snorted. "You will stand at attention and wait to be spoken to."

"Your Akari skills are doing very well," Rifun told him amenably. "Your combat is somewhat lacking. But that is why we are here to test and see where your skills are so we may know how to utilize them going forward." When Tommen smartly did not reply, he added, "Go to the infirmary. Get cleaned up. Then take a pot of stew and a medical kit down to the outer camp. Once you have run out of your supplies, then you may go home."

"Yes, sir."

And he limped away, a pitiful, whipped dog.

More vaovao came and went, each one more untrained and likely to die in battle than the last. Julianna was too happy to disperse for the evening and even happier when the testing finally concluded the following afternoon.

All of the testing judges took the evening off. Julianna headed to London for some people-watching, home-cooked cuisine, and even a bit of shopping. No one came looking for her. When she returned to the temple, no one came to check on her or tell her about some meeting or other engagement or catastrophe. The following morning, she was able to sleep in and, once she freshened up, able to leave the officers building for more than a quick stretch of the legs.

"Glad that testing is over?"

She paused where she stood in the street, looked around, and spotted Drinjin uh Ersik and Torbak Martin approaching. It was Torbak who had spoken.

"Quite," she answered, meeting them. "And you?"

"Certainly," Drinjin uh Ersik confirmed. "Although there remains some anxiety among those who feel they did not perform adequately."

"Hardly a novel phenomenon." She shifted her stance. "But what about you? You are the highest of instructors. Their success is directly tied to you, in a sense."

Both expressed a fair amount of confidence.

"Even so, we are also glad testing is over," Torbak finished.

She waved a hand. "Yes, of course. It was a droll few days, to be certain. And what is your opinion of things now? Are we ready?"

"Education and confined testing can only go so far. Eventually, we must take our skills to the field."

"Faharoa has called a meeting to discuss such things," Drinjin uh Ersik stated, his tone suggesting their small talk was concluded.

"Of course," Julianna said. "We mustn't keep him waiting."

If there was ever a time Julianna wanted to act like a petulant child, it was now as they returned, yet again, to the officers building. She hated it. She was tired of looking at it, the black stone and gloomy interior. The Akarin fortress was also underground, but it was still lighter and brighter than this place. But she said none of this out loud, just headed inside, making for Rifun's chambers.

Rifun and Godwin were already present, their demeanor suggesting they were just moving from their own small talk to serious planning. They barely acknowledged the trio's arrival except to motion for them to close the door and come in closer. As soon as the door was closed, a Sound barrier went up, and the five of them assembled around Rifun's desk which had been pulled out from the wall and cleared except for some notes and diagrams of the Akarin fortress.

"I know you left the officers building last night, as we all did," Julianna said, studying Rifun's somewhat haggard appearance. "But did you sleep at all?"

"I went out, as we all did," Rifun confirmed, not looking at her. "When I got back, I pulled Misik and a few others aside and we spent the night going over some of the testing results." Now he looked up. "I may not be willing to use the Borelians in battle, but I can still pick their brains for a few days, get the troops efficiently organized. We have a marvelous plan of attack for several Tacagan cities."

"No doubt aided by your masquerading as one of the governors."

"Indeed." He straightened. "And since you bring it up now, I was able to find something of particular interest. Apparently, Earth Time Agents have smuggled a chemical engineer to Tacaga in order to safely research Borelian toxins, trying to find a cure."

"Really?" Julianna felt her brows go straight up. "Any success?"

"Nothing that I've found. The engineer had only just collected samples on Earth, but increasing attacks made research dangerous and difficult. Now he is relatively safe on Tacaga, with access to their more advanced equipment, but he is still only one man. Any and all research is only in its preliminary stages."

"Better than nothing," Godwin commented. "Good on them. And it suggests that we may actually have to protect Tacaga in the end."

"Agreed," Drinjin uh Ersik stated.

"Has our unwitting pawn turned up anything else?" Julianna wondered.

"It seems Tacaga is playing host to meetings of various human Time Agents, all of the topics revolving around the Borelians in some fashion," Rifun reported.

"Is any of it relevant to our situation right now?" Torbak asked.

The mixed-blood shook his head. "No, unfortunately. Right now, we are still focused on the Akarin fortress." He returned to leaning on the table, indicating several loose papers. "We've made some loose plans in preparation, but now that we have the results of the testing and have our squads and battalions more appropriately arranged, we can make some concrete plans."

"And what is the goal?" Julianna jumped in. "What do we hope to achieve at the end of the day, other than territory?"

His expression said he knew exactly what she was asking. "After we kill the Borelians, I and a small team will go to the Akarin fortress, demand a meeting with their council. We will present the Borelians' heads—General Misik's especially—and make an offer of peace. If they surrender, they get to live. I have no illusions or expectations that they will accept. In fact, I am fully expecting them to reject with some flair and ceremony."

"Once the council rejects our peace, the primary ambany force will attack," Godwin said, rattling off a list of squads and other military terms Julianna did not fully understand. "It will catch them by surprise before they can rally a force, punch a hole for the bulk of the afovoany. No matter what, we still have only one point of entry and exit."

"What about the eighth floor?" Torbak asked. "I recall something about an emergency exit there?"

"And a self-destruct button," Drinjin uh Ersik commented gravely.

"That's where Julianna comes in," Rifun said, looking at her. "Once the Akarin realize what's going on, they're going to do three things: send forces to meet us; protect the council; secure the self-destruct button. You are going to beat them to the big red button."

"Me?" she echoed, bewildered.

"You're not a soldier, true, but you are not as unskilled as you may have others believe. As powerful as it is, that button will be low on the priority list; the Akarin will be more intent on and more confident in simply running us off. Anyone they do send to secure the button, it won't be their most elite force, and there likely won't be very many. If things don't go our way, it may act as a last-resort bargaining chip."

"And if things do go our way, you will be able to keep the council from escaping through that same emergency exit," Godwin added.

She nodded slowly. "Logical, I suppose. But do you really think I'll need to be there so soon? You're right that I'm not a soldier, but I'm not an idiot, either. I know that battles are not won in half an hour. I would either have to be there from the beginning to meet any guards or the council at any time when the tide turns, or I would need some sort of signal to know when to move."

"Signal is more likely," Torbak said.

"How do you think?" Drinjin uh Ersik wondered.

"If she is there from the beginning, there may be multiple instances where the Akarin send someone there. If they find her, it may be seen as us attacking from that place as well."

"That would divide their forces, force them to fight up as well as down," Godwin said, confused. "Even if that is not what we plan, that is how it would be seen. It would work to our advantage, at least for a few minutes while they are trying to figure out what we are doing."

"But it would only send constant reinforcements to the area," Rifun mused. "It would plant that paranoia in their minds about the self-destruct button, and as things go badly for them, the desire to use it goes up. Better for them to think that we don't know about the button or the emergency exit." He nodded. "We'll use a signal."

Drinjin uh Ersik made a sound of agreement. "Now, how do we get to that point?"

Rifun gestured to a diagram. "The fortress is, fundamentally, a giant cube. Four corners, four circular towers, four primary walkways, everything very geometric. The simplest tactic is to surround them, push into the interior, push up to the next floor, repeat. The real problem lies in the interior and the stairways. With exception of the bottom floor, which is fairly square and straightforward, those upper interior sections are giant mazes. We're going to be woefully susceptible to guerrilla tactics. Meanwhile, the stairways are not only a bottleneck, but an uphill barrel. Being so open, the Akarin will have a great opportunity to attack from above."

"So why don't we attack from above?" Torbak asked. "Start in the eighth floor, take the self-destruct button right away, and force the Akarin down?"

Godwin shook his head. "Too small of an entry point. The normal portal room is going to be difficult enough, the emergency exit is worse. A small force could push us back, and once we're back in the room, all they'd have to do is set up a lawn chair and pick us off, perhaps literally, one-by-one. The Akarin on the lower floors won't even know what's going on."

"The good news is, once we take the place, we can use all of these obstacles to our advantage," Rifun sighed. He shifted his stance. "The Shatai will be our main physical air support; they know the place the best, and they know the tactics the Iuri will use to help the Akarin."

"And we have several squads ready to go for ranged interception," Drinjin uh Ersik reported.

"What does that mean?" Julianna wondered.

"Identifying anyone who isn't on the front lines physically fighting, but is still using the Akari to attack from afar," Godwin explained. "Microportals and Gravity are the most common threats, but they could use anything. Similarly, we have more teams ready to intercept any Akarin trying to do the same to us, provide cover for our people to attack at range." He shifted his stance, expression thoughtful. "Physical occupation will win us ground, but physical fighting will only account for a very small portion of a victory. Unlike common battles where there is a limit to what the men in back can do, here, that limit is much, much higher. There will be more men fighting at the same time, though most of it will be non-physical."

As it always has been. Flesh is merely an extension of the spirit, the seen an extension of the unseen, and a terribly limiting prison.

Julianna would not say she understood everything they said. She didn't understand the fancy terms they used as they used models both intentional and improvised to fine-tune their plan of attack. And yet, she did understand that things were going to change. With the Borelians gone, they were going to do things as they were supposed to have been done from the beginning, the way she and Richard intended. With Richard now gone, she would reshape the Cult in her own image.

It appeared as though the ancestors and all the spirits in the universe hated the Borelians, too, or that was what Rifun told himself when he walked in the meeting room and found the general alone. His biggest fear had been that he wouldn't be able to get Misik alone and would instead have to fend off two or three or more Borelians at the same time. It seemed that the unseen realm agreed that this was a righteous cause and was giving him every advantage.

Misik was looking over some tablet screens and barely acknowledged Rifun's presence as he walked in and shut the door. In the dark temple, an old chamber used for sacrifice, only the fire in the hearth provided any significant light and heat.

"I see you are mobilizing your forces for Tacaga," Misik said, his tone suggesting he knew that was a lie, had always been a lie. He was waiting, fishing for information, formulating his own plan of attack.

Rifun could have Banded and killed the man. He'd done that for at least six of the others, and he was not above the practice here if things went poorly. And yet, he would admit that he wanted a real physical fight, real physical revenge for the scar on his cheek and everything Misik had put them through for years.

"We are mobilizing, yes," Rifun confirmed. "But before we go, I have a parting gift for you."

Although the general didn't move, Rifun saw his focus suddenly shift away from his work. He blinked, his mind evidently going over this new inquiry. Parting gift? What was it? What for?

Without being prompted, Rifun took the bag in his hand, turned it over, and dumped out the contents. Truthfully, Rifun didn't even remember her name, had never really cared to learn it. Still, he kept an eye on where it awkwardly rolled, teetering on exceptionally curly horns, noted where the blood stained the stone, unsure how potent her purple toxin could still be.

Misik stared at the head for a long moment, as if he couldn't believe what he was seeing. He blinked several times, then slowly looked up. Rifun drew a knife, one of the few he had kept from Cassius' collection, long blade glinting in the firelight.

"*Aleo hamarana ity.*" (Let's end this.)

Whether it was some residual effect from the emotional manipulation that was the purple toxin or honest rage, Rifun did not know. He could not afford to care as he focused his attention on trying to kill Misik without actually getting within the man's striking range.

Misik was bitoxic, yellow and gray. Yellow was cardiac in nature, which was why Rifun couldn't have simply healed the wound on his cheek. Gray was related to overall brain function and could cause coma and brain death. Currently he was yellow, but neither one was a pleasant option for poison.

Rifun was constantly moving from Band to Band, narrowly avoiding Misik's fist as it passed within millimeters of his jaw. At one point, Misik did make brief contact and Rifun suddenly heaved a massive blood vomit. It made him light-headed, but the sudden dizziness actually saved him as he stumbled and avoided a secondary blow. Misik's hand and arm went sailing by, and Rifun brought his knife up, aiming for the man's bicep. Perhaps his only saving grace was that Misik was dressed casually — or what passed as casual for a Borelian officer — and not in his regular armor. The knife pierced the fabric and struck deep into the muscle. He yanked the knife out, none too cleanly, and slipped to the side before Misik could appropriately react in his own Band.

Because of the Bands, the pain was slow in coming. Misik continued in his motion, fist finding empty air. It didn't hit him until he was coming around, searching for Rifun again that he had been wounded. He faltered for just a moment as his mind registered the wound, the pain, ascertained the severity, his attention taken from looking for his opponent. In that moment, Rifun struck again, this time in the man's chest underneath the opposite arm, right between the ribs straight into the lung.

Rifun could believe that Misik would be able to fight, and fight well, even with the stab wound in his arm. Hell, Rifun himself had that kind of training. Ignoring the air leaking from your lung into your chest cavity was a little harder to do, and Rifun couldn't deny he respected Misik for trying anyway.

One arm was injured, and moving the other only provoked a much greater wound. Still, the man came at him, reaching, grabbing, hitting or trying to. Rifun danced around him, making small cuts, waiting to see if the lung wound would weaken him further. It did so eventually, and Rifun recalled something Isthim had told him once, that a Borelian was immune to his own toxins. Entirely. Misik could not use his cardiac manipulation on himself, to stop the blood from filling his chest cavity or leaking out into the open. Finally the blood loss and adrenaline turned his fight into flight. He stumbled, staggered, and his swipes toward Rifun became half-hearted. His breathing became wet and bubbly.

He managed to orient himself in the room and try to get to the door, but Rifun lunged forward to slice the tendons in the back of his knees. Then he circled around to deliver a couple strategic stabs into the pelvic region, aiming for arteries and larger tendons. Misik went down, dying slowly.

"Damn, you have no idea how long I've waited to do this," Rifun hissed, walking to the door to stand in front of it. Misik was on the floor, just out of arm's reach. "Years of fear and uncertainty, being walked on simply because I am not you. But that's what you thrive on, isn't it?" He shook his head. "No more. We are going to be rid of you, then start doing things our way. As they should have been done from the beginning." Rifun squatted down. "I don't blame you for Cassius' poor choices. I just blame you for exploiting them."

Misik growled and made a pathetic lunge for Rifun, wiggling on the ground like a handicapped worm, reaching for him, toward his ankle, looking for bare skin. Rifun lashed out with the knife like a viper, the blade piercing his hand and driving it down. When the tip hit stone, it went sideways, ripping open the wound even more. Rifun added a little extra Force to the sudden change in motion, snapping Misik's wrist and lower hand bones. He used Sound to make the snaps audible.

After a moment, he withdrew the knife and thrust it into Misik's throat, then jumped back to avoid the blood as the man started to bleed out and finally went into his death throes. Even once he had stopped twitching, Rifun waited a good two minutes before moving. He would leave the knife for the time being, just because it was soaked in blood. That was all right, though, he had plenty more. And Misik was the only one he'd been intent on actually fighting. The rest could be dispatched via Bands and other sneaky means.

He was just reaching for the door when it opened and two Borelians stood there, weapons in hand.

Borelians were not telepathic, at least by the standards of most Earth media.

They could not hold silent conversations through their brains across impossible distances. Their abilities were more in the realm of tangible empathy within a certain radius. In this case, Misik had likely begun to project hazy images of his attack and the overall feelings of surprise, pain, and, ultimately, a slow death.

The two who had responded, hopefully the only two still in the city now, did not ask questions or bother with threats as they bulled through the door, going straight for Rifun.

As he had already decided, Misik was the only one he'd been interested in fighting. For these two, he had no qualms about Banding and just killing them outright, using Gravity to crush their spines.

By the time he was finished, he had thirteen heads which he put into bags and kept in his chambers. He hoped that each Borelian slain was also an evil spirit vanquished. Even if it wasn't the dragon, it would still send a message. Unfortunately, he could not account for the other four Borelians who typically showed up for training. He did not know their schedules, would not have remembered their names except for some of Misik's records, and could not even begin to guess whether they would be back before he left to meet with the Akarin. He could get away with waiting for one, maybe two, but how long would it take for all four to return? What if they were out on their own missions and wouldn't be back for days? He doubted they had days to wait. Misik likely sent regular progress reports, and someone would notice when those reports stopped coming.

A knock at his door interrupted his thoughts, but it was the knock Godwin used when approaching. A moment later, the man walked in. He carried a large sledgehammer in one hand and a man-shaped garbage bag in the other. The Borelian horns did not fit well into the bag and poked out on either side. This hole also allowed for a trail of blood.

"You'll want to clean that up," Rifun said, indicating the trail.

"Of course, sir," Win agreed, dumping the body. "Wouldn't want to alarm the rest. How many more do we have?"

"Three to go." Rifun knelt and, with an actual saw, began sawing away at the bag, hitting flesh and ripping through bone. "How'd you take this one?"

Win indicated the sledgehammer. "I was making some preparations of my own, just happened to have it in hand when I walked in the main hall there and saw him. A few Bands to disorient him, never knew what hit him."

"Excellent. If I'm right, the last three are all singular toxins, so no surprises."

"I'm a bit weary of surprises, sir, but I know battle tends to be full of them."

The head severed, Rifun stood. "It's in our best interest, then, to finish the battle quickly and minimize those surprises." He went to the table, Win following. "According to Misik's roster, the last three are a black, an urlo, and a white."

"I'll take the white."

Rifun gave him a look. "Hell no, I'm not letting you take the white. I've taken out thirteen of them, you got one and that was crime of opportunity only. I think I deserve a little something for my efforts today."

Win put his hands up, almost sarcastically. "I was simply volunteering."

"I know you are more than willing to be the hero, but I will take the risk myself. No, I've got the white. I'll take the urlo, too. You'll have your hands full with the black, I think."

"You're not wrong, sir. They are uniquely annoyingly difficult to kill."

Rifun straightened. "Well, let's get this wrapped up as quick as possible. We've got the troops assembling. Can't be late to our own party."

"Agreed, sir. Shall we meet back here afterwards for the final tally?"

"I've already won, but if it makes you feel better, sure. And maybe bring a few friends so we can carry all the heads at once. We can't leave them here for any other Borelians to find when they come looking for their general."

Win nodded, and the two of them left the room.

An hour later, they were back, handing out heads to the posse that would accompany Rifun to the Akarin fortress for the supposed peace negotiations.

"You look rather pleased with yourself, sir," Win observed. "Did you really get some before you killed the white?"

"Of course I did, how do you think I was able to get close enough to kill it?" Rifun replied, handing off a sack containing a Borelian head.

"With Isthim and the white Borelians all gone, what will you do now?"

"I'll think about that more on the other side of the battle."

"Fair enough, sir."

Rifun himself took five sacks, just for dramatic effect.

"Drinjin uh Ersik and the others have control of the army, just waiting for myself to announce peace, or Minic here—" He nodded to the appropriate member of the group. "—to announce war." He shifted the bags, his deficient right hand struggling to hold two bags while his in tact left hand easily handled three. "Let's go."

Win stayed behind to help the others manage the army when things went south. He also opened the portal to the Akarin fortress for Rifun and the rest of them now.

If a plan works, don't fix it, Rifun figured. While he was out killing Borelians, he'd had Julianna send out invitations to all of the Akarin and their sympathizing factions, councils and civilians and prominent members, telling them to meet in the fortress at a certain time. Maybe they expected something nefarious, but confusion and paranoia on such a large scale would only aid the Cult.

Walking into the fortress, this was exactly what they found. The fortress was not big enough to comfortably hold everyone of the main Akarin group, but to add in all their sympathizers made the place utterly claustrophobic, and Rifun had no reason to think that some of them hadn't decided to skip the invitation.

Not everyone knew Rifun on sight, but it only took one to spread the word, and even in the cramped quarters of chaos, the Akarin began to cut them a wide berth. Rifun walked in far enough to make a point, but did not allow his group to be cut off. There was still a fair distance between them and the staircase, but if he was right, the council would be coming to them any moment now.

"Well, I must say, it's been a long time since I was here last," Rifun mused. He raised his voice. "All right, who's in charge here?!"

"You can talk to me," a familiar voice said. A moment later, Aklaq White Bear pushed her way out of the crowd.

"Aklaq Durvin," Rifun stated, grinning. "To what do I owe the pleasure?"

"You sent the fake messages to get everyone here. What do you want?"

"Fake? Why, absolutely not. The messages themselves were real, and if you examine them, you will find no lies."

"It said the councils wanted to discuss matters relating to the division of the Akarin and the threat from the Cult."

"And I imagine they are doing so right now, as we speak, in one of their little meeting rooms. How quaint. Coming up with a battle plan, no doubt."

"You're not here with an army," she said. "Unless you truly are so arrogant as to think forty men can defeat everyone here."

Rifun shrugged. "I admit, Gideon is one of the lesser known heroes, but a man to admire."

She studied him, but he said nothing more. "Why are you here? What's in the bags?"

He looked down. "Oh, these? Nothing special. Call it...a peace offering."

With one fluid motion, he flipped the bags and sent the contents tumbling out. The space around him got even bigger, but Aklaq remained where she was. One of the heads stopped roughly two feet from her position, and she stared at it for a long moment, unable to contain an expression of surprise.

"Borelian heads," she stated, finding her tongue. "What is this?"

"As I said, a peace offering. And I have more where those came from—" He gestured to the others in his group who had bags. " — though they were not at all easy to acquire, as you might imagine." He shifted his stance to address the group at large. "The Borelians are a feared people, paralyzing any who try to defy them, whether it be humans, the Time industry, or the Cult and the Akarin. We spend more time worrying about—"

"You're the one who allied himself with them," Aklaq cut in. "It is not our problem that they are collecting a debt you can't pay. Humans have enough to worry about, but no one is going to worry about you."

"The Cult has the numbers. The Akarin have the power. The humans...have the cure."

He grinned and raised his voice so more could hear him. "The humans have discovered a cure for the Borelian poison."

"That's not true," Aklaq cut in, trying to make herself heard and quell the crowd. "We have less than a dozen trials and only the barest of research. We can't claim our work as the cure any more than aspirin can cure cancer. It might just be a coincidence. And who here is willing to face a Borelian, risk agonizing, drawn-out, certain death, in hopes that a guess might be correct?"

"Barring that, humans also have the defensive capabilities to keep Borelians off their world, is that not also true?" He went on before she could say anything. "The Borelians could come in here right now and wipe you out. I could call my army and we would conquer you. It may be a fight, but we would win. You know that to be true. You have nothing to gain by pretending to stand here, united and defiant. Everyone knows you are divided and weak."

"You propose an alliance in order to take out the Borelians," Aklaq stated. "To what end? More likely you just want our help to save your own skin after you failed to deliver on your promises."

"The Borelians would have a harder fight against us than you. Choose your words carefully. As to what end, well, we can go back to our petty wars later, once they've been dealt with." He held up a hand before she could object. "I recognize the defeat in the Wheel, and that is the only reason I am coming here today with terms first rather than an army. These are my terms. I am offering to spare you in your vulnerability, one warrior showing respect to another as it were. In exchange, I assume control and leadership of the Cult and the Akarin—"

Protests erupted around the circle. Shouts, yells, growls, snarls, and noises no human language had a name for. Rifun let it go for just a brief moment, then used a small show of Force to shake the crowd and settle them.

"—with my own officers as my council, with some representation for the Akarin as well," he went on, as though he hadn't been violently interrupted. "You are free to conduct your own internal affairs as it pertains to training and building new lives, but all affairs outside of the Akarin will be conducted through the Cult. Relations with the Time industry and other civilizations, for instance. And war. If we do move against the Borelians, it will be under Cult leadership and command."

"And when can we get back to our own petty wars, O Great One?" Aklaq sneered.

"Once the Borelians have been defeated, assuming you even have the power to launch a war against us."

"We do," one of the Upper councilmen declared, just now arriving and shouldering his way past Aklaq. "And we will. And when we are finished, we'll turn over whatever scraps are left of your heretical terrorist group to the Borelians and let them do with you as they please, seeing how you are the one declaring war on them. We will be glad to provide these heads as proof of your treachery."

Aklaq hissed something to the councilman that Rifun couldn't hear, but he could guess.

"And who will do that?" the councilman replied, giving her a cat's regard. "You? Me? Rest assured, no matter if we surrender or he wins, all of the leaders are bound for execution."

"So you're going to gamble against the odds in a senseless battle so you can keep your head? How many would die for you? No. How many would you die for?"

"I would die for the Akarin. We must learn from our enemies, which means we must understand their thoughts and values. For the Cult, death is always an option. Perhaps we should adopt a similar attitude."

"Life or death only. What about surrender? Giving our people a chance."

"Our people? Aklaq, you walked away. Micaiah is dead. Only because you are skilled and well-known do we not send you away now and even allowed you to continue negotiating on our behalf when you have no power to do so." He continued before she could speak. "Our votes have been rendered. Those who answered the summons—falsified though they may have been—are here to declare loyalty to the Akarin, which includes fighting and perhaps dying for it, the same as in the Wheel. If you are Akarin, you will be here. If you are not, go home now, because we have a war to end."

Rifun did not stop the few people who took the councilman's offer to leave, but his gaze never left Aklaq who did not bother to hide her horror or revulsion. Once the traitorous cowards had departed, they were again left standing there, staring at each other.

"So..." he said knowingly. "Do we have an agreement?"

It was unclear who fired the first shot so-to-speak, but the message was clear enough. Minic scampered off to rally the army while Rifun and the rest of the group engaged the Akarin.

It was only supposed to be a diversion, something to start the fight, engage the Akarin, distract them until the main Cult army could come through the portal for the real battle.

Three seconds, Rifun had dispatched two attackers and defended against at least three ranged attacks. No army.

Five seconds, he narrowly avoided what could have been a crushing blow by a massive alien. No army.

Ten seconds, four of his men were dead. No army.

Fifteen seconds, eleven of his men were dead, although there were probably fifty Akarin also dead. The rest were still pretty panicky. No army.

Thirty seconds, in his bid to avoid non-physical ranged attacks, Rifun had let his guard down against physical ones, and a rope tightened around one wrist. The perpetrator gave it a good yank and took him off-balance. No army.

Forty-five seconds, the alien with the rope knew a few good tricks and was busy binding his hands behind his back. The Akarin were calling for his blood. The rest of his men were now dead. No army.

Sixty seconds, the council debated what to do with him. Still no army.

He could have done any number of things to the rope. There was no reason for it to bind him except that he allowed it. Where the fuck was his army? Did Minic not make it? He glanced at the dead men, didn't see the messenger. Had something else happened? Had the Borelians attacked while he was away, perhaps hoping to catch them before they left for the fortress?

He could have escaped, rather than been put on his knees. He knew someone was behind him with a knife. They wanted to behead him and present his head to the Borelians. If they thought this would somehow save them, well, they deserved to be conquered.

The attention of the room suddenly shifted as a portal opened and in ran the army. When they saw the bodies of their dead comrades, the lack of fighting, and Rifun about to be executed, they slowed to a stop, infuriatingly confused.

Seeing his army, Rifun rolled his eyes. "A bunch of Johnny-come-lately's, I should think! What use are you now? Fucking hell, it's so hard to find good help these days." He looked at the executioner. "You see what I have to put up with? Some army they are, right? They are going to be in so much trouble when this is over, and I for one—"

With the ease of a snake, Rifun ducked his head, rolled to the side, wiggled around so he could bring his hands up in front of him, sliced off the bonds using the executioner's knife, grabbed said knife, and killed said executioner, one clean stab through the face. Continuing the motion, he swung around and killed the nearest council member as well, the one who had so fatefully rejected the peace offer, giving him a swift, clean, beheading.

Now the army got the hint and sprang into action.

Rifun melted back into the rush of soldiers, letting them flow around him like water while he pulled the rest of the rope off his wrists. Although he had sliced the rope with the executioner's knife, he found himself with at least two decent lengths. Giving them a quick strength test, he tied a loop in each one and took one in each hand. His right hand wouldn't be able to do much, but he would do what he could.

He pushed his way to the foremost of the physical fighting, joining up with a small group of ambony intent on punching a line to the staircase. He used a small Energy pulse to shake the ground before them, unbalancing the Akarin in their way. While the soldiers forced their way ahead, Rifun lashed out with his improvised lassos, hooking one Akarin around the neck and another around its body. Without even thinking, he managed to maneuver them together so they became entangled, the one with the rope around its neck stunned and struggling for air, as if it couldn't figure out how to use the Akari to free itself. Before it could devise such a solution, one of the ambony killed them both.

Unlike Antsranana Bay, and even unlike the Wheel, fighting could be accomplished from a distance with terrible prejudice. One soldier, his allegiances not immediately identifiable, used Matter to take the water out of one creature—so that he shriveled and died—and force it into another creature—drowning it swiftly. Another used the Energy of a microportal—perhaps tapping into some of the theories they had discovered from Julianna's rescue—to electrocute four enemies at once.

The ambony force met up with another Cult force coming from another direction, splitting the Akarin on the floor. Suddenly, the situation went from a surprise struggle to full-blown battle. The Akarin broke, tried to fight, tried to retreat, tried to form up. In their uncertainty, the Cult pressed hard against them, wave after wave coming through the portal room.

Rifun was struck from the side and went to the ground. He rolled and managed to stay at least on all fours, but he was not in an advantageous position. He again melted back into the crowd until he could stand and get his bearings.

The natural defenses of the fortress quickly made themselves known as fighting began to stall on the staircase. The large primary corridors to the north and east also began to clog with soldiers from both sides. The Shatai swooped overhead, but the manta-like Iuri kept them too busy to try and go higher.

The Cult continued to pour in, forcing the Akarin back. One battalion went clockwise around the southwest atrium, another counterclockwise. A third broke off into smaller groups, punching holes and dividing the Akarin into smaller and smaller groups to be picked off.

Rifun spotted Drinjin uh Ersik near the staircase and he headed that way.

"Faharoa!"

"Any rumors of my demise were greatly exaggerated!" Rifun told him. "We need to turn this bottleneck around. I want a perimeter around this staircase, put any Akarin prisoners inside. If their friends on the upper levels try to attack from above, they risk hitting their own people."

"Understood, sir!"

Drinjin uh Ersik immediately began shouting orders and moving people here and there.

Turning, he also spotted Godwin, right in the thick of things. He also saw a microportal opening up not two feet from his head. Rifun pushed his way forward and thrust a hand into the portal, the same way he had done for months trying to free Julianna from the in-between dimension. Grabbing the inside of the portal, he turned it inside out like a sock, trapping the perpetrator and several of his closest friends inside, then let go. The portal closed, the people now locked in the in-between dimension.

"Good to see you, sir!" Win shouted, one more voice in the din of war.

"Once we take this atrium, the Akarin are going to swarm us!" Rifun growled, fending off an alien that was more beast than man. "From the north, the east, maybe even the lower levels. Grab some men and make sure they don't overwhelm us!"

Godwin used a knife to open a hole in an alien, and he followed this motion with a manipulation of Matter as he punched his fist into that hole and ripped out some innards. "On it, sir!"

He ducked out and was gone, lost in the fray.

Indeed, as the Cult secured the atrium, the Akarin made another push, from the corridors and the lower levels, trying to surround them, cut them off. But Godwin and his men, whoever they were, beat them back.

The Akarin began to retreat and the Cult took the northwest and southeast staircases with ease. Rifun knew it was only a strategy, not true flight, and he kept this in mind as he worked to punch holes for his men. The Akarin would draw the Cult into the interior corridors and ambush them. But they had already planned for such things. More waves of Cult soldiers were still swarming into the fortress, the idea to make it look utterly endless, an infinite number of soldiers and allies filling in every gap like tar.

The Cult broke onto the second floor of the northeast staircase. Rifun watched the Akarin line break, another strategic retreat. The interior corridors up there were far more complex, far more vulnerable to ambush. There would be chaos. It needed to be organized. Looking around, there were plenty of wounded from both sides, and infinitely more were just exhausted. He wouldn't say he was not fatigued himself.

He made a decision and left the front lines. The first floor was taken. Prisoners were being kept in the center of each atrium, a bit of an insurance policy against aerial attacks. Wounded and fatigued Cult soldiers sat against the walls, nursing wounds or Banding each other through much-needed sleep cycles. He spotted

Torbak Martin in the northwest atrium and motioned for him to follow.

"Are you able to explain to me exactly what happened and why you were late?" Rifun demanded, turning south. "I could have lost my head."

"Someone messed with the portal and sent it into a black hole" Torbak reported. "We lost most of the ambony."

"Yes, I've noticed, seeing how we are still fighting and not making nearly as much progress as I might have hoped." He continued before Torbak could speak. "We'll investigate the matter later. Right now, we're going to set up a command post in the southwest stair, control the flow of people coming and going."

"Understood, sir."

"It will also double as hospital and prison for the time being, to discourage any attacks by the Akarin. Make sure we keep a couple active squads handy, in case the Lower Akarin try anything, or if something does go wrong."

Within an hour, Drinjin uh Ersik, Torbak Martin, and Godwin Lore were with him at the makeshift command post in the southwest stair. The three were rotating duties, between leading the security teams, helping wounded and exhausted Cult members, and assisting Rifun in keeping a hold of the situation. The Cult had taken most of the second floor and were working on the third, but it was still a much harder push than they had been hoping for and progress slowed to a crawl.

"Even with Banding and resting, we can't keep going forever," Rifun said. "The mind needs as much rest as the body. We should start preparing to dig in for the night. If we can hold the second floor, we'll at least have beds for some of them."

"Agreed," Drinjin uh Ersik murmured. "And—"

"Faharoa!"

The two of them turned to see a scrawny, velociraptor-like alien not more than four feet tall running toward them from the direction of the portal room with astonishing speed and agility despite the blood and bodies still on the floor. It wasn't until it got close enough for Rifun to see that part of one arm was missing that he realized it was one of the refugees from the camp outside the city in the Ruins of Meroian.

"Speak!" Rifun barked. "Can't you see there's a battle going on here?"

"It's the Tacagans, Faharoa!" the alien blurted. "They're attacking the city!"

"What?!" Drinjin uh Ersik hissed.

"They are turning the place inside out, killing the security force left behind, taking all of the refugees prisoner! I managed to escape so I could warn you."

"What about Julianna?" Rifun asked.

"I don't know, sir. I'm sorry."

"Did the Tacagans say anything about coming here?" Drinjin uh Ersik demanded.

"N-not that I heard," the alien stammered.

Drinjin uh Ersik turned to Rifun. "We're trapped here."

"Oh, really?" Rifun said sarcastically. He turned away and let out a breath, watching as one group of Cult soldiers came down, another group of rested ones going up to take their place. They couldn't keep this up forever, but now they didn't even have the option to retreat, not that they did before. And on top of that, now the Tacagans were their enemies as much as the Borelians. He sighed. "All right. We dig in for the night." He turned back to Drinjin uh Ersik. "We dig in, but don't tell the men what's happened. We can't divide their attention." He gave a pointed look to the messenger who made an affirmative gesture.

"We'll have to redouble our efforts," Dinjin uh Ersik stated. "We can send focused attacks through each interior and—"

"We don't have time to play games," Rifun cut in. "We need to push for the eighth floor, go right up the northeast staircase, break into the secret room, hold it hostage."

"Through the emergency exit, then."

"Yes and no." Rifun looked around. "The staircases are bottlenecks and the interiors mazes, but they are not the only defenses this place has. I would be…offended, really, if there were no traps set. We need to trip all of the traps, render them harmless."

"But traps themselves are not harmless; that's why they are traps."

"You are just full of stunning insight today, you know that? Yes, I am aware of the fact that traps cause harm. But, you can trip a foothold with a stick and do no damage to yourself. We trip the traps, push up to the eighth floor, keep their attention on us down here. Then we make a move through the emergency exit."

He did not wait for Drinjin uh Ersik's input. Instead, he waved over Torbak and Godwin and informed them of the new developments.

"Damn it," Torbak grumbled.

Win sighed. "So, what do we do now, sir?"

Rifun explained the plan, finishing with, "Drinjin uh Ersik is going to coordinate the troops still fighting. Torbak, oversee the digging in and make sure everyone knows what's going on; hand out assignments. Win, make sure the Lower Akarin don't try anything."

"And you, sir?"

"I'm going to get some sleep, see if I can't figure out where Julianna ran off to."

"You still plan on using her to secure the device?"

"If possible. I don't imagine she would let herself be taken prisoner or killed; she would have fled."

He could see Win looked uncertain, but the mercenary did not ask questions.

It was easily another hour or so before Rifun actually got a chance to sleep, and only his experience and training allowed him to even entertain the thought of sleep on the cold, hard, stone floor of the Akarin fortress. Either that, or he really was that tired. It had been a long time since he'd been on the front lines fighting. All the more reason to wrap this up quickly.

Whether it was because Julianna was not initially asleep at the same time he was, his own body demanded rest first, or the Energy of the power inverter on the eighth floor that kept them from tumbling into a black hole, he did not know, but it was some time before he was able to dream-walk to Julianna. He found her walking through a dream forest. Once she was roused to a dreamy lucidity, the minute activity of the forest ceased, even as the trees and ground remained.

They exchanged their respective stories of bad luck.

"Your excursions as Toros didn't reveal anything about this?" Julianna asked.

"No, but I didn't do much as him in the last few weeks because I was planning for our real attack," Rifun said.

She sighed and walked away a few steps, posture contemplative. "There is only one person who could have betrayed us."

"How do you figure?"

"The timing was critical, but not on-point. It would have to be someone who knew generally when we were attacking, but not specifically. And it would have to be someone who not only wanted to betray us, but knew to go to the Tacagans because they knew we wouldn't have influence with them."

Rifun shifted his stance. "The timing may be forgiven, because I didn't know when we would be attacking either. The peace negotiations were still highly variable. As for who could have done it, I would more suspect Misik or the Borelians in general. The Cult was becoming too unruly and we had to be dealt with, in spite of the Council of Ancrath's decision to go after humanity first. Send the Tacagans to attack and weaken us, if not wipe us out. The Borelians enslave whoever is left, and then they carry on their merry way to enslave the rest of humanity."

She turned to face him. "But Misik knew you were impersonating Toros. A governor would know about those plans, would have gone to those meetings." She put up a finger. "But you know who else has been having meetings with the Tacagans?"

Rifun blinked. "No."

Julianna strode up to him angrily. "Yes! Tommen did this! Your pet project nearly got us killed, has trapped the Cult in the fortress where win or die are the only options!" She went on before he could speak. "Tommen knew where we were hiding. He knew everything about our operations, knew we were going to attack. Whether it was him speaking directly to the governors or telling his father or someone else to tell them, I don't know and it doesn't matter."

"If Tommen isn't special enough to be more than vaovao in the Cult, why would he be going to secret meetings on Tacaga?" He cut her off. "It's not unreasonable to think there weren't other spies among us. Godwin Lore rooted out several.Whoever it was, they likely tripped the portal to the fortress, redirected it into the black hole, tried to wipe out the army, did a number on the ambony. Tommen doesn't have that kind of skill, as you enjoy pointing out."

"Skill implies conscious control over one's talents," she hissed. "Tommen has done far greater damage just by stumbling about like a fool than anything intentional."

Rifun sighed. "Well, we'll deal with traitors afterwards, assuming we have the standing and authority to do so. Our primary goal right now should be just to win. Win or die, those are our only options."

Her expression said she wasn't ready to give up on what she perceived to be a massive, "I told you so," but she reluctantly agreed. "What would you like me to do?"

"Come to the fortress. We've set up command in the southwest stair, but once we make the push to the eighth floor, I'm going to move it to the northeast stair. I will give you the signal myself."

She hesitated, then nodded. "Very well. I will meet you there."

The dream faded away to darkness, but it was some time before Rifun woke. He did not feel rested necessarily, but he was no longer bone-tired. It wasn't until he was upright that he started really feeling the stone floor. If he didn't have more pressing matters to attend to, he might have taken a minute to work out the knots in his muscles.

Around him, things were quiet. Most of the men were sleeping, others just sitting quietly, contemplating life. Up above, the Akarin seemed to be doing the same.

Rifun hated the eerie quiet of the battlefield. It was disconcerting how men could just wake up and start firing at each other. Then, eventually, they would decide that they'd had enough for the day, time to suspend the action and get some rest. But then, at some point, maybe at dawn, maybe before, someone would decide it was time to start the shelling again.

Drinjin uh Ersik was awake, consuming what he apparently thought was food. Nearby, Godwin was sound asleep. Torbak was nowhere to be seen.

"How long has it been?" Rifun asked.

"Long enough," Drinjin uh Ersik answered.

"Wake the men. We push."

Drinjin uh Ersik said nothing as he set aside his breakfast, stood, kicked Godwin in the ribs, and stalked off. Win startled awake. When Rifun offered a hand, the man grabbed it and yanked him down instead, shifting position and going for a pin and a broken neck. Rifun slithered out of the man's grasp. Only when Win was on his feet did he realize what was going on. He cleared his throat. "Sorry, sir."

"Damn it, now I know why I can never find a roommate," Rifun commented.

Win's expression turned cheeky. "I'll bet it was a hit when you and Isthim—"

"That's enough out of you. Get your men ready. We're moving."

In the stillness of the fortress night, every sound was amplified. Rifun half-expected the Akarin to be awake and ready for them long before they got moving. But when everyone got into position and Rifun and the others gave the order to attack, they took the Akarin completely by surprise. Still half-asleep, the Akarin surrendered the third floor without much of a fight and only started to really mount a resistance at the fourth floor.

Rifun did not have much by way of a command tent, but they had scrounged some papers and other improvised miniatures and models. These he was collecting into a small bag when he saw Julianna approach, clearly appalled by the sight of blood and battle.

"How are we doing?" she inquired, her tone deliberately neutral, gaze fixed on the far wall.

"The element of surprise worked well in our favor, but now the real challenge begins," he replied, gathering up the last of the supplies and starting down the south corridor. "Come on."

Some of the recreation areas were being used as improvised infirmaries or jails for prisoners. Julianna slowed a step as they walked by them.

"I thought we were conquering them," she stated, hurrying to catch up with him. "They rejected peace and all efforts of reason. Why are we holding them? Will they be questioned in some way for some information?"

"They might. They might not. They are not our biggest concern right now."

"The manpower required to guard them could be better used in the fighting."

"How do you think bottlenecks work? All the manpower in the world is useless against such a tactic. That's why bottlenecks are so well-loved by tacticians."

They reached the southeast atrium and turned north up the east corridor.

"Prisoners are of no advantage to us. They are mouths to feed, bodies to guard. No one is going to ransom them."

"If they're smart, they'll ransom themselves. Goal number one, right now, is the eighth floor. And that's it."

They reached the northeast atrium, the staircase spiraling powerfully into the air and stone. Rifun had only just begun to set up his new command post when the whole fortress began to rumble and shake. Fighting and the sounds thereof abruptly ceased. Then came the sounds of crumbling stone, rock slides and cave-ins. Cracks began to appear in shifting walls and floors. A thousand screams coming from the opposite end of the north corridor were sickeningly cut off. A large wind current brought a small dust storm, coating everything and everyone on the first and second floors.

"What was that?" Julianna wondered fearfully, wiping her face uselessly with a dusty sleeve.

A minute later, figures began to emerge from the dust lingering in the north corridor, all breathlessly telling slightly modified versions of the same story. Someone—no one knew who it was or even which side they'd been on—had collapsed the northwest staircase. Everything and everyone on or under it was dead, or most likely dead. Meanwhile, messengers from the northeast stair reported Akarin reinforcements keeping the Cult staunchly off the fourth floor.

Retreat was not an option. They had nowhere to go. If they broke and each returned to his own home, there would be no getting them back. The Cult of the Akari would be finished. There was only win or die.

Before Rifun could speak, the fortress rumbled again. He looked over at the staircase where enormous chunks of stone began crashing to the ground, killing the hostages kept inside the circle. More than that, hundreds of soldiers plummeted to their deaths, the stairs going out from under their feet. Rubble began piling up until it nearly plugged the hole and the stairs, making it almost impossible to climb up the staircase from the ground floor.

Furious, Rifun abandoned his planning materials and ran to the stairs. Jogging up to the end of the line, he used Gravity to move the boulders and chunks of staircase. It was a massive effort, but they couldn't let this stop them. They had to end this. They had to win. Either the Cult won or the dragon did.

If he'd had the time, he could have gently put the stone back in place, feathering the molecules together until they held. But for the moment, he just had to get his army from the third floor to the fourth floor. In the chaos, the Akarin had also retreated, not wanting to get caught in the falling staircase. But it was an excellent opening for the Cult. Once he got Gravity to maneuver the boulders in place, sweat pouring down his face, the soldiers began streaming onto the fourth floor.

When the majority of the army had crossed, he gently let the boulders back down to the ground floor, settling them less precariously and keeping them out of the way of the part of the staircase that remained.

He elected to take the long way back to the new command post. On the third floor, he walked down the corridor to the southeast stair. Some of the army had fled here after the staircase collapsed, and they had managed to push back the Akarin some and break onto the fourth floor. He might have joined them, but they needed to end this before the Akarin killed them all with their foolishness. Instead of going up, then, he went down.

Despite the scary looks of the cracks that now spidered through the fortress, the fortress remained largely stable. Stone was stone, no matter which way you sliced it.

He had just stepped into the northeast atrium when the fortress gave a massive heave and there came the loudest, most obnoxious sound of shifting stone.

More cracks appeared, floors and ceilings shifted, rocks large and small came crashing down all over the place. Rifun instinctively threw his arms over his head as he went to a knee. The place rumbled and shook as if from a massive earthquake. The light began to dim from the thickness of dust and rubble. Battle cries turned to whimpers, screams of pain, some of them mercifully and perhaps literally cut off.

Rifun began coughing involuntarily, trying to wave the dust away from his face. The battlefield quiet began to settle in once more, and only the coughing and groaning gave any indication of life.

"Faharoa!" It was Drinjin uh Ersik, though Rifun did not see him until they were at arm's length.

"Report!" Rifun coughed out.

"The Akarin collapsed the sixth floor onto the fifth. They also collapsed the stairs leading from the fifth floor up to the sixth and seventh floors on all three staircases. A fair portion of our army is trapped up there."

Only his continued coughing kept Rifun from swearing. Instead he looked around. "Is Julianna still here?"

"I'm here," a soft, British voice cough-answered. It was a moment before she was visible in the dim light. "I'm here, I'm all right."

"And Torbak and Godwin?"

"Unknown," Drinjin uh Ersik reported.

Rifun nodded. "All right. We end this now." He looked at Julianna. "You're up."

"Are we going to send someone with her?" Drinjin uh Ersik wondered.

"We don't have time to find anyone. The Akarin are as disoriented as we are right now. We take advantage of it now or never." Rifun looked at Julianna and nodded once. "Go. Now. I will see to the men on the stairs, and I will be waiting."

She dipped her head and started off down the corridor, heading for the southwest portal room. Hopefully it still existed.

"Start taking stock of who's here on the lower floors," Rifun told Drinjin uh Ersik. "Anyone maimed or in dire need of help, note who they are and send them home. No need to keep them here to die. Same for the dead, if you can. Make sure they have a chance at a proper burial."

"You don't expect this to go well?" the general inquired.

"Just rewarding loyalty with a chance at life, in case it doesn't."

Rifun walked away then, heading for the stairs. Any evidence of the clearing he had done just a moment ago was now buried again under more rubble. There were few soldiers on the stairs now; any who hadn't fallen to their deaths or been crushed had ducked into one room or corridor or another. The majority of those who remained on the stairs were stunned, maimed, dead or close enough to it. Out of pity, and with thousands of images of the Uprising flashing before his eyes, Rifun found himself delivering water and sending them down the stairs to be counted and dealt with.

He paused when he reached the chasm where the fifth floor used to be. The fifth floor was the Archives, the operative word now being "was." The sadness he felt was not so much that certain information had been lost, for anything the Akarin Archives knew, the Wheel Archives knew a hundred times more. Part of the sadness had to do with the loss of antiquity, the books and scrolls. Now it was all relegated to the cold, unfeeling Glass tablets of the Wheel. The other part of the sadness was the knowledge that the Authored Books were in there somewhere, likely destroyed.

Would the Author really destroy her own works? Or had this been the evil dragon spirit? If it was the Author, why? If it was the dragon, then who was responsible for summoning it? The Cult, in their ambition? The Akarin, in their arrogance? Who had initiated the earthquake that destroyed it? If it was the Cult at fault, Rifun wondered whether he was truly doing the right thing.

At the top of the stairs, at the edge of the chasm between the Cult and the Akarin above, Rifun found none other than Tommen Forbes. At first, the teenager did not appear to be moving. Suddenly panicking, that another chosen one of the Author had perished — under his care, no less — Rifun hurried to him. Within three feet, he saw Tommen was breathing, asleep like a rock, poorly trying to use his bag as a pillow.

Rifun reached for the teenager, then moved his hand to the bag. It looked enormous for a medic bag that should have been well-used by now. Peeking under the flap, Rifun grinned. The Authored Books. Tommen may have deserted his squad, but he had done the Author's work and saved the Books. Rifun breathed a sigh of relief.

He put a hand on Tommen's shoulder and the kid startled awake. Rifun held out a bit of food and water which he took readily.

"Eat up," Rifun told him. "How are you feeling?"

Tommen sighed, stared at his food, wiped his eyes. He swallowed and said, "I want to go home."

"I know. It's not safe right now, though, so just sit tight a bit longer. Are you hurt?"

"I don't know. I don't think so. Not bad, anyway. What happened?"

"The Akarin collapsed the sixth floor onto the fifth. They also collapsed the stairs leading from the fifth floor up to the sixth and seventh floors on all three staircases. Everything below us is in tact, but we're not going up and they're not coming down."

"Is that a wise idea? I mean, they'll starve, won't they?"

Rifun shook his head. "They have provisions up there on the seventh floor that will last them longer than we can outlast them."

"So then what do we do? Just turn around and go home?"

"No, not that simple. Even simpler. See, there's an emergency exit portal room on the eighth floor. It's how they brought in all their reinforcements. But they're not the only ones with a trump card. I've got one last little trick up my sleeve, slightly more subtle, but more powerful. This battle should be ended within the hour."

Rifun sat down next to him and put a hand on his shoulder. "It'll be all right," Rifun told him. "There will be no more fighting today. Not for you, not for anyone. Except maybe me."

"Then why not send me home?" Tommen asked quietly. "I didn't fight at all, and I'm a terrible medic."

"War is messy and complicated, and you won't remember half of what happened come next week. It will come as bad feelings and fleeting memories and a nightmare, but you won't remember. Which is good, because then no one else will, either. They might rag on you for a time, but if you can put it behind you, learn from it, grow from it, then you can shake off the fear and the shame and move on.

"As for not sending you home, that's more of a logistics reason. We're still here, technically still engaged, even if we aren't actively fighting. It's like asking why we didn't go home earlier after the first wave of battle. Because then it would have looked like we left, and the Akarin would have reoccupied the territory we so painstakingly won. Obviously we couldn't just come back the next day and politely ask the Akarin to leave so we could pick up where we left off. We won the ground; now we have to hold it."

"So why are you here? Shouldn't you be running humanitarian missions, making sure your soldiers aren't going to mutiny on you?"

"I've already made the rounds. Many are tired, weary, wounded, as is to be expected. But I'd say about ninety-five percent of them are still willing and able to fight, and they're very angry at the Akarin for pulling that little stunt. They want blood, and I don't think mercy is the name of the game anymore."

"I can see you're struggling to hold back the hounds."

"War is a tough game, as much politics as fighting, as much finesse as force. If I don't give them a little leeway, they are liable to turn on me. Give them too much leeway, they'll either desert or turn on me."

Tommen was not convinced. He was not a soldier, not like Rifun. At sixteen, Rifun had been running missions, gathering intelligence, and, yes, killing men. But it had been a cause he believed in. Tommen still did not fully believe in this cause. Even if he did, he didn't have the heart for it. Why would the Author write about someone who was so...ordinary?

"You'll be going home soon," Rifun told him. "I'm sure of it. As I said, no more fighting."

Before either could say more, there was movement from the Akarin, and the crowd parted.

"Rifun Ndolo!" someone called out.

Rifun stood and went to the edge of the crumbled stairs.

"Present!"

"You are requested here to discuss the terms of your surrender. Leave all weapons behind when you come."

"Of course, though I will be bringing someone with me."

"Leave all weapons behind."

Rifun gave a sweeping bow, then looked at Tommen and made a motion. "Come on."

"Me?" Tommen stood on wobbly legs, went down, got back up. "What for?"

"Insurance purposes. Let's go. Bring your bag."

To make a point of it, he again used Gravity to lift and twist broken slabs of stone into place for them to walk on. The angle was too steep for a direct path, so he maneuvered several slabs in a triangular pattern around the hollow tower. He went first, Tommen trailing. As they stepped off each slab, he maneuvered it safely back onto the staircase, significantly lightening the load each time. When they reached the eighth floor and entered the room with the power inverter, however, he took the last slab and settled it in vertically on the stairwell, trapping everyone up there.

"Now, I'm sorry, maybe I misheard, but whose surrender are we discussing?" he asked. "After all, it wouldn't be much for me to take those slabs and crush what forces you have left."

"No," the Akarin council member agreed, stepping back and moving into the only room on the floor, "but if that's the case, then we may as well take you with us."

Rifun followed them inside. The entire Akarin council, Upper and Lower, was gathered, as well as Aklaq White Bear Durvin, who stood with a knife to Julianna's throat just in front of the power inverter.

"Bitch thought she was going to hold us hostage to our own weapon," Aklaq said.

"What is it?" Tommen asked. "What is the weapon?"

"It's the Energy inverter for the planet," Rifun explained. "When the Akarin first built this fortress and inverted the Energy to ward off the effects of the black hole, they had to do it by sheer will alone, the power of the Akari. But they knew they couldn't hold it forever, so they built a machine to hold it for them. Press that button, turn it off, destroy it, the Energy reverts. If the planet itself doesn't explode from the Energy fluctuation, it gets sucked into a black hole. Do I have that right?"

"That is correct," a councilman acknowledged.

"So then if you're prepared to push the button anyway, what does it matter if it's me or you?"

"Because we would prefer not to die, as I'm sure you would agree."

Rifun shrugged. "Yes, but what does it matter to me if you kill her?" He gestured to Julianna. "Quite frankly, nothing happens one way or the other. You threaten her on the assumption that I'm going to grovel and surrender a war for the love of a woman—such love I do not hold, mind you. I'm more practical than that. So is she, if we want to be honest. You on the other hand are a little more sentimental, I think." He bent over and unlatched Tommen's bag, flipping up the flap and throwing out a few decoy medical supplies, revealing the Authored Books. "Now, I have possession of the Authored Books. All of them. Books burn very well. What would happen to the Akarin if these suddenly disappeared?

Tommen here has Books, and he's with me. Aklaq and Micaiah have Books. One's gone, the other is within range. They're gone, I take them. The Krydik, well, their defenses aren't even worth mentioning. And I have my Books tucked away, safe and sound."

"The Authored Books will always come back," another councilman said. "They always do. The Author protects her work."

"Yes, they will appear in their own time, true. But what will it do here and now?"

"It will break you," Julianna hissed, lurching against Aklaq's iron grasp.

"Shut up, bitch," Aklaq growled, pushing the knife closer against her prisoner's skin.

"As I said before," Rifun went on, "I can take those slabs and kill every Akarin here. As it is, I have more prisoners than bodies. With the council in here, I could kill all of you and not break a sweat. But that's not what I came here to do today. You claim to prefer life, and yet as you so obviously pointed out, you have control of the inverter there."

"You kill us, and the Akarin will never follow you," another councilman growled.

"Yes, there is that, which brings us back to everyone dying. Again, you are the ones preaching life while your finger is on the trigger."

They faced off for a long moment. Rifun did not look at Julianna, but he could sense her irritation. He didn't blame her, honestly. She didn't want to die, just like he hadn't wanted to die at the executioner's hand.

"How did you know I had the Books?" Tommen asked quietly.

Rifun raised a brow. "I looked while you were sleeping."

"You had this planned all along, then."

"No, not entirely. Some things I make up as I go along. If I plan too rigidly, then I have no room to account for the flurry and chaos of war."

"But everything you were saying about vague plans and bad ideas...?"

"Force and finesse, Tommen. You ought to have learned that after your case before the Hands. Perhaps you did, when you gave me this plan. A decent end goal, interesting means, just vague enough that I could modify it to my tastes." He gave a knowing look to the council, his gaze resting on Aklaq. "That's right. He's the one who conjured up this little plan."

"No, I wasn't!" Tommen blurted. "I wanted mercy! And alliance! Not this!"

"And genocide for the Borelians, but we won't go there." Rifun shrugged. "So then, one of your prospective recruits, driven away by political bullshit comes to me and offers a plan for peace, because he cares about both sides. I offer you that peace, but you turned it down, saying that maybe you ought to adopt an option for death. Well, here we are. Still offering you a peaceful surrender that one of your own former recruits came up with, and you are the ones with the big red button."

The council spent a minute or two just looking at one another, communicating through expressions and body language. Rifun could see the grudging assent ripple through the council even before they spoke.

"Name your terms," the lead councilman grumbled.

"First, you're going to release her," Rifun said. "In return, I will not burn your Books. Yet."

The council shuffled and grunted, uncertain as to his sincerity, but agreed. Aklaq hesitated for a long second, but finally put down her knife. Julianna stood up straight, smoothed her dress and her hair, and went to stand on Rifun's other side. A look passed between the women, one of pure hatred.

"Second," Rifun went on. "I want to hear every one of you, councilmen, swear your loyalty to me as your leader. If you won't do that, then there is no reason to continue further. Furthermore, if you don't do that, well, there's always the balcony."

"And what assurances do we get?" someone asked. "What do we get in return?"

"Swear your loyalty, and find out. These are terms now, not negotiations."

Again, the council glanced at one another, irritated, angry, uncertain. Rifun waited patiently. He and Julianna exchanged a look. Aklaq kept her murderous gaze fixed on the scarred woman. Tommen remained silent.

Then, reluctantly, one-by-one, the council members began to pledge their loyalty, though Rifun interrupted them.

"Do it like you mean it. I'm not convinced. And know that once we're done here, you're going to do it in public, in front of all your little followers out there. That's when it really counts, and seeing how war is messy business, I'd really like to drum up some enthusiasm, send everyone home on a hopeful note."

It was difficult to muster up any genuine enthusiasm, but they did it anyway, having to restart a second time after Rifun accused them of sarcasm. Then he turned to Aklaq.

"Your turn," he said.

She glared at him. "I'm not one of the council. They said so themselves. It doesn't matter what I say."

Rifun gave her a knowing look, but moved on, saying, "And that brings me to your little reward for your fealty. See, I'm faced with the new problem of having fewer numbers. I don't like that idea. Now, I could easily kill off enough Akarin to balance out the equation, but that's really bad for public relations. Instead, I'm going to have a census taken. Any who are injured and cannot fight will be permitted to go home, providing they do not come back unless they are prepared to swear loyalty and membership to the Cult. Depending on the number of those left, a certain number of those simply wishing to leave may be permitted to do so. I haven't quite decided how that's going to work yet, though.

"Those who are Akarin today will be allowed to remain associated with the Akarin. You may continue to self-govern your internal affairs, as I have already laid out. Any incoming members, however, will be referred to the Cult.

"And on that topic, I really don't appreciate the connotation associated with being part of a 'cult.' Again, bad public relations; people get the wrong idea. True, the historical name is the Cult of the Akari, but these days, it's not such a nice title to have. Therefore, effective immediately, we're undergoing a name change to become the First Order of the Akari."

"Does that make your members hors d'oeuvres?" Aklaq asked smartly. Tommen snickered.

"I admit your quick wit, I really do," Rifun told her.

"Why should we refer new members to you?" one councilman demanded. "We are permitted to self-govern, are we not?"

"Self-govern internal affairs. Bringing in new members is part of external affairs, which we will manage."

"And what about children?" someone else wondered. "Should a mother be forced to instruct her child contrary to her own beliefs and upbringing?"

"Children may be considered internal affairs for the time being."

"The Akarin may continue with whatever internal religious instruction and duties they are currently attending, but will also attend the training and instruction of the Order, including Akari instruction, journal studies, English studies, and combat training. We must learn to fight together."

"You do not wield the Akari," one council member growled, prompting agreement from several others.

"And I am certain you can debate that at length once the power transition is complete. Until then, as I have said multiple times, these are terms, not negotiations."

And on they went. Rifun had spent some time perfecting his spiel, and now he finally got to deliver his monologue, letting the Akarin know how things were going to be from now on. He was in charge. The Cult, ahem, First Order was in charge. This was mercy, and the Akarin should appreciate it. He would be leading the more physical and combat aspects of things, and Julianna would oversee the day-to-day affairs.

When all was said and done, it was time for the general public to be made aware of the situation. They left the power inverter room and one more time, Rifun maneuvered enormous slabs of rock into position so they could safely make their way down to the more stable staircase and continued down to the fourth floor. From there, they navigated the corridors to the southwest staircase. As they walked, Rifun spoke to various soldiers and sent some on errands, mostly just gathering everyone to the southwest stair on the main floor. Other soldiers simply fell in around the remaining Akarin forces, acting as an armed escort.

There was a bit of violence, as was to be expected. The First Order soldiers pushed and shoved and jostled the Akarin. Rifun did not stop them, though he did warn them off a few times for treating their prisoners too harshly.

While the earthquakes had been highly localized, the structural damage had spread and there was evidence of the destruction everywhere, even here. Cracks ran along the walls, the floors. A few chunks of the stairs were missing, and there were notable loose spots.

When they reached the main floor, the body of the Akarin was made to stay on the stairs, surrounded by Order soldiers on all sides. Rifun, Julianna, and the Akarin council went out to stand in the center of the atrium, with the bulk of the Order forces surrounding them, giving them about a fifty foot circle to move around in. Tommen and Aklaq got as far as the base of the stairs before they could go no further.

"As you may have surmised, the battle is won," Rifun began.

He didn't get further than that before the Order erupted in cheers and battle cries and other assorted noises. The cheering went on for a minute or two before Rifun made a move to quiet them.

"It was not an easy battle, and many of you lost good friends. Many more would have been lost had the fighting persisted. The good news is that the Akarin council has made a wise decision. They wish to spare their people further harm and bloodshed and are here to pledge their loyalty to the Order and to me as their leader. In my own mercy, I have granted them permission to self-govern their internal Akarin affairs. But make no mistake. We are one Order, we are one alliance. We will train together, study together, battle together. We will become an unstoppable force in the universe and the Order will take charge and lead, and wherever we go, new recruits will follow, because we are that mighty. We have conquered the Akarin, made them our allies. If we can do that to them, we can do anything to anyone."

One by one, the Akarin council again pledged loyalty to Rifun and the First Order. They were serious in their oaths, not sarcastic or silly, but it was clear that they were not happy about it. Did they second-guess themselves about the big red button? Were they even now plotting some treachery? He had no doubt on either point.

The last of the councilmen swore their fealty. The Order cheered loudly, though not as loudly as when the victory had been announced. Even some of the Akarin made gestures or noises of agreement. Yes, Rifun thought, looking around. This was how things were going to be. It was how they must be. One group of one loyalty, united under one ruler. Him. He had been chosen by the Author and the ancestors, a mortal capable of wielding the razana. With a little work, they would be capable of going after the Borelians and the evil dragon spirit Tujor together.

"I think some festivities may be in order," Rifun mentioned to Julianna. He glanced at the council. "But not for you. You just thank the Author you're still alive." He looked at Drinjin uh Ersik, Torbak, and Godwin. "Take the council and the high-profile prisoners below. We'll deal with them later."

Guards were summoned to escort the Akarin council to the sub-levels. Rifun walked with them to the edge of the circle and watched them go, feeling oddly self-satisfied. Once they were out of sight, he turned to go his own way. The men could celebrate without him.

Then, it was like Time slowed. Not as if from a Band or any artificial creation, but as if the Base Plane of Time itself slowed. All he saw in the moment was a white bear launching itself at him. It made contact with his shoulder, and he realized it wasn't a literal bear, but Aklaq White Bear. With one hand she grabbed his shoulder and began doing something to the Borelian battle gear he wore. With the other hand, she plunged a knife into his chest.

It was funny, he would later reflect. He didn't actually feel it at first. His mind was just trying to process the act itself and the strange object now sticking out of his chest. Had that just happened? Had that honestly, truly, really just happened? There was a knife in his chest. There was a knife...in his chest.

He tasted blood. Began choking on it. In his mouth, in his sinuses. He went to his knees, and that sudden jostle ripped open a tide of pain throughout his body. He went to his side, twitching from pain. Then it was like being hit by lightning as white spots exploded before his eyes just a second before everything went dark.

31 | Restitution
First Order Fortress, 2014

If you can't eliminate the enemies closest to you, how do you expect to do battle from far away? You expect it is easier to order others to do your bidding, that it keeps your hands clean. I assure you, this is not the case. In fact, you have the blood of all parties involved on your hands, dead or not.

Julianna sat at Rifun's bedside, knife in hand. She looked down at it, turned it over. A beautifully polished steel blade, the hilt made of exquisitely carved bone. This came directly from the whore's personal collection, maybe even crafted by her own hand.

Say one thing for Rifun and Cassius. At least they knew enough not to ask something of others that they would not do themselves. Even that whore has more courage than you do.

Aklaq White Bear had stabbed Rifun, then run away. It was nothing for her to be apprehended and dragged back. Before Julianna could cut her throat there in front of everyone, Tommen jumped in.

"Wait!"

She shouldn't have waited. She should have killed the whore anyway.

"Don't do it, Tommen," Aklaq said. "Stay out of this."

Tommen shook his head. "No. No more. No more fighting. No more bloodshed. I'm not going to see any more of my friends die."

"You would save him?"

He let out a breath. "I will not kill."

"His wounds are healed as much as they can be," one of the physicians reported, kneeling where Rifun lay in a pool of blood, still seizing wretchedly. "The poison needs to come out of his system before we can proceed, but he has no time to spare."

"What is it?!" Julianna demanded, turning on Tommen and storming over, knife leading. "What's the cure?!"

Tommen glanced past her, likely at Aklaq, swallowed nervously, and said,

"Sugar. Glucose. Dump it into his system and it will prevent the poison oils from bonding to the red blood cells which will take it to his brain and spread it through his body."

"Do it!" Julianna ordered wildly. "Now! Go! Save your Faharoa, you fools!"

The physicians and several guards sprang into action. While they scurried about looking for sugar, Julianna turned her attention back to Aklaq and Tommen, then to a couple guards. "Lock these two up. Together." She got in Tommen's face. "If he lives—" She pointed at Aklaq with the knife. "She lives. If he dies, she dies. Simple as that. Now then, you're sure the answer is glucose?"

"It's as much as I know. It's just a preliminary report, but it's promising," Tommen answered softly.

She nodded. "Good. I suppose you're not entirely worthless after all."

With a gesture to the guards, Tommen and Aklaq were taken away.

Of course, the whore got away, escaped right from her cell.

Should have killed her when you had the chance. Tommen has been broken; he would have given it up anyway. And he would have fewer contrary influences in his life.

He is still a traitor. Make an example of him and Rifun will have fewer contrary influences in his life.

She looked up from the knife back to Rifun as he started twitching and seizing again. She made no move to assist.

If you can't eliminate the enemies closest to you...

Borelian poison was immune to Time. His bare chest still had a wound in it where poisoned knife met flesh. It could not be Banded, and even Matter had to be used more creatively than normal. But there were still stitches there. There was still an open wound. Take the knife, slide it in one more time. For good measure, just a little tilt, a few centimeters lower, rip open his heart. Claim the Borelian poison finally took him. No one would be the wiser and he could die a hero. Everyone's reputation would remain in tact.

Except for his damn mercy.

If he died and she tried to cull the Akarin completely, this soon after the battle with everyone's blood still hot, they would fight back. More than likely, they would win or someone would push the button and blow everyone straight to Hell. She was not a soldier, but she was not an idiot.

He is very good at making himself indispensable, she thought, watching him calm down and go limp. A few minutes later, he weakly shifted position, whispered something unintelligible, and went back to sleep.

Once his initial wounds had been treated, he had been moved to more private quarters, the inverter room on the eighth floor of the fortress. Julianna left everything in the care of Drinjin uh Ersik, Torbak Martin, and Godwin Lore, and come to tend to Rifun. She had cleaned off the knife and had been waiting for at least three days now. How long did it take for the body to process out Borelian toxins? Even Walter Forbes seemed to have made a faster recovery, and he had marinated in the stuff for almost a week.

The door opened and a physician walked in, bearing cold water and a few rags.

"Is he well?" the physician inquired, not for the first time.

"He is better," Julianna replied, not for the first time.

The physician took away the empty dish and old rag. Julianna did not move for several seconds after it left. Even then, she moved slowly. She gently peeled back the gauze to inspect the wound. A little blood from the seizure, nothing really concerning. Unless she made it concerning.

Damn you, she thought, replacing the gauze and wetting a rag. *I can't let you die now, not while you have a chance to live and keep everything together.*

As she laid a rag over his forehead, his eyes opened. Unlike previous times, he did not have a glassy, distant look. He was sleepy and confused, two expressions of a truly conscious man.

"Inona...?" he whispered, sighing.

He struggled to sit up. Julianna grabbed an extra pillow to put behind him, then went to put the knife somewhere out of sight.

"You shouldn't be moving so soon," she told him, walking back and sitting down. "Your body hasn't recovered, and we still don't know if the poison will have any residual effects."

"What?"

He grimaced and looked down, apparently just discovering the gauze and the wound it hid. He peeled back the gauze, studying the unnatural hole in his body. And why should he? The rest of his tormented flesh should have been enough to erase the surprise of any wound.

"What is this? Why hasn't it been healed?" he demanded weakly.

"It has been healed to the best of our abilities," Julianna told him gently. "But Borelian poison is immune to Time. Your wounds had to be creatively stitched together using Matter, using the flesh that had not become infected by the poison. But they must heal in their own time."

"Who did this? Who stabbed me?"

"Micaiah's wife. Kayla."

He nodded slowly. "Yes, I knew that. Somehow. Where is she?"

"Escaped."

He let out a breath, wincing at the pain. "Which poison?"

"An unseen color called urlo. Causes seizures. You've been seizing and in and out of consciousness for several days."

"How was I cured?"

"Comes from an unlikely source. Research and results seem to indicate glucose as the cure for Borelian poison."

"Glucose? Sugar?"

"That's what we were told."

His expression said he was searching his last memories and trying to put it all together. "This kind of wound should have killed me quickly, if not the wound itself, the poison surely. You had to have gotten an answer out of her almost immediately. But if she did this, Aklaq would not have been so quick to give it up; she would have been prepared to die."

"Well, that's the thing. She wasn't the one who gave it up."

"Oh? Who, then?"

Julianna grinned. "Why, your star Apprentice. Young Tommen Forbes."

Rifun nodded and pushed the blankets back, wincing as he stood. "I want to speak with him."

She stood to meet him, effortlessly putting a hand to his chest and causing him to fall more than sit back on the makeshift bed. "Not yet you're not."

He looked down. He wore only a pair of boxers as the rest of his garments were either missing from the Tacagan attack or else discarded after being soaked in blood. "All right, fine, I need some clothes, but I still want to speak with Tommen."

"Not until we figure out exactly what we are doing with him," Julianna said forcefully. "He betrayed us to the Tacagans—"

"You don't know that for sure," Rifun interrupted.

"Maybe not, but he is still a disloyal coward, and a fool. It's not as though the Akarin hold him in any high regard, seeing how he saved your life."

"Exactly. He saved my life. As such, I am inclined to spare his."

Julianna blinked, feeling her mouth open in silent disbelief. Then, "He betrayed us! He betrayed the Cult to our enemies!"

"Our enemies already walked among us!" Rifun countered hotly, grunting and putting a hand to the gauze. "And how did they get there? Because you allowed them! You allowed an evil spirit to dictate the core and inner workings of the Cult!"

You should have killed him.

"My shortcomings don't excuse his treachery," Julianna said through gritted teeth. "If it had been anyone else—Godwin Lore, Torbak Martin, some nameless afovoany, you wouldn't hesitate to make an example of them. But because Tommen has some magical book, he gets a pass and I get a lecture." She went on before he could speak. "And if you are so sure that the Order is evil, why did you lead the charge to conquer this place? Personal revenge against the Akarin? And now that they are conquered, what is your next plan, O Great One?"

"The only plan that matters. The Borelians will come after us eventually. A target on our backs has become a target on the backs of the Akarin. They will have no choice but to fight with us. We simply need to take whatever time we have and learn to fight together." He stood once more. "As for Tommen, I'm not suggesting he be let off the hook. He will suffer punishment for cowardice. I only said I would spare his life. I did not say we couldn't beat him within an inch of it."

He made a few paces, stretching his muscles, picking at the gauze and looking at the wound several times. Julianna sighed and retrieved a small bag where she'd packed a change of clothes. She tossed it to him. "You'll forgive me, I had to guess on sizes."

She turned her back while he dressed, less for modesty and more so she could think.

Anyone else. If it were literally anyone else. But no. Tommen has a magic book. Micaiah's magic book didn't save him. Saul's magic book didn't save him. But Saul was bad and Tommen is good? Or Rifun thinks he can be made to join us? Rifun isn't even fully with us. One turncoat will not convince another.

If Rifun is a turncoat, make the example of him that you wish for Tommen.

It was tempting. It was oh, so tempting.

"Are you modest?" she inquired.

"If you've been watching over me for the last few days, I don't think modesty is a real issue," Rifun replied. "But the answer is yes."

She turned back around. Jeans and a button-up shirt, slightly more professional than a casual hooded sweatshirt. The gauze on his chest was nearly invisible. She tried to put on a good face. "Looks like I got the sizes correct, then."

"A bit long in the in-seam." At her look, he grinned and shook his head. "They're fine. Thank you."

Damn his charm. She folded her arms. "Now, about Tommen. You're not leaving this room until we've decided what to do with him. Seeing how you are unwilling, I will see to his punishment. But what about afterwards?"

"Oh, that's the easy part. We'll send him to retrieve the Book of Commands."

She blinked. "What?"

"The Book of Commands. The third journal? Less exciting than the Book of Abilities, more frustrating than the Book of Philosophy, still an important piece of the puzzle that has yet to make its way back into our possession?"

She tightened her arms. "Surprised you care about the writings of an evil spirit."

"Lies of omission are easily mended, but we still need the source material. If nothing else, simple possession will bolster our position while we figure out what Cassius got wrong."

"Yes, that's great and all, but what about the part where it's held in a Borelian temple in Ancrath? I just said Tommen isn't a soldier."

Rifun gave her a look. "But he is an excellent spy and traitor. You and I are too well-known, too obvious. And we're going to be too busy preparing for the Borelians. Send Tommen to 'find' the journal. He'll get his little Akarin friends to help him sleuth it out, or at least the key. We make a plan of attack, he gets to make a choice. He fights or he gives us the key."

"Or he hides the key for another hundred years," Julianna said distastefully.

"We're already attacking the Borelians. Our target is Ancrath; it's the only target that matters. I would have no problem pulling that whole temple down brick by brick. But it keeps him busy, makes him think he's doing something sneaky. And because it takes a Builder to open the Core of the Wheel, it might just bring a few interested parties out of hiding."

A wounded animal draws all kinds of attention. A big fish may eat a small fish, but the biggest fish of all devours them both.

"Fine," she conceded. "But he is not going to do it alone. I want some kind of guard on him."

"A guard?" Rifun shook his head. "No, a team. To help him navigate the social complexities of alien races and get him out of the tight spots he will inevitably get himself into. It will provide a safety net for him and perhaps bolster his ego if he is put in charge, it will allow us to know what is really going on when we ask them about it afterwards, and he won't be able to take any Akarin members with him."

She nodded. "All right. But I want more. Naturally, rebuilding the fortress and getting everyone to play nice is our top priority right now, but once things calm down and we can truly implement some structural changes, improving on what we had on Sadurnon, I want him to begin truly studying the journals. He may be resistant, but repetition is the most basic of indoctrination tactics."

Rifun did not disagree, but she thought his agreement was a little hesitant. Maybe she should have him go through the classes as well. She had considered getting rid of the Authored Books while he was down. Burning them or opening a portal into the void of space. Unfortunately, the peace they had going with the Akarin—whether it was a truce, armistice, ceasefire, or true peace, she could not say—was too fragile to play with that grenade just now. But, like Rifun killing the Borelians, maybe she could orchestrate his demise and make it look accidental. Not that she expected the Borelians to believe that Misik and the others all perished in the attack on the fortress, but the fact that they hadn't come calling just yet gave her some hope for a little breathing room.

"As for the attack on or from the Borelians, how much time do you think we have?" she inquired, changing the subject.

"Hard to say, I just woke up," he said, sitting back down on the bed. "I need to know what's going on here. I'm very curious to know what's been going on with the Tacagans, the meetings they've been holding, the research they're doing. If we're going against the Borelians, knowing more about their toxin research could be very helpful."

"Glucose saved your life. Isn't that enough? They attacked our city on Sadurnon."

"If we were comprised of only humans, maybe, but there are a few more species represented here." He rubbed his neck. "Some of them may not use glucose like we do, or maybe they can't tolerate it. It's something to look into. As for the attack itself, I intend to milk every second we have in order to plan. With Sadurnon and the Elif exposed, it's going to be another round of sweet-talking allies and making promises. Making more promises since we have to convince them to go against the scourge of the universe."

Julianna shifted her stance. "If you can do that, I'll hold down the fort here and keep things in line."

He nodded. *"Lavorary. Mahasoa."*

"Excuse me?"

He looked at her. "Good. Helpful. *Faire du bien.*"

"I see. Well then, seeing how you are up and around, I will retrieve Tommen for his punishment and then bring him here to speak to you."

He nodded and waved her off.

It was a maze to return to the main floor of the fortress. The northwest stair had been collapsed and teams were still digging through the rubble. Many portions of the northeast stair were also missing, some of the main corridors had seen significant blockages as a result of this, and she was forced to creatively wend her way through to the southeast stair. Cracks in the walls and ceiling made her nervous, and she found not a few loose stones, nearly twisting her ankle once. Even once she was on solid ground on the main floor, she was still a bit timid.

The portal room was the most undamaged part of the fortress, almost pristine except for some chunks missing from the entryway arch and some small cracks spidering from them. But it was still in tact and she had no trouble opening a portal to the bedroom of Tommen Forbes. It was a bit messy, as one could expect from a teenage boy, but of greater importance was that he was not present. Glancing at a clock, she saw that it was roughly four-thirty in the afternoon. Noises from elsewhere in the house suggested that someone was home at least.

A few minutes later, Tommen walked in. He looked pretty casual about it, but he froze instantly when he saw her.

"Relax, Tommen, I'm not here to kill you," she told him, trying to sound amiable, or perhaps just less hostile than when she had let him return home after Aklaq had escaped.

"Rifun is still alive, then?" he questioned.

"He is, and he has actually recovered quite well in the last few days. He wants to talk to you."

The already pale teenager went deathly white, but he made no hostile or cowardly moves. Julianna took the opportunity to open a portal, and he meekly followed her through.

Most of the rewards and punishment had already been doled out, an impromptu court being held in one of the old recreation areas. Julianna walked in confidently, leading a very anxious Tommen Forbes. Four judges sat at a table, and they looked up as the two of them approached.

"And who is this?" one of the judges inquired.

"Tommen Forbes," Berkloff, a judge, growled.

"Here for punishment for cowardice," Julianna told them, trying not to sound too enthusiastic about it.

"And treason?!" the Korin demanded, rising from his seat.

"Not here, unfortunately. Faharoa is going to see to him personally. You may, however, dole out any punishment you see fit, short of killing him."

This pleased the rhino man greatly. He was like the bucking bull held in the pen while the panel of judges formally issued the accusation, judgment, and sentence. Then, he charged.

"I've seen many vaovao in the infirmary with injuries from Berkloff," Julianna said, taking his seat at the judges' table, "but I've never known him to be quite so...boisterous. Tough, perhaps, but this does seem to be personal."

"His offspring died in battle," one of the judges explained. It gestured to Tommen. "This one was supposed to be with him. He has had nothing but vengenace on his mind since."

She nodded. "Ah. A son for a son, in perfect Korin balance."

And Rifun wasn't going to give him that balance, however much she may have implied so. Actually, she was surprised at how much restraint the rhino man showed, for any full strength blow from his horn probably could have broken every bone in Tommen's body. Not that the teenager wasn't suffering some broken bones anyway as he was tossed here and there like a ragdoll, but it wouldn't be enough to kill him.

Finally Berkloff got Tommen on the ground and held him there with his horn, staring at Tommen menacingly.

"Stay down," Berkloff commanded, backing off and returning to the panel.

Obediently, Tommen stayed down, gasping for air for a long moment. He managed to calm himself down, and Julianna watched as he likely used Matter to heal some broken ribs.

"Stand up," one of the panel members ordered.

Tommen did so, gingerly testing out all his limbs, being gentle with his right leg. He approached the panel and stood at attention as best he could, keeping his wrist close to his body.

"Tommen Forbes, your sentence for conviction of cowardice has been carried out," the head panel member told him. "This conviction and subsequent punishment will be noted on your record and can only be changed by the Faharoa or a designated agent."

"I understand, sir," Tommen replied.

"You have been able to heal yourself of most injuries. However, it is noted that some linger. Report to the infirmary for treatment. Dismissed."

"Yes, sir."

Julianna stood and led the way out of the recreation hall, Tommen following pitifully. After a trip to the infirmary to tend to the injuries he was not skilled enough to deal with himself, she took him on the long trek back up multiple flights of stairs and through a maze to reach the eighth floor. Although she tried to keep a good face, Julianna wondered if she might not try to convince Rifun to move his quarters to a more convenient location.

She stepped inside the room, noting that Tommen hesitated for just a second at the threshold.

Any hope she'd had of convincing Rifun to move to a lower floor disintegrated. She couldn't have been gone for more than an hour and he'd already turned the place into a bachelor pad. He'd moved in several dressers and other odd furniture, using them to section off room-like areas. The makeshift bed had been traded in for an actual bed, though it remained fairly utilitarian with only a bare metal frame and simple sheets. A half-whiteboard half-pinboard was already becoming cluttered with notes.

Clearly, this was where Rifun was setting up shop.

"You like it?" Rifun asked, looking around the room. Julianna wasn't sure just whom he was addressing. "I admit, it's not my best work—certainly not as great as what I accomplished in the Wheel—but it's cozy."

He began walking toward Tommen who was still only a couple steps in from the door. As he walked, Rifun began unbuttoning his shirt, a small chore considering his missing fingers. He pulled the one side open and peeled back the gauze. A single line of stitches, about an inch and a half to two inches long, just off to one side of the sternum.

"Thought you might like to see the damage," Rifun said. "Or all that remains of it. There's a similar mark on my back. I'm told I have you to thank for giving up the cure for the Borelian poison."

"Um...yeah," Tommen said. He cleared his throat. "Yes, sir."

"Please, Tommen, you don't have to be so formal." He gently replaced the gauze, smoothing the tape on all sides. "Say what's on your mind."

Tommen made a tight sound, then asked, "You're not going to rape me, are you?"

Rifun paused and looked at him, his expression completely baffled. Even Julianna blinked, surprised by the question. "Why the hell would I rape you? I wouldn't rape you. I wouldn't even hint a proposition, even if I were in a good mood right now." He shook his head, began buttoning his shirt back up, and walked away. "Believe me, Tommen, regardless if you had been the one to stab me or save me, I have no inclinations toward you. That's not how I get off." He leaned back on a dresser, elbows resting on top, facing Tommen. "Though it is a curious choice of topic. If I remember correctly, Christmas was the day you were supposed to finally get some." How or why he knew that, Julianna didn't want to know. He grinned as Tommen blushed. "That's what I thought. But why is it that you thought I was going to rape you? Between getting stabbed by your friend and you subsequently saving my life, that I would somehow seek either retribution or amusement?" He shook his head again. "No. As I said, you have nothing to worry about there."

Tommen's obvious relief was almost comical.

"Now for the real question," Rifun went on, more serious now. "Why did you do it? I know you've at least fantasized about my death, probably numerous times. Julianna gave me one explanation, but I want to hear it from you."

Tommen took a level breath. "I will not kill. Julianna was going to kill Kayla. If I wanted to save her, I had to save you."

"Please, Tommen, we all know Kayla can handle herself. Barring that, she was certainly more than willing to die in order to kill me. And you knew that. I can understand that battle can take its toll, and you certainly saw some terrible things. But only a fool believes that he can save everyone."

"Then perhaps I am a fool. Because here we are. You're alive. And Kayla's alive."

Rifun grinned. "Here we are." He shifted his stance, Banded briefly but did not appear to include anyone.

He is weak. He is nothing. He will never recover. His mind is fractured, his body now following. He must be disposed of.

"So here I am, once again, questioning your motives," He was saying. "I will give you credit. In the time that we've known each other, you've gone from being wildly predictable, to being just a touch unpredictable. I can respect that. At the same time, perhaps I myself am afflicted with a touch of survivor guilt, wondering why in the world you saved me."

He wonders. He doubts. He claims favor but then is suspicious of it. He is ungrateful. He is a traitor. He must be dealt with. If he does not want to be a survivor, he doesn't have to be.

Tommen said nothing

"He is learning," Rifun mused. He stood up straight and again approached. "Well, here's the thing. Mommy and Daddy aren't just screaming at each other anymore, they're going for the full divorce. In this case, Daddy is winning custody. And as in most cases, I have no problem with you, the child. I just can't afford to lose you to Mommy.

"To that end, you will be joining your vaovao friends on journal study nights. War is confusing, especially when you have no foundation of beliefs to either justify or rebuke it. You see me as evil; the Order sees the Akarin as misguided, if not evil. What does it all mean? I want to help you understand so that the next time Mommy and Daddy fight in front of you, you won't be the scared child in the corner, but can take a side."

"Your side, you mean," Tommen cut in. "Do I get education on Akarin beliefs as well? It would be a more well-rounded education. And if all they need is a small correction in order to come to your side and see the light, the flaws should present themselves. I am a huge skeptic after all."

"That you are. And while I appreciate the thoughtfulness of your suggestion, I don't think the Akarin would take it very well. You may have noticed, but relations are a little sour between us right now. Maybe wait a bit until things have cooled down and smoothed over, hm?"

"And make yourself the good guy," Tommen finished. "Train me, when the Akarin wouldn't. Offer peace to the Akarin and have them make the first move."

"Exactly. Make no mistake, however. I am exceedingly grateful that you chose to save my life, but I do not in any way believe that you are loyal to me. You have to prove it to me. Over and over and over again. But before you can trust me and I you, you must have an understanding of what is going on here, what we believe, why we did what we did. Otherwise, it's just a centuries-old cycle of revenge. Someone has to be right."

"How do you know it's you?"

"Clearly, the Author has shown us favor here. And if that's not enough, well, we could stand here all day and debate theology. I figure to let more learned men than me explain things. Go straight to the source material, as it were."

To which source material does he refer? He himself is a skeptic. At this point, he is bordering on treason.

Worse than treason. Heresy. Blasphemy to both sides.

It's going to get him killed.

So why should I do it? Let him dig his own grave, water the tree that will hang him.

"Do you know what they're planning, where they're going to attack?" Tommen was saying.

"Sadly, since murdering all the Borelians in our ranks, I do not. I am not privy to such information. I expect that, while it may take some time as the aftermath of this battle gets sorted out, the Borelians will hear of my treachery. Of course, like Charleston Police, I'm already at the top of their Most Wanted list. A few more bodies isn't going to make much of a difference. Except this time, I've lost all my insurance. Isthim, General Misik, all of them."

Rifun casually shifted his stance. "It's a similar situation to the one between Tacaga and Sadurnon, wouldn't you say?"

At least he's going to bring it up. I'm surprised.

Tommen swallowed. "I...did hear there was a raid."

"Did you really think you could get away with something that big? I will admit, it was very clever of you to use Tacaga—devoid of my influence—as a private conference center. I can only imagine the things you told your dad and Kayla. Oh, wait, I don't need to. Because Sadurnon is now lost to us. Seems this battle came none too soon, hm? Except I imagine you warned them about that, too. Perhaps they tried to head us off and arrived just a bit too late. I'm not entirely sure; I still have some catching up to do from the few days I was out. But rest assured, I will find out. Unless there is something you'd like to tell me now?"

Tommen took an even breath, let it out. "Honestly, I'm just tired of the fighting and the war and the threat of war. It feels like it's been a non-stop thing, ever since last year with the murders and the elections and everything else. Fine.

You won your war here. Now that it's over, I'd like to get back home to Earth and figure out a way to stop the Borelians. And if—"

"Are you done?" Rifun cut in. "Let me spell it out for you. The Akarin are defeated. The First Order won. You went out on stage and made a scene, defying Kayla and saving my life. You will never not be part of the First Order. That's a hard thing to take in, which is why I am sending you to journal studies, so you do have an understanding. To that end, I also fully expect that everything we say and do will get reported back to your dear Daddy and Kayla. So I want a little something in return. I want regular reports on their progress in defeating the Borelians, whether it be cures for their poisons, planetary defenses, everything. And because I don't trust you, you are going to report everything directly to me. It's easy to lie to Berkloff when the man hates you and you can't please him one way or the other. It's much harder to lie to the man who holds reward in one hand and punishment in the other, and who can read you like a book. And whom you saved."

"Yes, sir. If I may ask, are the Borelians the next target?"

"I only said you are reporting to me. That doesn't mean you get a promotion. I'm having a hard enough time with inter-faction politics. If I do have something else for you, I will let you know. Dismissed."

Tommen nodded, turned, and made to leave. He hadn't gotten more than two steps before Rifun called to him again and he turned.

"And just so we're clear. I am grateful that you saved my life. Never think I'm not."

"Yes, sir," was all he said. And he left.

Julianna huffed. "Well, you've certainly turned this place around."

"Wasn't difficult. Seeing how most all of my worldly possessions disappeared with the raid on Sadurnon, and seeing how this was not already conveniently set up for residency, I had to get creative."

She looked around. Mismatched furniture, odd layout. Something must have shown on her face because he added, "It doesn't need to be pretty. It just needs to work. You don't share my bed, so you don't get to criticize."

She put her hands up in mild surrender. "I wasn't saying anything."

"Good." He went to the pinboard and started copying some notes on another piece of paper. "I had a few ideas of who to put on his team. If you have any ideas of your own, feel free to add to the list."

He handed her the paper. She vaguely recognized a few of the names, but none of them stuck out to her. She also couldn't decide if the spelling of the names was true-to-form or just how his language rendered them. The only thing she could really discern was the universal coordinates, but only a few of the names had those. Interstellar geography was a little more complicated then normal geography.

He made a move as if to go somewhere else in the room when he slowed, stopped, squeezed his eyes shut, and sighed. He pinched the bridge of his nose.

"You've only just woken up from an injury that should have killed you," Julianna said, moving to stand beside him. "You've obviously been conjuring portals to move all of this furniture in here."

"It's just a headache," he said.

He'd barely gotten out the last syllable when he suddenly collapsed and started seizing.

Julianna couldn't stop a few nasty words from escaping as she scooted out of the way, then went to work on trying to move furniture. When that proved more difficult than anticipated, she used Gravity to move him out of the way instead. This was no easy feat with the way he was twitching, but she got it done.

A thought crossed her mind. If Borelian toxins were immune to Time, theoretically, they should be immune to other abilities. That was why they'd had to creatively stitch together flesh that hadn't been corrupted by the toxins. Now, maybe it was different with an Energy constant like Gravity, but what if?

She Banded. Just the two of them. It appeared to work. She pulled herself out of the Band. Rifun remained, and, as she would have expected, his seizure concluded inside the Band.

It's not a toxin anymore. This is real and natural.

She put a hand to his head, her fingers touching the bald indentation, the only exterior indication that he'd suffered a traumatic brain injury. Taking a breath, unsure what she would find, she Felt him.

With the seizure now concluded, brain activity was minimal, but she was able to discern that the greatest residual effects were in the area near his wound site. These effects lessened until his whole brain was, in effect, sleeping. Then activity started to increase and she could feel his consciousness start to reassert itself.

She retreated from his brain just as he was blinking awake, eyes rolling back in place, dilating and constricting, trying to acclimate to the light. She helped him to sit up, but he quickly rolled over onto one elbow. His other hand went to his forehead and he again squeezed his eyes shut.

"Inona no nitranga?" he mumbled. He sighed, tried to open his eyes, blinked several times, settled for an uncomfortable squint. *"Ai-je été touché à la tête?"* (What happened? Was I hit in the head?) He glanced at her, apparently used her as some kind of focus point as he gradually opened his eyes and got back to normal.

"You had a seizure," she said, unsure if he would even understand her.

She could see he was working through her words, matching them to concepts in his other languages. Then it clicked. "A seizure? The Borelian toxins should be out of my system by now."

"I don't think it is the toxins," she told him. "I Banded you. I Banded your seizure."

"What?"

"I think...I think it might be an honest side effect. Your old brain injury reacted to the toxins and this is a...natural feedback loop so-to-speak, even though the toxins are gone. Like the body manufacturing pain to get drugs."

He blinked again. "What?"

She couldn't decide whether his questions were from disbelief or truly not understanding such complex concepts at the moment. Gradually he got to his feet, but only inasmuch as he headed to his bed to sit down. She went to stand before him. His expression turned to disbelief as he stared at a spot on the floor.

"No. It has to be some residual toxin. Somewhere."

"Rifun, we know how fast Borelian toxins work. We know how potent just the gases can be. If you still had toxin in you, in the last hour, you should be well on your way to dead by now."

He looked up. "What if it's the glucose? What if it's just a temporary slow-down of the toxin?"

"It's not impossible, but once again, with how fast the toxin works..." She shrugged. "Maybe it is residual in some way. You've had several seizures in the last twenty-four hours. Maybe it is natural, but it's just an overreaction to the toxins. Like a racehorse, they don't just stop. Maybe they'll go away in time."

He rubbed his face and looked away. "By the ancestors, I hope so."

She shifted her stance and backed up a couple steps. "You looked like you had some sort of indication of it. An aura, I believe it's called?"

He nodded carefully. "A bit of a headache at first, a little pressure." He made a sort of five-finger flicking gesture with his left hand in front of his face. "Then it was like a sudden flash of light and white spots, almost the same as when the damn pickax hit me." He put his hand to the injury site. "The only pain I felt at first was my eyes, but nothing in my head. Then...nothing. Just...black. Then I realized I was unconscious, I was extremely tired, I had a wicked headache, and I was on the ground. It took a second to bring everything back into focus and see. I was a little nauseous when I first tried to move—still a little nauseous, honestly—but...I don't know." He looked up at her. "Are you sure it was a seizure?"

She raised a brow. "Believe me. I'm sure. One illness may be mistaken for another, but seizures are fairly recognizable, even for an amateur such as myself."

He lowered his hand. "In fairness, seizures are a symptom, not an illness, but your point is taken."

"Even so, we don't know what's going on for sure. If you want to hide up here and rest for a few minutes, I'll see what I can find for medication. Whether they go away or not, you can't risk looking weak in front of your men or the Akarin."

He sighed and lifted his legs into bed. "That I can agree with."

She managed a smile as she headed to the door and left the room. Interestingly enough, she caught up to Tommen around the fifth floor. He was taking his own sweet time leaving the fortress, but hurried his step when he saw her.

"Rifun will contact you when he is ready for you," Julianna told him as they stepped off the stair onto the main floor. "It may be for physical labor in reconstruction, journal studies, or because he wants a report. The aftermath of battle is always messy and timelines are nebulous, so you may have to be patient."

"Well, I'm not exactly in a hurry," Tommen said. "If possible, I'd really kind of like to spend this Christmas vacation not worrying about me dying, my dad dying, or anybody else dying."

"I'll be sure to let the Borelians know."

She opened a portal for him back to his bedroom, then opened one for herself to London. She did not immediately call a sympathetic Time Agent or Akari-bearer doctor or pharmacist for advice, instead choosing to take a walk around town for a bit.

If these seizures are natural and permanent, it is a huge liability. He can't afford to be seen as weak. The Order can't afford for him to be weak.

A ruler who cannot even control his body has no business trying to control others. If he were staunchly loyal, his mind might still be useful, but he is already a traitor. These developments will not change that. It may only worsen them, even if they are temporary.

Julianna sighed to herself. *The weak only get weaker. Iron has not been sharpened, it has been broken, cracked when plunged into battle and shattered when removed. It's time to clean house and start over.*

And yet, he did survive Borelian poison and what should have been a fatal injury in itself. He is still a hero of the Order. He cannot simply be removed.

It has been too long since his injury for it to be passed off as such, and likely he will make his grand re-entry soon. At this point, it would look like assassination. Within, without, it wouldn't matter.

He will have to be disgraced.

Public seizure.

Not enough. The reception to such a thing is too variable, and trying to plan for it too difficult, especially if they can be Banded. He must be exposed as a traitor. An incompetent traitor. And any loyal followers with him, like the mercenary.

Julianna crossed a busy street, still flowing with the masses.

The war with the Borelians, she decided. *He's going to attack Ancrath for the journal, but there is no way this is going to go well. Even if we do get the journal back, it's still full war on the Borelians.*

If he is hyperfocused on such a battle, and you are taking care of daily affairs, the rumor mill can be a vicious thing. Even the Akarin may be swayed.

Hyperfocused on a battle he can't win, costing thousands of lives — this after being so foolishly raided on Sadurnon and losing the ambony — covering up a medical condition that is obviously a punishment from the Author because of his unbelief.

Fits like a glove, doesn't it? And memories are as malleable with hatred as with Borelian toxin. There is plenty of hatred to go around right now.

She nodded to herself. For the moment, she would treat Rifun's seizures as being temporary and let the seizures themselves prove her wrong. If they were permanent, then she could figure out what to do about them, how to exploit them.

She called up a doctor she knew to be sympathetic to the Order. Strictly speaking, he was willing to treat anyone from any faction. He didn't ask questions, didn't take sides, just did his job.

It was just past noon in London, which made it early morning in the United States. After a few rings, a Southern American voice answered, "Dr. Haunstein speaking."

"Good morning, Doctor," Julianna greeted. "I'll give you three guesses who's calling, and the first two don't count."

He sighed. "Julianna."

"Henry."

"If you're not on my doorstep, I'm guessing you're at the hospital?"

"Actually, I'm in London."

"Oh, so this is a real emergency."

"I have a question for you, and I expect utmost discretion."

"When am I not discreet?"

"How would one go about treating seizures?"

"Seizures? Are we talking something like epilepsy or a drug reaction?"

"I think you would classify it as epilepsy. Seizures stemming from a head injury."

"Is this Rifun we're talking about?"

"It could be."

He sighed again. "The last time he was here, he had a documented seizure reaction to the medication he was given after the surgery for his hand. Again I ask, is this from a reaction to drugs or—?"

"He was recently exposed to Borelian toxins, specifically the one called urlo. It causes seizures. The problem is that the seizures have not stopped. I'm concerned that it did something to his brain where his old head wound is. A feedback loop of sorts."

Haunstein hummed a moment. "Not impossible, but it is rare for post-injury stimulation to cause such a thing, especially this many years later. Although, with the way the man scrapes by, it's a wonder he doesn't gamble professionally."

"Indeed. What do we do about it? We're not sure it's a permanent thing—too few survivors of Borelian toxin to say for sure—but it does need some management."

"Oh, of course. Is there anything else going on, by chance?"

"The toxin got into his body by way of a knife in his chest. Severed his pulmonary artery, just a few centimeters from ripping open his heart."

The doctor cursed. "All right. Anything else?"

"That's all."

He sighed. "All right. Here's what I'll do. I'll have a script for lorazepam waiting for you at a pharmacy." He gave her the address. "It'll be a seven-day supply. I imagine by then anything residual should be worked out and he'll know if they're permanent. I'll also do some research on my end, see if I can't find some...unorthodox treatments he might try."

"Thank you, doctor."

"Be warned, though. The pharmacist is a Time Agent, but less sympathetic than I am. He'll do his job correctly, but he may not be as discreet."

"I understand. Thank you."

"Script will be ready in about an hour."

He hung up without ceremony. Julianna put the phone away and made a nonchalant exit into an alley so she could open a portal and depart.

The pharmacy the doctor had mentioned was in Tennessee, about a hundred miles from the hospital where he worked. Julianna did not know the pharmacist, and if Haunstein hadn't said he was a Time Agent, she never would have guessed.

A couple of elderly patrons got their prescriptions and left. Julianna stepped up to the counter.

"Can I help you, ma'am?" the pharmacist inquired, his expression wavering as he tried to be friendly in spite of her appearance. His nametag read Jared D.

"Picking up a script from Dr. Haunstein," she informed him.

Now his expression turned knowing. He went to a printer and ripped off a small blue slip. "I see."

"Will you do it?"

His back still to her, he said, "Of course I will. But I'm not required to like it."

She waved a hand. "No, never. Of course not. Who would?" She glanced around the pharmacy to make sure they were alone. "And it's not like you're in a position where you could potentially switch medication, turn healing into poison."

He turned back around and studied her for a long moment. "You are Julianna Brown, right? You founded the Cult."

She put up a finger. "The First Order now. But let us consider that Calis Cutthroat first murdered my husband and came after me. He hijacked the Cult first. And now Rifun. I've only just been rescued from the in-between dimension. I am now in a position to return the Order to what my husband envisioned it to be."

He raised a brow. "Poison is a woman's weapon. What did you have in mind?" He looked at the slip. "Lorazepam. For seizures?"

"We're not sure if they're temporary or permanent. Haunstein is going to be looking into a few things."

The pharmacist shrugged. "I can swap them right now."

She shook her head. "No. There is too much instability in the Order, too unpredictable. Besides, he isn't the only one who needs to go. His supporters do, too. Which means spectacle. You don't have to worry about that part. But if these seizures are permanent, as I suspect they are, then you and I may have to work a little alchemical magic."

"I'm listening"

"We'll see if they're permanent first. And we'll see what Haunstein comes up with in his unorthodox research. Then we can talk about medication swaps."

He nodded. "Sounds like a plan. But I want my name left out of this."

She put her hands up. "I will say nothing. Your involvement is your own business."

He studied her again for a long moment. Finally he nodded. "I'll get this filled for you."

Interruption

First Order Fortress, 2014

He stared at the small pill for a good fifteen seconds before dropping it down his throat and chasing it with water.

Three days of the little pill. Two days without a seizure. Two days and he still couldn't come up with any way to see if they really were permanent.

They couldn't be. It just couldn't happen to him. Was it the dragon? The Author? Why? What did it all mean? It wasn't...fair.

They could be. Julianna had confirmed that she had Banded him during a seizure. That wouldn't be possible if it were the Borelian toxins causing this, and he hadn't consumed any unnatural sugars in the last few days. An apple, a small glass of orange juice, nothing so concentrated and potent as would be required for holding off the toxins.

They couldn't be. He might have believed it if they were accompanied by spiritual visions, some guidance from the ancestors, a touch of the razana. But there was nothing. Only bright lights, then darkness, then confusion accompanied by nausea and fatigue as he climbed back to consciousness.

They could be. Because he had no reason to think they weren't at this point.

But what did he do with them? He couldn't hide away in his tower indefinitely. He had a war to plan. But how could he run into battle again, knowing that he could drop at any moment and for the stupidest reason? Could he really trust these little pills to keep them at bay? How did he really know they weren't the cause, such as his reaction after the surgery for his hand?

He didn't know anything about seizures or epilepsy, and he'd been putting off any research. In an odd sort of way, he was a little afraid. If he did research on it, as it personally pertained to him, it might make it real. And yet, the universe never really cared what its inhabitants thought was real; it would continue to do whatever it wanted to, individual opinions be damned.

But maybe, just maybe, there was a way to reverse it. If the Borelian toxin urlo could cause the seizures, triggering something in the damaged part of his brain, maybe the engineer that had been smuggled into Tacaga to do research could come up with something that could undo the damage, un-trigger the seizures. Glucose could stop the toxin, but was there a way to fully reverse the damage?

The only way to know would be to attend one of the many secret meetings that humans had been holding on Tacaga. The only way to attend would be to impersonate one of the governors. He had grown fond of Toros. Might as well keep up that charade.

He donned his Toros Disguise, which unfortunately had to include the clothing seeing how the actual clothing he'd taken from the man's closet had probably been destroyed in the raid.

Would they have recognized the clothes as belonging to Toros? He imagined they would have been identified as Tacagan at the very least, but since the Tacagans did not believe in magic or religion—and regarded the Akari as both— they wouldn't understand the concept of Disguises, right? He didn't exactly have a whole wardrobe full of Tacagan clothes, so what would they make of it?

Only one way to find out.

Rifun headed to the emergency exit area but paused before he actually conjured a portal to Tacaga. What if the pill didn't work? What if he had a seizure and blew his cover? He would be completely vulnerable, and there was likely to be more than one person there who would love to kill him. He couldn't hide here in his tower forever, but was he taking too big of a risk too soon?

He didn't have a choice. The Borelians weren't going to wait for him to be comfortable, and if this engineer had discovered some way to reverse the effects of Borelian toxins, sooner was better than later to do so. Besides, Win was waiting for him.

He went to Tacaga.

Well, Win wasn't exactly waiting for him, but Rifun had sent him on a short mission specifically to keep the real Toros away from the meeting so Rifun could go instead. With his Disguise well in place and heart hammering in fear, he headed to the governmental building where he quickly met up with Milay, another governor. Unlike Toros who had pale white skin, her skin was jet black.

"The rest of them have already arrived," she sighed. "The sooner we get down there, the sooner we can have this meeting—"

"And the sooner they can leave," Rifun-as-Toros finished. "My thoughts exactly. Let's go."

He let her lead the way to an elevator that took them to a sub-floor. Although everything here was outdated by Tacagan standards, they were still well-advanced compared to what Earth had to offer. Down the hall and to the right, a room that might have housed an entire lecture hall was now used for roughly two dozen people from various human worlds.

The Krydik, from Hlohi, displaced Native Americans as outlined in *The Lone Wolf*. The Xalani and Etlawa, from Ehani, African and South American tribes simply thrown together and told to play nice. The Dorigisi, from Dorigis, Vikings and Polynesians and other sea-faring peoples. The Aleisi, from Aleis, pilgrims, Puritans, and Amish, eeking out a simple, God-honoring lifestyle. The Sakarians, from Sakaria II, dwarfs and giants and others with physical deformities that might have gotten them killed as heretics or monsters or devils. The Vin Lay, from Vin Lay, Orientals seeking escape from Genghis Khan, Pol Pot, and other tyrants. Earthlings, from the home world Earth. And now the Tacagans.

To Rifun's dismay, Aklaq was part of the Krydik delegation, or else she had simply invited herself to the party. She would be able to see right through his Disguise. That part didn't bother him. In fact, it amused him to spite her just by living. Stabbed in the chest with a poisoned blade, and here he was. But what if she found out about the seizures?

At the front of the room, an Asian man was working with some piece of technology that displayed some kind of presentation on the wall. When he finally got it to work, he called for quiet.

"Thank you for coming to this meeting. I apologize for not being entirely prepared. I have been busy and lost track of time. My name is Do Chien. I am from Earth. I was born in a small country called Vietnam where I studied chemical engineering as it relates to the human body and medicine. I then moved to a country called China where I continued my work.

"As you may know, several months ago, I was approached by a Timekeeper who proposed the idea of researching the Borelian poisons. I agreed. This research soon turned dangerous. Because Tacaga is a safe and technologically-advanced world, I was smuggled here and allowed to continue my research in this lab, which I have done with, I believe, much success.

"First I am going to address what is probably on everyone's mind: How does the Borelian poison work, how much time do we have once we've been touched, and is there any true cure? Even better, is there any way we can protect ourselves?"

What followed was a fairly lengthy and incredibly detailed lecture on cellular biology. But, while educational, it didn't tell Rifun anything he didn't already know, at least as it related to the toxins. Yes, they were all considered deadly. Yes, they affected different parts of the brain and body. Yes, glucose seemed to be the answer, at least for humans. But that was where it all seemed to end. No one knew how the Borelians seemed to be able to control them. No one knew what long term effects ther may be. Was there no hope of reversal? Was he really stuck with this condition?

The engineer paused his lecture as Aklaq put up a questioning hand. "What about the quick turnaround time? Walt was on his deathbed, but up and walking around by the end of the day after being given sugar, barring the actual, physical injuries. What about the tissue damage?"

The short answer was that the doctor didn't know, and Rifun found his hopes of reversal growing slimmer by the second. The oils just weren't powerful enough to last so long. They either killed or they died. Considering how long the Borelian heads had lain out by the time Aklaq poisoned her knife, even that oil probably hadn't been especially potent. Delivering it directly into his bloodstream had done a number, but this long after, especially with treatment...

"Is there any way to test this theory?" Milay interrupted, startling Rifun-as-Toros. "Can't you infect some of the Borelian oils with the hasax oil?"

Do Chien frowned and folded his arms. "Now we're getting into a gray area. See, in spite of all the climate control available in the lab, the Borelian oil, without the ability to spread and multiply, degrades very quickly. Nitrogen neutralizes it the quickest, but it will break down regardless. I estimate that since the acquisition of the first sample, it is only at about nine percent potency right now, which makes testing on it very difficult to do."

"Do you need more samples?" someone asked.

"How would we get them?" another person shot back.

"What would make it the easiest on you?" Aklaq inquired of the doctor.

"Obviously, the easiest way to test it would be if it were fresh," Do Chien sighed. "The problem is, the Borelians are currently sitting quiet and merely sending out cryptic messages. I fear that once they decide to mobilize, the time for testing and theories will be long gone."

"What about capturing one of them?" one of the Ehani delegates proposed.

"How would that be done?" one of the Xalani sneered. "Are you going to capture it?"

There followed some arguing over the feasibility of capturing a Borelian to study.

"My studies on the oils have cleared this stage of research," the engineer interrupted. "The next logical step is a live test. Walter Forbes from Earth has already survived two Borelian attacks, which has provided a solid foundation for the study of the oils on a living human. All that remains is to study the oils as they are, fresh from the body. I understand that this is less than ideal, and perhaps you would wish to turn your attention to your defenses, but if you want more work on the oils, I need a live subject."

Had Walter suffered any residual, lasting side effects? Narcolepsy? Asthma? Persistent gout? Dry mouth? Something, anything else? Tommen hadn't said anything. If Walter had suffered any lasting effects, Tommen would have no doubt tried to beat Rifun over the head with it. Was this truly all on him, because of his stupid head wound?

The Vin Lay were the ones to finally call an end to the gathering, citing things they had to do at home, both in terms of regular chores and passing on the information. The others reluctantly agreed, and they began filing out of the room.

Milay stood quickly, eager to leave the company of the barbarians. Rifun-as-Toros followed, hoping his expression did not betray his dismay and mild panic. Halfway to the elevator, there came a familiar voice.

"Toros, if I may have a word?"

The Tacagans paused and looked at Walter Forbes walking quickly toward them. Rifun-as-Toros looked at Milay. "Go on ahead. I'll deal with him." She left, and he turned his attention back to Walter. "Yes?"

"Mostly, I just want to thank you for opening up your lab here for our engineer, and sending the teams to install the defenses on each planet. It's a kind gesture, and it's nice to know that we can all set aside our differences for a common goal of not being exterminated or sent off to Borelian slavery." Walter held out his right hand as if for a handshake. He knew. Likely thanks to Aklaq.

Rifun did not give himself up right away. Instead he sighed in the Tacagan way and said, "You are...welcome. I trust our deal still stands." He looked at the hand and raised a brow. "Do you expect something from me?"

"Oh, no. My apologies. It's a local custom. A handshake, an expression of gratitude or brotherhood."

"I see."

Walter went for meek embarrassment. "I realize that you see me as inferior, and I'm probably carrying any number of foreign germs, but humor me for its own sake."

For a long moment, Rifun considered ignoring the gesture. But he needed to know, somehow, if Walter had suffered any long-lasting effects. He held out his left hand.

"The other hand," Walter corrected gently.

Rifun-as-Toros gave him a look and switched hands, reaching gingerly for him as if reaching for a dirty sock. He had almost no return grip as Walter clamped down hard. Walter put his left hand over Rifun's hand, then gave a small compression at the base of his thumb, over the index and middle fingers. The fingers were solid at a brief touch, but when he applied pressure, they vanished.

Rifun Banded himself as he took the opportunity to Feel Walter. With luck, Walter wouldn't notice that he was poking around. Brain, heart, lungs, kidneys, liver, skin, muscle, bone, anything and everything. Rifun did not know Walter well enough to say what his normal baseline was, but he found nothing out of the ordinary. But then, would anyone find anything unusual about him, Rifun, if he was not actively seizing? He didn't know.

He dropped the Band, heaved a sigh, and looked Walter in the eye as he threw up a new Band around the two of them. "You figured me out."

"Lucky Kayla is still around," Walter replied smugly.

"Lucky indeed." Rifun shed his Disguise. "Not so lucky for me. First she stabs me in the chest, now she gives away my Disguise. She's a real nuisance, you know."

"Why are you here? To lay a trap to kill her?"

"Had the opportunity arisen, I will not say I wouldn't have taken it. The same way you would no doubt take the chance to kill me for attempting to kill you. Every man sees his own cause as noble."

"What cause are you advancing here by parading around as a Tacagan Governor?"

"The cause of information. I was dead, but now I live again, isn't that how it's supposed to work? Your son brought me back to life, and I'm grateful. But I want to know the what and how and why. The Borelians are coming for my people, too, and I want to keep them safe."

"So safe you led them into war against the Akarin."

"The Akarin chose their fate. I offered them peace, and they wanted none of it."

"And now you're on a humanitarian mission to rid the universe of evil."

"The thought had crossed my mind."

"No doubt in those last few moments before the darkness closed in around you. But now you're back. Why are you here?"

"As I said. Information."

"And what's to keep me from killing you right here?"

"The fact that you couldn't if you tried."

"Kayla almost killed you."

"I admit, she got the jump on me. And yet, here I am. Thanks to your son." Rifun went on before Walter could speak. "Now then, we could spend all day here, threatening each other, making demands, asking questions and beating around the bush. But I think that would get very old very fast for both of us. So let's cut to the chase. I'm here for information. Same as you. From past experience, you ought to know well that I'm not just going to stand here and monologue my evil schemes. I'm not even really in a mood to kill anyone right now. And seeing how my Disguise has been discovered, I think anything else may have to wait."

With that, he donned his Toros Disguise and dropped the Band. He resumed his air of Tacagan superiority. "You are...welcome. I suppose."

Then he turned and left, striding down the corridor to meet up with Milay.

"What did it want?" she sneered.

"Oh, some form of flattery and bestial display of gratitude," he said, waving a hand. They got on the elevator and started up. "I think once we get back upstairs, I will have to take the time to wash myself of his filthy influence."

"Understood. I may have to do the same, and I was only in proximity to them."

They reached their floor and left in different directions. As soon as he was alone, Rifun returned to his chambers in the fortress.

That hadn't been so bad. He'd used a Disguise, gone to a hostile environment, listened to a rather lengthy science lecture, and held minor conversations, all without blowing his cover to the Tacagans or having a seizure. Whether it was because of the pill or because the seizures really were temporary, he did not know. Either way, he had done it. Maybe the universe wasn't ending after all. Maybe things really would be all right.

He still had trouble focusing his attention on plans to attack the Borelians. Their only real option was Ancrath, but that didn't mean it would be easy. And still his thoughts always came back around to, What if?

He looked up from his work as the door opened and Julianna walked in, papers in hand.

"I took a trip to Tacaga," he told her before she could speak.

"Oh? And what did Toros reveal to us today?" she wondered, approaching.

He gave her a summary of the discussion. "In short, you may be right. They may indeed be permanent. Because of my fucking head wound." He lightly hit his fist on the table and turned away.

"But if your head wound were to be healed...?"

"People with otherwise normal brains and no injuries still have epilepsy."

She frowned. "I'm sorry. I don't know what to say."

He sighed. "How about you say what you came up here to say?" He made an indication. "What are those papers?"

"Yes. I figured we should get started on sending Tommen on his little errand —" Her tone suggested she still didn't like the idea and would rather execute him for treason instead. "—and I made up a list of people and places he might like to investigate, who may have had some interaction with the Book of Commands."

Rifun took the papers and looked at the lists. "Give him the dots, let him connect them. Men will believe something they have discovered more readily than something they are told."

And what have I discovered lately?

"Precisely," Julianna beamed.

He nodded and returned the papers. "Of course. I suppose that means I should retrieve him as soon as possible."

"You don't look enthusiastic."

"There are a few people I can think of who would love to see me in a vulnerable state. I don't think Tommen is one of them, but he knows those who are."

"You go get him. I'll meet you down in the portal room when you get back. Seeing how your seizures can be Banded, I will hide them as best I can."

Covering up a vulnerability, one that couldn't be cured. *Damn it.*

The stairs just outside his chambers had been fixed so they were more stably connected to the rest of the staircase. The fifth floor was still missing, but otherwise the three stairs that were still standing were safely usable, and Rifun had no trouble reaching the ground floor. He noted how every look he garnered, every greeting thrown his way, were all tinged with awe. Even the Akarin, who hated his guts, were amazed by his ability to recover from Borelian poison. But had he really? Sure, he was alive, but was this any way to live? Armies tended to have standards when it came to recruitment. Back in the day, he had almost been rejected because of his believed age. Now, it didn't matter how young he said he was; his seizures would disqualify him every day of the week.

He kept his gaze fixed firmly ahead, hoping his posture spoke of a determined mission that should not be interrupted. He reached the portal room with no trouble and opened a portal to Tommen's bedroom. The teenager was not in presently, but it was the middle of the night and Rifun heard noises in the bathroom. Rifun helped himself to Tommen's bed, sitting back and relaxing, hoping to not give anything away.

A moment later, Tommen appeared, his demeanor saying he was ready for bed. When he saw Rifun, he froze, unsure what to do. When he opened his mouth to speak, however, his phone rang. He gave Rifun a smirk and answered the call.

"Hi, Dad," he said loudly, pointedly. There was some murmuring on the other end. Then, "Just fine. About ready to head off to bed." Pause. "What did you find?"

The kid's smirk quickly disappeared. "Actually...he is kind of standing right here."

A few seconds passed, then Tommen handed the phone out to Rifun. Curious, he took it.

"Walter, how are you?" Rifun wondered, trying to stay upbeat. "It's been, what, a few months, hasn't it? At least?"

"I don't know what you're planning tonight, but if something happens to my son—"

"Yes, yes, I understand all 'if you ever's and 'when I catch you's and all the threats that go with them," Rifun interrupted, sighing dramatically. "Please, save us both some time and get to the chase. You didn't want to talk to me just to threaten me."

"I'll threaten you as much as I please. But you're right. That's not why I'm calling."

"I'm all ears."

"Tommen told me you were saying something about going after the Borelians. How true is that?"

"As true as the fact that they are coming after us. Timelines have yet to be worked out, however, though with how quiet they have become and New Year's upon us, well, as they say, something's got to give. Why do you ask? You may not have heard, but there are unfortunately no Borelians left in my army; I do not have knowledge of their dealings."

"Doesn't matter. War is war, slavery is slavery, no matter which way you slice it. But I have an idea to put us on the offensive, maybe stun the Borelians into not attacking on New Year's, though it could also fully ignite this war or a full invasion."

"And you're coming to me for help."

"Quite frankly, you're the only one either dumb enough or brilliant enough to pull it off. Seeing how I don't think you'd pass up a chance to attack the Borelians and show off your limitless talents and brilliance—"

"All right, what's the plan?" Flattery annoyed him on a good day, now it just felt like needling.

"The Borelians can't sow their own soil; Brelix is too unstable. Ninety-nine percent of their food is grown off-world. We may not beat them technologically, maybe not even in hand-to-hand combat. But we can hit them where it hurts. In their stomachs. Torch their fields, they have no food, they can't fight.

"I'm going to make some calls and get some people ready. I want to have a meeting tomorrow morning on Tacaga. Normally I wouldn't, but as much as it could send the Borelians scrambling, it could also be the catalyst for an invasion as they seek to take our food. Obviously, we're not the only human world, and the impact goes beyond our borders; I want the others to know."

"And you want me there?"

Walter let out a huffy breath. "I do. You're a genocidal maniac, but a brilliant one with an army. More to the point, your army consists of non-humans. If non-humans torch the fields, it could confuse the Borelians and stem the impending invasion."

Rifun was silent for a long moment. Finally, "Walter, if I didn't know you and Tommen were family, I would say that the odds of both you and your adopted son being so brilliant and conniving are astronomical. But we both know better. Yes, I'll be there. Even if the whole thing turns out to be a trap for me, it sounds exciting at the very least."

"Two missing fingers and half a heart don't seem to have slowed you down any."

"Very true, but then, what was that phrase you loved to parrot? Only injured, not helpless. Now then, if you will excuse me, your son and I have a few things to do tonight."

He hung up, then handed the phone back to Tommen.

"What was that all about?" Tommen asked.

"Your dad will tell you about it in due time, I expect," Rifun said, opening a portal back to the fortress. "Most likely tomorrow morning once he gets home. Given the task he's laid out, I am suddenly inclined to make this a very brief trip tonight."

As Rifun stepped through the portal, he noted a sudden wave of vertigo overcome him. He stayed upright, and he hoped it was just from overexerting himself. Not that portals were difficult, but—

"Julianna said your pulmonary artery had been severed," Tommen began cautiously. "How long does that take to heal?"

"Longer than a week and a half," Rifun countered irritably.

Even a teenager could see he wasn't well. Damn it, he had to get a hold of this. If he couldn't go about his normal day, he wasn't going to be running into battle.

He had just spotted Julianna walking into the room when his head suddenly pressurized and his vision exploded in white spots.

Fucking hell.

When he came to, he noted several things. First, he came around a lot quicker than he had before, and didn't feel quite as bad. Was that because this seizure wasn't as bad, or was he simply becoming accustomed to the feelings and repercussions? Second, he noted that he was in a Band and everything around him was stopped. That was it. This wasn't Borelian toxin. This was real. This was permanent. This was just a part of his life now. But he had to get a hold of things. Why didn't that little pill work? Were Borelian seizures somehow immune to normal pharmaceuticals, too?

Grudgingly, he gave himself a once-over and got to his feet.

"Are you all right?" Julianna asked.

"What do you think?" he snapped back.

She blinked, then dropped the Band.

"Are we going?" he demanded of Tommen, though the teenager hadn't really moved except to turn and look at him.

"You're still having seizures," Tommen stated. "Julianna has to cover them up because otherwise you'll look weak in front of your men, and the Akarin. You can't risk mutiny or an overthrow. But Borelian poison is fixed in Base Time and you've been cured of that, which means these are naturally-occurring, maybe a side effect of the poison that could stay with you."

"And you're a perceptive little brat with a big mouth," Julianna hissed, moving to stand close to Rifun.

Damn it. Damn it damn it damn it.

He was done. Tommen was going to tell his dad, probably the remaining Durvin twin, and Aklaq was going to hear about it. And she would lie in wait like a predatory cat, anxious for him to drop. On the other hand, if a dumb teenager could figure it out, it was only a matter of time before everyone knew.

Dear Author, why have you done this to me?

Rifun Banded, just himself and Julianna.

"When we're done with him, send Drinjin uh Ersik and Torbak Martin my way," he told her. "I have something for them."

She nodded but did not say anything. He dropped the Band.

They only went to the third floor, to one of the meeting rooms. Julianna entered last, closing the door behind them.

"All right, to answer the question that is no doubt on your mind, we're here to discuss your performance during the battle last week," Rifun began. He leaned back against a table. "Quite frankly, it was even worse than pitiful. You are absolutely useless. Medic, soldier, doesn't matter, you are useless to us in a fight."

He could see both uncertainty and relief in the teenager. He wouldn't be called on as a soldier anymore, but what else did they have in store for him?

"Instead, we—Julianna and myself—came up with a mission for you, something that blends what you need with what you want. Think of it as gaining valuable work experience before ever applying for the job you want most in the Time industry. And we both know it's not Timekeeping."

Tommen gave him a look. "Scouting?"

"Exactly. Not to worry, though. You won't be going alone, but with an experienced group of people. They'll get you through the local customs, politics, all that. At least, to an extent. There is no telling where this could lead. You may very well reach worlds untouched."

"Where am I going? What am I doing?"

"Your mission," Rifun continued, "is to find Richard's third journal. Julianna can give you the details as to when she last had possession of it and what happened, and there are several rumors you may wish to investigate as well regarding its location."

"Richard's third journal?" Tommen echoed.

Julianna nodded. "The Book of Philosophy opened everyone's eyes and minds to the existence of the Author and the greater universe; it kept the Cult alive for over a hundred years. The Book of Abilities strengthened the loyal followers and gave them the power they needed to overtake the Akarin.

"The Book of Commands is what's missing. It details the more day-to-day affairs of conducting business internally and externally, especially in dealing with the Akarin. I have quite a bit of it memorized, but just as the Akarin draw strength from the Authored Books, so the Order will be strengthened by having all the journals together. It will also provide a more solid, reasonable basis for our claims, far more than just hearsay and rumor. If we conduct business with the Akarin according to the details set out in the Book of Commands, then we will be without fault according to our own rules."

"Why send me to find it? If I'm going with a group, then it's not like I'm your only hope."

"You're not," Rifun told him bluntly. "Quite honestly, I'm trying to find a job for you where you aren't rendered useless and menial. I'm trying to give you a career, not a day job at a bakery, as it were. If you think you want to be a Scout, or something like it, this will be an excellent test to see if you have what it takes. You are the spearhead of the search; you are responsible for gathering information and following leads. You just also happen to have a safety net at your back for social niceties, political dealings, and the ever-possible threat of violence. This time around, you are the hero. You have a sidekick, or a posse. You call the shots. You are the one chasing the priceless artifact.

"Furthermore, if you pull this off, you will have standing among your peers. Human, hero, globetrotter extraordinaire. You may even become more of a celebrity than me. It will also serve as a solid foundation for future assignments as you learn to navigate the tricky details of cross-cultural niceties. In the process, you will learn many essential skills for the Scouting lifestyle. More than just politics and religion, we're talking about picking up languages, wilderness survival on a strange planet, and general ethnology, reading others without making a scene.

"You're right; you are not our only hope. You're not even our best hope. But we want to give you a chance to prove yourself, to make an investment, both for us and you. You don't want to be a soldier, and I don't want to throw you in the kitchens. We're giving you a lot of leeway and extending a lot of trust to give you this opportunity."

He could feel Julianna's eyes on him. Rifun wanted to give him a chance. Rifun was making the investment. Rifun was giving him a lot of leeway.

Come on, Tommen, don't fail me again. I can't protect you from what I've created.

"I can see the wheels turning," Rifun goaded. "He wants to do it. But he's uncertain. What if the others in the group don't listen to him? Is this some kind of test? What if I fail? A cowardly soldier, a useless medic, and a worthless treasure hunter. How can I show my face after three strikes?"

"I'll do it," Tommen cut in.

"Excellent." Rifun straightened. "Well then, I have many other things I need to do today. Julianna will give you the rundown on how to begin tracking the journal."

"Wait, I have to do this now?"

"Quite frankly, I would hope not. There are a few things you need to learn before you just go gallivanting off across the universe. Surely your experience with Sifura taught you that much. Normally, I'd say you got lucky, but seeing how this is all unfolding makes me think the Author had this planned all along."

Julianna gave Rifun a look as she escorted Tommen out of the room. A minute later, Drinjin uh Ersik and Torbak Martin entered.

"Faharoa," each acknowledged.

"Gentlemen, we have a plan, but it must be carried out swiftly." Rifun filled them in on the idea to burn a Borelian farming world. "I want as many teams as possible, but I want no two members of a team to be of the same species. We have to confuse the Borelians and deal damage, but we don't want anything coming back on anyone if we can help it."

"Of course," Drinjin uh Ersik said. "When do you plan to launch the attack?"

Rifun quickly did the calculations. It was less than twenty-four hours until Earth started turning into New Year's Eve, but Walter still wanted to hold a meeting about it in a few hours. Well, it wasn't as though the two generals here would be able to put together that many teams in ten minutes. Finally he decided, "Twelve hours. That will give you time to round up the teams and hand out assignments."

"And which world are we targeting?" Torbak inquired.

"Rindik, in the Othmin system. Lush farming utopia worked by the slaves the Borelians trust the most. More slaves, fewer guards, less resistance." The only reason he knew that was because of Isthim. Borelian pillow talk was a little less romantic than human pillow talk; they didn't believe in sweet nothings.

"Of course. Are there any special orders or missions?"

"This is a mission of destruction. Burn it, tear it down, whatever it takes to decimate the food on that world. Crops, wild plants, if it grows, it goes."

"Understood, sir," Drinjin uh Ersik said, sounding rather eager.

"Anything of use, pillage it. Weapons, armor, medicine, we're going to need it for ourselves. I will leave the specifics in your capable hands. Meanwhile, I have a meeting to attend."

He left the room and headed to his chambers, conflicted. How much did he want to risk? He'd taken a pill but had a seizure anyway. Did the pill not work? Had he somehow overexerted himself and the stress caused it to happen? What were the rules here? Did he really want to risk a second meeting on Tacaga? Should he send Godwin instead this time?

No, he couldn't do that. He couldn't hide. But he couldn't let himself be exposed either.

Damn it all, but this was just so...inconvenient!

His fears were in no way assuaged when he showed up to Walter's meeting and most of those in attendance expressed some desire to inflict great bodily harm on him. If stress was a factor in his seizures, well, this was not helping. True, he didn't have the stress of holding a Disguise, but how did he know how much stress was too much? And what other factors might he need to consider? Diet? Sleep schedule? Lighting? How many different pills was he going to have to try? What if none of them worked? Would this biochemical engineer know any way to help? Could he come up with something new? Maybe the Tacagans knew something, if he could get into the correct computer.

Aklaq was at the meeting again, and she made no mention of his seizures, though her hatred for him was unquestionable in her demeanor and attitude. When he attempted to leave the meeting after explaining the idea, she stormed after him. She caught up to him at the elevator, striking him in the back where the tip of her dagger had punched through. When he staggered, however briefly, she grabbed his arm to turn him, then struck the knife wound in his chest to get him to stumble back against the wall.

"As much as I like aggressive women, you're really not my type," he told her, trying to shrug off some of the fear that flared through him.

"You murdered one husband," she hissed. "I will not have you slander the name of another."

He nodded once. "Of course. That was an unfair blow, and I apologize. However, I can honestly tell you that I did not kill Micaiah."

She glared at him. "I don't believe you."

"You don't have to believe me, it's the truth."

"Someday, I will make sure you pay for what you've done." She pushed on his chest wound again, harder this time, and stepped back. Instead of getting on the elevator, she returned to the meeting room, standing outside the door.

Rifun initially got on the elevator and went up to the main floor. He was halfway to the train when he reconsidered and returned to the sub-floor. When the doors opened, Walter and Tommen stood there. Cautiously, they got on and hit the button.

"So," Rifun began, "here we are. The question is, why are we here, really? Do you honestly believe you need my help?"

"If I didn't think so, I never would have asked," Walter told him sternly.

"I see. But you would still like to see me dead, whether by your hand or someone else's, you don't care."

"You deserve it."

"Well then, here I am."

Walter shook his head. "I'm not an idiot. I learn from my mistakes. You'd lay me out flat without breaking a sweat. Even Kayla proved that you have to be taken by surprise."

"Then why continue to hold a grudge if you can't act on it?"

"Do I really need to remind you of your crimes?"

"Seeing how you seem to enjoy recounting them every time we meet..."

"Then why do I need to remind you again? How do you not understand why some people might be a little irritated with you?"

He did understand. He understood very well. The problem was that he was just one man, one soldier working with incomplete information. They needed to retrieve the Book of Commands, then get to work on removing the dragon's taint from it. Only then would people start to understand, once the fog of the Shadows had been lifted. But that didn't mean the current work was unimportant. Incomplete information did not preclude the possibility of very real enemies in the vicinity.

"Then I guess I'll just call off my men from torching the Borelian corn fields," he decided casually. "Granted, one act in itself will not cause the downfall of their civilization, but if it works, humans are going to be jumping on this idea, and others. And just think, you would have been the mastermind behind it all, if and when the Borelians start dying—from starvation, from battle, doesn't matter. And then what, hm? I never actually killed anyone in the Wheel during my reign. I may have given the order, but I never touched anyone. This all goes down with the Borelians, what separates me from you, hm? Is it because of our preconceived notion of evil, that the Borelians are a blight that must be wiped from the universe? They see us the same way. We're enemies; it's what happens. Same with the Order and the Akarin. History is written by the victor, and the Author is one who decides the victor.

"Dust and logs, Walter. Given the state of things, I might be a little irritated with you." Rifun lifted his right hand for emphasis even as he released the Band he'd erected around the elevator car. "But I've decided to forgive and put it behind me for the sake of this little endeavor we've got going on." The elevator stopped at its destination and the doors opened. Rifun stepped out first. "Now if you'll excuse me, I have some corn fields to burn."

He got off the elevator but didn't even bother with the show of getting on the train and leaving the city before opening a portal directly to the eighth floor emergency exit and leaving. Again, when he went through the portal, he knew a wave of nausea. He made it to his bed, but the nausea was as far as it got. There was no vomiting and no seizure.

He had to get this under control yesterday. He had tried praying at the small shrine he'd set up. He had tried pharmaceuticals. Neither seemed to be working, and cutting back on stress was not in the cards right now.

He figured he must have slept at some point, because the next thing he knew, someone was entering the room. Rifun leapt out of bed, ready for anything, but it was only Drinjin uh Ersik, Torbak, and Godwin.

"What is it?" Rifun asked, unable to come up with anything else.

"The mission was a resounding success, sir," Drinjin uh Ersik reported. "The entire planet is burning, millions of acres of crops and other foodstuffs turned to ash."

"Lovely. Now make sure we have a plan of attack and defense if they do somehow track it back to us."

"Of course, sir."

Drinjin uh Ersik and Torbak departed, but Godwin remained.

"Something you needed?" Rifun wondered, relaxing a little and working on making himself a little more presentable.

"A question, sir. More of an observation," the mercenary began, sounding hesitant as he shifted his stance. "You don't seem to be...yourself. Since you woke up. I can understand some disorientation, but this...is unusually extended."

Rifun glanced at the closed door, then erected a Sound barrier. "Have others noticed?"

"I don't think so, sir. The only reason I noticed, I believe, is because I am expected to, as your decoy, your bodyguard. But seeing how I have never found someone wearing a Disguise of you, I can only assume that it is you every time."

"For the sake of the universe, I hope I don't have any more doppelgangers running around," Rifun said mildly, leaning on a dresser.

"I agree, sir. Makes it very difficult for mercenary work."

He said nothing more, but his expression was asking. Rifun frowned and stared at his hands clasped together in front of him. "You know I was hit with Borelian poison."

"Everyone does, sir. Glad to see you've made a recovery."

Rifun shook his head and looked at Win. "Except I haven't. The toxin was urlo. It causes seizures. Those seizures haven't gone away. The toxin is gone, but they haven't. I fear..." He looked down. "I fear they are a permanent fixture of my life now."

Win shifted his stance. "Has such a thing been documented? These long-term effects?"

"The prevailing theory is that the toxin seizures reacted with an existing head injury. The toxins are gone, but now that part of my brain is stuck in a kind of feedback loop. And there are too few survivors of Borelian poison to draw any long-term conclusions."

Win frowned. "I'm sorry to hear that, sir."

"So if I seem a bit distracted or not myself, well, I'm trying to figure out ways to protect myself. Medications are not working as I might have hoped, and any gods or ancestors out there seem to be just as deaf."

"Sounds like you need a decoy, sir."

Rifun smiled joylessly. "I just might."

"Your biggest threat is going to be the Akarin," Win stated. "I can deal with them while you plan our assault on the Borelians and go to any meetings on Tacaga."

"Ha! That's an even more dangerous prospect, I think. If I drop here, it might be construed as an attack by the Akarin, the Order may come to my aid. I drop on Tacaga, I don't have such loyal allies. And Aklaq White Bear is out for my blood."

"Would...you prefer that I go to the meetings on Tacaga?"

Rifun hesitated for a long moment. Then, "No. Stay here and keep a strong face in front of the Order and the Akarin. If it does get out—through the Tacagans or Tommen or Aklaq or someone else—then maybe it will be dismissed as the foolish ramblings of a rival."

"Good thought, sir."

Now Rifun straightened. "Well, seeing how this little campfire idea worked, I suppose I should round up the peons and collect what little thanks I can, and decide what to do next."

"Agreed, sir. And if I may, I've been following Walter around for a bit. Curiosity, mostly, seeing how modern police work is compared to what I knew."

"And how is it?"

"A bit pathetic, honestly. His partner tonight is worthless, but he himself handled a bar fight all by himself."

"I'll keep it in mind. Thank you, Win."

The mercenary nodded once and took his leave. Rifun dropped the Sound barrier and watched him go. Then he looked at the emergency exit. Then at the dresser drawer where he kept the little pills. The last of the little pills. Did he take one now? How long had it been? Wasn't Haunstein supposed to come up with something by now?

Reluctantly, he took the last little pill, then opened a portal.

On what he perceived to be the suggestion from Win, he headed to Earth to track down Walter. It wasn't hard to get his attention, just cause a little mischief in his area. A prowler around a widow's home, oh no. Pretty soon, Walter was out in the dark, looking for some intruder. Rifun kept himself hidden for a bit, getting some amusement out of the futile search. Then, just when Walter was ready to call it off, Rifun sneaked up behind him.

"Boo."

Walter whirled around, drew his gun, and aimed. He was half a second from firing before Rifun sliced through his Band and clamped down on his right wrist. His grip faltered just enough that Rifun was able to use his other hand to break the grip on his gun and snake around his left arm. Then Walter did something a little unexpected; instead of trying to pull away from the grip, he put his full weight behind a sudden shove. Rather than stumble back, however, Rifun went low, releasing his left arm and instead twisting around to grapple at his old right thigh injury. When Walter's leg reflexively jerked, Rifun went in for the takedown, crumpling his knees and getting him on his back.

With Walter subdued, Rifun released his wrist and moved off several feet, chuckling.

"You son of a bitch," Walter hissed, getting to his knees, finding his gun, and reholstering as he stood. "Did you enjoy that?"

"I have to admit, I did," Rifun said, still grinning. "I have to make sure you're still alert. After all, New Year's Eve is a pretty hectic night for you, isn't it? I saw your bar brawl earlier, and I will say that I was thoroughly impressed. I hope you get a commendation for that."

Walter brushed sticks and leaves from his uniform. "Why are you here? Is this another trap?"

"Not a trap that I know of, certainly not one set by me. Now, whether or not I was Mrs. White's potential prowler is another matter."

"If you wanted to talk, you could have just called."

"Yes, but I had to get you alone somehow."

"Great. Here I am. What do you want? Did your plan work?"

"Your plan, you mean. And yes, it worked. Seeing how my men were only ordered to start the fires and not to put them out, I imagine that most of them are still burning. It makes California look like a matchstick."

"Good." Walter nodded.

Rifun put a hand to his ear. "Do I hear a...?"

Walter sighed. "Thank you."

Rifun bowed. "You are most welcome." He straightened. "Now then, I'm sure we'll all want to get back together for group therapy sometime soon to discuss what happened. We can also discuss the matter of my payment. Obviously, I am not speaking of monetary compensation, but favors and the like."

"Your payment," Walter interrupted, "is your secrecy."

Rifun raised a brow. "I'm sorry, I don't understand."

"Tommen told me about your seizures."

Now he folded his arms and shifted his stance. "What about them?"

"If you have to cover them up, it's because they're naturally-occurring, outside of whatever may have been done to you by the Borelian poison which was cured. You cover them up so as not to look weak, but also to minimize your vulnerability. If you dropped right now, you would have no defense if I decided to kill you. You don't like being helpless. How many people out there in the universe want to see you dead? Word gets out about your seizures and that vulnerability, and you'll have assassins practically at your doorstep, just waiting for you to go down. Not to mention what your men might think about you, their fearless leader, shaking uncontrollably, pissing himself on the floor."

Walter continued before Rifun could interrupt. "Payment for your services is keeping that secret. Only Tommen and I know—aside from Julianna and whomever else you've told, that's beyond us. We're willing to keep it that way. If you make a move against either of us or try to pull anything clever, well, Kayla might get a second shot at her revenge."

"And what's to keep me from killing both of you?" Rifun countered, internally panicking. "Men kill for information all the time. I have no real need for either of you. Neither of you is essential to anything I'm doing. You're not particularly useful anywhere else. You are special only to each other."

"Because you may be a cold-blooded killer, but you don't do anything senselessly. Kayla and a lot of others know that. You kill us, they'll go digging, looking for the reason why. It's only a matter of time before they figure it out, too. As it is, it may be only a matter of time before your little secret gets out anyway, just the luck of the draw when they decide to hit. But it won't come from me or Tommen."

Rifun grinned. It was all he could do. He could see all of his hard work disintegrating before his eyes, his chances and ability to defeat the dragon turning to dust. "Now you're negotiating. And what is it you expect from this little bargain?"

"A little cooperation would be nice."

"Cooperation? This does sound interesting. Please, explain."

"You seem pretty eager to go after the Borelians, maybe as a human, maybe as the Cult leader, whatever it is, you're in. You may or may not have heard, but there are rumors in the Wheel that you're gunning for the Zero Hour again, having taken out your greatest opponent."

Rifun nodded slowly. "Ah...I see...and you want me to make some special announcement or other spectacle that lets everyone know that I'm not, that I'm going after the Borelians solely. In fact, you want me to make a big deal about perhaps allying myself with the Hands, a joint venture as it were. Just as your son proposed, a three-way alliance between the Order, the Akarin, and the Hands, all joining noble forces and defeating the scourge of the universe, like a bad novel and worse movie."

He shifted his stance, trying to keep the anxiety out of his voice. "Now, as to the matter of my seizures, certainly the secret to end all secrets. I will make an effort to get the word out that the First Order is going after the Borelians. Anyone asks, we have a mutual interest alliance, the Order and the humans, brought together because I am both. I won't claim that you are my allies in the same way that Sadurnon was, we just happen to be working toward the same goal. Similarly, you will not seek to conquer or otherwise overthrow me and the Order. You're not going to storm my castle or sell the fortress schematics to the rebel alliance. If you do, well, Earth will see an invasion; it just won't be the Borelians.

"Furthermore, I expect you to not only guard my secret, but defend it. If Julianna were unavailable, such as right now, I would expect that you or your son would shield me if something happened."

"And about not going after the Wheel or the Zero Hour?" Walter asked, folding his arms.

"Let me put it this way, Walter. I've already conquered the Wheel once. I've conquered the Akarin. If I defeat the Borelians, what is the Time industry really going to do about it, even if they do discover my secret? I put the First Order in that position of power with that track record and no further enemies — or no credible threats is what I should say — they will fight to hang onto that power, regardless of whether I'm alive or dead. I am merely the cornerstone of that empire, the Founding Father if you will. I get them where they need to be, and they take it from there."

But was he even going to make it that far? It wasn't even two weeks and his vulnerability was becoming public knowledge.

"Well," Walter said at last, "it's like you said. I imagine we'll need to have a debriefing to discuss what happened and how to proceed. Perhaps in the next day or two, try to analyze how the Borelians are going to react. Once they've put out the fires."

"I'm glad we see things eye to eye," Rifun said. "Now if you'll excuse me, I have a few more things to take care of this evening."

He got out of there as fast as he could. The only thought in his head was, *I'm a dead man.*

33 | Machination

First Order Fortress, 2015

It had to be the tarka root tea that finally wrangled Rifun's seizures under control, because it certainly wasn't the Dexedrin.

Haunstein had recommended the tarka root. Native to Dorigis, it was a depressant similar to cannabis, though without the THC of marijuana. Not quite a dedicated anticonvulsant like lorazepam, but a reasonable natural alternative. Haunstein had rolled his eyes over the phone on the last bit and muttered something about primitive superstitions around pharmaceuticals.

It was Jared the pharmacist who swapped the lorazepam for Dexedrin. It was a low-dose version. Julianna didn't need to kill Rifun right away, but if she could introduce the amphetamine into his system a little bit at a time, she trusted that his body would do the rest in good time. Too much too soon, and it was assassination. A slow buildup, and he just wasn't that smart about his medications.

Obviously neither Julianna nor the pharmacist told him it was an amphetamine. Rather, it was generic midazolam. Easier for the pharmacist to fudge or lie on his records because it was so much cheaper. Same medicine, they assured Rifun, just not owned by a greedy, fascist, Western corporation.

And so, all she had to do was wait.

"And you are prepared to take over military operations should something happen to Rifun before we attack the Borelians?" she inquired of Drinjin uh Ersik. They met in one of the meeting rooms, Torbak also attending.

"I am," Drinjin uh Ersik confirmed. "Though I still question why we are being so...lenient. Cautious, perhaps, is a better word. Traitors should be dealt with swiftly and severely, not left to slowly rot and snuff out like a candle at the end of its wick."

"He's too popular," she explained. "And seeing how he just won us this fortress, it would be difficult to make such assertions of treason. Showing mercy to the Akarin, his fascination and even reverence for the Authored Books, maybe he's changed sides. A foolish attack on the Borelians on their home world where none can survive long without suffering horrendous, permanent injuries—"

"To obtain the Book of Commands, yes?" Torbak asked.

"That's not a publicly known operation at this time. All anyone out there will be aware of is that they are attacking the Borelians on their home field. I'm no battlefield strategist, but it seems to me that such an act flies in the face of every reasonable strategy out there. And even if the journal operation were known, why do we need to attack Ancrath to get it?"

She continued before either general could speak. "Rifun's...condition...makes him unfit for battle. It is a sad thing, but true. A horrible fate I would not wish on any strong man. Were he more loyal, he might still be a teacher, in the journals, in basic combat. He is very smart, believe it or not. And for a long time, I had hoped that his spiritual endeavors would strengthen and solidify his faith in the Akari and the Author and the First Order. Instead, it seems to have done the opposite. But I think we all know that he will not be dismissed quietly."

"Assuming he does survive until the battle, shall we do as he did to Misik, try to make it look like a casualty of war?" Drinjin uh Ersik asked.

"It may be for the best, but I will leave it to your discretion, whether you wish to eliminate him or bring him back for trial. I would personally favor the trial as it will bring out any traitorous followers as well who may seek to defend him."

"Am I correct to assume that we should spend the time in between swaying those followers away from him regardless?" Torbak ventured.

"Naturally, and that is where I have incredible leeway. I am in charge of the domestic affairs, including the restructuring of our ranks. Not everyone is fit for battle, but some may find fulfillment as scholarly types. It is no difficult feat to manipulate the educational system, and the more diverse the crowd and whatever core values they bring from their home worlds, the better. Instruct them in the ways of the Akari and the journals, and make subtle points about Rifun not following those ways, his desire to change the journals, his belief that they are evil and corrupt. Revolutions are rarely planned from the bottom, but that is where they are carried out."

"Would that not only open us up to attack from within? From the Akarin?"

"I expect so, which only serves to bolster our position. If Rifun can't keep the Akarin under control, then it was a terrible idea to let them live, never mind live and work and study alongside us. But even if this does happen, the Borelian threat should always be the foremost thought, the greatest threat, the closest goal."

She could see Drinjin uh Ersik was not impressed. "Something you want to say, sir?"

"I support you, Madame Brown, but I must admit some confusion."

"Oh?"

"Are you here to direct this coup operation, or turn it over to us to handle?" He indicated himself and Torbak.

Julianna blinked and gave him a hard regard. "I had assumed this was something of a mutual interest."

He made something of a frustrated, apologetic gesture. "How much planning are you planning on doing? Right now, you have given only a goal and a general outline of what you wish to accomplish. Do you have specific plans, backup plans, contingencies, insights, advantages, weaknesses? What milestones must be reached in this plan and by when? When we leave this room, what is our first step in accomplishing this goal? What if we are unable to?"

She nodded. "A fair question. Let me say first that anything related specifically to battle or fighting, I leave to you. As I have said, I will plan and lead the domestic affairs."

"The two are intertwined for the time being."

"They are, yes." She paced a few steps. "Reconstruction efforts are a necessary priority, but progress is being made. Some scholarly classes have begun, others are a bit late in their commencement. I will take care of the education system. I have already put loyal instructors in place to sow the seeds of doubt. Strength and loyalty concerning the Order and the journals, doubt over Rifun.

"As for you, for the moment, simply start grumbling. Small things. Where has Faharoa been? Why is he locking himself away in his chambers—?"

"But he hasn't been," Torbak interrupted, confused.

"He did for a while, and things are so chaotic that most people don't see him anyway. We only need to plant the seed. Give the people an idea that Rifun is not around and this is what they will think about when they go about their business. Where is he? Why isn't he here? Add in some grumbles about the Akarin. Why are they here? Why were they allowed to live? Why have some been permitted to return home? Always question, always doubt. And if you two are wondering, the underlings will notice. Why don't the highest generals know these things?"

"We may also find sympathetic idiots among the Akarin," Drinjin uh Ersik mused. "Those who are too confused by their own beliefs to hold any steadfast loyalty one way or the other, and those who are willing to cause a little trouble."

"Now you're thinking."

"We can't incite anything too soon," Torbak said thoughtfully. "Immediately after the battle, that would be understood. But that time has passed. Now the Akarin are waiting for us to become lulled into a routine. Work with any who are confused, get a deeper feel for the Akarin grumbling, and twist that to our advantage in its own time."

"We will need a pre-picked force to deal with it," Drinjin uh Ersik decided, "those who will say and do just the right things to maximize the doubt, wondering if Faharoa really can bring us together or keep us safe."

Torbak shifted his stance. "There is one matter we should also consider. What do we do about Godwin Lore?"

Drinjin uh Ersik evidently did not think this an important matter as he waved it off. "Mercenaries can be bought."

"Only if we have more to offer," Julianna told him. "Threatening him won't mean anything. At best, he'll just walk away. At worst, he'll tell Rifun and start working against us."

"Being close to Rifun, though, he may be more susceptible to the doubt," Torbak offered. "Or he may be able to persuade Rifun to step down."

"Being repentant does not excuse the crime. Stealing money from your mother's purse, perhaps. Leading thousands of men to their deaths, abandoning them in their hour of physical and spiritual need..." She shook her head. "Far too egregious to let stand. As for Mr. Lore being susceptible to doubt, that may be an avenue to pursue. He will notice any...changes within Rifun as soon or sooner than we will. See if and how he reacts to the initial grumbling and questioning. That will tell us where his loyalties lie."

As the conversation continued, Julianna quickly decided she really didn't like planning, not to this degree. She liked establishing the goal and working toward it. Markers and milestones and contingency plans, that she just wasn't cut out for. Not like this.

The attitudes that got you where you are, are the attitudes that need adjusting. You will stay and you will plan and you will learn. Or this all goes away in another spectacularly massive fire of failure.

Isn't that what delegation is for?

Delegating to whom? Cassius? Isthim? Rifun? All failures. Some of them more catastrophic than others. If you want something done right...

I can't run into battle.

Maybe not, but you can direct its goals. Retrieve the journal, be rid of Rifun. And after that?

Then I rule the Order.

Then what? Don't be Cassius. He was the Zero Hour and did nothing with it. Because he had no real goals, no ambition. Keep your eyes forward. There is always more.

We're already in a war with the Borelians. But if I'm criticizing Rifun for a foolhardy attack, we can't do something similar so soon. The Time industry, then. Secure the hub of the universe, attack the Borelians wherever they are.

Too low. Aim higher. What went wrong last time?

The Akarin. They will need to be dealt with. Not subjugated, not imprisoned. Executed. Every last one of them executed. All of them here, and especially all of them who have Authored Books.

Now you're talking. Keep your eyes forward, always look ahead. What will get you closer to the goal? Just don't trip over your own two feet.

Drinjin uh Ersik was very meticulous about having or gathering information for planning, but Julianna was able to excuse herself from the discussion eventually. She headed up to the eighth floor where Rifun was organizing some notes, an enormous sheet of paper featuring a hand-drawn map of a city. The only reason she knew this was from the label in corner reading "Anakrat" in letters that were less than elegant.

"Honestly, Rifun, if we're trying to teach everyone the language of the journals, you could at least use it yourself," she told him mildly, making a mental note to bring it up later to her instructors. "And why the middle 'a'?"

"English is not my first language, nor my second. I may be considered well-versed, even fluent according to some, but when it comes to things like war and battle and my life, I want no confusion or mistakes on my part," he replied, not looking at her. "As for the middle 'a,' there is a middle 'a' because that is where a middle 'a' must be. Does it matter that much?"

"If I recall, English has the largest lexicon of any language in the world, allowing for stunning nuance. You may try to employ such nuance in order to separate your ideas and plans."

Now he looked up. "Did you come all the way up here just to insult me?"

She waved a hand and managed a small smile. "Of course not." He returned his attention to the map and she slowly got closer to the table. Holding down one corner of the map was a thermos, the logo on the side too faded to tell who it was supposed to be advertising. She mildly indicated the thermos. "Is that your tea?"

"It was. Right now it's my paperweight."

She picked up the thermos. The corner of the map curled over slowly, then reached a breakpoint where the whole sheet began to roll up until it hit Rifun's outstretched hands. He gave her a look.

"Apologies," she said meekly. "Shall I make you some more tea while I'm here?"

He sighed. "Might as well. Then maybe you will see fit to inform me why you came here at all."

"I just came to check on you. My goodness, you find some relief for...how many days in a row now?"

"Five."

"Five days and suddenly you act like everything can just go back to normal. It's too soon to tell."

It was nothing to use a micro-portal to take fresh spring water from Earth and fill the thermos. A quick manipulation of Thermodynamics heated the water while Julianna prepared the tarka root, shaving off a bit of the root and stuffing it in a tea infuser ball which she dropped into the now almost-boiling water.

"It's not too soon to work," Rifun was saying, his back still to her. "You know about it, Godwin knows about it, anyone who is likely to make the trek up here to see me knows about it. Even Tommen and Walter know about it. At this point, does anyone not know?"

"Your underlings. Your enemies. The former may be forgiven for coming across the knowledge, but the latter should never find out."

Rifun sighed again. "True enough, but I still have work to do. I will take all the time I am given to plan the assault on Ancrath."

She set the steaming thermos on the table. He looked at it, hesitated, picked it up, hesitated again, took a drink, grimaced to the point where she thought he was going to spit out the drink, then swallowed and allowed the thermos to resume its position as a paperweight.

"Haunstein hates me," he growled, clearing his throat several times. "It may work, but in the most foul-tasting way possible."

"His personality does leave much to be desired," Julianna acknowledged, "but at least he is willing to help." She leaned on the table. "So, what's going on here? What's happening on Tacaga?"

"Tacaga. Earth. Dorigis. Aleis. Hlohi. All of the human worlds have been infected with a disease. As far as Earth is concerned, New Year's may have been about infection rather than invasion."

"Weed out the weak before they're auctioned off."

"Exactly. Plans have been somewhat stalled because of it."

"You think it's retaliation for burning their crop fields? Now they're turning our attention inward?"

"Not impossible, but unlikely. The coordination required is too great, would take too long, even for them. Actually, they may have infected the worlds before but we're only just now seeing the effects due to the exponential spread."

She frowned. "Hm. Not a comforting thought."

"So burning the crop fields would be our retaliation against them. But, it doesn't matter now. Our own progress has slowed to a crawl."

"Is there no way to help it along? Does Tacaga have the technology to find a cure?"

"Of course they do. Strictly speaking, we have the cure that they could replicate. Burning the crop world wasn't just about the crops, but salvaging anything that might be useful. Medicine was part of it. Problem is, no one seems to want our help." He shrugged. "More for us."

Once the Borelians are dealt with, the Tacagans will need to taste justice as well. Murder by negligence and pride.

"So what do we have so far?" she inquired, looking over the map. She couldn't read the writing; they could be generic place labels or specific location names.

Rifun's expression turned unreadable. "We?"

She met his look. "Yes. We. The First Order." *He insults you.* "Honestly, Rifun, is it a big secret for you?" She went on before he could answer. "Fine, so maybe I don't have much to offer, but speaking your plans out loud to someone could help."

He considered this for a moment, then nodded. "Well, Tommen recently got back from Turit. They've agreed to stick with us. They raised their price, but..." He didn't look overly thrilled, Julianna thought. "For the moment, I'm thinking they will do best in the Borelian shipyards. Commandeer the ships, give us air support, or air defense if the Borelians bring down their orbiting vessels."

She nodded. "A good precaution."

"Our primary goal should be the journal, but we can't let the Borelians know that. The complex where their holy pyramids stand is a wide open battlefield, but the pyramids themselves are too easily defensible for them. If we can draw their attention to the city itself and their primary structures — the governmental building, their intelligence archives, things like that — then we can send in a special team to retrieve the journal."

"Again, why not just retrieve the journal in a small operation? Why the battle?"

"Because we are at war," Rifun said sternly, straightening and looking at her. "You and I are at war with them on two fronts. And they have almost every advantage. We could tiptoe around the Borelians, taking this or that, but it amounts to nothing. They don't care about the journal. With this key situation and the vault in the temple, they probably wouldn't even notice it missing."

"So why the grand spectacle? How is anyone even going to survive long enough on Brelix to attack Ancrath?"

Rifun reached for something and produced a translator, as from the Wheel. "Generates a small atmospheric shell beneficial to the user. It won't stop the toxic air completely, but it will buy more time. Our attack will also have to come in waves so we can get people out before they suffer such permanent damage. As for the why, Ancrath is home to their leaders, their generals, their heroes. We may not take the city, but if we can cut down their top brass in their own town, it would hold the same significance as burning the Authored Books in front of the Akarin."

But the Akarin are still alive. As is most of their council. The Authored Books still exist; they were not burned. And Rifun himself has suffered permanent damage from the Borelians. He is going to send men to die for no significant gain.

"I trust you are also discussing this with your generals?" she ventured.

He nodded, still staring at the map. "I am. And I trust them to do their jobs of organizing the men as they believe best, then bring those determinations to me so we can weave this plan together. And hopefully execute it a little better than we did here."

Julianna folded her arms. "On Sadurnon, we only had one traitor. Here, we have plenty more. How are you going to stop the Akarin from sending you into a black hole?"

"By sending them first to attack the governmental building." He pointed to the spot on the map. "Their odds are as good as ours. The enemy of my enemy, and the Borelians do not feel the same way."

"Well, we know they're too cowardly to push the big red button, so it's unlikely they'll mess with a portal. If they must die, might as well take a few Borelians with them."

"My thoughts exactly." He looked at her. "I want you to gather any of your people, the scholarly types, and if they are able-bodied, get them back into combat training."

"They're scholars for a reason, Rifun," she told him. "They fulfilled their contract, so-to-speak. They're civilians now."

"And that would be just fine if it were any other foe on any other battlefield. We need numbers."

Broken promises to his men. A way of life, a new beginning. Life as each man sees fit under the words of the Author and the journals. He forgot to mention continuous military service, whether or not you have other hobbies or desires. At least he's only limiting it to able-bodied members. For now.

"I will tell them about it, but I will only tell them to inquire with military leaders. I will not be the one to take blame for this order."

"No, of course not," he murmured.

She could tell he was deliberately ignoring her look as she said, "Drink your tea."

Still not looking at her, and not moving except his arm, he grabbed the thermos and took a sip. Then his facade broke as he reflexively contorted, as if trying to outmaneuver the taste.

"Damn it," he hissed, replacing the thermos. He looked at her, his expression almost accusatory. "You're British, can't you do anything about the taste?"

She shrugged. "I suppose I might be able to come up with something. What is the flavor?"

He gave her a look. "Try it, find out."

She made no move to touch the drink. "Honey is typically the first tea additive people try. You might also try fruit juice. Licorice is popular. Being from Madagascar, you may have better access to fresh, natural vanilla." She ignored his glower. "Or certain flowers may work to alter the taste to your liking. Mint, lemon or orange, cinnamon, ginger, nuts, cocoa, the possibilities are endless. Some people add milk, although I personally find this rather odd and disgusting."

He made a kind of grunting sound, though its meaning was lost on her.

She huffed. "Well then, I suppose I will leave you to your work. Shall I send up Drinjin uh Ersik and Torbak? Or Mr. Lore if I find him?"

He shook his head. "No, not yet. There is a meeting coming up on Tacaga. I want to get a feel for how things stand there."

"You really expect the other human worlds to fight for us? I know the show you put on for the weak patrons of the Time industry, but you actually believe it?"

"I don't expect they'll fight for us so much as with us. Tacaga is the only human world capable of truly standing up to the Borelians. They're installing planetary defenses on all human worlds. Once those defenses go up, Time portals will not be able to go in or out of those planets. This may be the only chance humans get to really strike at the Borelians."

And he would sacrifice them, too, in this absurd plan of his.

"I see. Well, I will leave you to it."

He said nothing as she departed, making her way back down the stairs, avoiding construction work as much as possible. The first two levels were almost completed with exception of the northern staircases. Some of the recreation areas on the first floor, those not set aside for combat training, had been converted into classrooms for the time being, and most classes were in session.

Julianna floated from one class to another. She made a sign to let the instructor know she wanted to speak afterwards, but otherwise just silently watched from the back of the room.

There were two scholarly disciplines at work: the philosophical, and the practical. The philosophical classes studied the Book of Philosophy from a more esoteric point of view. Who was the Author, and why was she unknowable? What was this universe that she had made? Why had she made so many different species? Was she actually human, or was that just how she appeared in this dimension? And why be human when there were other species that were bigger, stronger, faster, and generally just better in every way?

The practical classes studied the Book of Abilities, but for more practical, everyday uses, rather than combat. Heating up tea, for example, or coordinating a kitchen so all dishes finished at the same time. Mending a child's booboo or preventing an accident in the first place. Investigating one's body for sickness or defects and correcting them.

At the thought, Julianna's mind wandered to Rifun's cousin and not-quite-girlfriend, Lalao. Sickening that he not only had such feelings for her, but that he'd also slept with her. His cousin for God's sake. Oh, and don't get her started on royal incest. At least the monarchy had good, pure genes to reinforce excellent traits. If Rifun had anything going for him, he at least had some French genetics to add into the equation. Thank God they hadn't actually reproduced.

But it was something she might introduce into her equations. Rifun had spent hours to cure the woman of cancer, rather than let her die in the arms of her family. Perhaps Julianna could convince him to step away quietly, go live with this now much older woman. He'd spent so much time in Madagascar, forced her, Julianna, to parade around as his fictional daughter, he clearly wanted to be there. He didn't want to be here. With his seizures, he wasn't going to run into battle anymore. Retire quietly and don't cause trouble. The Order would protect him from assassins as long as he sat quietly. If he tried anything, those same bodyguards would kill him themselves.

Death demands justice. Treason demands justice. It demands death. He cannot be allowed to walk free so easily. He got his respite. He finished his story. He celebrated his own funeral. That life is gone for him now. The only path open to him was the path of the steadfast servant, and he has failed. But the woman may still prove useful.

If nothing else, if he gets wind of several potential threats, perhaps by Akarin who may have somehow gotten a hold of his Authored Books and read them and know of her existence...it would divert his attention, only adding to his betrayal of the Order.

Richard's sacrifice was necessary. Rifun will have to decide the worth of this woman. Is she worth more than the Order?

Hm...but if he isn't going to war, he may try to defend her himself, or investigate it himself. He would turn over the plans to attack Ancrath onto Drinjin uh Ersik and the others. Then the fault would lie with us. He needs to lead the charge into failure himself, even if he does not physically fight. But the woman could still be useful. We'll see. It's not a priority right now.

The classes began wrapping up, the instructors slowly flocking to Julianna like wayward chicks. There were about forty of them today, and her first instruction was that word get around to all of the instructors for all of the classes.

"As you may know, Faharoa and his generals are preparing for an assault on the Borelians," she began, then paused to let the news sink in for any who didn't know that. Judging by the reaction, only a few of them didn't know. She continued, "I have been sent to deliver orders that every able-bodied member of the First Order is to report for combat for this assault, just as they were for the attack on this fortress."

Now the reaction was a bit more noticeable, and it was exactly the one she had been expecting.

"This is not what we were promised," one instructor said at last.

Julianna nodded. "I understand that. I do. However, Faharoa believes the Borelians are too great of a threat to let anyone sit out if they are able to help."

They would have a hard time arguing the point, but that didn't mean that they were happy about it in the first place.

"The order went through the generals and the military first, so if you have questions, you can ask any of the...sergeants." She wasn't actually sure what they were being called. "The ones in charge of the smaller units." She tried to put on a good face, but not too good. "Of course, you may think of these as...reserve forces. They will need to know what they're doing and they may have an assignment, but they will likely not be part of the main fighting force. They will be waiting in the wings, should they be needed."

The instructors still looked rather annoyed by the prospect, and they dispersed in groups of three or four, grumbling amongst themselves. Julianna watched them go. After a moment, she left the recreation area. She ran into half a dozen more instructors out and about and gave them the same speech. Only one instructor looked optimistically intrigued by the thought, but the instructor had been maimed in battle. He still had plenty of fight left in his spirit, but things tended to get difficult when missing two of his six ambulatory appendages; even just getting around the fortress looked like a chore for it.

"Faharoa and the generals ought to consider a silver stone unit," he suggested sincerely.

"A silver stone unit?" Julianna questioned.

"A unit for those who know they cannot or will not return, and they will honorably sacrifice themselves to take out as many enemies as possible for the benefit of the primary forces."

A kamikaze regiment, she decided. She dipped her head. "I will pass along the suggestion. I do not imagine you are the only one to think in such a way. But do not think that you are somehow unimportant or useless because of your deficiency."

"Maybe not, but there is honor in service and victory. Against such a foe, we will need every willing soul and every advantage."

"Of course. As I said, I will pass along your idea."

The instructor ambled away. He would be one of Rifun's supporters, Julianna knew. No, he might not be especially staunch or radical about it now, for he clearly perceived everything as being mostly unified, but when push came to shove, he would stand in support of Rifun.

Hm...a kamikaze unit might not be a bad thing. Although the instructor was maimed, he was still quite a bit larger and stronger than Julianna. He was still a threat, at least to some. Depending on his Akari abilities, his deficiency might not mean much outside of physical warfare. A lot of soldiers supported Rifun because of his willingness to fight on the front lines, to run into battle, in spite of his missing fingers or having to fight Borelians or, perhaps now, his seizures. If she could rouse that same attitude in his followers, especially the maimed ones, well, as the saying went, the housecleaning might take care of itself. And, seeing how she was the one in charge of domestic affairs, which used to include the refugee camp, she could very quickly find out who Rifun's less triumphant supporters were.

The best part was, Rifun himself no longer mattered. If he succumbed to the drug mixing before the battle, his supporters could be rallied to fight — and die — in his honor. If he didn't succumb but didn't fight, he could be made into a coward. If he did fight, well, Drinjin uh Ersik already had his orders.

This part is already taken care of, then. Keep your eyes up. What else needs to be addressed?

Drinjin uh Ersik and Torbak would be working to needle the Akarin and provoke a calculated rebellion, so she didn't need to interfere in that. She had everything under control with the instructors and classes and non-soldiering types.

Tommen, she decided. Tommen was the last major wildcard that she could reasonably influence. After saving Rifun's life, he would have no support from the Akarin at large, he wasn't in the greatest standing with most of humanity after giving up the research efforts and toxin cure, and he was pretty well bowed to Rifun's will. And yet, he could still have some friends trying to help him undermine the Order's grander plans. Sending him with a team from the Order was a decent security measure, but unless they kept Tommen here against his will, they couldn't monitor him so exclusively at all times.

If he did manage to bring Nathan Wilde and Andrew O'Dell out of the woodwork, to try and take the key out of the Core and use it for their own purposes, there would be a window of opportunity to be rid of them once and for all, punish them for their meddling.

And yet, we may still need them to free the key. I can't do it. Rifun seems to think he can't do it. That window of opportunity would be very, very small.

Would it, though? Those men are out there in the universe right now. Somewhere. If they scurry out of their holes to do this, there's a chance they will scurry right back to those same holes, if they think it's safe. So why not let them think it's safe?

Because we don't know where they are in the first place.

Maybe not yet, but they have to come for the key at some point.

Risky and intensive. If they suspect anything —

Of course they'll suspect something. They would be fools not to suspect something. But if they suspect something and come anyway, it's because they're either confident or desperate. The Akarin will be sent to fight in the battle, so they will have little or no backup. This will make them desperate. Desperate, and willing to take intense risks that you can exploit.

Julianna considered this for a long moment. *We've held the Akarin for a while now. Nathan and Andrew aren't here. Seeing how no mention of them has been made, even in passing, they haven't been here for a while. And Tommen isn't the smartest kid out there. If they come to him, or if he does manage to find them, it's because they want to be found. Which means they're keeping an eye on things somehow. It could be by proxy, for their own safety, but with how important this war is, and this upcoming assault, they may not want third-hand information. They may be willing to risk exposing themselves in order to get close to Tommen and hear what he has to say about what he's finding on these little missions of his.*

And where is the best place to get such first-hand information?

The meetings on Tacaga.

Of course. Right beneath their noses the whole time. But were they really? Rifun had said nothing about Nathan and Andrew being at the meetings.

Either he is foolish enough not to Test any of them, or else his betrayal of the journals is keeping him silent on the matter. He knows what you will do to them if you find out. Maybe they are working together, but to what end?

First I will force them to release the key from the Core. Then I will feed them to the Borelians myself.

Suddenly irritated, Julianna made her way to the nearest staircase. She was growing weary of these games.

And what if it isn't true? What if Nathan and Andrew aren't at the meetings? You risk making a fool of yourself.

I spent too much time in the in-between dimension to believe that. I traced every move they made. I saw them take the journal and disappear. Years I watched and waited for them, pored through more years of history just in case I missed them. If they're not on Earth, they have to be on one of the colony planets. The colony planets are far less engaged in any Time or Akari business. They have to be getting their information from somewhere, and this is too important to entrust to some errand boy or unwitting pawn.

And what if they aren't involved at all?

No. They're involved. The only way they aren't involved is if they're dead, and I think we would have heard about that, even a minor rumor.

But if they weren't? Then what?

Then Tommen isn't getting his key.

Which means?

Which means...Rifun isn't getting his key. Which means we're not getting the journal.

Not in the conventional way, no. But what else does that mean?

It means another failure for Rifun. Another charge of treason, sending everyone on this mission for no real goal.

So either way...

Either way, we win. And Rifun is out.

There is always a way to spin things.

Julianna still had a hard time believing Nathan and Andrew weren't directly involved in affairs in some way. If she thought she could get away with going to the meetings on Tacaga, she might go and see for herself. Problem was, she wasn't wanted in the war tent so-to-speak, and she wasn't likely to get along with at least a few of those in attendance. The whore Aklaq White Bear, for starters.

By the time she made it to the eighth floor, most of her anger had cooled. Some of it had to do with conversations she had with herself, some of it had to do with how long it took to get there, and some of it had to do with the simple physicality of it, walking through the corridors and up all those stairs. She knocked on the door.

"*Hiditra,*" came Rifun's reply.

She opened the door. Truthfully, it looked like he hadn't moved since she'd left.

"I know married couples who don't spend this much time together," he commented, not looking at her.

"Those married couples likely aren't waging interstellar war."

"True enough. But, considering that you are in charge of the more domestic affairs of the Order..." He looked up, his expression a mixture of curiosity and irritation.

"I had a thought," she said, "about Nathan Wilde and Andrew O'Dell."

"What about them?"

She explained her line of thought, about them being at the meetings on Tacaga, finishing with, "Have you Tested the others at the meetings?"

"Interestingly enough I have." His demeanor said that while he could appreciate the line of thought and was perhaps considering its merits, he was not overly impressed by a theory alone. "Everyone is exactly who they pretend to be."

"I know you weren't around to meet them originally, but does anyone match the description of either of them? Nathan, brown hair, brown eyes—"

"I have brown hair and brown eyes."

"—Andrew, an Irishman, black hair, thick black beard."

Rifun sighed. "Ancestors help us if you ever have to give witness testimony in a trial."

She gave him a look. "Well?"

"No!" he insisted. "There are no Disguises. Andrew and Nathan aren't there." He straightened. "Yes, there is a delegate there named Andrew. Yes, he has black hair and a black beard. But he is Aleisi. Pilgrim, Puritan, Amish, whatever you want to call them. Pacifists, all. Hardly someone who would go messing with God's Creation."

"It would be a perfect cover."

He rolled his eyes. "If you can find me some concrete evidence that this man is Andrew O'Dell, then we can do something about it. Maybe."

"Maybe?"

"Andrew O'Dell is a Builder. We need a Builder to get the key out of the Core. Once we have the key, O'Dell no longer matters. Once we have the journal, none of them matter."

Julianna nodded, but before she could say anything, the door opened and a messenger scurried in. It carried a messenger bag on its body and dug out several sheets of paper.

"Faharoa," it greeted, saluting.

"What is it?" Rifun sighed, looking grateful for the distraction.

"Multiple messages for you, from the other human worlds."

It handed over the messages. Rifun took them but did not dismiss the messenger right away.

"Multiple messages?" Julianna inquired, taking one out of his hands. "This one is from Dorigis, asking if we have anything to do with why they can't get to Tacaga."

"This one is from Vin Lay," Rifun murmured darkly. "An operative in the Wheel discovered a report that Tacaga was under attack from the Borelians."

"Under attack? Any other news?"

He shuffled through the papers. As he set aside one letter or another, she picked them up and did the same.

"Can't reach Tacaga, can't reach the Tacagans, Tacaga under attack." She shook her head. "Nothing beyond that." She set the papers down and looked at him. "Has Tacaga fallen?"

"Serves the bastards right for a lot of things, but fucking hell if it's true," Rifun said softly, shifting his stance back.

"I'm guessing there was supposed to be a meeting now or soon?" Julianna guessed.

He nodded absently. "Soon enough. I guess I lost track of time."

"Sounds like it might have saved you. Message from Dorigis indicates they didn't get caught. Who else?"

They looked through all of the letters again.

"Looks like they're all accounted for except for Ehani," he observed. "My guess is the attack happened earlier, but we're only just now finding out about it."

"Could the Tacagan planetary defenses be keeping them out?"

"I imagine that's exactly the case. The Tacagans don't have to worry about the Borelian fleet. Tacaga is in Quadrant Five, Brelix is in Quadrant One. Brelix and Earth are only separated by four Sectors and the Borelians still can't reach Earth."

"What do we do? Shall I summon the generals?"

He thought a moment, then nodded. "Do that. Let them formulate a plan if they so choose, but don't send them out just yet. I'm going to go take a look around, see what we're up against."

"Alone?"

"Only a quick observe and report at this point. I will find out very quickly, I think, where we stand."

He did not consult her opinion, just left the room, briefly relaying an order to the messenger to find Drinjin uh Ersik, Torbak Martin, Godwin Lore, and a couple others and bring them to the room to discuss and prepare. The messenger saluted to his back and scuttled off to do just that.

It didn't take fifteen minutes for the generals and others to assemble.

"What's this about?" one of the slightly lesser officers inquired. "Faharoa summons us, but he himself is not here."

"He said he will be scouting the situation," Julianna said. "Tacaga has come under attack from the Borelians."

"Under attack?" Drinjin uh Ersik echoed. "What's the situation?"

She opened her mouth, but it was Rifun who spoke.

"And in a dramatic turn of events, he conveniently walks in the room at just the right time to answer the question!" Rifun helped himself to the head of the table around which the group had gathered. Some had been studying the maps he had drawn, but all looked at him now. "Tacaga's capital city of Lip was attacked. Once the planetary shield was activated, it cut off any further invaders, but the battle continues.

"I am here only long enough to let you know so you can stand down from an immediate threat, for the Tacagan ground forces are more than adequate. I am going to round up the rest of the human leaders and proceed with the meeting that was originally scheduled for this time, and we'll see if we can't learn something from this episode. In the meantime, feel free to mull over some ideas for any similar future interruptions."

And he was gone again.

"I mean no insult to you," Drinjin uh Ersik said, looking at Julianna, "but why should we be concerned with the human worlds when we have our own problems here?"

"I understand the concern," Julianna told him. "But Tacaga may be one of the best allies we have right now. They are hosting the engineer who was studying the Borelian toxins and had the preliminary research for a cure, the same cure that saved Faharoa."

"A retaliatory strike," another officer suggested.

"Possibly."

"I suggest we limit our scope to our own defenses," Drinjin uh Ersik decided. "The only problems we should be focusing on are the ones we are certain exist and can strengthen. We cannot spread our resources so thin as to encompass the whole universe."

The rest of the group agreed, even Godwin Lore. They made to leave, but Julianna called back her two bodyguards.

"Something the matter?" Torbak inquired.

"Is this about Faharoa?" Drinjin uh Ersik guessed. "Calling a war meeting yet not attending."

"As strange and improper as that may be, no, not this time," Julianna said. "Actually, this has to do with a couple of Akarin Builders and a couple of humans." She again explained her theory. "I need proof that Nathan or Andrew or both are attending these meetings. So far, the only lead is Andrew from Aleis."

"You are certain this Andrew from Aleis is the same Andrew O'Dell?" Drinjin uh Ersik did not look convinced.

"It has to be. The Akarin have too much riding on this."

"All humans do, for this is your war. But how would it help them with the Core of the Wheel?"

"While we're distracted by the assault on Ancrath, they sneak in, take the key, sneak out, make off with it yet again, and we are left without the journal."

"We could just pull the temple down completely," Torbak commented.

"Time and extra effort, two things not found in abundance in war," Drinjin uh Ersik said, not exactly rebuking Torbak. "And the idea is sound, given the history of this journal in particular." He made an affirmative gesture. "We'll look into it."

"Thank you. The sooner it can be proven, the sooner we can keep track of Andrew and the key and intercept him before he can disappear."

"He can disappear. Once we have the key and we're through with him, we'll make sure he stays disappeared."

Lip was a city the size of the American state of Texas. So while it was tempting to imagine that the whole city lay in fiery ruins after the Borelian attack with bodies piled high, crows circling ominously, this simply was not the case. There was some damage, yes, at the entry points to the domed city where the Borelians had launched their attack, but with the shield in place, the Tacagan forces had little trouble picking off what few Borelians remained.

There appeared to have been a separate attack on the governmental building, perhaps to free several Borelian prisoners who were held in the research lab, courtesy of the Order's attack on the farming world. As the elevator door opened, Rifun's suspicions were confirmed.

The whole floor was trashed. The glass wall that allowed for observation of the research lab had been shattered. The decontamination unit, normally the only means of entry or exit, was damaged and useless, very much like the rest of the laboratory equipment. Machines both heavy and delicate had been ripped apart, papers scattered about, torn, burned, soaked from the fire suppression system that was no longer spraying. In the midst of fading Band wakes, Rifun spotted the biochemical engineer dead on the floor.

He also spotted two dead Borelians and a third held in the air by a Band controlled by Walter Forbes, though he could also see that she herself held a Band, perhaps trying to get the jump on him. She had her arms outstretched, polydactyled hands reaching for his throat. A gun lay on the floor, perhaps out of bullets. Carefully, Walter maneuvered away from his attacker and took up a shard of glass, perhaps to kill her.

"She can still kill you," Rifun said.

Walter startled, almost cutting himself. He looked around the Borelian as Rifun picked his way through the remains of the decon unit.

"As soon as you touch her Band, she'll touch you. And she will kill you," Rifun told him. "That would be a bad day for everyone, I think. Would you like me to do it?" He held out his hand.

"What's to keep her from killing you?" Walter surrendered the glass. "Or are you just going to use your revolver?"

"Oh, I could use my gun, true, but when the opportunity arises, I enjoy making my enemies suffer, just a little bit. As for how I'm going to keep her from killing me, well, you seem to have forgotten. I've done this before."

Rifun embedded thousands of tiny Bands and other inhibitors all along the Borelian's arms and head, her entire body, rendering her completely immobile. He set them in her spinal cord, to separate the time between messages firing off and when her body would respond. Then he set a Band in her throat. He couldn't cut off the air, but he could cut off the muscular response, keep her from inhaling and exhaling. Finally, he set a Band in her artery, and Walter watched as Rifun pulled the knife across her throat. In the end, not a drop of blood was spilled as it simply clotted in the artery, nowhere to go. The backup would cause congestive heart failure. Rifun took a step back, released all the Bands at once, and the Borelian dropped dead, with not a defensive wound to show. He hated that he knew how to do that, how reminisce it was of the women Cassius murdered in Charleston for his own pleasure, but it appeared to have served a purpose now.

"Do I hear a...?" Rifun goaded, trying to take his mind off it.

Walter sighed. "Thank you."

"You are most welcome. I look out for my own, after all, and you are one of my body guards. Or perhaps a mind guard. I'm not sure. Either way, it still benefits me to keep you alive."

"Good to know I'm still wanted. How the hell did you get in here? I thought the Tacagans activated their shell or whatever their planetary defenses are."

"They did. The catch is, it only keeps out Time. But even the most powerful shield cannot hold back the Akari. And comparatively speaking, their shell is pretty weak. To that end, I've brought the other leaders. Seeing how it's a bit of a mess down here, they're meeting upstairs. Would you like to join us?"

Walter agreed, but not before he'd cleaned himself up first. Rifun didn't blame him. Once the man was as clean as he was going to get without the decon unit, they set out for the elevator.

"So, who really did kill those women, Rifun?" Walter asked.

"Cassius always wielded the knife," Rifun replied levelly. "I was simply an observer."

"An accomplice, you mean."

"Perhaps."

"What's the status of the bridge?" Walter wondered as they got on the elevator. "Or any other roads in and out of the city?"

"The army is keeping the Borelians from infiltrating," Rifun answered. "With the shell active, reinforcements can't help them. The Borelians are losing numbers and hope. That's a quick summary of things."

Walter shifted his stance and folded his arms. "That's it? No detailed explanation? No quick wit or sarcastic comments? Not even a smirk? Are you all right?"

"Priorities are a wonderful thing, Walter. Given the circumstances, I prefer to focus my attention on keeping my people safe and not dying."

"And here I thought your charming sense of humor came naturally."

Rifun gave him a look. "Sorry, sweetie, but you know how the pill messes with my hormones."

Despite the inference Walter would get, Rifun was actually referring to the midazolam. It had to be the midazolam because he didn't think it was the tarka root tea, however repulsive the taste. He didn't like how the midazolam made him feel. Excited yet sluggish, having the energy and ideas of a thousand men, but with a head clouded like sickness and the drive of an elder on his deathbed. He didn't take it every day, or even most days, and on the days he refrained and drank only the tea, he generally felt better. A little slow, still, head a little foggy, but without the jitters and anxiety and feelings of his body being tightly bound. Sometimes he wondered if it might not be better just to embrace the seizures.

They made for a small conference room where the other planetary leaders, including Milay and Toros, the real Toros, were already gathered. Presently, it seemed as though Milay and Aklaq were having an argument over the effectiveness of the shield. Aklaq tried to explain that the Akari was different; Milay dismissed it as foolish religion, technology that primitive apes called magic.

"You can't ignore something you've seen with your own eyes," Aklaq was saying, giving off the impression of a snarling dog, hackles raised. "The Akari is real. The only good news is that the Borelians don't use it, are untrained in it."

"The ones who were," Rifun interrupted, announcing his entry into the room, "are now dead, thanks to me." He cast her a pointed look and put a hand over his chest wound as he bowed. "You're welcome, by the way."

"What news from other worlds?" Mi Chin inquired.

"The Borelians were attacking Ehani when I went to get Xoris and Tambu," Rifun reported. "Xoris was dead, the Xalani dead or enslaved, Tambu and the Etlawa not far behind." He continued before Milay or Toros could speak. "I did not see the Tacagan engineers, nor did I inquire after them. I was simply happy to make it out alive myself. But I think it's safe to say that Ehani is lost to us."

"Attack the strongest and the weakest of us," one of the Vin Lay stated. "Weaken your strongest enemy while crushing your weakest and foraging on their resources."

"They took one of our worlds just as we took one of theirs," Aklaq said, folding her arms. "Ehani is the most plentiful in game and forage, good for farming I bet."

"What is their next most likely move?" Andrew from Aleis wondered. "Where will they go?"

"Brelix has very little water and only one small ocean. They are very inexperienced when it comes to naval warfare. They will not attack Dorigis yet," the Dorigisi woman said.

"Sakaria is a wild card, unpredictable in war," a Sakarian giant said. "We are unlikely."

"Vin Lay is industrializing, which means their mines are open," Walter mused. "But Aleis and Hlohi are still largely primitive and undeveloped. Given the choice, with Aleis having some mining operations, my bet would be on Hlohi, work their way up the chain."

"I disagree." Mi Chin spoke. "The Borelians have taken Ehani as payment for the world we attacked. But there is nothing to be gained by a prolonged siege on a city, and no country has benefited from prolonged warfare."

"Sun Tzu," Rifun stated.

"Brelix prohibits active drilling and mining, and it takes a long time for the volcanoes to push the metals to the surface, to say nothing of the long excavation and refining process. Operations on their colony worlds is what keeps them breaking even on their needs. Vin Lay is the richest planet in many metals with a very stable crust, and many mines are already open. If they hope to continue the siege on Tacaga and engage in open combat, they will have to manufacture weapons and armor faster and on a larger scale than they already do."

"Why attack Tacaga at all, though?" Toros wondered, sounding genuinely clueless.

"Psychology and practicality," Aklaq answered spitefully. "Psychology, because then all other human worlds are going to be looking to you, to make sure that your defense technology works, that it can save them, too. Practicality, because in launching a simultaneous attack on Ehani or any other world, you can't come to help. If you send troops to reinforce Ehani, you leave yourselves open to attack. If you put up your shield, Ehani falls. I'd be willing to bet that the force that attacked the city today wasn't very big, because they wanted to see what you would do."

"We're doing things reactively," the Sakarian giant lamented. "Three worlds gone, and who else must die or be enslaved before we are able to fight back effectively?"

"We took the fight to them once, and this is what it got us," one Dorigisi said.

"It was coming anyway. That's what war is," Aklaq shot back. "Maybe this was their plan all along, and it has nothing to do with the planet we burned."

"Maybe we ought to burn more," another delegate from Vin Lay suggested. "Rifun, you have enough men to burn all their worlds, don't you?"

Rifun raised a brow. "If a tactic works, we might as well keep using it. We should, however, consider what we will do if that tactic ceases to be useful. There is also merit in figuring out what the enemy is planning and proactively reciprocate their efforts." He glanced at Walter.

"We shouldn't be forced to depend on him," Aklaq growled. "What can we do? If we're fairly certain that Vin Lay will be their next target, how do we protect them? I highly doubt the Borelians are going to wait until the planetary defenses are up."

"Is there any way to create the defenses on a smaller scale?" the first Vin Lay wondered. "If the Borelians are after our mines, what if we made smaller shields to defend the mines?"

"They would only have to dig new mines," Mi Chin answered. "And unless all your people were under the shield as well, they would slaughter you and destroy the defenses. If you did hide under the shields, they would only have to wait you out, starve you."

There was a pause. Surprisingly, it was Toros who spoke. "There may be a way."

All eyes turned to him, Milay's the most hostile of all.

"Having conquered Ehani, the Borelians will require at least a few days to process the influx of slaves. In that time, small defenses may be installed to protect the larger mines as well as the teams working on the larger defense system. Being so close to finishing, they are not traveling and moving around as much; it's more about coordination and finishing than engineering and building." Toros looked at Rifun. "I don't understand how you got in here through our shield, and we can debate it later. But if the Borelians can't do it, then we have nothing to lose by using it ourselves."

"Except our souls," Aklaq muttered.

Toros continued, "We can send supplies and store them in the areas where the small defenses will be erected, but it would be up to you and your men to take them anything else they need, through the shield, especially if it becomes a prolonged event. We anticipate that the defenses will be completed within the month."

"And what about the people outside the shields?" the Dorigisi woman asked. "The larger shield may be protected and it may go up as planned, but if everyone outside has been killed or enslaved, we've accomplished nothing. Even now, the Borelians have access to the defense technology left on Ehani. If they figure it out and figure out how to disable it, get around it, whatever, we're done. None of this matters."

Milay lifted her chin indignantly. "Our engineers had strict orders to destroy the defenses if such a thing ever happened. The Borelians will find nothing."

Apparently the only ones who didn't have doubts about this were the Tacagans, Rifun noted. Nevertheless, Vin Lay needed supplies, reinforcements, and time, and the Order was going to give it to them. The planetary defenses should be operational shortly thereafter, and they could decide what to do next.

After the meeting was dismissed, Walter caught up to Rifun in the hall.

"What's this bullshit mission you've got my son on? You wouldn't send him after some holy artifact if you didn't think you would win in the end."

"I always win, Walter, but we're on a bit of a timeline," Rifun told him. "Julianna and I have simply decided to tie up some loose ends in the aftermath of the war, though small skirmishes do still happen, I will admit, between the Order and the Akarin. It's a messy, complicated business. The easy things, we're outsourcing."

"If finding your sacred text was that easy, I think you would have already done it. It took the murder of a dozen people before you found the second journal in a damn museum. What is the cost of the third journal, I wonder?"

"Higher to the Borelians than to us, I hope."

"Still not given to monologues, are you?"

"Sadly, no. Now then, if you will excuse me, I have other appointments to keep."

He left before Walter could say anything more, returning to the fortress where he found his chambers mercifully empty. He wouldn't say he experienced his aura necessarily, and he didn't black out as from a seizure, but he certainly didn't feel right. The left half of his body felt fairly normal, if a bit fatigued from all the portal travel. The right half of his body felt like it did when he took the pills. Energetic, but tightly bound, like a taut rubber band. He'd done some research and knew that it was possible to have half a seizure, but if this was what it felt like, he'd rather take the whole thing and be done with it. But could he Band himself since he was still conscious?

He didn't get a chance to find out before it subsided. For a moment, his right side felt limp and exhausted, though not unusable. Then, strength returned, and it was like it never happened.

He would have to talk to Haunstein again, or maybe the pharmacist. Something wasn't right; he just didn't know what. But he couldn't run into battle with his body and mind the way they were. Just getting supplies to Vin Lay could prove a challenge for him.

Once he was confident that his body had no other surprises in store for him, he stood and headed out to find a few officers to coordinate a supply chain. Vin Lay would need basic necessities so they could move their population into the mines, and possibly some physical defense in case the Borelians attacked before the Tacagans were ready to launch the shields.

The idea did not go over well with the officers.

"We have our own troubles with our own supplies to worry about," Drinjin uh Ersik informed him. "We need access to weapons, but we can't risk the Akarin getting their hands on what they shouldn't have. Yet we are expected to fight together. As for the basic necessities, with the Akarin whom we are holding prisoner, they require such necessities. And we have a lot of those prisoners."

"Then send those prisoners to defend Vin Lay, fight the Borelians, and earn their necessities," Rifun said. "Show them what they're up against, teach them to fight with us and for us and treat this as a test run of sorts. On Vin Lay, the Borelians won't have the home field advantage. Once the shields are up, they're completely cut off. If we can't beat them there, we stand no chance in Ancrath." He went on before anyone else could object. "As for replenishing our supplies, make note of what is being used. There is a whole universe out there; we won't have trouble replenishing our stock."

None of the officers looked enthusiastic, but the idea of a test run seemed to have sealed the deal. Indeed, if they couldn't do anything about a small force on an alien world, what were they going to do in Ancrath, really, besides die?

"Some enthusiasm would be appreciated," Rifun said as they began to break up. "A military with purpose is a military united. We have a goal, now let's start taking real steps to accomplish that goal."

No one replied and only Godwin remained.

"And what's your opinion on the situation?" Rifun asked, only half-sarcastic.

"A little slow on the draw, sir," the mercenary said. "Your accident and recovery notwithstanding, you let the war machine come to a stop. Now it's taking more effort to get it moving again."

"We've had to assimilate the Akarin and repair the fortress, what do you expect?"

"My repertoire of skilled solutions is fairly limited."

"How about unskilled ones?"

"Couldn't say for sure, sir. I don't know what I don't know."

"You're over a thousand years old; that's bullshit."

"You can wear a noticeable path in the forest in only a couple weeks. Imagine the rut than a millennium can produce."

Rifun just sighed.

Godwin shifted his stance. "I'll go scout out the situation on the ground, get the lay of the land, draw up a few maps and ideas."

Rifun nodded. "I'll come with you."

"Are you sure, sir?"

He nodded again. "I need to get out of here. This place is driving me insane."

Twenty minutes later, they were standing just downhill from a mine on Vin Lay. It wasn't the biggest, but it was comparatively the richest. The landscape overall was quite rocky, gorges sundering the hills, ocean cliffs not half a mile away.

"Well, sir, we have a few advantages," Godwin began.

"Bottleneck at the entrances to the mines, should the Borelians get that far," Rifun said, looking around. "Narrow passes act like a secondary bottleneck. High cliffs make it easy to set up an ambush."

"My thoughts exactly, sir."

"If at all possible, until the planetary shield is in place, we should use Vin Lay forces to attack the Borelians. Make them think this is a simple fight. Once the shield goes up and they're cut off, then use Order and Akarin soldiers. It will keep Drinjin uh Ersik happy that we're not wasting our men unnecessarily, but it should still provide a good test run."

Win pointed vaguely and started moving. "I think we should take a look down this gorge, sir, see if there aren't any caves we might utilize."

In spite of the grumbling, things worked out remarkably well for Vin Lay. The Tacagans provided smaller shield generators for the mines deemed most likely to be targeted, and the teams working on the larger planetary shield worked double time to get it up and running. Before they could finish, however, the Borelians arrived.

Rifun elected not to fight, choosing instead to remain behind, take reports, and analyze the data as it were. He claimed it was so he could get a better feel for how Ancrath could go and adjust accordingly. Although he did do this, standing at the table in his eighth floor chambers, he also hadn't quite broken through the fear that was his seizures. They did seem to be coming under better control, but they hadn't faded into the background enough for him to want to risk a minor fight turning into a major problem for him, that is, death. Or worse, slavery.

The Vin Lay lasted longer than he expected without needing Order intervention; Rifun would admit he was impressed. The Borelian siege ran into some unexpected resistance.

"Faharoa."

Rifun looked up from his table as Godwin entered the room through the emergency exit portal room.

"The Tacagan engineers are ready to launch the planetary defense, but they're going to need a quick escape."

Rifun nodded. "Go to your post. You know what to do. I'll handle the rest."

Although there were six mines in total under siege, protected by the smaller shields, there were eleven larger generators needed to power the planetary defenses. Eight of them were safe, tucked away in obscure geographical areas that the Borelians hadn't discovered. The remaining three happened to be very near or even inside the besieged mines.

Godwin left for his post, but Rifun made a quick detour to pick up Tommen. The teenager was basically the only able-bodied Akari-bearer who wasn't overworked at the moment. No one trusted him to fight, no one wanted his help on any mundane project, and no one really understood what secret mission Rifun had for him.

It was late in the eastern time zone, and Tommen looked like he was fully intending to get into bed when he entered his bedroom. He stopped when he saw Rifun.

"What did I do this time?" he wondered.

"It's not what you've done, it's what you're going to do. The Tacagans are ready to launch the planetary defenses on Vin Lay. Once that's done, you're going to help me evacuate the engineers."

"What about the Borelians already there?"

"The Vin Lay will take care of them. Food and medicine aren't the only things I've been taking them."

Tommen nodded. "Okay."

"I'll get us there, but you'll be opening portals of your own from Vin Lay to Tacaga. It's a little more difficult because you are inexperienced, but it's not much different than the portals from your bedroom to the fortress."

"What about the shields?"

"You'll feel the resistance, but it's cake to break through. The Akari cannot be bound by such feeble means. Let's get moving."

They landed on a hillside looking up into enormous rock formations and cliffs. The sun was well below the horizon, but there was still light in the sky. Looking around, there was little evidence of civilization except for carvings in the stone around the mouth of a cave and steel supports to keep the roof from collapsing. Behind them, in the valley, an enormous war camp with tents as far as the eye could see—which wasn't far considering the expanse of rock formations, but Godwin's reports had made it clear that the Borelians were a formidable presence. The only thing that separated them was a shield that could only be seen in the right light.

"I'll take you in to meet this team," Rifun said, starting up the hill, "then I'll go meet the team I'm evacuating in another mine. I have other operatives ready to evacuate the rest of the teams. Once you're done, go straight home."

"What if something happens?"

"Do what you can. I'll check on you. I have a feeling that I'll be done before you."

He took Tommen deep into the mine where a team of six Tacagans were working around a large metal apparatus that was one of the shield generators. They did not like being watched in their work, especially by primitive Earthlings, and Rifun pointedly ignored them.

"This is your team," Rifun told Tommen. "They'll tell you when everything is in order and they're ready to go. I'll see you in a bit."

He left, walking a short distance away, then opening another portal to the generator he would be defending. This one was situated on a hilltop. Down one side of the hill, the entrance to a mine was invisible. Slightly farther down the slope, the waiting Borelian army was not. A cloud passed over the sun and Rifun wondered if the cast shadows were as innocuous as they looked.

The generator was dome-shaped, but the color allowed for more natural camouflage. Assuming anyone could see them up here, they would appear to be oddly enamored with a small boulder, one of many that dotted the landscape.

On the other side of the hill, opposite the army, thin trees eventually turned into a forest of squat trees. They were bonsai in shape, but had easily double the leaf count of even the fluffiest tree on Earth. Enormous ferns made it almost impossible to see the ground while vine-type plants snaked their way here and there, wherever they could find purchase. That would be an excellent ambush point, if the smaller shield generators hadn't kept the Borelians away.

"*Initios,*" one Tacagan said suddenly.

Rifun turned to watch. All but one stood back from the machine while the one who had spoken began tapping. Invisible keys suddenly came to life in an array of colors with Tacagan words on them. The dome began to hum and glow, and a round port suddenly opened up at the top. A second Tacagan took a spot on the opposite of the dome and tapped more buttons. A panel opened up, revealing several dim lights. Gradually, they began to light up. One, then two, then five, then all nine, all yellow.

"*Domosi ete parati,*" a second engineer reported, looking at all the green lights. "*Esspetos vox sui.*"

"Pink," a third began, *"quasse, tre...do...eno...jam!"*

More buttons were pushed, and suddenly the whole dome lit up green for just a second before some camouflage programming kicked in and quickly turned into the same stone pattern as the rest of the dome. One by one, the yellow lights on the one side turned green, then vanished into the camouflage.

Then the Tacagans were running, sliding down the hill, rocks skittering before them. Rifun followed, keeping one eye on the Borelians at all times. Nothing happened, the shadows remained where they were, and the team reached the mine without incident. There the engineers began dismantling a camera-like apparatus, the smaller shield generator for the mine.

"Parato?" one Tacagan inquired as pieces and parts were distributed amongst the group.

The rest gave an affirmative answer and looked to Rifun who opened a portal to Tacaga, straight into the governmental building, the same meeting room humans had been using to collaborate for weeks now. Stepping through, Rifun saw half a dozen more portals from the other generator sites. The Tacagan teams stepped through, followed by the Order member who got them there.

Milay and Toros, already in the room, started counting heads. One team was no sooner realized missing than another portal opened and they appeared as if by magic. Once everyone was verified alive and well, the Tacagans broke out into cheers. Rifun half-expected a champagne cork to pop across the room.

He didn't mind the celebration. He was happy for them, in a sense. But the way they deliberately shoved the Order members aside was a tad annoying. Rifun shuffled his men out into the hall, leaving the Tacagans to their merriment.

"You've done well today," he told his men. "Truly, you have. Today, and in the days past, for those of you who have been fighting, or been prepared to do so. You have my commendation, and my blessing to take a well-deserved rest."

No one argued, and all but Godwin headed for the elevator. A minute later, the Tacagan teams also exited the room. A couple bumped into Godwin whose expression said it took everything in him to not snap at them. It didn't stop the Tacagans from grumbling and complaining that he was in their way, but it never got further than that. Milay and Toros were the last to exit, though they motioned for Rifun and Godwin to join them.

"Our end of the bargain has been fulfilled," Milay began.

Rifun put up a hand. "Before you start making speeches, demands, or threats, it may be prudent to bring the other leaders here to discuss the matter."

It was the last thing Milay wanted, and they all knew it, but Rifun left the room so he could open some portals and do it anyway. Because it was not a scheduled meeting, it was a little harder to interrupt daily lives and bring everyone together. The Vin Lay were the last to arrive but first to speak.

"Thanks to the Tacagans, our world is protected," they reported cheerfully. "Some Borelians remain, and there is yet fighting. But, we have every confidence in our own men and in reinforcements from the Order and the Akarin to drive them back."

"This would give us a good opportunity to collect more toxin samples," someone suggested. "Do Chien may be dead, but the Tacagans still have the technology to study and dissect it."

"Why?" Milay asked flippantly. "The whole universe knows the cure by now. Does it matter what the toxin is made of?"

"Reverse engineer it," Win piped up. "Figure out what makes them tick, why the Borelians can be affected even by each other's toxins. Then, synthesize a brand new toxin, one that none of them have immunity to, preferably one that will not harm us in the process."

Others jumped on the train of thought and started adding in their own ideas of what the toxin could or should do. Instant death in a variety of ways, neutralize the Borelian toxin system completely and permanently, act as a physical means of Suppression so they couldn't use Time, and so on. Rifun watched from where he leaned against the wall. After a moment, Godwin joined him.

"You're quiet, sir," the mercenary observed.

"I have a splitting headache from all the portals I've been managing today," Rifun told him. It wasn't a lie, either. His head was pounding, his old injury feeling fresher than he would have preferred. Everyone was talking too loud, the lights in the room were too bright. He wasn't even sure what the discussion was about presently. Something about the planetary defenses on the rest of the worlds being operational within the next seven to ten days.

"I'll send them home, sir, if you need to get out of here," Godwin offered.

Rifun shook his head lightly. "It's just a headache, Win."

The mercenary did not argue.

By the time the meeting was wrapping up, Rifun wanted nothing more than to crawl under a rock. The pain from his old injury had spread to encompass the entire back of his head and neck. He used Light just so he could shield his eyes and Sound to stop his inner ears from pulsing. Nausea was not yet in the picture, but if he had to send everyone home, it would be.

Was this just from excessive portal use, or was it somehow tied to his head injury or seizures? He decided it was just from portal use. Even the most greatly talented Time Agents and Akari-bearers tired of portals after eight or nine jumps, and he'd been ripping open portals right and left, more than two dozen if he counted correctly. Of course he might be a little sick. The fact that he was still upright was amazing. And he still had a few more to go tonight.

"We should all remain vigilant as the Tacagans finish their work," Andrew from Aleis said calmly, his tone suggesting the meeting was over. "I would suggest that we do nothing hasty until the shields are in place and we are more secure in our positions."

Rifun studied Andrew the best he could through throbbing eyes. Was it absolutely impossible that this was Andrew O'Dell? No, but it was highly unlikely. Even if the man had run off to another human colony to hide, Rifun would have expected him to run to Dorigis or maybe Sakaria II. Even Treman and Trebald were likely options. Maybe he had and he was dead now, since they were fallen. Who could say for sure? But Rifun was not feeling well enough to launch such an investigation here and now. Right now, he had to wrap up a few chores and get to bed.

"I'll send them home, sir," Godwin repeated, his tone saying it was no longer a friendly offer. "You get out of here."

Rifun may have said something or made some motion of gratitude; he couldn't remember. What he did remember was ducking quickly out of the room and opening a portal for himself. First he had to make sure Tommen had gotten off Vin Lay. His team had returned, but he had not been with them. If he hadn't, well, chances were good he would be hunkered down in the mine with the women and children, like a coward. But the first spot to check would be the kid's bedroom. As long as he was there, safe and sound, Rifun would let him be.

When he came back to consciousness, he was indeed in Tommen's bedroom. The light was on, the teenager was looking at him with some concern in his eyes and a bottle of isopropyl alcohol in his hand. If Rifun's head had been pounding before, it was stabbing now with a particular, arduous flare. Rifun also realized he was looking at something. His hand, with just a little bit of blood. He'd cut his head on something.

"What the hell happened?" he asked.

"My guess, you came to my room, had a seizure, hit your head on the corner of my desk there." Tommen indicated the corner in question. "You forget to take your meds this morning?"

"The meds and tea only serve to keep the seizures under control; it doesn't stop them completely. And I've been doing a lot of running around today." Damn it, he hoped it wasn't a seizure but just passing out from opening yet more portals today. He didn't recall having an aura, but then, he didn't remember leaving the meeting on Tacaga either.

Rifun got up from the floor, but only made it as far as sitting on the edge of the bed, resting his head in his hands.

"You okay?" Tommen wondered. "Like, the seizures aren't getting worse or anything, are they?"

"No, I expect not. Or not that anyone's told me. But a splitting headache is bad enough when it's not compounded by a secondary head wound augmented by a generous amount of alcohol." He gave Tommen a look.

"Would you have rathered I call an ambulance?"

"I suppose not."

"What's the word from Vin Lay?"

Rifun let out a breath. "They're going to be fine. Some areas are going to be under siege for a short time, going back and forth between Borelian and Vin Lay forces, but the shield is in place. No more Borelians can get in. Of course, if any of the Borelians manage to break into the mines and disables one of the shield generators, that could be called into question. From what I understand, though, that's not likely to happen."

"I assume there was another meeting on Tacaga following the activation of the shield?"

"There was. Our gracious Tacagan hosts were humbly grateful for the return of their beloved engineers." He shook his head.

"What about the defenses on the rest of the worlds?"

"Up and running within the next week to ten days."

Tommen studied him. "Let me ask you something. Other than this whole seizure thing, which I think is becoming less and less of a factor seeing how you have meds and seem to be getting used to it—" He ignored Rifun's glare. "—do you really think helping save humanity from the Borelians will absolve you of your crimes against the universe and those you murdered?"

"Does it matter? The Borelians will enslave all of us, regardless, and they'll take particular joy in enslaving me, I think. I'm saving my own skin as much as everyone else's, and as it has been pointed out, I'm the only one crazy, stupid, and brilliant enough to pull off half of what we're doing. And I have an army."

"But you're hoping that, if we succeed, some people out there might be persuaded to look the other way."

"The Elif did. The Turitians do. There are others out there. That's the wonderful thing about morality being subjective throughout the universe."

"And you hope to bring them all under the absolute morality of Richard's journals."

"It's a lofty goal, I admit."

"Yeah, but...what if the Author's morals are different from yours? I admit, I'm only in the first stage of the first book and we have a test coming up, but what if?"

Rifun smiled tiredly. "I like you, Tommen. I really do. Always questioning. Always wanting to know, to understand, to be anchored in something." He sighed and stood deliberately. "But all answers do not come in a single night. Keep studying for your test, and be ready to leave on your mission soon after."

"Are you good to open another portal?"

The man nodded. "One last one, straight into bed."

And he did just that, or as close as he could get, landing in the emergency exit portal room just off his chambers. From there he stumbled his way to his bed and lay down, his heavy head leading the way through the room lit only by the faint glow of the power inverter. His equilibrium had apparently not come through the portal with him and he fell into bed more than lay down. But, since he was now in bed, he could get some sleep and hopefully not have to deal with the nausea that was sloshing in his brain. He took an even breath, closed his eyes, and tried to focus on the darkness, on sleep. The worst of his sharp pain dulled, and the throbbing lessened from a booming firework to a small drum. His eyes still hurt, but the pulsing ceased, and the quiet of the room was welcome relief to his ears.

For as wretched as he felt, sleep itself remained elusive. He tossed and turned, searching for any position of comfort, the discontent shifting from his head to his neck and back again. And through it all, Tommen's question echoed in his mind. *What if the Author's morals are different from yours?*

Every time he leaned hard into the Order, every time he pressed into the journals, what they said, what they stood for, what they meant for the universe at large, he himself experienced rather intense suffering. There were setbacks, there were obstacles, and then there was this. Missing fingers. Seizures. A brush with death that was far closer than anything he'd experienced so far. War with the Borelians.

On the other hand, his head injury had occurred before he even knew what Time was. He had been tortured before hearing about the Akari at all. For the longest time, he had been convinced that it only served the ancestors' purpose, to prepare him for even tougher battles to come, to prepare him for this interstellar, perhaps even interdimensional war with the Borelians, with the Akarin, with the dragon and the Shadows themselves. He still believed that this was all preparation, but what if it was preparation for something entirely different?

They were about to attack the Borelians in their own home, in one of their greatest cities and strongholds. They were going to break into a temple and loot it. If they could bring down the temple and break the dragon's stronghold, it would send shockwaves through the unseen, spiritual realm, not just the physical universe.

And yet, there was the journal to consider. Was this journal—and by extension, the other two—really considered good, then, because this whole adventure was leading up to breaking the dragon's stronghold on Brelix? Or was it evil, inspired by the dragon and now protected in its own home? Was it possible that it was better to leave it there, let it rot, let it burn, let the Borelians do whatever they wanted with it? What about the other two, then?

The Shadows were the enemies of the Whites, the enemies of the Author. It was reasonable to think that they held two different sets of morals. But where did that leave him? He already suspected that the journals were incomplete because of Cassius' interference. Wasn't it a good thing to get them back and set them to rights?

He wouldn't say he didn't understand Julianna's hesitation on the matter. She loved her husband, believed in his work, didn't want to even consider that they had both been duped. In the midst of turmoil and the fallout from a splintered Akarin, it had been easy for the dragon to confuse what the Author was trying to tell them and so write the journals in its own image as it were.

Except the Author already had the Authored Books. It was why the Akarin splintered, why Richard and Julianna had left in the first place.

Because the dragon couldn't write such books, because the dragon didn't have the same intimate knowledge of Creation that the Author had. It could only copy, not create. Then things started to get out of hand. The following was growing, but Cassius was, too, more unstable. Before the dragon could whisper any more journals, things erupted into chaos. Journals were lost, Julianna and Cassius were lost to time for a while, and everything spiraled out of control. So while the dragon and its mortal minions scrambled to find and keep track of three little journals and a scattered following held together only by the dragon's most elite soldiers, the Borelians, the Author continued to quietly release her own Books.

Of course, the dragon didn't need mere mortal books to have power over this three-dimensional realm. It had survived for countless years without them, through empires of total authoritarianism and total chaos. It had a claw in every pie: the Borelians, the Tacagans, the Time industry itself, the First Order of the Akari, maybe even the Akarin now that they were fractured, and who knew how many more?

And now, it was maneuvering everyone into position to face off in war, like professional sports teams playing for a championship. One slow elimination at a time. The Order conquered the Akarin, now they were moving up to face the Borelians. After that, the goal was the Time industry. The Time industry, the Wheel of Time. What's more, the Core of the Wheel. And Rifun, the only non-Akarin Builder who had access to it. Who had almost given the dragon access.

Rifun still had his eyes closed, and he stared into the darkness, begging for sleep. He couldn't decide whether his thoughts were rambling and incoherent because of his stagnant yet still-powerful headache, or perhaps the clearest they'd been for some time. What if it was true, and they were about to make a massive mistake? The Order had suffered from failed leadership for a long time; this could be how the dragon finally got rid of both them and the Akarin. On the other hand, what if it was a lie, and the dragon was trying everything it could to protect itself and its Borelian minions from being razed by the Order and the Akarin?

He rolled over, still looking for a position of comfort. He toyed with Matter a little, trying to relieve some of the pressure in his head and neck. It did not go away completely, but, like deflating a balloon, everything began to settle, and pain slid into fatigue. He'd think about it more in the morning, when his head was a little clearer.

Just as he was on the cusp of sleep, a new sensation crept over his body and he felt himself tense up and freeze. For a moment, he had a specific instinct that a *halamenavody*—a black widow spider—was crawling on his arm. His chest tightened as he tried to use Matter to pinpoint its location. But why would there be a spider on him? And why a *halamenavody* specifically?

Then there was something like a thought or an impression placed in his mind. There was no spider, but the danger and wrath he was provoking was just as deadly.

The sensation vanished, leaving him feeling tired and shivering. Now entirely unwilling to open his eyes, he rolled over again and finally found sleep.

35 | Maturation
First Order Fortress, 2015

The rumor mill and discontent with Rifun started to take on a life of its own, like a machine that was beginning to run under its own power. Julianna didn't even need to plant the seeds of dismay as Rifun practically ignored a small skirmish with Akarin rebels and instead spent Order resources on a single human planet. It might not have been so bad, except Vin Lay didn't really have anything to offer the Order. They weren't the bigger threat, and saving them produced no great gains. With the discovery of the vast network of rich mines, which the Borelians had targeted, Vin Lay had finally hit an industrial revolution and was well on track to invent things like mechanized factories and rail systems, hardly anything to jump on.

Meanwhile, the Akarin fortress was very nearly rebuilt. The staircases were all functional again, and the fifth floor had been resurrected, the fourth, fifth, and sixth floors now sitting in their proper places once more. There was still plenty more work to be done as the floors were still very unstable and off-limits to the general public, but it was an enormous step in the right direction. Julianna was just on her way there to see how things were coming along when she spotted Tommen meandering his way down the staircase, likely just finished a meeting with Rifun after going on another adventure in his mission to rescue the journal. She changed course and intercepted him.

"Good morning, Tommen," she greeted amiably. "I trust your adventure was productive?"

"Haven't decided yet, but it would be nice to know why I'm being sent to places you can't go yourselves seeing how everyone already knows you there," he replied shortly.

So, he was annoyed that Rifun wasn't doing this himself, or that the man seemed to know a lot more than he let on and was jerking Tommen's chain.

"We aren't sending you anywhere, Tommen. You choose where you think you need to go. Rifun probably told you about having the means but not the time?

Well, it is true. Merely gathering the rumors took considerable time, never mind having to figure out which ones to pursue. I'm behind on my work, and he is behind on his, whatever his work is these days."

Tommen blinked. "What do you mean?"

Julianna sighed and lowered her voice. "The seizures have taken a toll on him, not necessarily the convulsions themselves, though that takes a considerable physical toll when they do happen, but the psychology of it. Likely they will be with him the rest of his life."

"Hm...can't imagine what that's like." Tommen intentionally scratched around his ears, intentionally indicating the hearing aids he'd worn since being partially defeaned by Rifun firing his gun next to his head. No sympathy, then, that Rifun was maybe getting a small taste of his own medicine.

"That's another reason why we want you to do this. You are known as the Faharoa's favorite. As long as you are out there and active and pursuing this, it makes him look busy and involved as well. He's a field general, meant for war. Between the seizures and the desk job, I think he's lost heart."

"It's called depression. He'll get over it."

"This war with the Borelians seems to be the highlight of his life right now, even more so than the journal."

"Then why doesn't he track it down himself? Purpose, meaning, hooray. Seemed to help him when he went blind."

"All faith goes stagnant at one point or another, no matter how zealous the follower."

Tommen shrugged. "Once again, he'll get over it. Either the war with the Borelians will enslave or save us all, or I'll find the journal, one or the other. Then he'll be back to his usual self."

She hoped her expression conveyed some measure of concern as she nodded. "I hope you're right. If the men ever got wind that their fearless leader was depressed—to say nothing of the seizures themselves—it could cause them to question him, me, our cause. The Akarin would see the weakness and they may try another uprising."

"Shouldn't they have faith in the Akari, not Rifun?" Tommen wondered innocently.

"True, but with exception of the core group who has been with us through the revolution and many years prior, most here are in just the earliest stages of personal faith. Rifun is still the face of victory. He led them against the Akarin and survived Borelian poison. He is practically a god to them." She paused for some dramatic effect. "Find the journal. It may bring Rifun back around, help get him back where he needs to be, and it will strengthen the men. Then we can go after the Borelians whole-heartedly."

The teenager looked like there were a thousand things he wanted to say, but in the end he merely promised to do his best, but only after he went home and got some sleep. Julianna got out of his way and watched him go.

He could just be tired, but she had a sneaking suspicion that Tommen was not overly impressed by the way things were going either. Not that he'd ever been what one might call a willing participant, but considering the leeway he was being given in this, even he sounded frustrated and confused. He would be running to the Akarin soon enough, looking for help, looking for a way to pull one over on the Order and maybe get back in the Akarin's good graces. If he could deliver the journal, it might spark another uprising attempt, and what leverage they would hold, assuming they did get their hands on journal.

With Tommen now gone, she resumed her original course, meeting with Torbak on the platform of the fifth floor. They ducked under the veritable rope and made use of a small nearby nook. The general public would not bother them, but it would be easy enough to leave if the construction workers chased them out.

"What have you found?" she asked, putting up a Sound barrier.

"The spies weren't willing to swear on their lives, but they believe there is a strong chance that Andrew of Aleis is Andrew O'Dell," Torbak reported. "Physique is very similar, and he is an outsider come into Aleis only in the last few decades. He was not born and raised there like the rest. Similarly, while he does hold some local authority and lives the local lifestyle, he does not observe all the local customs."

Julianna frowned. "The Aleisi are highly religious and do not easily suffer dissent in their ranks, especially among their leaders. If there is an outsider who does not keep all of their ways but is still permitted authority, even just local authority, there is a damn good reason for it."

"Also makes it hard to keep track of him," the general told her. "Towns are small, families are large and intermixed —"

"Everyone knows everyone, and everyone will know if something's off, whether a stranger comes to town or if someone isn't acting right." She nodded slowly, mostly to herself. "He chose his disguise well."

"What do you want us to do?"

Now she shook her head and looked at him. "You and your spies have done well; you don't need to do anything more. This is a human matter now."

"And you will not waste our resources as Faharoa did."

"Exactly." She dipped her head. "What else did your spies discover?"

Torbak handed her a few sheets of paper. "A map from the town to his house. A map of the land around his house. Some rudimentary observations of his actions compared to others the spies believed similar to him. And some other notes of interest."

"Very good. I will look over these and get back to you if I have any questions."

The general took his leave, sliding out of the nook, exiting the Sound barrier, and returning to the staircase with no trouble. Julianna, meanwhile, sifted through the papers. The maps were not exactly satellite images, but they were well-detailed and would get her from one place to another. She glanced through the observational notes. Some of them were clearly nonsensical, but she did not hold it against the spies; they were not versed in human customs enough to know that some of these things were entirely innocuous. Other observations were more interesting and more astute, but hardly sinister. Andrew would sing in church and read the Bible, but he was not fully one of them. Likely raised Catholic, he would not easily allow himself to be associated with any other religion or denomination. Because of this, he might not have been permitted to marry, or no woman would have him. On the other hand, if he did fully convert, he might have been expected to marry. Did he view such a family as a potential liability, for a time such as this? Or was he too afraid of having to watch them grow old and die well before him?

She decided on the former, because it meant that he still kept one eye out for the Order, for the Akarin. It was the only way he could be such an outsider but still hold local authority.

But, as she'd said, this was a human matter now, and non-human notes and observations could only go so far. She needed more information, she needed to be absolutely certain, and she would have to do it herself.

She kept her Disguise simple: cover the scars on her face, bring out more of the recessive features from her father, change her hair color, and maybe add a few pounds for good measure, make it look like she'd had a few kids. She couldn't do much about clothing until she saw the local fashion, but seeing how her normal preferred clothing was a couple centuries outdated, she didn't think she would look too outlandish if someone did happen to spot her.

Torbak's spies might not have had the best drawing skills, but they were remarkably accurate in their technical skills, such as reporting the exact planetary location of the town Andrew was associated with, as well as his house. Judging by the map, the landscape was generally wide open in every direction, large swaths of crop fields, wheat and hay and corn.

Corn would be her best bet, she decided as she started opening up microportals, looking for a corn field close to Andrew's house. She found a corn field, and it wasn't what she would call close, but it was the closest she was probably going to get, and she wasn't inclined to waste time looking for a better opportunity.

Stepping through the portal to Aleis was no different than any other trip through a portal, but the fresh air, morning dew, and brilliant sunrise did make it easier to bear. The din of activity from the fortress faded away, leaving only a mild breeze that ruffled the long leaves on the corn stalks that were only just taller than her. Overhead, a sudden twittering caught her attention as two small birds danced overhead, darting at each other in either a courting ritual or a minor scuffle, she could not tell.

She stood on a relatively flat piece of ground, though in about twenty yards it began to slope away, down toward a wooden fence that separated the corn field from a wheat field. A house that was not Andrew's sat off to the left. Beyond this wheat field was another fence and another grassy field, whether wheat or something else she could not tell at this distance. On the other side of that field was Andrew's house, set near the road. She started that way, hoping that distance and a little manipulation of Light would hide her from any happpenstance glances. Although she remained a distance from the first house — south, she believed it was — she could hear the noises of morning chores on the wind as it shifted. Milking a couple cows, gathering eggs, feeding chickens, dealing with a stubborn goat, and trying to corral a few rambunctious toddlers.

No alarms were raised, no greetings called as she slipped from the corn field into the wheat field and continued to the fence where she easily slid over and continued on. This field was not wheat, but hay, and she had to erect a Sound barrier to cover a sudden bout of sneezing.

She avoided the barn so as not to alert any animals to an intruder. She saw four enormous Belgians in a pasture on the other side of the road, but she could hear more movement in the barn. More by smell than sound, she was able to identify a flock of chickens and at least one billy goat. They may not raise an alarm for a stranger, but they might get fussy about wanting breakfast.

Through it all, she did not see or hear any indication of human life either inside or outside. No movement, no lights, no talking, nothing. Still circling the home area, she came upon a smaller barn-type structure and found it empty. Tracks indicated this was where the buggy was kept.

Early riser, she thought, *and already on his way to town.*

She remained cautious as she approached the house and let herself in, noting that the doors didn't even have the option to lock, neither keyhole nor bolt nor exterior padlock. Just a perfectly trusting knob. Once inside, she Banded and did a quick search of the house to make sure Andrew wasn't around. Satisfied that she was the only one here, she dropped the Band and was less paranoid about being sneaky.

She wasn't sure what she would be looking for here. Her better bet was probably to follow him into town and hope he was going to some council meeting. The problem with that was, one, she was a woman, and two, there was every chance that even if there were a meeting she could get into, it would be just mundane business. Clearly it was almost harvest time; they would be coordinating manpower and resources to get the crops in before winter. They could be worried about the Borelians all they wanted, but if they didn't have food for the winter, they weren't going to last long.

Besides, she mused, carefully opening up every cabinet, cupboard, and drawer, Andrew probably didn't flaunt his past life. If he was hiding, he wouldn't parade himself around and separate himself any more than he already was.

The kitchen was unremarkable, if cute and tidy. The wood bin near the stove was missing a few logs but was otherwise full, the small wash basins were upside down to dry, a few dishes on a towel nearby. The rest of the dishes were put away, a place for everything and everything in its place.

The living room offered the first clue, a rifle hidden in the base of the couch, the secret compartment accessed under the cushions. This might not have intrigued her, except the rifle was not what one would call Old World craftsmanship. It wasn't exactly an automatic military rifle, but it wasn't designed to plink squirrels and rabbits.

There were four bedrooms and six closets in the house. Two bedrooms were used for general storage. Julianna lightly pawed through some of the stuff, but found nothing of interest. Judging by the dust and general disarray, nothing here was intended to be retrieved quickly. A third bedroom was more properly set up, though it had no singular purpose. A sewing machine sat in one corner, but tables along the wall were populated with a variety of small projects, from sewing to minor woodcarving. In this room's closet, she discovered a pistol, again clearly not of Aleisi origin.

Finally she made her way to Andrew's room. The simplicity of Aleisi life meant she didn't have to go digging through endless baubles and trinkets and extraneous entertainment. It was in the closet where she found her first lock, on a chest on the floor. While the chest itself was designed to have a loop that could be used to thread a padlock, Julianna deduced that such a feature was intended to simply keep the lid shut while moving the chest, not deter burglars.

The lock was not magnetic and entirely unaffected by Magnetism, but this was nothing a tiny bit of Force couldn't handle. The pins clicked and the lock popped open.

"I found you," she sang softly, opening the chest and examining the contents.

Clothes not of Aleisi origin or style, a bag of supplies including more guns and ammo, and a small container of multiple currencies and bogus documents. Only one of the official documents actually read Andrew O'Dell, but the pictures were all the same, and it was all she needed.

Very clever, Andrew. You've been keeping your head down and still managed to keep an eye on everything going on. Was this just the most clever thing you could think of, or do you actually expect to find forgiveness for your sins?

She put everything back the way she found it and quietly crept out of the room, as if too loud of a sound might make the man suddenly appear. She left the way she entered and retreated into the nearest field where she crouched and waited.

And waited.

And waited.

The sun rose high over the landscape and the air grew warm. The morning dew was long gone and the breeze had given way to stifling humidity. Still Andrew did not appear. She saw and heard no buggies, no horses, nothing but the faintest hint of activity from the neighbor.

Eventually, she gave up and returned to the fortress. Stifling humidity was replaced with stale stuffiness. The sounds of nature disappeared, sharply giving way to the din of activity in a crowded building. Beautiful sunlight dimmed to whatever it was that this place used to see by. It was a bit disheartening, but also a problem for another day. She had confirmed Andrew O'Dell's identity, now she had to figure out what to do about it. First she should make sure he didn't react to her being in his house. Other than a little disturbed dust in the extra bedrooms—which, her experience with men said he wouldn't notice anyway—she had done her absolute best to ensure everything went back exactly how she found it.

Killing him was out of the question at the moment. He was working deep cover, and whatever contacts he had outside of Aleis, at this stage in the game, it would be treated with great suspicion, and she didn't feel like having to deal with any time-consuming ramifications. With his skills as a Builder, even trying to make it look like some farm accident would be too tricky to pull off unless it was a last resort. Similarly, it was far too late to try and persuade him to switch sides, or at least be a little more sympathetic to the cause.

Was there anything he could be threatened with, coerce him into certain actions or inaction in their favor? He didn't have a family on Aleis, but maybe he'd pulled a Micaiah and squirreled one away somewhere else? He obviously valued his life if he was going to such lengths to conceal himself, but he couldn't be a complete coward if he was still involved at all, and with the stakes so high, he might be willing to give his life if he thought the cause great enough. Was one little journal really that important to him? Or would he look at the Borelian backdrop, lump the two tasks together, and decide that death was the same in any form?

Could they entice him into the open in some way, provoke him to violence like Drinjin uh Ersik provoked the Akarin and subsequently beat down? They would have to get the key, then deal with Andrew, in that order. They could not let him get away.

Accomplices. Did he have any accomplices? Indirect ways of reaching him, but also possible avenues of escape. Was he still in contact with Nathan Wilde? It was reasonable to think so, assuming the man was still alive. Unfortunately, if he was, he seemed to have pulled off a better disappearing act than Andrew.

You can't let your plans and ideas slide into nebulous obscurity. You must work with what you know and what you can reasonably suspect.

Andrew from Aleis is Andrew O'Dell. That much I can prove. He hides on Aleis and is blended in with their culture and lifestyle, but he does not fully commit, even has a bag all ready to go in case he needs to flee quickly. And yet, the Aleisi allow it. Or they don't know about it, but I doubt that. The Akarin have never so much as hinted at him, suggesting he isn't sneaking off to see them or rally any troops. If he is truly an integral part of life in his town, he can't be doing too much heavy lifting about the journal, the key, the Order, or any other matters, so he must have outside help of some form. He helped to hide the key, so he can't not suspect that Rifun intends to go after the journal and will need said key.

And...?

Tommen is the one going after the journal. No doubt he is keeping his dad and probably others apprised of the situation. Last I knew, he said he'd hit a wall and didn't know quite what to do. If he continues to flounder, something will have to give. Either Rifun will have to tell him where the key is, or the Akarin — Andrew or Nathan, if he's alive — will. Rifun is counting on the Akarin coming forward, the Akarin can't risk Rifun coming forward.

And...?

Rifun seems to think that he lacks something necessary to get into the Core of the Wheel and retrieve the key, something that Andrew and-or Nathan possess, be it a talent or a physical object. If that were true and obvious, Andrew and Nathan have no cause to worry; like watching a dog try to dig through concrete, they only have to sit back and watch the futility. So either it's not true and Rifun is simply unskilled and cowardly, or it is true but Andrew and Nathan don't know this little hiccup.

Julianna sighed and paced a few steps. She felt like she was going in circles. On the one hand, she felt like she had to do something. On the other hand, it seemed like the only meaningful course of action was to do nothing.

Waiting patiently is not the same as doing nothing. A predator waiting for its prey to move within striking range is not doing nothing. And considering one's actions can save much time and headache later. What would you do with Andrew if you did catch him before you had the journal? You have stated that it is useless to kill him, maybe even counterproductive. Coerce him, threaten him? What would you want him to do?

Open the Core and give us the key.

So, he does this, and you have the key. Now what?

He doesn't matter anymore. If he escapes, it is frustrating, but not especially consequential. Or we can kill him and be done with it.

And what of the key? If he has help, they will find out what happened, by his words or by his death.

They provoke the Akarin to violence and uprising against us, or they try a more subtle method of stealing it back.

And there is one more thing to consider. What if they decide to simply destroy the key? No more hiding, no more capture the flag, just straight up destroy it? One key to a lock, and one lock to a key.

Then we would have to go with the backup plan, use Matter or Energy to force the door open. Or just tear down the entire temple.

And in the middle of a battle, which plan is the best use of resources? What is going to require the least amount of planning, the least special treatment? Which is going to have the most significant impact?

Tearing down the temple. We're not going to conquer Ancrath, so we might as well destroy it, and it sends a message to the Borelians.

And...?

And it renders Tommen's special mission entirely obsolete. No more chosen one nonsense.

Or...?

Or we can combine the two. Send Tommen to get the journal, then, once we have it, bring the temple down on top of him. Capture Rifun, if he isn't already dead, and blame him for that, too. Can't even keep his favorite minion safe. She sighed. *But for it to get that far, we have to wait. Patiently.*

You waited for decades in the in-between dimension, learning history and acquiring extensive knowledge. Shake off the urge to run after everything that moves just because you can, and learn to pick your targets and pick your battles.

If I don't move against Andrew now, if they think they can pull off this heist in secret, then he will only return to his safe little hole afterwards, pretend nothing happened, and try to blend in like before. But now I know who, what, and where he is. I will find him, and I will kill him. Just like I killed Micaiah and Foyez and soon Rifun.

Still, she wasn't thrilled about the waiting part. She had done nothing but wait for decades, and here she was, still waiting. The problem was, she didn't necessarily want to rush Rifun. The longer he dawdled, the more restless and dissatisfied his men grew. On the other hand, the longer he dawdled, the greater chance the Borelians would attack the Order first, or go after another human world. Planetary defenses were great and they offered a fair amount of breathing room, but they were not infallible. They couldn't just sit back and let the Borelians continue to attack without getting in at least one good swing.

Maybe she could push him into a rushed, foolish attack. No, that wouldn't work. The Order was too large by itself to mobilize everyone instantly, and their operation—attacking Ancrath plus trying to include the Akarin—was far too enormous. She had faith that Drinjin uh Ersik could muster some men in time and get things moving, but it would not have the same power that it would with a more stable plan. She only wanted to take out Rifun's supporters, not her own.

She set off in search of Drinjin uh Ersik. When she did not find him easily and could not find anyone who was certain of his whereabouts, she decided to change her focus to Rifun and headed up the northeast staircase. When she reached Rifun's chambers, she found both him and Drinjin uh Ersik, as well as a handful of lesser offices, standing around the table, studying a huge, much more detailed, printed map of what she assumed to be Ancrath. At least this time the labels were in English, although there were still some non-English notes scribbled here and there. There were also several smaller sheets of paper with what looked like graphs and charts, but she was not in a position to be able to read what they were depicting.

"Julianna," Rifun acknowledged. "Something we can do for you?"

She approached the table, briefly noting that the chart nearest her was detailing how much time a certain alien species had before the toxic Borelian atmosphere started to do damage, and how long until that damage became permanent.

"I was just coming to make a general inquiry," she replied. "Naturally, the artists and philosophers among us are less than pleased that they are again being called to war. I promised them I would inquire as to a timeline of when they are expected to fight and also, perhaps, if they might have...lesser assignments."

Rifun opened his mouth to speak, but one of the lesser officers cut him off. "I do not know how things are among humans, or among those whose lavish societies permit such things, but among my people, there is a saying that the head and the body cannot be separated if the person wishes to live."

"Yes, that is a rather prudent observation," Rifun commented mildly, his tone suggesting this was not the first time he had heard this speech.

"What one wants and what one is capable of must be in alignment," the officer went on. "A man may wish to be an artist, but if his strengths, especially his physical strengths, are more appropriately applied elsewhere, then he must obey the call. You may tell your artists and philosophers that entertaining the head is secondary to utilizing the body."

"Enough!" Drinjin uh Ersik barked. The officer shut his mouth, but his expression said he stood behind every syllable.

"Lo'Pak isn't wrong," Rifun told her. "We cannot let a Grunjor hide in the back because he enjoys oil paintings more than war. He is a Grunjor, he is more suited to the front lines."

"But a Miamo, the smallest alien among us, not much larger than a common rat, you would send to the front lines if he were enthusiastic to do so, rather than keep him back because he is more suited to preplanning spying or espionage?" Julianna challenged.

"The Miamo cannot go to Brelix; even with a translator providing an atmospheric shell, he would be brain damaged in five minutes, dead within ten. To your point, were that not an issue and he able to go, would be set to a task requiring his size and dexterity. For example, cutting the wires and damaging the circuitry of the Borelian ships in the shipyard. As it is, they are the ones keeping an eye on the Akarin downstairs, reporting any further...disgruntlement."

Provoking further disgruntlement, Julianna thought.

"As I have said before," Rifun went on, "if it were any other enemy or any other battlefield, they could go about their business as desired. We don't have that option right now."

"The Borelians don't know we're attacking. We can change anything we want!" she blurted. "Why not choose a more hospitable world to attack, another farming world? Divert their military there, sneak into the temple on Ancrath and steal the journal from under their noses."

"The Ancrath Archives will have more useful information," another officer told her. "Movements, strategies, weaknesses, strengths. We cannot stay on the defensive forever. Such a bold move this early in the war will shake them and may open up more opportunities."

So he was both rash and delayed. That was rather impressive, actually, but twice as frustrating.

"Now then, was there something you actually needed?" Rifun asked.

Public humiliation in front of all his friends. How quaint. And what if he were to have a seizure now? Would you still shield him?

We need to out his supporters, too, make a public spectacle of it.

Trying to keep him alive, then? Why switch his meds? Why not go straight for the battle and the accusation of treason?

We will see whom the Author favors. If she sees fit to kill him, then it will be so.

One day, you will learn to kill. To pull the trigger, to wield the knife, and to not hesitate. But you are learning.

She Banded herself and Rifun. "What do they know of the journal and the key?"

"They know about the journal, but not the key," he told her, his expression unreadable. "As far as they're concerned, the journal is in the temple somewhere, but they do not know about the vaults."

"And what do they know of Tommen and his mission?"

"Right now, they consider him my errand boy. A few have an inkling that he is up to something important, but they don't know exactly what. They will learn eventually, but I want something a little more concrete from him before I parade him around as anyone helpful to us."

She nodded once. "Well, you're not wrong there." She dropped the Band and addressed the group at large. "Has anyone heard any rumors about the Akarin Builders Andrew O'Dell or Nathan Wilde?"

"No, why?" Rifun asked, unimpressed.

"Andrew O'Dell has been located."

"Yes, you said you suspected that he was one of the Aleisi leaders."

"And I confirmed. I went to his home on Aleis." She described what she found. "He is the Builder who stole the journal years ago."

"Did you find anything at his residence indicating some planned treachery or sabotage when we launch our attack?" one officer inquired.

"I did not. I—"

"Everyone get out," Rifun cut in. He looked at Julianna. "Except you."

It took a moment for the command to register, and another long minute before everyone finally left the room. Even once the door was shut, Rifun erected a Sound barrier and Banded the two of them.

"What are you doing?" he asked, his tone uncomfortably level. "I'm trying to make a plan of attack."

"And I'm trying to get the journal back. Or is Tommen's little quest to get the key out of the Core a silly little diversion for me as well as him? Because it may just draw Nathan and Andrew out of the shadows. And if Andrew is a leader and he's going to all these meetings and getting all this information...He's not Aleisi or Amish or whatever. He's not some meek and mild pacifist who's turned over a new leaf and is going to let this go. He wants to be involved. As soon as Tommen figures out the key, he's going to be all over it." She spoke before Rifun had a chance to open his mouth. "Again I ask, was this little quest intended to keep Tommen busy, or me?"

"Either, neither, both. Take your pick. It is intended to be taken seriously. As much as I would love to just rip apart the temple brick by brick, we don't know enough about them to do so. Wanton destruction, we could, but I don't want to damage or destroy the journal in the process, or make it more difficult to access. We don't know what kind of security we'll be facing and a more sneaky approach with a key may be more appropriate than even dismantling a single door."

"What, your girlfriend didn't give you the secret password?"

"I count us fortunate that we got such information at all. She did it because the Borelians were cocky enough to believe us beat whether we had the information or not. I think the Author gave it to us because she knew we wouldn't roll over so easily but maybe still needed a little push. Honestly, if not for the journal being in that temple, we probably wouldn't be going to Brelix at all right now."

"So why not—?"

"*Mijanòna! Aza miteny intsony!*" he snapped, turning and walking away a few angry steps. "*Arrêtez! N'en dis pas plus!* Stop. Talking." He paused, maybe ten feet between them, and turned to face her. Taking a deliberate breath, he said, "You wanted to be in charge of the Order. Fine. You are. You have full control over everything that happens in this fortress, but you don't have skill in war or battle. I am trying to manage a war, and a battle and battlefield where we are sorely outmanned and outgunned. In order to find a journal that you want and need for your operations here. Meanwhile, I am also trying to play politics with a faction who isn't the friendliest toward us right now. Maybe instead of sticking your nose in business where you have nothing to offer, you could instead take your charm— and you have far more charm than I do—and try to build some bridges to our enemies right downstairs and convince them to fight with us with some enthusiasm.

"We are coming up on mobilization. We aren't just sitting here playing cards and pretending to plan; we are actually planning. We have determined a course of action that we—as a collection of military veterans and leaders with over four centuries of combined experience—believe is the most appropriate for the situation and our goals. That is what is happening. The details are still being ironed out, but the big picture is already clear.

"Now, if you have something useful to offer, such as discovering treasonous activities or other major obstacles or developments, by all means, let us know. If you find out that Andrew, or his mystery helper, is secretly rallying a force to attack us here in the fortress while our attention is on Brelix, let us know. But enough with this fretting and worrying. Let us do our job. I don't ask to see your teaching curriculum and ask you to constantly change it. Please, give us the same respect."

Julianna studied him for a long moment, trying to discern his motives.

"I know you question my loyalty," he went on, calmer now, as if reading her thoughts. "But I only wish to see the Order thrive. That means getting rid of what is evil, yes, but it may also mean considering that we may be wrong on some points as well. And who knows? The Book of Commands may hold something that will clear up some issues."

"And what are your plans for the Akarin?" she wondered. "Assuming we do get the journal, assuming we do survive this assault and have the luxury of letting the artists be artists?"

"Once we establish what is good and true of the journals and the Books, then everyone either conforms or serves."

At the mention of the Books, Julianna scoffed and shook her head.

"We can discuss it afterwards," he said, his tone turning blandly professional. "Right now, we have a battle to fight."

She said nothing, just let the Sound barrier dissolve and the Band drop, then left the room. Outside, the officers were milling about, uncertain whether they should wait or else go about some other business. They looked up as she exited. She simply waved them in without a word, then started down the stairs.

He was still on about the Authored Books. Still thought they could be salvaged. No. This just wasn't going to work.

You can't serve two masters. The Author may be one being, but viewed in contradictory lights. The human range of vision is one hundred eighty degrees for a reason, to face only one way, the true way. Turning to try and view both at the same time means you cannot see either, not for as it truly is.

Plans are already in place, and more are in motion. All that remains is to wait and continue to water the seeds already planted. Trying to plant too many seeds will only choke out what would have grown with more careful cultivation.

So many years in the in-between dimension. Waiting. Lurking. Gathering information. Dreaming of what she would do with it once she was free. All these plans, these desires. And yet, she was still waiting. The gates flew open, the bell sounding madly, crowd cheering, but the maximum allowed speed was a walk.

Keep your eyes up. Ignore the immediate vicinity, for it is clear. What lies ahead? What will you do once the journal is recovered and Rifun deposed?

Go after his followers and show no mercy. You cannot serve two masters, and a house divided cannot stand. Make an example of them first, then go after the Akarin. Tear them down, dismantle them, destroy them until they are nothing but dust. Destroy the Authored Books so that no record of them remains, and rewrite the journals to exclude them as well. Make it so the Akarin never existed.

No. They will always have existed. Covering them up only indicts you.

Then they went extinct. Through theological disarray and military inferiority.

Natural decline is easier on the minds of future generations than horrible violence. Eventually, they become just another ancient civilization with no bearing on anything of importance.

And if Rifun could learn to be a Builder without being Akarin, others can learn as well. They might even learn better because they don't have the divided loyalty that he does. The Core of the Wheel will be no challenge for us and we will have no further need of the Akarin Builders.

It was nice to have a plan, a destination, but a mountain fifty miles away might be visible, but it was still fifty miles away. And she was still only walking.

The meetings on Tacaga were never pleasant. They might have been civil, but no one ever arrived or departed feeling like something might actually be accomplished as a friendly, cooperative endeavor for the greater good. No one really felt confident that the people who called themselves allies would actually have their back. So it wasn't much of a surprise when Hlohi announced that they were going to take the fight to the Borelians with some new allies. It was even less surprising to find out that Aklaq White Bear was the one spear-heading the effort.

The allies she had found came from a planet with no universal name and was populated by a multitude of races, all of them animalistic humanoids. The world itself was Scientifically Primitive and Unengaged, which was the first mistake. Aklaq's contact with the planet and people came from Sifura, who was, in fact, a Hand of the Time industry, and who had been the one to help Tommen find a cure for his ailing father after Cassius rejected his petition before the Hands. Her people were called the Xur, and they resembled lions and tigers. Other interested races included the D'Bok, like a bear crossed with a komodo dragon; the Gin Jor, with head fans like some lizards; the Rupi, bird-like in appearance, a bit like the Tibidi; and the Ouin, having a distinctly fishy appearance.

"So," Walter said, looking over each tribal delegation. "These are your allies."

"They are," Aklaq stated. "And with a combined army of nearly a quarter million."

"With sticks and stones," Rifun said casually. "And no Time abilities to speak of."

"Before we get too far ahead of ourselves, how about a status report from all the worlds?" Walter suggested. "That way we have a platform to work from."

It was a short report. All the Borelians that had been on each of the planets before the shields were activated had been killed, and no new ones had come through. Each world, except Tacaga, had a small force of Akari-bearers who could get through the shields to take the Time Agents where they needed to go, most often to the Wheel. Tacaga still denied the Akari, denounced the Akari-bearers, and demanded to know what new technology or abilities they were using, but were simply told that it could not be taught to hard-headed atheists. The Akari was powered by Faith, something the Tacagans greatly lacked. Well, that spawned a whole new philosophical argument, but the bottom line was, the worlds were safe.

"So why do you want to mess it up?" one of the Sakarians wondered. "If we are safe here, or on our worlds, and have nothing to fear, why would we do this?"

"We made a promise to not stop until the Borelians were destroyed," Aklaq said harshly.

"Promise to whom?" Milay asked. "Each other? We promised to deliver the planetary defenses, and we have. Our agreement has been met. Our status as an autonomous race is being debated even now."

"We are spear-heading this effort. I have brought the Xur, the D'Bok, the Gin Jor, the Rupi, and Ouin. I have little doubt that Rifun has been busy securing his alliances, though they are not so selfless, I presume—"

"So you do intend to remain with us?" the Aleisi not Andrew asked. "You are not going to attack the Borelians on your own?"

"We will if we have to. I will not abandon this mission." Aklaq turned to Walter and fixed him in a glare. "You've said often enough that people fear the Borelians, yes, but they love to hate them, they admire how untouchable they are." She looked around at those gathered. "And what are you all doing now? Reveling in your own safety? Sleeping now? Have you forgotten the fear you once lived under, that your world could be next? What would have happened to Vin Lay if we could not get the smaller defenses up to shield you? What if the Borelians had taken your world?

"Should we do nothing to avenge Treman and Trebald, lost to us before we even understood the threat? Ehani, who perished maybe or maybe not because we took the fight to the Borelians? Because that's what war is."

She paused to take a breath, continuing before anyone could object. "The Borelians are not going to go away because we've decided to hide under our rocks and pretend the threat no longer exists. They don't give up. Remember when the Wheel was closed off to us because the Borelians were hunting for human portals and entering that way? I don't know why they aren't doing that again now, but it is a hole in the defenses. What happens if they don't send an invasion, but just enough to come in and disable the shields? Who here knows how to repair them? Who can do it in time? What if the Borelians pull off an operation like that, with their armies ready to go as soon as the shields go down?

"We got in a great victory when we burned the Borelian farming world. Hundreds, thousands of species looked upon that monumental task with fear when it was proposed, and awe when it was accomplished. All over the universe, they watched as their greatest foe was wounded. Too big to hurt, or too big to miss? Now that the Borelians have figured out the connection between that attack and the human war, word has spread. There are allies out there, but because of politics in the Wheel, many are too afraid to speak up. Unless we give them reason to hope, reason to think that it wasn't a one-time operation, a one-time victory. We must have more victories. More victories means more allies means more victories."

"And you thought you were going to accomplish this by discarding my army of Akari-bearers and going with primitive spear throwers?" Rifun wondered. "Tell me, Aklaq, how well did that work out among your people facing the Russians, or any Native American—even my people—fighting the Europeans? The Borelians are only Engaged Privilege, true, but one Timekeeper in a thousand soldiers can still do more damage than the nine hundred ninety-nine he fights alongside, if the enemy cannot fight back. One skilled Harvester—a Triage, for instance—can do exceptional damage at just a touch."

"And for that matter, how do you expect your allies to respond?" one of the Dorigisi inquired. "They are not only primitive, they are Unengaged. They have never seen an alien, never seen this kind of technology, never seen Time. It is far beyond their military and psychological capabilities."

"We are many races," Sifura said, stepping forward. "We share one world. You all here, you are but one new tribe to us. The Monkey tribe, as Tommen Forbes once claimed. You are strange, but not so different. And the Borelians, the Ram tribe as he called them, yet another tribe. Many tribes, all unique, but still sharing a common goal. Many days, it is simply survival. Caring for one's family, one's clan, one's community. Food, water, the necessities of life. Defending against this atrocious enemy."

"Great. Now how about where it really matters in this instance?" Toros asked. "On the battlefield. One Timekeeper catches you, you are all dead."

"And that is where you all underestimate me," Aklaq said slyly. She slapped a folder on the table and opened it. "Profiles for every Borelian Time Agent, their activity, base location, current location, rank, training, everything. Including all the Grandfathers, past and present. Even now, I have assassins going out and killing these motherfuckers one by one. Thirty-seven are already dead, and that was just today. By the end of the week, I estimate over a thousand should be dead. The week after, ten thousand. The week after, who knows? Engaged Privilege means only their higher-ranking officers are trained. Kill them, and the army itself will begin to break down. Put the fear of God in them. Get rid of them. Take out their strongest while we still have the advantage to do so. The battlefield will easily balance itself out, if not tip in our favor."

"That's assuming they just stand there and take it," a Sakarian said. "They'll catch on pretty quick, I think. Then we may not be taking the battle to them. They'll be coming after us. Any of us, doesn't matter which. Or, if they catch on too much and figure out the Xur and the D'Bok and all them are now our allies, I'm pretty sure their world doesn't have the same planetary defenses ours do. It took months to get our defenses in place. And we can't just let them into our worlds as a roommate for a couple years while the Borelians pummel us. What would you have them do? Where do you expect them to go if things get bad?"

"Xur do not flee," Sifura hissed, flattening cat-like ears and baring cattish fangs. "We stand our ground and die defending it."

"That's nice when it's your ground," an Aleisi commented. "Would you do the same for someone else's ground?"

"When the Gin Jor declares an ally, we are allies for life," the lizard man hissed, tongue flicking out, not quite human but neither was it solely reptilian. "We are brothers. We do not flee."

"Where do you expect the battlefield to be?" Milay asked slowly. "We're not going to lower our defenses in hopes of enticing them onto a battlefield here. I would hope you people aren't stupid enough to try anything similar. And taking the Borelians to their world—" She mildly gestured toward Sifura and the others. "—would be, as Walter has pointed out, suicide, if not worse."

"Assassinate the Time Agents," Aklaq stated. "Burn the farming worlds. Do what has worked. Force the Borelians to react. How they do will determine our next move."

"So you haven't thought about this at all," a Dorigisi said. "Burn their farms, they'll raid someone else's farms."

"The enemy of my enemy is my friend. Burn their worlds, gain victories, gain allies. If the Borelians torch someone else's cornfields, more allies for us. Get closer and closer to home, eventually, we'll be on the steps of Ancrath itself."

"Except in their home system, the Borelians have support from above, and I'm not talking the God kind," Rifun pointed out. "Space ships. War ships. Reinforcements. Slightly less bad than an army full of Timekeepers, but no arrow is going to clear the stratosphere."

"Then we'll have to work together to disable them, or keep them busy. The Krydik, those from Wolf Clan, are trained in the Akari as well."

"Barely. To most, it is simply magic."

Aklaq ignored him. "The Tacagans are the most advanced of us. I'm sure you could come up with something. A bomb, perhaps. A computer virus."

"Fine," Rifun said, cutting in. "So the Tacagans give the Borelians a space war to worry about, and your little friends here are beating the Borelian ground army to death with clubs, spears, arrows, and a little magic. How exactly do you plan to win? Borelians have a societal structure, true, but every single one of them is trained to defend and die for their people and their world. They don't run and hide with the kids. When the civilians start getting involved, that's a lot more soldiers shooting at you. And they know their home turf better than you. More than just the lay of the land, they know the streets, their buildings, their homes. They know where the guns are stored in closets and under pillows."

"Then that makes it easy to know who the enemy is," Aklaq retorted, glaring at him.

"And I've noticed that my army is conspicuously absent from your plan. What are my men doing at this point?"

"Minding their own damn business. And you with them. Or maybe I'll offer you up first, see if they'll just take you and go home, call an end to the war."

"Doubtful," Rifun mused, but he was drowned out by the others, all talking over one another.

"His army brought us our first victory that you want to duplicate!"

"They are talented, gifted in Time and the Akari!"

"Many species bring many talents, many strengths to utilize!"

"His army is powerful, conquering those who conquered them until I believe they are undefeatable!"

"He is monopolizing the balance of power in the universe!" Aklaq cut in. "The Borelians are the only foe they haven't defeated. And we all remember what he did in the Wheel. Who is going to keep him in check then?"

"Who is keeping him in check now?" a Vin Lay asked simply. "For one man to keep another in check, both must have an agreement about it. Each man must allow the other to leverage power over him, to tell him to stop. No one tells a Borelian no, for he shall be enslaved. No one tells the Hands of Time and the Grandfathers no, for he shall have his clock broken. No one tells Rifun and his army no, for he shall die. Each one is constantly trying to dominate the other because he will not be told no, he will not allow power to be leveraged over him. And so each has proven to be true. So in a way, each one has his own monopoly."

"Very philosophical of you. What happens if Rifun's army does defeat the Borelians? We've gone from three powers to two, and one has already conquered the other in the past."

The Vin Lay, Lin, was not fazed. "And was conquered. That foe may have been conquered himself, but was he not viewed as unconquerable at one time? And yet he was. No kingdom lasts forever. Except, perhaps, the Borelians. But we cannot stop them if we do not use all our resources."

"A rabid dog once released will devour his master as surely as his enemies," Andrew from Aleis recited. Rifun thought his expression was a little too knowing.

"And be devoured himself in time," Lin continued. "The Borelians have ruled for a long time. How did they come to power? Did others fear their rise? Were they once fighting against a great evil in ages long past? Was it a similar situation as now? Who can know? But those who feared their rise, feared they would have eternal power. And we continue to give it to them." He looked at Rifun, his expression oddly calm. "We must use all of our resources." He gestured to Rifun. "Those who have great talent to match our enemies on the field of battle and Time warfare." He gestured to Aklaq. "And those who have great talent to match our enemies on the open battlefield. Or in the shadows, as the case may be."

Aklaq would not be swayed. "We have our plans. They may not be perfect, but they are our own. Ally yourselves with this monster if you wish. Sell your souls to him for thirty pieces of silver while you're all gathered here. But we will be carrying out our mission as we see fit. With or without you. And definitely without him or any of his men."

Aklaq and her allies turned to leave, but before she walked out the door, Walter asked, "Does that mean you would reject Tommen's help if he offered it?"

She left without answering.

"Well, this isn't going to end well," Rifun said, stepping away from the wall and moving off. "I better go have a word with her."

No one tried to stop him as he left the room, about five yards behind Aklaq and her new allies as they headed for the elevator. The tribal peoples were looking around like children trying to take it all in, too in awe to even ask questions.

"Pride will get you nowhere," he said casually.

She stopped. Her allies stopped. He stopped. She turned slowly and deliberately made her way back in his direction. He continued before she could speak. "You're just going to discard your greatest asset because you don't like me very much?" She stopped again, just out of arm's reach. "My people had pride. We had endless pride. In ourselves, our heritage, our ancestors. We had spirit; no one will deny that. But spirit does not win wars. Even numbers and home field advantage didn't mean much. Because we had no weapons, no means of defending ourselves or attacking our enemies. We came onto the battlefield with spears and improvised clubs and farm tools. The French came with guns and machinery. And fire. The only ones who stood a chance were the military defectors in the north, but even they didn't last long. By the time we were able to get weapons, we had already lost. Oh, we held out for a fair amount of time, holed up in old college dorms full of hunger and disease, but that wasn't life. That wasn't freedom.

"We got our freedom, in the end. France granted Madagascar its independence, albeit only under international pressure. But even that took a long time. Over a decade." He shook his head. "The Borelians...they're not going to grant humanity 'independence.' They will not call for a truce or a ceasefire or an armistice. They will kill us, if we're lucky. Handing me over would only satisfy your personal vengeance, but it will not help humanity. You think I want to work with the Tacagans? I don't. But they have the technology we need. They have the technology we need in order to even entertain such asinine discussions as whether we should even do anything because we have planetary defenses."

"So what's your grand plan, hm?" Aklaq challenged. "Throw the Akarin out front as fodder? Sacrifice all of them in the name of some noble cause and at the end of the day, you are all that's left?"

"If you're really that interested, if you are willing to listen to any semblance of reason, then come and see what we have planned. If we end up having to lead separate armies on the same battlefield, so be it. But this truly is one war where we cannot afford to fight each other." He hesitated. "The French knew that. They stoked the fears of the coastal peoples, claimed that the Merina would enslave all other peoples if they won the war. We ended up fighting each other for a time, which cost time and resources and men that we could not afford to lose." He gave her a serious look. "Don't make the same mistakes we made."

"I never make the same mistake twice," Aklaq hissed.

She lunged at him, but one of her allies, the lizard man, intercepted her like a viper. Sifura joined in and the two of them dragged her backwards. Rifun sighed but opened a portal to Hlohi. The tribal peoples walked through. As soon as Aklaq was through, still being held by Sifura and the lizard man, Rifun let the portal snap closed.

He returned to the meeting room where food and drink had been brought, an uneasy intermission to a tense meeting. Rifun did not announce himself, but he did not get much more than a plate of hors d'ouerves — internally snickering at Aklaq's comment about Order members being called such — before Toros spoke up and called the meeting back to order.

"Well, now that you have returned, perhaps we can figure out what our response is going to be. The first question becomes, do we want to try and stop her? I don't know how, but do we want to try? Yes or no?"

Half the room said "yes" at the same time the other half said "no."

"We can't afford to lose another world. Two, if the others truly are allied with her," one said.

"We will not lose anything the Borelians won't take by force if we don't try something," another pointed out.

"I say let her try," a third said. "Certainly doing something is better than doing nothing."

"That may have been true while we were yet helpless and without the shields. Now that the shields are in place and we can relax a little, we have to plan on how to do the right thing, the effective thing. Something that will make progress in this war in our favor," a Dorigisi threw in.

"She is making progress," someone unknown mentioned. "She has assassins working to dispatch Borelian Time Agents. Yes, they may figure it out, but as long as our losses are none, we are still making the greater progress. If they have to stop because they are discovered, then they stop. We still have the shields. We have lost nothing by trying."

"But what about her terms?" someone else wondered, maybe one of the Vin

Lay. "Rifun has been our best hope, militarily, so far. Do we really want to get rid of our only great general, in favor of a hot-headed widow? Regardless of his past, he has the tactical mind to see a problem, map a plan, and execute it. The Borelians know he and the First Order are in on this. They are as vulnerable as we are when it comes to the Borelians' fury."

"He has the better army and the technology," Mi Chin grudgingly agreed. "While I do not doubt the purity of intention that Aklaq and her allies possess, strength and numbers win wars."

"Rifun, what are your thoughts?" Toros inquired stiffly.

Rifun swallowed the last of his food and regarded the rest of them. "The quiche is delicious. That's my thought." He swallowed again. "But if you're asking about the plans going forward, I will answer honestly that I am generally unconcerned. As it has been pointed out, the Borelians know the Order is involved. That is not a bad dream, it is a fact. My people know it. To that end, we have our own worries and our own operations which we will be conducting here shortly. Large operations. Whether or not you want to be a part of it is up to all of you, assuming you can get your acts together."

"And what are you planning?" Milay wondered.

"Nothing you would be interested in, I assure you," Rifun replied with a look. "The details are still being worked out, as I believe we will only get one chance at success. If anyone is truly interested, beyond a passing curiosity, and wish to, as Aklaq said, sell their souls to me for thirty pieces of silver, then you may contact me. At a later date. I don't want anyone here to feel rushed into a decision."

"Can you tell us anything about this big plan of yours?" the Aleisi not Andrew asked, although Andrew did look very interested.

"I would really rather not. I fear it may conjure up an unfair advantage in my fanbase, and I want to give Aklaq an equal chance at garnering support. For now, just consider whether you want to help me or her."

"How did it come to this?" a Dorigisi wondered. "Now that we have the shields, why do we have to split like this? She was more than happy to go along with it until the shields were in place."

"Perhaps the Tacagans ought to decide, then," a Sakarian suggested. "If this is the thanks we're giving them for saving our skins — that we're just going to split into squabbling factions — perhaps they ought to decide whose plan we go with."

"We have been prepared for this for a long time," Milay said haughtily. "And we will remain here long after the rest of you have gone. How you choose to go and whom you choose to follow there are of no concern to us. As for the gratitude concerning the shields, while we appreciate even the acknowledgment of such help — only now is it being brought up —" She sniffed. " — our payment is being decided before the Hands. With luck, we won't even be having this conversation because we will have fully separated ourselves from you."

"You think the Borelians are going to care?" Walter piped up. "Human or not, just like Sifura and the others, you aided us. You aided us in such a way that the Borelians, presently, can't even touch us, or not easily. Whether you decide to call yourselves Tacagans, Better Humans, or Masters of the Universe, the Borelians will still come down on you."

"They can try," was all the dark-skinned woman had to say.

"Well, if they're not going to decide for us, then perhaps this is going to come down to individual preference," the same Sakarian decided. "Those who follow Aklaq, and those who follow Rifun. Maybe more will be accomplished if we are on separate teams. Each one has strengths and weaknesses. Maybe they can't work together, but having them both working at all may prove to be advantageous."

"Following that logic, why not leave it every world for himself?" someone wondered grouchily.

"Because we don't individually have the numbers," Walter answered. "And only a couple of us have technology past the Industrial Revolution. Time is a wonderful thing, but having the firepower to back it up isn't a bad idea either."

"Vin Lay will back Rifun," the delegation said after a long minute of silence.

It was the only official decision made. Aleis and Dorigis had to take it to their ruling councils while Sakaria refused to speak on the matter.

"Was there anything else anyone wanted to bring up while we're here?" Toros asked, sounding fatigued.

It was a Dorigisi who spoke. "I assume you are hurrying through your emancipation just as quickly as possible, and no doubt you will send grand, embellished letters to the rest of us once it is complete and you have successfully separated yourselves from your Neanderthal cousins. If that happens before our next meeting, where do we want to meet? Where can we meet?"

"Without Do Chien, there's no real reason to have it here anyway," a Sakarian commented dryly.

"And that's another thing," Walter cut in. "What do we want to do about all the research? Everything was destroyed. Anything we want to do will have to be done from scratch, barring whatever was saved in your computer systems." He looked at the Tacagans.

"I vote for Dorigis, to have our meetings," Rifun said. When they looked at him, most of them confused, he clarified, "It's as you said. Brelix has only one small ocean, and they navigate primarily by space ship anyway. They have no naval experience. It may be our safest bet."

"What about your fortress?" someone asked. "Seems pretty impenetrable."

"Obviously not, seeing how I conquered it. And I am suggesting a human world inasmuch as we can all agree that we are human. The Order fortress will remain for use of the Order and its business. That way we can actually get stuff done here without going down all sorts of religious and political rabbit holes."

Pause.

"I second the motion," a Sakarian said finally. "Dorigis as our new meeting world."

"Aye" seemed to be the prevailing response, though the Dorigisi did not look prepared in the least. Eventually, they simply said that they would bring up that issue with their councils also and get back to them.

As for the research, no one had an answer. They knew enough about the toxins to be able to counteract them, and the lesser illnesses that had been loosed on their worlds were more readily curable. Did they really need such extensive research?

"Well, we can all give it some more thought and reconvene at a later date," Andrew suggested calmly. "I would ask that the Dorigisi be the ones to call the meeting, if indeed that is where we are moving the meetings to. In the meantime —" He yawned. "—I should like to get some sleep. It's near harvest, and there is much work to be done."

Rifun sent all of the delegations home, then returned to his chambers in the fortress. He headed over to the table, buried under layers of maps, charts, graphs, and innumerable notes. The preplanning was done. They had their targets and they were working out which units should be sent where. As they had explained to Julianna, they needed to utilize everyone's strengths, not just their desires.

Over the next couple weeks, those strengths grew as the human colonies declared their allegiances. Those who sided with the Order submitted their estimated numbers, with appropriate strengths and weaknesses.

With more and more time spent plotting the assault, Rifun did a little redecorating of the room. The personal living space shrank and disappeared behind makeshift walls, and the war room grew until it was no longer a mismatched conglomeration of garage sale leftovers and whatever they could scavenge. Maps became more detailed, the maneuvers more deliberate.

As things started to come to a head, Rifun found himself throwing back more of the little pills, about once a day like he was supposed to. He hated it with a passion. It was as bitter on his conscience as the tarka root tea was on his tongue, but now more than ever, he could not afford to show weakness. And yet, sometimes he wondered if the pills weren't doing just as much damage. Only Tommen had really outright said anything about it, but he did not miss the looks others occasionally gave him. He didn't understand why, really, and he pushed it aside, telling himself that minor opinions of his personality and disposition mattered little in the face of impending battle. Now, he had to focus. Or focus as much as he could with the way his mind seemed to pull in two different directions: one that demanded action right now, and one that desired no action at all.

He almost didn't notice Tommen standing there in the middle of the room, looking around at the new furniture.

"My young Apprentice returns," Rifun commented, trying to keep his head on straight. "I trust you got my gift?"

Tommen had expressed some boredom in his journal studies classes, mostly because none of the other students spoke English, which meant the class was more of an EFL class than a journal study. So Rifun had bumped him up to a point where the students could at least communicate.

"Getting moved up to level three? I did. Thank you. What about the second class, though?"

"Second class?" Rifun glanced at the teenager, then meandered over to the whiteboard to jot down some notes.

"Apparently I'm taking on a second class, level one in the Book of Commands."

Good to know Julianna had enough faith in the operation to already craft a study course around a book they didn't have. Not that she hadn't been doing that already, with heavy improvisation, but Rifun chose to take it as a vote of confidence. "News to me. Certainly wasn't my doing. But I suppose it will do you some good. It will keep you occupied, anyway, if level three of Philosophy bores you as much as level one."

"I don't expect it will bore me, but the Book of Commands class ought to be interesting. Especially if the journal itself were to be part of it."

"Found it, did you?"

Tommen answered calmly, "I did." He didn't want to admit to it. Still felt like a traitor.

"Do you have it?" Rifun questioned.

"Unfortunately, no. Turns out, it is held in a Borelian temple. On Brelix."

"Yes, that's where most Borelian temples are located. Do you know which one?"

"Uh..."

"I'm only kidding. A prize that valuable, there is only one temple they would hide it in. The Temple of Tujor in Ancrath."

"Are you sure?"

"Of course." Rifun finished his notes and capped the marker. "They would offer it up to their death god in hopes of gaining the power within it. Cosmic osmosis, I suppose. The Temple of Tujor is where they'd hide it."

"They have other temples?"

Rifun faced him. "The Temple of Power, the Temple of Victory, the Temple of Money, the Temple of Labor, the Temple of Pleasure, the Temple of Despair, the Six Facets of death, or so they somehow believe. Tujor rules over all of them, of course. The Borelians, those who are religious, may make specific requests at any of the smaller temples, or petition the god of death himself, hoping for a larger reward."

Tommen frowned. "Guess Isthim forgot to go to Black Mass the day she died, huh?"

"The Borelians do not fear death. They welcome it. In battle is the only good way to die, as much their salvation as the crucifix is Catholic salvation."

Tommen shifted his stance. "So what do you want me to do? Going on adventures with my little team is one thing. There is no way we'll be able to pull off going to Brelix and getting inside one of their death temples and stealing a prized commodity and getting out. I'm sorry, but it's impossible. And I'm not willing to risk myself for a suicide mission."

"There won't be a suicide mission." Rifun moved around the huge meeting table. "At this point, with the location of the journal confirmed—and you are absolutely certain this is where the journal is?"

Tommen nodded. "The ones who hid it there told me themselves, told me exactly where to find it and how to get to it."

Andrew and Nathan. They were involved, just as Julianna said they would be. He would have to act on it, but he wasn't about to tell her she was right. He didn't need to listen to that "I told you so" right before battle.

"With the location confirmed, there is now only the big plan."

"The one you've been working on for a while now."

"That's correct. Only the final preparations need to be made. Then, once everyone is comfortably moved into their new beds, well, we'll see who gets to actually sleep in them."

"And what is my part in this?" Tommen inquired nervously.

"You've done your part," Rifun told him. "You located the journal, using your team and superb sleuthing skills. That is what I asked of you, and you have delivered. Not exactly post office material, if you catch my meaning, but you'll do. And you're done."

It was what the teenager had always wanted to hear. And really, Rifun wasn't trying to bait him into anything. The kid was a piss poor soldier and medic, but Rifun was beginning to see that his real worth might lie elsewhere. But he had confirmed the location of the journal and the key, and no doubt Andrew and Nathan were going to jump on this.

Nevertheless, he said, "No. I'm not done. I need to get the journal."

"It's in the Temple of Tujor," Rifun told him. "We'll send in a special force."

"You can't do that; it won't work."

"Why not?"

For a split-second, Tommen was a deer in headlights. Then, "The faith of a skeptic. Finesse, not force. Your men will storm the temple, ready to die for the cause. It's a temple of death. That's what the Borelians are expecting; that's what they want. You have to send someone afraid to die, but more than that, you have to send a coward. 'In looking for a way out, a coward only hastens to his death.' It's a Borelian saying, but it's also very applicable. Force a coward into the temple. He will be able to follow a string of clues that will lead him deeper and deeper into the temple, into its vaults, to the heart of Tujor himself. It's just the way the temples are built. That's where the journal is being kept."

It was a string of total bullshit, yet it intrigued Rifun. Here was this well-known coward and traitor who had begged not to fight, had begged to do anything else, had betrayed the Akarin and the human race, and now he wanted to run into battle on Brelix? The Builders had a plan, and Tommen needed to be there more than he wanted to not be there.

"And you're hoping I choose you to be my coward," Rifun stated slowly, going along with it. "While I admire your sudden courage to go that far, I have no shortage of loyal cowards who would do the same. What does the faith of a skeptic have to do with anything now?"

"Because as a skeptic, I will be looking for every way to betray you and the Order. The Borelians have the highest standards of loyalty among their own, and to an extent, they expect it from their adversaries as well. Mutiny is not well-received by the god of death, and it will only lead to Tujor's wrath. In the heart of the temple."

Well, he wasn't wrong. "I admire your cunning. Your reasoning puts me in such a position that I cannot tell you no, though I suspect most if not all of what you just said is total bullshit. I suspect there is more to the story, more to your reasoning, why a failed soldier and traitor to all wants to venture into the heart of a Borelian temple. I think there is more down there than you let on, and whatever your source told you is very compelling to you. I'm curious to know what it is. Therefore, I accept your request to be to the one to retrieve the journal. I will bring in my advisors, finish up the plans we have, and then let you know what we expect of you."

"Fair enough."

"Good. Now then, why don't you go home before this gets any more interesting, hm? I will send for you when I am ready."

The teenager scurried away before his big mouth could get him into any more trouble. Rifun watched him go, mildly amused. Then he frowned.

Andrew, and likely Nathan, were going to get involved. Involved in what way? He thought about calling Tommen back and asking, then decided against it. They knew he was working for the Order, working closely with him, Rifun. They wouldn't want to be interrupted or intercepted, so they probably wouldn't tell him. And yet, they couldn't realistically expect that Tommen would be allowed to walk into the temple alone, even if his arguments had been silver-tongued perfection.

An ambush, then. Were they expecting him, Rifun, to want to retrieve the journal himself, or at least be present? Well, they would be right. Two against one, hardly what one would call impossible odds except they were all Builders. What's more, they were Builders of the Akari who would be in a Borelian temple of death while a battle raged outside with the very real possibility that something could happen to bring said temple down on top of them.

Rifun leaned against the table, studying everything laid out before him. Planning was over. It was time to act. But they couldn't return without their prize.

He said nothing about it for a full day, instead deciding to think about it himself without input from bickering officers or a nagging woman. He needed a way to ensure that no matter what, the journal returned to the Order at the end of the day.

More than that, he needed to figure out how to defeat the dragon. Maybe that was the whole point. This wasn't about Tommen or Andrew or Nathan. They were just incidentals. This was the Author maneuvering her most powerful pieces into play. They were going to destroy the dragon together. Rifun couldn't do it alone, and Andrew and Nathan never would have helped Rifun by themselves, but with Tommen acting as glue, they might just have a chance.

It wasn't much later when messenger came bearing a letter from Aklaq White Bear. Reading it, Rifun couldn't decide if she was remarkably restrained with how formal it was, or if she had dictated the letter and the person writing had a little more discretion with what to include. He'd put money on the former, actually. The Krydik had no reason to like him after what he did to Sabelu. If Aklaq was inflamed during a dictation, the scribe would be as well, and he would have no qualms about expressing them twice as passionately. No, Aklaq herself wrote this, and it was remarkably formal.

She was ready to negotiate an alliance, even outlining the date, time, and venue, which happened to be the fortress. This was, she was careful to reiterate multiple times, a formal meeting and negotiation of potential alliance. It was not surrender or subjugation. It was a temporary truce. Therefore, she would expect basic hospitality and no hostilities against either herself or the Akarin while she was there.

"Hm," he mused.

"Faharoa?" the messenger wondered.

"Wait a moment, and I'll have you take a reply."

He went to a desk and brought out a sheet of paper and pen. His off-hand penmanship was improving, but it still wasn't as elegant as his natural handwriting. *Voix ambiguë d'un cœur qui au zéphyr préfère les jattes de kiwis. Hetezo voankazo fotsy mangatsiaka lehibe dimy ao anaty akanjonao rahampitso,* he thought ruefully.

When he was finished, he handed the letter to the messenger. "Tell her I accept her invitation."

The messenger saluted and scampered off.

It would be a few days before the meeting, before they launched the assault. Considering how many weeks and even months they had spent planning, things should go pretty smoothly, from an overarching, logistics perspective. But there was always that chance of death. He didn't mind it, so long as it came with a roar of defiance and not a twitching whimper of a seizure making him vulnerable before his enemies.

The next thing he knew, he was home in Madagascar, in the spot he always used when opening portals near Lalao's home. Within just a few minutes, he was at her front door.

"Rivotra!" she cried, grinning. "Oh, my dear, come in!"

"Would you prefer that I come in, or would you like to go out?" he asked, matching her smile.

"Oh, come in. Tomas has gone out for a while and I was just thinking about making an early dinner. Come, come!"

He obediently entered the domicile, noting that she had cleaned recently.

"It's been at least a couple weeks," she said, heading into the kitchen where several assorted food items were laid out, untouched. "Last time we talked, you were saying something about planning for battle!" She glanced at him as she got out a few more items. "I assume you were victorious?"

"We've not fought yet, but in the next few days," he admitted, suddenly feeling the weight of it. "I wasn't going to leave without saying goodbye."

Her body language and expression said she wasn't sure quite how to respond. She opted for, "So this is your battle against the evil spirit? The dragon?"

"Yes," he said, sitting at the dining table. "We're going to defeat the dragon and tear down its temples."

"Good. Very good. And I know you are just the man for the job."

"Don't laud me too soon, and don't make that pedestal too high. I may fall." He tried to smooth out his chuckle, but he knew some anxiety leaked through.

She shook her head as she did this and that in the kitchen. "No. You will be victorious. I know you will."

"What if I'm not? As a hypothetical."

"Then you will try again. And again and again. As many times as you must."

He wished he had her confidence. He knew his mission was righteous, but the resistance was so great. He was bringing a literal army to bear against the dragon and its minions. If there was any good news, it was that there was no ambiguity about his enemy here. His mind went to Sabelu. Had he murdered an innocent man?

"...spicy or not spicy?" Lalao was saying.

He shifted in his chair and cleared his throat. "Sorry, what?"

"Do you want it spicy or not spicy? Or maybe I should ask how spicy you want it."

"At least a mild spice," he told her, "but I'm not picky."

"Ha!" she laughed. "Men say that, then get upset when it's not exactly how they want or expect. You may be the bane of evil spirits, but you are still a man."

"You should know."

She laughed again. "Yes, I do know." She sighed dreamily. "Ah, so many years ago. What would our life have been like, do you think?"

He thought a moment, then replied, "Complicated. Communism already took a toll on your family. Now add in my mission to defeat an evil spirit. I don't think things would have gone well."

"Hm...I suppose there is some truth in your words." She glanced up from where she was dicing up some vegetables. "When you have defeated the dragon, would you consider getting married and having a family? Not with me, obviously, but with someone?"

He sighed. "I don't know. Maybe."

"The world is not what it once was, Rivotra. No one who matters really cares that you're a mixed-blood."

"A very minority opinion, unfortunately."

She shrugged. "I didn't say it wasn't. I also said that those who matter don't care. So if you find a woman whose family doesn't care, you'll know that she matters."

"Maybe," he assented.

"Children?" she wondered after a moment.

"I expect so, in time."

"You know, some fathers brag about going hunting or whatever it is they do for a living. Imagine the stories you could tell your children! Fighting dragons and evil spirits, how exciting!"

How dreadful. Failure after failure after failure, losing eyesight, losing fingers, losing wars, losing his mind. His life was one big object lesson.

"What have you been up to these last few weeks?" he asked, intentionally changing the subject.

She gave him a look, but soon wandered off into a number of short stories of an otherwise mundane life. A normal life. Soon enough, she was scooping out food onto a couple of plates, still talking as she served.

"And I made sure that was the end of that," she concluded, sitting down. She stared at her food for a moment and huffed a sigh. "Forgot the utensils."

Rifun stood. "I'll grab them."

She gave him a warm smile. "Thank you, dear."

He retrieved a couple forks and spoons, then sat to eat.

"Delicious, as always," he told her after the first bite.

"Even if you don't think so, you're still kind about it," she told him cheekily. "I hope that one day whatever woman you fancy, you give her the same loving treatment. And remember, she's your wife, not your mother. Sometimes I think you get the two mixed up in your head with me, but with my age, I can't say I don't understand why."

"Maybe so, but from what I've seen, you have been a very good mother."

She hummed a sigh. "Thank you, love. Now eat up. I imagine that fighting evil spirits is hungry work. You'll need all the energy you can get."

He did not argue, and he saved himself from having to reply by taking another bite.

37 | Confirmation
First Order Fortress, 2015

Julianna had been warned to stay at the third floor or above the day that Aklaq White Bear was to visit, and yet, she just couldn't resist sneaking down the staircase as far as she could to sneak a glance at what was going on at the main level. She was just below the platform leading to the second floor. Crouched behind the short wall that functioned as a railing, she could just make out the forces on the floor and the gate to the lower levels.

Drinjin uh Ersik's carefully crafted force had the Akarin surrounded, while a small unit led by Torbak blocked the stairs. Down on the floor, Julianna could smell blood and other, less pleasant, odors, suggesting some sort of skirmish had broken out. The gate to the lower levels was down, Order soldiers keeping the Akarin away from it from both sides.

When Rifun had announced Aklaq's (alleged) flag of truce and possible negotiations, even Julianna was smart enough to come up with a minor sabotage. She talked to her generals about it afterwards. They not only agreed, but they had four different plans already in their heads. This was just too easy. Clearly the Author was favoring them; she was just dumping ways to discredit Rifun in their laps. First, another Akarin revolt. Whatever grand ideas he had about taming them or converting them, obviously it wasn't working. Second, an alliance with the very one who stabbed him in the chest in front of everyone. Third, she was going to demand the release of the Akarin in exchange for the cooperation of her army, and he was going to give it to her. Julianna just knew he would. In spite of the revolt, Rifun was going to let them go. After the battle on Brelix, maybe, but he would.

All of this on top of the general discontent rippling through the ranks. Why was it taking so long to attack? Why did it always take so damn long? They weren't even testing this time. The longer they waited, the more likely it was that they would be exposed and possibly undermined, just like last time with the loss of the ambony. Was Rifun trying to destroy the Order? He was far too friendly with the Akarin. He had Authored Books and he believed in them. Was it possible that he was an Akarin plant? A spy of the deepest order?

Julianna wondered that herself sometimes. She'd first met him when he was looking for a way to heal his scars, but she was not the only one he talked to. And for all his arguments with and misgivings about the Akarin, he had always maintained a small spot of courtesy and respect for them. Could he be a spy sent to uproot them?

She blinked back to the present moment at the sound of grunts, metal, and assorted noises she could not readily name. Down below, what little she could see, an argument turned into a shoving match with a little steel involved. Things calmed down for a moment. She heard grunting and roaring, its intonation suggesting that they were words rather than mere noises, but she did not bother to use Sound to listen to everything verbatim. She knew very well what was going on.

Then things ramped up again, more people and more steel involved. There was some movement on the stairs, a sudden piercing shriek that cut off rather abruptly. The smell of blood intensified. Things calmed down yet again, though the atmosphere remained volatile. There was more shouting, more grunting, a few roars.

Behind her, Julianna sensed a growing group of curious onlookers, the artists and philosophers who had no real interest in fighting. Not that they were keen on having the Akarin around, but they weren't soldiers anymore, or they weren't supposed to be.

"What's going on?" one whispered.

"Are they attacking?" another wondered.

"I think they tried," Julianna told them. "But Drinjin uh Ersik and Torbak have them at bay."

"Will we have to fight?" someone asked, sounding anxious.

"No," she answered calmly. "No, the generals have this all under control."

Everyone will choose their side when this is all over. If they choose correctly, they will be free to pursue their desires. If they choose poorly, well, they may end up as an unwilling soldier for another side. And then a dead soldier. An enemy combatant, not an artist, not a philosopher. Just dead. An example to the rest.

More movement down below, another skirmish, but this time, the Order soldiers did not give up just because the Akarin backed off. This time, they pressed harder, moving in closer, forcing the Akarin into tighter and tighter quarters with nowhere to go. A few screams rose into the air on waves of copper and other smells.

For a long moment, it was as if the entire fortress balanced on the head of a pin.

The Akarin relented. The lower gates opened and they were forced inside. Whatever chores or tasks some of them might have been sent to do, whatever they were entrusted with, it was all suspended for the time being. Julianna watched and waited for anything more to happen, that one guy who would try to bolt for the door.

"Why don't they open portals and escape?" someone behind her wondered.

"Because they know if they leave, they're not coming back," someone else answered. "As long as they stay here, they can try stuff like this."

"Why can't they come back?"

"Portals to this place must be done by feel," Julianna explained. "If the Akarin leave, even just a significant group of them, Faharoa will scramble the energy here, and they won't be able to come back. They think that by staying here, they can still fight for this place."

"What about their families?"

"I don't know. I guess that shows how selfish they are, on top of having been willing to blow us all into oblivion."

"So, was it a good thing that Faharoa spared them? And why keep them here if they can do stuff like this?"

Julianna opened her mouth to speak, but someone else replied, "To keep them from rallying against us somewhere else, to keep them under control."

Before anyone could say more, the gate to the lower level slammed shut with a clang and the Order soldiers began to disperse, many of them grumbling amongst themselves. Before they could get too far, a familiar voice rang out.

"What do you mean there was a fight and I missed it?!"

The whore, Aklaq White Bear. Even from her poor vantage, Julianna could see she strode into the fortress as pompous as you please. Many of the soldiers turned to look her way, and some of them even stopped to regard her with hard stares. It was Drinjin uh Ersik who approached and spoke to her while Julianna made her way down the stairs.

"I have an appointment with your leader," Aklaq was saying, unbowed by Drinjin uh Ersik's size. "He might have told you."

"Indeed he did. And it seems they—" He gestured toward the gate where the Akarin pressed heavily against it, straining to see her. "—knew of this as well. Isn't that a lucky coincidence? Or maybe not, since you are late."

"Then it is coincidence only. I have an appointment, and I intend to keep it."

"General," Julianna said, walking up and inserting herself into the conversation. "Go up and inform Faharoa of Aklaq's arrival. I will escort her."

"You don't need to," Aklaq told her with a smile and a glare. "I know where I'm going."

"And I'm going with you."

Julianna nodded to Drinjin uh Ersik who grunted, turned, and started walking away, steps unnecessarily heavy but not quite a childish stomp. She turned her attention back to Aklaq whose demeanor turned a bit grouchy.

She wore exactly what Julianna expected from a savage such as herself: soft leather clothing of unremarkable style and nonsensical designs formed with shells and stone beads. She also wore a soft fur about the shoulders, trying or perhaps not trying to hide heavier leather plates, like crude pauldrons, or the caricature of such. Her hair was styled in two tight French braids on her head, then braided together into a single braid once it hung loose. It was perhaps her only redeeming feature. Julianna might have wondered what Micaiah ever saw in her, but then, he was an Irishman, hardly a model of elegance and standards himself. She wouldn't be surprised if the whore was sleeping with his brother now, or if she had been before.

Julianna opened her mouth, but Aklaq was already speaking. "Save it. Don't pretend like we're friends or that you're some meek and mild bystander. You're not. You are a vile, malevolent bitch. I may not want to work with Rifun, but I'll still take him over you. Now, you can still pretend to be a servant escort, or I can make my own way just fine."

She started walking, not waiting for Julianna or even looking back to see if she followed. Julianna considered letting her go and carrying about her own business, but decided against it at the last minute and quickly fell into step beside her. She also considered telling her about Rifun's seizures, just to see if it would spark anything, a plan, an idea, another assassination attempt. She decided against this as well. She needed to oust Rifun as a traitor, not make him a god-martyr.

"Looks like the reconstruction went well," Aklaq observed, looking around. "At least you've taken care of the place."

"I notice you've come alone," Julianna stated. "The other humans I can understand being...skittish. But what of your new allies Rifun told me about? It sounded like they were ready to prove themselves, yet they don't show their faces here."

Aklaq gave her a look. "We don't even know if there will be an alliance between us. I'm not bringing more hostages here. I am here to negotiate, and they are training their warriors as they see fit."

"Hostages? The way Rifun tells it, they're little more than primitive barbarians. But then, it takes one to know one, I suppose."

She'd barely gotten out the last word before Aklaq threw up a tight and powerful Band, put one hand around Julianna's neck, and started walking her back, leaning her over the side of the stairs. By now, they were easily twenty stories high.

"I swear to God, I will kill you," Aklaq hissed. "If we weren't going against the fucking Borelians and didn't possibly need this alliance so fucking much, I would throw you over and use Gravity to ensure your entrails splattered over the entire floor."

Julianna, now recovered from the initial stun of the maneuver, lashed out with one hand. She only just touched Aklaq's chest, but she put Force behind it, knocking her back. What she wasn't prepared for was for Aklaq to not let go and instead drag her along by the neck. Aklaq stumbled back but did not fall. Julianna managed to maneuver her shoulder around, loosening the grip around her neck, and driving Aklaq back until she hit the wall of the fifth floor. Aklaq released Julianna's neck, but before Julianna could do anything, a knife was suddenly between them, angled at Julianna.

"I'm not stupid," Aklaq said breathily.

Julianna backed off, hands up just a bit. "At least this one doesn't have Borelian poison on it." She chuckled and let her hands drop. "Not that it matters anymore."

Aklaq grinned, and not in a nice way. "We have the power of the universe, but you're still afraid of a knife." She replaced the knife and dropped the Band.

"I'm not overly fond of them, no," Julianna said, again moving to walk beside her. "Surely you might understand why."

"You and knives. Rifun and fire. We're at war with the Borelians now; you both need to grow up."

"So can we expect an invitation to your next wedding? I'm assuming your partner of choice is your late husband's lookalike."

Julianna expected another lash with the knife, or perhaps another grab for her throat. She was unprepared for an elbow jab in her ribs, and she was thankful Aklaq did nothing more. Perhaps it had something to do with a few bystanders who stopped to see what was going on. None of them intervened.

Because they're artists and philosophers. But we'll get to that later.

"Like I said, if we didn't potentially need this alliance so fucking bad..." Aklaq let herself trail off, conscious of the audience.

Julianna straightened. This time she led the way up the stairs. Once they got past the sixth floor, the general population thinned to almost nothing and the stairs were empty.

"What's it like being such a spiteful bitch?" Aklaq wondered. "Honestly, part of me wonders if Rifun regrets saving you. Have you tried to kill him yet, or are you saving that for later, after the Borelian war? Maybe he incited this war, in part, so you would constantly need him, made himself too valuable to kill."

"What's it like being such a whore?" Julianna retorted. "If I recall correctly, your Authored Book is divided up by the men you slept with. Is that true?"

"Thought you didn't believe in the Authored Books?"

"I do not believe in them having any sort of religious authority nor any infallible authenticity, but, like any historical fiction, they must be based on something true, even if it's just a few names. Seeing how sexual partners is a rather odd choice for division, I can only assume that it was true. Or else the Author really does hate you. It says so, in the back, where it says she hates female leads."

Aklaq grinned. "Jealous?" She glanced over and raised a brow. "She may not like it, but she did it anyway. For me. Two centuries and two Books later and you don't have shit. If she hates either of us, it's you."

"Ha!" Julianna barked a laugh as they reached the eighth floor and stood outside the war room which doubled as Rifun's chambers. "Chaos. War. Ruin. Picking and choosing different lowly, savage peoples to write about, each one jealous of the next." Julianna shook her head. "No. The Author dictated the journals to us. To Richard and myself. Proper English, superior citizens of a grand kingdom."

"Oh, would you come off it?" Aklaq sighed. "You are nothing. I'm here to meet with Rifun, not you. And if you were a model citizen of this grand kingdom, you would have remarried by now and you'd be serving your husband and taking care of domestic affairs. You'd be down in the kitchens or the infirmary, or maybe just at home taking care of children. But you're here. And even so, you're acting as an escort while the rest of us deal with things that matter. I think you are jealous. You hate your place in the grand kingdom and are trying to figure out ways to make it serve you.

"I'm kind of curious. What would you do if you did have an Authored Book, or even just a small part of one? Just one little chapter. An epilogue, even. What then?"

Julianna shook her head. "Never happen. Because the Author only inspires the truth. Not some flippant fiction."

"I don't think you would have felt that way if the first Authored Book were about your grand kingdom. You would have taken it and lorded it over everyone else as proof of your superiority. Behold, the Author has chosen her people." Aklaq shook her head. "You chose yourselves, like bratty children pushing their way to the front of the group. And when the Author chose someone else, you threw a temper tantrum and went to form your own club."

Before either could say more, Rifun made himself known, saying, "I mean, she's not wrong."

Julianna didn't know how long he'd been standing there, or when the door opened. The best she could do was, "What?"

"Aklaq isn't wrong in her observation," he said, very matter-of-fact. "If the first Authored Book had been about the English rather than the Krydik..."

Julianna had a mind to tell Aklaq about Rifun's seizures right then and there, maybe see if she couldn't do something to induce one. If he had one on his own at that moment, she wasn't sure she'd cover it up. He was a traitor, plain and simple. Maybe he really was a deep cover spy for the Akarin, as some of the Order thought.

"On the other hand," Rifun went on, "power in the hands of such narcissists never ends well. Bringing the journals to Richard and Julianna through Cassius may have been the Author's way of still imparting wisdom while keeping them humble."

"You're deluded," Aklaq stated, unimpressed. "But still brilliant."

"Hm, with that first comment, I thought about rejecting your offer. But your flattery there at the end saved you."

The whore was still unimpressed as she entered the room.

"If you wanted to round up the generals and officers, that would be most helpful," Rifun told Julianna.

"If I wanted?" she wondered, brow raised. Then, "All right. I think they're pretty well done cleaning up."

She turned away and started back down before either could say more. No, she didn't want to. She wanted this to be done and over with. She wanted Rifun gone, the journal returned, the Akarin dead, the Borelians dead, and everything exactly as she wanted it, as she and Richard had planned so many years ago. The finish line was in sight, but it was still so far away.

Not a finish line. A checkpoint. Simply an indication that you are on the right path. Once you have achieved all of this, then you will be ready for the next step, and it will far surpass Rifun's so-called Building.

The thought felt hollow as she descended the stairs, occasionally picking up an officer and sending them Rifun's way.

At the bottom of the stairs, a crowd had gathered. Some were cleaning up the blood and other fluids from the earlier skirmish, but most were there for the spectacle. She ran into Drinjin uh Ersik and Torbak just down from where she'd hidden earlier.

"Faharoa awaits you," she informed them, trying to keep the sneer out of her voice.

"Of course," Drinjin uh Ersik grunted.

"More going on?"

"Merely attempting to find the ringleaders of today's operation, and discern if Aklaq White Bear was a part of it."

"Hm. Well, I will be standing by once you are finished with Rifun."

The generals merely grunted some form of affirmation, then started up the stairs.

Julianna didn't expect the meeting to last too long. Reject Aklaq's offer, blame her for the skirmish here, execute her and a few ringleaders, dishearten the Akarin a bit, send them out front to die in battle.

She managed to keep herself entertained for a little while, but when the war room let out for a brief recess, she couldn't help but walk in to ask Rifun what the holdup was.

"We're planning," he told her. "We're having to suddenly incorporate a lot of new units."

"You're actually agreeing to this?" Julianna wondered. "Please tell me you have something up your sleeve, some ulterior motive."

"To what end? Yes, the Akarin may be used as a certain kind of insurance, but I'm not going to just outright murder them. Besides, with Aklaq here, we have a way of ensuring the journal gets back to us and doesn't go running off again."

"Oh? And how is that?"

"Tommen has suspiciously volunteered to be the one to retrieve it. I have set Aklaq as his bodyguard of sorts. Tommen, the journal, and Aklaq must all come back to us or else the Akarin downstairs will die."

Julianna folded her arms. "And are you prepared to follow through on that threat? You just said you're not capable of murder."

"I did not say I was not capable. I just prefer it to mean something. Cassius' first and only threat was murder. He did kill a lot of people, yes, but the threats themselves got very old. Very uninspired. And he didn't even carry them out in the end, just whined about the unfairness of it all and how he was going to maintain his power or something."

A foolish plan, flawed, easy to bypass. What's to keep the Akarin from fleeing the battlefield? Then there will be no one left downstairs to execute.

She relayed such questions to Rifun.

"Never underestimate the power of honest men. They'll fight. And they'll come back. Because this place is home. Because it is familiar. Those who do not plot to rise against us and catch us in the ass, such as they tried today, will instead maintain their morals in an effort to show that they are separate from us, that they are different. They see us as a bunch of barbarians, but they thrive in such adversity, desperate to prove to themselves that they are better. Maybe some will flee. I expect some of ours to flee, for the Borelians are a powerful foe. But some will return. There will be prisoners to execute. Count on it."

I do.

The officers slowly filtered back in from their break, and Julianna saw herself out. She did not go very far, but was determined to wait and catch her generals as soon as they were finished. But as the minutes ticked by, her resolve began to waver. Rifun said she didn't understand, but he never saw fit to really include her so as to make her understand.

Some people are just incapable of teaching. Others simply do not understand the necessity of teaching. They think that once they have learned a thing, everyone else has magically learned it as well. They look down on those who have not yet had such a breakthrough.

And to come from one such as him...

She waited quietly for the generals but by no means patiently. Her body was calm, but her mind was active. She wanted to know what was going on. She wanted to know how Drinjin uh Ersik and Torbak planned to be rid of Rifun. She debated whether to skip the trial and go straight for the execution, except outing his supporters was more important than petty vendettas.

Politics is about balance, keeping your eyes up, your goals in sight. Marring the view with immediate blood lust or selfish wants will only steer you off-course, and only the very lucky can recover from such fatal mistakes.

Well then our luck as a whole has long since passed into divine intervention.

Considering what is about to occur, do you really want to waste this chance to set things right, then?

No, but would she ever have the chance to indulge a petty vendetta? Even a little bit? Seeing how she would be imprisoning Rifun, could she interrogate him a bit? Maybe use a bit of force? Maybe show him that the French weren't the only ones who knew how to wield a blade or a flame?

Are you an honest man, Rifun? Would you take the chance to escape and only prove yourself a coward? Or would you stay out of some misplaced notion of nobility and courage, some sort of savior? You failed to save your people then, and you will fail to do so now.

The power of honest men, he said. And how did he view himself?

The door opened and the officers filed out, each one looking intent on some mission. Julianna and Aklaq exchanged hateful glares but nothing more as the whore strode by. Drinjin uh Ersik and Torbak were no exception to the urgency in the air, but they slowed and stopped to meet her, none of them speaking much more than light pleasantries while the last of the officers hurried by. Even when they were gone, she put up a Sound barrier.

"What's the plan?" she asked. "Specifically?"

"Rifun intends to join the team going after the journal," Torbak reported. "Defending Aklaq and Tommen Forbes."

"The plan is to attack and secure the temple where it is being held," Drinjin uh Ersik explained. "I am personally leading the assault. As far as they know, we will simply hold the temple, wait for them to return with the journal, then bring the whole thing down before returning here. Separate teams are under orders to attack and destroy the smaller temples if at all possible."

"Lovely," Julianna said. "Now what's really going to happen?"

"We're going to attack and secure the temple, as planned. Once inside, we capture Rifun, Aklaq, and Tommen Forbes, bring them back here and keep them under guard. Then we rip that temple apart to get the journal and any other goods, bring down the temple and grind it into the dust of history. Again, the smaller temples will suffer the same fate if we have the time and resources."

She looked at Torbak. "And where are you in all of this?"

"Also with the team assaulting the primary temple, but I will be the one to bring the prisoners here and keep them under guard until everyone has returned."

She nodded. "Good. At least there will be a couple competent members on the team. And you have men ready to handle all of this? They're not going to go quietly. Well, Tommen might, but Rifun and Aklaq will fight, only Rifun has a physical weakness with his seizures, and he and Aklaq aren't emotionally predisposed to each other. I don't think she'd mind it all that much if you killed him, but she herself won't go along with you."

"The team taking the temple is comprised of loyal men," the general promised. "Rifun will be alone. Aklaq will be alone. And Tommen Forbes is already a known coward."

"I am less interested in Tommen than the others," Julianna told them seriously. "His reputation is tarnished, his abilities non-existent; we can go back for him if necessary. Rifun is priority number one, Aklaq priority number two, though the margin between them is infinitesimally small, you understand?"

"Very well."

"Good." She nodded once and almost managed a smile. "I suppose the absolute specifics will only be known on the field of battle, and those I will entrust to you. After all, in the fog of war, well, who knows what happens, really? It's who's standing in the end that matters. Good luck."

The generals made sounds of assent and continued on their way down the stairs. Julianna let the Sound barrier dissolve and turned her attention upwards, towards Rifun's chambers. She only had to keep up the charade a little while longer, and part of that was, perhaps, attempting to talk Rifun out of fighting. Who knew? Maybe she could do it. Then he could simply be arrested here for cowardice. Maybe she could induce a seizure at an opportune moment. Maybe she could close a portal on him and condemn him to the Land In Between for a few decades, see how much he liked it.

Only a little while longer. And part of the charade was making nice to Tommen Forbes when she spotted him on the stairs as well. His demeanor said he'd probably seen her speaking to the generals, though he obviously couldn't have known their conversation.

"Ah, Tommen," she said, forcing a grin. "Rifun told me about your desire to volunteer to retrieve the journal. Very noble of you. A noble coward."

He shrugged in that disrespectful teenage way. "If by 'noble' you mean 'foolhardy' then sure, I guess I'll agree."

"Well, regardless, once you get it and Rifun is done parading you around with it, make sure you get it to me before something happens to it. I imagine the celebrations will simply be uproarious, and I don't want it to get damaged before we have a chance to read and study from it."

"Yeah, I heard you wanted me in your class."

"Of course. I hand-picked my first crop of students, from the beginners to the experts. You've come a long way, Tommen, and I want you to get the full experience once we have all the journals."

What that experience would be, however, was entirely subjective.

"Flattered. Listen, I...have my own appointment I have to make. Doctor's appointment."

She waved a hand, actually glad for an out. "Of course, of course. The uprising did put a bit of a delay on things, and it's not as though we have a ton of time to waste, not like they do in the Wheel. Yes, go on, go talk to your doctor or dentist or whomever you need to see."

She continued up the stairs without waiting for a reply and she entered Rifun's chambers the same way. The worst she got was an annoyed look as he gathered papers, notes, and appeared to be packing them up.

"Running away on us again?" she wondered, trying to keep the tone semi-light.

"The idea sounds better every day, but I fear my sense of duty prevents such a thing," he replied wistfully, not looking at her.

"You consider yourself one of those honest men you spoke of, then?"

"Well, I'm not a liar, so in that sense, I am an honest man."

She raised a brow. "Is there another sense in which you are not, or are uncertain?" She could only burn someone at the stake once, so she might as well throw as much fuel on the fire as she could.

He slowed a bit in his organizing of things. "Actions can be dishonest. Even if they are not illegal by any reasonable standards, whether they are merely unethical or just individually uncomfortable, actions can still be dishonest, or considered dishonest, if they are reasonably misunderstood."

"You think someone might misunderstand war? Or battle? Or what we're trying to do here?"

Instead of answering, he shook his head and turned his attention back to the task at hand. "I am going out to gather the other human leaders on Tacaga, inform them of the situation, make any last-minute tweaks, and we move out tomorrow."

"Tacaga? I thought meetings had been moved to Dorigis?"

He waved a hand. "Oh, someone somewhere didn't like something, there were other problems. We don't have time for the bureaucracy of minor counties. And Tacaga made some mention about having a parting gift for the human worlds. I assume it has to do with their ultimate emancipation from the rest of humanity. Whatever, I can't concern myself with it now. We'll use Tacaga this one last time. Assuming we survive, then next time, when we don't have battle breathing down our necks, we can go to Dorigis."

Julianna briefly considered her role in this. Yes, they would accomplish their mission to get the journal—of this, she had little doubt—but the war would continue to exist afterwards. The Borelians would continue to go after humanity. The Order would still have the most powerful and reliable army. She would probably have to go to Dorigis for at least some of the meetings, at least the first one immediately afterwards. She would have to explain that Rifun was no longer around, that she was in control of the Order, and Drinjin uh Ersik and Torbak were her primary generals and representatives in the matters and details of war.

She knew how it would go. There would be questions, which she would ignore if at all possible. Likely Walter Forbes himself would finally volunteer the information about Rifun's seizures. Maybe they just got the better of him in battle. Or his men turned on him because of them. Who could say for sure?

As for Aklaq, well, the only ones who would really be offended by it were the Krydik, and Julianna did not give two shits about the Krydik. In fact, if the Borelians could stay at arm's length for half a day, once the last of Rifun's supporters were gone, the Krydik were going to be her next target. The first so-called chosen ones of the Author, the first Books to appear, well, it was time to test that theory. If the Author truly had chosen them, if she truly had written those Books, surely she would save her precious people. And if not, well, no time like the present to burn a heretic. At least Rifun had already taken care of Sabelu.

Keep your eyes up, always looking forward. When one target is secure, move on to the next. Do not lose momentum.

"If you could ensure that your able-bodied artists and philosophers are also ready, that would be beneficial and time-saving," Rifun was saying, cutting into her thoughts. "I have full faith in the officers to carry out their duties, but I don't want to have to deal with duty dodgers and complaints of unfairness."

"Of course," she replied levelly. It was all she could say. As much as she might have wanted to help some of her artists and philosophers dodge the draft as it were, she would pinch her nose and do such a task to completion. Every person who could be made to hate Rifun would only help her own cause, and it was never too late to learn to hate. "Was there anything else?"

"Nothing I could say seeing how we're not married," he answered cheekily, looking ready to leave. "You won't even pretend to be my daughter."

Now she glared at him. "God, I hate you sometimes." More than sometimes, but it was the diplomatic thing to say. "Do you really intend to fight?"

"Of course I do. I can't send a million men to fight on foreign soil and not be there with them. I couldn't send a million men to fight on home soil and not be there."

"This isn't Madagascar, Rifun. The Order are not your people, the B—..." She honestly couldn't remember, her mind drawing a complete blank.

"Betsileo," he informed her gently. "Malasay, really. And it's true, we have few humans in the Order as it is, and I am the only one from Madagascar. But that doesn't matter. Those who I lead are at least my responsibility, and if they want me to lead them, then they are my people, and I one of them. Full stop. The Order are more my people than most of humanity itself because I am more welcome here than in the meeting I am about to attend. Considering that the Akarin still hate me, I think that says something."

It says he is ignorant and living only on hopes, wishes, and fanciful ideals. He has barely been present since moving in, preferring to skulk around up here, in fear of his seizures, going to meetings on other worlds, sending others to put down rebellions in his own home while he spends resources on distant skirmishes.

"Of course," Julianna said again. "That is very heartwarming and all, but what about the seizures? Are you feeling up to it? War isn't something to play with."

"I know more about that than you do," he told her sharply. "I will be the judge of my own fitness."

There was nothing more to be done. At this point, they were only spitting empty words at each other. The only thing left was the battle and the trial. Julianna nodded once and watched him leave. Gone to some human meeting on Tacaga apparently. One last pep talk for the other half of the army that refused to cooperate in any other way.

And so you see, Rifun, that your attempt at catching flies with honey has yielded nothing but trouble, and it will not make things any easier for me later. They will run. They will abandon this place and hide in the farthest reaches of the universe. Because they are cowards, not honest men. Cowardice is a form of dishonesty. There may be a few noble souls, but not enough for a satisfying execution.

She sighed and broke her gaze away from the emergency exit, sweeping around the room as if expecting to see something new or different. At least he had cleaned it up a little so it didn't look like a flat for a hopeless bachelor.

She approached the personal living side of the room. Although the paperwork from all the planning and battle had spilled over into this side, everything else remained crisp, clean, ready for military inspection. She started going through every cupboard and drawer. Everything was neatly arranged, though the exact method of organization eluded her.

She found the Authored Books, stashed away in a cupboard, looking as pristine as ever. First thing she'd do was burn them, see how many Akarin and Order heretics she could entice out.

How many Books were here? How many more promised? All of them about the low-lifes of the universe, all of them thinking they were something special. Well, time to put that to the test.

Leaving the Books, she soon found some of Rifun's more interesting things. Locked safes proved no challenge for her, though she was careful to note how things were arranged. Passports and other forged documents, currency, a few travel guides and language phrase books—and not just for Earth places either. Official missives and special letters from dignitaries of note.

Then she discovered an envelope containing a birth certificate and small stack of pictures. She could not read the writing on the back, but she could pick out the names easily enough. Rivotra Andilan. And his mother Lalao Andilan.

Julianna studied the pictures. Lalao was short, slender, brown skin, hair that might have been brown or black, brown eyes, fully unremarkable, primitive but not entirely unfortunate. Had Julianna come across this woman running around with the infant in her arms, she might have suspected a kidnapping. Rifun very clearly took after his French father with exception of his skin which was just a bit too dark. It was too bad he'd elected to use his Malagasy language over his French to color his English, or else he could have passed almost perfectly, even romantically.

Hm, but that was neither here nor there. She'd burn these, too, right in front of him, right before she had him executed.

She put everything back the way she found it and left the room.

There was nothing more to do. It was a bit like a child waiting for Christmas, she thought, the anticipation. Except, perhaps, Christmas was too joyful of a thing. Waiting for judgment. Waiting for news. Waiting for a particular type of news that, when you do see the postman approaching, your heart simply stops. Waiting for Cassius to tell her that Richard was free, only to realize that it wasn't true.

Richard was the chosen one of the Author. We were the chosen ones. But he fell prey to ego, the thrill of early success. He invited Cassius and his murderous chaos into what the Author was trying to build. And now I am about to be rid of the last of the infection. Only then will we see what the Author really intended.

Keep your eyes up and keep moving forward.

No. We're about to start moving forward for the first time.

Rifun hated the pills. He had come to loathe them. And yet, he needed them now more than ever. He couldn't afford to risk a drop on the battlefield, not if there was any way to avoid it. At least the battle would allow him to, hopefully, work off the tightly-bound energy he would feel. So, he pinched his nose, took a double dose of the pills, then brewed two large thermoses of tarka root tea which he hastily drank while he donned the battle gear so generously donated by General Misik.

Aklaq's forces were already on the move, aided by the first waves of humans and Order. It killed him not to be there with them. He wanted to destroy the city, tear down every last brick and stone, shatter every window, uproot every last scraggly plant. And yet, he was going to be on a slightly more important mission. He was going to have to trust his officers to sack the city while he searched for the journal. If he had any consolation prize, at least he would be helping take down the pyramids.

He shrugged on the shoulder plates, trying to adjust them and keep them in place as he secured the tactical vest that was the last part of the set. It was also the most uncomfortable, but whether it was intentional or just because it hadn't been tailored to him, he did not know.

He should have done this earlier, he knew. He probably should have been wearing this when he went to gather up the human part of the army. At the very least, he should have had this on when the first waves of soldiers started marching through the portal to Brelix. On the other hand, it was only armor, only good against direct physical contact, and even then it had weaknesses. He felt the spot where Aklaq had weakened the material and plunged the knife into his chest. He had managed to repair the area somewhat, but it, like his chest, still bore the scar.

Unlike Aklaq, however, Rifun didn't intend to miss when he finally stuck in a knife into the dragon. He didn't know how this was all going to turn out. He didn't know what he expected to find when they breached the temple, and the spirits had been silent in spite of his many prayers. Considering that the dragon had to know what he was coming to do, would the dragon itself be waiting for them, ready to defend its territory?

With his hair tucked protectively inside the gear, Rifun left the room. With the army waiting downstairs, every battalion, every unit, every squad having a planned departure time, he had taken up residence on the second floor with those who were coming with him to the temple.

"Any sign of Tommen or Aklaq?" he inquired of the closest officer.

"No, sir."

Rifun nodded and walked away several steps. He could feel his heart begin to race, his muscles tightening, seeming to squeeze against an invisible bind. He rolled his shoulders a bit, shifted the gear. No, it was definitely loose enough for movement. He balled his fists and let them relax, but could find no relief. He felt a kind of tingle shiver through his body yet it never quite reached his bones to be able to move him. His body said he had to go, do, now, yet his mind felt sluggish. It was like watching everything happen from a distance and being unable to react to it. And still he needed to do something before his body burst out of this armor.

Damn it, he hated the pills. He might not have a seizure on the battlefield, but this tampering with his perception and reflexes and overall self-control could easily be the death of him. Maybe he should have taken a regular dose, even half of one, just enough to cover him for a few hours. After all, humans couldn't stay on Brelix for more than a few hours, so preparing for an entire day was a bit overkill.

"You all right, sir?"

Rifun turned to see Godwin standing there. When had that happened? Damn it, he shouldn't have taken those pills. Did he dare use Matter to try and speed up their metabolization in his body? Would that only cause worse problems? They couldn't afford to lose time on Brelix or have gaps in coverage.

"Any sign of Aklaq or Tommen?" he asked instead.

"Not yet," Win reported, looking unconvinced. "Something I can do for you in the meantime?"

Could he ask Win to manipulate the drug in his body? No, that was too fine, too delicate, and it was too late for what was surely a lengthy procedure. Rifun put up a Sound barrier. "Stay close to me if possible. There's something...I'm not right."

"Not right how, sir? A seizure?"

"I don't think so. I don't know how to describe it, and no one is more frustrated than me by saying so."

"Poison? We've got a lot of strangers walking around here."

"No. Unlikely. Too many variable species, and we're all in the same battle, all dealing with the same consequences of failure."

"You take your meds today?"

Rifun hesitated. Then, "Yes. But I don't normally, and today I doubled it."

"Sir?"

"I don't like how they make me feel, so I don't normally take them. But I can't risk it going into battle, so I took twice as much."

"Dangerous thing, sir, you're not accustomed to them."

Rifun gave him a look. "Oh, really?" He tried not to react as something in his vision shifted. It wasn't his aura, but it didn't feel any better. "Just stay close to me. Please."

Win did not reply immediately, and Rifun could feel the Sound barrier enlarge. He looked to see Julianna approaching. Because she was really who he wanted to talk to.

"Something the matter?" she inquired.

She was supposed to have stayed out of this today, but she just couldn't help herself it seemed.

"Faharoa hasn't been taking his meds," Win said. "But today he did, and he doubled it, and now he doesn't feel right."

The look that crossed her face was indeed one of surprise, but there was something about it that was very disquieting. On the other hand, it could have just been him.

"And you still think you're going to fight?" she questioned. "No, you can't." She wasn't pushing very hard in his opinion, which was both a minor blessing and a tad suspicious. "A seizure is bad enough, but it's predictable. Who knows what could happen with unfamiliar drugs in your system?" She tore down the Sound barrier, as if she might bring in some outside reinforcement for her argument. "It's a bad idea. Your place is here, what if something happens?"

"Then it's a good thing my little bodyguard will be close to hand. My place is out there, on the battlefield, leading my men, leading by example. You stay here and read and study and learn and teach. I can't sit in an office any longer, pretending I am a general who only leads from his desk. A warrior's place is in the field of battle."

"But your—"

"I've already taken the meds. I will be just fine. Besides. It's a battlefield full of Borelians. Who is going to know the difference?"

He didn't know who he was trying to convince. Godwin was only one man. What if he was busy or they got separated? What if he was killed? They were running into battle. And where were Aklaq and Tommen? He'd planned for a lot of things, but desertion wasn't one of them. Tommen, maybe he decided to be a coward after all, but not Aklaq.

"I hope you're ready for the consequences," Julianna growled finally.

"I don't have much of a choice now, do I?" he retorted. His words were gruff, but his mind was suddenly exhausted even as his body demanded action.

Behind Julianna, he spotted Aklaq and Tommen approaching. He took the opportunity to ignore Julianna.

"Good, you're here. Slight change of plans," Rifun began. "I will be going with you."

"With us?" Aklaq questioned.

"Yes. I will be with my men, forging a path into the temple, and then I will go with you and Tommen to retrieve the journal."

It sounded like a big change in his head, but as he voiced it aloud, it seemed less so. The expression on her face reflected this. Had anything about the plan actually changed? Suddenly he wasn't sure. Damn it.

"What, you don't trust us?" she challenged.

"I have no reason to, darling," he told her.

"You think I would just abandon my people? I'm doing this for them, not me."

"So we're on the same page, then, excellent. Don't worry, I'll keep my end of the bargain. You can be Moses and free your people at the end of the day."

"What's to keep you from stabbing me in the back?"

Rifun moved his right hand and put the gap where his two fingers should have been in the spot where she'd stabbed him only three months ago. "You have my word of honor."

"Your word means nothing."

"Well, regardless of your opinion, that is what is happening, and you better come to terms with it because I predict we'll be moving out in..." He pretended to check an invisible watch. "Less than ten minutes. Maybe less than five. Come on, then, I'll introduce you to our security detail."

"Security detail?" Tommen wondered.

"They'll be in charge of getting us to the temple safely. After that, everything is up to us."

Once he began moving, taking Aklaq and Tommen down to the first floor where it was nearly time for them to burst through into battle, Rifun's body demanded to move even more. His skin felt tight and his muscles tense. He thought Tommen might have said something, but he wasn't paying attention as he opened up the portal and stepped through.

There was no cheer on Brelix, no real joy whatsoever. Ancrath was the origin and center of the Borelian empire, and to be social was to be militant. This was astutely represented by sharp, angular construction jutting up from black, rocky cliffs and hillsides littered with brown, stunted plants. The variety of Borelian skins provided the only real color contrast to this dismal scene, and it was like having the targets on the range lit up.

Rifun had never actually been to Brelix, though he knew Ancrath well from all the maps he had been studying for months now. His only intent when he opened the portal was to get as close to the temples as he feasibly could without walking directly into a line of fire, and he trusted the Author to do the rest. Maybe it was a foolish test, but it seemed to work.

Immediately he Banded to take in his surroundings. They were in a building, facing what could reasonably be considered the front door. To compare it to anything on Earth, it might have been something like an art gallery or a live modeling studio, but with a quaint cafe for spectators. His knowledge of Borelian culture as well as taking in more of the scene quickly painted a little different picture. This was an indoor slave gallery, and the "models" were those kidnapped from the field of battle, already being put up for sale and spirited away for hard labor. Those doing the buying appeared to also be slaves, probably highly-trusted household managers or some such, while the Borelians themselves acted as guards in case the prisoners tried anything.

Cassius would have had a field day with this place, Rifun thought. *He would have ripped the planet in half.*

But that was neither here nor there as Rifun picked his line, picked his targets, and dropped the Band.

Step one, allies. With a swift leap, Rifun propelled himself into the line of prisoners being auctioned off, using Matter to dissolve any and all bonds.

Anthropomorphic bear lizards launched themselves into the crowd that suddenly began to panic, angry lions and lizards and birds hard on their heels. A few found weapons, but most were angry enough to make do with their own biological means, claws and teeth. Slaves ran while guards engaged.

Step two, clear the building. This was not optional, and Rifun reacted reflexively as something moved in his peripheral vision. He knocked the barrel of a rifle-type weapon away from his head, then hooked his arm around it, locking his opponent with him. When the Borelian's gaze flickered toward Rifun's arm on the gun, Rifun took a cheap shot at the Borelian's opposite leg. He put the Borelian's knee on backwards, and it started to crumple. Rifun used a bit of Gravity to force it down faster. It was still trying to keep its good leg in position, but this only kept the gun up at an awkward angle, making it almost useless to the user. Fortunately for Rifun, it was in a perfect position for him to ram the butt of the gun into the Borelian's face, which he did so with great prejudice and a little Force, just enough to crush the skull.

From there, he yanked the weapon out of the bloody skull and turned it on the closest Borelians he could find, getting off four expert marksman shots in rapid succession. Apparently the Borelians didn't believe in high-capacity magazines. As the next Borelian ran up on him, he used the rifle as a club, again augmenting the motion with Force. While it killed the Borelian, it also broke the gun.

He dispatched two more attackers with ease, although it was more from muscle memory than conscious effort. His body felt better for constant movement and action, but he still didn't feel quite right overall. As long as he was moving, he felt faster, sharper, and stronger than ever. Whenever he stopped, his brain began to slosh and his body felt tight. He said nothing of this as he looked around and assessed the situation. He had his revolver, but in the interest of conserving his own ammo, he picked up a Borelian sidearm, too.

Between himself and his team as well as the now-freed almost-slaves, the building occupants were neutralized swiftly. Even once things appeared calm, they waited a good three seconds to see if more would come running in from another area, but things seemed quiet. As if on some silent cue, everyone moved to the middle of the room.

"Everyone here?" Rifun demanded. "Is anyone dead or dying?"

A handful of Aklaq's bestial allies had died or been badly injured in the attack. A couple more volunteered to return them to their world. Aklaq knew the location of their camp and sent them home without a fuss.

"Anyone else injured?" she asked once the last had gone. "Has anyone been terribly exposed to Borelian toxins?"

Her concern was her allies, but Rifun's team also reported a negative.

"We should get your allies home," Rifun suggested. "They've served their time."

The bear-lizards — D'Bok was their species? — wholly rejected the idea, as did the lion-like Xur. Apparently insulted by the idea, or thinking they'd been called weak or cowardly, the dozen or so animalistic creatures moved off to have their own conference where they evidently chose a leader and headed out into the street to look for a fight. Rifun did not stop them, although he did go out to see where they went and if any trouble was currently coming their way.

When he ducked back inside, Aklaq was sending the rest of the allies home. Not all were injured, but they'd clearly had enough. Whatever they believed about the war before, this was not it. Rifun had tried to warn them, everything else was on them.

"Everyone else is going to the temple, right?" he inquired irritably. They only had so long to complete the mission.

"We're ready," Drinjin uh Ersik reported.

"All right, it's about two miles north to the temple complex," Rifun said, deliberately slowing his breathing. He felt his body tightening even more, desperate for more action. "We buy time for Aklaq and Tommen to get the journal, then unleash hell."

No one objected. As they fell into formation and walked out into the street, Rifun encased them in a Fast Band.

The largest of the pyramid-shaped temples was visible from the slave gallery, the only angular monstrosity of its kind, with some kind of statue or relief spiraling around its peak. After watching the animal squad jog off to pick a fight, Rifun had determined their location and knew how to get to the temple complex, even when the temple disappeared amid a wall of large buildings.

The city was eerily quiet here, not just from sound as might be expected from being in a Band, but also in movement. With exception of a few innocuous items in suspended animation, it was hard to tell they were even in a Band. There were no civilians, no conflicts, nothing. The governmental building and the archives were all to the west, the shipyard to the east, and there would be fighting at the common points of entry. All Borelian forces would be concentrated in those areas. But not here, not in this common neighborhood.

So far, everything was going according to plan. But then, the plan was pretty simple; everything was basically one big distraction so they could steal the journal and infiltrate the temple.

Rifun glanced up at the pyramid, the peak just barely visible above a building. He couldn't decide whether the dark mist he saw was naturally-occurring or something only he saw because of the Shadows and the dragon. How could anyone not see it? How could anyone not tangibly feel the darkness of this place? How were the Borelians super majority atheist when they lived like this? Every door and most windows were adorned with artifacts known as bone spirits, the bleached and decorated bones of the Borelian dead. If Rifun could attribute his physical suffocation and discomfort to anything at this exact moment, it would be the evil exuding from such horrible trinkets.

It was this distraction that nearly cost him his life as a squad of Borelian soldiers barreled into them from the west. The leader was using a Time Band. When it collided with Rifun's Akari Band, his distraction caused the two to burst apart like shattering glass. Everyone stumbled, which proved to be the best outcome for the moment. The attackers, intent on a particular direction, were thrown off and most unable to complete their present mission. Those being ambushed were knocked out of the way of weapons fire, physical blows, and any exposed Borelian skin.

Rifun stumbled to one side, quickly picking up on the situation and deciding to go with it. He forced himself to go as limp as his body would allow, rolled swiftly, and came up in a low stance. Trained reflexes more than conscious thought saved him as something reached for his head. He twisted painfully and drove himself into the body of his attacker. He used Force to off-balance the first attacker, but was not able to do anything more as a second was soon on him. He slithered away, saving himself but giving the pair the opportunity to get to their feet and in ready position. Both had firearm-type weapons but were very lightly armored, with several areas on their arms and legs open to the skin.

They raised their weapons and fired. Rifun Banded so he could study the firearms and find the exact moment when the projectile was loosed, but before it left the barrel. When he found that moment, he shrinkwrapped his Band to the weapons, leaving himself and his attackers in Base Time. He launched himself at the space between the two. His attackers were unprepared for him to not only not die, but then rush them. They pulled on their triggers again, but nothing happened. By now Rifun was close enough that they had to make a decision. Each one stepped to the side and faced him, their posture suggesting they were going to make a grab at him as he went by.

He Banded himself as he got close. They kept their weapons up, as they had probably been trained. Before they could drop them and make a physical grab for him, he stopped himself and released the Bands on the guns. Two shots struck each attacker. Whatever kind of gun it was, whatever the ammo used, two was enough to kill, even if they hadn't been perfect shots.

Rifun dropped all Bands and looked around. Their group had been somewhat separated, but not perilously isolated. Aklaq had taken out three, Tommen another one, Drinjin uh Ersik four, Torbak three. But they had also lost three, there were still more in the initial ambush force, and reinforcements were likely on the way.

Just as quickly as they had been ambushed, a new force came barreling into the street, this one led by a few Sakarian giants, flanked by Turitian special forces, and filled in with a squad of Dorigisi. The remaining Borelians, about eight of them, retreated from their individual targets and tried to regroup, their formation somewhere between old French and modern Hollywood. They were slow to act, however, apparently having some trouble figuring out who or what they were supposed to fire at first. The Sakarians were the biggest target, but the Turitians had armor.

Their indecision cost them their lives. They got off one shot each, but most were ineffective. Rifun couldn't say that any of them were immediately lethal as the Sakarian giants crushed the Borelians, the Turitians sacked those who managed to dodge the giants' hands and feet, and the Dorigisi picked off anyone who remained.

"Well, you certainly are a welcome sight," Rifun said to one of the Turitians, breathing heavily.

"Our plans have been betrayed," the Turitian said, its voice slightly marred by its helmet.

For half a second, Rifun stopped breathing. He cast a momentary glance at Aklaq, then Tommen, then looked back at the Turitian. "What do you mean, they've been betrayed?"

"The Tacagans sold out, allied themselves with the Borelians and the Hands of

Time."

"How do you know this?"

"One of the spaceships was damaged when we attacked the shipyard," one of the Dorigisi said, "but we entered and started pulling information anyway. We found the general notice in the computer."

Months of meetings and planning, every idea, every strategy, every strength and weakness, every number, every movement. All of it straight through the Tacagans to the Borelians.

How long had this been going on? Had the attack on Lip been a setup, too, or had the Tacagans been coerced because of it?

The Borelians would be waiting for them at the temple. And everywhere else. How many men had they lost already? In this instance, was no news...bad news?

"The good news," the Turitian went on, "is that we were able to commandeer four of the six ships. Once the other two are dealt with, the pilots will fly over the temple and the governmental building and take out as many enemies as possible."

"I don't think you're going to have just two ships to contend with," Aklaq mentioned, pointing to the sky as hazy gray objects quickly turned into the outlines for spaceships descending into the lower atmosphere. Then they broke through the clouds and zoomed over the city.

"Rest assured. The pilots will do their best. They will wreck the city on their way down if they must."

They weren't here to take the city. They couldn't hold it if they did. Everyone knew that, yet it now suddenly felt very unfair. Images of burned jungle and decimated villages flashed through Rifun's mind. Total destruction. Necessary in this instance, for he held no illusions of mercy from the Borelians, especially now. And yet, he found that he was having trouble separating the two incidents in his mind.

They were going to the temple. They had to. They had to complete the mission.

"If our plans have been betrayed, we must fall back," one of the officers said.

"We may never have another opportunity," Drinjin uh Ersik countered. "We should do as much damage as possible while we're here."

"We'd be slaughtered."

"Death is always an option."

Rifun put a hand up and both men fell silent. He gave both of them a stern regard. "If you're afraid, run now. And pray I don't catch up to you later." He roamed among the Borelian bodies, taking their guns and ammo and other weapons and distributing them among the group. "The full temple attack force will be arriving shortly, if they're not there already. We continue that way. We expected that by this point, they would have some kind of mobilization of their forces, and that is how we shall navigate this sudden turn of events." He glanced back and forth between Tommen and Aklaq. "We are still going after the journal if at all feasible. Just understand that we won't be following a polished yellow brick road."

He did not wait for a response, simply headed off.

They were here, on Brelix, in Ancrath. They were going to the temple of Tujor, and they were going to take back the Book of Commands, wherever it was hidden. They were in very real danger here, from the Borelians. The Borelians had the home field advantage, in addition to advanced weaponry and their natural toxins, but they didn't have the advantage of Time or the Akari. Very few possessed Time abilities, and Rifun had killed all those who were in the Cult. Even if they had taught anyone here at home, such abilities would be paltry. Plus Aklaq had done well to decimate the higher chain of command, which was probably the only reason they were faring as well as they were.

They didn't get a hundred feet down the road before they all hit the ground. Two spaceships roared overhead, might have deafened them except for a Sound barrier. Only the ships' size prevented them from racing down in the streets, though one clipped the top of a building, bending steel and sending stone crashing to the ground about fifty yards ahead.

The ships weren't especially large, most likely just personnel transport between the ground and the larger vessels in orbit, probably didn't have much by way of weapons or armament. But they were fast, though not quite supersonic at the moment.

Rifun got his feet under him and was moving even before he was fully upright. Behind him, the rest scrambled back into some semblance of formation and hastily followed.

One might have been forgiven for assuming that, being in a cold stone city, Rifun would have no trouble ignoring the memories and flashbacks of a jungle. But that wasn't the only place the rebels had fought. Once they were more secure in their victories, they had set up their headquarters at the university in

Fianarantsoa. When they began to lose ground, they holed up in the university. And when they lost, they fought in the streets.

Around every corner, he first expected to find French uniforms. Thankfully, he was never confused when he found Borelians instead, and he did not hesitate to put them down. And yet, he still couldn't quite shake the images or the feeling of looking for French uniforms.

Underneath it all was now a current of confusion, betrayal. The coastal peoples had been recruited away from them, their own people made into enemies. No, it was the Tacagans. The Tacagans had willfully betrayed them. Hadn't they? But if it was willful, then why continue with the planetary defenses? There must be more to the story. There had to be.

They rounded a corner, now less than a block from the temple, and ran into a small Borelian squad, likely a scout or perimeter troupe. He couldn't be concerned with the Tacagans just now. Treachery or not, they were in a war zone, and they had a mission to complete. If there was any good news, it was that he had never really brought up the journal at the meetings on Tacaga. That was a mission solely within the realm of the Order, not pertinent to the human war. So things might not be all bad. Only Aklaq's plans to assassinate the higher officers had any real consequence, and that had been more icing on the cake than primary plan.

The group easily knocked down the perimeter troupe, then huddled at the edge of the temple complex. It was a massive area, easily the size of the university campus and then some. A pyramid the size of the largest of the great pyramids of Giza loomed in the center of the complex. Each side was covered in bones decorated with gems. During the day, it was probably a glittering masterpiece. Snaking its way around the edges and finally perched on top was a statue of Tujor, the dragon itself. They were at the southwestern edge of the complex, and the statue faced north. But Rifun did not need to see its head to imagine its face or what it was doing, lording itself over any and all worshipers, looking down on them with narrowed eyes, scrutinizing its prey. The black mist, whether real or not, hovered over the entire area.

Six smaller pyramids were arranged symmetrically around the center one, each one laden with gem-covered bones and topped with a dragon statue. The smaller dragons were each perched atop something that represented one of the Six Facets: money, pleasure, and so on.

Rifun had a brief thought, wondering if they were all Tujor, or if there were more evil spirits like it. What if the thing that had inhabited Cassius was only one of these lesser evil spirits, lesser dragons?

Didn't matter, he quickly decided. He would kill one dragon, he would kill seven of them, he would do whatever it took to vanquish this evil spirit and set things back to rights.

From what he could see of the situation, Order forces were at the northernmost temple, with Borelian forces likely guarding the center temple. Neither army wanted to dance out in the open if they could help it, but they couldn't just sit around waiting for something to happen. The Order forces might be on borrowed time, but the Borelians didn't have Time at all.

"What do you think?" Torbak inquired. "Sneak around the perimeter or straight to the center, catch them from behind?"

"From the side at best," Rifun informed him, "and I don't want to get caught inside with Borelians between us and our reinforcements."

"Do we want to do anything to these lesser pyramids?" one of the Dorigisi wondered, looking a bit eager to do some demolition.

"If you attack the lesser pyramids, you run the risk of becoming trapped."

"We'll be fine," a Sakarian said, eliciting nods from his fellows.

Rifun considered this for a moment, then nodded. "You take it on yourselves, then. And it may draw their forces away from the center pyramid." He looked over them. "The Dorigisi and Sakarians have leave to carry out this mission. The Turitians stay with us."

No one argued, and the Dorigisi and Sakarians darted toward the nearest pyramid while Rifun and the rest skirted the edge of the complex, heading north toward the main fighting force.

Rifun elected to take it as a compliment that even with the Tacagans' betrayal, Order and human forces were still putting up a good fight and carrying out their designated tasks. To his knowledge, no one had ever attacked the Borelian home world, never mind the capital city. Even with advance knowledge, the Borelians just didn't know what to do.

Everyone looked up as the rumble of spaceships grew louder. Rifun spotted half a dozen of them higher in the sky. He judged it to be four on two, bets that the two were on their side. But they made no maneuvers towards the temple complex at the moment, and the group continued to make their way north.

Order forces were currently clustered around the northernmost pyramid, facing off against Borelian forces guarding the central pyramid. Rifun slowed his pace and let himself be swallowed by the crowd. It took a moment for the men to realize just who had joined them, but when they did, he saw relief and encouragement swell through them. He took the time to pat backs and murmur some encouragement, all the while looking for those in charge.

"All right, what are we looking at?" Rifun asked.

"Welcome, Faharoa," Torbak Martin greeted. "We regret to say that our plans —"

"Have been betrayed. This I know. I have been so informed. But I'm not willing to give up so long as we have a fighting chance. We need that journal."

"Of course, Faharoa."

"So, what are we looking at?"

Rifun peered through the darkness at the mass of Borelian soldiers standing guard at the central pyramid. They didn't want to be out in the open, didn't like the idea of possibly being pinned inside the complex or maybe the pyramid itself, but there was nowhere for them to go and still guard their charge. It was both necessary and unnervingly stupid. With the Tacagans' betrayal, they couldn't have come up with anything better? The Borelians knew they ruled primarily through fear, but was that all they had to their name? Was Rifun exposing a colossal weakness in the Borelian army? Well, he'd consider that later, once they had the journal and were safe and sound in a more tolerable atmosphere.

"Difficult to estimate the numbers," Torbak reported, "but few wield any sort of Time abilities. Getting in should not be a problem."

Rifun frowned. "That's what I'm worried about. I don't like bait. But on the other hand, that's what portals are for. Any idea what the inside looks like?"

"If it's anything like these smaller temples, when you go in, it will open up into a main atrium with a great statue in the middle, both art and engineering as it is structurally necessary. The whole interior is circular in shape, with altar-like constructions at all compass points and on each side of the center statue, and there are enclosed corridors around both walls leading to a large library-like room at the rear. There are also stairs along the walls in the atrium leading to a second floor balcony. Things could be different in the Temple of Tujor, but I would imagine that the basic layout is the same upon entry."

"Understood. Do you think your men can hold it once we get in?"

"You would not have chosen me as your general otherwise."

"That's what I like to hear. All r—"

He was cut short by the deafening boom of an aircraft coming out of the speed of sound, followed by the shrill shriek of a novice violin player. Two spaceships danced in the sky, high up to start, but heading directly for the temple which spiraled into the air a good five hundred feet or better. One ship was in pursuit of the other, firing wildly. Several blasts ripped open the ground in the temple complex, shaking the pyramids, blasting small rocks, and filling the air with heavy black dust. The pursuing ship abruptly ceased fire, but the lead ship wasted no time in taking it up, making a beeline for the largest temple and firing madly.

Huge chunks of stone rained down over the complex. Rifun threw his arms up as everyone scattered, each person looking for some kind of shelter in an infuriatingly open field. There was a thunderous crash as a flying boulder struck the dragon at the top of a smaller temple and more boulders came tumbling down. Many got clear, but not all, and nothing remained of them as they were driven into the rocky ground like tent spikes.

The spaceships zoomed overhead, clearing the temple complex. The pursuing vessel again opened fire. The lead ship banked to the right, toward the governmental building, and flew off.

Dust hung in the air, and with the gloom of night, visibility was limited to about two feet. Only the vague shapes of the pyramids lent any sort of helpful landmark for orientation. The whole attack had lasted less than twenty seconds, and Rifun didn't like wasting time. His whole body was shaking, desperate for action as he slammed a clip into his Borelian firearm.

"We're not going to get another opportunity like this," he declared. "We move now."

He did not wait, did not look to ensure anyone was following as he started into the dusty gloom. He did not want to move too fast and run directly into the Borelian soldiers he knew were in here somewhere, but he felt like he just could not move any slower than a jog; his body wouldn't let him.

Something came at him in the darkness. He registered the Borelian's horns only after he pulled the trigger. The attacker dropped to the ground, revealing a second one just behind. Rifun fired again. He either missed or else hit armor, for this attacker did not go down. Instead, it fired its own weapon, a rifle-type firearm. Rifun Banded and dodged. The Borelian, moving in slow motion, took something out of its rifle or off the side, he could not tell which. It appeared to be a bladed implement, having the shape of a glaive but being only the length of the rifle.

The Borelian swung at him with a wide sweep of its blade. Rifun bent backwards and ducked in, still moving in a Fast Band as he got close to his opponent. The Borelian noted his movement and executed a crisp change of direction with his weapon, but it was all for show anyway, as far as Rifun was concerned. With the Borelian's arm still in its wide arc, Rifun raised his small firearm, right up into the Borelian's arm pit, and fired. The Borelian and his rifle and his small, fancy glaive fell to the ground.

The air was still thick with black dust, the pyramids the only reliable, discernible shapes in the gloom. Around him, Rifun could hear the sounds of battle: screams, snarls, grunts, groans, weapons fire.

A light suddenly pierced the darkness, like that of a flare. In the reddish light, an odd sensation struck Rifun and he looked down in front of him, half-expecting to see Tommen bound to a chair, waiting for his father to come for him in the warehouse.

The sensation lasted for only a heartbeat. Only the thickness of the air protected him in that moment he was sure, because as the flare sputtered out, the shadows seemed to lengthen twice as long as they were before. He looked up at the central pyramid where he could have sworn the dragon statue at the top had moved and was looking directly at him. It knew what was coming.

Rifun turned toward the pyramid and broke into a jog, for he could do nothing less.

What did death look like for the spirits? Was the dragon truly afraid, or was there something more beyond all of this? There were alien creatures in the Time industry whose natural lifespans were no more than a few months. Did they view longer-lived creatures, like humans, in a similar fashion?

No, he decided, recalling his many months of prayer and meditation at the family tombs. Death was something far more sinister for the spirits. It was utter non-existence. Even he, when he died, would eventually blend with the ancestors within the razana and continue to bring life to the universe. But for the spirits, they could be cut off from that, rendered truly dead.

And yet, nearing the temple, looking up at the eyes which seemed to glow a sinister blood red, Rifun couldn't help but feel a twinge of doubt. He pushed it away as hard as he could. He could afford no doubt, not now. Now, there was only action, only reality, where he would pull the fourth dimension into this three-dimensional realm and slay it. Tommen and Aklaq would be there, and Andrew and Nathan would be, too, somehow. They would vanquish this demon together.

If only you knew...

It was unclear where the thought came from, but Rifun knew it wasn't his. He swallowed once as he approached the steps to the temple, three black stones leading to an enormous set of doors, one of which was already open. Inside looked as dark as outside, and the odd acoustics made it difficult to pinpoint what he was hearing or where it was coming from. He didn't know where anyone was, and he could feel the doubt return, mixing with fear and a little despair.

He forced himself to walk inside, gun first. Crossing the threshold, his doubt snapped into confusion as he was hit with a sensation he was unprepared for and had not expected to find here. He could not explain it except as some kind of powerful electromagnetism. The left side of his head began pulsing like an impending migraine, and he was convinced that only his confusion staved it off. His equilibrium shifted in that direction and he couldn't stop himself from lowering his gun and putting more focus on just reorienting himself to his surroundings.

Eventually his eyes adjusted to the light, which was little more than a few dozen candles marking a staircase, a ladder, the center pillar, and providing a general ambiance. All around, Order soldiers stood or milled about like automatons. Some talked to the air, some cowered in fear, some waved weapons around menacingly, but all were clearly mesmerized by something invisible. He spotted Tommen a short distance away, talking to the air. No, not the air. The dragon, or the dragon carved into the center pillar. Tommen shook his head, saying, with full conversational intonation, "No. I can't do that."

Rifun would not deny that he was more spiritual than most, but when he walked into a temple and he didn't see anything while everyone else did, he smelled fish. Even if he wanted to stroke his own ego and suggest that the rest were being terribly deceived while he alone walked in truth and light, he would still expect to see the shadows. Knowing the truth didn't make the shadows go away; in fact, it only tended to make them more pronounced.

Electromagnetism. He looked around, using Light to amplify the candles and make the invisible spectrum more visible. Indeed, there was technology at play here. If he had to hazard a guess, it was a neuroelectrical field similar to the one used in the Seat of the Hands, when those desiring to be Apprentices and Masters had to undergo a psychological exam.

Rifun looked around, using Sound to get a better feel for his surroundings. The Borelians outside had regrouped and were moving in for the kill. *La baudroie,* Rifun thought, the fish that uses a bioluminescent light to lure in other fish to kill.

It was nothing for him to overpower the field, but the flash that resulted did not help his headache any. He made his way over to Tommen, pulling the teenager out of the way of the doors toward one wall.

"What?" Tommen asked, clearly dazed. "But—"

"A neuroelectrical projection field," Rifun said roughly. "The same one they use in the Wheel for reviews. Shows you what you want to see, what you expect to see. Worshipers of Tujor expect to come and meet with the god of death. Well, the priests couldn't arrange that on a truly spiritual level, so they went with the next best thing. Technology."

The Order soldiers had been blinded by the flash and subsequently taken by surprise by the Borelians, but they soon had the situation under control.

Tommen looked at Rifun. "But then, how did you—? You aren't affected by it."

He shrugged. "I can't see what's not there. The most it will do is give me a headache as my eyes and brain try to reconcile the two. Those of you with in tact brains are much easier to fool."

"That's how you were able to look at the Core of the Wheel and not go insane."

No, but it wasn't a discussion for the present moment. "Precisely. Now then, we just need to find Aklaq and get this show on the road. You have the key?"

"Yeah."

"Good. Keep it close. We're going to need it."

Rifun spotted Aklaq on the far side of the pillar. Commanding Tommen to stay put, he reloaded and slid out of hiding. He didn't get farther than that as the whole temple rumbled, as if from an earthquake. Fighting came to an awkward pause. It started as a low rumble, then grew to the volume and frequency of a machine gun belonging to a god. Rocks and dust dislodged inside the temple and tumbled to the ground. Then there was a direct strike, and another, and another, straight up the north face of the pyramid. Inside the temple, stone rumbled and creaked. The pillar cracked and began to slide. Another string of direct hits saw the dragon's head and one foreleg come sliding off, breaking off the pillar and crashing to the ground below, killing a dozen or more.

As the assault from the spaceships died down, fighting resumed, albeit cautiously at first. The pyramid hadn't collapsed with the breaking of the central pillar, but that didn't mean it could hold up well to another such direct strike.

Rifun knew better than to grab Aklaq as he had Tommen, and he could only be thankful that she decided to kill her current opponent instead of him, then agree to continue the journal mission. He didn't like her being behind him, or beside him. He wasn't sure he would have been comfortable with her in front of him either. He glanced around. Where were Andrew and Nathan? Weren't they coming?

Suddenly, Tommen jumped from his spot and began waving his arms, his motions indicating an attack from behind. Both Rifun and Aklaq turned, raising their weapons, preparing to fend off some sinister force.

But it was not a Borelian whom they faced. Rather, it was Drinjin uh Ersik. Rifun knew a moment of relief, initially figuring that either Tommen had mistaken a motion for an attack, or was perhaps trying to warn them to get out of the way of the large alien who had been engaged with a couple of Borelians.

His relief was short-lived as Drinjin uh Ersik pushed Aklaq out of the way and turned on him. Rifun could not detect any trace of the neuroelectrical field still active, and he didn't like the look on the general's face.

"What is this?" Rifun demanded. He was here to fight an evil spirit, not his own men. Could Tujor have possessed Drinjin uh Ersik as he had Cassius? Was the dragon itself not even going to show up but instead force Rifun to slaughter his own men? Coward!

"In the heat of battle, working with one who has already tried to kill you and another of questionable loyalty, who's going to know?" the general said. "Then we will have a real leader in place, and we will get back on the right track."

On the other hand, who didn't enjoy a good old-fashioned mutiny every now and again?

In a regular fight, Rifun would have been crushed in a single blow. But he had the Akari and the Author on his side. A sudden change in Gravity forced the general's first blow off-target, and it was a powerful enough change that the whole man was momentarily put off-balance. Rifun took the opening, using Force to augment the wobble. The unsteady general went to a knee. Rifun hopped up onto the general's back, glancing at Tommen and Aklaq who watched with wide eyes.

"Go! Find the journal! I'll take care of this!"

Before he could implant a Band into the general's nervous system, Drinjin uh Ersik rose, using Force to attempt to throw Rifun. Rifun reached for Gravity and managed to save himself from smacking his head on the hard stone floor at least. He rolled and got his legs under him just in time to invoke Magnetism and deflect Drinjin uh Ersik's next blow via his metal gauntlets. The general followed up one failed blow with another attempt, leaning into the magnetic change and swinging at Rifun again.

Was this a mutiny, or was this possession? Drinjin uh Ersik had been a good, loyal general, and a good student of the Akari. It had to be possession. They were in the Temple of Tujor, and the general was arguably the largest, strongest creature in here. Was Rifun really going to have to kill his own general? Was there a way to save him?

"I came here for the dragon, not you," Rifun said, hoping to elicit some spiritual response as he dodged another blow, still trying to assess the situation.

"That's your problem," Drinjin uh Ersik replied.

"And so are we," another familiar voice stated.

Rifun looked around. The Order had cleared out the Borelian forces and now turned their sights on the fight. Torbak was the one who had spoken, and the rest appeared to agree.

Drinjin uh Ersik and Torbak, Julianna's bodyguards and confidants. And mutineers.

Pressure began to build up in his head.

No, no, no, no, no, not now!

Torbak moved in to attack half a second before Drinjin uh Ersik did the same.

Rifun scampered into a more advantageous position, trying to avoid the edge of the circle and the equally enraged supporters. The sight in his left eye began to fade.

No, no, no. It can't end like this.

Stars erupted in his vision.

39 | Confrontation

First Order Fortress, 2015

After Rifun left for Brelix, Julianna headed up to the eighth floor. She had never had such aspirations as to make her residence in a castle tower, but now that she was confronted with such a prospect, she couldn't deny it did hold some romantic appeal, almost like a storybook.

Certainly she would decorate it with greater taste than Rifun had. Oh, it had improved some with more appropriately matching furniture, but it was still terribly bland. And the living side of the room was still very much a cross between a military barracks and a bachelor flat. Plain, dull, but at least it was neat. She would give Rifun that credit; he was not a sloppy keeper.

She had little else to occupy her time while the battle was underway, and, like when they attacked the fortress and she awaited the signal to leverage the power inverter, she now awaited the return of her generals. Her mind did her few favors, however much she tried to corral her thoughts. Too much could go wrong; that was what war was, really. Something, somewhere, went horribly, horribly wrong. Rifun could die in battle and become an instant martyr. He might not succumb to the drugs or a seizure at all, discover her plan, and kill the generals and their immediate supporters. Her generals could perish in battle, in which case she would ensure that they were remembered well. But anything could happen on the battlefield.

What would Rifun do, she wondered, when he found out? Whether he discovered it on his own and came to confront her, or whether he was captured and put on trial, they would be speaking again. Would he try to kill her? What excuse would he give? Straight mutiny? Was she possessed of an evil spirit? Surely he knew the case he would have to make in front of the entire First Order. He had failures and detriments and a whole list of things to point to why he was an unfit traitor. She had no such thing. She was loyal, talented, intelligent, had never stopped working for the betterment of the Order, even when she was trapped in the in-between dimension. The worst mark she had against her was Cassius, but that was easily explained away.

She didn't like waiting, not like this. She could keep her eyes up and keep looking up and up until her eyes rolled back in her skull, but it wouldn't make the battle move any faster or in any more favorable direction.

The door opened and she turned, hope and dread mixing in her bosom. It was not Drinjin uh Ersik nor Torbak nor Godwin Lore nor Rifun. It was an officer, but not one she was overly concerned with.

"Yes?" she wondered, unsure what else to say. Was it possible they had all died?

"I thought it proper to report, seeing how you are human, the Tacagans have betrayed us," the officer said.

"What?"

This was not even in the top ten list of things she expected might go wrong today. Not impossible, she supposed, but still not the racehorse with the best odds.

"The Tacagans have reportedly allied themselves with the Borelians and —"

"Sold out every plan we ever made in their presence," she finished. She sighed and nodded. "How are things on the battlefield?"

"Still raging, going about as expected, I suppose. No word from Faharoa or his officers."

"Well, let me know if something develops."

The officer made a gesture of assent and left the room.

This was an unfortunate turn of events. What was she supposed to do with this? Of course, anything she wanted. She'd already counted Rifun out, which meant she was in charge. Without her generals beside her, she had to make the immediate decisions. Problem was, they were still fighting half a galaxy away. Schrodinger's soldiers, simultaneously alive and not alive. There wasn't much she could do, really.

She could visit the returning wounded, she supposed, offer some words of comfort, maybe stoke a few flames of discontent against Rifun that he continued the fight in spite of their plans being made known to the enemy. And yet, she just couldn't bring herself to leave the room. She wanted to sit here and imagine and dream, just a little longer.

When there was no fast followup, she relented and left the room, heading down, down, down, to the first floor. She was no judge of military camps, but if she had to hazard a guess, things were wrapping up. There were no more waves prepared to deploy; everyone was either on Brelix fighting or else returned and sucking in sweet, breathable air. Even those who showed no obvious signs of injury were heading for the medic camps in the old recreation areas to get checked out. Julianna could not speak from experience, but she imagined that it was easy to lose track of time on the battlefield; how many were now permanently maimed because they couldn't get out in time?

"Generals returning!" someone shouted.

The call got bounced around through dozens of people so that it continued even after Julianna spotted Torbak Martin. Well, at least he was alive. She made her way through the crowd. The rumor mill was the only instance in the universe that she knew of where sound could beat light, and she knew even before she got close to the general that he had Rifun with him, apparently unconscious. She fell in step beside Torbak who was currently heading for the lower levels.

"I'll take him," she said, using a Gravity track to remove Rifun from the general's arms. "He needs care." At the general's look, she put up a Sound barrier. The two of them stopped, a sizable group gathered around. "I will take him for care, as is to be expected. You start complaining and spreading rumors. When I come out of the recreation area, we're going to have a meeting. Then we imprison him."

Torbak agreed wordlessly.

"Any sign of Godwin Lore?" she asked.

"Lost track of him," the general admitted. "With any luck he's dead or on a Borelian auction block."

Behind him, Julianna spied Drinjin uh Ersik also just returning. She nodded and looked up at Torbak. "You have your orders."

The general turned away. Julianna dropped the Sound barrier, adjusted her Gravity track, and took Rifun to the medics, the whole way calling out that the Faharoa needed help. The crowd parted, but everyone wanted to see. Had he been stabbed again? Poisoned with Borelian toxins again? Something else? He survived once, he could survive again, right?

To her eyes, he really didn't look that bad, barely injured in any way. He was exceptionally dirty, stinking sweat coated in black dirt and bodily fluids, but physically he looked fine. No broken bones, no bruising, nothing more than a few small cuts. So, the drug mixture had finally worked, and, hopefully, with an excellent sense of dramatic timing.

Eight medics were waiting for him as Julianna forced her way into the medic camp. Most of them had assisted in his previous knife and toxin injury, and their body language suggested they were ready for the same. Once they determined that there was no knife and no apparent toxin, the tension and worry in the room deflated faster than a popped balloon.

Sorry, Rifun, Julianna thought, moving to his head. *It's been fun.*

She touched his hair in a gentle, almost motherly way. The medics paid no attention to her. She Felt inside him, felt the damaged skull, the damaged part of his brain. She knew a moment of pity, imagining the migraines he must have endured, simple headaches augmented tremendously by broken bone and misfiring neurons. His brain was still a bit sluggish, but it wouldn't stay that way for long, not unless it had help. Julianna didn't know quite how seizures worked, but she had a good idea of where they started for him.

She couldn't say exactly what she did, flicked a neuron just right or fed a little bit of her own body's electricity into it, but Rifun began to contort violently like a man possessed. Julianna stood and stepped back, letting the medics do their work. As before, when he was recovering from the Borelian toxin, there was little they could do. They had no drugs, would not know what or how much to give if they did. And the brain was a delicate thing on a normal day; this sudden surge of activity would not go well for anyone who tried to Feel it.

"Do what you can," Julianna said wistfully, leaving the room. She answered no questions on her way out of the recreation area, and Drinjin uh Ersik and Torbak were faithful to intercept her as soon as possible. They hastily retreated to a meeting room on the third floor.

"He's alive," she reported. "He'd be fine if we weren't about to send him to trial and execution."

"There was already plenty of discontented muttering without our intervention," Drinjin uh Ersik said, "but the revelation that the Tacagans betrayed us and Faharoa still ordered the fight did not go over especially well."

"Some details may have been, how you say, fudged," Torbak threw in.

Julianna nodded. "Good. And Godwin Lore?"

"Some people claim to have seen him return, but we ourselves have not."

"He may try to visit Rifun in the medic camp, but otherwise, we will simply have to count him as one of Rifun's supporters that we are trying to flush out. He is not the important one here, just a very annoying one."

"Rifun's support has dwindled considerably," Drinjin uh Ersik stated. "It can only continue to do so."

"And what about the journal?"

Now the generals glanced uneasily at each other.

"Well?" she pressed. "That was the whole reason you went."

"Tommen Forbes took it and ran," Torbak admitted slowly.

Julianna didn't know if her shriek of frustration or her use of Force to throw the generals across the room came first, but she figured it didn't matter. "Are you kidding me?! An entire squad of traitorous soldiers and you couldn't keep track of one coward?! What about Aklaq White Bear?"

It was Torbak who answered again, carefully picking himself up off the ground. "She was captured and brought back. She is currently imprisoned in the lower levels."

"Well, at least we have that going for us. But how fucking incompetent do you have to be to be hoodwinked by a teenager?" she hissed. She paced back and forth a few times, noting that the generals got up slowly but did nothing more. Finally, "We're going to continue with our plans to execute Rifun and Aklaq and the Akarin. After that, you two are personally going to pursue Tommen Forbes and retrieve the Book of Commands. Do you understand?" The generals murmured assent. "Good. Now then, get down to the medic camp and arrest Rifun before he starts walking around."

The two left with barely a word.

How does this happen? What have I done that I should deserve this level of incompetence? One trickster stealing the journal and eluding the Akarin is one thing. But to have a second trickster, a cowardly teenager, pull the exact same stunt is…there is no word to describe this situation or my feelings about it.

Feelings don't matter. This is the situation. There are actions to be taken.

And questions to be asked.

It was a couple hours before she could get down to talk to Rifun. She had to spend that time pretending to be shocked by the betrayal and Faharoa demanding that they fight anyway and so on and so forth. Drinjin uh Ersik was right, the crowd was plenty unhappy on its own, with no real prodding needed from them or her. But she prodded them anyway, with useless, innocent, yet pointed questions and leading conclusions and accusations.

The Akarin—those who had returned to the fortress, anyway—were unusually silent as she entered with a small escort. They didn't know what was going on, why Rifun had been brought down and imprisoned with them, and they weren't going to ask, not her.

Julianna did not post guards on Rifun's cell, figuring the Akarin would be happy enough to attack should he try to break out. She had actually expected Rifun to try and make a break for it, once he was conscious. Either he would fight his way out to the main fortress and expect some secondary battle, or else he would quietly open a portal somewhere and slip away. It came as a surprise to find him still in the cell, no surprise to find him bowed in prayer. He had been cleaned up some, or so it appeared as his back was to her.

"After everything that's happened, you still expect your ancestors to save you?" she said.

He paused in his praying and turned his head, but his back remained to her. "I'm not praying for them to save me. I can do that well enough on my own." Now he looked at her. "I am praying for them to curse you, to pay back a thousand times the wrongs you have committed. Against me, against the Order, the Akarin, the Author herself."

"Ah, is that it? Well, I think we have seen very well whom the Author favors. And it's not the one with divided loyalties and divided blood."

He visibly flinched at the last bit, but he stood and approached to try and cover it up. "Is that what this is about? Your own superiority?" He shook his head. "Because you just can't stand the thought of not being the favorite, not being the best, not being the center of the whole fucking universe. You want to be, not a chosen one, but *the* chosen one. The *only* one. And you would tear down everything and everyone around you to get there."

"And wasn't that the whole point of taking over the Wheel, not once, but twice?" Julianna countered.

He put a hand to his chest. "I sought to make the Akari, the Author, accessible and available to everyone. Yes, wipe away that which was wrong, because it is wrong, but make that which was right openly available." He made a sweeping gesture. "This..." He shook his head. "You want exclusive access to the Akari and the Author. You will dictate who is worthy to see and to know and to learn. You may allow everyone crumbs, but you will save the loaf for yourself and your superior friends. Isn't that right?"

"Even a stopped clock is right twice a day." She gave him a look. "Not everyone is smart enough to govern themselves, so it falls to the superiors to do it for them. It's no different than being a parent."

"Something you know nothing about."

"Nor do you!" she snapped. "You who sees yourself—and your disgusting people—as equals when you have no right—"

"The Author gave us that right!" Rifun cut in. "Because we exist! But you can't stand it! It burns you! Every night you fall asleep and are tortured just by the thought of someone other than you existing. And it haunts you." He shook his head. "But your imagination has created your own worst enemy."

She shook her head and grinned. "I think not. Because we're about to execute them. Publicly. As we should have done a long time ago."

She walked away before she had to listen to any more of his prattle, and she did not check in on Aklaq beyond ensuring she was where she was supposed to be. The whore glanced her way but did not appear to want to talk either, except with her middle fingers.

As soon as she was safely back on the main floor and the Akarin locked behind bars, Julianna summoned her generals.

"We're moving now," she told them. "Get as many here as you can, Order and Akarin."

They agreed wordlessly and set about the task. It took a couple hours before Julianna was satisfied with the size and mood of the crowd.

Learning from Rifun, as well as to make a point, she stayed above the crowd, addressing them from the staircase, Drinjin uh Ersik and Torbak on either side of her with several more officers keeping everyone off the stairs.

"Welcome, to those who have returned!" she began, projecting her voice as best she could and using Sound to amplify it even more. It took a few minutes for the crowd to quiet.

Julianna would be lying if she said she didn't feel even a small power rush, looking out over the crowd. This was what she had envisioned all those decades ago, when Richard first put pen to paper. She wished he could be here with her. She was glad he wasn't.

"You have fought hard, and well," she began calmly. "It has been a difficult time and an even more difficult fight. Many of you were asked to sacrifice time and comfort for the sake of this fight, and I commend your willingness to adapt. But I know some of you have questions, and there have been some rumors going around.

"You know that for this battle, the Order allied itself with human worlds, for humans are engaged in war with the Borelians. It served a common interest, which I know most of you can appreciate. We would be fools to turn down such help."

She raised her voice. "But then, the Tacagan humans sold out! They allied themselves with the Borelians!" She went on before the outrage could grow too loud too quickly. "All of our plans, laid bare before our enemies! The Tacagans turned their back on their own brethren! The Tacagans not only turned their backs on their own people, but they allied themselves with the very ones we were fighting against. And furthermore, with the Hands of Time, creating a nearly unstoppable force. I say nearly because we all know that their strength comes only from their numbers and paltry Time abilities."

A subtle wave of agreement rippled through the crowd.

"But even the Borelians had less than this by themselves. By themselves, they had only numbers. They barely even had Time. Even with knowledge of our plans, we were still the greater force! We had great numbers, fearless warriors from many races, many factions, many peoples! We had not only the Akari but the Author's blessing as well! We had a noble mission!"

Louder agreement.

"And still we lost."

Nods stopped cold and grunts of agreement turned into grumbles of discontent.

"This is not the first time we have been so let down, losing to a lesser foe. In the Wheel, one lone Akarin managed to cage you, cage us, in our own castle while he devised a plan to end our reign before it could truly begin. If that mission had been conducted properly, there would have been no need to attack this fortress and lose even more men. And even though that was still successful in the end, there was yet a traitor who sold out our allies and saw them punished for helping us. Now we come home from battling another lesser enemy, failures once more.

"Was it our numbers? No, for we have fought against even worse odds and won. Was it our power? Of course not, for we wield the greatest power! Was it our faith? Surely not, for we fought under the banner of the Author, seeking Richard's third journal. We even extended mercy to the Akarin, and they fought honorably beside us. So then, where did we go wrong?"

She paused to look over the crowd. She had them. She absolutely had them.

"Each of you here," she said gently, "fought nobly. You have been into the maw of Hell itself, battling the universe's most feared beings. You knew, even before the treachery, that there was every chance you may not return. You could have died. You could have been sold into slavery. And yet, each of you also lost someone. A leader, a mentor, a friend, perhaps even a family member. There is nothing that can be said to ease the grief or bring them back. But how many more of them would be here today if there had been even an ounce of care?

"No man can control the battlefield entirely. No man can control his enemy entirely. Else there would be no such thing as war. But an army is only as good as its leader. And there are certain qualities expected of leaders, especially those who command the lives of hundreds of thousands. You. Which is why I submit to you today that Rifun Ndolo, the man we have called Faharoa, Second, only to the Author herself, is unfit to be leader of the Order and must be held accountable for all who died senselessly on the battlefield, not only today, but through all of his blunders, even the Zero Hour Revolution."

The gate to the sub-levels opened up and Rifun stepped forward. He was not bound or shackled in any way, and Julianna could see that the guards who walked on either side of him still deferred to him somewhat. Was it uncertainty, loyalty? She couldn't see from this distance. He walked confidently through the crowd that had parted, most of them with open mouths and uncertain expressions.

He walked confidently up the stairs and was bade stop when he was at but a polite conversational distance. He would kill her, she knew. He wasn't going to get such an opportunity.

"Rifun Ndolo," Julianna started again, using Sound so everyone below could hear, "you are unfit to be Faharoa of the First Order. Your battle plans have failed time and again and you have cost thousands of lives unnecessarily. We have gotten nowhere except running around in circles, attacking anything that moves. This time around, we were betrayed and still you insisted on the attack, rather than listen to your advisors to fall back and plan again. The Borelians managed to surprise us and wiped out more than half of all the forces fighting on the ground. Your stubborn determination has seen failure after failure. Even when one of your own generals turned against you, you were unable to defend even yourself before a mysterious, previously-unknown medical condition destroyed you and made you vulnerable. And how much more vulnerable did it make your army once you were unable to lead?"

Even before she was completely finished, there came a small uproar of support for Rifun. His supporters, outing themselves. She cast a glance at Drinjin uh Ersik who made a small gesture. Names and faces, all bound for execution.

"The goal," she interrupted, her voice carrying across the entire room, "was not to conquer the city of Ancrath. We can accept that because of the toxic atmosphere which would have killed everyone eventually. But the goal was to retrieve Richard's third journal. Your men had it in their hands and were returning when the traitor Tommen Forbes—who has betrayed us and the Akarin multiple times and cannot be trusted, yet you keep him close to hand at all times anyway— ran off with it. Was he betraying us?" She lowered her voice menacingly. "Or were you?"

"I have the journal!"

The shout was barely heard above the crowd, and Julianna might not have paid attention, except she knew that stupid voice and accent anywhere. She looked down where Tommen Forbes pushed his way through the crowd, bulky backpack bouncing along behind him. He made it to the stairs and sheepishly approached. The guards stopped him, but he never broke eye contact with her. "I have the journal."

She nodded to the guards who let him through. He was slow, cautious, and he made sure to stand directly between Julianna and Rifun.

"Prove that you have the journal," Julianna commanded.

Tommen dipped his head meekly and slid the pack off his shoulder. He unzipped the bag, opened it wide, and brought out a leatherbound journal. He glanced at each of them momentarily, then opened the journal himself. Julianna immediately unlocked the Imprint, and both she and Rifun looked it over.

"It is the original," they both declared.

The crowd erupted into a roar, yelling and shouting. Most expressed support for Julianna, but she was a bit dismayed that Rifun still had as much support as he did. She again glanced at Drinjin uh Ersik who gave an almost imperceptible nod.

"I have never attempted to usurp you," Rifun told her evenly. "I have always remained loyal to the Akari, the journals, the Author herself. If anyone here is a failure and a traitor, it's you."

The crowd below was ready to erupt.

"I think the crowds have spoken," Julianna declared. "You are no longer wanted here."

"Fine," Rifun said shortly. "Guess I'll just take my little traitorous minion and leave."

"Excellent. But not before he hands over the third journal to me."

Tommen swallowed.

"Tommen, give me the journal," Julianna ordered.

"Don't do it," Rifun cut in. "She can't do anything about it if you don't. Not like she has any kind of military prowess or battle experience whatsoever. What would she know about the hardships of war?"

Julianna grinned. "I may not know too much about war on the open battlefield, but I do know a thing or two about leverage." She looked at Torbak and made a motion.

Aklaq White Bear was brought up from the lower levels. She was not bound either. Julianna made a mental note to have a discussion with her prison guards later.

"Bitch," Aklaq said, stopping beside Tommen.

"Whore," Julianna replied. She looked at Tommen. "So then, this is how it's going to go. You give me the journal and they both go free."

"Give me the journal," Rifun interrupted. "Julianna dies and Aklaq goes free. And the Akarin. Even I am not so cruel as to force them to suffer at this woman's hand."

"Give me the journal, Tommen," Aklaq told him. "They fight it out between themselves, we take the opportunity to rescue the Akarin and steal all the Books and the other two journals."

"Yes, please do," Julianna said. "It would probably be the only thing that would reunite us here today."

"I have the rights and the success of the military," Rifun declared.

"And I have the rights of succession," Julianna countered. "I am Richard's wife!"

"And I am his general."

"And I am sick of listening to you two bicker," Aklaq snarled. She grabbed the journal out of Tommen's hands and threw it mightily off the staircase into the crowd. "Fight it out yourselves!"

Immediately the crowd erupted into chaos. Julianna uselessly jumped toward the stair railing as if she might catch the journal out of thin air. At the very least, she might see it somewhere in the sudden mob and be able to use Gravity to retrieve it. She did not see it, and when she turned back, Rifun, Tommen, and Aklaq had all disappeared.

"No!" she shrieked, slamming her fist on the stone. She looked at her generals. "Get it back! We can't lose it again!"

Drinjin uh Ersik and Torbak were already moving. Julianna turned back around and looked out over the main floor which had erupted into chaos. Her supporters, Rifun's supporters, and, when she peered closely, the Akarin as well. Glancing at the lower levels, she saw the gate was completely gone, Akarin swarming out like angry bees. Looking back at the crowd, there was almost no way to tell who was who, where loyalties may lie. Her supporters would be fighting themselves, the same for everyone else.

Well, let them, she decided, making her way up to the second floor where she, like the officers, had taken up temporary residence for the assault on Ancrath. Her possessions did not amount to much, but she made sure to grab a knife, the one the whore had used to stab Rifun. Then, just for good measure, she opened a microportal to Ancrath. It took a few tries, but she eventually found something like a morgue. No one paid any attention to the hands working in mid-air to carefully scrape some oil into a small vial.

It wasn't much, she thought as she screwed the cap securely on the vial, but it would be just enough for her intended target.

She looked up as Drinjin uh Ersik and Torbak entered the area. Torbak held out the journal.

"We found it, but the fighting cannot be contained or subdued," he reported.

She grabbed the journal and again verified its authenticity, then stooped to gather up the other two lying amongst her things. "Leave it for a moment. It needs to happen, I think. We're going to find the whore and the coward, and I have an idea where they might be."

Her first thought was the eighth floor, looking for the Authored Books. Her second thought was the fifth floor, the Archives, where Julianna had planned to keep the journals once the renovations were complete. Considering the distance between the two, and the climbing required, she checked the Archives first. Drinjin uh Ersik, Torbak, and a handful of loyal soldiers followed.

Aklaq and Tommen were indeed in the Archives, staring forlornly at the empty glass case where they had evidently expected to find the journals.

"Shit," Aklaq was saying. "That can only mean that—"

"Looking for these?" The whore and the coward turned. Julianna held up the three journals. "I admire your spirit. I admire your loyalty. But it can only take you so far in the face of imminent destruction."

"Yeah?" Aklaq drew a knife. "Tell your dogs to stand down and let's me and you have a little discussion about imminent destruction."

Julianna wasn't much of a fighter, but with everything going on, well, she couldn't pass up an opportunity to teach the slut a lesson. She handed off the journals to Torbak and drew the knife. Then she produced the vial of poison and dabbed a few drops on the blade.

"Borelian poison loses its potency very quickly, I'm told, even with climate-controlled environments," she said lazily. "Good thing it's only been a couple hours. But even so, you still won't be able to survive once I cut out your heart."

The whore was so easily provoked to a fight. And yet, Julianna could not deny her speed, her determination to get in the first blow. Julianna ducked and twisted, bringing her knife up to stick it under Aklaq's arm, but the whore smoothly changed her direction and bounced off to the side. Julianna tried to find a stable position, but Aklaq was more accustomed to thinking on her feet and was already coming for her. The best Julianna could manage was a step back and a wild swing at the back of Aklaq's neck as she went by. Aklaq, sensing this move, ducked and rolled forward.

Julianna could hear the grunt and sigh of effort as Aklaq got back on her feet and turned around. She was a fighter, but she had also been doing just that, and she was exhausted. And yet, Julianna couldn't help but admire her spirit. After all, she had to know that if she did actually harm or kill her, then the soldiers standing not ten feet away would surely attack and kill her, too.

Aklaq lunged again. She reached for a Band, but when Julianna went to counter it, it vanished. Suddenly thrown off-balance, mentally if not physically, Julianna was almost unable to knock Aklaq's arm away as she went for the kill. Her next movements came almost as a divine revelation, or maybe a dream. She knocked Aklaq's arm away, then used her fighting arm to grab Aklaq's body. She slipped around behind the whore and pulled her close to chest. With her off-hand, she grabbed the whore's hair—she probably liked that—and put a knife to her throat.

"Well now, this is a bit familiar, wouldn't you say?" Julianna asked, breathing heavily. "Is there anything you'd like to say before I send you to see your husband?"

Aklaq grinned and chuckled. "I will still be better off than you."

Fifteen feet away, Tommen shrieked as Julianna pressed hard and drew the knife across Aklaq's throat. His shrieking died down as the blood suddenly turned black and the Disguise dropped just as readily as the body. For a long moment, they could only stare at the alien, plated in rock like a Grunjor, yet not a Grunjor. What was this? Who was this? It sure as hell wasn't Aklaq. She might be a slut, but even Julianna wouldn't consider her a coward. Which meant she'd had some other plan all along. Could she and Rifun have conspired to all of this?

Tommen was the first to speak.

"Jali," he stated. "She was a Builder, one of the Akarin."

Julianna turned and stormed out of the room, the soldiers following, Tommen irrelevant. She did not come this far only to lose everything!

"If they're Akarin or a supporter of Rifun, kill them!" she ordered her generals. "Forget the trials, forget any formalities. Just kill them. And if you find Rifun himself, kill him and make sure he's dead!"

There was evidence that the fighting had reached the second floor, but it had since receded back to the first. Looking out over the mess, Julianna could see that the movement of the mob was simply retreat. Akarin, Rifun, probably some of her more fearful supporters as well. No one knew what was going on, so the next best thing was to just go home and hide out for a while.

Torbak handed the journals back to her, then followed Drinjin uh Ersik and the others down to the first floor.

This wasn't happening. This couldn't be happening. She had everything planned out, both in the immediate, the medium-term, the long-term. She had kept her eyes up, looking forward, not bothering with nitpicking details. Where had she gone wrong?

You haven't gone wrong. You are simply paying the price for everyone else's foolishness. After all, if Rifun had forcibly dismantled or executed the Akarin like he should have, how much of this could have been avoided? You would have killed the real Aklaq, not an impostor. And you wouldn't be losing men to them right now as the Akarin flee like roaches. This isn't you. Sometimes, you just have to deal with the natural consequences of things.

Well, I'm not just going to sit idly by and let it happen. Perhaps now, in this moment, but it must be rectified. The Akarin have to go, and their rosters are still available in the

Archives. Rifun's supporters will also have to go. If not for my own due diligence, there probably wouldn't be any lists of them. Plus we still have to eliminate all of those in the Authored Books.

She returned to her temporary quarters, a bit dismayed to find things kicked about and scattered, but relieved that nothing was broken or truly destroyed. It took a few minutes for her to find everything and gather it up, but it was nothing to move it up to the eighth floor. No time like to present to move in and start redecorating. And she might even make use of some of the office stuff Rifun left behind.

Arriving in the inverter room, she could only sigh. She assumed it was Tommen and not-the-whore who had been here. The room had been ransacked, cupboards, cabinets, and drawers all thrown open and roughly pawed through. The cabinet where the Authored Books had been was now empty, and who knew where they were now? Some broken safes also indicated petty theft, but she wouldn't know what would have been taken. They just had to make everything that much more difficult, didn't they?

This is what happens when you can't control the people under you.

She set her things aside and started cleaning up. Rifun had done a fair amount of work, but almost all of his notes were in Malagasy, entirely useless to her. So loyal to the Order that he couldn't even write in the language of the journals. Oh, there was plenty of technology out there that could translate it, but why bother? She didn't have time to sift through his blithering heresy. She would write her own notes just fine. After all, her plans were different than his anyway. She found a few things in French, though it was a little more advanced than she was comfortable with—probably some local, savage dialect or creole anyway—so she tossed those aside as well. At least the handful of English notes she found were more easily sorted into useful and useless, heavy on the latter. She would rewrite them later anyway; his handwriting was atrocious, though she couldn't fully blame him for that. She'd seen his old handwriting, and it had been quite nice.

She didn't know how much time passed, but her generals eventually made their way up to see her.

"No sign of Rifun," Drinjin uh Ersik reported hesitantly. "Nor Godwin Lore or any of his more staunch supporters."

"Aklaq and the Akarin?" she inquired.

"No sign of her, and most of the Akarin escaped. It seems as though Rifun's supporters and the Akarin helped one another escape."

"Of course they did, for there was little difference between them. That's the whole reason this happened, because Rifun couldn't separate us."

"Of course."

Clearly they were expecting some sort of punishment. While it might bring some personal satisfaction, Julianna elected to forego such a thing for the time being. They would have to work it off, and they wouldn't stop working it off until every single one of their enemies was dead.

"Any sign of Tommen Forbes?" she asked, knowing full well the answer.

"None," Torbak admitted.

She sighed and folded her arms. "Well, the good news is that he's incredibly predictable. He's also too weak and cowardly to pose a threat. His consorts, however, are a different matter."

"We already have teams going out after those who escaped," Drinjin uh Ersik offered. "Tommen Forbes is not the only predictable one."

At least someone around here is thinking. "Good."

"Everyone is under orders to take a special interest in locating Rifun or his close confidants. Someone must know where he is likely to go."

Julianna nodded. "We can hope. And what of the Borelians? We can't forget about them. Are they reacting in any way to the attack?"

"Nothing we've been able to discern."

"Well, don't lose sight of them. Continue sending out hunting parties, but don't let the Borelians slip away quietly. Nor the Tacagans. Their interests may lie in betraying humanity, but we were there, too."

"Of course."

She paced a few steps. "There are too many Akarin and Rifun supporters. There are likely to be a lot of leads. To prevent wasting time and resources, we should set some targets and priorities."

"Agreed."

He looked like he had some suggestions, but she cut him off. "We start with anyone in the Authored Books, the subjects and main characters, those who have perspective chapters, those the Akarin look up to. Micaiah is dead, as is Cassius and Sabelu. Now it's time to go after the rest, and I suggest we start from the very beginning with the Krydik."

"We may find Aklaq White Bear among them," Torbak mused.

Julianna nodded. "I'm counting on it. Once the Krydik are taken care of, then we can set our sights on the rest. Any questions?"

"We will redirect our teams accordingly," Drinjin uh Ersik promised.

She dismissed them and stared after the spot where they disappeared.

Reflection

Rifun, Win, and a handful of other humans spent the night in a motel in rural Belgium. It was as inconspicuous as Rifun could think of in the two seconds he'd had to decide, while still being somewhat culturally accessible, at least to himself. They took turns showering, caring for wounds, eating, sleeping, and standing guard, just waiting for some kind of cleanup crew to find them and finish them off. Rifun knew he would be the number one target, but after two days, he dared to breathe.

"What a bitch," one man, Sergei, grumbled, leaning against a wall. "Sending us running like rats after everything we've done."

"Fought in a fucking war we did," another man, Mark, agreed from where he sat on the bed farthest from the window. "Multiple fucking wars. And what did she do? Get stuck in another dimension, play with art and philosophy. And she thinks she can just—"

"Well, she did just," Win cut in irritably, standing in the middle of the room. "Because that's what women fucking do. Especially ungrateful cunts like her."

"So what do we do now?" a third man, Andor, wondered, sitting in one of the chairs in the room. "We might have helped them some, but we're not Akarin. We're not First Order anymore."

"No, but you are still *miaramila*," Rifun said. He sat on the edge of the bed nearest the window, looking out at a rather drab, rainy day. "Still soldiers."

"We're scattered, and we have an enemy who would very much like to kill us," Win stated. "What are your orders, sir?"

"My orders?" Rifun could barely comprehend the thought.

"Last I checked, you were *adjudant-chef*. That makes you the ranking officer, if Faharoa isn't enough."

"Don't give me that shit, Win, you've been a soldier longer than I have."

"Mercenary, sir. Mercenaries having pecking orders, not ranks. And I'm no leader."

"Obviously neither am I."

"Bullshit," Sergei said. "Our plans were exposed to the enemy and we still kicked their asses. That's the kind of shit that leaders do."

"And you did it with a fucked up head," Mark added.

Rifun sighed.

"I would bet ten thousand pula that she knew about your seizures," Andor said, glancing at the script bottle Rifun no longer bothered to hide. "Am I right?"

Rifun nodded. "She knew about them very well. She was one of those I trusted to cover them up when I was out and about." He made a vague gesture. "Godwin, too. And a couple others."

"And yet, we're still here." Sergei shrugged.

"But we can't stay here forever," Win said, his tone a little pushy.

"What's the matter, tired of Belgian waffles already?" Rifun asked. Win gave him a look. He sighed. "You're not wrong. The prudent thing to do would be to meet up with other small groups like this, regroup, figure out who and what we have available, go from there." He rubbed his face as if it might get his mind working. "There aren't too many humans in the Order, and fewer still were soldiers."

"Miaramila," Sergei interrupted.

"Yes, that's what that means," Rifun said, puzzled.

The Russian shook his head. "No. That bitch still has soldiers. At least two traitor generals, too. But they are soldiers only. We are Miaramila."

"How about we come up with a name for our club later?" Mark suggested, eliciting a grunt of agreement from Andor.

"Do we know of any other humans, for sure, who would be with us, and where they might be?" Rifun wondered.

Mark and Andor only gave blank looks and shrugs.

"I only know of Angel and Tiana," Sergei said. "But they're from Colombia, and God knows where they'd be. Chances are good they're doing like us, hiding somewhere completely different."

"But not completely foreign. Take Mark and Andor and start looking," Win ordered.

Sergei glanced at Rifun who merely nodded. The three men stood or straightened, gave themselves and their paltry gear a once-over, then departed, leaving only Rifun and Win in the room.

"What would you like me to do, sir?" Win inquired, sounding earnest.

"A personal favor, if you would, because it would be too dangerous, I think, for me to go." Rifun grabbed the pad of paper and pen on the nightstand and scrawled out an address. "Check on the woman in this house. I know Julianna will have expected me to go there."

Win took the address and studied it. "You're not hiding a wife on us like Micaiah did on his friends?"

Rifun shook his head but couldn't quite muster a smile. "No. But she should have been."

"I'll look in on her."

And he vanished through a portal.

With the room empty, Rifun determined the cardinal directions and knelt in the northeast corner to pray. He hadn't been down more than thirty seconds before he paused. What was the point? Was anyone listening? And, perhaps most important of all, who was he even praying to? Forget whether anyone was listening at all, for he knew that someone was, but who was it? Who was out there to listen and hear and say yea or nay? He had studied everything, learned enough to qualify as a shaman, knew far more than any living mortal. He had gone into the lair of the dragon spirit with full intent to slay this demon, and it hadn't happened. Hadn't even gotten a chance. And now it felt like the rug had just been pulled out from under him in every other aspect of his life.

What more could he do? Or say? Or learn? Where did he go from here? His entire world felt like it had shrunk to just this room, and even his roommates were all gone now. Who knew when they would be back, assuming they returned at all? Julianna wouldn't let them just escape; she would be hunting them down. Him, any of his supporters, and undoubtedly all of the Akarin. Hell hath no fury like a woman scorned, except he still couldn't figure out why she felt so. Except, maybe, that she just wanted to be special.

As Sergei said. What a bitch.

Sighing, Rifun ended his prayer — he wasn't even sure what he'd been praying — and stood. He had to get out of this room, had to walk around.

The first day they'd been in Belgium, the group had done a little petty thievery, Banding and stealing some food, clothes, toiletries and other small necessities from the local stores, just enough to replace their dirty, stinking battle clothing, blend in, and tide them over for a few days. Rifun had also made a trip to the pharmacy where he'd been getting his seizure pills. His off-the-books script was kept in a specific, locked location, along with a small tarka root. He took what he needed and departed, not even bothering to speak to the pharmacist in case Julianna came after him, too. Even so, he'd had at least one seizure every day in the motel.

Rifun brewed some tarka root tea, filled his new thermos, grabbed his coat and shoes, and headed outside. He had no real destination in mind—quite honestly, he wasn't entirely sure just where they were except rural Belgium. The motel was at one end of a one-road town. Rifun walked down to the other end of town and then kept going for a couple miles, trying to enjoy the wet landscape. All the while, he just waited for someone to jump him from the bushes. Or an alley. Or the open street. Why should he think Julianna's men would care about stealth and not being seen?

He stopped into a small diner-type establishment, making sure to sit in a far corner not near the windows so he could observe the goings-on of the restaurant and the street, hopefully without being easily seen.

"Qu'est-ce que je sais vous passer?" the waitress inquired. (What can I get for you?)

Rifun glanced over the menu. *"Je voudrais...des boulets à la liégeoise."* (I would like...Belgian meatballs.)

"Ça va. Autre chose? De l'eau? Du café ou du thé?" (All right. Anything else? Water? Coffee or tea?)

"Non, merci." (No, thank you.)

Ten minutes later, she returned with the meal. *"S'il vous plaît, des boulets à la liégeoise."* (Here you are, Belgian meatballs.)

He ate slowly, still keeping an eye on things outside. He wasn't three bites in before the door to the diner opened and Godwin walked in. If he was trying to blend in and generally keep a low profile, he wasn't succeeding very well. He was clearly agitated and clearly looking for someone. He visibly relaxed when he spotted Rifun and crossed the diner in four strides to join him.

"You could have at least left a note," the mercenary chastised.

"I did think about that," Rifun said lamely. "What news?"

"She's fine," Win reported. Rifun breathed a sigh of relief. "But your hunch was correct. Found some of Julianna's goons hanging around, obviously waiting for you to show up."

"I trust you took care of them?"

"Of course. I won't bore you with what I did to them, but they won't be reporting back to Julianna."

Rifun nodded. Before he could speak, the waitress returned and inquired after Win's choice of meal. The mercenary sighed, clearly unprepared and not even having looked at the menu. He glanced at Rifun's plate. "I'll have what he's having."

"*Un autre des boulets,*" Rifun told her. "*Et l'addition.*" (Another plate of meatballs. And the check.)

She moved off.

"So you just decided to come out and get meatballs?" Win wondered.

"I had to get out of the motel in general," Rifun said, munching on a side of fries. "It was getting a bit dull."

Win gave him a look. "You all right, sir? You seem off."

"No, I'm not all right!" Rifun hissed. "I've just been overthrown in the middle of a fucking war and now I have basically every major faction hunting me down! The Order, the Akarin, the Borelians, the Tacagans, humanity, my own fucking body giving me away..." He sighed and chomped angrily on another fry, looking out the window across the room.

"No one here is hunting you down," Win said after a moment. "The waitress is kind of cute. Obviously she doesn't think the same about you because she's not coming after you either." Rifun gave him a look. "The Order, well, that much is obvious. The Borelians, you could make a case for that. I don't think the Tacagans care about you specifically, and I think the Akarin have their own worries right now, much like we do."

He produced a piece of paper and slid it across the table. Rifun looked at it. It was a scribbled note addressed to him, telling him to be at Forbes Cave at a certain date and time.

"Found that when I was checking out your lady's house," Win explained. "My guess is a trap."

Rifun shook his head. "I don't think so. The trap was already there; you dismantled it yourself. Besides, I have an idea whose handwriting this is."

"Aklaq White Bear?"

"Please, she's from a time like mine, when good handwriting was an essential skill and strictly enforced. No, this comes from a more modern era."

"Could still be a trap."

"Only one way to find out."

The waitress brought Win's food and the check which Rifun paid for with cash he had pilfered from here and there, all in the safety of a Band. She took the cash and wished them a good day, her gaze resting on Win for just a moment, just long enough to notice.

"She's not coming after me, but not for the reasons you thought, I think," Rifun said, giving Win a knowing look.

"No," Win said, shaking his head. "She's just doing her job."

"Come on, you said you've had families before."

"That's a pretty big leap, don't you think? You just said it yourself, we're at war and people are hunting us."

Rifun sighed but couldn't not smile as he shook his head.

"I'll admit, these aren't bad," Win said, sticking a meatball with his fork.

"The little pleasures of life," Rifun agreed. He stood. "But it looks like I have a time to keep."

"Are we meeting back at the motel later?"

"Yes. Hopefully Sergei and the others have news of the others, good, bad, or otherwise."

Win grunted an agreement and turned his attention back to his food.

Rifun left the diner and returned to the motel room before opening a portal to the United States. It was early morning in the eastern time zone and the mountains only shaded things even more.

Forbes Cave was completely blocked off now, no thanks to the boulder that had sat there for eons, almost covering the opening but not enough to deter determined adventurers and small children. He suspected that the quest to free Julianna and Tommen had some bearing on this cave-in. He also suspected that no one had discovered the cave-in yet, as the useless chain and stupid sign still hung across the old opening, warning curious onlookers about non-existent toxic gases inside.

After about half an hour, he heard rustling behind him, on the overgrown trail. Judging by the gait and the breaking of wood followed by a hushed curse, it could be none other than Tommen. Rifun turned his stance just a bit to bring the teenager into his peripheral vision, but he remained largely where he was, facing the old cave, his thermos in one hand which he reluctantly sipped on.

"I thought that was your handwriting on the note," Rifun chuckled. "Come to join me at last?" He couldn't be bothered to even try and cover up the sarcasm in his voice.

"Hardly," Tommen told him. He held out a large manila envelope.

Rifun took it cautiously, opening it up and examining the contents. He brought out three passports, several hundred dollars in cash of various currencies, a smaller envelope, and a folded piece of paper. He unfolded it. His birth certificate. Rifun Felix Ndolo in typed letters, Rivotra Felix Andilan in bold marker above it, the penmanship distinctly feminine. He refolded the paper and peeked in the smaller envelope. All of the pictures Lalao had given him, the ones saved from the farm. Most were of his mother, but there were a couple of him, too, on the rare occasion they visited the farm outside of Fianar. Rifun bit his tongue to keep himself grounded in the present moment as he put everything back together, and slid everything back in the manila envelope.

"I know you were looking for the Books and the journals," he said. "Why save this? More to the point, why give it to me when you have to imagine the leverage potential behind it?"

"Julianna will come for you eventually," Tommen told him. "Think of this as a chance to get a head start on her."

"Far away from you, I imagine."

"I've forgiven you for what you did to me. I don't know that anyone else has or ever will. Call it a gesture of good faith."

Rifun stared at the manila envelope a moment longer, then let his hands drop to his sides. "I suppose I always suspected someone would try something. Maybe a splinter group of soldiers, maybe the Akarin would inspire something in the Order, I don't know. But looking back, while it all makes sense, I still can't put the pieces together in my mind. It's almost as if I can't see them clearly." He took another drink.

Tommen dug an orange script bottle out of his coat pocket and shook it. "It's because of these. And that." He nodded to Rifun's thermos.

"I don't understand."

"Tarka root is a mild depressant, similar to alcohol, maybe marijuana. On its own, it's probably good for your seizures, to keep them in check. But these—" He shook the script bottle again. "—are not the pills you think they are. They're not Versed. They're Dexedrin, an amphetamine, an upper. One of the worst things you can do is give uppers to someone with a seizure disorder. So you drank your tea to stay ahead of it, mixing uppers with alcohol. Your brain was so fucked up you couldn't see straight even if you had your sight. On top of that, tarka root loses its potency when exposed to air, so every time you opened your bag of powder, or just opened your drawer and exposed the solid root to air, it was less and less effective. By the time the battle came around, it was almost completely useless, leaving you medicated only by amphetamines. It gave you the strength and willpower to go through with the battle, but the social and political damage within the Order had already been done, and uppers plus seizure disorder means you were a ticking time bomb for a drop, which was exactly what Julianna's minion general was waiting for."

It sounded so ridiculous, and yet, it all made perfect sense. He thought of the pills he'd gotten from the pharmacy, thought of all the seizures he'd had just in the last few days. "I got my own medication from a pharmacist who is also a Time Agent and Order sympathizer. But he was loyal to Julianna the whole time."

Without so much as a grunt, Rifun hurled his thermos at the side of the cave. Being cheap plastic, it cracked, and black liquid began leaking out, staining the snow.

"Take the money and run," Tommen said. "I don't know what you believe, but whatever you're looking for in this life, I hope you find it. Without needing to kill anymore."

Rifun did not reply, but he found his hand migrating toward his revolver. He didn't know what he was going to do with it if he did draw. There was no reason to shoot Tommen. The kid had been through enough, and he had worked out a mystery that had nearly gotten everyone killed. Maybe he should point the gun at himself and save everyone any more future trouble. Except he couldn't bring himself to that point just yet. Maybe later, when he'd had time to digest the news a little more.

He looked around, but Tommen had gone, leaving him alone. A teenager, a chosen one of the Author. He was never meant to be a soldier, and he wasn't much of a medic. And yet, in spite of everything, he had come through and become great in his own way. Tommen had saved Rifun's life more than once. But for what reason? If the Author liked him enough to keep him alive, why did it feel like she was taking everything away? What about slaying the dragon?

He returned to the motel. Win was there, but Rifun ignored all inquiries in favor of, somewhat violently, disposing of the tarka root and the bottle of pills.

"What's going on, sir?" Win demanded, watching Rifun open up microportals to anywhere in the universe and tossing the pills through, angrily, one at a time. Only when they were all gone did he relay what Tommen had told him about the pills and the tea.

For a long moment, neither of them spoke. Then, "What a cunt." Win shook his head. "What an absolute cunt. And very predictable."

"Everything is predictable when you're looking back on it," Rifun said. "Otherwise I might have hoped you would have told me." He shook his head. "Honestly, I very rarely took them. I hated how they made me feel. Now I understand why."

He sighed and folded his arms, looking out the window where fragments of blue sky could be seen amid the clouds.

"I would imagine, sir, that getting rid of the pills will help," Win offered after a moment. "And maybe the tarka root, too. Flush out your system, see if there even is a problem. You may not even have a seizure disorder; it could have been straight poisoning all along."

Now Rifun nodded. "That's kind of what I'm hoping." He looked at Win. "Unfortunately, such experiments would not only be risky on my part, but it could endanger the rest of you, with Julianna's murder squads out there. Has there been any word from the others?"

"Not yet, sir."

Rifun sighed and sat down. "We'll give them another day or two to make some kind of report. Maybe my brain and body will sort itself out by then."

Win raised a brow. "You intend to just sit here for a day or two?"

"You want to go back to the diner for more meatballs? Or the cute waitress?"

"Either is fine with me."

Rifun snickered and shook his head, but made no move to leave the chair. He looked up at Win. "Why are you here?"

"Sir?"

"I brought you in as advisor, decoy, doppelganger, spy, and a bit of a confidant. But all of that is gone now. We're wanted men. You would be fully within your rights to either save yourself or carry out some other mission, help Sergei and the others look for Angel and Tiana, or look for any others. Why are you here with me?"

Win pulled a chair close to himself and sat down, facing Rifun. "You might think that being so long-lived, my sense of loyalty, especially as a four-time-married mercenary, would diminish. Actually, I think it's become enhanced, more defined. I have learned to slow down a little and enjoy my longer life. This commander or that regime will not last forever. My families did not last forever, and so I cherished every moment I could, knowing that I could. I have learned to become more discerning in whom I choose to support, because I am not some unknown young man desperate to make his mark on the world before he dies. And I have learned to appreciate that I will not last forever, that just because I have more natural years does not mean I am guaranteed to live them. And so, I have become even more discriminatory, deciding whom or what I am willing to die for.

"Simple curiosity may expose me to certain people or ideologies, but I am not a simple man. I chose to stay with the Cult. I understand that you may have seen me — may still see me — as a simple passing mercenary, whose interest and loyalty must be bought anew each day, and I accept that. You are not the first, and hopefully not the last. I will prove my loyalty to myself, if no one else. If I am expressly dismissed, I will go. But as long as I believe in something or someone, I do not let it go easily. And in my years, I have seen men stumble, falter, lose faith, and I have seen them rise again. Because nothing lasts forever."

Rifun would admit that he was stunned by such a thoughtful admission from the mercenary, and then he knew a moment of shame at himself for being so shallow in his assessment of the man. Daniele Ivolo came to mind. The problem, then, lay with him, Rifun, unable to see and appreciate trust and loyalty. Perhaps his own paranoia created his own worst fear in Julianna. Or maybe it was something more. How could he know?

"It has been an honor to serve you in this manner," Win continued. "Your own loyalty to the Author, the Akari, the journals and the Books, even with things going to hell, it strengthens my own loyalty and confidence in the cause." He shifted position. "Too many idiots with power think that they have somehow achieved something, if they walk down the street and men flee from them. In fact, a leader should be one whose intelligence and wisdom and skills are sought after, where men come to him because they want him, they need him, and they want to need him. I feel that you are one such leader."

Rifun glanced at his hands in his lap. "Thank you." He nodded at the man. "That is very kind, and inspirational in its own right. You don't know how much I needed that."

Win shrugged. "With respect, sir, I've been around long enough that I think I do."

"All the same, thank you."

"So, now that we've had our heart-to-heart pep talk, would you mind telling me the plan?"

Rifun couldn't help but laugh, and he didn't even know if there was any humor to be found. "Plan?" He let out a breath. "Ah...the logical thing would be to find the others and regroup. And not get killed by Julianna's minions."

He stood but was immediately driven back to the chair by a sudden pressure in his head.

"Shit," was the last thing he remembered before the explosion of stars in his vision right before everything cut out.

When he came to, it was still just him and Godwin in the motel room.

"You all right, sir?" Win's voice was garbled and distant.

As Rifun sat up, the room began to spin and his stomach lurched. He wasn't able to do much more than a drunken crouch to get to the bathroom and offer up the meatballs and fries from earlier.

Forty-five minutes and a shower later, Rifun was back in the chair, holding a washcloth wrapped around ice to his head. His eyes were closed, and the only real plan in his head was just getting into bed.

"Whether or not this is simply poisoning from mixing drugs or a full, permanent disorder, I have to get a handle on this before I can be of any use to you guys," he mumbled.

"How do you expect to do that?" Win wondered. "You spend any length of time in a hospital, Julianna's going to find you. And you are still a wanted man. Using a Disguise to cover up your missing fingers might help a little, but it can only take you so far."

"I'm not going to stay in a hospital if I don't have to. The first thing that is going to happen is withdrawal." He cracked an eye open to look at his free hand, trembling mildly in his lap. "I think it's already started, honestly." He closed his eye. "Is it possible to have withdrawal even if I only took a couple pills here and there?"

"Yeah, but you were guzzling that tea by the gallon," Win pointed out. "I'm no chemist, but I don't think that mixture did you any favors. And again, how do you expect to do this, especially if you're not going to a hospital?"

"By going straight to the doctor himself."

"Haunstein? That son of a bitch?"

"That son of a bitch took care of my missing fingers for weeks. He's taken care of a lot of injuries under the table for any and all Time Agents, Akari-bearers, and the occasional homeless person."

"And what do you expect him to do, just let you sleep in a spare bedroom?"

"If he's willing. Do you have any better ideas? I'm not going to ask you to babysit me. You're a good mercenary, maybe even a good field medic, but that's not what I need right now and not where your skills are needed."

The mercenary huffed a disgruntled sigh.

"To that end, when Sergei and the rest return, I am leaving you in charge of things. Find the others, regroup, hopefully find a safe location where you can actually rest and relax a little, and go from there."

"You think you're going to be gone a while?"

"Withdrawal is a pain. And now that I'm thinking about it, I can't be sure that the tea wasn't laced with other things. Would have been nothing for Julianna to Band and slip something in the drink while I was drinking it. It already tasted awful, how was I going to pick out one more awful taste?"

"How do you know she won't go straight for Haunstein? Everyone knows him, everyone goes to him. Why wouldn't you? Especially if you have to lay low for a while."

Rifun didn't have the energy to shrug. "I don't know that. Maybe she's already been to see him. Maybe she's killed him so I can't go to him. Maybe she's got eyes on him just like she did Lalao. It's a risk I have to take."

"I don't like it, sir."

"Neither do I, but what choices do I have?"

The mercenary didn't have an answer, nor did the other refugee soldiers when they returned the following evening, Angel and Tiana in tow. The group stayed overnight in the motel and checked out the next morning, trying to pretend like nothing was wrong. Godwin took charge of the others and was already busy making a plan. Meanwhile, Rifun found a secluded spot to open a portal, straight to Kentucky.

It was the middle of the night in Kentucky, and he wasted no time going to the good doctor's house and knocking on the door. After a moment, a light flicked on.

Rifun silently prayed that it would be Haunstein who answered the door and not one of Julianna's minions.

It was Haunstein. The first thing the doctor did was curse. Then, "Do you know what time it is?"

"I need your help," Rifun said.

The doctor blinked, rubbed his eyes behind his glasses, and sighed. "Damn it, I've been hearing some weird rumors. What the hell is going on?"

"Can I come in?"

Haunstein sighed, grumbled a little, then stepped aside so Rifun could enter.

"You don't appear to be missing any more appendages," he observed, "nor do you appear to have any unauthorized intrusions into your skin, muscle, bones, or organs."

"Julianna's been poisoning me." Rifun again relayed what he had been told, the tarka root tea and the swapped medications, including his own theories that she may have laced the tea with more drugs. "I've got to get it out of my system."

"I would say so." Haunstein, dressed only in shorts and a ripped T-shirt, studied him for a long moment. He gestured to the small kitchen table. "Sit down. I'll draw some blood and do a workup."

Rifun sat, putting his hands on the table. His heart was racing and his hands were now visibly trembling. How the doctor expected to do a decent draw, he didn't know. But, somehow, he did it.

"You obviously haven't been homeless," Haunstein observed, "but you also haven't had a proper rest in a while, I can tell. Where are you staying?" At Rifun's look, he sighed. "You were hoping to stay here." He looked at the vials of blood. "Because you don't know how this is going to go and I should have figured that." He mildly shook his head. "All right. I can understand it for the time being, at least until we know what the labs say about what's swimming around in your blood." He stood and made a vague gesture toward a door. "I got a bedroom downstairs. Gets a little cold, but you can use it."

Rifun stood, thanked the doctor, and headed downstairs. He found the bedroom, didn't even bother with the lights, and laid down just as soon as he got his shoes off.

He didn't know what to do. He didn't know how it had come to this. He had taken the power of Building straight to the lair of the dragon, ready for anything, and he had failed spectacularly. He hadn't even seen the dragon, not even a glimpse. It had never bothered to show up. Why was that? Had it been afraid? Had he been misled somehow? Maybe the drugs and poison had somehow interfered with things.

He Felt himself, intending to go down into his blood and —

He couldn't Feel himself. It should have been easy, something he'd done a million times without ever thinking about it. Gone. The knowledge was there but it was like having the necessary tools taken away. He looked at a small night light near the door, tried to reach for Light to amplify it. Nothing.

He could have cried. He might have. Or he might have fallen asleep. He didn't know. He just didn't know. He had failed. And now, the Author had abandoned him. Rescinded all use of the Akari.

He felt pressure in his head. Then stars.

Then nothing.

Author's Note

Michigan, 2024

S o ends *The Hands of Time,* with Julianna's victory and Rifun's defeat.

The temptation to split this into two books was incredible. I knew right where I'd split it (after Cassius' death), and I was considering it all the way to the end, right up until, basically, I started writing this last tidbit, the Author's Note. There are a few reasons I ultimately kaboshed the idea.

First and foremost, it would dilute the focus of the story in a sea of unnecessary fluff. The whole focus here was Rifun taking the fight to the dragon, desiring only to slay the beast while still holding onto his humanity and good standing with the ancestors. Now, splitting it at Cassius' death, having the dragon get away in one story and turning the second book into the hunt and the confrontation would make a lot of sense. The problem is that filler thing again. Rifun spent the last book in endless meetings and training to become a Builder. He has the plans, the tactical mind, the power, the knowledge, etc. etc. I didn't need to spend yet another book going over meetings in the war tent or reiterating that he prays—a lot. This time around, I wanted to show off the actions, the consequences, and not spend so much time on the thought processes that caused them. At a whopping 325,000 words, I couldn't justify adding even more.

This extends into the second reason, which is that Julianna just isn't that interesting, comparatively speaking, and I didn't want her chapters to plod along like a middle school girl working the rumor mill. Because that's really what it boils down to on her part. She's in charge of domestic affairs and she plots rebellion with Drinjin uh Ersik and Torbak Martin. More meetings, more rumors, and, other than a brief stint to investigate Andrew O'Dell, quite dull in its execution. This does not make her unimportant, as she very clearly has a role to play, but no one wants to read about the excruciatingly mundane details. As much as I hated writing Cassius' last few chapters, his high-octane insanity, I wasn't fond of the idea of writing out conversations between Julianna and her instructors, setting up philosophy classes.

The third reason for not splitting the book is that it is kind of already split. This is the corollary of the first eight books of *The Chivalrous Welshman*. If you have already read those books, you may have recognized some of the conversations and other scenes. As far as political intrigue, you already know what's going on. Trying to integrate it any more into this series would make it both redundant and a bit dull, again with meetings and planning and such. It would also take this book far out of its scope, focusing too much on Rifun's obsession over Tommen as a chosen one when this is already well demonstrated in that series. Again, this book — this entire series, really — is about Rifun and his journey to take out the dragon spirit. It is about his character, his growth, his fanaticism, and his final, perhaps too late, realization that maybe he's been batting for the wrong team the whole time. I could have easily written out the entire corollary book for book, but there would have been no real point to it.

Finally, the overarching story found in the whole of *The Timekeeper Chronicles* would not well allow for the split, and Aklaq references this when she is talking to Julianna on the stairs going up to meet with Rifun under a flag of truce. What would happen if Julianna did have her own Book? Or just a part of a Book?

All this to say, don't think I didn't consider splitting this book in two, because I did consider it. Heavily.

Although this series was, fundamentally, about Rifun, this isn't where the overall story ends. He may be defeated, in the throes of detox and withdrawal, but Godwin Lore and the remainder of Rifun's supporters are still out there, and now Julianna is in a position to do things as she thought they should have been done from the beginning. The story will continue, tangentially picking up in *Turning Point*, the ninth book of *The Chivalrous Welshman*.

Thank you for taking this journey, Reader. Maybe we'll see each other again soon in a different book.

- Brooke